ADVENT OF ASCENSION

New System, Who Dis?
Volume One

By

Ryan DeBruyn

Ryan DeBruyn

TABLE OF CONTENTS

DEDICATION

To my loving wife, and burgeoning family that I hope to be adding to
soon.

FOREWORD

Hello everyone. Ryan DeBruyn here.

I just wanted to start out by thanking everyone who has picked up the book. I'm so thrilled that you are reading it and hope you enjoy it as much as I did writing it.

For anyone reading on Royal Road, or Patreon: Please know that while the story contained in these pages are similar, they are not the same. Only the book you see in front of you now can be considered Canon for the series. Everything else is just a rough draft.

Still, I hope the people supporting me over on Patreon are enjoying the conclusion to Book Four.

Check in at the end of the book after the bloopers for links to Royal Road or Patreon to continue your journey if you're desperate for more!

CHAPTER 0

Tuesday, March 26th, 2069

"We're here with Abbas, the last survivor of the Sayyad Guild's main attack force," Fleece said.

The news anchor was dressed in his usual woolen suit, which rumors said had something to do with his Skill. The outfit was a stark blinding white which contrasted heavily against his black skin, hair and dark brown eyes. Fleece introduced a very dour but well-kept Arab man. After the man gave a nod, Fleece asked a question, the one that I'd been waiting for since the segment started on my line-mate's tablet. "What happened in there, Abbas? Sayyad is one of the top Guilds in the World. What did you find? What attacked you?"

Abbas looked off camera for a moment, before it panned out and revealed a second man sitting beside him. Eva, my beautiful companion in holding our places in line, saw my confusion and simply whispered, "It's a translator, Brodie," even as the other man leaned into Abbas' ear.

Abbas then turned to the camera and responded in English, surprising me. I guessed that the translator was only there to make sure Abbas fully understood the question. "My Guild was mighty, yes. What we found in the Dungeon in Qatar was nothing Sayyad could have expected."

The translator leaned into Abbas' ear again, and I began to think that Eva was wrong in her assessment. Public Relationship Manager maybe?

Abbas continued once the man leaned away. "The rank of the Portal was only B and we didn't send our *main* attack force. What we ran into was certainly a creature of at least A-Rank, if not higher. What me and my fellow Hunters fought was a creature of Myth and Legend. Something that the Faris quested to root out from our World in those Legends. We fought a Dragon!"

I sucked in a breath, while Eva beside me did the same. I was a second year Portal Management and Materials major and, while I still had a lot to learn, I felt like Dragons should have been the first thing teachers mentioned. Surely that would get a class's attention, but only if they knew they actually existed, I guessed.

"You're saying that Dragons actually exist, Abbas?" Fleece asked, leaning forward in his seat, mirroring my own thoughts.

"Yes, Flek, they exist, and they guard treasure beyond your wildest dreams." The translator or PR Manager leaned forward and Abbas' excitement seemed to dry up, just as his mouth turned down inside of his bushy, black beard. "My team died fighting it, and they didn't have to. If we had more Mana Banks, perhaps the Healers could have lasted longer. Nonetheless, their sacrifice wasn't for nothing."

I wasn't sure if I could hear the forced enthusiasm or if it was my imagination. Still, in Abbas' eyes I could see the pain of losing his friends and Guildmates. So, false or not, he likely wanted to give them a legacy. There probably was an amazing weapon or Monster Core that came from the encounter. Something that might one day—

"Are the rumors true then?" Fleece asked, in a dramatic stage whisper. "Did your team uncover the first permanent B-Ranked Portal, Abbas?"

I blinked. Unable to control myself, I exclaimed, "They what?"

Eva jumped from the unintended volume of my voice above her shoulder, then slapped at me playfully. "Don't scare me like that, Brodie! Abbas did say the Dragon guarded treasure…"

Her giggle and playful tone made my unintentional jump-scare somehow okay. Still, a Permanent Portal of that rank could be a blessing as she mentioned or a curse for the world. To Eva I said, "I'm sorry, but what happens if that Portal Breaks?"

Eva had already paused the news story, and her giggling cut off as she went deathly silent. Her tanned face was at least two shades paler when she spun to look at me with a forced smile. "Surely we're far enough away here in Canada to not have to worry, right?"

"He said there was a Dragon, Eva." I raised an eyebrow. "Those things can fly."

Her unblemished skin grew even more pale before she tsked and slapped me on the arm. "Stop trying to scare me!"

I could only nod with my own forced smile.

B-Rank wasn't something that usually would be considered a catastrophe waiting to happen, but the fact that Monster Fields and the containment around them existed for lower ranked Permanent Portals didn't seem to provide much hope for this thing not having a Break someday.

"Maybe they're wrong and they'll find a way to close it?" I said, truly hoping that might be the case. While a permanent B-Ranked Portal would provide ample Monster Cores and limited Portal Resources to the world—it was still a ticking time bomb.

Eva nodded, while she visibly swallowed. "Plus, we're here to become Mana Banks, so maybe that will help in the future!"

I could tell she shared the sentiment about the dangers of a B-Rank Portal but still, I nodded at her point. It was my utmost dream to become a Mana Bank and make a difference in the world. Sure, I wished there'd be a re-Awakening too, but if I could help fight against the Monsters—then I'd be happy.

That was why both of us were here, after all. To get noticed.

* * *

<u>Prologue</u>
(Not the MC)
Saturday, March 30th, 2069

Morgan Hallsbrad pulled out a pen from his breast pocket, opened a small notebook using the fabric bookmark, and crossed out an entry about midway down the page. The thin sheet of paper held a simple list, not even filling up half of the small page. As he lifted his pen, Morgan breathed heavily out through his nose—the ink was black, and yet there was a red smear glinting freshly above the entry.

Turning over his gloved hand, he found a small smear of sticky red on one of his knuckles. That was the culprit of untidiness. He licked his teeth and then peeled off his two gloves, turning them inside out before stowing them in an outer pocket of a practically brand-new jacket.

Inhaling deeply, he examined the page one more time—at least the stain was above the crossed-out line of the page. The next not crossed-out line read 'Tara Isand,' but the one before it, the recently crossed-out entry, was for a 'Craig Chaput.'

Morgan looked down at Craig. Another of the far-too-abundant single Skill Awakened. One of the unchosen, unlike him. He shook his head.

The young man lay on the ground, face as white as the paper in Morgan's book—his eyes wide but unseeing. Atop the corpse, right above its heart, was a small blue sphere. Morgan put on a fresh pair of gloves, pulled from a different pocket of an entirely different interior jacket, before picking it up.

In a practiced motion, he turned this pair of gloves inside out as well, with the small blue sphere inside of them, and then placed those into a plastic bag before sealing it. Morgan took one slow look around the dimly lit alley, seeing nothing but the corpse as proof or witness he had been there. He spun on a toe and strode away.

As soon as he got out of the alleyway, he pulled out a cigarette from the breast pocket of his inner spring coat, lit it up and exchanged his lighter for his cell phone before sending a quick text one-handed. The text simply read 'complete,' and went from sent to 'read' before his first drag on the cigarette ended. He was holding his breath, savoring the taste of the pull when his lowering hand felt the phone begin buzzing.

Reversing his elbow's direction, Morgan glanced at the phone and was surprised to find that he was receiving a phone call and not simply a text. He glanced back across the street he had just crossed, toward the alley he had just exited and deemed the distance to be insufficient to answer. He hit the red 'do not accept' button, sending his contact to his inactivated voicemail. People were much more likely to make note of a man talking on a phone than one just passing by.

Just as he finished his cigarette and was preparing to flick it into a road a few blocks away, the phone buzzed again. Morgan hadn't bothered putting it back in a pocket, knowing that the broker on the other end would be calling back. This time, however, he was several streets away and could talk, so he answered.

"What's up?" he said by way of greeting.

"You know I don't like that particular idiom, Mr. Hallsbrad," the modulated voice on the other end said dryly, but then continued as if he hadn't just scolded Morgan. "I've got a high-priority target for you."

Morgan simply waited to allow the silence to stretch. He wasn't exactly a huge fan of the anonymous person on the other end of the phone. He always corrected Morgan's word choices and had a snobbish way of speaking that the voice modulator couldn't hide. If he knew who the asshole was, he would probably at the very least punch him in the face. Although, it was only at the other man's 'teachings' that he'd gotten this good at his job. Yet, he debated if the teaching, constant information, and money were actually good enough to save Mr. Anonymous from Morgan's wrath if they ever met.

Morgan actually believed he'd met the anonymous caller in the past but had somehow forgotten the interaction. He didn't know why he got that feeling—but he had a new Skill that would likely prevent something like that from ever happening again.

He lit up another cigarette and let the silence stretch.

"Alonzo Mars," the voice on the other end of the line finally gave in. "That's just his SwiftGram alias, his real name is Brodie Flacarada. He has a high-demand Skill that I can flip for hundreds of millions."

"Okay," Morgan answered simply.

"Before you hang up, make sure you don't use any Skills or siphon Mana from him. Understood?"

"Sure," Morgan responded, even as he rolled his eyes. The fact that the person on the other end said stuff like that didn't support his theory that they'd met. That just wasn't how his Skill worked. "Can I go now?"

"Mr. Hallsbrad, I can't stress enough—" Morgan hit the end button, not happy with the tone and the way it paired with the usage of his name.

Does this husker think he's my mother or something? He silently mouthed into the air.

"Well, he certainly knows he's smarter than *you*," a somewhat squeaky voice said from the awning of a late-night pizza shop. Morgan glared at the gargoyle-like creature but continued to walk past the building before turning into the alleyway that ran behind it and many other shops in the area.

He saw what he was looking for immediately and adjusted his path to move directly toward the dumpster. A third pair of gloves slipped onto his hands, and he stripped out of his second jacket, tearaway pants, and even his shoes. He slid into a pair of crocs that seemed to be placed there just for him—because they had been, and he had done the placing. He continued down the alley after balling up everything and depositing them into a corner of the half-full container.

"You know I don't like it when you speak without me addressing you, shit-stain," he said over his shoulder.

The large gargoyle, which no one else but him could see, floated there, not even using his wings to stay aloft. Morgan hated that he couldn't hurt the creature that came with his Skill—but this had been his life for over twenty years now.

Well, the Demon had grown a bit, since Mr. Anonymous helped him figure out how to best use his Skill. At least he and the gorilla-sized Demon had a bit of an understanding now.

As he walked toward the other exit of the alley, he again pulled out his notebook and flipped to a new unused page before writing 'Alonzo Mars' and then 'Brodie Flacarada' under it.

He circled both and added a star next to the name.

CHAPTER 1

Thursday, March 27th, 2069

"Take down another button," the photographer stated. Two assistants came by and helped me get the white silk to sit right as I clumsily got the button undone on the shirt. A cool breeze from the overworked air conditioning made my skin prickle as it swept through the now larger gap and over my mildly muscled chest.

This wasn't something I did on the regular. It wasn't like I was some sort of A-list celebrity. I wouldn't even say I enjoyed this sort of thing. However, this was a photoshoot that could lead to something fantastic. Something I wanted—maybe desperately needed. Ever since I was young, I wanted nothing more than to make a difference in the world, and other than being best friends with a Hunter that awakened with a Skill—this was the only other path I could see.

It was even a competition of sorts—one I didn't truly care for. Some of the others would be here for glitz or glamor, but not me. Sure, I wanted the chance of re-Awakening that came along with being a Mana Bank—but I'd be happy if I was useful—or I hoped I would be.

To remind myself of the people who were here for the wrong reasons, I scanned my gaze over the room, seeing the line of other hopefuls who had paid for the SwiftGram photographer's photoshoot today.

Just like I had done, the next person in line was going through a fitting. Another assistant—this one a very stylish gay man—held up different blouses and short skirt combos, assessing them against the Egyptian woman's skin tone. With only her bra and panties on, there was a lot of skin to contrast the garments against.

How did I know she was Egyptian? Well, we'd spent about forty-eight hours waiting in line for this. On and off, of course, as our families held our place. Me looking to remind myself of the people here for the wrong reasons, backfired when I saw her—she was undoubtedly here for the right reasons.

"Tease me, make me want it. Better! Now lean forward slightly," the photographer directed me, and I complied. This was Arnando Moreza, and he had millions of followers online. If I could impress him or have the best shot of the day, he might post about it. That would ensure an increase in my follower count and jump-start my hopeful career as a Mana Bank. "Good, Mister Mars, that young look to you is going to be irresistible. Now run your tongue over the right incisor and give me your best bedroom look."

That was something I'd heard my entire life. I looked young for my age. Being twenty-one and in my second year of college but looking like a teenager was

14

annoying, but others seemed to envy it. I morphed my smile, turning it seductive in the best way I knew how, and placed my tongue as instructed.

It wasn't like I was some sort of expert, but I had been watching online MeTube documentaries. Part of me wanted to cringe at my actions, but those same MeTube videos agreed that this was my best shot at contributing to the war on Monsters.

The photographer grinned back at me, and a few women and men nearby tilted their heads in appreciation. A flush of heat ran up my back to my neck and then over the crown of my head, leaving goosebumps in its wake at the response I was getting. Maybe all my hard work would finally pay off… Maybe I'd make a difference.

"That's fantastic, Alonzo. Flex a bit. Not that much. Dial it back," Arnando instructed. "No. Not quite right, I think. We need something more. Bring in a Magic Staff!"

"Which one?" someone shouted. I looked for the speaker but there were too many racks of clothing and armor around to find them from such a short exchange.

"Blue, to compliment his eyes," Arnando commanded.

Almost instantly, I was handed a rod of black metal with a sapphire triangular prism glinting from its top. I was pretty confident this was a prop and not true magical equipment, since the latter was so damn expensive. Still, feeling good from the reactions I was getting, I put the rod over my shoulders and draped my wrists over both sides, attempting to play to the camera. Arnando's smile grew and the shutter speed increased, telling me I might have managed *something* special.

Muttering broke out from the line and the attendants. Some in appreciation, but most in discontent. Everyone wanted the same thing, I supposed, and my success could mean their failure. I'd shared a few mutters of grievance myself with Eva, the Egyptian woman, while waiting in line. So, I understood the feeling all too well.

"That was fantastic, Alonzo." Arnando flipped open a compartment on his camera, took out a small disk, and traded it with an empty one from an assistant beside him. "Morena here will do the editing and transfer the pictures to your DropDisk. I wish you luck. Next!"

My flush of excitement slithered and morphed into a wiggling mass in the pit of my stomach. That was my fifteen minutes with Arnando, and he was moving on to Eva. I swallowed the lump that began climbing my throat and followed Morena. She made her way to a Pad-desk and placed the small DropDisk atop it.

The top of the table instantly became a folder filled with photos. Due to the size of the table, each picture was large enough for me to make out. Morena began clicking on thumbnails, and I followed her finger. Each photo she touched was of me blinking, licking my lips, rounding my shoulders, or committing some other 'travesty.' She dragged them all to the trash, and I felt a flush creep up my neck when I saw a hundred and fifteen pop up in a bubble before she cleared them. I wasn't exactly an expert model or anything like that. But I had been working on it.

I just wanted to form a Mana Bank pairing so *badly*. That, and *this* somewhat distasteful SwiftGram shoot, was my only real chance to not have to follow my parents' wishes of becoming an office worker. My only real chance to help people. Sure, the glitz and glamor might be nice—but I just wanted a good pairing.

And perhaps, deep down, to re-Awaken a secondary Skill.

Next, Morena touched the bottom of the desk nearest her and navigated various menus. With each finger tap, the pictures changed. Filters were applied and blemishes smoothed by an AI program she expertly managed. She paused in her tapping and looked up at me.

"Hmmm. I don't want to wash you out with light colors. How about a beach background?"

I blinked, not realizing that she was asking me a question until the silence stretched long enough that it highlighted her pause. "Oh umm, sure."

She smiled and nodded, clicking some more buttons that effectively turned the green background of each picture into something different. No two pictures were the same, but each one was now taken on a beach or a boat. The pose with the staff over my shoulders was on the deck of a frigate now, with a huge hovering aquamarine Portal contrasting the dark blue of the water below. The silver of the ship and the military fatigues of milling people told me this was a shot of me 'in the field.'

I could almost recognize the shot. It was eerily similar to one of the first images the public had seen of a Portal after the Advent on December 14th, 2045. High school classes had driven the image into my brain as we'd studied and examined the days leading up to its appearance and the days after. Still, this wasn't exactly the same picture, and if I was honest, I barely recognized the 'teenager' standing on the Frigate.

My twisting stomach got worse. While I could still tell it was me in the pictures, I could also tell it wasn't. I looked at myself in the mirror every day and knew my blemishes like old friends. To see these doctored pictures was like a strange fantasy I never wished for. A look I wouldn't achieve even with the best makeup. Something I never wore—save for today.

Morena finished up a few heartbeats later, while I studied the changes she was making. Somehow, the pictures became even crisper in appearance. "Alright, anything else you think I should do?"

I scratched the back of my head, feeling the coarse shaved hair there as I considered her question. I couldn't tell her to replace some blemishes to humanize me, right? Surely, they were the experts—that's why I'd asked my mom and dad to save up and send me in here, not to mention drive me. Sucking in a deep breath, I shook my head. "No, they look excellent."

Morena frowned for the briefest of moments before she shrugged ever so slightly. Then she made a motion above the table. Holding her open hand above it, she made a fist and then positioned it above the DropDisk. All the pictures vanished and she picked up the small disk.

"Okay, if you're satisfied, head over to the receptionist and she'll handle your final payment. The disk is encrypted, so don't even think about trying to pocket it and walk out. You'll never get the pictures that way and just lose your fifteen-hundred-dollar deposit."

I held out my hand and she dropped the DropDisk into it. She held the small disk and her fingers in my palm and met my eyes.

"I hope you find yourself a good, Selfless young man."

Thanks to her endearing look and smile, I recognized she didn't mean the comment as an insult. She was likely in her mid-thirties and was using a compliment that had morphed into something snide since. Plastering on a smile, I responded with enthusiasm, "Anything but a Greed!"

"To the best partners," she said and let go of the disk. I held my smile until I turned away. I knew she hadn't meant to imply that I was a simp, but being reminded of the different categories of Mana Bank partners was always a bit depressing, regardless of intent. Sighing, I made my way to the receptionist.

"Fifteen hundred dollars more for the pictures. Five hundred if you plan to keep the outfit," the bored-looking receptionist said flatly as I approached. I looked down at the white silk shirt and off-white dress shorts before flinching. I'd forgotten all about them.

Making a face, I excused myself and immediately changed into my ripped jeans, black t-shirt, and 'vintage' jacket I'd worn to the shoot. I wish I could say they were old by design, but they were thrift store purchases. Then returning, I paid the other half of the money my parents had given me.

The receptionist took the disk and placed it into a slot beside the register before handing it back. "All good. You have full access. Have a wonderful day."

I put the disk in my pocket and then turned to watch Eva pose. The designer had chosen to dress her in a turquoise blouse and peach-colored skirt. The choice made her skin tone pop in a way that accentuated her stunning beauty even more. Arnando barked orders and Eva smoothly moved to follow. I hoped I had looked as good as she did up there.

There was a moment where I considered waiting for her, but I was tired and had her contact information. Plus, I'd spent the last two days chatting with her and was now competing against her for the picture of the day—which might make the conversation after the session awkward. Instead, I turned on my heels and left.

The shoot was on the fifth floor of the Merceda Sports Center in Toronto, and as I made my way down the stairs, I studied the tents and campers that filled the entire parking lot. Arnando probably had another ten to fifteen *days* of people lined up outside, and I couldn't help the new sigh that escaped unbidden. Sometimes this life felt like a rat race, an endless, self-defeating, pointless pursuit. All these people were competing for the same thing, to become a Mana Bank to a Hunter or the Stars—and I was one of them…

The real problem was that without enough popularity, you wouldn't get to pick the right Hunter. For me that was an active one—but for most it would be the one with the most star power. There were several horror stories out there about Portals and Pairings in general, which is what prevented most people from becoming Mana Banks.

Growling, I started jogging down the stairs. I knew better than to let negative thoughts rule like that. Mindfulness and finish-line thinking was the way to win in the end. I just needed to believe I would come out on top, and I would. Or at least that's what my school guidance counselor had said.

I jogged out of the door at the bottom, keeping my thoughts positive and a smile on my face. It felt good to be walking the opposite way of the long snaking line—like I had accomplished something that had meaning. My eyes were fixed on that long lineup when something—no, *someone*—ran into my chest.

Even as I registered the discomfort the collision had caused me, a waft of stale alcohol hit me in the face. At a glance, I could tell that the guy was drunk. On closer inspection, his yellowing skin and eyes suggested that he might be someone who operated in a constant state of drunkenness. I was no medical expert, but thought there was a name for the condition. Something to do with the liver.

The man's face started to go red as he looked around. Clearly still trying to process what had happened, but already stoked to anger. I decided to leave— not wanting to deal with an unreasonable drunken man. I glanced back, just to make sure he wasn't seriously hurt, and found him trying to throttle a kid in line while shouting. Thankfully, I didn't have to go back and help, since security was already rushing over.

Sighing, I doubled my pace and focused my eyes in front of me, not wanting the accident to happen again. It didn't take me long before I reached uncle Jarred's old, borrowed tow-camper. My parents were in chairs under the awning.

My mother, Clara, stood up at my approach. "How did it go?!"

"Why don't you see for yourself?" I answered, mirroring her excitement and fishing in my pocket for the DropDisk. I handed it to her, and she touched it to her phone. A moment later, she was flipping her finger over the screen and wearing a proud mothering smile. My dad, Gary, stood up after a time and looked over her shoulder. He wore a strained smile, which told me how he truly felt about my current pursuit, but at least he didn't voice his feelings again.

"So, which one is your favorite?" he asked instead. "Which one will have my son becoming a Mana Battery to the Stars?" I could hear the forced enthusiasm in his tone, but only because I knew him so well.

I appreciated his attempt.

"The accepted term is 'Mana Bank,' sweetie, Mana Battery is for Monster Cores turned into Mana Pools," my mom corrected for me. "You know the ones the Specialists use at work."

"The one on the boat in front of the Gate. With the Sapphire Staff over my shoulder," I answered, cutting off their sidebar. I didn't have to feign the genuine excitement in my voice, but I did avoid correcting the misconception that I was aiming to be a Mana Bank to a Star. It took a few minutes of flipping, but I could tell when my mom found the photo I was talking about, because her face lit up and her eyes widened.

"Oh, that's fantastic. You look so good!"

"Are you sure that won't confuse the Hero Awakened?" my dad asked as he studied the picture over her shoulder. He looked up at me, his eyes conveying the earnestness of his question. I hadn't looked at it from that perspective yet. Magic equipment was only used by Heroes, otherwise known as Hunters, so he was asking if a picture of me holding the fake gear would make me seem like one.

"That's a good point," I answered, feeling my smile slip. My hand came up toward my mouth but my mother placed her hand on mine, helping me to remember not to bite my nails.

"It's a great picture!" My dad said quickly after receiving an elbow from my mother's other arm. Clara mildly shook her head and flipped backward through the photos.

"If you're that worried, then I'd suggest this one," she said and turned her phone around. The display held a picture of me looking genuinely happy. I nodded, and she flicked a finger which sent the photo to her phone. "In fact, I might just hang this on a wall at home."

Smiling and slightly red in the face, I took back the DropDisk and started thinking about which photo I should post to SwiftGram first. I owed my small following an update. Would this photo be a good option for that post? It had been a few days since I told them about this shoot, but I'd definitely like to sit down and think about what I wanted to convey to them now. Most books I'd read agreed that as a small business, which was what I was trying to become, you needed to brand yourself.

The four-hour drive home to Windsor would give me the time I needed to think...

"Let's get out of here," I said as I motioned to the old Ford Escort in front of the trailer. We'd been here for two days already, and I had school on Monday morning, so my rush didn't seem to offend anyone. That or they were as eager to get home as I was.

I helped load up the chairs and grill, my mind whirling. What should my approach be for my upcoming post? Usually, I went for the eager and earnest approach, but my five hundred followers may be proof that it wasn't working. That or I had no hope because of my F-Rank—

"Stop it!" I scolded myself under my breath.

My followers didn't even know that the UNMH had scanned me as an F-Rank. I climbed into the back of the car and buckled in. Then I began creating a post on SwiftGram. I hadn't even uploaded the picture when a notification for a new message came in. I clicked the button and found a name I'd been seeing everywhere for the last two days.

I probably should have just blocked him after the flame war we had in the comments of a different post—but I figured one more follower wasn't a bad thing.

With a sigh, I clicked in, expecting the worst.

> The Shop: Hey, be honest,
> what would it cost for a one-
> time mana-connection?

I shook my head. This was not only a common request and considered beyond rude, but it had also been the exact topic I had been fighting with him over in the comments. The exact reason I needed popularity so I could pick the right Hunter to pair with.

I clicked over to The Shop's profile and found what I remembered. A relatively 'new' account, with low posts, low followers, no pictures, and a heavy number of follows. I reported the message and was about to flip back to my profile when another message came in.

> The Shop: You must have a pretty high-ranked Skill if you're hoping for a Selfless lifetime bond.

My jaw clenched as I read. He was taking my profile introduction, twisting it, insulting me, and using it to poke at me for a response. Unlike Morena, he clearly was calling me a simp or sub. My profile simply read I was looking for a lifetime bond to grow with. A true partnership bond… which many believed was something of a fairy-tale.

Before I could click the 'more actions' button and block the asshat, he sent another message.

> The Shop: All you stuck-up morons are the same. You all think you're hot shit, that you'll find a prince or princess charming out there for you! News flash, you'll probably get husked.

My eyes widened. Husking was the greatest fear of a Mana Pool Awakened like me. Essentially, the threat of losing your Gift and becoming an unAwakened. A husk of your former self. Most people who lost their Gift committed suicide shortly after because they felt out of place in a world full of Gifted. Even if ninety percent of those Gifted only had an unused Mana Pool…

Scientists theorized that having a Gift gave people a deeper connection with the current world. Like somehow it was an anchor. And while humans had survived for thousands of years before the Awakening, now everyone had a Gift otherwise known as a Skill.

That first pull from a Mana Pool always carried with it the greatest risk. So, everyone wanted someone who was going to be careful—going to take it slow and have the restraint to stop before permanent injury came to their Bank. Essentially, someone who either knew what they were doing already or at least had trained in the theory of it. The phenomenon of Husking was still pretty common, and the term 'Greeds' was coined to describe the people who became Mana Drunk upon the first pull. That's why one-time pulls were relatively rare—you just never knew what type of person you would get.

I knew I should let it go and just move on, but the comment hit a bit too close to home because it called my dream into question. Reiterated my fairy-tale aspirations. Personally, I knew my desire to be *a someone, and to make a difference,* was

20

a long shot. My urge to contribute to the fight against the Monsters wasn't probable, but I didn't want to be a Normie either.

One of the seven billion, and then some, who had a Mana Pool and just let it go to waste. Abbas' interview was a prime example of the desperate need for more active Mana Banks in this fight.

The Shop's comments cut extra deep because I was not even a high-ranked Mana Pool talent. No, I was an F-Rank, according to my assessment. This guy was a piece of shit. Plain and simple. Probably someone lucky, who Awakened with a Skill but no Pool—and thus thought himself above people like me.

Growling, I clicked the response box.

Alonzo Mars: What's your problem? Are you so ugly that no one wants to let you touch them? You're likely a Greed that doesn't know how to control his pull, and so anyone who has worked with you can't work with you anymore. So, instead, you come on here and pray to find a one-time Bank. Just to feel that rush of power again. Have you ever thought of the Banks you've hurt along the way? People like you disgust me.

I hit send hard, and the anger seemed to drain out of me a bit as I re-read my response.

Admittedly, it wasn't my best work. Insulting, yes, but this person was likely in a similar situation to mine. Everyone Awakened on their eighteenth birthday. The issue for me and people like The Shop was that on the *extreme* average, people Awakened with one Skill. I'm talking about one in hundreds of thousands awakened with dual Gifts. Meaning that most of the world only had a single one. There were rumors of people having a single Skill that didn't need Mana, but those may only be rumors. As far as I knew, each gift required Mana to use, and only if you Awakened with a Mana Pool and a secondary Skill could you be totally self-sufficient.

The only other way was to put yourself in situations of extreme stress, usually within Portals, and re-Awaken another Skill.

But those two situations were beyond rare… like rarer than Awakening two gifts to begin with. Except people could compound the odds in the re-Awakening by going into Portals over and *over* again. There were still further complications, too. Even if you got a good Skill, getting into a good Hunter University to train yourself on its usage wasn't a guarantee. All in all, that's probably what happened to this Shop character… Lucky enough to Awaken with a Skill other than a Mana Pool, but never properly trained.

The fact that ninety or higher percent of the population Awakened with a single Gift was also why people like me, who Awakened with only a Mana Pool and no secondary Skill to use it, were in high demand. The chance of re-Awakening was why so many of us Pools wanted to be a Bank. It might be rare—but it *did* happen.

It was the real reason I was getting pictures taken today and attempting to make a name for myself. Sure, I didn't have the biggest Mana Pool to start, but rumor said it could grow with the right partner. With someone who would be cautious and not husk me. After a few years and slow growth, I could contribute to the fight as a Bank. Or, *hopefully*, I would be one of the lucky few and re-Awaken a new Skill.

It was that or get a degree and work, which I was also pursuing—reluctantly.

I glanced at my parents in the front seat. They were the ones who insisted I get a degree. They were both Normies, otherwise known as people who had a mostly untouched Mana Pool. So, while they supported me in my dream, they didn't really understand it.

Gary, who was driving, smiled back at me in the mirror, which effectively took the edge off any of my remaining anger. They truly cared for me, and while I knew that the chances of becoming a Bank to a Hunter or a Star was slim, they wanted me to realize my dream. Gary just insisted I have a backup plan, which was why I was in my second year of Monster Material Management at Phoenix Academy.

My mother noticed my father and I smiling, and joined us with a wide, brilliant grin. Then she pointed to the traffic we were joining on our way out of the stadium. "Glad we got here so early, or you'd never have made it to the first day of summer semester on Monday!"

That was a very nice way of her saying that they both took a vacation to sit in a parking lot with me for the last three days. Even then, being here three days early hadn't made us anywhere near first in line.

"No kidding," I said and, in a much quieter voice, added, "Thank you both." I knew they both heard me, but they chose not to acknowledge it. Instead, Gary reached out and clasped Clara's hand. She squeezed back, and I returned to my phone to give them privacy.

A new message made my heart clench in my chest.

> The Shop: I'll see you around Brodie Flacarada.

My name on this account was Alonzo Mars. Brodie was my given name by my parents, but I'd decided long ago not to use it online. There were a multitude of reasons, but primarily amongst them were people finding me or my family through it.

I hurriedly reported The Shop again and then blocked and banned the account from my page. How had he found my real name?

Cold sweat ran down my back. Trying to be inconspicuous, I looked through my eyelashes at my parents. Should I tell them? I shook my head. I was an adult now, and a person finding my real name didn't mean anything. Right?

After checking all my privacy settings and account information to ensure it was private, I calmed down a little. Surely, this Shop was just trying to scare me or something. Maybe it was even an old highschool classmate, just trying to husk with me. Either way, I wouldn't let them.

I moved back to my profile and finished my post, consulting an app I had for trending tags.

CHAPTER 2

Monday, April 1st, 2069

"Good morning, students," Miss Chavez said from the front of the auditorium style classroom.

No one returned the greeting, and I wasn't the only one who took a sip of coffee. Chavez was my teacher for Portal Materials and Common Uses II, and she always had a habit of being a bit too high-energy. Since this was a late-night class and my final one of the day, I was just hoping to get through it—hence the extra-large cup of caffeine.

My only response, other than the sip of coffee, was a sigh. At least she wasn't making a poor attempt at April Fools' humor like my morning teachers.

I didn't think of Miss Chavez as particularly attractive, but I was clearly in the minority. This class was required for my bachelor's but was a common elective for many others. It only took a quick glance around the room to highlight the male to female ratio of the class's attendance and correlate just how many males enjoyed Chavez's' bubbly personality and appearance. I guess I could see the appeal. She wasn't hard to look at but was a bit too short for my tastes.

Not that a tall, too-young looking guy, with a single Awakened Skill and living at home with his parents really had room for tastes…

I shook myself off my tangent and took another gulp of coffee when I realized Chavez had continued speaking. I tuned back in as she said, "— the course curriculum is listed on the outline. If you didn't get an outline, they were available on my desk on your way in. If you lose yours, or prefer to save paper, you can download another one from your WhiteBoard Portal."

A hand shot into the air, and Chavez turned a withering stare at the offending student. "If you don't have access to your WhiteBoard, then you might want to drop this *second-year* course, since you clearly shouldn't be here."

The hand dropped faster than it went up and Chavez smiled sadly for just a moment and noted something on her clipboard. My gut twisted for the owner of that hand. I guess Chavez was done babying us, like she had in our first year. Still, it wasn't like getting access to your WhiteBoard Portal was anything difficult.

"That's a good enough segue, I suppose. I didn't want to start the class on this note—but—as you all just witnessed, this is a second year course. So, mistakes that you may have gotten away with last year, won't fly this year. As an example, things like capitalization on your reports. Everyone at this point of schooling is *aware* that Portal related Materials, Professions, and Creatures must be capitalized to distinguish them from their old world counterparts. Understood?"

Chavez used the same tone she had when rebuking the student who'd raised his hand. The class was eerily silent. Many people gave a shallow nod, not risking saying anything and becoming the target of Chavez's ire. She was normally so cheerful...

She smiled and the class drew in a collective breath of air. Like a stay of execution.

"Good, now that I've gotten that out of the way. Where was I? Oh right, last year, we focused on two things: the logistics of collecting Crystals, Ores, Flora, and Corpses commonly found in low-ranked Portals and...?" she let the question hang in the air.

A student in the first row put their hand up, and Chavez nodded at one of the few women in the room. "We also discussed the rarity of certain goods based on the Gifts or Skills needed to acquire them."

"Correct," Miss Chavez said. "Can you remind the class of what that means?"

"Sure," the front-row student answered and then, with a deep inhalation, continued. "It means that certain *adults* Awakened with Gifts unsuited for combat." The student emphasized 'adults' to further convey a point that everyone on Earth knew. Everyone eighteen or older Awakened.

She continued, after a brief pause to collect her thoughts since Chavez put her on the spot, "Those like the Hunters that fight on the front lines are rare. Even rarer if they Awakened a Mana Pool and a Gathering Skill. *If* they have no Pool, and only a single Gift, then they too need to use Mana Banks or Batteries to perform services, which increases the rarity of goods they collect."

I silently snorted a breath out of my nose. That wasn't the whole story. No self-respecting Mana Bank had chosen to work with *common* Gatherers in nearly fifteen years. Once a Gatherer with a proven Skill came about, some Banks did form partnerships for the money, but that was still less common. Mostly because, to date, not a single Mana Bank had ever re-Awakened a second Skill working with Gatherers.

For my part, I'd be willing but wanted to contribute more meaningfully. Plus...

Re-Awakening was the primary reason people *wanted* to risk their lives and become Mana Banks. Well, that was what I assumed—because that was what *I* wanted. Perhaps, I should give others more credit. I did also want to become a Mana Bank to make a difference, after all.

Still, to re-Awaken... Chavez coughed, taking me out of my daydream.

"Can anyone tell me what we call these individuals, and what percentage of the population Awakened as Gatherers?" Miss Chavez asked and then pointed out a new student as they began to raise a hand.

"We call them Specialists, usually. If ten percent of humanity Awakened with a Combat Gift, then another ten percent awakened with Gathering Gifts. However, it's far more common, at nearly double the amount, for Gatherers to have also gotten a Mana Pool."

The student almost stopped speaking then, but after scratching his chin he added, "The UNMH is still conducting research into the why of that phenomenon. This number was further skewed because of something else though…" the student faded off, clearly not remembering one of the exam answers from first year.

"Because some Awakened who feared the Monsters inside Portals chose to use Combat Skills for Gathering," Miss Chavez said. She nodded while the student she'd called on nodded in appreciation, seeming to recall that part of last year's lessons with the simple reminder. I wanted to sigh—those numbers were heavily contested and likely inaccurate.

Well, maybe they were accurate, but the Read-it forums, which I often perused, told a less biased tale—or, I guess, *I believed* they might tell something closer to the truth. People on Read-it claimed that at most ten percent of the population *total,* Awakened with Gifts that weren't Mana Pools—leaving ninety percent like me.

"The first student alluded to it, but what skews the number of Gatherers that work in Portals further, which does *also* help lower the rarity and cost of goods?" Miss Chavez asked and then pointed me out as I raised my hand.

"Many Mana Pool Awakened," I began using the more acceptable term for Normies. "—also enter Portals as part of Gathering Teams and Mine, Garden or Clean with regular gear or become Specialists with Enchanted Gear. Specialists can also use Mana Batteries more easily than Combat Hunters because they have less to fear from the Batteries running out mid-combat or breaking if overused."

"Correct," Miss Chavez said, gracing me with her beaming smile. "You did forget about the Lumberjacks, and Fishermen, but they rarely work with other Gatherers, so I guess that's a pretty common mistake."

"What was the reason Hunters and Specialists can't just pull Mana from the Mana Crystals?" someone from behind me asked their neighbor. I could tell it was meant to be a whisper, but unfortunately for them, an auditorium was meant to carry sounds, not muffle them.

Miss Chavez smiled at someone above me in the tiered seating, and I turned around in my seat trying to find the culprit of the 'whispered' question. Surely, the idiot shouldn't have made it to the second semester.

A group of five guys sat close together, one of them extremely red in the face. Two others gave him looks that threatened some good-natured ribbing for making them the center of attention. One even gave the offending boy a Charlie Horse.

Seeing that she wasn't likely to get an answer from the young men, Miss Chavez opened the question up to the class by saying, "Anyone?"

She didn't bother repeating the question, since if she'd heard it, it was likely they all had. No hands shot up, and I sighed. Come on. The faster we got this over with, the faster we got out of the first late-night class. Everyone knew that first classes were just an introduction. I was about to raise my hand when another student beat me to it. The same girl in the front row who had answered Chavez's first question.

Once indicated, the girl said, "The Mana is different than personalized Mana from within your pool. It's theorized that there may be a way to harness it, but currently all humans can do to extract Wild Mana is burn the Crystals and convert the intense heat into energy."

"Good," Miss Chavez said with a beaming smile. "What's the difference in Crystal grades to energy output?"

Another young man, a single row in front of me, raised his hand. "It's unknown for some of the highest ranks of Crystals, but a single B-Rank Crystal is something akin to a Fusion Reactor. C-Rank would be a Nuclear Reactor, I think. Then D and E-Rank are essentially Electric Dams of varying sizes. F-Ranks are just Gas-Powered Generators for a single intact Crystal."

"With those levels of Power contained in a single Crystal, why do Guilds not always mine low-rank Crystals whole?" Miss Chavez asked. This time, no one raised a hand, and so I did. She motioned at me again, giving the same appreciative look she'd given the girl in the front row. The only other person to answer multiple times so far.

"Sharding is done for time efficiency, as well as demand. Just like you don't need Jet Fuel in a car—some engines can only handle Sharded Crystals of F-D-Rank. However, the more prevalent reason is the time efficiency for the Guilds. Each Guild only has so many Hunters that they can field. When Gatherers enter a Portal, those Hunters are often required to be present to protect them. Part of Union rights. So, instead of wasting too much time harvesting full Crystals of low rank, they'd rather get what Ores and Crystal Shards they can and move on to the next Portal."

"Excellent, once again!" Miss Chavez said. "Anything else you'd all like me to go over?"

She paused for a moment, then seeing no questions or further hands in the air, sighed and held up a piece of paper, which had been one of a larger stack that was on her desk. Most students had grabbed one on their way in, and I was among them. "As you can see from the Course Outline, we'll be moving on to the actual resources and how to recognize them this semester. We'll start each lesson with ways to identify the items and spot fakes before we move onto quality-grading tips and tricks. Finally, we'll discuss uses and economic implications of availability and large purchases of said material. Understood?"

The student that had put his hand up earlier to ask about WhiteBoard access grumbled something I couldn't hear from my spot, but thankfully Chavez was the type of teacher that didn't like interruptions. "A bit louder for the class, *Mister Hessir.*"

There was a long pause before the clearly embarrassed student grumpily called out, "What's the point of learning how to *identify* material if someone the System gifted an Eye Skill can just look at them and tell?"

"Does anyone want to tell *Frank* here what's wrong with that *assumption*?"

No hands went up, and so I eventually put mine up again, wanting desperately for the class to move along. Ms. Chavez didn't take her amused but also scolding look off Frank but still indicated in my general direction.

"The existence of a System is still largely unproven, and people who Awakened with Eye Skills with the ability to Identify Items, Weapons, Enchants and Portal Materials are exceptionally rare. It's why the UNMH Awakening Assessment is done by machines that are far from accurate."

"Exactly," Ms. Chavez confirmed. "If people like that were common, then there would certainly be no need for this class, but since they aren't, and all of these wonderful people are here—I think we can *assume* that this class has *some* value, is that not correct, Mister Hessir?"

Frank Hessir didn't respond, and even from here I could see his head hanging down in embarrassment. I felt slightly bad for the part I played in his scolding, but thankfully Ms. Chavez did get the class back on track, thanks to my *noble* sacrifice. "Does everyone understand the curriculum for this class?"

Chavez took the late-night class's silence as agreement and moved on. "Normally, today would just be that recap and an introduction to each other before I let you go, but I can't think of a better beginning to our lesson than watching the news segment from last night."

She clicked around on her desk in a professionally practiced manner before the screens behind her changed from a black chalkboard to uniform blue and then resolved into a picture. It was clearly a news segment from the UNMH, and I leaned forward in my seat. The video was labeled, "With the New Permanent Portal in Qatar: Is Hero Retirement a Pipedream?"

I looked around to see if other people were as lost as I was. Most of my news came from SwiftGram or SmileBook, which often clipped videos such as this into smaller sections, highlighting points that may or may not be contextual. Still, I didn't think I had seen anything from this video yet. That was probably because of what Chavez had claimed; it was aired last night. Someone would have had to be quick on the editing to have it up in under twenty-four hours. Plus, after The Shop's scare a few days ago, I was kind of avoiding social media until I figured out how my name leaked. Or if the account belonged to a high school 'friend.'

Well, other than responding to comments on my post from a few nights ago. *Okay,* and I'd also checked who got the picture of the day for the last five days.

The victor for *my* photoshoot had been none other than the gorgeous Eva, who had been right after me in line. I wanted to hate her but instead had sent a quick congratulatory message. Normally I would have studied the picture, appreciating her curves and the way she worked them for the camera, but knowing that she got the chance I coveted, it was hard to keep my internal dialogue polite and positive.

I'd tried hard before distracting myself with how many new likes and followers I'd received from my own results.

Seventy-five likes and five new followers. It wasn't anything to brag about, but growth was growth. Chavez had been talking again, and I missed it as I ruminated on my last few days of freedom before school restarted. I should probably start hitting the gym right before this class if I wanted to pay attention till nine pm.

The news segment jingle was what snapped me out of my own daydreaming and tuned me back into the video as it started playing.

"For years, Mana Crystals have been the safe investment for Heroes, but a sudden spike in mid-rank Crystals availability may have changed everything," Fleece, the host and anchor, of the segment stated as an opening call to action. I knew it was a shock and awe tactic but still felt my gut clench at the statement.

"Could this be the next Gold Crash? Let's go to Echo in the field for more."

The LED lighting of the studio changed to the turquoise glow of high-grade Light Stones. Echo, a relatively well-known retired hero, was center-frame of the shot. Echo was tall with silver hair and looked to be in his thirties despite being at least *eighty*. His eyes were a vibrant green, and he was clearly wearing make-up to accentuate them and his cheekbones.

A constant discordant clanking could be heard from the video, and I immediately recognized the sounds of Miners doing their work.

"That's right, Fleece. We may be looking at a drastic market shift as supply of mid-quality Mana Crystals flood the market. If you look behind me, you'll notice I'm in the newest permanent Portal in Qatar. What you hear is, of course, the sound of Miner's Picks and tools. What isn't immediately apparent from your sneak peek is that this is the fifth day of continuous Mining."

The camera panned over dirt-covered Miners as they worked. Everyone, whether they were male or female, was well muscled and sweating profusely. A few people in the class made noises that indicated disgust. I pursed my lips and lightly shook my head. Mining was considered a high-paying, low-brow job that required no intelligence to perform. For some reason, this meant that Mana Pool Awakened Miners were looked down on by people who considered themselves intelligent. My thoughts on the matter were that the *real* smart ones were the ones doing what they needed to do to take care of their family and responsibilities.

My dad was a Miner, and while he often came home bone weary, with just enough energy for a meal, shower and to crawl into bed, it paid extremely well. By the continued sounds of mockery, I was in the minority of people who considered Mining a respectable job…

The camera returned to Echo, who was now walking through the Mining cavern. The camera had panned out to show nearly his entire body. He was wearing a silver suit that matched his hair, with a vibrant blue undershirt.

"Right now, I bet you're thinking, 'But Echo, they can't have mined continuously for five straight days. Everyone knows that Permanent Portals don't reset resources.' You're right, and until a few days ago, that *was* a known fact, but not only have the Draconic Kobolds that inhabit this place respawned overnight, so have the Crystal Deposits!"

"Wait!" a student near the front exclaimed. "Draconic Kobolds? Is this the Permanent B-Ranked Portal?"

Chavez paused the video, giving the young girl a stern look that rebuked her for not raising a hand. Still, after only a moment to get the point across, she waggled her brows and smiled. "That's exactly it! It turns out that fighting a Dragon truly yields amazing results!"

The class gasped in unison. I couldn't speak for the rest of my peers, but my gasp was because I was not only terrified of the B-Rank Portal having a Break, but also imagining the value of such a Portal. That would be like having a money tree in your backyard. The other student had hit the nail on the head. *Each B-Rank Crystal* was like a fusion reactor! Not that Echo said these were B-Ranked Crystals. In fact, he'd said mid-rank, which meant anything from D to C-Rank, but even if they were just mid-rank they'd be extremely valuable. I wondered if this was owned by the United Nations Monster Hunters, UNMH for short, or by the Sayyad Guild in Qatar…

This Portal was becoming more and more of a goldmine, and if it was owned by Sayyad and not the UNMH, I worried that they might not protect it well enough against Monster Breaks. I could further see the already war-ridden Middle East breaking into far larger conflict over the thing.

My mind raced with the terrifying possibilities and the amazing benefits of this new Permanent Portal. Permanent Portals were already rare, at less than one percent of found Portals. Likely less than point one percent, since the world had hundreds of thousands of Portals covering its surface—many of which were too far outside of civilized areas to be explored in the twenty-four years since the Advent.

That was its own larger issue that I wouldn't get to think about, since Ms. Chavez restarted the video.

"While this sounds great, Specialists are immensely worried. A permanent source of Crystals of this grade could create a Bear Market. This, of course, means that 'safe' investments into Crystals or companies that deal in Mana Technologies could go belly up, Fleece."

The screen became a dual video as Fleece came back onto the left side. "Echo, I think what most of our viewers want to know isn't about the Bear Market—but about whether this Permanent Portal is safe?"

"Good question, and something that has been talked about a great deal in the last week, Fleece. As our loyal viewership might already know, this Portal is owned by Sayyad, but the UNMH stepped in a few days ago to ensure that proper practices of creating Monster Fields around Permanent Portals would be maintained."

Fleece nodded along and as soon as Echo finished speaking, he followed up with a new, clearly rehearsed question. "So, what measures is the Sayyad Guild taking, Echo?"

My mind drifted back to the PR Manager that had sat with Abbas. Surely, he was working overtime lately. "The Sayyad Guild is sparing no expense, Fleece. Last time I was outside, trucks were arriving hourly with A-Ranked Portal Metals and Building Supplies. This Field is going to be the largest and strongest ever created."

I noticed that they didn't show the outside of the Portal to the viewer, which could mean nothing, but did make me slightly suspicious about the clearly contrived dialogue between the Anchor and the Reporter.

"That's all the new information on the Field and Portal, Fleece. Let's head on over to Admin and see what the Hunter Association Leader has to say on this subject." Echo said, segueing back into the story about the Crystals.

The screen changed from split to full screen Fleece for a transition. "Thank you, Echo. I know I'm not the only one who wishes that Portal popped up in my backyard, am I right?" Fleece said, mirroring my earlier thoughts about its immense value but adding a tone of humor to play to the audience and diffuse the tension from a moment ago.

He chuckled to himself, and the class chuckled along with him. I didn't join them. The rank alone was terrifying, but the fact that the UNMH showed up to ensure anything meant that this Portal was beyond *unique*. Even more so than before, I worried over the state of the countries and Guilds in the Middle East. Surely, this Portal could cause a war. So, re-thinking of it popping up in my backyard made me shiver.

Fleece continued, "This next clip is from a press conference in which Admin answered concerns over this new permanent mid-rank Mana Crystal supply."

The camera shifted again, showing a press conference underway. We didn't hear the question, but Admin was sitting at the center of a long table near the front of a full room. Behind him was a blue screen that cycled through numerous logos and companies that were clearly sponsors or partners of the UNMH.

Admin was what had been repeatedly described as a 'grandfather on steroids.' The few ladies in the classroom made noises of appreciation, reminding me of his other nickname. GILF, or Grandfather I'd Like to *Husk*.

"Concerns of market crashes are premature. UNMH is carefully watching the Stock Exchange and the ZMU price point. It has risen eight points over the last week, showing an increase despite what *experts* have been saying. I caution Hunters and Citizens from jumping to conclusions based on rumors surrounding Mana Crystals. A mass sale of stock will certainly lower the value of current Mana Crystal stock, but our experts here at UNMH believe that a more consistent stock of mid-grade Crystals is something the world desperately needs. This is a simple issue of supply and demand economics. As the price point lowers, access to Mana Crystals will become more available to a wider audience. This greater access will lead to a boom in innovation and quality of life across the globe as more people gain access to resources. This is not a Doomsday, it's an Independence Day—a time for celebration."

The screen turned off and all eyes in the room turned to Chavez, who was raising a finger from the stop button on her Holodesk. "There's more to the story, and I encourage you to watch it on your own. Still, for the purposes of our discussion today, that's about all we need. My question to you is, from a Portal Material and Economic standpoint, what do you all think?"

There was a moment of hesitation as people took in her meaning. Clearly she didn't want the discussion to get sidetracked and focused on Portals, and the danger or wealth it might represent. After the gears of the student's brains finished turning, a few hands went up. Chavez called on a girl from earlier. The one sitting near the front of the class. "I think Admin is blowing smoke up the country's ass. The UNMH is in full damage control mode, trying to avert a panic. He practically said everything but 'fake news' up there."

The class chuckled, and Chavez smiled before responding. "Very astute, but what's the core of the issue?"

I raised my hand after a few moments when no one else did. Chavez indicated me with a point. People in the class turned to look at me for the third time, which made me a bit uncomfortable, but I gave my answer all the same. "The market on Portal Materials is volatile and can change drastically based on current economic factors."

Chavez raised an eyebrow, holding up the textbook. "Thank you, Doctor Beast," she said as she pointed to the author's name of the book. I flushed, and she chuckled. "That is the textbook wording of the problem, but what does it *mean*, Mister...?"

I coughed sheepishly and cleared my throat. "Flacarada," I answered her final question with my last name and then continued, "to me it means that a new Dungeon opening can change the value of Materials. Since we can't predict Dungeons—"

"*Portals* are the proper term, Mister Flacarada, and I expect you to use *proper* terminology in my classroom," Chavez interjected, looking around to include all the students in that rebuke.

I nodded.

"Right, sorry, *Portals*. Since we can't predict Portal openings, we can't forecast expected values of the materials inside the Portals. We can't create the necessary logistics ahead of time for capitalizing on these new arrivals, either. Add to that how many Portals are outside of human reach? Well, we basically must have workers on hand that can travel to any given reasonable location and establish the necessary outposts, roads, and other infrastructure. None of this accounts for the geo-political issues of Portals showing up in locations that are politically problematic. No one needs more cartel or blood-diamond equivalents. Plus, the Magical Market and its Commerce have only been around for twenty years, so we likely haven't even discovered everything of value."

"Good enough!" Chavez stated. "Thank you, Brodie." She clearly had consulted her class list to get my first name, since I hadn't interacted with her overly much last year. "Homework—" she began and then cut off as the entire class groaned, "—or I can keep you here for the allotted class time?"

Rustling was suddenly audible as everyone including me went into bags and pulled out Tablets, Computers, Phones, or other scheduling devices. In moments, Chavez had everyone's full attention again. "I figured," she continued with clear humor in her voice. "For the next class I want a single page assessment of a Portal Material that is commonly found and used in industry. Then I want a quick forecast of what could increase its value or decrease it. Dismissed!"

Chavez clicked a few buttons on her Holodesk and the black of the chalkboards returned. Students started to stand, and many rushed out of the room. A small number went to introduce themselves to Chavez, and I mentally labeled them as the try-hards as I walked by and out into the hallway.

This was my last class today, and since it ended a whole two and a half hours early, I had some decisions to make. Knowing that this was a possibility, I hadn't packed a dinner and instead planned to grab something with friends on campus. I pulled out my phone and messaged Dave, my closest friend who stayed in residence:

Class is done. You still in yours?

Dave Disaster: Nah, didn't bother. I just printed the Outline from Whiteboard. Want to come by the dorms? I'm making my famous iron Grilled Cheeze with Amazing Bread and American Singles.

His response was almost instant, and I smiled as I hurriedly typed out my own. I would love a Grilled Cheeze, who wouldn't?

I also confirmed he was still in the same dormitory as the previous year. Turns out he was now on the third floor since the first and second were for first years. I began making my way to room three hundred and five of the dormitory.

I took a shortcut between the Quad and Cafeteria, as I opened up SwiftGram to see if I had any more followers or likes. There weren't many people on the path, and I assumed that was because this was more of an alley, which contained dumpsters.

Still, it was by far the fastest way to the dorms. Only if it was winter would I take the paths through the buildings. Since the snow had recently melted, the path was wet and the night air chill but not unbearable.

Even with the climate shift after the Portals began arriving, Canada still suffered from short summers and long winters. Far milder in winter if you listened to the old folks complain and the news channels boasting, but still long. At least in comparison to other countries.

The climate shift wasn't anything huge, in the grand scheme of the planet. Not like the Global Warming scare history said it should have been. In essence, the Advent made hot areas slightly cooler and cold areas slightly warmer. That change did melt the ice caps for example, but the fear that the land masses would flood was somehow diverted. The why of that was unclear, since according to all science it should have happened. It just didn't.

Shaking off that first-grade history lesson, I registered as a guest at the security desk and made my way up the stairs to Dave's room. It was already propped open with the deadbolt, and so I entered with a knock to at least warn him.

"If you're rocking out with your cock out, I'm reserving the right to take pics," I called out loudly as I pushed the door open. "I just got done doing a shoot with the best in the business. I'm basically a professional now, so you don't need to be shy."

Room three-o-five was an exact duplicate of Dave's room from first year. Or at least the shared kitchen and common area with four doors off it was.

From behind one of those doors—the one that had led to a shared bathroom last year—Dave shouted, "I knew you only wanted me for my body. Taking a shit, be right out."

"Maybe slip into something a little more comfortable while you're in there," I yawned. "Don't make me come over here and leave with nothing."

My only reply was an impressively loud improvised fart that I could hear from across the entire apartment.

Touché.

I rolled my eyes and made my way over to the couch. The TV was on and displaying the home screen of an XStation Next. I debated starting up a game of Monster Piece Z or something but grabbed the remote and changed it over to MeTube. Once there, I searched for the news segment title we'd watched in Miss

Chavez's class. Once the results returned, I moved the selector over the first entry and hit play.

The time of nearly sixty minutes on the video let me know that I'd selected the full segment and not just the piece about Mana Crystals, but I didn't bother exiting back to the search results. I was a bit behind on current topics thanks to the photoshoot, and now I was having to play catch up on current events.

Of course, as videos tend to do on MeTube, I was forced to watch an ad. The screen showed clips of well-known S-Ranked Hunters battling Monsters, and then one in particular known as Mr. America woke up in bed. The commercial cut quickly away to him coming down the stairs, with his shirt still off, and moving about his kitchen. "Even heroes need help waking up in the morning. Get Vitamin SSS today, it's what the pros trust!"

Mr. America tilted his head back and presumably took one of the Vitamins and a swig of a liquid in a coffee cup. He then looked into the camera with his ocean blue eyes and smiled. "Who knows, with Vitamin SSS you might just Awaken a power like mine!"

Corny commercials like these were the new norm, since the Advent and marketing shifts. Thankfully, it was short, or I might have thrown the remote at Mr. America. Awakening a Combat Skill was already rare, but to try to sell a Vitamin with the notion of it helping Awaken an S-Rank Skill was beyond frustrating. The chances of S-Ranked Skills Awakening were a miniscule percent of a percent.

I managed to unclench my fists from around the remote, and thanks to the news segment starting, I lowered it from behind my head. Huskin' stupid marketing, if you asked me. Vitamin SSS—more like Vitamin Mana Pool, here we come. It probably wasn't even made with Portal Materials…

"Good evening and welcome to Worldwide News at six," the anchor, Fleece, said. "Top news today is once again focused on new UNMH satellites helping estimate how many Portals remain undiscovered."

A corner of the screen showed the new satellites that were made from Portal Materials, or at least a rendition of them, behind Fleece. The man continued giving a bit of context to the report. "Current UNMH estimates are even more optimistic about the Portals that seem to have opened beneath the oceans. Currently, less than one percent of the hundreds of thousands of Portal signatures the satellite discovered shows living Monsters escaping. It is believed by UNMH Researchers that only a few Portal Monsters are suited for life under the Sea.

"And yet, as more and more Portal signatures light up the specialized cameras on the satellites, scientists finally must admit that there is far more of our World that humans never conquered than we'd like to have believed. Now with the estimate of nearly two hundred thousand unreachable and undiscovered Portals, the UNMH must concede that we, as a species, can only lay claim to about one-third of the planet."

I listened to Fleece with half an ear. This wasn't truly news since the estimates on Portals were constantly shifting. As were the theories as to why the unreachable Portals that were in the ocean weren't overwhelming us with

Monsters already. It was a long-held theory that most Monsters drowned during Breaks or were crushed by the pressure.

The next few pieces were kept somewhat local—meaning the Greater Toronto Area, which Windsor was only tenuously considered a part of. Each segment spoke about the graduating classes of high school students. Or the kids who'd just turned eighteen! Each piece focused on those adults that had the highest potential to move on to Hunter Academies. The fact that high potentials were anyone from D-Ranked Awakened up to a single A-Ranked, showed the truth of my earlier thoughts on Mr. America's commercial.

The Greater Toronto Area was home to nearly ten million people, and not a single eighteen-year-old Awakened with an S-Rank Skill. In truth, news like this was very common and seemed somewhat boring in comparison to the first undiscovered Portal estimates Fleece made and the small clip of a permanent Portal in class. I continued to listen with half an ear, while simultaneously going through Chavez's course syllabus on my phone's Whiteboard App. It was probably about fifteen minutes before I heard the toilet flush, and not even five seconds after, that Dave exited the bathroom in his boxers—not even having pretended to turn on the tap to wash his hands.

Dave was a tall young man, with blonde hair that bordered on platinum and an extremely skinny frame—which his current near-naked state only emphasized. His skin was pale enough that I'd be concerned for him on a sunny day—and his eyes were a greyish blue.

"Sup Bro-deez," Dave said by way of greeting. "Whatcha watching?"

"Local news," I answered. "We've already got homework from Chavez."

"Husk dude, that blows. Well not the Chavez part—I'd let her husk me, if you know what I mean. Literally break my Mana Pool if I got to be that close to her." I must have made a face because he gave me a raised eyebrow. "What? She not looking as good as last year?"

"She's as bubbly as ever…"

"And as *perky*?" Dave asked, his emphasis followed by waggling his eyebrows suggestively. I rolled my eyes before shrugging noncommittally. He took that as an affirmative. "Dude, you know you wouldn't say no to some after school 'tutoring'! I wish I had her for my electives."

"Good thing it's required for my course, because from the queue to get into the class, I needed that priority registering thanks to people who share your way of thinking."

"See? Total smoke show, the mob agrees with me, and if there's one thing I've learned in my long years on this earth, it's that when shit goes down you always want to be on the side of the mob." Dave had only let his butt touch the other couch cushion for a second before he hopped back to his feet. "Right, Grilled Cheezies!" he said excitedly.

"Wash your hands," I said pointedly and then chuckled when I saw his cheeks flush slightly red. He made his way to the sink and used the dish soap there to lather up.

"I just moved in and don't even have a roommate yet, so like I don't got no soap in the bathroom yet, k?" he mumbled as an excuse. I just let him have that one and instead focused on the other side of his comment.

"No roommate? You think you'll have this whole place to yourself then?" I asked, feeling jealous of the dude's family wealth and, by extension, his freedom.

"Nah, I'm guessing that there'll be some shifting going on after the first week. Remember last year when Wayne Bruce moved out of my room because he didn't like how many people I had over?"

"Oh right. Whatever happened to Man Bat?" I asked, recalling the nickname we had for the rather prudish individual.

"He dropped out, I think?" Dave said as he got out the bread, cheese, and iron to start making us food.

"—let's go to reporter Skulk in the field to find out more about this gruesome murder." The TV cut off Dave's and my conversation. Well, it didn't exactly cut us off, but the mention of *murder* had us both turning to the screen with interest.

"If you've been following along, this marks the fifth murder attributed to the same killer here in New York. The police have yet to release the information on the victim but have confirmed that the M.O. of the killer fits with several other bodies found in similar conditions." Skulk wore a black suit and even had a black half-mask covering his face all the way up to the bridge of his nose. The only parts visible on his zoomed in face were his jet black hair and brown eyes. He likely wouldn't have made a great reporter if it wasn't for his soft, menacing voice. It sounded like a whisper from a dark figure right behind you and just fit with this kind of horror story.

"The man found in an alleyway a few days ago is the fifth in a string of murders that span back over the last few months. Police warn citizens in the area to stay inside after dark whenever possible and urge anyone who might have information on the perpetrator or victims of the previous crimes to come forward.

"This suspect has a particularly grisly and chilling calling card, leaving his victims Husked or *Skill-less*, physically beaten and heartless without a single incision on the body. Police believe that the individual is using a Skill and powering it with the victim's Mana Pools, since each one was a relatively high-leveled single-Gift Awakened."

"That's code for common Mana Pool gifts in the mid C-Ranks," Dave commented, adding context that I already parsed together. I just nodded and kept listening intently.

"There are some similar cases in other states that make local authorities worry that this killer may be on the move. The trail stretches south through Pennsylvania, Virginia, and North Carolina, making authorities worry that he may have already exited New York. They also warn that his timeline is progressively speeding up and urge all citizens in the area to be vigilant and aware but also want to reassure citizens that their special Hunter task-force is on the case."

"Good thing that's happening so far from us," Dave chimed in as the news segment ended with a wide-view shot of a dark alleyway between two buildings that could have been anywhere in the world. Dave's eerily timed comment paired with such a shot made me shiver.

Sure, the events on the news happened in New York, which was nearly the entire province of Ontario and country line away, but that shot of the alley could have been the same one I walked through to get here. Or close enough. I looked to Dave, who was now busily making grilled cheese, and said, "You don't think he could keep coming north, then?"

"What? You think a murderer's going to chance crossing a border?" Dave asked distractedly.

I nodded and felt the goosebumps my internal thoughts raised stop prickling. Dave was right, and I was just probably thinking too hard on it. Probably because of how creepy Skulk's voice made the news sound like the killer would be right behind me as soon as I walked outside.

The news continued speaking of more world events. I only got a chance to listen with half an ear because Dave said, "Still, I can't believe you want to risk your Skill, man. Getting husked is a real possibility, even with a good partner."

"I know that, man, but like if you don't take the risk—how the hell are you ever going to become a Hunter?" I retorted playfully. This was a common argument between us. Mostly because Dave did want to become a Hunter but was too scared to take the risk I was. Those first uses of Mana Pools just ended in Skill breakage or damage far too often.

Dave stopped making the grilled cheese and took a deep breath, which let me know that this time he wanted a more serious conversation on the subject. "Brodie, I know you're determined to become a Bank, but do you remember the day you turned eighteen?"

Of course I did. The moment a light illuminated from within my chest, and I suddenly felt it. I closed my eyes remembering that moment, remembering the euphoria of receiving a Skill. "Yeah, it's cliché, but how can anyone forget the moment they can finally *see.*"

"That's what I mean, Bro. I know that it's now just something we all intrinsically understand and are used to—that connection to something more. I just—" Dave floundered for a moment, clearly lost for words. With a sigh, he spoke plainly, "Why risk losing that? To use your own analogy—why go up to a guy with a laser and minimal training to improve your eyesight, when he might make you blind?"

It wasn't Dave's finest metaphor, but I did understand it. This was a conversation I'd had many times with my parents. It was why they had 'untouched' Mana Pools. It was why most of the world did. How could you risk losing that connection? How could you return to being a 'true' Normie again.

Smiling sadly, I shrugged at Dave. Softly, I asked, "Do you know of another way to contribute to the fight? A better way to re-Awaken?"

Dave went silent after that, and I tuned back to the MeTube news video. After a bit more talk from the anchor, on the last video about Wildlife Evolutions, the familiar start to the segment I watched in Chavez's class sounded out, and I truly tuned fully back into the TV while pulling out my tablet to make a few notes.

Dave joined me about midway through the piece and handed over a plate with a sandwich and a healthy glob of ketchup. I could tell by his sheepish smile he was somewhat apologizing for his earlier question.

"Man, this Portal is husking crazy, right?" Dave said quickly when he saw an opportunity to fully change the subject. He used his bitten grilled cheese to indicate the screen. "Can you imagine how much the Sayyad Guild will make owning that thing?"

"I'm more worried about whether a Monster Field can even contain it!" I interjected, thankful for the return to our normal banter. I paused the video.

"Good point, but the UNMH being onsite means they'll take it away if Sayyad doesn't meet the criteria."

"Sure, but like didn't Abbas say they fought a husking Dragon, dude?"

Dave shivered and shook his head. "It could have been an anomaly or something. The UNMH rarely gets a reading that wrong, right?"

"No clue, I've never been in a Portal before."

"Me either," Dave said around a bite of his grilled cheese.

Other than his continued interruptions to voice his desire for a Portal like the one in Qatar to pop up in his parent's estate, he watched along quietly with me. The rest of the piece that I hadn't seen yet spoke to two 'experts' in economics, who both claimed that this could be the start of the end—or similar apocalyptic statements.

I noted their names when the segment ended, so I could look them up later, and then paused the remainder of the video to give my sandwich my full attention. Soon Dave and I were playing Monster Piece Z, an online MMORPG where you could join parties and quest as a powerful Hunter. Its setting was present day Earth and allowed Mana Pool Awakened like us to fictiously live out our dreams.

Before I knew it, my watch read nine pm and I groaned. "My parents will be expecting me to be getting on a bus. I gotta get going."

"Dude, why don't you just crash here tonight?" Dave said and pointed to the right-most of the three doors that used to lead to bedrooms in his old room. I assumed they still did here.

"Husk, if I'd known I would have packed a change of clothes and a toothbrush," I answered, truly meaning the words. "Tomorrow?"

"As long as no one moves in. Or you know, if a girl wants the old Dave Disaster special."

"Yeah, how many girls did you have over last year so you could 'give 'er the D'?" I asked pointedly.

"Too many to count, Bro."

"So, none?"

"Well, Rebecca came for dinner that one time," Dave countered.

"So, still none staying the night?" Dave's red face was answer enough, and I chuckled as I patted his shoulder. "It ain't like I'm any better," I added to assuage his hurt ego.

"Yeah, but you live at home and the girls are *still* all over you," Dave said sulkily.

"No, they aren't!"

"Man, now I *know* you're delusional. Get out of my room before I punch you."

I laughed good-naturedly even though I still disagreed with my friend's assessment. Then I made my exit giving him a bro hug, which was slightly uncomfortable since he was still bare chested and in his boxers.

"Send me a text with your schedule," I said as I opened the door. "I'll check if we have any classes together on my limo ride home."

"Yeah, enjoy your extra-wide, extra-tall, earthquake-simulating stretch limo, bro!" Dave scoffed, even as I heard him resume playing Monster Piece Z.

I made my way back downstairs and then, thanks in large part to the news segment and Skulk's creepy voice, decided to take the long way through the buildings toward the bus stop. It only added maybe five minutes and before I knew it, I was looking across the street toward the under-tunnel of the bus stop. I was just making my way across the campus crosswalk when a shadow separated itself from a nearby wall. I spun to face the man who was wearing a far too thick black jacket for this time of year.

Eyes trained on the man, I spun again, head now canted over a shoulder and increased my pace. I made it another two steps before the guy pulled a terrifyingly familiar-shaped object from a holster or pocket near his waist. He kept the object close to his side, but its outline was still clear.

"Brodie Flacarada, we told you we'd be seeing you," he said as he adjusted the pistol at his side, pointing it in my direction.

I froze. The matte steel of the gun had little to reflect against the backdrop of the dark-garbed man. My breath hitched in my throat, my heart hammered in reply as my eyes dilated at the sight of the muzzle, tucked in close to his black jacket, trained on me. The gaping opening of the barrel put all the surrounding darkness to shame. It was the blackness of death. I wanted to run, but my legs felt numb. I might have managed to escape if I hadn't been looking over my shoulder and seen the weapon. Maybe, even if given a few more seconds, I would have built up the courage to try and sprint away, but soon enough the man reached me and drew in close, pressing the gun discreetly into my side.

It was only then that the man's words caught up to me. He said my name. My real, *full* name. Terror crept into the edges of my vision.

My fear morphed when the sensation of the hard metal pistol dug into my abdomen just below my ribs. The man didn't even bother speaking again as he draped an arm around my back and latched onto my other arm's bicep, effectively trapping my right arm between his body and mine, and my left arm with his grip. He then steered me away from the bus stop's tunnel and back across the street. My brain attempted to find a means of escape, but the painful sensation of steel under my ribs continuously reminded me I was a finger twitch away from being bullet ridden.

As if the man sped up or time skipped throughout the campus, soon enough the very alley I had cut through earlier today came into view. We were heading directly toward it.

My usually active thoughts were nothing but loud static.

CHAPTER 3

Monday, April 1st, 2069

"Why me?" I asked stupidly, my voice trembling in a way I didn't like but wasn't in control of. I felt a surge of pride that I got words out but immediately brow beat myself for that feeling. My life was at risk, and I needed a way to escape, not useless questions.

"I already told you twice now. Did you think you're special? That you get to skate through life without consequences? Maybe the third time's the charm. We told you we'd be seeing you soon, Brodie Flacarada. Well," the black-garbed man responded, jamming the gun deeper into my ribs, forcing out a grunt of pain, "here we are." His voice was colder than the receding chill of the Canadian winter.

"I pissed you off? That's what this is about?" I answered and then realized what he must be referring to. This was The Shop from SwiftGram. I blinked a few times, trying to decide if that was a good thing. Thanks to the news article, I had feared this was the serial killer, but surely a disgruntled Swiftie was better to deal with, right?

My brain couldn't truly decide, and The Shop didn't respond to my squeaked question. I was left floundering with my own stupid mental back and forth. Surely, I should be thinking about more pressing concerns, like the gun currently digging into my side.

We entered the alley, and soon took a turn I didn't know existed, moving further off the already less-frequented shortcut and into the deeper recesses of the backs of the school buildings. I tried to stiffen up and drag my feet, but The Shop simply walked a bit more purposefully, half dragging and half carrying me.

"Come on man, you don't want to do this!" I shouted over the sound of my rubber soles scraping on asphalt. The pressure of the gun in my side withdrew, and for a split second I thought I'd gotten through to the man with my simple plea, but then something hard and sharp smashed into the back of my head.

My world spun, and I lurched forward as he released his hold on my arm. Thanks to the hit, and without the support he was giving me, I took three stumbling steps before gracelessly crashing face first into the wet alley asphalt.

I fought to stay conscious and either won against the intrusive darkness, or hadn't been hit hard enough to succumb, because I managed to spin around and begin crab walking in the same direction of my fall. I somehow managed to keep a good awareness of my directions because I was in fact gaining some space between myself and my attacker. Right up until my back bumped into a wall.

"No shouting," the man said with a wave of his pistol, "and no trying to escape, or I put a few holes in you and then Husk you."

My body froze up again as my mind helpfully tried to decide which of his threats was worse. Losing my connection to the world by becoming Skill-less, which would lead to a slow, agonizing death in a downward suicidal spiral, but might be survivable—or bullet ridden?

To say that I was less than impressed with my body's current response to danger was an understatement, and I used that surge of negative emotion at myself to get my feet under me and stand up.

"Easy there, *big guy*," The Shop said as he trained the muzzle of his weapon back to the center of my chest. I could tell he was being highly sarcastic—but it did highlight that I was physically larger than he was. Not that it mattered if he had an Awakened Skill and Stats, but I doubted the latter. The Shop continued, "We don't want any mishaps. Look, there's no guarantee that me using your Mana will hurt you. I just need a bit to activate my Skill, and then I'll let you on your way, deal?"

My eyes narrowed as they took in his gloves, tearaway pants, and boots. He looked more like a murderer than someone who was assaulting me for a bit of Mana. We'd been told how to spot Mana addicts, people who may attack you to steal your Mana. People who didn't think of the consequences of their actions and often left broken Skill-less people in their wakes, from what they viewed as something 'harmless.'

This guy didn't have a single one of those signs I'd been taught to look for.

"You don't look like a person who's out here for a quick Skill activation," I said, surprised that my voice came out so calm.

"You dare compare me to those filth? I'm not some useless single-Skilled Awakened. I'm a *Paragon*, one of the chosen few. Someone that is already above ninety-nine percent of humanity. I'm the one who can make other Paragons and will one day stand atop this world! Now, did you know that a Mana Pool's Gift is still active after death?" the man retorted with a bored wave of his gun.

I instantly felt faint. That psychotic monologue conveyed so much more than I ever wanted to know. It did more than simply suggest that this Shop had killed someone and taken their Mana from them afterward. It also conveyed that he was likely one of those beyond rare people who had multiple Skills Awakened. I'd never heard the term Paragon before, but through context, I figured it was something he was using to make himself feel superior. That thought was even more terrible. He was thinking of me as some sort of ant, below his notice. The fact that he got two or more Skills without a Mana Pool was devastating. Comparing him to a Mana Addict was unfair to the addicts…

Somehow, this final injection of fear spawned something primal and ferocious in me. I growled as I felt a wave of heat rush outward from my chest. I wasn't going to let this guy have his way. "Then why haven't you shot me already?"

His eyes, the only part of his face I could see, glinted with amusement and I could just tell my question had made him want to smile. The wave of heat grew, and I didn't even shiver looking into that frosty gaze.

"Look at you, being observant," he said, and I could hear the smile in his words. "I'll tell you a secret: the Mana starts to fade quickly in death. It puts me on a timer, and I need something of a more permanent connection to activate my Skills."

Even with the growing, strange heat, I shivered.

The man moved then, seeming to close the few steps to me in a blink. I realized then that his left glove had the palm cut out of it as he grabbed my wrist. "Plus, since I'm being honest, I need to draw from you while you're alive to fulfill the conditions of my Skill."

I opened my mouth to scream but a jab of his other hand still holding the gun impacted into my stomach, effectively driving the air out of my lungs and silencing my intended shout.

My teeth clicked together, and I almost bit my tongue as I tried to double over. Now that he was closer, I could smell the greasy sweat and even see a bit of it on his forehead and the bridge of his nose that was just visible inside of his hood. He was definitely a Mana Addict…

One of those who desperately needed to feel their Skills activate just one more time. If Dave's earlier analogy about 'seeing' could be used—then Skill activation was said to be the next level of bliss.

My shaky inhalation through my nose brought with it a horrible stench and I wondered if I had wet myself, or if someone had recently used this part of the alley as a restroom. If it was the latter, I hoped another individual might do the same, and soon. I prayed desperately just for such an event. Then my brain blanked.

That part of me in my chest. The piece that changed on my eighteenth birthday shuddered as The Shop mentally seized it. I felt the moment he formed a connection between his Skills and my Pool. It was like an electrical circuit being completed. I felt the connection but blinked as nothing happened.

This was how it felt when someone accessed your Mana Pool? Had I been concerned for nothing? I'd always assumed there would be danger or pain involved with someone accessing your Pool. You know, with the risk of it breaking and leaving you husked—

Then the switch was flipped, and the pain began. It was the exact opposite of my eighteenth birthday. I felt the moment that my Pool began to crack. I could tell in that moment that The Shop was attempting to pull all my Mana out in a single go.

The fracturing pieces of my pool shook, and I heard what I could only describe as a low humming growl. Instantly, I knew it came from inside my chest. Was it the sound of my Skill shattering? Was I going to be one of the Skill-less?

An awareness wrapped around the 'conduit,' the fracturing Pool, and my chest. Like a fist, it squeezed, creating a pressure that closed the cracks in my Mana Pool. In that moment, I thought I understood what activating a Skill felt like. Was this just by association because the Shop was activating his Skills?

"Ten Mana, that's it? How is this a highly-valua—"

The Shop's words cut off abruptly. Simultaneously, the force from the pistol pushing into my stomach lessened. The two in conjunction made my eyes fly wide. They were still filled with water from the earlier pain, and so I wasn't surprised to see stars. Yet the stars I saw didn't behave like I would have expected. They acted like real lights hovering atop the black-clad man's jacket. I saw three orbs overlaying his chest. One was fist-sized and orange—it looked like a small sun—and the other two were marble planets orbiting around it. They glowed gray and green.

As I blinked, the stars doubled. Then the newer three spheres seemed to be gripped by the invisible pressure that I was still exuding. The pressure almost looked like the jaws of some terrifying creature made from nothing. It was impossible to discern the 'outline' of black on moonlit night. A growl was still reverberating through my chest. The smaller two stars collapsed into the larger sun before shooting toward me. Almost seeming to be 'swallowed.' I might have flinched if I didn't think I was imagining everything.

The gun's muzzle, which was still pressed against my stomach, slipped further as The Shop's mouth dropped open and his face paled. The slipping continued and the pressure let up. Was he distracted enough that I could disarm him? I took Muay Thai, was physically larger than him, and went to the gym to maintain my physical appearance, so surely, I could use that—right?

His eyes seemed to spin, and what little of his face I could see paled further. Multi-Skilled attacker or not, I needed to *move*.

Now!

In a quick motion, I grabbed the gun's muzzle and shoved it out to the side of my stomach, sucking in my abdomen as much as I could. The Shop's muscles tensed spasmodically, but thankfully the man's finger had slipped out of the trigger guard. So, the gun didn't fire. I brought up a free knee to ram it up between his legs. I felt the impact that resonated through my own body.

His mouth had been opening to shout something at me, but instead a crying groan of pain escaped. I used my bracing leg to hop and brought my grounded leg's knee up, even as my other leg returned toward the asphalt. Either I was more Skilled at Muay Thai than I thought, or I got lucky. The Shop was in the process of curling up around his injured groin, which meant he was dropping his head. My knee drove up into his falling face, meeting the softness of his nose before colliding with the skull behind it.

There was a moment of resistance from the skull before it gave in as well. Any tension in the disgusting man's arms drained away as his body went limp. He fell to the ground like a dropped stuffed animal. The gun slipped through his fingers, remaining in mine. I flipped it around and pointed it at the downed man.

I could still feel the strange pressure and hear the low, humming growl. But the imaginary image of the dark shape was gone. Had this man broken my Skill? My stomach lurched, but I bore down against the nausea with everything I had. I would *not* throw up. Not right now, at least.

My hands shook violently, making the muzzle of the weapon jitter on and off his unmoving form. A part of me wanted to pull the trigger. To shoot him for what he might have done. Another part wanted to rush off to a UNMH assessment center and find out if I was indeed Skill-less. Instead, something else took the reins of my actions, and whatever was growling cut off all my other thoughts.

As if I was watching someone else in control of my body, I watched as the gun instantaneously stopped shaking, and one hand removed itself from the grip. Somehow, I'd adopted a shooting stance that I only recognized from movies that had won awards for their high level of technical proficiency on-screen. The freed hand calmly reached into the pocket of my jeans and pulled out my cell phone, bringing it up to my face to efficiently unlock and dial one-nine-nine.

"One-nine-nine, what's your emergency?"

"I—I," My voice, unlike my cold and detached body, didn't seem to be capable of stringing together words, let alone explaining that I had just been held up at gunpoint for a Mana Connection.

"Calm down, miss," the operator on the line said. "Can you tell me your location?"

Miss? Was my voice that high pitched? It startled me enough that she got a response. "Phoenix Academy."

"Good, good. Can you try to explain what's happened?" the operator coaxed.

I opened my mouth, but my throat seemed to have inherited the earlier shaking of my hands. I felt my vocal cords constrict and relax in rapid sequences as I began to try to explain.

"I—held at gunpoint—Mana Addict—between class and dorms." I managed to get out.

"Okay, sir. Can you give me your exact location? We've already got units on campus."

At least I was back to sir. I took that as a win, even as I thought how strange it was to focus on that in a situation like this.

"Alley—Quad and Cafe…" I stuttered out.

"Okay, stay on the phone with me. Officers are en route."

She kept asking questions of me, and I attempted to give responses, but eventually I broke down into nervous sobs. What if I was husked? Skill-less? It was a strange thought considering I felt even more connected to the World currently. Still, it felt like I was watching my body from outside of it, and so I couldn't be sure. It reacted and I just watched. Whatever was going on, I didn't even manage to form two coherent or logical thoughts together before I heard booted feet approaching, followed by a shout.

"Put the weapon down!"

With a snap, my out of body experience ended. I found two cops holding hands at the entrance to the alley. The lead cop's hand glowed with blue light in a threatening manner. It looked like a magic Skill, and it was pointed right at me. I dropped the gun and the phone, placing my hands immediately high above my head.

"I called you! I called you!" I shouted repeatedly.

Again, I must have lost track of time because I suddenly felt a hand on one of my arms. I jumped and pulled away, the memory of the greasy Shop's hands on my wrist too fresh in my mind. The grip grew harder as I tried to pull away and then wrenched my hand behind my back.

I fought it, until I realized that it was the cop. Then I let him move both arms behind my back without a fight. I heard clicks as something tightened around my wrists. The officer helped me to a nearby wall and sat me gently against it.

He looked me in the eyes and gave me a weak smile. "Just a precaution," he said gently. "Just so you don't accidentally hurt me or my partner, okay?"

His eyes were a light brown that held a real warmth in them. I nodded once and then a second time in quick succession. His partner knelt beside The Shop and held two fingers on his neck.

She grabbed a radio from her chest and clicked the button. "9L31. Suspect down. Pulse reedy. Request Ambulance."

"9L31, 10-4. Ambulance en route."

"9L30, 10-4," this time the officer nearest to me responded. He looked me in the eyes again after he released the button. "Are you going to be okay here for a moment while I lock this alley down?"

I swallowed audibly but then looked at the female officer kneeling above The Shop. I was safe if he was being watched, right? After a moment, I nodded. I stared blankly at the nearby wall, losing track of time once again as I tried to piece together my scattered thoughts. The darkness of the alley suddenly bloomed into a bright red-and-blue light show as cop cars and first responders drove cars into the space. The alley was necessarily wide to allow garbage trucks to get in and out to access the campus trash cans, so it wasn't a problem for the many emergency responders to pack into the space.

The next indeterminate amount of time became a blur of flashing red-and-blue. Officers put caution tape at each entrance to the alley and blocked them with diagonally parked vehicles. More and more bodies in uniform seemed to appear out of nowhere.

First responders carefully turned The Shop over before getting him situated and locked in on a hard stretcher. They strapped his body in place and put something over his neck and face to either keep him from escaping or protect him from further damage. I didn't know which, but I watched the procedure dully from my seated position against the wall.

A few officers tried to come talk to me throughout the process, but for some reason I couldn't make sense of their words anymore. I stared at the speakers, trying to put meaning to the sounds they made, but failed time and time again to hear them over the increasing sounds of growling in my ears. Eventually, the original officer came over and together with his partner helped me to my feet. Then they escorted me to a cop car near an entrance to the alley. The words 'Police Interceptor' stood out in stark relief across the passenger side door. What a weird name for a car. Were police really 'intercepting' so many things that it needed to be written across the car?

"I'm going to cover your head with my jacket," the woman cop said. It was the first clear words I'd heard in some time, but the sudden absence of the growling made me doubt my hearing. Cover my head? It wasn't even raining outside. Suddenly, a small jacket was covering my head, neck, and back, leaving a small opening around my face. "So the other students don't start snapping your picture."

A bit of force between my shoulders bent me forward and under something as they continued escorting me.

"Brodie! Brodie, is that you?" I heard a shout nearby. It sounded like Dave, but turning my head didn't move the jacket. The cops must have noticed my reaction though because they stopped for a moment.

"Do you know him?" the male officer asked.

"Umm, I think so. Brodie was on his way home after hanging out with me," Dave's voice responded.

"Do you mind coming with us?" the officer asked. "We haven't been able to get anything out of him. Do you have any contact information for his parents or guardians by chance?"

"Yeah, Clara and Gary. That's his mum and dad. Is everything okay? Is *he* okay?" Dave responded quickly.

"We'll explain in the car. Get in."

The officer lifted the 'Police Line Do Not Cross' tape, letting Dave, or at least his legs, duck underneath and move toward a police car.

It wasn't long before the female officer put a hand atop my head, and with a bit of force guided me into a cushioned seat of a different car. The smell of urine changed, morphing to urine mixed with a sterile car's interior. At least that told me that I had in fact peed my pants. That fact somehow fit right in with all the other things that had happened to me over the past… however long it had been.

The seat thankfully had some sort of plastic coating over it that my hands behind my back stuck onto. I felt the strap of the seatbelt get put around me gently, even as the cuffs got removed.

"We're going to get going very soon. We just need to fill out some paperwork with the help of your buddy, Dave. Okay?"

I nodded, the jacket moving with my head. She didn't take the item back, thankfully. The confinement steadied me somehow.

When had the growling stopped? When had words started making sense again? I could recall this officer speaking with Dave. Maybe her words to me about the jacket?

I leaned forward after I heard the door close, pressing my forehead against the cool plexiglass dividing the front and back seats and allowing the small jacket to shade me even further.

My all-consuming thought now that I was left alone?

Did I still have my Mana Pool, or would I soon start feeling my loss of connection to the world around me?

CHAPTER 4

Monday, April 1st, 2069

Steel chairs bolted to the floor weren't comfortable. Even worse when they were directly in front of a matching steel table that confined my personal space. The officers had at least taken off the cuffs they'd reapplied for the jaunt between the car and the station, which allowed me to stand up and pace the room whenever I grew too claustrophobic, which—given the *accommodations*—was often.

Somehow, I felt fully in control of myself again—no, that wasn't completely true. Oddly, I felt *better* than I had even before… I left that thought unfinished. Surely, I'd know if my gift had been drained and broken, right? If I had been Husked?

I figured that my newly found emotional control was probably a good thing. Sure, I still felt victimized by The Shop's attempted robbery, but I wasn't embarrassed. Instead, I felt angry and exhilarated. I'd been here for over an hour, or at least that's what it felt like. I was strangely confident in my timekeeping, given that I'd 'lost the show' after the… *incident*, when time had become more of what I imagine Doctor What meant when he called it 'wobbly-wibbly'. At first, I thought perhaps I was still running high on Adrenaline, the hormone masking my Skill-less situation, but surely this feeling was lasting too long for bio-chemics to be the answer.

Forcing myself to sit down, I examined the feeling. It felt familiar, almost like when that—creep connected a conduit to my Mana Pool. Like I was filled with energy from a source outside myself. Was I just proud that I had stood up for myself? Doped up on endorphins that I'd won a fight against a man with a gun? All those things were certainly true, but I didn't feel any wavering in my seemingly unending energy levels as I picked up and examined my actions.

That was enough sitting, I decided and stood up to pace again. Just as I spun on my heel to change directions at the first wall, I heard the handle of the door rattle.

The first person in the door was my mother, Clara. I could tell that she wasn't supposed to be the first person to come in by the sounds of protest from the people behind her.

Her dark hair may have got caught in the door if someone's, likely my fathers, hand didn't catch it. She like me had a tanned complexion even in the early spring. She was tall for a woman at five-foot nine, and had a skinny build that made her seem smaller.

She rushed over and gave me a hug.

It felt good but highlighted, at least for me, that my body was *vibrating*. She held on for a long moment before pushing me to arm's length to look at me. Tears openly flowed down her cheeks, but she didn't sob. She wore an expression of such depth of emotion that I couldn't even try to unravel it. Her eyes lingered on the orange pants that the officers had changed me into, and another emotion I couldn't recognize crossed her face, joining the others.

By the time I managed to look away, my father was closing in, which turned my mother's scrutiny into a family hug. My father was where I got most of my looks. He too had blue eyes, if lighter than mine—and the same darker skin that was common in Italian men. While he was tall, I still had a few inches on his six-foot four frame.

I closed my eyes and tried to sink into the love they had always provided. I failed as that energy deep inside my body hummed—no, growled? Either way, it felt like I physically vibrated. Thankfully, a polite cough forced my parents to let go before I felt compelled to push them away.

"How are you feeling, Brodie?" a man in a suit asked. I didn't recognize him at a casual glance. Nor did I recognize the smaller Spanish man who was sitting down with a folder in front of him. He was in a suit as well, and the two almost matched with there dark complexion and militaristic haircuts. They must have sensed my hesitation because the first taller man added, "I'm Detective Flair, and this is Detective Volt. We were in charge of the crime scene, and we've been speaking to your parents outside."

"I'm feeling *better*," I responded hesitantly as my parents subtly guided me back to the bank of metal chairs. They sat me between them protectively.

"That's fantastic news. Let's ask you again, since you seem responsive now, can we get you anything? Coffee, water, something to eat?" Detective Volt asked as Flair stayed standing. I twitched in my chair from the exhilarating energy and shook my head in response. The last thing I needed was *more* energy.

"On second thought," I said as I saw my parents glance concernedly at each other. "I could go for some water."

Surely water would help, right?

Flair moved back out of the door and was back before the silence became awkward. The door didn't even fully shut, which made me think they had a table of refreshments just outside the room. I looked around, trying to decide for the fifth time if this was an interrogation room or just a space meant for casual discussions.

Sure, it looked a lot like many Hollyhood depictions of interrogation rooms, but it had two clear windows. One beside the door, with its blinds mostly pulled, and one on the left wall, which seemed to show a hallway. Still, the bolted furniture—

"This isn't an interrogation," Flair said as he placed a plastic water bottle in front of me before taking his seat. "We just need to have a quick chat with you surrounding the circumstances of the altercation tonight."

"Okay," I responded dumbly. I wasn't exactly keen on rehashing the moment The Shop found me and guided me into that alley. However, with my current nearly-bouncing-out-of-my-seat energy, I was willing to blaze through a retelling.

"How did you know—" Volt checked the folder's first page, "—Morgan Hallsbrad?"

"Who?" I asked, looking first at both Detectives for a clue and then my parents.

"He may have had a few other aliases," Flair hurriedly added. "What were they again, Volt?"

"Let me see here," Volt answered the other detective as he scanned through pages in the folder.

I tried to get a look inside and read them, but it was upside down and on sheets that were clearly streamlined for the purposes of people who understood them. I did see multiple pictures though. They all seemed to be of a building, but the front of it kept changing.

First it was a 'Comic Stop,' and then a 'Comic Library.' The more Volt flipped, the more names the building took on. I hadn't bothered to count at first but knew that the building had at least twenty different names by the time it reached one that made my skin prickle with goosebumps despite the heat of the room.

"The Shop."

The backs of my knees collided with the metal chair, painfully, as I stood up. The feeling of energy morphed inside me, and I finally recognized it. It was a muted feeling of when that *Greed Pig* began using my Mana. My parents both stood beside me and placed a hand on my shoulders, even as the detectives looked first at me and then at the folder.

Volt reached the conclusion first. "I think that was the name of a Business Account on SwiftGram. Can you confirm he was using it? Do you recognize it?"

I closed my eyes and swallowed a lump that was forming in my throat. With my parents' support, I returned from my crouching stand back into my seat before nodding.

"Someone with that name contacted me on SwiftGram almost a week ago. I reported him, blocked, and banned him from my page."

"You had no other interactions with 'The Shop'?" Detective Flair asked. I made a face that clearly told the answer they already knew.

"I also had a disagreement with him in the comments of a post on Mana Banks a day or two before that."

They both nodded, confirming that they already knew.

"That's the only contact you've had with Morgan Hallsbrad?" Flair asked as he noted something down on a small ringed notepad. This note I could read since it was just two letters, 'SG.'

"Well, umm, assuming that you mean Morgan Hallsbrad *is* 'The Shop,' then… yeah?" I answered. I'd made that same connection in the alley, so figured it fit. Then in the silence that followed, I felt the urgent desire to explain the situation to my mother and father as they squeezed my shoulders in support. "He sent me a message asking about getting the price of a one-time Mana Connection—" my mother gasped, and I looked at her, hurrying on. "—I didn't even respond. I just reported him on the spot!"

I glanced at my father on my other side as my mother's mouth firmed into a hard line.

"I swear, Dad, I didn't respond until he started insulting me, and then, yeah, I sort of told him to screw off. It seems like he didn't appreciate me standing up for myself."

My dad's eyes widened even as he squeezed my shoulder again. A hand on the other side grabbed mine and threaded smaller fingers into my own. Since I'd already started, I finished telling the story, even admitting the fact that The Shop knew my actual name.

I didn't go into the events of today. I told myself it was because the Detectives didn't ask for that. However, the moment of silence after I finished my admission made me question my own reasoning. Was I still scared of the man?

"Would you mind if we took a look through your phone and saw those messages?" Volt asked. At my nod of approval, Flair stood up and exited the room. "We have a suspicion that Morgan used a third-party app to gain access to some of your personal information after you responded to him on Swift."

Uncomfortable silence followed this statement, and for some reason I couldn't meet the eyes of anyone present. I should've told someone about the interaction. This was all my fault.

The only thing that stopped me from wallowing in that thought was the energy humming in my Mana Pool. It was heady—a feeling I didn't know I was missing my whole life. I studied that feeling as my parents squeezed my hand and shoulder. I wasn't even sure myself what had happened in that alleyway. What had those multiplying orbs of light been?

Flair came back in with my phone. He slid it across the table, and I unlocked it, before going to SwiftGram and pulling up the deleted messages from the trash bin. The Shop's messages would have likely removed themselves in about a day more, if I understood the social media's protocols on deleted messages correctly.

"May I?" Volt requested and I passed him the phone. He read it quickly and then passed it to Flair before looking at me. "Can we take a screen capture of the conversation?" I nodded and watched as Flair held two buttons down. He then clearly sent a text, email or e-dropped the picture to himself.

"Thank you," he said before turning to the second detective. "Make a note of every app he has on there. We'll want to see if any of them have any suspicious connections with e-crimes later."

My fingers itched to get the phone back, but the detective continued before I had a chance to ask for it. "If you think you're up for it, can you describe the events from tonight?"

It took what felt like hours, but with some prodding and a great deal of support from my parents, I got the story out. In the end, the two Detectives pulled my parents outside and spoke to them in view of the window while I waited in my chair. The energy that helped sustain me through this 'not-interrogation' was slowly drying up, and I wondered if I would ever feel my Mana Pool again.

The thought struck me as strange. Surely I wouldn't want to go through something like this *ever again* and yet, the thought came unbidden. I wanted this powerful feeling to not—no, to never stop…

Flair handed my phone to Gary, and then Volt stuck his head in the door. "Your parents are going to take you home, okay?"

50

I nodded and practically jumped up from the metal seat.

The drive to the house was eerily silent. I kept debating about asking my dad for my phone but then chickening out at the last instance. He was driving and I shouldn't distract him, right? My mom kept looking at me and attempting a smile that looked hollow. Was she disappointed in me?

When we made it home, she finally broke the silence. "Want me to order your favorite?"

I shook my head, my stomach too knotted to think of eating. "I think I just want to go to bed."

Without my phone, I couldn't check the time, but it certainly felt well past midnight.

"You've got to eat—" my mom began before my father cut her off with a hand on her shoulder. He shook his head ever so slightly.

"Do you want us to come check on you at all? Maybe order something for you if you wake up hungry?" he asked in her place.

I felt a sob try to escape my throat as I nodded my head. For the first time, I saw my parents bumping head-first into a problem without answers, and it hurt. It broke something deep inside of me. I rushed up the stairs instead of voicing my reply.

I practically dove onto my bed and under the covers. It took about thirty seconds before I realized I wasn't going to be able to just fall asleep. I grabbed my pillow and screamed into it.

What the *husk* happened today?

Surely, I would wake up in a moment to realize it was a dream. Surely.

The clarity of my thoughts dissuaded me of that delusion. I was sweating thanks to my Mana Pool still seeming to 'supply' me with a trickle of something.

I needed a shower.

I stripped out of the orange pants that made me look like a criminal and glimpsed myself in the mirror. Despite the events of the day, I still looked pretty put together, thanks in large part to how much work I'd done in the morning to style my hair and choose an outfit.

I felt completely disgusted with myself in that moment. Was my attempt to be *useful* as a Mana Bank the cause of all of this? I just didn't want to be a nobody. I wanted to help in the fight—at least that's what I had told myself, but I had an F-Ranked Mana Pool...

In that moment—with that thought I intrinsically felt like I was just trying to foist myself onto some Hunter.

My highest goal was to become a charity case, thinking it was something I could be proud of.

My family circumstances screamed at me to stay a nobody, but I reached for more. I tried to use my looks and social media to find a good-hearted partner talented enough to raise my station. To maybe even awaken another Skill...

And I told myself that I would be helping?

What the husk was I thinking?

I turned the water on and stepped under the stream while it was still bitterly cold. The sensation was soothing against my skin—against my hot rage.

Just as the water warmed and then became hot, my steady stream of energy seemed to completely vanish. My legs wobbled and my knees grew soft. I could have steadied them, but instead I allowed myself to semi-collapse onto the old-tiled floor of the standing shower. I fell out of the hot stream and quickly slid myself back until I was under it again.

I let the water flow over me as I studied the patterns the drips made as they fell from my gelled hair. I watched them join the stream and circle the drain. As I looked on, the water first wet and then puddled atop the aged grout of the tiles. I might have imagined it, but I swore I could see greasy oil mixed with the water swirls. The image made me shiver.

I considered berating myself some more for my fault in all this but held it off.

Was the situation that bad? I thought to myself. Tomorrow I could go back to school and pretend none of this had happened. *What really* had *happened?*

"A piece of shit attacked me, and I kicked his ass," I said to myself, my voice a low growl. "I defended myself against a man—no, a Multi-Skilled Awakened with a gun. That's a husking *good* thing!"

I was staring at the shower tiles and allowing water to fall down the sides of my face. I jerked involuntarily when my vision went a vivid blue—similar to the color of the chalkboards earlier that night as they shifted to video.

A blink later and the sudden shift in my vision returned to the dark gray and black tiles. I swallowed hard against that resurgence of my earlier fear of being husked but felt my saliva catch in my throat as it happened again.

Skill Copy Canceled...
Full Skill Acquisition Requirements Met

Low A-Rank *Mental Fortitude* Skill Transferred
Mid C-Rank *Recovery* Skill Transferred
***Ex-Demonic Vault* Skill Transferred**
Error Insufficient Contribution for acquisition of *Demonic Vault* Rank
Downgrading...

What in the hell was going on? The screen flickered and changed colors going from vibrant blue to an amber tone.

Checking current Operating System
OS-6.1.4 Corrupted.
Downgrading
OS-5.0.18 Corrupted.
Downgrading
OS-4.3.4 Corrupted.
Downgrading
OS-3.2 Corrupted.
Downgrading

OS-2.0.0.1 Corrupted.
Downgrading
OS-1 Default (Downloadable)
Downloading…

This time the screen changed tone with each line from amber through various tones of orange before arriving at red. I watched in fascination as the three dots after downloading continuously reset to zero before growing to three and starting over. It probably only took, at most, ten seconds because I held my breath through the entire scrolling message until a new red screen popped up. Was I somehow Awakening new Skills?

And not just one!

Skills transferring…
Low A-Rank *Mental Fortitude*,
Mid C-Rank *Recovery*,
High E-Rank *Demonic Vault*,
Transferred.

I felt a *weight* settle onto my chest and spread out from there, making my body go cold and lethargic despite the heat of the shower. When my eyelids suddenly felt like they each were holding up a twenty-pound weight, I knew I needed to get into bed or fall asleep right there in the shower.

"Why are you wet and sitting on the stone floor naked?" A screechy voice asked, and I realized how tired I must be if my internal voice suddenly didn't even sound like my own.

I got to my feet and stumbled my way out of the standing shower. I didn't bother with a towel and managed a few more steps before aiming my inevitable fall at my unmade bed. I felt my face collide with the comforter before the battle with my twenty-pound eyelids was lost.

* * *

Greb-Shak blinked from a spot above the strange naked *human* that was half sprawled, but mostly collapsed, onto a soft massive cushion, covered by more soft fabrics. He didn't understand how he had arrived here. As far as he knew, he should still be training on Crendalar Five to become the guide of the second *Demonic Vault* Skill his Sect was making.

He looked down on himself, having known that he wouldn't come across the Divide in his Felguard-esque body, but not having expected to arrive as a full-fledged skin-sagging Imp. He wanted to bite and claw at something but had enough training to know that he wasn't truly in this plane and thus couldn't interact with it.

He scratched behind his own pointed, saggy ears, hating his current appearance. How weak was this child to have Summoned him into this *stupid* body? Even as a *weak* researcher, he was twelve feet tall, muscled, and capable of fighting all but the strongest entities on his planet.

Still, none of that answered why he was here, wherever *here* was. The System had jammed some information into his head. Like the name of this planet: Earth, and the race of the pale, weak-looking creature—Greb-Shak amended that thought slightly. Right now, the *human* was larger and stronger looking than he.

His question of where here was meant on this planet in general. It certainly didn't feel like he had appeared in a stronghold. Not with these flimsy, almost cardboard walls.

He moved about, traveling through walls and checking out the building he had appeared in. Two other inhabitants were in another pillow-like structure on the top floor like the naked boy, but they weren't asleep and instead laid there talking about someone they called 'Brodie.' It was an easy assumption to arrive at; Brodie was the naked boy. Greb-Shak flew on, trying to find something of value in the domicile.

After a scan of each room, he decided he would try moving outside. He did so but barely made it past the next house before he felt a strange *tug* and somehow popped back into the room with the naked, sprawled child. He remembered then that he had a tether to his Summoner, one that wouldn't let him move further than a hundred yards, if he recalled correctly.

After a few moments, he remembered his notifications and checked on them. He read the last three lines.

Your Master, Morgan Hallsbrad, has died.
You will be returned to Crendalar Five.
ERROR:

Compatible Tether recognized.

Transferring your Mastery to Brodie Flacarada.

"Huh?" Greb-Shak said. "But I haven't had a master before?"

However, his notifications claimed he had, and if there was one thing he was sure about, it was that the System—the same System that had conquered his entire planet—no, all *five* of their planets—couldn't lie.

Was this naked child his new Summoner then? Had he truly come that close to destruction? He swallowed. The creation of the first *Demonic Vault* Skill had cost his Sect almost everything—despite him and the other researchers cutting corners and costs—and if the Skill was destroyed upon death, then they could lose all that wealth and sacrifice just as fast!

Greb-Shak needed to be careful.

CHAPTER 5

Tuesday, April 2nd, 2069

I woke up cold the next morning and had the distinct urge to just pull my covers over my head and return to the safety that sleep offered. Yet, a very sensible voice in my head told me that would only make the situation worse. While this voice was certainly right, it didn't make me hate it any less. Plus, why was the sensible part of my brain so loud today?

Like it somehow had center stage when it used to be a relegated voice of discontent...

I flipped the covers off me and got up before I'd fully examined my new-found clarity of thought. I picked up my phone, which my dad must have put in my room while I was in the shower and clicked the button that changed the phone from Sleep mode to active. I'd also tied that into my room's lighting, which immediately caused me to squint as the lights flared.

"Moogle, lights to ten percent."

They dimmed, allowing my watering eyes to begin clearing, but not before I saw a shadow of a bat on the wall. The shape immediately reminded me of my fevered vision of the bat-Demon thing in the middle of the night, when I'd woken up to find myself not under the covers and in desperate need of a pee. Last night I was tired enough to ignore it.

Now, the shadow was still there but with the muted lights it was far less dark, and so I tried to tell myself to ignore it. That too-sensible voice in my head scolded me for cowardice, and I turned my head.

Why was I listening to it?

"Husk," I cursed as the ugly foot-tall bat-gremlin came into focus.

It was watching me from the right headboard post of my queen-size bed. Our eyes met, and the dark pools of its gaze made me shiver again. I internally cursed the part of my brain that peer-pressured me into looking. It calmly explained that *not* seeing the creature would be worse than confirming it was there... probably.

That last inkling of misgiving wasn't doing my blood pressure any favors.

"Husk? That's all you've got to say? I guess a mental fortress doesn't help if what it's protecting is deficient from the get-go," the creature said, its voice whiny and lispy at the same time.

It took me a second more to realize it just called me stupid.

"Hey, what the husk?! Not only can I see you, but you can *talk*, and the first thing you do is insult me?" I asked, moving to point at it accusingly but then thinking better of it. It wasn't attacking me at the moment, and it hadn't in my sleep either, but that didn't mean it wouldn't.

It just meant that it *wanted* something.

"You really need to work on your vocabulary," it responded and pointed a long thin finger with a talon at its end at me. I narrowed my eyes at the creature. It was holding the same posture I wanted to use a moment before—to point at it. This was certainly surreal.

I kept my eyes on it as I backed up, feeling behind me for my desk or chair. I eventually bumped my hands onto the corner of the desk and felt around it until I arrived at my chair. I turned it and then lowered myself down, while keeping my eyes pinned to the Gremlin with wings. My hands remained clenched on the arm rests, ready to use the thing as a weapon if it came to that.

Its spindly arms looked like they were bone and skin without enough muscles to even move the extremities. So, maybe I could take it. While I could see some hints of red in its black skin, it was more like seeing a red light glinting off something dark than it was a true skin tone. Its wings looked ratty and dry, almost ready to tear.

The bat-thing in turn watched me with its black eyes. Perhaps I was getting better at reading its expression because I saw a great deal of derision in its tight-lipped smirk.

To my surprise, I began to calm once I felt the chair under my bare ass. That didn't mean I released my death grip on my improvised chair-weapon, but that same strange clarity upon waking returned, seeming to allow my brain to stop whirring and focus.

I assessed my situation.

While feeling disturbed that I'd gone to bed and was still naked in front of a Monster, I was calm. Yet, why was I equally worried about my state of undress, being interrupted, and the husking MONSTER in my room? While I'm sure my parents would have questions if they walked into my room and found me naked and staring at a Monster, how was my brain able to calmly assess the chances of that happening, while simultaneously preparing a self-defense plan if it lunged at me?

On top of that, a corner of my mind was assessing if this creature was simply a figment of my imagination. Dissecting the situation, our interactions so far, the Monster's actions, and the fact that the talons of the bat-Demon weren't attempting to rip out my jugular—I was oddly leaning towards the conclusion that I was possibly insane.

So, maybe my parents would only have questioned my nakedness if they walked in.

I crossed my legs protectively over my manhood.

"So, have I gone insane?" I asked the creature and, by extension, myself.

"Doubt it. With what you just got in there," the creature gestured vaguely toward my head. "I really *do* want to know what could make someone like *you* go insane, though. Can we test it out?"

"With what I 'just got'?" I asked, scanning the room for something that didn't belong, while simultaneously not taking my eyes off the sharp-toothed Gremlin. It wasn't very effective, and I didn't find anything out of place. Other than my far-too-calm brain cataloging each item in the room.

"It isn't a physical object. Just check your Skill Cards," the thing said.

With an eyebrow raised, I slowly turned back to it. "My *Skill Cards*?"

Then of course I recalled the strange windows I received while in the shower. Was that what this thing was referring to? Still, it began answering my question, confusing me further.

"Yeah, surely you have a mid-rank Spent Mana Crystal around here somewhere," the demonic thing said as it gestured around the room but included the whole house. "Maybe not, since I couldn't find anything through the night…" it drawled. "What sort of shit Summoner did I get bonded to?"

"Bonded? Summoner? Can you start making sense?" I spat, and then realized that if I was insane, as I was becoming more and more convinced that I *was*, it likely wasn't going to get better. Still, how could I pull back up that strange red window from last night?

"Hmmm?" the creature said as it tapped its thin purple lips. It seemed to notice something either on its talon or in its teeth because it began using one of the two deadly implements to clean the other. I just watched, fascinated by the scene. It was a morbid inspection because I was beginning to understand that the trauma from yesterday had somehow broken me.

I probably hadn't even seen the red hovering window in the first place.

Yet somehow my head felt clearer than it had in a long while—my emotions calmer. Normally, I would have a million questions racing around in my head. Even on my best days that was something I battled with, but now? Now, it almost felt like my brain was filtering those questions and prioritizing them based on this imaginary creature's responses and what I needed most in this moment, right here, right now.

Perhaps that was why I asked another question before it even formulated a response. "Let's start with this then. Are you real and how did you get here?"

"Of course I'm real, at least, for values of 'real.' Only you can see me," the creature said, its voice indignant. "As for the second part of the question—I don't really know. I was Summoned using a Skill Card, but it was by a guy named Morgan Hallsbrad, according to my logs."

I blinked. My body reacting to the Demon's words by starting to curl in on itself.

The Shop! I stopped the physical flinch even as my fingers attempted to release my hold of my totally 'bad-ass' chair-weapon I was bare assed upon.

Why was I flinching?

Wait.

Surely, I should feel fear or anger toward the man he was talking about, but I wasn't afraid *nor* angry. My brain was chugging along and telling me I had nothing left to fear from a man in police custody. Unless he'd sent this Demon— even then, though?

"So, he sent you to kill me?" I followed up.

I could feel my body attempt to tense even as my far-too-calm brain urged it to remain calm. Only with a calm mind could I react to the possible incoming attack. That was the best way I would be ready to react if the creature leaped at me.

The Demon scratched a long, pointed ear and tilted its head.

"Nope. If I'm being honest, I can't even recall that guy. According to the log, he's *very* dead now, though. So, no orders to try to kill you. Not that I could kill anything anyway." He swiped at the lamp on my nightstand, and I tensed briefly, readying myself to catch it before the creature's taloned hand passed right through it.

After its little demonstration, I was finally able to unclench my muscles. Really relax, and with that feeling I could breathe slightly easier.

Then the doorbell for my house rang and I flinched again even as my brain scolded the physical reaction. What in the actual *husk* was going on? Why was my own mind scolding me?

My phone buzzed in my hand, and I checked the doorbell camera to find a snapshot of the two detectives from the previous night. I looked between the Demon and the recording doorbell camera. If this thing was telling the truth, they were likely here to inform me of The Shop's death. Shouldn't I feel a certain… something about that?

My brain remained calm, however. They'd already assessed the case as self-defense, right? So, what would change if the asshole died, except perhaps the *degree* of me coming to my own defense? As if I wanted an answer to that question, my far-too-calm mind pulled it out of thin air.

The severity of the case would increase, and they would have to make sure that I didn't use excessive force for the situation. Or something like that. Did this mean I could be charged with manslaughter?

Still, unperturbed, I clicked into the camera to listen as I heard one of my parents answer the door.

"Hello, Detectives," my mother greeted, her voice stiff. "Is there anything I can do for you?"

"I'm afraid what we talked about last night, that could be a possibility, has happened, and we need to take Brodie back in for follow-up questioning."

My mother gasped in surprise but didn't follow up with a response. Surely, I should be even more worried than her, but I was calmly going over the situation. There was *surely* no way I could be charged with anything since the asshole had a gun, and I was unarmed. I had hit him two times, once in the groin and once in the face to put him down.

I tapped my lip. It wasn't like I'd beaten him repeatedly once he was incapacitated or anything. A good lawyer would immediately be able to have this case assessed as self-defense. Because that's what it had been. Right?

I stood up from my chair, thinking I should change out of my birthday suit before I was forced to go with them. A small cough reminded me of my crazy, demonic delusion on my bedpost.

"Since you claim to be real, can you stay here while I handle this?"

"No can do. I cannot get further than a hundred yards from you. However, because I'm a Skill Summon with no combat capability, I'm kind of between phases of reality. As I said, I doubt anyone can see me," the Demon said before tapping a tooth with a claw. "Well, they *can* see me if they have high level Space Skills, or maybe there's a way I can make myself visible?"

"What happens if you get more than a hundred yards from me?" I asked, ignoring the question he seemed to be asking himself, as I hurried to my closet. I quickly found underwear, socks, jeans, and a t-shirt.

"If I was physically in this dimension, we'd both likely experience severe pain at any significant separation. Since I'm not a Combat Summons, I just get sucked through space back to your side. At least I think that's what happened last night when I tried it."

Having a conversation with what could be a figment of my imagination while dressing myself calmly so I could go speak to two detectives about a possible manslaughter charge should have felt off, but it didn't. I blinked twice in quick succession, my only reaction to the current situation.

"Do you know how to pull up that red window from last night?" I asked as I snorted some air from my nose and pulled my shirt over my head.

"Red window? You shouldn't have been able to see The Shop yet?" the Demon-Imp said, and I just blinked at it. "Well, you just supply the *Demonic Vault* with Mana…"

The Demon, which I realized I was getting tired of calling 'the creature,' made that sound extremely easy. I tried to mentally command my Mana to supply the *'Demonic Vault'* Skill and nothing happened.

Since there were two detectives waiting downstairs, I grabbed a pair of socks and handled my other annoyance with the creature.

"Okay," I said, stretching out the word, "well, it seems like I'm stuck with you, so we'll talk about the Mana thing later, okay? Now, what should I be calling you?"

"Pick a name. I won't be giving you mine. Names have power, and you already have more over me than I care for."

"Okay," I responded dryly. Then realized that if he wanted to play a stupid game, he'd win a stupid prize. I could at the bare minimum give him a fitting name. "Okay, you'll be Smegma."

I almost felt bad as Smegma grinned at the name. Clearly it had no idea of its derogatory nature. Still, it had chosen to not tell me its name, and it hadn't exactly had a great attitude so far. So, what little guilt I felt was easy to push aside.

Plus, if it was just a figment of my imagination, I didn't particularly like that it existed in the first place.

After I was fully dressed, to my surprise, Smegma didn't follow me out of the room or down the stairs. I wasn't too concerned though since, if it was telling the truth—wait—why was I so sure it *was* telling the truth?

Whatever.

If it was telling the truth, I couldn't possibly get a hundred yards away from Smegma while in my parents small two-bedroom rent-controlled house. It was with that thought that I turned the corner on the stairway landing to find my parents hugging each other in the center of the living room while the two detectives sat on the couch.

Still, it was the image of Smegma's head phasing through the ceiling and staring into the room that my eyes were glued to. I took a deep breath and closed my eyes before transferring them to the detectives.

"Good morning," I said to the room, attempting to add a bit of enthusiasm to my voice. I failed.

My parents released each other and looked at me. Their faces were twisted into pitiful masks of such a mix of emotions that I couldn't even begin to unravel them. However, right at the forefront for both was sadness, pity or worry. Maybe even all three.

"Good morning," Detective Flair said as he stood up. "You don't seem surprised by me and my partner in your living room."

"I saw you on the doorbell camera," I answered. "I'm not really sure why you're here, but if you don't mind my saying so, you being here at all doesn't seem like it's a good thing." I lied while I pointed to my parents. Both now had tears silently running down their faces.

"I'm afraid that the case has become a bit more complicated," Detective Volt stated, which caused my mother to begin sobbing openly.

My dad reached out and pulled her into a one-armed hug, even as he took the liberty of explaining.

"The guy who—the guy…" he faded off for a moment, seeming to try to find a way to continue without talking about the events from yesterday. After a pause he simply whispered, "he died."

A part of me wanted to glare up at Smegma, because I was sure that the reaction I had upstairs would have been more fitting at this moment. Instead of my muscles going limp, or even my face changing, I stood there staring at Volt. He blinked first, seeming to be waiting for something before his eyes narrowed.

"You don't seem surprised by that news."

"I told you that I saw you on the doorbell cam. The wonder of technology that it is—the thing has audio, too. I heard what you said to my mom. It wasn't hard to piece together what 'that thing that we were afraid could happen, happened' means. There are only a few things it could mean, given the situation, and my mother and father's reactions confirmed my speculation," I bold-face lied. Somehow, instead of being flustered in that moment, my brain had pieced together a near perfect fib. One that was entirely plausible. After my pronouncement, silence stretched as my mother's sobs intensified.

Volt's eyes narrowed further, making me think that the lie wasn't as perfect as I'd believed.

"*Well*, that *does* make sense, but you aren't showing a hint of remorse," Flair said, his voice not full-blown skeptical but close.

The only response I could give the man in my current state was a blink. After which I moved further into the room and closer to my parents. My dad extended an arm, and I moved into it, accepting the hug. Tears did come then, but upon examination, I realized that they weren't in response to the death of Morgan Hallsbrad, but because of what this situation was doing to my mother, to my father.

The detectives waited patiently as my family clung to each other. I would never know what they were thinking about, but their faces looked less suspicious now that they were seeing a reaction from me. After a few minutes, Flair stood up.

"I'm sorry to do this, but you'll have to come to the station with us, Brodie."

"If you have a lawyer, I suggest you call them," Volt said to my parents before pulling his cuffs from his waistband. "Brodie, you're under arrest. You have the right to remain silent. Anything you say can and will be used—"

I tuned out the rest of what he was saying as I allowed him to maneuver my hands behind my back for the third time in two days. I stared up at the ceiling, watching as Smegma slowly phased fully through the stuccoed drywall. I followed him as he began hovering ever lower. I held my breath as he got level with the officers' heads. No one reacted.

My dad was already on the phone with someone, and my mom was staring at the detectives with a mixture of murderous rage and deep sadness written upon her face. I wanted nothing more than to give her a hug. Thankfully, she rushed to me and wrapped me up in a tight embrace.

"Don't worry, your dad is calling the Miner's Union. They'll get a lawyer assigned through his insurance. We'll meet you at the station. I love you!"

She practically shouted the last bit. I leaned into her hug, unable to use my hands to squeeze her back. The officers thankfully let us have our moment before I felt a gentle tug on my arm. A glance over my shoulder found Volt with an uncomfortable smile on his face.

"Sorry, we need to take him now, Mrs. Flacarada."

I was escorted to the unmarked cruiser parked at the curb. It was early enough that no one was on the cul-de-sac, which my supernaturally calm mental state assessed as a good thing.

Still, that didn't bar out people watching from windows. I took a slow glance around as my brain categorized everything I saw.

Thankfully, I didn't see anyone as I was guided into the back seat. Perhaps that would help prevent rumors from spreading.

CHAPTER 6

Tuesday, April 2nd, 2069

"What did Morgan Hallsbrad say to you in the alleyway?" Flair asked again, his voice curious.

I opened my mouth to immediately answer before realizing that I should check with my lawyer first. I turned to Ms. Stovall, who sat right beside me, and she nodded—confirming that this question was fine to answer.

Ms. Stovall was a very interesting woman. A study in dichotomy. She was short, when compared to someone like my mother, but infinitely more imposing. It wasn't like she was physically intimidating—but the no nonsense air about her and the way she styled her blonde hair; even the way she hid her blue eyes behind designer glasses, all leant themselves to a woman who exuded authority. Despite her lack of stature.

"What would happen if you claimed you weren't even there?" Smegma said offhandedly and I pointedly ignored him. He was perched on the top of an empty chair on our side of the table.

This wasn't the first question so far or Smegma's first interruption. Still, after a quick one-on-one with Ms. Stovall, she'd deemed that I didn't need any coaching in answering questions but that I should check with her to let her object to certain lines of questioning. I'd forgotten to check with her early on, and she had placed a hand on my elbow in a quiet but friendly reminder. Sadly, she'd done it twice already.

"He told me I pissed him off," I began. "Then he told me that he just needed a 'quick connection' to use his Skill as he pointed his gun at me. Although, something was off with the way he said it. Like he was meaning something different than what those words typically meant."

I shivered and paused for a second as the hair on my arms rose at the memory. I hadn't realized it at that moment, but in retrospect I thought I could see the insinuation. He just needed to use his Skill to send me on my way—to the afterlife. I shook off that tangent with relative ease as my mind focused me back on the question.

"He also claimed that he could still pull Mana from me even as a corpse—which really creeped me out. Umm—I think that's pretty much it…"

"How did you manage to distract him before you attacked him?" Volt asked the follow up with the same nonchalance, but a hand on my elbow told me that Ms. Stovall would be answering this question.

"So let me get this straight. Even though he was attacking you, you can get in trouble for attacking him back?" Smegma asked incredulously before Ms. Stovall could answer.

"I would like it noted that my client defended himself against a C-Ranked Awakened with a gun and did not *attack*, but merely defended himself from an ongoing assault in the form of an involuntary Mana Connection, which—I will remind you—is a felony. The situation justifies *any* level of reprisal from an unarmed victim."

I gave Smegma a quick warning glance, hoping he would get the hint and shut the husk up.

"Our apologies, how did you distract your attacker as you *defended* yourself?" Flair clarified, with a nod at Ms. Stovall and a curious glance to the chair I just looked at.

A quick glance toward my lawyer got me a nod and I told an abridged version of how Morgan got 'distracted' once he pulled on my Mana.

"He must have been surprised when his Skill activated," I finished.

"Bullshit," Smegma said, and I tried not to react but might have failed.

Flair and Volt looked at each other skeptically before making notes. Still looking down at his papers, Flair asked, "What rank were you assessed at again?"

"My client Awakened as an F-Rank," Ms. Stovall answered on my behalf. "As you can see, he was out-ranked and held at gunpoint—" a sudden scramble behind the door made her stop mid-sentence as both the detectives turned in their seats. The door flew open and a third detective, who was breathing hard and practically sweating, made a motion for the two sitting in the room to join him outside.

"If this *interruption* pertains to the case, I'll remind you of my client's right to know," Ms. Stovall said with a raised eyebrow.

The detective in the hallway gave her a distasteful look and simply waited for the two detectives to stand and join him in the hall. The door of the interrogation room closed behind them, and I sucked in a large lungful of air. It felt stiflingly hot in here.

Ms. Stovall stood up and moved to the door before opening it and grabbing two water bottles from the cart I'd seen on my way in. She passed me the first, and I realized I'd already finished the one I'd been given when she first arrived. I scanned this room and immediately knew that the detectives had told the truth that the room I was in last night was not an interrogation room. While they looked similar, this one was smaller and had no windows to the hallway or workspace. It had a camera in each of the four corners and markedly bad lighting from two lamps that either needed new bulbs or better placement.

"That was definitely strange," Ms. Stovall commented offhandedly as she drank from her bottle. "Normally, they will avoid interrupting detectives that are mid-interrogation." She looked at me and blinked, before changing tones. "Nothing for you to worry about, I'm sure. You're doing great."

"Do they really think *I* attacked The Shop?" I asked, a little lost. I felt off balance now that the questioning had let up for a moment. It was truly strange to be questioned in such a manner.

"This is just their jobs," Ms. Stovall answered. "I can tell that they know that it was self-defense, but I think they're both feeling like something in the case is off. Something doesn't add up for them, or you wouldn't be here."

Smegma phased back through the mirrored glass, his dark black eyes wide.

"They're talking back here," he said as he half phased back into the window. "According to them, Morgan Hallsbrad may be a 'cereal-killer'—something called a 'Snatcher.' He had a book in a pocket with a list of names. Your name was in it, but all the names crossed out have now been proven to belong to victims all along the eastern 'United States'—whatever that means."

I wanted to ask Smegma what a *Snatcher* was, but I couldn't really say anything to the Demon-Imp with Ms. Stovall in the room. Or with the cameras, I supposed. Also, with the way he said the word, I didn't think that he knew what it was either. All indications seemed to point that the Demon didn't even come from this world. What I *did* realize though, is that this may prove if the creature was real or not. I certainly had no way of hearing what was going on behind that glass—so if the Imp's words proved true, like this morning, surely that would be proof, right?

"Flair is still claiming that something is off with you," Smegma continued. "Volt agrees and says even more so, if Morgan was a cereal 'Snatcher.'" There was that word again. "They're both looking at you through the glass. The third detective, too." Smegma glanced in my direction and then chuckled. "Yeah, now I see why they're bringing it up; you are staring at the window—right at them. Even the well-dressed chick next to you is giving you an odd look."

I blinked and shook my head to stop myself from continuing to stare at Smegma intently. Instead, I looked at Ms. Stovall.

"What do you think is going on?" I asked to cover up my momentary distraction.

"If it pertains to this case, we should know soon enough," Ms. Stovall said, even as the door opened again to admit Flair and Volt.

They sat back down, and I realized that they were now carrying a folder they didn't have on them the first time. Ms. Stovall gave it a cursory look before she retook her seat beside me.

"Some new information has come to light in the case," Volt said as he sat down.

Ms. Stovall immediately held up her hand to stop any questions that might have followed that statement. "If that's the case, I would like to have some time to go over the new facts in private before we go any further."

"As you wish," Volt said with a tight-lipped smile. He then slid the folder over to Ms. Stovall. "These are the facts that your client is privy too. Please read them over, and then we'll continue."

The two detectives stood up and left the room again. A moment later, the window became see-through, and the small red lights on the cameras blinked off. I looked around in confusion as Ms. Stovall flipped open the first page of the folder.

She appeared to begin reading, but at the speed she was flipping through pages, I wondered if she was skimming. Smegma hovered over her shoulder, his wings not even flapping before giving me a look.

"I can't read your language, yet," he said flatly after a moment. "So, if you want to know what this says, get over here or start asking questions."

I realized this wasn't the time to laugh and so morphed my chuckle into a cough. The fact that I could laugh in a situation like this at all startled me a bit. I really wanted to ask the damn thing how it could *speak* English, but not read it. But still, I took Smegma's advice and asked, "What's it say?"

"It says that Morgan Hallsbrad is suspected of being a Snatcher-for-hire. That he is suspected of targeting you in a manner similar to his other victims through a phishing app on your phone and initiated contact through SwiftGram. This says that you're without a doubt the only surviving victim of a terrifying individual, which just turned this entire line of questioning into a farce." She snorted. "Excessive force? Against a *serial killer*?" Ms. Stovall stood up, eyes hard and glanced at me. Then in a firm, calm voice she said, "I'll be right back."

Smegma rubbed his hands together and followed her through the door, leaving me totally alone. A moment later he popped back into a space beside me looking chagrined. "Dammit, I really wanted to see that. She looked like she was going to tear the detectives a new asshole. Why couldn't she be my Summoner…"

"Hey, I'm right here!" I complained, while silently agreeing with Smegma's assessment of the fiery woman. She definitely was a badass and I felt lucky to have her on my side.

CHAPTER 7

Tuesday, April 2nd, 2069

"Would you like your parents here for this?" Ms. Stovall asked. She had come back to the interrogation room and immediately had me transferred back to the far friendlier meeting room I'd been in the night before. Afterward, she'd explained that I was no longer being held for questioning, and that she would be right back. She had just re-entered the room after a brief discussion with my parents. In fact, I could see them both in the lobby through the window. They were holding hands while staring into the room, right at me.

In truth, I wasn't sure I wanted them here for this. If Morgan Hallsbrad had been a serial killer, I didn't think my parents were going to take that news well. It meant that the threat last night was not only to my Mana Pool—that what happened wasn't just attempted Mana Theft—that last night my parents could have lost a son. Plus, I still didn't know what a 'Snatcher' was, but I was starting to think it might be even worse than a *serial murderer*, which couldn't be 'good.'

The tone of my lawyer conveyed what might be expected in this situation under normal circumstances, though. So, I nodded, and she motioned them to come inside.

They nearly jumped toward the door before entering and sitting down beside me. Ms. Stovall smiled at us. It was a reassuring look that seemed to bode well.

"First off, let me assure you the actions taken by Flair and Volt are going to be highly scrutinized. While it was just protocol to bring you to the station to answer some follow-up questions, it certainly *wasn't* protocol to treat you as a criminal.

"The good news is that Brodie is free to go. From the evidence at the scene and Brodie's retelling of events, the Police *believe* that it was self-defense. They have now dotted *all* of their I's, or rather—I've dotted them *for* them and this will *surely* be dismissed in the pre-trial before it goes to court. They will *not* be permitted to take you in for further questioning without extenuating circumstances."

Her voice was hard at times, like she was displeased with the police force for their handling of the case so far. Her emphasis of certain words made it very clear that the police would be toeing a line from now on in this case, but also that the forecast she predicted wasn't set in stone. It was a strange study in contrasts—so sure and confident while simultaneously hedging her bet. Perhaps it was a lawyer thing. Nothing was true until it was proven to be.

She flipped a few pages in her folder and pointed to a line I doubted anyone but her could read. "Morgan Hallsbrad was assessed as a C-Rank Awakened and is suspected to have been even higher than that. He never retook the assessment due to his criminal ties—"

"Criminal ties?" Dad asked, cutting off Ms. Stovall with the startled question.

"Morgan Hallsbrad is suspected of as many as forty murders, with possible others yet undiscovered or linked. Have you two heard of the Heartless Killer?" she asked as their faces started to pale.

"The guy on the news, from New York?" my dad asked, his voice hoarse.

"That's correct. According to evidence found in Morgan's possession—he is linked to every name of the known murder victims and many more besides. The police believe he might have been a Snatcher."

I saw my opportunity and took it. "A Snatcher?"

My parents looked at me before each one placed a hand on a shoulder in near unison. They then looked to Ms. Stovall for an answer as well.

"Yes, it isn't exactly a well-known term. The media is told to steer clear of it—so as not to raise a panic. Perhaps it should be more surprising that they actually *do* what they're told."

She paused for a moment and then sighed. "There are two classifications of Awakened Skills that are not widely publicized. They are Cannibal and Snatcher. The first of the two means that the individual can consume and then use a Skill from an individual after they die. They do this with their own Skill and it usually results in a single, very powerful Hunter. Most of these Cannibalistic Skills have drawbacks, Limits or other parameters to them, such as a maximum capacity for how many—or perhaps, how powerful—Skills they can 'take.'

"The second type of Skill is usually far more dangerous. That's the Snatcher. They can literally create a vessel that holds the stolen Skill, which will then allow them to transfer it to someone else. Again, they can have a great deal of Limits and Parameters, but since the person doesn't have to take the Skill for themselves, some of that Limit is instantly removed, making them far more dangerous. They usually sell them through black market back channels. Interpol and the FBI monitor these back door deals and usually catch Snatchers when they move to make a sale."

I swallowed hard. It was somewhat easy to forget that Ms. Stovall was talking about murder and not just stolen property. Stealing someone's Skill was nightmarish. It was like condemning the person to a literal Hell where they lost a connection to the world around them—becoming husked, what some people described as a Zombie. Dead but still animated. Yet, the price of a secondary Skill would be astronomical, right? It was so rare to Awaken with more than one, but to be able to purchase a Skill of 'your' choice? The cost was unimaginable and could motivate a person who possessed such a Skill.

"So, why was Morgan Hallsbrad not caught before he assaulted our son?" my mother asked, her voice hiding tears and anger in equal measure.

"The Police have handed that investigation off to Interpol, and they are looking into it. As of yet, they can only speculate but believe that Morgan may have been collecting the Skills as personal trophies without selling them at all."

"Or using the same buyer," the newly analytical part of my brain pointed out, and I spoke almost without realizing it.

Ms. Stovall raised an eyebrow. "That is quite possible as well. It would drastically limit his exposure and is likely one of the first lines of inquiry the investigators will look into." She turned back toward my parents. "I understand your anger Mrs. Flacarada, Mr. Flacarada, but I can only convey that I am not a part of the investigation into Morgan Hallsbrad. I am simply here to defend Brodie and will continue to do so. With this recent evidence and suspicions, Brodie's case should never see a courtroom."

She looked from my mother to my father and then to me. "With that in mind, do you have any questions for me about Brodie's case?"

My parents had plenty. All of which were about what we would have to do from here. Ms. Stovall was confident in her answers, which all seemed to say we just had to wait for the pre-trial court date to be scheduled and then she would have it dismissed. There was one question they didn't, or couldn't have asked but my overly calm mind wouldn't let it go. Like a dog with a bone.

"Would anything change if I was no longer F-Ranked?" I asked.

All heads turned to me and three sets of eyebrows raised. Ms. Stovall was the first to recover and ask, "What do you mean?"

I kept my eyes on her despite wanting to turn my head to the back of the chair beside her. The chair that Smegma was perched on. He looked bored. Thankfully he had remained mostly quiet throughout the rest of the interview. I could feel his eyes on me and somehow felt his warning before he spoke it.

"I wouldn't tell her about me, if I were you," Smegma stated. "First, it's not going to help your case, and second, people with Demonic Summons aren't exactly viewed favorably, not on most worlds. I doubt yours is any different, at least not based on what I've been trying to read." The demonic bat motioned over to a police force's cork board. It had a ton of wanted posters hanging on it that I couldn't read from where I was seated. Not that the illiterate Demon could either, but the warning was probably a good one.

I might have rolled my eyes in any other circumstance—not believing the Imp—but instead I calmly sat regarding Ms. Stovall. She wore an expression of confusion, so I decided to clarify.

"I felt a surge of something after—" I cut off and swallowed deliberately before continuing quickly as if I hadn't. "—after the attempted theft. It was like I was filled with some sort of power."

Why was I intentionally acting nervous about the attack yesterday? Well, my mind insisted that I act as expected of me in this situation. I'd already drawn enough attention to have Volt and Flair suspicious of me. I frowned at my own calm thinking. Something was definitely off, and I once again considered if the Mana Connection had broken me in some way.

Was I that Zombie?

Ms. Stovall smiled and lowered her eyebrows. "Oh. Not to worry. Re-Awakenings are beyond rare. Even more so when outside of a Portal. So, there is less than a one percent chance that you re-Awakened. Not to mention the flash of light that you couldn't miss. It always accompanies a re-Awakening. The feel of *power* was just a response to your Mana being used. It's extremely common. It's kind of like an adrenaline high and likely helped you build up the courage to save yourself."

My parent's looks of concern changed to that of comprehension, and I let the question drop. "Ahh, yeah—I've had it a few times when Mana Leeches get a bite in," my dad said in an understanding way.

Had there been a flash of light in the shower? It was possible, but I recalled what happened on my eighteenth birthday. Ms. Stovall was right; it was impossible to miss. Another point in the column of my insanity.

Before he grew too concerned with my faraway look, I gave my father a hurried nod and a small, forced smile. If what Smegma said was real, then I knew it wasn't just my Mana Pool, but it wasn't like I even understood how Smegma had gotten here. The strange messages I had seen indicated that something more had happened. I didn't yet know exactly what, or what the other two Skills I got were.

Still, after hours of sitting in the interrogation room by myself waiting for the lawyer, I was pretty sure that I'd somehow inherited Morgan's Skills. I now also knew how he could have gotten such high-leveled Skills, even if he was C-Ranked on his original assessment. He was a Snatcher—I shivered at the realization that he had likely been after me for my Mana Pool.

If only he knew I had an F-Ranked Pool—he probably wouldn't have even bothered.

Still, now I had a Pool and multiple Skills! I really needed to see what Smegma could do. He'd already claimed multiple times he wasn't a Combat Summons. So, what exactly was he then?

I tuned back into the conversation as Ms. Stovall stood up and said she'd bring in the detectives.

Volt and Flair followed her back in a few moments later, and after they both apologized, she took control of the conversation in a very firm but professional manner.

"I know you're both veterans at this job and therefore must be well aware of the facts of this case." She placed a hand on the closed folder. "Since my client isn't a flight risk or guilty of anything save self-defense, which led to a Justifiable Homicide, I request that Brodie Flacarada be released into Clara and Gary Flacarada's care until the pre-trial, where the Judge can rule on his risk if required."

Volt and Flair looked at each other and nodded before Flair turned to Ms. Stovall. "That's acceptable. However, your client must be made available for further questioning if the need arises. He will have twenty-four hours to bring himself to the station once contacted. Agreed?"

Ms. Stovall glared at the detectives, but eventually transferred a much softer look to my parents. They nodded at the unspoken question. They would ensure I made it here in a timely manner.

"I want it noted that any request for further questioning be directed to me, and I will pass it on to the Flacarada's. Understood? Any contact outside of me as an intermediary will be identified as, and *prosecuted* for, harassment." Ms. Stovall said, with more than a hint of a threat in her voice. The two detectives nodded with sour looks on their faces.

I raised my hand, and the two detectives turned to look at me with mild amusement written on their less than happy faces. Ms. Stovall explained the smirks as she said, "No need to raise your hand Brodie. This isn't a classroom. What do you want to ask?"

"Can I still attend school?" I asked.

"I'd suggest you—"

"We have no problems with you returning to your day-to-day life, Brodie," Volt responded, cutting off Ms. Stovall. There was a hint of something in his voice. It felt ominous.

"It's a trap," Smegma said scornfully, as he made faces at Volt and Flair. "They want to see if you'll just return to your life like nothing happened. It would indicate something missing in your head or the like."

I'm not sure that line of thinking made any sense, as it seemed to me that anyone in a similar situation would want a return to normalcy in their life. However, I nodded to Volt and discreetly included Smegma for the astute warning.

I turned to Ms. Stovall instead and offered an explanation. "I'm just worried about failing due to extended absence, or wasting the money my parents and I spent on tuition."

Ms. Stovall smiled at me and my parents before turning her gaze on the officers. "Very considerate, Brodie. Probably a good idea to have the *detectives* here write something up to explain your absence. Your parents or you can probably go see the Dean of your program with that."

The meeting went on for another hour, but it became less talking and more filling out paperwork. Once everything was done, the detectives shook my parents' hands and the lawyer's but left the room before shaking mine. It was strange but easy to dismiss.

Ms. Stovall gave my mother and father a hug before fixing me in place with a look. I was halfway standing from the metal chair when I saw it and debated lowering myself back down. I chose to continue to push myself to my feet while meeting her eyes.

"I suggest," she began, before finding me calmly meeting her gaze. She stuttered slightly as her mouth firmed. Then she coughed before continuing as if nothing had happened. "Take some time. While you seem to be handling the attack well, it has only been a day. Your father's union benefits will cover a psychiatrist.

"I strongly suggest you have a few sessions with one of them before you make a final decision on returning to school *or not*. Otherwise, wait for a call from me or the police. With a case like this, we should get a pre-court date within the month."

Her look paired with her words let me know that she, like the police detectives, was sensing something off with me. I also heard what she left unsaid. There was no guarantee that my current calm wasn't numbness or the like. Something that would and could suddenly vanish. To everyone else, the attempted theft—no, murder—was a huge deal.

"I think she's also thinking that attending sessions with the psycho-person will help you look normal…" Smegma offered, giving me something else entirely to think about.

He probably wasn't wrong, but what if this was just an illusory calm? Then I may find myself angry, scared or depressed in short order. That, of course, could make me unpredictable. So, I should see a psychiatrist to help me dig deeper into my current state—what Ms. Stovall seemed to be implying was only a coping mechanism.

Was it? I had a few suspicions that it might be one of the Skills I'd gotten along with *Demonic Vault*, but I had no idea what each one did. Plus, didn't skills require Mana to work? Just how many times today alone had I already questioned my sanity?

I nodded and sidestepped away from the bolted table and chair. Something landed on my shoulder. While it wasn't heavy, I was still surprised that Smegma had any weight to him at all since he was able to phase through any object he wanted. Then again, he *did* stand on chairs and bed posts. How did that even work, anyway? I didn't look at him, and instead made my way to the door. My parents gushed a series of thanks and appreciative comments toward Ms. Stovall, and she fended off their praises magnanimously, claiming she was only doing her job.

When I opened the door, my parents excused themselves and rushed to join me. Ms. Stovall gave me a relieved look, like I had just saved her from something she found particularly distasteful. I gave her a tight-lipped smile and exited the room. I really needed some time to myself to figure out what in the *Demonic* Hell was going on.

I turned my head to Smegma as I walked out into the hallway. Someone led me and my parents out of the station, and we got into the family Ford Escort. The trip home was mostly silent.

From time to time, my mother would bring up how blessed we were to have Ms. Stovall on our side, and my dad and I would make noises of agreement, but otherwise no one spoke.

The only break from the silent ride was a bit of levity in the form of Smegma phasing his head through the rear window of the Escort as we drove down the highway. The Demon's mouth was open, tongue flicking in and out between his fangs, as his head spun from side to side, taking in the sights. I realized that the magical tether he had to me meant that he was unable to explore the entirely new world he'd found himself in. How would I feel if I were placed in the same position?

Certainly not good, but I kind of was in a whole new world myself. A day ago, I would never have thought I'd be in and out of a police station after an attempted theft of Mana—with a winged Demon-Imp as perpetual company. The realization reinforced my desire to get a grip on the changes that occurred and what the benefits, drawbacks, and limitations were. I needed to figure things out soon.

* * *

"Okay, without bringing up checking my Skill Cards or Skills with a Crystal again, which I don't have and can't afford. What the hell do you do— other than annoy me?!" I asked Smegma as soon as I sat back in my office chair inside my room. I kept my voice to a whisper, not wanting my parents to think I was talking to myself. I'm sure they were both stressed enough with everything, and the last thing they needed to cap off recent events was to see their son talking to himself.

Especially since I had just finally escaped their over doting and awkward silences at the dinner table.

"I'm a Demonic Trader. I can connect you to my Sect on Crendalar Five. You can purchase things with Mana or Mana Crystals," he answered plainly.

"Okay," I answered slowly, trying to understand what that might entail. It wasn't like I couldn't buy things at the local mall using Mana Crystals. Sure, the dollar was still more widely used, but Mana Crystals were accepted worldwide. "What are the Skills *Recovery* and *Mental Fortitude* then?"

"Oh, so you're aware that you got both of those? With your response earlier, I wasn't sure. You probably would have been a real mess today if you didn't have that combination..."

I gasped. Not only had I re-Awakened and gotten this *Demonic Vault*, but Smegma just confirmed that the two other messages in the red window were in fact two other Skills. I shivered as I recalled Morgan's words about being a 'chosen one,' a 'Paragon.' The goosebumps rising because that implied statement somehow now applied to me. Four Skills, if I included my Mana Pool.

Wait—the combination of *Recovery* and *Mental Fortitude* was doing what? Was that why I felt so calm, so clear-headed? I wanted to be upset with Smegma, but thanks in large part to that feeling of clarity, I didn't feel the need to. In fact, my mind simply acknowledged his statement as true and then wanted to move on. I took a deep breath at that realization.

While I was glad that I could examine the events from yesterday with a mostly calm detachment, I still felt small twinges of anger. Yet to not feel haunted by the assault… It wasn't natural—wasn't *normal*. No wonder I had been getting such strange looks.

It wasn't as though I felt like it hadn't happened—more like it had definitely happened, and I had somehow gone through all the stages of healing from overcoming the possible husking and risk of imminent death. It was only that the time required for that healing had been condensed down to hours instead of requiring a more 'normal' time frame of days, weeks, or even years. My brain seemed impatient with wanting me to 'move on' from this subject—almost seeming to say 'get over it and pay attention to what's important.'

What *was* important?

Well, my calm, rational mind pointed that out for me, too. It was along the same line of thinking that had made the comparison between the Demon's words and shopping at the local mall from a moment ago that suddenly stood out in stark relief.

"Wait. Can I buy Skills from your world?"

"Skill Cards, yes. I'm a Demonic Trader. And no, before you ask, I don't *think Demonic Vault* can turn someone into a Snatcher."

"Then how did Morgan take Skills?" I asked, thinking it odd that if I inherited his Skills when he died that I didn't have one that fit that particular criterion. Then again, the fact that I took his Skills might mean I was—what had Ms. Stovall called it? A *Cannibal...*

I felt like throwing up at that thought and decided, if I was somehow a Cannibal, that I wouldn't be taking any other Skills from people. Never again. The thought of purchasing Skills from *Demonic Vault* sat better with me, so I asked, "Can you show me what you have to offer?"

"Do you even have any Mana Crystals to convert and spend?" Smegma asked pointedly. I didn't respond and eventually he sighed. "You'll need to provide me with Mana, so I can manifest the Inventory Pages."

My eyes opened and closed and then picked up in pace as I blinked rapidly. I needed to provide him with Mana. Did that mean he was going to connect with my Pool like Morgan had? My disgust must have been apparent because Smegma held up both of his three-fingered, taloned hands.

"Don't get all worked up. I don't take the Mana from you, *you* give it to my Skill Card. I don't fully exist on this plane from a certain metaphysical perspective and can't force a connection to your Mana," Smegma explained.

"Okay, so how do I do that?"

Thus began my first extremely frustrating lesson from a small, wisecracking Imp-Demon named Smegma.

CHAPTER 8

Wednesday, April 3rd, 2069

"**Y**ou said that you'd be better after a night's sleep," Smegma accused as I attempted to glare at him through blurry, crust-filled, tired eyes.

We'd stayed up far too late last night with Smegma attempting to teach me how to infuse Mana into the *Demonic Vault* Skill. The slight narrowing of my already squinted eyes didn't seem to affect the rude little Imp, and so I gave up and blinked.

"Why did you decide that six *AM* was a good time to wake me up?" I countered; my voice filled with as much whispered heat as I could muster this early in the morning.

"Your body had released all the hormones required for your biological wellbeing and repaired any damaged or senescent cells. Additionally, you were at peak energy efficiency," Smegma answered and I blinked, not having expected such clear biological terms as a response. I truly had thought the Demon was just being a little shit.

"Well, first of all, let's get one thing straight: it's not me who's the shitty student here—it's you who's a shitty teacher. How am I supposed to 'feel' the magic when I don't know what it feels like? It's like saying 'just *see* the color Demonic Red.' How do you expect me to sense something I've never experienced before simply by telling me to do it?"

"You'll know it once you find it. As for Demonic Red, only the most profound of our race ever found it," Smegma said, his voice sounding sagely.

"Really?" I asked, wondering if I had somehow accidentally guessed a color from the Demon's world.

"No, that's the stupidest name for a color ever, plus why do you humans have different names for all these colors? That's green, and that's a light green with some blue. Husking moronic race."

I wanted nothing more than to punt him out my window.

With a growl, I tried to search inside myself as instructed. I had tried meditation once before in my life, and this felt a lot like that. Similarly to when I'd dabbled in meditation, my thoughts raced around in my head—most of them accusatory and belittling.

I will admit that this process was better than the meditation, but that was only because the racing thoughts included somewhat helpful suggestions, probably thanks in large part to my new *Mental Fortitude* Skill…

Still, it isn't very helpful when the thoughts were directing you toward a feeling you had when your Mana was forcibly taken from you, reminding you of the risk of husking and simultaneously highlighting how calm and rationally I could examine that experience.

It felt like I had a car. That car worked fine and I had maintained it with oil changes, fed it gas when it was sucking fumes, and generally knew the ins and outs of the vehicle like a best friend. Sure, the car was older, like the family's Ford Escort or maybe even my mom's rust bucket, but it worked and I was used to it. Then, out of the blue, I went out to my driveway, got into that car and discovered that all the parts had been replaced with that of a Formula One race car. The exterior looked the same, but everything under the hood wasn't.

It was as if this 'car' was mocking how terrible my old one was just with its presence. I couldn't even feel weirded out by the change, thanks to the engine and premium fuel chugging along—taking me to my destination while cruising over a smooth road that should be pockmarked or at least covered in occasional speed bumps.

Even when I thought of the risk of the Mana Theft, my anger wasn't generally because of Morgan Hallsbrad and his actions in particular. No, my frustration was due to my own failing. Despite the instructions of Smegma and my own internal direction, I couldn't latch onto my Mana Pool. I knew it was there, my body could intrinsically feel its presence, and Smegma was even able to direct me to its location inside of me, but I felt like a toddler trying to catch air.

My 'hands' swiped through the space feeling resistance but phasing right through it. I tried waving my mental awareness back and forth through the area and felt the Mana Pool like thick smoke—present but ephemeral.

Frustrated, I tried flicking it like I would an object with my index finger. As though a church bell began ringing from a few feet away, I felt my body vibrate. I did it again, and again, enjoying the strange sensation because it felt like progress. After the tenth to twentieth flick, I opened my eyes in frustration.

While the mental poking was getting a new response, it wasn't advancing me toward my goal.

"How the husk am I supposed to supply you with Mana when I can't access my Pool?" I complain-asked. Somehow, I was more frustrated now that I found something new about the strange well of power inside of me, but it turned into another failure.

"I'm starting to question the intelligence of your entire race. It looked like you were causing ripples there in the Mana. So, you were close. Try creating a *conduit* between the two areas where your Skills and your Mana reside. Honestly, if this is the best you 'humans' can do, your race is doomed."

I gave Smegma a withering side-eye—trying to convey my disdain for his race of 'bat-Demons' in turn. His dark eyes simply regarded me, before letting out a loud fart. The staring contest continued, and eventually my brain's insistence to move on won—and so I blinked and shook myself.

Okay! I let my 'supercar' of a brain guide my thoughts.

This wasn't his first time speaking about the topic of impending doom. Each time he did, it sounded like he was foreshadowing the inevitable. Like he was a history teacher claiming that everything always repeated itself. Cataloging it as a question to ask him later, I returned to mentally 'ringing the bell' that was my Mana Pool.

"A conduit," I whispered to myself. "So, like electrical wires, piping or…" I faded off as I attempted to visualize the examples I was naming. Then a simpler example struck me. "A straw!" I emphasized, and as if the area of my Mana Pool was a KapiSun, I jabbed the sharpened end of my mental straw into it.

Instantly I got a reaction, but not the one I was expecting. My mental hands holding the straw felt the tip pass into the layer of ephemeral Mana. However, a building resistance grew and I frowned. It felt like I was fighting a marshmallow. Suddenly that counter force buckled and then popped, like a membrane of a balloon. Thankfully, something that felt like a piece of rubber sealed around the circular straw. But a straw has a hole at the other end, and I quickly realized that the contents of my Mana Pool were under some sort of pressure. I felt the Mana from my Pool rush down the interior and spill out the other side, flooding my body with energy. For a moment it felt good, right until that euphoria morphed into nausea. Mentally, I plugged the end of the straw with a 'thumb' as I fumbled, somewhat drunkenly, to find the place where I intrinsically knew my Skill for Summoning the *Demonic Vault* resided.

I finally located the tiny area that seemed to resonate with the feeling of the Skill I was searching for. The straw's end with my mental finger plugging it passed through a slight resistance at the location where my mind was telling me the Skill was located, multiple times, but it was such a small area that the straw moved into and out of it again in mere fractions of inches. The nausea and energy shaking my body was going through slowly calmed down, and that helped me guide the mental straw to the right spot.

It wasn't simply that the rampant, spilled energy disappeared, but that *Demonic Vault* or something else seemed to slowly suck the energy moving through my body into itself. Finally, my 'thumb' found the spot and released the second end of the straw.

It fixed itself in place, and I watched as two stars seemed to blink into existence behind my closed eyelids. On closer inspection, however, one appeared to be a galaxy with about seven blue dots circling around it. Then there was a hollow tube that led from the edge of the galaxy to a red blinking, growing sun in the distance. It reminded me of the sun and stars that had been pulled from Morgan Hallsbrad, duplicated, collapsed, and then were seemingly transferred into me—somehow. Still, I only had a galaxy of small dots and a distant sun—so, it wasn't exactly the same. Once I examined them both thoroughly, I opened my eyes.

Smegma was flapping his wings and looking at his three-taloned hands. I wondered why he was so still and quiet after my success, and then I saw it. The wrinkles that made him look like one of those hairless skin-cats, Sphinxes I think, were slowly firming themselves. It was like watching a filter move through a SwiftGram picture, but in this case Smegma started to look more healthily terrifying with each blink of my eyes.

I shuddered as I watched the gremlin grow half a foot taller, as well as taking on the appearance of a verifiable killing machine. I hoped he was still unable to interact with much of the physical plane, and if not—well, my body might be in for a rude shredding. That definitely wouldn't be a fun way to die…

"That's it?!" Smegma shouted once the transformation ended.

He was clearly upset, verging on angry, and my eyebrow raised unbidden in question. Smegma stared at me before closing his eyes. I felt a presence in the space I had just exited and closed my eyes to watch what was happening. The red star sent a strand of red 'hair' down the straw toward the Galaxy. The string attempted to enter my Mana Pool, but that very membrane I punctured earlier with the sharpened straw's end seemed to somehow exist inside the straw as well. It rebuffed the hair-thin, red strand back toward the Sun.

"Hey, you said you can't connect to my Mana," I accused.

With a growl, Smegma asked, "I'm not *taking* Mana you moron. Just trying to figure out why I look like *this*. How large is your Mana Pool?"

"Umm. Ten points, assuming that bastard told the truth back in the alleyway," I responded with the number that Morgan Hallsbrad had seemed surprised about.

I was still watching as the red strand attempted to find a way past the membrane to the Galaxy of blue stars behind it. An eighth star popped into place, and I realized that my Mana Pool was also reabsorbing some of the spilled Mana in my body. The star's reappearance also indicated that the blue, far smaller, suns circling around the black void in this Galaxy were points of Mana.

"That doesn't make any sense," Smegma complained. "Are you mentally blocking me from examining your Pool?"

I opened my eyes to find Smegma still standing on my bed with his eyes closed. I didn't think I was blocking him, but then again, I wasn't sure why he wanted to examine my Pool. I didn't quite believe his reason and felt it was far more likely that he was trying to take it for himself, like Morgan had.

I raised a skeptical eyebrow toward the Demon. "You just watched me flail around to establish a link that you yourself said was so easy that you started questioning the intelligence and survivability of my entire race, and yet now you think I have enough control over whatever this is to actively manipulate it and 'block you?' So which one is it, smarty pants? Am I too dumb to breathe or so amazing that I'm somehow better at this than you are?"

With a growl, his eyes shot open, and he flinched to discover me staring at him. His frustration seemed to drain from his face, and he began tapping a talon on his sharp teeth. A gesture I'd come to recognize as him thinking.

"No, you're definitely right that on the scale you mentioned, you're much closer to 'too dumb to breathe' than the savant at the other end of the spectrum. There's no way you can be blocking me from a simple examination while not concentrating on doing so. Still, it can't be a higher ranked Skill than *Demonic Vault* with just ten points of Mana. You sure about the ten points?"

"Well, not really. The Shop seemed surprised and said something about 'ten points, that's it,' or something like that when he connected to it."

More talon-on-tooth tapping followed. After a few seconds, Smegma threw his hands above his head. "Well, I guess I'm stuck like *this*," he gestured at himself, "until you die! Husk it. Send a drop of Mana across and I'll display the windows."

The exclamation surprised me for a second before I remembered the straw and the whole point of connecting the two Skills. I mentally shot one of the glowing stars down the straw and saw a red screen pop up in front of Smegma. "What in the husk is this?" Smegma shouted. "These are all the F and E-Ranked trash!"

"What?" I asked dumbly. "That doesn't make any sense." I distinctly remembered the *Mental Fortitude* Skill being A- Ranked on the weird message window, as well as the *Recovery* Skill being Ranked C. "Show me!"

His tiny fists clenched into balls and his face scrunched up, but he waved a hand, which seemed to force the screen to rush to a place in front of me.

When I realized that I couldn't read it and why, I rolled my eyes and said, "Can you flip it around?"

"Yeah, yeah, whatever. This is total bullshit anyway," Smegma complained even as he complied.

Demon Vault 1.0
Crendalar Five – Abyss Sect's Wares

<Skills>
Consumables
Weapons
Armor
Miscellaneous
Currency: 2 mC

The first thing I noticed was that it was obvious he hadn't been talking about *my* Skill ranks earlier. I was hoping that he'd found a way to show me some sort of Video Game recap page on myself. One that I could examine. The second thing I saw was that I had two 'Coins,' which was unexpected.

I looked away from the screen to Smegma and asked, "Do I just provide Mana to the Skill to build up currency?"

"Like it matters. It will take you forever to get anything good with only ten Mana. Plus, all the good shit that I've been training to sell isn't even there! I've spent a good portion of my husking life preparing for this!" Smegma answered, well—*complained* was more like it.

I felt slightly bad for him but couldn't find too much empathy for the little shit. I had been dreaming of being a Hunter my whole life but Awakened with a single Skill, and it was not only the most common, but the lowest ranked Skill at that… Between the two of us, I think I had it worse.

I realized he kind of gave me an answer and so started *mentally* clicking into the options, starting with Skills. I instantly discovered why Smegma was upset. The list of Skills were things I didn't even know *could* exist. Things like Aid, Alarm, Alter, Animal Messenger, Arcane Armor, and Augury were listed. I clicked into a few that seemed interesting and grew even more discouraged when I saw the price.

Aid Skill Card
Aid
(1)
Skill Type: Healing
Skill Rank: Low F-Rank (Evolvable)

Magically apply first aid to an injured individual. This Skill will remove some status ailments such as bleeding or burning. It will also aid in recovery of the injured person, increasing their rate of healing by 1%.
Cost: 1,000,000 mC

Not only were the effects lackluster, but the cost was astronomical. Another issue popped into my head, and I turned away from the screen to look at Smegma.

"Is there a limit to how many Skills a person can have?" I asked reluctantly, recalling the conversation about Cannibals. I didn't really want to know the answer if there was a limit, but needed to.

"There is and it's based on Soul and Magic Capacity. So, a wastrel like you will probably only be able to have ten."

"Hey!" I complained and saw Smegma's face scrunch up slightly. He didn't apologize for his derogatory choice of words to describe me though, and I frowned. I asked my next question instead of dwelling on it. "What does the number one beside the Skill mean?"

"Skill level. You can level up a Skill the more you use it. Something like Aid will just have its healing rate increase as it levels, until you can Evolve it."

"Evolve it?" I asked, immediately excited. Didn't that mean my Mana Pool would grow the more I used it?

"Evolution is a very complicated process and requires a System Opportunity. Skills Evolve based on the use and desired direction of use of the owner of the Skill. For example, Aid can become First Aid, Minor Heal or even something like Bind."

"Okay," I answered, trying to understand how a 'healing' Skill could become Bind. Then it struck me. The bandage tying could possibly be used to tie someone up, I supposed. That seemed like a good enough deduction for now, so I asked the much more pressing question. "Doesn't that mean my Mana Pool can grow?"

With a sigh, Smegma manipulated the screen in front of me.

Mana Pool Skill Card
Mana Pool
(1)
Skill Type: Resource Pool
Skill Rank: See below (Evolveable)
Will create a well of Mana inside of the owner. This well can be used to power Skills and Spells. Only one Mana Pool can exist inside an individual. The Mana Pool's ranking determines its size and it cannot grow.
Recharge rate increased by 1%.
F-Rank – random assignment of 1-10 Mana – 2,000,000 mC
E-Rank – random assignment of 11-50 Mana – 20,000,000 mC

I sighed. But then realized that just because this Skill description didn't seem to allow the Pool to grow didn't mean I couldn't Evolve the Skill to grow. I was pretty sure some famous SwiftGrammers showed that they had grown their Mana capacity. "So what if I Evolve the Skill?"

"Sure, but if you really have an F-Rank Skill to begin with then it will be difficult to grow. Plus, it will be limited in Evolutions. Not to mention the difficulty involved in coming across an opportunity to Evolve the Skill."

While Smegma's words were discouraging, they didn't completely remove the small bud of hope that seemed to be growing in my chest. Plus, with the *Demonic Vault*, couldn't I just replace my low-rank Pool for a higher one?

"So, can I buy a higher-grade card and replace the one I have?" I asked.

"Yes, but you'll lose the levels in the Skill you have. Plus, how's a dumb-dumb like you going to get twenty million Mana Coins?"

"Even a *dummy* like me knows there has to be another way to increase my Coins. Right?"

With a scoff, Smegma gestured around the room. "I've already told you. Mana Crystals! Do you have a Mana Crystal safe I wasn't able to find?"

"Nope, but I might know where to get some."

Of course, I was thinking about my father's Mining job. I'd helped part-time over the summer and carted out bags of mined Crystal Shards. Surely, I could sneak one or two, right?

As it always seemed to happen, it was then that I saw the man who loaded the bags in a new light. He'd marked each Bag of Holding with a number, and the porter, who I had previously worked with, would double-check at the truck with a scale that I dropped the bag onto. So, then I would have to be a Miner to pocket a few? There was no chance of becoming a loader, those people were paid extremely well and often friends of the owner.

"You know where there's an unattended Portal?" Smegma asked, sounding excited for the first time.

"No. I was just thinking I could get hired as a Miner and sneak a few Crystals to The Shop," I responded.

Smegma went back to tapping a talon on his tooth. Then the screen in front of me changed.

Miscellaneous Professions Gear
Miner's Pick
(1)
Item Rank: Low F-Rank
Durability: Unlimited
Damage: 1-3 (x100% to Mineable minerals)
This Miner's Pick will use the Mana run-off from the Crystals to repair and strengthen itself, making it unbreakable. It will also store excess Mana to intermittently create a Mana Crystal of appropriate rank.
Current progress to Mana Crystal: 0 of 1,000 Mana
Cost: 10,000 mC

"Why is this so much cheaper?" I asked, having read over the description with growing excitement.

"Because it's a Miner's Pick?!" Smegma said incredulously, like that was answer enough. I supposed it was. I guessed that Demons also looked down on professions like Miners. I continued to scan through the Miscellaneous section and discovered numerous other Profession Tools. Skinning Knives, Alchemy Lab, Engineering Toolbox, and Tailoring Kit being a few among them. What I discovered was that certain tools were vastly more expensive than others. Like the Enchanter's Kit or the Alchemy Lab.

"Do the prices on these reflect how large the physical size of the purchase is?" I asked, staring at the multiple million-Coin price tag on the Lab and Kit.

"Somewhat for the Lab, sure. But nope on the Kit. Do you not have Potions and Enchanted Jewelry and Gear on this world?" Smegma asked. I gave him a look that questioned his intelligence, and he got the message. "Well then you know how expensive those things are. This is Crafting versus Gathering, thus, the price tag, idiot."

I ran a hand over my patchy stubble. "Who sets the prices?"

"My sect did, obviously."

A smile came over my face. So, the prices were based on what the Abyss Sect thought was valuable. Since they likely had far more experience with the value of magical, and perhaps even mundane, materials than Earth, they were probably pretty accurate. However, that disconnect could be exploited if I discovered instances of things on Earth that were relatively common or easily accessible—hopefully both—and that the Abyss Sect valued highly.

"Can I sell items for Mana Coins or credit?" I asked.

"Yes, but we'll only give you about half the value," Smegma answered.

I nodded in understanding and started scanning the lists of weapons, armor, Skills, miscellaneous and consumables. As I searched, I funneled the remaining eight points of Mana to the Skill. A new star popped up about ten minutes later and I sent it across too, arriving at eleven Mana Coins. This would be a good test to see how fast my Mana regenerated as well.

As I combed through The Shop, I began cataloging items I found interesting, trying to arrive at what my first goal should be. Right at this moment, I was leaning toward an E-Ranked Mana Pool Card, but to make the necessary twenty million Mana Coins, I would need a Miner's Pick and to join my father on a job.

Could I convince him to bring me with him? It would be tough. He was the prime factor in me attending University because he didn't want his son to be a Miner like him, or god-forbid, a low-ranked Hunter with a gun against the threats out there with powerful Skills. My mother, who worked as a secretary for the same company as him, wanted me to attend school as well, but with a bit less vehemence. So, the real question was how do I convince my father?

I realized then that my supercar analogy from earlier wasn't accurate. It wasn't like my intelligence had increased. More like the engine was a more efficient model. Something like a hybrid or maybe even a Mana Crystal converter. I was able to think logically without much distraction, but that didn't make it so I could solve problems I couldn't before.

Or in this instance—the insurmountable problem of a way to convince my father to join him in the Portal Mines… I looked at Smegma pleadingly and he shook his head derisively. Under his breath, the Demon muttered, "All the guile of a husking *Mirror Fish*, this one."

CHAPTER 9

Wednesday, April 3rd, 2069

"**L**ike we practiced, moron!" Smegma coached, his body sticking out halfway through the ceiling. I really wished he could understand social cues, particularly ones around when his presence would be a distraction.

My parents were both teary-eyed, and my father, the man who needed convincing, looked so crestfallen that I wanted nothing more than to give him a hug and renege on my request. Still, despite my low assessment on Awakening, I hadn't given up on my dream of becoming part of a Hunter's team.

Now with the chance at my fingertips to better myself, contribute to the fight, and my future prospects, I was going to chase it like a dog with a bone. Despite my parents clearly thinking that my mindset and future were headed down a toilet-like spiral if I joined the Miners. I could see in their eyes the slow-death of their desire for me to live a better life than they had for themselves. Asking to join the Mining team was clearly, to them, an admission that they had failed a fundamental part of their goals in raising me.

"It's only for a semester," I said again. "I'm going to need to take time off until pre-trial anyway, and if I go back a month behind, my grades will suffer."

"All of your teachers already told me that they'll accommodate you, Brodie," my mother countered.

"It isn't the same, and you know it. Sure, I can read and even watch the lessons online, but if I'm supposed to be taking a break like Ms. Stovall said, then shouldn't I not be reminded of the place where the assault happened? I shouldn't constantly have the thought of returning to already underway classes hanging over my head." I knew that this was a low blow, considering I wasn't too shaken up about the whole thing. I assumed the reason I was okay with using it in such a way was also because of the high-rank *Mental Fortitude* Skill that I'd received.

That and the horrible influence that was Smegma.

Wait—Why couldn't I find that Skill in my mindscape-universe-thing? I figured it would have turned up when I was looking for *Demonic Vault* earlier, but I realized now that I hadn't seen any indication of it while I had been searching around. I made a mental note to try to look for it later.

My mother opened and closed her mouth a few times before looking at my father.

"You could let him work with you until the first appointment with the psychiatrist. It would get you back to work and you could—" she cut off and glanced at me. I could tell she had been about to say something along the lines of 'keep an eye on Brodie,' and had thought better of it. I just hoped that my father would agree, and not keep 'too close' of an eye on me.

"When's his first appointment?" Gary asked my mother.

"Next Monday, so five days from now," my mother answered.

"Okay Son, you can join the crew for four days. As you know, we don't work Sundays usually. You'll work as my assistant, which won't pay well but will start teaching you about the Mines and how to do the job. Then whatever the therapist says, we'll follow, deal?"

I could tell he was banking on the therapist telling me I should continue with my schoolwork from home but wasn't too worried about that. Even if that was the conclusion, I figured I'd have accomplished my first goal. Or at least hoped I'd have done so by then. Smegma had claimed that F-Ranked Mana Crystals were worth anywhere from sixty to just over a hundred points—depending on clarity and size.

So, in theory I would only have to sneak away about two hundred of those to get the Miner's Pick. If my dad's crew happened to be Mining in a higher ranked mine, then I'd need even less.

I doubted the last, but I could dream. It would be beyond rare for Mana Pool Miners to end up in high-ranked mines. Mostly because mid to high-ranked mines were so rare. At least, if I understood what my dad did correctly. It all came down to the fact that even in high-ranked Portals you often found low-ranked Mines. The opposite of discovering high-ranked Mines in low-rank Portals? *Forget about it.*

I nodded enthusiastically and rushed upstairs. I'd felt my Mana Pool fill in the middle of the discussion and hadn't wanted to close my eyes to will the points to the *Demonic Vault* Skill. Once in my room, I closed my eyes and entered my… Internal Universe? I found my Mana Pool with twelve stars surrounding the black void. My eyes couldn't open fast enough. I found and then glared at Smegma. "You said Mana Pools didn't grow before they Evolved."

"I said nothing of the sort. I showed you the Mana Pool Skill Card."

"Semantics, asshole!" I harshly whispered.

"Regardless. Low-ranked ones usually don't grow. Why? Do you have more than ten Mana Points now?"

"Twelve!" I said excitedly.

"And you think some shitty Snatchers initial reading was one hundred percent accurate?" Smegma answered leadingly. I got his message and closed my eyes again to gain my twelve Mana Coins.

"No, I trust my own 'eyes,' asshole. I *saw eight* mana in my little galaxy thing and had already spilled two to the *Demonic Vault* accidentally. Now there's twelve! Plus, I awakened as F-Rank! Now, how long has it been since I drained all my Mana?" I said absently as I began looking for a space within the Universe-thing that the *Mental Fortitude* Skill might reside.

"Just to let you know, low E-Rank and high F-Rank can look identical to a low-quality reader. As per your question," he paused, then answered, "Probably about ten minutes of worthwhile conversation and another two-plus hours of worthless emotion." Smegma sneered and shivered like his body was covered in ick. I rolled my eyes.

Two hours to fill twelve points of Mana. I began doing some quick math. When I realized it would be well over a hundred days till I reached the ten thousand Mana Coins for the Miner's Pick, I groaned. So, stealing Mana Crystals it was…

"You know I can feel the way you're justifying the theft, right?" Smegma said casually.

It was my turn to shiver like I had ick on me. "You can read my mind?"

"Not really," Smegma said with a back-and-forth motion of one his three-taloned hands. "I can hear you when you're mentally talking to yourself, though. It's actually how you can talk to me, without speaking aloud."

"So, are you saying you have a problem with my reasoning?" I asked, trying to cut off my habit of internally debating things in my head.

"I have no problem with theft to begin with. I just find it odd that you're justifying it at all. Not to mention claiming that it might help you become a Hunter, which in turn will help the world, it's a bit thin, in my opinion…"

I mentally thought, [Then I'll just pay back the value later—when I can.]

"Why bother?" Smegma laughed. His laugh was anything but pleasant. He sounded like an evil character high on helium. "I don't even live in this world, but I know enough about greed to understand what the likely outcome of a valuable resource appearing in a random location is. It means that the closest power with the biggest fist is going to gain control of that resource. The chances of that powerful group or individual being a 'good guy,' are practically nil. So, what do you care, even if you took every scrap of value from under their nose? You're not stealing from a poor innocent soul here; you're likely stealing from a blood-drenched warlord out there somewhere in the world who's using the most socially or lawfully appropriate form of slavery they can manage to leech every drop of materials they can get."

I frowned at the Demon. That was a very dark outlook to have and not wholly accurate. Still, it probably wasn't far off. The guy who owned my father's company was certainly well off when compared to my mother and father, right? Definitely not blood-drenched, though. Right? Eventually I shrugged. I didn't have to justify my reasons to Smegma anyway. I would pay back what I stole…

I returned to searching my 'Mental Universe' for *Mental Fortitude*. By the time I had recovered five points of Mana, I still hadn't found it or the *Recovery* Skill. I converted the Mana to Coins and gave up. Five points would roughly mean an hour went by and if I hadn't found either Skill—*Mental Fortitude* was better hidden than I thought. So was *Recovery*, for that matter.

Opening my eyes, I asked, "Do *Mental Fortitude* and *Recovery* work without Mana?"

"Of course, they do. Otherwise, you'd have to activate it. They're called *Passive* Skills for a reason, stupid."

"Thanks for that. What I meant to say is—is that common?" I asked as my face flushed.

"Then maybe you should have been clearer. There are probably more Passive Skills than there are active ones. However, I never took the time to count."

"Some merchant you turned out to be."

"Shut up!" Smegma glared. "I *am* a merchant and a researcher. You're thinking of a scholar."

"I'm just saying, merchants should know their wares," I countered, feeling pleased that I was getting a reaction out of Smegma. He'd called me a few names today, and while it didn't bother me, I wanted to return some of the razzing.

"Yeah, sure, whatever. I spent most of my time as a researcher," Smegma mumbled as his reddish cheeks seemed to gain a shade or two. I thought he might have rolled his eyes too, due to the movements of his eyelids, but because his eyeballs were entirely pitch black, it was tough to tell. I celebrated the 'victory' all the same and realized I did so through mentally talking to myself when Smegma glared at me.

That was something I was going to need to work on.

I spent the rest of the day scanning through screens and writing down Skills that I thought I could use to become a Hunter. Thanks to my excitement about the end-goal of my actions, the day quickly turned into night. I grabbed my phone and made a SwiftGram and then a SmileBook post before setting a two-hour timer. I figured I would wake up and dump my Mana into *Demonic Vault* before restarting my timer and going back to bed. Closing my eyes, I got ready to do just that. I paused as I counted the stars, feeling that something was off.

Sure enough, there were thirteen now.

"I gained another point of Mana," I said to Smegma, who had switched places with me and was on the back of my office chair.

Shaking his head, Smegma said, "No, you didn't."

"I'm looking at my Pool right now. There are thirteen points!"

"Then it wasn't full earlier!"

"I know it was. I felt it!"

"Yeah, the idiot who found his Pool this morning is suddenly the expert."

"I'm going to punt you out the window. I'm telling you it increased—*twice*, now."

"And I'm telling you I've never heard of a Skill that starts the Pool capacity in the F-Ranks and has the capability of that kind of growth, and if it existed, I assure you that I'd have heard of it."

"What the husk?! Like you 'heard' about the number of Passive Skills in your own damned shop? I think you've already clearly demonstrated that you don't know and haven't seen as much as you'd like me to believe. I'm literally looking at it—" I cut off as my door opened. I realized I had raised my voice more than I had intended.

"Everything okay in here?" My father asked, his face pale.

"Sorry, I was just getting ready for bed but was having trouble falling asleep."

My dad came into the room and sat on the bed beside me. "Your mother and I were talking downstairs. I'm glad you're going to get out of the house with me. I know I argued against it, but your mom made me see how good it will be for you. We both just want you to know that you can always talk to us. We promise to hear you out, no matter what it is." He took a long pause and then looked me straight in the eyes. His own were glassy with unshed tears. "I can't help but think this is our fault, somehow."

I reached out and hugged him. I felt my own tears threaten to come then. It was strange. While I wasn't dwelling on the assault, my parents were. "It isn't your fault," I soothed, hugging him tighter. "It isn't anyone's fault but that asshole's. You heard Ms. Stovall. He was a Snatcher and a murderer…"

My dad tensed as I reminded him of the less than pleasant terms used in the Police Station, but then gripped me harder. "Just know that you can tell us about things like what happened on that Instantgram thing."

I chuckled. "It's SwiftGram, Dad," I said in a mock annoyed voice. "*Instantgram* would be a stupid name. And don't worry, I'll be more careful."

My mom came in and joined the hug soon after. I consoled them both, trying my best to convey that I was okay. I could tell that it wasn't effective, but in time they'd probably understand. It didn't help that they both had the Mana Pool Skill but had never truly tapped into it. So, they could only imagine what it had felt like to have it used forcefully against my will. That, of course, muddied my feelings on it as well. Without *Mental Fortitude*, would I be a complete wreck?

Certainly, a Mana Connection against a person's wishes was a serious crime, and even now I never wanted to have anyone touch my Mana Pool again, but was it that bad? I had no reference point to use because I was simply over it. Or at least I was coping with it far better than even I thought I should be.

By the time my parents left my room to let me sleep, the only conclusion I had was that I understood why certain individuals with Mana Pools actively lent their Mana to anyone. Even now, as my Mana was neither refilling nor being used, I could feel the energy—no, the *power* that was literally sitting inside me.

I could see how that rush could be addictive.

As soon as the door closed, I mentally said, [Are there no low-ranked Mana Pools that can grow?]

"Not that I, nor my entire race, was aware of when I started training to become a Trader," Smegma answered. He spoke aloud since no one could hear him anyway.

[You mentioned a way to check my Skills this morning, do you sell anything that can do that? Or can you just look at mine for me if I let you?]

"No, I can't tell you, even if you let me—or I would have already asked you to let me see, moron. On the other side, yes, my Sect sells Spent Mana Crystals of all ranks. I'm pretty sure that the low-rank Spent Mana Crystal will be a waste of money. It's just going to show you that you have a low E-Rank Mana Pool."

[Is that how you identified Skills back on your planet?] I mentally asked.

To my surprise, Smegma didn't instantly respond, making me search around for the Imp. I found him staring out my window. I couldn't tell what he was looking at and mentally prodded him.

The Imp started and then turned the dark black orbs of its eyes on me. "No, we could simply pull the cards from our chests and examine them. I'm not sure how I know that Spent Mana Crystals can read the Mana Signature of a person—and create explanation cards—I just *do!*"

I frowned at his tone. It was clearly a bit lost. Like Smegma was admitting to having forgotten something. Or possibly scarier—finding knowledge stuffed into his head, by something else. I shivered at that thought. Still, if any Spent Mana Crystal could read Mana Signatures...

[Why are you distinguishing a low-rank Mana Crystal if all Crystals can read Mana Signatures?]

"The higher the rank, the more sensitive it is," Smegma answered, his voice hollow, causing me to grab my biceps as goosebumps rose. "Spent F-Rank and E-Rank can handle up to C-Rank skills. D and C up to low A, and so on. If you try to force it to identify higher ranked Skills, it will shatter."

By the end, his voice sounded more natural, almost returning to his haughty know-it-all tone. He made a gesture with his hands and a screen popped up.

Low-Rank Spent Mana Crystal
Consumable
Item Rank: High F-Rank:
Mana drained (Previously High F-Rank Mana Crystal)
This Mana Crystal can identify the Skills of the holder up to C-Rank.
To use, infuse your Mana into the Spent Crystal for five minutes. This will allow the frequency of your skills to reverberate and be identified. The Crystal will then create Cards that identify the user's Skills.
Cost: 100 mC

"Smegma..." I drew the Imp's name out with a faux-arrogant lilt. "Turns out I now know something you don't."

"Lies," the Imp snorted.

"No, for real. I know how the Mana Crystals' identify Skills." I gestured at the prompt in front of my face that he, for obvious reasons, couldn't see.

Smegma glared at me, clearly refusing to ask me to give him the information. I stared back. The standoff went far longer than I'm comfortable admitting before I started to feel guilty about holding back information, with the firehose of knowledge the Imp was giving me. I cleared my throat.

"It looks like a person's Mana has a sort of 'fingerprint,' or as the System prompt calls it, a *frequency* that, when injected into a Spent Mana Crystal, allows the System to interact with the information inside of the Mana to identify its inherent properties.

Smegma blinked. "That... makes total sense, actually." For just a moment, he looked like he might thank me, then he smiled wickedly. "I can probably sell that information to dumb humans like you after I take over this planet and become your intangible, unknowable God-King."

I choked on my spit a bit, thinking about a Demon who wouldn't even be able to prove to a group of amateur ghost-hunters that he even existed, taking over the world. After a moment, I turned back to the prompt, frowning. I *really* wanted to know what my Skill Cards looked like. Sighing, I mentally closed the information window.

Since I couldn't even afford the hundred Mana Coins, I reset my two-hour timer and funneled the thirteen Mana Points over to *Demonic Vault*. I now had thirty-nine mC, which meant I'd be able to purchase a Spent Crystal sometime tomorrow.

"When I use a Crystal to gain Mana Coins, does it become a Spent Crystal after?" I asked, realizing that I probably would be at the Mine by the time I managed to save enough Coins. Which meant—if I was right—perhaps I wouldn't need to spend any Coins at all, and get to have my cake and eat it, too…

"Yes, but if there's too many flaws in the Crystal, it might break when you try to use it to identify your Skills, once all the naturally present Mana's been drained from it," Smegma stated, his voice still not quite losing the deep melancholy that had been present since he began talking about his world.

I tried to dismiss the uncomfortableness of the last few questions and answers. That the System or something could shove information into the Demon's head disturbed me. No matter how much I rubbed my arms, the goosebumps and shivering wouldn't recede. My mind asked me a pertinent question that I hoped the Demon didn't hear.

'Is the Demon even real, or part of a System Skill?'

That didn't exactly make me more comfortable with the notion of knowledge being inserted into what appeared to be a creature with its own thoughts and personality, but it did help. I managed to get my shuddering to abate by telling myself that the System couldn't do that to *me*.

Right?

I pulled my blankets over myself a little too quickly and said, "Moogle, lights off."

CHAPTER 10

Thursday, April 4th, 2069

"**W**hy are we passing all of these Mana Signatures?" Smegma asked, sounding aghast. "It's really inefficient to drive by Portals."

Since it was practically pre-dawn, I wasn't really in the mood for much conversation, and neither was my father, as evidenced by his white-knuckled grip on the steering wheel. After a long pull on my double-double coffee, I blearily checked where we were in the city by gazing out the window.

Mid-town?

Blinking, the buildings came more into focus and I found one of the Steel Stadiums sitting in a mostly abandoned section of the city. Smegma was staring at it and then at me, waiting for an answer.

[It's a Monster Field,] I answered, my mental voice sounding half asleep even to me.

"What in the actual husk is a Monster Field, dumb-dumb?" Smegma retorted instantly.

The question woke me up. I was operating under the assumption that Smegma was Summoned here from a planet that was at least somewhat similar to Earth. Seeing that Smegma's knowledge, and even what his Sect sold, was leagues ahead of Earth, I'd also assumed that his planet was further along in the process than we were. Whenever I brought up Crendalar Five, Smegma changed the subject though, so it was tough to be sure. How, though, would he not know what a Monster Field was then?

[A Monster Field is an area that surrounds a Portal that has no clear conditions—] I began.

"*Every* Portal has a clear condition for closing. I'm starting to think that calling you stupid is unfair to the human race…" Smegma stated over the top of my explanation. "It's looking like the problem is genetic and generalized to your entire species, if this is 'common knowledge' among your kind."

[Shall I finish?] I asked. Smegma spun a taloned finger in a gesture that likely meant 'keep going.' [When we've conquered a Portal's boss multiple times and it still won't close, we erect a Monster Field, also more simply known as a 'Field' around it. Then when the Portal begins allowing the Monsters to come out, they are contained. Fields then allows Hunters to enter and capture Monsters. Hunters are paid bounties for each Monster killed, and they can sell the corpses or materials on site, as well.]

"While that sounds sensible, you know that Portals grow stronger the longer they stay open, right?" Smegma asked, but more told me.

I looked at the Steel Stadium and nodded. [We're aware that the creatures are going up in strength, yes. But I don't think they've ranked up?]

"They will in time. Even just knowing that they're getting stronger is a bad sign. Your race is fine with that?" Smegma asked incredulously.

[I already told you we haven't found a way to close those Portals yet and Permanent Portals are pretty rare…]

I scanned the other direction to the Detroit River. It was behind a few houses, and a massive ten-meter-thick wall, but I wasn't really looking at it. I was looking behind it to the city of Detroit. It was one of the largest Fields on the planet. In truth, it had likely been at least five years since someone had entered the mid-rank Permanent Portal in its center. Maybe longer.

I was pretty sure a few more Permanent Portals had even sprung up since… That or some new Portals have had breaks because of humanity's limited access.

Smegma followed my gaze and his dark black eyes widened. "There's multiple Dungeons in that direction. Are you telling me that you idiots left them all to *grow*?"

I didn't bother responding. The massive ten-meter-high wall should be answer enough. Plus, Smegma's tone was curdling the milk I'd drank in my cereal and coffee this morning. I took another sip of my double-double coffee, hoping it would beat the grumble into submission.

It wasn't like I made the decision or even had a say in things of that magnitude. Still, maybe with—

My dad made a left turn, which surprised me. Startled, I asked, "Wait, are we going to the Field of Detroit?"

"Yes, we're meeting the teams at the wall and then convoying to one of three cleared Dungeons," my father answered sleepily. He yawned, and a moment later I did too. He smiled at me when I did so, likely finding the contagiousness of yawns amusing. "Don't worry. We're being escorted by the Snowbird and Lynx Guilds."

My eyes widened at the names of Windsor's two largest Guilds. Still, in the time it took for him to answer, the Wall had already grown larger. Smegma was eyeing my father with a suspicious narrowing of his eyes.

"Is he trying to reassure *you* or himself?" he asked after a moment.

[Both,] I responded. [He always says there's a reason Miners get danger pay.]

"And the other Miners only have a Mana Pool too? No other Skills to go along with it?" Smegma asked cautiously.

[That's the most common Awakening Gift, yes, but a few of them could have a different Skill and no Mana Pool beside it.]

"It seems that the System is acting differently upon your world than it did on mine in more ways than just the *cards*," Smegma said as he jumped onto the dash and phased his head through the windshield for a better view of the Wall.

[On Crendalar Five, you mean?] I asked mentally, hoping he might be willing to share more this time.

After a few moments of silence, I realized he was acting as though he couldn't hear me with his head outside of the car. I wasn't exactly a hundred percent sure that wasn't how mental communication worked, but I was somewhat confident that he'd heard the question.

My father pulled into a parking lot that I hadn't noticed but should have. While a parking lot was nothing to make note of, the massive military vehicles inside of it were. It wasn't like I hadn't seen the things before, at least on television, but to see this many together, and with my own eyes, should have immediately gotten my attention.

In high school we had a history class that covered the World Wars and advancement of military technology. Still, the jump the technology had made since the Advent of the Portals, Monsters and Mana was more akin to a quantum leap than a steadily achieved advancement.

The vehicle wheels alone were easily four times the size of my dad's Ford Escort. Four times bigger than the entire *car*, not bigger than our car's tires. They also were made from Monster Materials that would help to prevent punctures and promote traction over almost all terrains. That was just the start when it came to the new technologies. The 'metal' or 'rock' on the exterior didn't gleam or shine in the rising morning sun. No, it actively seemed to take the sunlight and convert it into shadows that wreathed the vehicle in a seemingly dark cloud.

My first-year class on Portal Materials with Miss Chavez discussed a few of the extraterrestrial metals, and I guessed that this one I was seeing was Necrograph, a 'metal' whose composition was more similar to diamond and coal than it was to metals from the periodic table. Some argued it wasn't even a metal at all and that it was more of a rock, but regardless, someone had discovered how to shape it, and it was now used as armoring and protection for vehicles. No Hunters used the stuff for armor though. It was simply too heavy and dense.

Though, considering the nature and ranks of Skills, I wouldn't be surprised if someone out there, like Gamonji, had the sheer passive Strength to lug around armor made from the stuff. That got me thinking about what Smegma had said about Passive Skills being more abundant than active ones, as well as his comment on how the 'System' worked differently on our planet. I immediately understood that his people probably didn't merely get only one Skill Card, or that they had some way of easily accessing more—perhaps through this Shop of theirs.

Regardless, since humans rarely Awakened with more than one Skill, it made me think that, at least initially, the best possible first Skill for a single-Skilled human, as things stood, would be to gain a Passive Skill. It completely bypassed the problem of either needing a Mana Pool to activate an Active Skill, or needing a secondary Active Skill to utilize the Mana inside your own Mana Pools.

Were there more people out there with such Skills, given that Smegma said they were more common, or were they merely more common for Demons than they were for humans? I couldn't help coming back to the thought of some Superhero-esque jacked physique of a man with a high-ranked Passive Skill increasing his Strength Stat just walking through a hail of bullets, wrapped head to toe in Necrograph.

I returned to studying the vehicles with a childish smile at my daydream. The varying densities along with the new properties of these new 'metals' was another reason for our planet's technological leap, however this one was in Engines. Fossil fuels were still used by common people like my family, but Mana

Engines that could run off Mana Crystals were the height of wealth and power. These monstrous military vehicles could only be powered by one of them. Nothing else could move the several hundred tons of military-grade, mobile destruction.

Smegma landed on my shoulder as I exited the Ford's passenger seat. It was strange, because despite knowing the demonic Imp was there, this time I didn't feel a shift in weight. I wondered if Smegma could stand on the air if he chose to and just hadn't 'chosen' too a few times in the past. My dad moved to the trunk and, after I took a quick count of the Military ATV's, I joined him. Sixty-five of the huge vehicles idled in the shadow of the Wall.

"I don't have a set of protective gear for you with me, or a pick. We'll have to get you a loaner set from Mitch." My dad's voice was muffled as he pulled on an old, highly worn leather chest piece. If I remembered correctly, it was made from Kobold hide, but thanks to massive dust and dirt build-up, I couldn't even make out the small scales I'd recalled made up its surface.

After the chest, he strapped on thigh guards, stepped into knee pads, and tucked a pair of shin guards into his socks and under his stretchy jeans. He then reached back into the trunk and placed two small elbow guards into a helmet, grabbed his terribly worn pickaxe and hung the helmet strap over the spike. He motioned to a large cooler with his free hand. "Mind grabbing our lunches, Bro?"

"Sure, *bro*." I rolled my eyes but couldn't stop the chuckle that escaped my throat.

My dad used to always call me Bro, until I grew old enough to hate it in elementary school. Mostly because I met a kid that called *everyone* bro, and the way that kid had made it sound was douchey, at best. Still, after many years of maturation, I found I didn't mind it as much, since it also doubled as a short form for my name. I grabbed the cooler, and my dad used his free hand to close the hatchback.

We walked in the general direction of the ATVs as my father pulled out his cellphone and checked something. "ATV Forty-One is my crew's transport. Mitch should be checking people in."

We walked side by side as more cars came into the parking lot behind us. My father waved back to a few people that I didn't know as we passed ATVs, crews, and administrative workers. The air was filled with the buzz of half a dozen ongoing conversations, all of which were too far away to make out more than a word from. I studied each ATV and the groups that were forming up beside them.

[Those are the Cleaners,] I mentally said to Smegma. He was staring at the same people I was, and I figured he might want an explanation.

"Cleaners?" Smegma asked.

[They butcher what's left of the Monster Corpses for meats, skins, components, and reagents.]

"What about them?" Smegma asked, pointing a talon at a group of what looked like beekeepers.

I frowned, unsure myself. I pointed them out to my father and asked, "What do they do?"

"Ahh, the Herbalists or Gardeners. You wouldn't have seen the new uniforms, I guess. Remember a year ago I told you about that guy who died from a Dungeon insect bite?" At my nod, my father continued. "Well, the insects only attack if you disturb them, and the only places the ones with stingers seem to congregate is in flora-rich areas. So, using Widow silk, the herbalists have created protective suits to prevent further casualties."

"That clothing has to have about zero resistance against any Monster attacks," Smegma commented in response. I nodded to my father first, conveying that I had been listening to him.

Mentally to Smegma I explained, [The Monsters, other than the boss, are supposed to already be dead. Plus, Hunters go in with the Gathering teams to make sure no mishaps occur.]

Smegma pointed at another group with an eyeroll at my answer. The people he pointed at made my steps hitch. The air suddenly felt a bit colder as I examined the group. They all wore smiles and conversed jovially, but every single one gave off a palpable aura of something dangerous.

[Those are the Hunters from Lynx Hunters,] I mentally said, trying but somewhat failing to hold back my excitement.

"Those are the famous Hunters?" Smegma responded, sounding disappointed. I glanced at my shoulder where he rested and then back to the Hunters that all had a white stylized cat somewhere on their armor. I found them beyond impressive, but Smegma made it sound like they were barely worth his notice.

[Why are you frowning? What's wrong with them?]

"Half of them don't even have Mana Pools!" Smegma said, disgust clear in his voice. I turned back to study the group. The two to three people surrounding nearly each of the dangerous looking Hunters had kind of faded into the background on first inspection. Mana Banks. They were the ones with Mana Pools that those with powerful Skills could draw from in order to use their abilities. Intrinsically, I knew that they had to be there, and until the incident with Morgan, I had wanted nothing more than to be one of them. Now, with Smegma's Shop options? I wasn't sure what my future goals would be.

First things first, I needed to see if Mining with my father was a reliable source for Mana Coins. My father made a small adjustment to our path, and I followed along, scanning in front of me to see the reason. Sure enough, a piece of bristle board was nailed onto plywood and staked into the ground. It read 'forty-two.'

We still had a few hundred yards of walking, so I asked a question of Smegma. [How exactly do you expect them to gain a Mana Pool? They Awakened with what they got and are making the most of it. The people with them are Mana Banks—and are trained to feed them Mana at a *reasonable* distance.]

"What?" Smegma exclaimed, then examined the Hunters and Banks again. "No distance is 'reasonable,' a Monster would chew through those Banks in seconds… And of course they can get a new Skill. Monsters drop Card Shards. Portals reward full Cards on clears. Not to mention simply killing others with Powers and pulling the Skills from their Heart Deck?" Smegma retorted. He was using a voice that I associated with an owner speaking with a pet. One thing was certain, I didn't like the condescension that came with his words.

[We get Monster Cores as Monster drops, and after a Portal closes there is a Portal Core,] I responded mentally matching his tone. [The part about pulling

Skills from other human's sounds exactly like what Morgan was doing and I just heard of the existence of these 'Snatchers' because he attacked me—so I don't think it's exactly common!]

Smegma's earlier comments, as well as his confusion toward humanities' issue of Awakening with only a singular Skill and never gaining more were beginning to make sense. His people didn't necessarily *start* with multiple Skills— their Portals gave them access to them. No wonder they could build a whole economy on the buying and selling of those Skill Cards.

Smegma jumped off my shoulder and hovered right in front of me with flapping wings to stare me in my eyes.

"What?! I just assumed a pathetic moral compass was the only thing stopping you from killing someone and taking their Skill, and Morgan Hallsbrad had risen above it," he said incredulously. "Show me one of these 'Cores.'"

"You've got to be kidding me?" I said aloud, and immediately realized my mistake. My father turned to regard me as we kept moving and I pointed to a woman on the edge of the group. "Sorry, I haven't seen aunt Willa in ages. Mind if I go say hi?"

"Not at all," my dad said with a huge smile. "I'll talk to Mitch and get you a loaner set of gear for the week. After that you should have enough wages to buy one if you aren't going back to school."

His tone said that I *would* be going back to school, but I appreciated him at least allowing for the possibility of me choosing not to.

I nodded and rushed off. As I jogged, I responded to Smegma hotly, [There's no way someone like *me* would have a Core! Do you think I moonlight as a Monster killer in my down time?]

"Okay, but we're about to enter a Dungeon with Monster Corpses, right? Is there not a way you can get close to one, even for a moment. I want to see these Cores," Smegma countered.

[I said the Cleaners butcher what's *left* of the Monsters. The Cores have so much value that the Hunters rip them out on the spot!]

"Valuable how?" Smegma asked, sounding sincere. That tracked, what with him being a merchant and all.

[Well from my understanding, crafters use them to create weapons and armors with Skills or effects built into them. With proper Enchantments, some can even be used as Mana Batteries, but good quality Batteries are very rare and Hunters won't use bad quality ones in case they break. Umm, there's probably more things you can do with them, but I've never really looked heavily into it. In any case, a Core of an F-Rank Monster starts at twenty-five hundred dollars.]

"So, the Cores impart Skills to the crafted gear or weapons?" Smegma said while tapping a talon on his fangs. "It sounds like they are similar to the Cards of my world…"

"There is *no way* that be Brodie!" Willa shouted as she first stopped and assessed, then recognized me jogging toward her.

I hadn't seen her in about five years, so I wasn't surprised that it took her a minute to recognize me. However, I looked enough like my father at this point that it probably wasn't too hard to piece together.

"I heard you were joinin' us mole rats today, kid. How ya feelin'?" Willa said as she pulled me into a very tight embrace. Her accent was always funny. It came and went depending on how excited she was.

Willa was muscular even compared to any man present. She had dark olive skin, with black hair and brown eyes. She used to come over to my house for dinners, but since she now had small children of her own, she hadn't made the trip in a long while. Still, her tone conveyed that my father was still very close with her. Close enough to disclose the circumstances around my presence today.

I smiled at her concern and then said, "My dad has probably made it out to be worse than it is. I'm spending more time consoling my mom and him than I am about worrying over myself. I'm sure I'm not one hundred percent over it, but I'm feeling better than people think I should. If that makes sense."

She pulled me into another hug, and whispered, "We all handle stuff like dis in our own way. It be like a roller coaster, though, and just because you be okay right now don't mean you will be tomorrow. If it get bad, just make sure you talk to Gary or Clara. Obviously your parents care about ya. Ya can even call me. Don't think I didn't notice that you ain't callin' anymore."

I pushed her off with a smile, as she tried to kiss my cheek affectionately.

"Eww gross!" I mocked, even as she tried a bit harder to land a third kiss. She was stronger than me and managed to shower me with at least ten kisses before I fended her off.

"You used to love Aunty Willa kisses, kid," she jested as she lightly punched my arm. I made a show of wiping the slobber from my cheeks. She made a hurt face and the attack resumed.

It felt good to laugh with someone who took me at my word. While it had only been a day of my parents walking on eggshells around me, it was already getting old. My laughter died as Smegma made a wet raspberry sound while 'kissing' my cheek.

I froze and stared at the Demon-Imp, wide-eyed. [What the husk, dude?]

"Ahh, sorry, I couldn't figure out the significance or humor of the action. Plus, are the noises necessary?" Smegma asked as he eyed Willa skeptically.

Willa in turn was looking at me. I realized I must look like I was staring off into empty air. With a shocked expression, I pointed at the Hunters. They were a little off from my field of vision, but I was sure that would be hard to discern for Willa.

"Are those the Lynxes?"

"You know damn well they are," Smegma shouted.

"Yep, they had an excellent draft year!" Willa answered, pointing out a few individuals that looked like they were either in newer armor or better-kept ones. "That's Zerker an' that there is Flash. From the rumors, they'll likely be A-Ranks once the first-year assessments are finished."

"What, really?" I said, not having to feign my interest.

"I shit you not. They're one of the reasons that the Lynx Guild is tacklin' the Detroit Field again. Supposed ta be that both of them Awakened with two or more Skills."

"Why would she 'shit' you, to begin with?" Smegma asked, looking confused. Then he looked over to the two hunters Willa was indicating. "They don't look like much and they have those stupid Banks with them," Smegma said and then flew off in their direction. I hoped he was just going for a closer look. He soon popped back into a position beside me. I glanced at him but tried not to stare, due to Willa. "They're farther than a hundred yards," Smegma explained sheepishly.

I almost burst out laughing at the shame in his voice. My dad walking over, carrying a rucksack with a Mining pick attached, allowed my chuckling to go mostly unnoticed. Willa still gave me a side-eyed look, but I ignored it.

"Get this on and load up," my dad said.

He held the bag out to me, and I quickly pulled out the ancient looking armor within. Clouds of dust formed above the bag as dust fell off each piece. Smegma sneezed a few times as he tried to get a closer look inside the bag.

I wondered how dust could affect him but not things like walls or *physics*, but then dismissed it. It wasn't like it mattered. My dad and Willa helped me put on the patched gear, working together to understand straps that seemed to have been done away with on newer iterations. It only took a few minutes before I had everything but the helmet and elbow guards on. By the time they were done, the dust had mixed with my sweat and began coating my skin.

"Good, you'll fit in better with a bit of mud on ya face," Willa stated with a wide smile.

"Maybe a bit more will help," my dad added, and then reached back into the bag before blowing on his hand. He didn't direct the dust toward me, but instead emphasized just how much there was. "We're storing bags and lunches in the fifth bulkhead," my dad added with a gesture toward our lunches and the large, opened storage bin on the side of the ATV.

"Ya ready for this, squirt?" Willa asked, grabbing the dust filled bag and her own, far smaller, lunchbox.

I shook my head as I followed her and my dad up the drop ramp. "Probably not, but it's what I signed up for, right?"

She punched me in the arm with a bright smile. "There be the spirit."

The ramp lifted up as the last of the Mining crew and protective detail boarded the massive vehicle, eventually cutting off the sunlight and the view of the remaining battle-ready Hunters outside.

CHAPTER 11

Thursday, April 4th, 2069

"Is—it—always—" I began, my teeth rattling around in my mouth at the jarring impacts of the huge moving vehicle.

My dad shushed me without making a sound. Instead, he placed his finger over his lips in a sign that was understood worldwide, but was also somewhat infuriating. I felt like a child being scolded, and that mood clearly shone through my expression.

"While these be pretty sound proofed and probably make more noise than we could speakin'," Willa whispered from her seat on my other side. She even went as far as to lean to my shoulder to keep her voice down. "For some reason words attract *'em* more than crick-cracks an' ATV noise."

She clearly was meaning the Monsters in the Field, but likely didn't mention them because for her and my father a Monster was far more 'common' than for me and the rest of humanity that didn't work directly with Portals.

Despite the constant jarring ups and downs of the ATV, she seemed to be completely unaffected, both in her whispered words and in general. I tried to mimic her, my father, and the other experienced Miners. I could tell they were somewhat bracing with their legs and the lower half of their bodies to act as shock absorbers. A closer examination showed me that most were even hovering their butts above the seat.

I gave it a try and felt my legs burning after just a few minutes. I collapsed back to the chair and saw my dad give me a smirk.

Rolling my eyes, I mentally asked Smegma, [You don't happen to sell a body-strengthening Skill for cheap?]

Smegma was hovering near the roof and scoffed at my question. "We have plenty, but they're all higher than E-Rank, which is all a wastrel like you has access to. Plus, they aren't cheap."

My mouth twisted and I looked up through my eyebrows at the Demon-Imp. I had been trying to lighten the mood, but then realized that it was getting close to time to dump my Mana for Mana Coins. Plus, I had a timer set on my phone, which I should probably turn off, if my father's shushing was any indication of proper Miner-etiquette.

I did that first, accessing my phone and silencing it before finding my timer. The silencing was likely wholly unnecessary since I had no reception, but you never know…

I closed my eyes and entered my Mental Universe before willing the Mana stars toward *Demonic Vault.* As the first point moved across my mental bridging straw, I frowned. I still had thirteen points, but I couldn't help but question if I had been 'full,' or if it was just my imagination that I could have possibly gotten another point. The thirteen points did bring my Mana Coin total over a hundred, though, which made me consider purchasing a low-grade Spent Mana Crystal, but since I was about to Mine a bunch of *unspent* ones, I figured I'd wait.

[Wait—how come I've never seen 'Spent Mana Crystals' for sale on Earth?] I asked, realizing for the first time that they should be readily available on almost every street corner with how much we relied on Mana Crystals for energy.

Smegma narrowed his eyes.

"That's a good question. They said this thing runs on Mana Crystals, right? Be right back." Smegma flew off and phased through the door that led to the cockpit, or whatever the cab of an ATV was called. He returned a moment later, "How the *husk* is your race even still alive?"

Because of his incredulous tone, I almost responded aloud before thinking better of it. [What's wrong?]

"That *'engine,'*" he enunciated the word, clearly showing his distaste. "Is literally *burning* Mana Crystal *Shards*."

[How else would we get the energy out of them?]

"Oh, god's no. Please tell me that you've heard of Ritual Circles, Mana Circuits and the like?" Smegma asked, his face earnest despite his aghast tone.

[I've got a feeling this is going to upset you, but I've never heard of them. That doesn't mean they don't exist.] I added the last hurriedly when thunderclouds seemed to roll over the Imp's small face.

No response came for an awkwardly long time. Finally, I prodded Smegma mentally and he twitched. I gave him a look with both my eyebrows raised, hoping he'd take the hint and explain. He did but his tone was beyond frustrated.

"I've been sent to the ass end of the universe, summoned by a low-ranked human, who can't even access my good wares, and the entire race is literally wasting Mana. A precious resource. I *literally* would have been better off with the drug-dealing Llamas than on this backward ass rock!"

It wasn't really an explanation, and it brought up a great deal of questions, not the least of which was—*drug-dealing-Llamas?*—but I got the message loud and clear. Smegma was upset about Earth's lack of strength, technology, and progress. He was probably seeing this as a useless waste of time. I wasn't going to disabuse him of that notion. On one hand, if he took it into his head that we were stupid and could be 'fleeced' in trade, it would become infinitely more difficult for me to increase my Mana Pool Skill rank or purchase an offensive Skill to become a Hunter.

On the other hand, his bias could work in my favor…

The distinctive sound of air brakes firing perked me up, as well as everyone riding in our ATV. The group of ten Lynx members and their Mana Banks closest to the drop ramp began tightening straps on their gear and adjusting weapon straps for use. The scene made my heart stutter for a moment. Were we stopping because we were at the Portal or because a Monster was outside?

My father tapped me on the shoulder and pointed to the green light near the door. Beside it was a red and an amber light. I assumed green was 'good,' which meant we'd likely simply arrived at the destination Portal. The drop ramp soon cracked its seal with an audible hiss before it began lowering on its massive hydraulics.

I could tell that the ATV was still moving, but coasting to a controlled stop. The Lynx Hunters unclipped from their seats and stood up in near unison. They braced with a forward lean toward the drop gate just as the ATV jerked to a stop with a particularly loud screech of the air brakes. Only then did the Banks stand up to join the Hunters.

In fascination, I watched as the opening widened, but that fascination soon morphed into something else. I was certainly captivated by what the 'window' to the outside world revealed, but it had shifted into something that was more morbid. Disturbingly shocking, actually.

No wonder the ATV was jumping all over the place. It looked like an industrial dump or landfill. Maybe the site of a recent demolition before cleaning up? Concrete, rebar, glass, brick, wood and so much more littered the area in various states of destruction. Planks of wood were reduced to long sharp splinters. Some windows were whole while others were square shards seeming to be in the process of returning to sand. Concrete dust surrounded concrete blocks and even walls, and structural bones of what used to be sky-rises.

Is this where Hollyhood gets its scenery for apocalypse movies? I thought. I didn't mean to send it to Smegma, but my thoughts weren't really private anymore thanks to the shitty Imp.

"What the husk is a Hollyhood?"

Like with the question about 'shitting not,' I just shook my head and continued to stare at the ever-enlarging scene. I felt like I could stand here and study the small amount I could see for days and still find new horrors that would give me nightmares. The view had layers. Starting with what was nearest the door, I could be shocked by the state that a city could be reduced to, or I could scan into the distance and never sleep again.

It felt like pictures I'd seen from ships at sea, with water in every direction but up. It felt isolating. It felt like there was no end, that what we had left behind no longer existed. I couldn't see the walls in the distance that contained the Field. I couldn't see any structure that would indicate an intact human civilization. Instead, no matter where I looked, I found signs of human ingenuity in ruins.

Then the smell hit.

The air we'd traveled with, or perhaps due to the ATV's air filters, had neutralized the smell. However, with the ramp down, it washed into the space, displacing the 'clean' air. It was a scent I couldn't place, but it 'tasted' awful. It reminded me of a landfill, swamp, dying forest, and slum all at the same time. I began breathing through my mouth to avoid the nauseating experience. It remained in my memory, and I imagined the 'taste' still with each breath.

Was this a glimpse of what was to come?

"If your race doesn't start figuring some shit out, then yes," Smegma answered gravely, despite me not meaning to ask the question to him.

His answer only made me more anxious. My watch beeped a warning at me, and I looked at it to see that my heart-rate was at about one-eighty. Since I was sitting down, and had been for the last half hour, that wasn't a good thing.

My dad squeezed the back of my neck. Willa saw this and squeezed my shoulder nearest her. She whispered, "Don't worry, Monsters usually steer clear of the ATVs when they be stopped. Any that still be alive, in any case. Pull up your faceguard."

She deliberately pulled her dust covered faceguard up from around her neck and I looked down to find a similar, dirt-filled one attached to the chest piece I wore. I pulled it up and felt my breathing grow easier. The smell changed to that of old dry earth, which allowed my inhalation to return to my nose if I chose. A hint of the decay still came through, but it was tolerable.

They both misinterpreted the reason for my anxiety. Sure, Monsters were a worry, but Smegma was making me question the methods and future of our entire race. Still, I tried to use their comforting gestures to remind myself that I wasn't alone, and I was in a rather remarkable piece of human ingenuity. My heart did at least begin coming under control with that line of thinking.

The Lynx members rushed down the ramp and their well-armored Mana Banks were right on their heels. I focused on their actions as they swept the immediate surroundings near the bottom of the ramp. The fact that the Mana Banks had trained to supply Mana to fighters without touching, like the cops in the alley, made me instantly more comfortable. Their thoroughness further helped, and I managed to unclip my seatbelt with slightly trembling fingers.

My legs protested standing after the bumpy trip but soon recalled what they were meant to do. I waited for the others onboard to gather their gear and prepare. The experienced Cleaners, Miners, and Gardeners all shuffled to the top of the ramp before waiting. No one spoke, and I took my cue from them thanks in large part to Willa's warning on the trip. Moments later, a short but intense beep sounded. It came from two small speakers on each side of the door. It was clearly a signal because the leaders nearest the door jogged down the ramp. Each subsequent line of people took a moment to react, but the group moved like a sluggish military formation, which honestly surprised me.

"So, you're Mining in a Sective Agora Portal," Smegma said, and my brow furrowed.

A what? I had just made it to the side of the ATV and looked at him, which brought the large shimmering green Portal into my peripherals. He was staring at it. Why was it green? All Portals were blue, weren't they?

"Sective Agora Portals are much better for medicinal herbs and other fauna than they are for minerals or Crystals. I wouldn't expect anything other than low-grade Mana Crystals."

I wanted nothing more than to ask questions but decided to wait. Even Smegma's minor distraction had made me fall a step or two out of line with my father and Willa. I quickened my steps and focused on staying in the formation. Something told me that a group of civilian workers acting this way were doing so because it was important.

The people in the front of the line began entering the Portal, creating ripples in the energy, as if it was a pool of green water that sat on a vertical plane. It was strange that it took me until this moment to realize that this would be my first time inside a Portal. As a porter in the past, I'd remained outside and first packed, then carted the boxes or bags to the transport vehicles.

Just as the verdant water grew to take up my entire field of vision, I made another realization without even having to look around. We had no porters, at least not in the way I had performed the duty, today…

A chill seeped through my armor, feeling at first bearable and then like a cold dip in a near frozen lake. My skin under the armor prickled with goosebumps as a humid heat wafted over my chest, even as the intense cold froze my head and back. My nose and face suddenly flushed as it, too, entered the Dungeon.

"A god damn rainforest Dungeon," my father said as he stepped out beside me. Willa groaned from my other side, and I couldn't help but marvel at their casual banter after having walked through a Portal. I guessed that was because the Monsters were all dead except for the boss… Or they were just used to this mind-altering moment.

[Is this the Agrano whatever Portal you mentioned?] I asked mentally, trying to distract myself from reminiscing on the strangeness of the sensations I'd just gone through. It was surprisingly easy, probably thanks to *Mental Fortitude.*

"Sective *Agora*. That's what the locals call this planet, yes." Smegma casually inspected the trees, forest floor and then seemed to bolt up into the canopy. I stared up at him, which luckily wasn't too strange since the trees were huge and captivating. Had he just insinuated that the Portal took us to another planet?

[We're on another planet?] I thought pointedly at him. I saw Smegma look down at me and then decide to fly further up, before disappearing and poofing back into existence at my shoulder.

"Humans have never run into one of the locals?" Smegma asked just as pointedly as I had.

I slowly shook my head, then wondered if I had missed a news article about intelligent creatures being inside the Portals. After a moment, I shook my head more firmly.

Making his thinking face, which consisted of a face scrunch and a talon tapping on a tooth, Smegma mumbled, "How is that possible?"

"All Miners to Jeral, all Cleaners with team three, and all Gardeners spread out in the immediate vicinity. You can begin harvesting anything you find. No one is to go more than two kilometers north, as that's the location of the boss. Understood?" a new Hunter I hadn't seen upon entering shouted from gaps between the bodies in front of me.

I shifted from foot to foot to get a better view and almost gasped when I recognized the speaker, and even the name of the one we Miners were assigned to suddenly clicked. Beastmode, the B-Ranked Hunter, was standing not more than twenty feet from me, and we, the Miners, were supposed to *ignore* him and find *Sturdy Jeral*, a B-Ranked Tank?

Beastmode was wearing black leather armor, that had animal or Monster hair adorning the joints. On his hip he had two long daggers or short swords. His arms looked dark primarily due to the copious black hair. From here I couldn't see his eyes but knew they were grey with red from TV. The one surprise was just how 'short' he was, standing near the five-foot mark—at least without his hairstyle that stuck up on both sides of his head. It made a strange u-shape in the middle.

"Let's go, Son," my father said, placing a guiding hand on my back. I gaped at him.

"Close your mouth," Smegma said. "The air isn't edible."

My mouth did close, but only so my jaw could clench tightly. Mentally I shouted, [But that's Beastmode and Sturdy Jeral!]

"They can't be stronger than C-Ranked, surely." Smegma moved to Beastmode and hovered inches in front of his face, studying the short but extremely muscled man. Was something clenching my heart in my chest? My feet hit a root, and I would have fallen if my father's second hand didn't steady me.

"I know it's your first time in a Dungeon, but surely you can walk, right?" he laughed, as I transferred my earlier frustrations with Smegma to him with a scowl. "That's better. The Hunters are just doing their job, and extraterrestrial scenes like this become everyday things once you've been through enough. Just keep your head on straight, okay?"

His laugh allowed my scowl to turn into a smirk. Willa held out a Mining pick, and I realized I had forgotten to grab mine before departing the ATV. I opened my mouth to thank her, but she chuckled and punched my arm. "We all started where you be now, kid. Don't worry 'bout it. Your father did the same for me."

"What was that, a hundred years ago?" I teased.

"Ya little shit!" Willa said and punched me harder, making it very clear that she had held back last time. I rubbed the spot she hit and then stumbled on a root again when Sturdy Jeral in full armor, minus his helm, came into view leaning on his door shield.

He smiled at the group and my body reacted with an awkward wave before I could stop it. My father and Willa facepalmed on both sides of me, but Jeral's grin widened. Jeral in comparison to Beastmode was a tall man. Even, in comparison to me and my father he was tall. He had dirty blonde, almost brown hair, and a face I was sure women found attractive.

I couldn't see much of him due to the full plate armor, but the very fact that he was standing there so casually, likely meant he was jacked under it.

Unfortunately, Smegma was hovering nearby. "Oh, are you smitten? I didn't know your tastes lay in this direction."

[I like women, Smegma,] I mentally corrected the Demon even as my cheeks flushed. Admittedly, Jeral had a very rugged charm to him, and thanks to Smegma's comment I momentarily considered him as an 'option.'

Jeral pointed to me and included Willa and my father in the gesture. "First time?" he asked.

"Yep. This here is my son, Jer." My dad added a slap to my back and wore a look that contrasted his long years of pushing me to attend school. He was clearly proud to introduce me.

Jeral moved around his shield and stepped toward me. Maybe it was all of the new experiences today, but I suddenly felt faint as Jeral extended a hand to shake. Smegma flying to examine the man's standing shield helped shake me out of my stupor.

Hesitantly, I extended my hand and jumped a bit when the mitt of the much larger man seemed to envelop mine. From this distance, I had to look up to him, which was rare for me because I was taller than most men.

Is this how people felt when they met me?

"You *are* smitten!" Smegma crowed from his perch atop the shield.

[Shut up!]

"Introduce yourself," my dad encouraged with a chuckle, which emphasized that we were standing there in awkward silence. Or I supposed I was.

"Hi! I'm Brodie!" I said with far too much enthusiasm. Jeral took it in stride.

"I'm assuming by the look on your face that my reputation precedes me, but I'm Jeral. I've worked with Gary many times. He's a good man, but looking at your frame, you might be even stronger than him one day, no?" Jeral added the last bit to Gary while reaching out a hand to grip my bicep. My dad's face broke into a grin usually reserved for my mother, and me when something wonderful happened. I of course smiled wider.

"He's just on a hiatus from University, but he certainly got the best of mine and Clara's genes!" my father answered, his voice filled with paternal pride. I felt my face heat up and knew I was flushing.

Jeral released my hand, shook my fathers and then Willa's before he made an apologetic face and excused himself. He clearly wanted to chat more but was supposed to be taking charge of the group that was slowly accumulating around us.

He was only a few steps away when I turned to my father and hissed, "You never told me you knew Sturdy Jeral!"

"Want him to set you up on a blind date?" Smegma teased. I ignored the obnoxious Demon.

"More than just him, my boy," my dad said even as his smile slowly fell. "I didn't want you dreaming of joining me as a Miner…" he explained softly. "You should be joining *them* in a different, more managerial role. Or their *personal* salesman!"

Willa reached behind me and lightly tapped my dad's shoulder in an imitation of her earlier friendly assault of me. "Yeah, 'cause kids dream of vacations like this or of bein' a personal salesman, Gair!" she said before looking me in the eyes with firm resolve. "There's nothin' wrong with Minin', kid, but your da' just wants more for you. That's all."

My dad socked her back in the shoulder. "Don't go putting words in my mouth."

Since Beastmode had given his directions, a low hum of conversation had been constant from the Miners, but now it died down in slow spurts. My father and Willa looked around and their eyes, along with mine, landed on Jeral, who had a raised hand.

Silence fell.

In the hush only interrupted by steady breathing, I finally realized that my mask had fallen when my mouth had dropped open at Beastmode's appearance, and that my nose was delighted in the surroundings. The air felt fresher and more vibrant than anything I had ever experienced. Like I had been smelling imitation candles or colognes my whole life but was surrounded by a real forest. Because that was the only way to describe the earthy richness of the aroma.

"The cave with the minerals and Crystals is a kilometer east. It was filled with nature slimes and may still have some hiding. So, do not leave my sight as we descend. Everyone good to go?" Jeral announced from behind his shield. I nodded and others must have as well because Jeral heaved up his shield, which made a sucking sound as another foot of it exited what must have been semi-soft ground.

I tapped a foot under me and found the ground to be far harder than 'semi-soft.' Just how strong was Jeral? Armor clanking, the man in question spun the shield onto his back like it weighed nothing, before turning and leading the way between trees to the intended destination. I noticed that no Mana Banks seemed to be following close behind him.

CHAPTER 12

Thursday, April 4th, 2069

Unleash Hell!

I don't know how others would act in my current situation, following behind the massive wall of a shield, but I couldn't help picturing myself as a Hunter. Imagining myself following a Tank like Sturdy Jeral as we conquered this Rainforest Portal. My eyes only left the large shield on the man's back to marvel at the changing scenery for a few moments before they coasted back to it, and my daydream.

It wasn't hard to picture the Monsters that could be attacking us. I'd seen pictures and byproducts of the creatures my whole life, played video games, and even played with action figures the way my parents supposedly played with Barbehs and G.A. Johns. In my imagination I wasn't afraid, but I will admit that in my heart I questioned whether I was simply lying to myself.

Then again, maybe the *Mental Fortitude* Skill would make it true?

Regardless, at that moment, it felt like my father was more than just downplaying his job as a Miner.

"I can hear your increased heart rate from here!" Smegma commented. "You want to be a *Hunter* but you can't even hike a mile in Miner's gear. It's kind of pathetic."

[Stop being a dick!] I said to my Demon companion.

"Stop broadcasting your thoughts like some sort of reality love story!" Smegma countered. "He's just a man, and a rather weak one at that. If he's a B-Rank, then his abilities and Stats are the lowest I've ever seen."

[Stats?] I asked, wondering what he meant. Sure, I knew that certain Skills awoke a 'Stat'—you could increase how much power that Skill could use by increasing it—but unless you had multiple Skills—wait—was that—

"See dat over there," Willa commented from slightly behind me, stopping me from mentally questioning Smegma.

I followed her finger and saw a massive mountain that looked wrong. It was like someone had turned on a sepia, black-and-white filter, changing the mountain into a painting or some artistic masterpiece. My head tilted involuntarily as I tried to understand what I was looking at.

"It be what we call Scenery in da Portals," Willa explained. "There's a kind of film—"

"Barrier," my father corrected, and Willa gave him a look that both thanked but threatened him. I noticed he made a face that seemed to suggest he feared interrupting Willa again.

"I call it *film*, 'cause it kinda looks like we be inside a bubble of soap when you're near it. It looks like a casual poke should pop the thing, but it only gives a few inches before it becomes impossible to move. That and everythin' on da other side looks like it ain't real. Almost like it be frozen in place, under water, or just drenched in black soap, oil or stuff like that. No wind be blowin' the leaves. No sound be reachin' your ears. It be real disturbin'."

"We don't usually go near it," my father added. "Only if our Mining spot happens to border it." I nodded along but had my eyes on Smegma and the black-and-white landscape his eyes were glued to.

[What's up?] I asked mentally, wanting to know what the Demon was so intently focused on.

Smegma looked up, scanned the area above him and then looked at me, his expression conveying his confusion. "Up? I have no idea. I don't know what the locals of Sective Agora call their sun or sky," he answered, his tone also confused.

[No,] I mentally said while avoiding a physical sign of exasperation. I failed because my father and Willa both looked at me.

"What? You don't believe us?" my dad said.

"I'm tellin' you kid, you don't want to be goin' near the *film*," Willa said, her voice filled with both humor and performance to try to make the warning seem more profound.

I laughed. "I believe you. I just can't believe how different yet similar it is in here." I answered them. Then sent, ['What's up' just means 'what's wrong,' or what are you thinking so hard about,] to Smegma.

"That's an oddly specific idiom for this particular situation," Smegma answered, giving me a piercing look.

[Idioms are kind of our thing; it feels like we have one for every occasion— okay? So, what's going on?] I responded to him but realized I needed another response to Willa and my father. They were both looking at me funny. "I'm just overwhelmed."

They both shrugged, as if they shared the same mind and then even nodded to themselves, like they were deep in their own thoughts and memories of their first time in a Portal. I let them stew there so I could hopefully get a response from Smegma. However, the Demon-Imp was gone when I looked back to find him.

I scanned my immediate area under the guise of taking in more of the scenery but couldn't see him. For a moment, I worried that something had gotten him, or he was somehow un-Summoned or something like that. But a quick check in my Mental Universe showed me a connection from the *Demonic Vault* Skill existed. Where it led, I couldn't discern, but Smegma was certainly with me still, but hiding. [I'm going to remember the question,] I mentally sent. [You can't avoid me forever.]

No response came, but my scanning for a sign of the Imp allowed me to find the likely site of our Mining before my dad or Willa. I pointed to the rocks that seemed out of place in the rainforest. The two snapped out of their introspection and followed my finger. Sure enough, the large black structure only grew the closer we got, right up until the entrance to a cave became apparent.

From a distance, the darkness of the entrance could be mistaken for the dark rock that surrounded it, but the sun gleamed off the stone in a dappling pattern, suggesting that the stone itself might have a metallic quality to it. The entrance, however, was more like what covered the ATVs and consumed what light filtered through the canopy. A few Miners pulled out Cores of some variety upon seeing the darkness of the cave—my father and Willa amongst them.

"Just stay close to us for today," my dad responded to my scrutiny of the item. "These are Light Stones. Mine's cheap and only lasts a few hours, but Willa's is better and can usually last for a few days. They always pair people with someone who has a good Light Stone like hers, so we'll probably get one or two more Miners assigned to work with us. I'll only use mine for entering and exiting."

My frown must have conveyed my confusion to Willa because she explained further. "This Light Stone ain't 'mine' per se, it's *ours*, Gary. Your kid is goin' to think you're leechin' off me if you say it like dat."

"Well, I mean, I kind of am. Half the days I forget to take my stone out of my gear so it recharges—or I'll forget it in the car. You have *our* stone because I can always count on you to bring it. Plus, have you ever taken a sick day?"

"I'd rather get paid out for unused sick days than take 'em," Willa whispered to me. "Plus, once ya be Awakenin', do ya really get sick?" she added with a smile.

It was true. Sick days were kind of a hangover from before the Advent of Portals on Earth. Not to say that they didn't still have value, but the name probably was due for a change. Most illnesses were entirely eliminated from the planet with the Awakenings—so 'sick' might be better as injury or mental health days. Since I didn't have a lot of experience with work, I shrugged and dismissed the conjecture. Someone smarter than me should be revamping that stuff.

However, there was a caveat. Now when people were sick, it was *always* serious. So, forget about taking a few days off and getting paid. If someone had an illness or disease, it meant an emergency trip to a hospital and fighting for one's life. Some illnesses even required a certain-ranked Healer to treat them. I'd read plenty of articles on SmileBook about that change to the health industry. Most of the articles were complaints about the massive cost those trips entailed.

Since my family still lived in the borders of Canada, the people who took those hospital trips and were now in massive debt simply from getting 'sick' complained loudly, and often. One of those 'back in my day, healthcare was free,' sort of deals. However, most survivors were only alive because a sufficiently ranked Awakened Gifted with a healing Skill was at the hospital the day they were rushed in. So, the question was: would it be better to be alive and working off a debt that insurance couldn't cover or... the alternative.

That was also why if you were Awakened with a healing gift, it pretty much meant you were set for life...

Sturdy Jeral didn't even hesitate, and neither did the Mana Bank group that followed him into the dark cave. To my surprise, the Miners didn't even have a hitch in their steps either—unlike me. Illumination sprang from people's Light Stones as they activated them at the threshold. From my place only a few rows back, it looked almost like auras around the people in front of me. Curious, I watched as Willa pressed on an embossed circle on the core of hers. I didn't catch my father engaging his, but noticed a similar circle as I quickly panned my gaze over. It would seem these Light Stones, made from Monster Cores, stored internal Mana and could be activated by anyone, which likely made them more expensive than ones that needed a Mana Pool.

Still, the difference in price between one that ran on internal Mana, or recharged and used its own, wasn't important to someone like me, who didn't have the funds to consider either option.

They transferred the stones to a prepared slot on their leather chest guards, which allowed their hands to be free. It did block the light at about a hundred and eighty degrees, and I couldn't help but wonder how this light would work when we started Mining. However, that thought was dismissed when I saw the light reflecting off the numerous clusters of Mana Crystals that seemed to spring out of the stone walls, ceilings and floor like weeds.

I pointed them out, unsure why we weren't collecting them. My father chuckled. "This isn't a low-ranked Portal, it might be a low-ranked Mine, but that doesn't mean it won't be huge. So, these dregs at the front aren't worth the effort, my boy. Just wait…"

I frowned but tried to follow his words and remain patient. I was only successful because I used the time to try another attempt to find my missing Demon Trader. I failed and assumed he was somehow phased through the walls. The tunnel was too small for him to be elsewhere.

It didn't take long before the lights from the stones of people in front of us indicated a widening in the tunnel. My eyes grew larger as the light appeared to change color, first becoming the blue of Mana Crystals, and then changing to refracted rainbows. A moment later, I thought my eyes might eject from their sockets.

The group in front entered the room and moved to the side. I had a moment to wonder why they stopped but soon found out. The floor was almost entirely covered in the sharp relief of Mana Crystals. The walls and corners of the room looked like bladed carpets of the Crystals, only broken up by veins of varying shades of metal.

I looked first to Willa and then my dad, and finally at the other Miners. We were supposed to get through this entire room, *today?*

Jeral returned across the cavern, a group of other Hunter's and their Banks in tow behind him. He coughed politely and then said, "Four teams here, the rest follow me to the next cavern."

"There's more than this?" I said in utter shock. Then added, "We have what? Forty Miners?"

My dad smiled. "Just me and Willa could likely clear this room if we spent the day. Those four teams will be done in three hours at the most. Watch where you step now though, Son. These Crystals can cut through the sides of your work boots if you aren't careful. The soles are reinforced with ET41, so you can step directly on the Crystals or in an empty spot but watch out for diagonal jags."

"How about I follow your lead today?" I suggested.

"We might be havin' ta carry you out on a stretcher if you be doin' dat. Your da' be the clumsiest guy in here. But he's also the only one near your height, dat has canoes for feet. So, I guess that works," Willa teased and received a light punch in the arm from my father.

"Willa often tries to get lost, so she doesn't have to work. That's the real reason I gave her the Light Stone," my father retorted, and Willa returned the shot to his arm, along with a hurt face.

"I would never *try* to get lost," she said before laughing. "Except if we have ta mine Palentine. Husk that noise."

"People don't really use that saying anymore," I said, trying to coach her out of using the old slang of 'husk that noise.'

"Na, I literally be meanin' the noise it makes. It be feelin' like your eardrums are goin' to shatter if you be in the same cave system when someone's pickaxe collides with da stuff."

"Oh," I said stupidly while blushing. She jostled my shoulder, letting me know she accepted my 'apology.'

Our group was left in the next cavern, which looked a hell of a lot like the last one, just a quarter of the size and obviously deeper in. Sure, some of the metals were smaller or larger, and different shades, but it had the same density of Crystals poking out all over the place.

Willa transferred her Light Stone into a metal cage and then pulled something out of her pants pocket. With a click, it extended up into an eight-foot staff that looked dangerous. She hung the Light Stone on it, and my father turned his off but left it in the slot on his chest. With a grunt, Willa drove the point on the staff into a gap between Crystals. The metal scraped audibly before thumping into the rock or loose dirt below.

Willa wiggled the staff a few times before wedging it into a place she was satisfied with. She then looked up and behind me. "Miguel, Fat Gary, good to have ya with us. This be Brodie's first time, so why don't you two work on that side to avoid Crystal Shards hittin' ya. He mines like he be tryin' to pay back the Crystals with all the ills in the world."

"Hey," I hissed. "You've never seen me mine."

Willa smiled at me then whispered back, "Trust me, you ain't going to be a savan', kid."

The way she said 'savant' confused me for long enough that I didn't respond in an appropriate amount of time.

The two men nodded seriously, Fat Gary not seeming to take offense to the nickname. I guessed it was because he wasn't fat, just wider and more muscular than even my father, who was taller and more lithe. Both were muscled far beyond my teenage frame, though. Still, the necessity for the nickname obviously derived from my father, and the fact that my dad wasn't 'tall-Gary' was likely because he was here first.

Fat Gary had other features that would distinguish him from my father but wouldn't be polite to call out. For instance, he was black and had a shaved head that gleamed in the light from the Light Stone and Mana Crystal's that were refracting the emitted light. He was also a tall man standing over six feet in height, which might also explain why my dad didn't get 'tall-Gary.' The way he stood with Miguel suggested a long-time friendship.

Miguel on the other hand was a small man, closer to five feet. He looked like he could be of Mexican descent but that was hard to place. His dark hair and features matched his darker skin tone, and his eyes were the typical brown of most Spanish men.

Without a word of acknowledgement, the two spun and moved to the edges of the light the stone gave off. They un-shouldered their pickaxes and swung almost in step with their arrival.

"They're like robots," Smegma said from beside my right ear. I jumped.

"Don't worry, you be gettin' used ta' the noise," Willa said and pointed to the nearest wall. "The ones on the wall be a better place to start. So, try ya hand there. Your father and I will be over there," she pointed to an area opposite Fat Gary and Miguel. "The only tip I have is don't be hittin' yourself with the pointy end, okay kid?"

I snorted out an exhale in amusement through my nose. That would be a shitty way to get injured. My dad gave me a look that told me I shouldn't find that thought amusing, and instead very possible.

"Son, I don't care how slow you work today. But don't get cocky and try to do too much. That's how newbies get carted out of here with a pickaxe in a foot or leg."

I gulped, and he nodded like that response satisfied him more. Carefully, I started to move to the wall, but my father held up a quick hand. "Oops, forgot you don't even know the basics. Let me clear out the spot you can stand."

Willa moved off to begin working on her area, and I scanned back to Miguel and Fat Gary, who had moved into the area they had just been 'attacking' with their picks. I could see a pile of Shards from the Crystals surrounding them.

Smegma hovered closer to my father as he began chipping out Crystals in a small circle clearly intended for me to stand in. Smegma scoffed and then with outrage in his voice stated, "Your dad and all these Miners are just shattering the Crystals with no care for quality maintenance!"

[What do you mean?] I asked. My father had been at this for nearly twenty years. So, if anyone knew what they were doing, it was him.

"The first couple are fine, but now that he has a clear avenue to the stems, he shouldn't be Sharding a perfectly good F-Rank Crystal." Smegma responded.

[Maybe it's just for the clearing of a standing spot?] I suggested, but Smegma made another noise of disgust.

"Nah, the ones in the other chamber and over there," he pointed to Fat Gary and Miguel, "are only marginally doing better after clearing a spot to stand."

My father finished, which forced me to hold onto my response to Smegma's outrage. "Alright, so stand here and clear off as much of the wall as you can. Call me when you're finished, and I'll show you again how to clear a new area to stand, like I just did."

"Nope, I'll be the one showing you things," Smegma said as he hovered back to me with crossed arms.

Nodding to my father, I fought to keep a neutral and serious face, thanks to Smegma's condescension. I needed to show my dad I understood his instructions. He thankfully seemed to interpret my nod the way I wanted him to because he patted my shoulder and seemed to consider saying something more before pulling me into a quick hug. The moment didn't last long, and he moved to join Willa in the area she was still clearing. I transferred a glare to Smegma.

[Don't think I forgot about you leaving my earlier question unanswered! Also, you're trying to tell me you, a *Trader*, are a more knowledgeable Miner than my dad—who *Mines for a living*? Not to mention many of our Engines can only handle Shards!]

"Admittedly, I've never Mined before, but I've read about the way to do it properly, and if this is a discussion on whether or not your people or mine are better Miners? If the quality comparison is similar between your Hunters and ours, then yes—I, as a proxy for my people, know *vastly* more about how to Mine than your vocational Miner of a father. I *could* shit all over everything I've seen of your race, but I'm trying to be generous. How long have you had the System in your world? One? Two Decades? You think you know more than a civilization that's had it for thousands of years? How about you open up your ears and just maybe you can learn something and start making some real changes and advancements for your entire race. With my help, of course."

Smegma almost stopped there, ending his rather imperious speech arrogantly as he normally did, but I saw the moment he thought of something more to add. He pointed a talon at me.

"Also husk off with that shit about answering all your questions, I'm certainly allowed some time to myself. Not to mention, if you haven't forgotten, I'm still a *merchant*. I don't *owe* you anything. You want to know things I haven't voluntarily offered?" He held out a hand, rubbing his fingers together. "Everything has value, and information has more value than most things in the wide universe."

I sensed discomfort in his voice at first, which he tried to cover up with the sales pitch. I quickly turned my mental teasing tone off. [Is the reason you needed time something bad?]

Smegma rubbed his face with his hands as though considering whether to answer. After a moment, he straightened, clearing his throat. "Crendalar Five has completely fallen to the System's Portal Invasion. My people are barely surviving underground, and it's been nearly a generation since a new Portal off world formed on our planet. So, no one has seen a Time Bubble like the one Willa was pointing out earlier in centuries. At least not from *this* side—It hasn't exactly brought back good memories..." Smegma explained softly.

[Okay, let's just take a big step back here for a second.] My mind was spinning. I subtly gestured toward the 'Bubble' distorting the skies in the distance. My current point was obviously at a wall of the cave, but I hoped he'd get the intention from my thoughts. [Willa called this thing a 'Bubble,' sure—but you're calling it a 'Time Bubble' with the kind of emphasis that makes it seem pretty damned significant. What exactly is a Time Bubble, and how does it work?"]

Smegma froze at my question, slowly turning towards me, shock and exasperation written across his features. "Are you trying to tell me that you've had the System for two decades and you don't know how Portals work?"

I chose not to correct the Imp and add the additional four years he was missing. Instead, I took a quick look around to make sure the other Miner's weren't watching me and noticing my distinct lack of work. They weren't, so I figured I had a bit more time to get to the bottom of this. I did make a show of studying my pick and the Sharded Crystals my father worked on as we continued talking.

[If by 'you,' you mean me, Brodie Flacarada, then yes.] I nodded, pointing at myself. [If you're talking about all of humanity, then I have no idea how much we know about Portals collectively. This is my first time inside one, and I don't work in that scholastic field, so I'm not aware of everything we may or may not understand.]

"Brodie," Smegma shook his head. "I've been here long enough to learn about the existence of schools. I'd be stupid not to, since you're a student. Basically, what you've just told me is that your world's education system is in as bad a shape as the rest of what I've seen."

[Yeah, yeah.] I clenched my fists, unable to make too much of a scene despite my frustration with the Demon's constant negative comments about humanity in general. I also wasn't sure how to explain to Smegma that humanity was somewhat still stuck in the past, fixated on lessons about important topics that happened or were discovered before the Advent. Frustrated with my lack of a path forward that wouldn't lead to more arguing and not get me an answer to my original question, I sarcastically added, [We're all dumb, and your race is the best, smartest, and greatest. Now, I've stroked your ego, can you please tell me about the Time Bubble and how it applies to Portals?]

Smegma sighed. "Fine. Basically, a Time Bubble *is* where the Portal leads. Always. No matter what Portal you go through, or to what World, you will always be within *a* Time Bubble." The Demon stared off toward the wall and the shimmering barrier beyond it. "Think of a Portal as a connection between your world and a portion of another planet that has been sectioned off by a System created Time Bubble. In this Dungeon's case, the connection is between Earth and this portion of Sective Agora."

[That's it?] I frowned. There was no way that was all it did.

"Of course not, but don't give me that look. Even if that *was* all it did, it would still be pretty badass. Spatial manipulation across the vast reaches of the Universe? Connecting one planet to another? That's mind boggling on its own. But you're right. There's more.'

[I'm guessing it's not called a *Time* Bubble, for no reason, for example.]

"No. It's called a *Time* Bubble, because time works differently inside of Portals than in the Worlds beyond their barriers. The Worlds that connect to yours are all failures. They have rampaging Monsters upon their surface and struggling races desperate to survive."

[That's why you were surprised humanity hadn't met any locals?]

"Yes, now stop interrupting. Fat Gary and Miguel have looked over twice. I'll give you the abridged version. It's called a Time Bubble because it freezes time inside itself and opens for about four hours a day to re-establish its connection to the world it's on. In those four hours the System resets something so the Time Bubble stays strong. In some cases it resets the things inside as well. Needless to say, it's a Time and Space Bubble. Good enough?"

[Come on, that can't be—]

"Enough with the bullshit. We've got work to do. Swing here!" Smegma cut me off and pointed at the base of a Crystal.

I frowned, unsure whether to be upset or thrilled that conversation was finished. If I was honest with myself, I didn't want to delve any further into the topic. Time and Space were concepts far too complicated for my mind to wrap itself around—*Mental Fortitude* or not. I let my aforementioned Skill pull me back to the more straightforward task of Mining. I looked at the wall where he'd gestured.

Wasn't he pointing to the tiny speck of black stone wall visible between the Crystals? I looked at the point of the pickaxe and then at the small opening there. *It would have to be a perfect swing.*

Smegma noticed my scrutiny and likely heard my internal thoughts. "This one is the hardest. It'll be good practice, so just give it your best shot. You can't do worse than these other imbeciles."

I hefted the pickaxe and wedged the point into the indicated gap between Crystals before pulling it up and to the side of my head. I swung it down and somewhat found the opening. My aim was remarkably good, but the point jumped on contact with the stone and cracked the bottom of the Crystal.

"Not great," Smegma commented. "However, it still lost less Mana than if you shattered it. Quite a bit less. I thought your people were dumber than a box of rocks for burning Crystals like they were logs, but it's becoming clear to me that everyone on this planet is woefully ignorant and unprepared for what's coming. *You* can change that." He turned away with a sigh, but not before I heard a, "you're going to have to," in a tone that made my skin go cold from the unsaid 'or else' I could hear in his defeated voice.

Smegma turned back toward me, rubbing his forehead as though he had a headache. "Go again but use your body more, and don't raise the pick to the side. Choke up closer to the business end of the pick. It'll give you more accuracy at the cost of power, but in this business—accuracy *is* power. You don't actually *want* to smash everything apart as hard as you can, get me? The best sculptors on my planet will often talk about how stone speaks to them. When they carve—they say they just remove the pieces of stone that don't belong and free the sculpture from its entrapment within the stone. What you want to do here is similar. Your goal is to free the Crystals from their prison, not execute them for their crimes."

I chuckled at that last bit and followed his instructions… and missed the opening entirely. Another Crystal deflected the point of the pick by contacting the long, thinning metal a few inches from the point, which turned the blow. Luckily, it turned it toward my target, but instead of hitting the same crack I already made with the pickaxe, it broke the large Crystal in two. With the second blow, though, the original crack opened up, making the two halves of the blue Mana Crystal fall off the wall and to the floor atop others. Smegma made a disappointed noise but then pointed to a much wider area of stone. "Not bad for the first one. This gives us some needed room. Now target here."

This time I managed to dig the tip of my pickaxe into the stone wall. However, the sound it made was vastly different from my first swings. This time, instead of a twang of metal on reinforced glass, the pickaxe made a dull crunch as it bit into the wall. A spark even formed and the pungent scent of ozone quickly

114

burned my nostrils. The change in tone made my father pause and look over from the corner of my vision. He watched as I levered back and forth on the pick to free it.

"Oh, my mistake, Brodie," he called. "These are just going to be used in Mana Engines, and since it's easier to carry out Shards, that's what we're aiming for. Don't bother keeping them in full—"

"Don't listen to him. Sharding the Crystals is wasting over ninety percent of the stored Mana." Smegma said over my father.

"—leave the Shards on the floor and someone from Lynx or Snowbirds with a Storage item or Skill will eventually come by to collect 'em."

I missed some of the middle of his speech but hoped I'd gotten the gist of it. I nodded and gave Smegma a look with a single raised eyebrow. It was just like I'd said in class. [See, they have their reasons!]

"Yeah, but those 'reasons' are frankly stupid. They're degrading a perfectly good F-Rank Crystal, and not just one." He gestured at all the shattered Crystal around the Miners. "Think about it. Over ninety-percent of the value of everything you see here is just… *gone*. It's not *ninety percent* easier to carry, as in— it's certainly not worth destroying the value of this sort of resource. Your dad's a nice guy and all, but he's dead wrong here, *Bro*. Think about it like this—would you rather get one or two Mana Coins from each Sharded quarter or fifty to a hundred from a full Crystal?"

I knew the answer but couldn't figure out how I was supposed to mine as instructed without my father hearing the difference and coming over to scold me.

[I don't think I have a choice,] I answered and Smegma looked over to my father.

After a moment, he pointed to the base of the Crystal. "Nicking the Crystals on the edges here is about the best you can do and not make it obvious that you're not listening to your dad's advice. It'll sound normal to them but you won't have to completely shatter everything. It will likely halve the efficacy of the Crystals but that's better than the ten percent you'd be getting otherwise. I'm almost wondering if it's worth ignoring your dad's advice even though, yeah— he's your dad, but right now you have some leeway being new and can 'discover' how much more Mana undamaged Crystals have, and then maybe we can convince the others to do away with this whole process of just smashing everything to bits entirely."

Smegma was clearly not understanding the power a single human voice carried. I wondered for an instant if things like this changed drastically on his planet all because one person said so. Surely that was impossible. Was the Demon naive because he was a researcher?

[It won't work like that,] I mentally said. [Plus, I already told you that a lot of our infrastructure is based on Sharding…]

Smegma ignored me, clearly not wanting to waste Mana and I made a decision. Naive or not, I still wanted more mC rather than less…

With Smegma's direction, I began again. This time, I targeted the very base of the Crystals where they exited the wall. I missed multiple times, cracking many Crystals in half, completely Sharding others, and even hitting only air once or twice, but with each swing I started to get marginally better. Finally, I managed to knock a large Crystal off the wall in two swings and in one solid piece.

"That's better. Put your hand on that piece and I'll tell you the sale price," Smegma directed. My fingertips barely touched it when Smegma said, "Thirty-five mC. Shit, that's horrible. Likely only a third of the actual value."

[What happens to the Crystal after sale?] I asked.

"Normally, it becomes clear and this quality would maybe make a low-grade Spent Mana Crystal. However, this particular one will just become clear and useless because you've damaged it. Plus, since you likely don't want evidence of tampering, I'll port the Spent Crystal, damaged or not, back to my Sect in Crendalar Five. I won't even charge you a disposal fee," Smegma said this all in a very uninterested manner. I stood back up and kept Mining for now, not wanting a huge break in noise. Not after the long chat we'd had at the start. "What are you doing?"

[Thinking,] I answered.

It wasn't like I could just *sell* every Crystal and get away with it. The question was how many I could get away with. So far, I had struck down around ten from the wall. But even as I swung my pick at the next Crystal, I saw a problem. Each fallen Crystal left behind a small blue part of itself embedded into the wall. So someone could easily count those marks and know how many Crystals should be on the ground, especially with the full Crystals Smegma wanted. However, I was supposed to be Sharding the things— which would make a count impossible, right?

I changed my next swing, copying what my father had done, and hitting the dead center of the Mana Crystal I was aiming for. It shattered off some pieces and I raised my pickaxe to do it again. Smegma flew into my path and said, "What the husk are you doing?"

Smiling, I swung the pick right through him, even as I responded, [Covering my tracks.]

Smegma didn't react to the pickaxe going through his skull, which was disappointing. He looked at the floor, with its blue pieces and the Shards falling to it, then the wall, and scowled. "I guess the Crystal roots are a bit too obvious, but what a husking waste," he said with a dejected sigh.

It was another fifteen minutes before I was willing to try for another Crystal. This time, because my father, Miguel, Fat Gary, and Willa had moved farther away, I followed Smegma's direction and aimed for the rock wall. When the Mining pick hit, I glanced toward my father and Willa, smiling when they were indeed too far away to notice.

It took three swings before I felt and heard the Crystal being released from the surrounding rock, like the snap of a shattering Prince Rupert's drop—and then the Crystal simply fell from the wall. I hurriedly bent down to place a hand on it.

"Seventy mC, that's a mostly intact Crystal," Smegma said, excitedly. "It may even be undamaged enough to become a low-ranked Spent Mana Crystal once the Mana inside it is sold off."

Suddenly, it started to feel like we were making progress. Slower progress than my Demon companion would like, but progress!

116

My feeling joined his when I discovered that I had damaged the Crystal a bit too much to use it to identify Skills.

CHAPTER 13

Thursday, April 4th, 2069

[What would happen if I tried to sell you a Crystal still in the wall?] I asked Smegma as I bit into a sandwich I'd prepared this morning.

We had just taken a break for lunch. The Mining team was still in the cavern that we began in this morning, but it was nearly entirely cleared of Mana Crystals. My contribution was lackluster, mostly consisting of a cleared space about the size of a large master bathroom.

No one was giving me a hard time over it though, which was likely either because they remembered their first times, or because my father and Willa were here. Those two were responsible for the two largest cleared portions. Still, if my relation to them was protecting me—well, it surely wasn't by physical proximity.

My father was eating his sandwich while examining a golden colored vein in a distant wall. Looking around, I realized that the metallic ore veins were the only reason we were still 'working' this cavern. Willa was also studying something near one of the two tunnels leading off our cavern. From here, it looked like a massive crack in the wall but could easily be a dark metallic ore.

Miguel and Fat Gary sat nearby quietly eating. I was just glad that they weren't engaging me in a conversation, which allowed me to study the *Demonic Vault's* red screen.

Specifically, I was staring at my number of Mana Coins. For every fifteen Crystals I Sharded, I had been attempting to mine one that I would sell to Smegma. Thanks to that, and me moving to Mining full Crystals as my father moved away, my mC total had climbed to three thousand and forty, but my hopes for purchasing a Miner's Pick by the end of the day were drying up fast.

Maybe I could speed up a bit in the afternoon, though. My nerves at getting caught in the morning hadn't let me go particularly quickly or take as many Crystals as I might have otherwise. Although when the Lynx member with the Spatial Skill or Item came by and started taking the Shards, he hadn't seemed to notice anything amiss.

This could really work, it seemed.

Still, I doubted I would get to ten thousand by the end of the day. That was due to the second, far sadder reason why my attempts to collect enough mC were currently below my expectation. Mining was far more difficult than I expected.

The first hour was relatively manageable, but each hour afterward saw me slowing down considerably. I stared at the peanut butter and jelly sandwich squished between my numb fingers. Squished because I'd dropped my first one onto the cave floor, thinking I was gripping it sufficiently. I didn't even know that repeated jarring impacts on the object held in your hands could cause this sort of malalignment.

No matter what, I had a new appreciation for what my father did.

Smegma phased through the floor before floating back to me.

"You can try to drain them while they're in the walls, but then you'd be leaving the 'evidence' of Spent Mana Crystals in the walls. Since I could only theoretically buy the Mana inside and not the actual Crystals themselves. I even doubt that would work because they're kind of living things, but sure, give it a shot." The Imp said in answer to my mentally thought question from a few moments ago.

Smegma's tone wasn't what I would call encouraging. He sounded disinterested, almost angry. He'd gotten more and more like that slowly over the course of this morning's four hours of Mining. At first, he'd been slightly excited, but my dwindling efficacy with each hour also seemed to drain something from the Demon Trader. It took me a moment to fully register his words, but when I did, I nearly choked.

[They're what?] I said, thankful it was a mental communication, or I might have swallowed a piece of sandwich into my lungs.

"Crystals are essentially Flora. Don't ask me how that works, because no one knows. They essentially absorb Mana like sunshine and gas and they grow. They don't have cells or biological living tissue as the Demon race knew it," Smegma answered with a shrug. Then he saw the peanut butter and jelly sandwich on top of the bag and covered in dirt. "What happened?"

I took another bite and smeared the raspberry jam and peanut butter around in my mouth, allowing the sugar to wake me up a bit.

[I don't want to talk about it, my hands are numb.] I responded before changing the subject. [The Miner's Pick says that it absorbs and stores Mana though, right? So won't it take more when I'm Sharding? The excess Mana lost from Sharding doesn't just disappear, right? Do you think the pick could absorb all that extra waste and form whole Crystals out of it?] I said as I studied the screen for the item in question.

Miscellaneous Professions Gear
Miner's Pick
(1)
Item Rank: Low F-Rank
Durability: Unlimited
Damage: 1-3 (x100% to Mineable minerals)
This Miner's Pick will use the Mana run-off from the Crystals to repair and strengthen itself, making it unbreakable. It will also store excess Mana to intermittently create a Mana Crystal of appropriate rank.
Current progress to Mana Crystal: 0 of 1,000 Mana
Cost: 10,000 mC

"You need the Miner's Pick first," Smegma said with such boredom in his tone that I wanted to kick him. I definitely would have if I could, and my two lunch companions could think what they will.

Since Smegma was such a bore, I turned my attention to Fat Gary and Miguel. "What's the usual plan for after lunch?"

"After lunch?" Fat Gary asked, looking up and meeting my eyes with a bit of skepticism. "It's already impressive as hell that you made it to lunch, kid!" He pointed to the first peanut butter and jelly sandwich. "How can you even feel your hands?"

I blinked and looked at my numb hands. Even as I held them in front of me, I thought I felt some feeling return to them. I was working under the impression that after lunch they'd be fine again. I looked between Fat Gary and Miguel, a bit lost.

Miguel smiled at me but went back to eating. I furrowed my brow at his seemingly strange response to Fat Gary's shock and my pleading look. "Miguel's English is poor. He only speaks after he's known you for a little. Still, are you being serious? Are you really going to try to keep working after lunch?"

I nodded and watched as Fat Gary's face became defeated. He reached into a pants pocket and pulled out his wallet before handing a twenty to Miguel. He said something in Spanish to the man, and Miguel's smile grew even bigger. "Miguel bet me you'd keep going, but I thought it was easy money. Most new workers only Mine for the first quarter of an hour."

Fat Gary clicked his tongue as I watched the two with raised eyebrows. I hadn't thought about just how physically demanding Mining would be. Surely, they were right—nothing I'd done in my life to date would lend itself to this kind of work. Not my gym sessions, or my Muay Thai.

It doesn't take a rocket scientist to figure out what was going on.

"Your *Recovery* Skill," Smegma said, finishing my thought for me, just before Fat Gary got over his frustration at losing a bet and turned back to me.

"Usually after lunch break, we go back to work, but in this case, we'll likely head to another Cavern and leave the mineral deposits to those two, or the Specialists."

"Specialists?" I asked, not having seen anything to distinguish Miner's apart.

Fat Gary raised an eyebrow and then pointed in the direction that my father had been when I last saw him. For a moment, I thought my father was considered a Specialist, but that quick glance showed someone speaking to my dad. Fat Gary gave some context a moment later. "That's Bruce. He Awakened with two Skills. Mana Pool and something to do with Mining, or at least it's useful in Mining. He's one of our team's Specialists."

The man looked like any other Miner I'd seen on the way out here. In fact, I thought I could recall him in the ATV and from just inside the Portal. He was smaller than even Willa but had corded muscles that seemed to be trying to escape his tight hairy skin. My father was gesturing to the golden-colored vein and Bruce was nodding.

Either Fat Gary sensed my confusion at the situation or just felt the need to explain further. "That could be the magical equivalent of Fool's Gold or True

Gold. Right now, your father is asking Bruce his opinion. True Gold is rare and exceptionally valuable, but if Mined improperly, useless."

Without looking back, I asked the obvious. "So, why wouldn't Bruce just Mine the vein to be sure?"

"He's got an F-Ranked Mana Pool. Sure, he's getting more efficient but he still can't handle too many ore deposits in a single day. Same goes for our other Specialist. So, if they use their Skills to Mine something useless, they'll be done for the next five hours. Normally, we catalog all the potential minerals first and have the Specialists work on the most profitable."

Something bothered me about that. My father had been with this Mining crew for my entire life. "Why don't they try to hire a Bank, or why haven't the Specialist's Pools Evolved if they are using them everyday?"

Miguel looked up, startled—saw my genuine confusion on the matter and chuckled to himself. Fat Gary also responded with clear amusement in his voice. "It isn't that easy to just hire a Bank. Most willing want Hunters—and those willing to settle on Miners want well-off Specialists. So here at P-Cubed, when Specialists get better, they head for greener pastures. If they manage to find a Bank, they'll get bought out all the faster. No one would choose to stay either. Like, why would you stay with a crew of Normies when you can join one with mostly Specialists and get higher pay from bonuses?"

"The company can't provide them with Mana Batteries?" I asked, thinking of the Cores that could be turned into Mana Storage devices. Surely, they'd get a great deal of use out of those, and I always thought they were more common in Mining and other Professions because if they broke they wouldn't cause too big of a problem.

Fat Gary smiled. "Have you met Jagger? Guy's cheaper than a Wandering Hunter—at least Wandering Hunters realize they need to take care of their teams. Jagger makes his money when the Specialists move on, though—I'm pretty sure of that."

My lips firmed. That made a great deal of sense—if Jagger had the contracts, then he could sell his 'trained up' Specialists to others for an immediate profit. Then the new company could get that Specialist set up with Batteries or Banks. Well, at least we had some Specialists while they trained up their Skills.

Then another thought hit me.

"Why can't we just camp out inside the Portal and work until everything in here is stripped?" I asked the question that had been sitting at the tip of my tongue.

Fat Gary and Miguel both hissed from beside me, which drew my full attention back to them. To watch them go from amused to terrified made me snap out of the lethargy I currently felt.

Miguel was making a gesture, crossing himself in the religious way that Catholics did, and Fat Gary was clutching a ring on his left index finger tight enough to cause the appendage to change color from lack of blood.

"Kid, Portals ain't safe at night. If the area within is big enough, sometimes entire clearance teams, and sometimes even Mining teams, are forced to camp for the night, but *our* team has strict contracts that state we won't ever do that. Too many teams and Hunters have died in Portals when they camp overnight."

121

If the two hadn't both reacted so vehemently, I might have suspected that they were hazing the new guy with 'ghost stories,' but both still looked shaken by my casual question. "How come I've never heard about this on the news?"

"You have," Miguel said, speaking for the first time. He had a very heavy accent that I couldn't place. "Every tragedy in Portals on da news is overnight campders."

I blinked. *What? But the news never mentioned anything like that, how come?*

"It's the Time Bubble." Smegma cut in. "I told you this earlier. For four hours at night, Dungeons are synced with the planet's geography. The process takes down the Time Bubble, which you can think of as the 'fence' separating the Portal from the rest of this world. With the Bubble down, creatures from the planet that weren't originally part of the Portal can enter the area until the System re-establishes the Bubble. You have to remember, Brodie, that these planets are ones that failed and were overrun by Portals and Monsters. Monsters are not like you humans or Demons like me. They don't need Mana to keep growing stronger. It helps, and speeds up that growth sure, but they'll grow regardless. So, it comes down to luck after that. In some cases, nothing enters. And in the worst cases, a creature far exceeding the zone rank finds its way inside," Smegma explained, and I transferred my look of shock from Miguel to the Demon Trader.

"It's all over the Read-it forums, and I don't think the United Nations Monster Hunters wants the public to know about it, so of course it won't be in the news," Fat Gary said, seeing me seem to have an epiphany. To him, it must look like I was staring into empty space with wide eyes when pieces of a puzzle came together or something.

I was, of course, still paying attention and instantly recalled the Snatcher and Cannibal criminal distinctions. Just how much was the UNMH keeping from us?

With an effort of will, I looked away from Smegma and that knowledge bombshell he just casually dropped. Somehow, the look of the empty cavern and the smell of wet stone was far more intimidating than it had been all morning. It was like the undercurrents of sulfur that had been on the breeze were ignited and turned the place into one giant match in my mind. It affirmed for me that no Portal would ever be truly safe, whether they'd been 'cleared' or not.

Gulping audibly, I nodded to the two Miners, showing my understanding before I looked back to my dad and the Specialist, Bruce. I found my father returning to the group.

"Willa, don't bother with that vein either. Bruce says they found a lot of Thorium in a deeper cavern. The Specialists won't have time for 'True Gold' or Necrograph."

Willa waved from her place near the tunnel, showing she'd heard my father but didn't make her way back to the group.

My dad sat down with me, across from Fat Gary and Miguel. He pulled out a second sandwich and before taking a bite, addressed the three of us. "You two are going to take the Light Stone deeper and work with another group to begin clearing it of Mana Crystals. Willa and I will remain here and use my Light Stone to attempt to mine a few of the ores."

Miguel and Fat Gary nodded but Fat Gary motioned at me. "Just the two of us? Kid says he's going to keep going."

My dad turned his head to stare at me, looking incredulous. "Brodie, you've already done more than I would have ever expected. Any more and you probably aren't getting out of bed tomorrow. The reason you're getting paid next to nothing as my assistant is that it will take weeks for you to build up the muscles and resistance to the constant hammer-like impacts."

I flexed my muscles comically, choosing to turn it into a joke instead of a direct argument with my father. "Remember what Jeral said, Dad, I might be stronger than you!"

My dad rolled his eyes, and his face morphed into a look that seemed to be questioning if he should just let me learn my lesson. I jumped in quickly to let that be his final thought on the matter. I *needed* ten thousand mC!

"So, you're going to try to mine that even if it's True Gold?" I asked, not understanding how Thorium was more valued than a potential True Gold vein.

"I've successfully extracted one usable ingot of True Gold before," my dad explained, his face still stuck on the last conversation. Eventually he let it drop, firmly deciding that I could learn the lesson the hard way.

Noticing my confusion at that answer, he continued answering my unspoken question, "The problem isn't that we're not sure if it's Fool's Gold or if it's True Gold, it's that both of them tend to exist in the same place and they're nearly impossible to tell apart. There's likely to be some True Gold in here among the fake, but none of the Skills we have access to would allow us to identify what's what. The chances of extracting Fool's Gold is too high to waste the Specialist's Mana. So, the crew would rather get the assured bonus for grabbing what we can of the Thorium vein than to gamble on the less than ten percent chance of finding True Gold in that vein."

I looked at the vein and then scanned to the open window for the Miner's Pick.

[Smegma, would the pick be able to help a non-Specialist Miner take on Thorium or True Gold deposits more successfully?]

"At level one? Unless the guy has a Skill or absurd experience, no husking chance," Smegma stated. He did give my father a quick up and down, seeming to appreciate that the man had Mined a usable ingot without a Skill. "Maybe Thorium at level ten, and True Gold between twenty-five and fifty." A smile came onto my face and Smegma did a double take. "What the shit are you smiling like that for? You look like a pedophile who saw a new boy."

I gave the Imp a warning look for his offensive reference, then wondered how he knew that our world had issues like that. Or did his world also have a similar moral structure? Shaking off that question, I looked at the three present Miners and the picks they used.

[What would happen if I supplied all of them with these kinds of picks?]

Smegma narrowed his black eyes. They widened a moment later. "If you don't hand over the Keystone—"

[The what now?] I interrupted not having heard the term before.

"Don't interrupt me, moron. The big brain is at work. Plus, wait till you buy the pick. It's husking self-explanatory! Where was I—oh yes—without the

Keystone, they won't be able to take out the accumulated Mana as a Crystal. They'll level the picks and be essentially supplying you with—wait, that won't work. Once they see how beneficial the new equipment is to their work, they'll just take the picks home with them, and that's completely separate from the little problem of you explaining where a student with no Mining experience, and who isn't some kind of legendary blacksmith, got them in the first place. Imbecile!"

Just like that, Smegma's excitement shriveled and died, but not mine. If I started with my father and claimed I needed to maintain the object with oils or something, would he listen? Then as the pick leveled and became better, would he convince his crew to use my picks? I thought he would, and it wasn't like I had to buy the picks if he didn't. I could just buy two. One for me and one for him. Or maybe three if I included *aunt Willa*...

An idea started to form. It certainly needed work, but I was about to go back to mindlessly swinging a pickaxe—so, I had time.

I must have projected some of those thoughts to Smegma because he was now grinning evilly. "You little entrepreneur! If we figure this out, it could be huge!"

[I've still got to buy the first Miner's Pick,] I said, throwing his earlier drab words back at him.

He made a rude gesture with his three-fingered hand. I assumed it meant the same thing as a middle finger but didn't want to ask. What was a demonic equivalent of a husk you?

CHAPTER 14

Thursday, April 4th, 2069

Once in the new cavern, I instantly discovered that my earlier 'brilliant idea' was impossible. I couldn't sell Mana from Mana Crystals that were still attached to the wall.

The removal of a fast and easy solution caused me to grumble. Right up until I managed to successfully hit the 'stem' of a Crystal for the second time, but this time perfectly. Between one swing into the rock and another, the Crystal simply seemed to roll free with a strange crackling pop, similar to the ones before but more pronounced. Once I had a full undamaged Crystal and could still see the stem in the wall, it was clear that Mana Crystals were like a plant, as Smegma had explained. They even had a root system and everything.

Discovering the simplicity of the task made me confident I could do it again in the future. Sure, not with every attempt—but it was definitely repeatable. Plus, once you looked at the entire cavern and Crystals like a front lawn, you had to wonder just how much like plants the things were. A quick question to Smegma got me an answer. It turned out that, in theory, all the damage the Miners did in these tunnels would eventually regrow—as long as the planet had Mana.

But 'eventually,' meant after hundreds, if not thousands, of years. Smegma was bitter as he explained this piece of Mana Crystal trivia to me. I saved my question about why he was in a mood for now. Not that I expected him to answer it with his track record. Instead, I chose to examine the perfectly intact Mana Crystal I had just mined.

Knowing it acted like a plant made my study of it tilt heavily toward a biological assessment as opposed to staring at a mineral or a rock. But the Crystal was not easily classified in either of those categories. If I was to compare it to a plant, it seemed similar to lettuce, containing an almost rounded bottom that narrowed to a single point above the stem. The 'leaves,' however, were nothing like lettuce, and instead were made up of sharp edges and points that looked like that science experiment I'd done in elementary school. It was a pretty simple one where I combined sugar, water, food coloring, and a popsicle stick. I guess there was also heat involved somewhere, since I recalled getting help from my mom with the stove. What *was* clear, however, was the 'rock candy' that had formed on the popsicle stick back then closely resembled what I was seeing in the Crystal, which reinforced for me that the 'leaves' were more like mineral deposits.

"You might want to sell that to me, Miguel is about to finish with his section, which will move him to another," Smegma commented dryly.

[But this one for sure will work as a Spent Mana Crystal, right?] Smegma nodded so I continued. [Then I want to keep it to check on my Mana Pool.]

Throughout the day, I'd continued to convert my Mana to Coins through *Demonic Vault*. So, I wasn't sure if the Pool had grown further, but I had a niggling suspicion it had. Since it kind of felt like Smegma was gaslighting me or calling me crazy when I brought it up, I desperately wanted proof that I wasn't insane.

Smegma shrugged and a notification popped up offering to buy the Mana from the Crystal for eighty mC. Smiling, I accepted it and was left with a clear Crystal in my hands. I spun it through my fingers while keeping my hands affixed to it. Smegma had said I only had to hold it for five minutes to have my Skill assessed, hadn't he?

"Don't bother with those," Fat Gary said. "The clear ones are useless."

Thinking fast, I answered, "Does that mean I could take it home?"

"We've all taken souvenirs from time to time, kid. I don't think anyone will care about that, but ask your da'. I don't think he wants you fantasizing about Mining."

I could only grimace and nod. Maybe he would change his mind after I got the Miner's Pick. Then again, from his point of view I'd just been through a traumatic event and any plans that involved Mining might look like I was desperate to drop out of school…

I put the Spent Mana Crystal on a clear patch of stone and soil beside me before resuming my work. [Is it just me or does it seem like people don't know the value of Spent Mana Crystals?]

"It isn't just you. You're an idiot and you're noticing it. Someone much smarter than you, like me, has already formed many possible scenarios for this by using the clues around me…" Smegma let his leading sentence hang in the air. He clearly wanted me to ask his opinion.

[Oh, good, at least I'm not the only one,] I answered instead. My reward for ignoring his hints that were practically begging me to ask him what conclusions he'd come to was seeing a small amount of tension form around the Imp's black eyes.

"Gahh, you're so husking boring! I'll educate you then. So far, every piece of technology I've seen you humans use burns Mana Crystals. Meaning it consumes the Mana *and* the Crystal. How much do you know about your world's Mana Engines and other Mana Technologies? Is my speculation close?"

[Practically nothing, but history class did teach me that fire and humans have a deep-rooted history. In some folklore, it's what was gifted to us by the Gods and took us out of the Dark Ages. In that myth, fire was associated with enlightenment—with the impartation of the Divine that allowed humanity to survive, thrive, and ultimately led us on a path toward building a civilization.]

"Took you out of the 'Dark Ages'? What the husk? You idiots are still *in* the 'Dark Ages' from my point of view. My people pooled their resources for generations all for a small chance to change our fate and Ascend. To take a step and get one step closer to the Divine, and instead of that I've ended up on this Podunk piece of shit planet!"

[Do you want to talk about it?] I asked, hearing the frustration in his words more than the insults.

"Talk about what?"

[Well, I mean you've been pretty sour on and off all day. I get the feeling that you aren't angry at me or this planet. Not really.]

Smegma stared at me for long enough that I was forced to return to my token show of Mining. Luckily, I had the completely physical and unintelligent work of Sharding another fifteen growths before attempting to negotiate a stem again, which gave me the opportunity to give the Demon time to consider whether or not to confide in me. I could still feel Smegma staring at me as I worked. I ignored him, trying my best to give him space to decide for himself.

"Mana, in enough abundance to refill Mana Pools through osmansis, only appears on newly integrating planets or in planets that successfully Evolve or Ascend. Crendalar Five failed to Ascend. Actually, any planet that is used for Portals has, by definition—failed to Evolve—and its people are left with Mana Pools that don't refill and thus Skills that can't be used. Understand?"

[Then how are we on Sective Agora and Mining Mana Crystals?] I asked but continued my Sharding of nearby Crystals.

"This has to do with why the powerful Monsters and creatures often enter an area inside the Time Bubble when it drops for those four hours. That area has residual Mana and resources. The Time Bubble brings with it Mana, Crystals, and an overabundance of other resources. My research team in the past hypothesized that the Time Bubble kind of progresses the area inside of itself and floods it with Mana—that's why there are so many Crystals, Fauna, Flora and Monsters.

"Plus, it usually kicks out any local Monsters or stragglers from the other world if they aren't out by the time the Bubble comes back up… there are some exceptions to that, too."

[So, can't your people just fight for those areas, refill your Mana Pools, and collect anything that isn't captured by our Hunters and their teams?]

"We've tried that for many years. It certainly works, but it's even more dangerous for us than it is for your Hunters after the Bubble goes down. First, we have to fight the same creatures and the local wildlife, which are far more powerful, but we also have limited resources on initial contact. Second, if we are found by the lifeforms pillaging the Portal, or Hunters, as you call them—they are often also enemies, if only because we'd be competing to access the same resources. Plus, we are not the only Sect on my planet and the other Sects are also competitors for the materials in Bubbles. My Abyss Sect is down to a few fighters after years of competition. We have been forced to use what resources we have left to secure our gates against surface Monsters and other sects. It's been like a siege. In desperation, we came up with this plan…"

[Okay, so your people need a lot of Mana—thus the existence of Coins you offer in trade for it?]

"That's right, good job getting there." Smegma's bitterness came back with a vengeance.

[I feel like I'm missing something. I'm working toward providing Mana, aren't I? In fact, nearly six thousand at this point! Why are you still bitter?]

Smegma gave me a withering stare. Then scoffed and deigned me with an answer. "Six thousand won't even fill my Pool, and I'm a researcher. Our Sect Leader needs hundreds of millions of Mana to fill his."

My mind boggled at the implications that admission brought with it. So, his planet failed to Ascend even though it had someone with that kind of power, and the people there had the ability to pick up more Skills. A further piece of information made my mouth drop open. Smegma hadn't come right out and said it, but if you read between the lines, his Sect was on the verge of collapse. It was likely one of the weaker ones on Crendalar Five. So, was his Sect Leader with hundreds of millions of Mana also considered 'weak'?

My next strike failed to hit the stem of the Mana Crystal I had been planning to put up for sale, thanks to my turbulent thoughts. I Sharded it and paused, hoping to be in a better headspace before I tried again. My stomach was in knots, but I knew that my only option was to ask. I hated doing it, but I summoned my courage before saying, [Smegma, do you think our planet has a chance?]

"It's been what? Under fifty years since the first Portal formed?" he replied.

[You were closer with your first guesses. It's been just a bit more than twenty for certain, as far as we can tell.] At my response, he tapped a talon against a tooth.

Several taps later, he tilted his head back and forth while oscillating his hand. "You've got plenty of time left if we go off of Crendalar's history, but from what we discovered in the five-thousand-plus years of history of Portals in our world, there isn't really a pattern to the Ascension deadline. Some planets lasted longer than us before ultimately succeeding or failing, and some were deemed failures in less than a decade."

My emotions went through a roller coaster as he spoke. In the end, I was left with another question that I probably should have asked earlier.

[What does a planet need to do to Evolve or Ascend?]

"You have to conquer a sequence of Portals that you don't even want to think about. We called these Portals the Seven Deadly Realms—and if you fail even a single one, the Portal sucks your planet dry of Mana and vanishes."

[And if you succeed?] I asked as I swallowed.

"You did pretty good for your first day," my dad interrupted from right beside me.

I'd been so distracted that I hadn't seen him approach. I registered his words and glanced at my watch. It was two thirty, and a few hours short of quitting time. It took me a few moments more to understand why he said what he had. I had to examine myself to get it. I was breathing hard, leaning against the haft of my pickaxe with the head grounded, doing no work.

"Just taking a break, Dad. I'll get right back at it."

"Brodie, I'm telling you if you push yourself too hard—" My dad said but then cut himself off with an odd expression that I couldn't read. He changed what he had been about to say, and asked, "What's this?" He indicated the Spent Mana Crystal.

I tried to act excited and landed somewhere in between tired and strained enthusiasm instead. "It's a clear Crystal. I thought it was something special, but Fat Gary told me it's worthless. So, I thought I could take it home?" I turned it into a question with intonation and then added, "Please."

128

My dad licked his teeth, which was never a good sign, but surprised me when he said, "If you manage to work consistently for the next two hours, I'll let you take it. Deal?"

I nodded, even as my brain turned over his abrupt change in feelings on my continued Mining. Hadn't he been about to tell me it was okay to stop? Shrugging, I changed the subject. "How'd the Mining up above go?"

"Fool's Gold," my dad answered simply as he moved toward Miguel. "How's everything been down here?" he asked.

"Good, good. We may be sixty percent done. Willa and you rejoin?"

My dad nodded and moved over to Fat Gary next and had a quick conversation with him that I couldn't hear.

As I went back to working, I repeated my earlier question to Smegma, [What happens if you succeed?]

"How would I husking know that, dumb-dumb?"

He did have a point there.

I managed to get another stem after four more attempts. This time, I sold the Spent Crystal as well, not wanting it to look like I was finding an abundance of the clear type, which in truth I had yet to even see.

Smegma bought it and the Mana for a hundred mC.

Two hours later, our group had cleared a second cavern of Crystals and the Specialists had dismissed the Ores. My dad was sufficiently impressed by my perseverance to let me take home the Spent Crystal. I picked it up with my gloves and asked, [Smeg, will it still activate if I'm wearing gloves?]

He gave me a look that questioned my intelligence. "You need to insert your Mana into it, dummy!"

Flushing with heat, I chose to keep wearing my gloves due to the sharp edges. Either way, I wouldn't be attempting to use the thing till I got home. I wasn't sure what would happen when the Crystal activated and told me what my low-ranked Skills were, but I wouldn't want it to happen in front of others. Even if it wasn't flashy. Having other people see my Skills would be like exposing my dick to them or something. At least that's how intensely personal it felt.

Our group started moving all the Shards to boxes to help the Lynx Guild Member with the Spatial Skill. Once we were finished, it was about ten minutes after five, and my dad led the way back to the surface. Outside the cave entrance was a man I didn't recognize but sported the Lynx's logo. He glanced at the large watermelon-sized Crystal in my hands, but quickly dismissed it, likely after noticing its see-through clarity indicating the absence of Mana.

A few groups were already outside waiting. Everything seemed normal until my dad approached the waiting Lynx Hunter. "Any reports?"

"Two minor injuries to your crew. Four major acid burns that required a Healer. Unfortunately, the cost of heals wiped out about nine-tenths of your bonus, but currently you still have a hundred thousand to split amongst the workers."

A hundred thousand?!

That's when I remembered the size of the crew as a whole and realized that only equated to about two thousand dollars each. I scoffed at my own thoughts. *'Only'* two thousand dollars plus hourly for a day's work? That's half a month's wages for some lower-class families. Wait, would I get a share of that? Willa socked me in the arm. "Don't be worryin', kid. Everyone gets a share, but newbies be starting at a half percent. That be meanin'—"

Echoes of shouting laced with screams echoed up the tunnel, cutting Willa off. Everyone outside spun to face the entrance as four men carrying a package between them rushed into the remaining light of the rainforest. It took a moment to realize the 'package' was moving and—*screaming*. I inhaled sharply through my nose in surprise.

I began to cough as the sulfur-like, sour odor of burning skin attempted to climb down my throat. The man who had just answered my father pointed in a direction and the four men kept jogging while supporting the mangled body between them. My eyes weren't sure what they were seeing. The reason it had looked more like a *package* than a human at first was because the leather armor looked like it had melted into the man's flesh. Where one might expect blood, instead there was something that resembled moss but shone like metal, and finally, but most confusing, was the lack of two limbs. Suddenly, that two thousand dollars didn't seem like quite enough.

"Well, shit," my dad said. Willa grimaced from beside me and slumped down onto the rainforest floor with a disappointed exhalation of held air.

"I really could be usin' dat bonus," she complained.

"So, we don't get it anymore?" I asked, still watching the spot where the four men and the terribly injured one vanished.

"Not a chance," my dad stated plainly. "In fact, our group's insurance is probably going to take a hit. Better than Silvia dying, though."

My father's face was whiter than I'd ever seen. A quick scan showed me that the whole Miner's group looked the same. It was only then that I realized that this could easily have happened to me.

CHAPTER 15

Thursday, April 4th, 2069

The trip back was the opposite of what I expected. First, the quiet introspection by the Miners only lasted perhaps five minutes, or until everyone was confirmed to have exited the Mining caverns. Then we were led back to the entrance of the Portal. Once the exterior of the Portal was cleared by our Hunter guides, we were sent through, and I experienced my second trip through a Portal before we were efficiently loaded back onto the ATV. Once aboard, we met the group who had carried away the man who had been missing limbs.

The mood instantly felt turbulent right up until people noticed the fifth member with some very red skin on his *intact* limbs and parts of his body. While there wasn't cheering or loud exclamations of joy, each member took a moment to go pat the man on a shoulder, head, or knee. I was the odd man out here, not feeling comfortable approaching a person I didn't know, but I definitely felt the simmering undercurrent of relief that I assumed everyone else did. It was good to know that if you got injured, you would be healed.

"The Healing this meat sack received is surprisingly good. Not many Healers on Crendalar could regrow limbs, and the ones that could were beyond expensive." Smegma commented, his voice speculative and clearly not meant to start a conversation. He paired his introspective comment with a motion that looked like he was squeezing biceps that he didn't currently have.

For my part, I was too busy tightly clutching my 'trophy' from the day—the clear Spent Mana Crystal. I was also busy funneling each regenerated point of Mana I received into *Demonic Vault*. It was rather enjoyable to watch the mC number climb ever closer to ten thousand. While I say ever closer to ten thousand, I was still over five hundred points away, which wasn't exactly achievable, at least not tonight.

That thought depressed me a bit because if I couldn't grab a Miner's Pick tonight or in the morning, I would have to wait till tomorrow night. My reasoning was that if I suddenly pulled my own pick out of mid-air while Mining, there would be questions, one of which would be ownership. If I got it at home, all I would have to do is leave the house for an hour or two tonight and borrow the car. Then come home and claim I bought it. Then when I arrived at the site, I'd be in possession of my own pick, which would put a stop to all questions of ownership.

Suddenly, I had an idea. Smegma was a merchant, right? The world was full of different things, and after talking to the Imp, I realized that there were things we likely valued very little that Smegma or his Sect might value very highly, or vice-versa. Could I become an interplanetary Silk Road middle-man between his world and mine? I did have some savings…

[Smegma, would you accept other objects for Mana Coins?] I asked mentally, thinking about taking that shopping trip but purchasing objects with another form of currency.

Worldwide Greenbacks. The world-wide accepted currency, which—let's be honest—was just American Dollars with a name change. According to history, the name change was ceded to assuage other nations when the Awakening Advent occurred. It was somewhat amusing since the currency was identical to previous US dollars, with one change so far. The twenty-dollar bill print had a new face, and that was Connor O'Gorman, the Hunter Unions president and world's first double-S Hunter. Plus, he was, unsurprisingly, American—so I wasn't even sure if that wouldn't have happened either way.

It also didn't help that the term 'Greenbacks' never really caught on, and that most people still called the global currency 'dollars', but they tried, I guess.

"If it has any value, but I doubt you can buy anything I'd be interested in. It isn't like you can send a Healer over…"

I looked at the Healed man, who looked exceptionally tired from the day's ordeals, and then rolled my eyes. Even if I could purchase a person, there was no way I'd be sending them to Crendalar Five after Smegma's admission. Still, I loudly heard Smegma's stance on Earth's everyday items and technology. It didn't mean I wasn't going to try, plus there were always credit cards to max out for something of true value…

[You've been floating around and annoying me long enough that I've realized a few things. You're not impressed with our technology, and you seem to roll your eyes at how we are utilizing the newly available resources, but *I* was thinking that the raw resources we're using *so poorly* might be worth more to your people than to us, at least for now,] I began to explain.

As I floundered for more to say, more that would truly highlight just how far spanning this idea could go, I glanced over at the Imp. Surprisingly, he was smiling. It was… terrifying.

"You forgot one… *little* thing in your fledgling plans of world domination." His voice was smug. I hated it already. "You see, *I'm* the merchant here. I'm the one connecting entire worlds through my sheer awesomeness. The *merchant* makes his money through the margins, not the seller."

I frowned. Smegma smiled cheerfully and added a final line that turned my frown into a scowl of distrust. "It's still a good idea, though. Definitely *worth* exploring."

He basically just told me he would try to rob me blind on any transaction, hadn't he? Sure, I'd likely get some value out of the trades still, but this felt like it should be a relationship of mutual benefits. At least to me. Wait—

Was he already doing that with the Mana Crystals? My eyes narrowed and I ground my teeth as silently as I could manage. I'd keep that little slip up from the Demon in mind for later.

The ATV came to a stop and then slowly inched forward as if suddenly stuck in rush hour traffic. The silence in the cab lessened as murmurs of conversation sprang up. Willa and my dad were no exception. My dad started by directing a question to me, "So, how are your hands feeling after your first day?"

I released the Crystal with one of the hands in question and looked at the thick Monster-skin glove that covered it. Opening and closing my fist made me realize just how odd my hands felt. I had expected *Recovery* to have fully taken care of any problems, but my hands did feel quite numb after the day of work.

"Not great," I said as I stared at my own hand that didn't feel like it was totally under my brain's control. "Numb and weak."

"Oh my god, yes!" Willa exclaimed. "Mine are feelin' the same but that be because I tried my hand at that Necrograph deposit. That stuff needs a magic jack hammer or a Specialist, I think." Willa opened and closed her hands, mirroring me, though she no longer wore her gloves.

My dad noticed the difference and reached over to help me take off my gloves.

It took me a second to realize his intention. I spoke up. "No, not yet. There are a couple sharp places on this Crystal. I don't want to cut my hands."

"I already told you, it isn't just touching the thing that activates it," Smegma groaned from beside me. He sounded like he was talking to a child. Unfortunately, I had once again forgotten that point, and it was too late now—so I stuck to the lie.

My dad blinked then nodded. "Okay, but once we get in the car, I'll need to take a look. My guess is your hands are covered in blisters." At my widening eyes, he chuckled. "Don't worry, I have a salve in the car that will instantly heal them but leaves behind the calluses. As for that Crystal, we'll have to file it down later, I don't want your friends getting hurt if they come by to study. I've got a grinder in the basement."

I nodded, even though there was no chance of him using the tool to ruin *my* Spent Mana Crystal. While it was true that there were some sharp edges to the thing, that wasn't the real reason I hadn't wanted to touch it. I wanted to hide my face in my hands but fought the urge and instead turned to Willa and asked, "In school we learned that there are better picks out there that turn an experienced Miner into a Specialist. Is that true?"

"Oh sure, but they be stupid expensive. Plus, they break quick. So, it be a gamble."

"Gamble?"

This time my dad answered the question. "Yeah, you get higher pay as a Specialist, and the group could get a higher bonus with more people able to mine deposits like True Gold, Thorium, Necrograph or even stronger materials. However, as you saw today, bonuses are anything but guaranteed. Then, when you have to repair your pick, if you don't have enough money—it's coming out of your pocket. We've had a few people give it a try, Willa and I included. I think I was in the black by about a hundred bucks when mine broke for the fourth time, and I just gave up. Willa, how much did you lose again?"

"Husk Gary, ya be knowin' better than ta bring that up." Willa glared at my dad, then softened the look when she saw me intently looking at her from my seat between them. "About ten thousand," she answered sheepishly. My eyebrows rose.

"How much does one of these picks cost?" I asked, trying to understand how she could have gone that much into the red.

"Anywhere from five thousand to a hundred thousand, depending on the quality and what it will do," my dad nonchalantly quoted.

"That's because you are walking apes and can't figure out how to create a self-repair Enchantment," Smegma said insultingly. It allowed me to know that he had returned to this side of the cabin, but I ignored him, more interested in what these expensive pickaxes could do.

"What could make the most expensive one worth that kind of money?"

"They aren't really, unless you're Minin' in higher rankin' Dungeons. There be multiple problems with buyin' an expensive pick. Primary among them be that a Miner's Pick ain't always the best tool for da job. You'd gone to da next cavern already, but sometimes you be wantin' wedges and sledges. Or a jackhammer. So, yeah, a Miner's Pick can work for all deposits and Crystals, but if ya really want to be doin' it right, ya need a whole set—that or you be breakin' the Miner's Pick early, and in debt—"

"—Nah," Smegma interrupted, cutting off some of what my father said next. "A Skilled Miner can do with just the pickaxe, well at least one of *my*—"

"—answer what on a pick to make it worth that kind of money. Sellers claim that the higher-end models can help guide you to existing cracks and strike points while you swing. The heads are also made of metals from C-Rank Dungeons, which means that they are absurdly durable. However, it usually isn't the metal that breaks, but the Enchantments, so the better the Enchants, the more expensive the repair..." My dad said while looking wistful. I could tell he wanted a pickaxe like that, but simultaneously couldn't justify spending a quarter of our house's mortgage on the thing. Not to mention the possible millions it might be to get a whole tool kit.

I glanced at Smegma, thinking over his interruption. I couldn't see how additional tools wouldn't be helpful for various situations... It took me a second to notice that the Imp was practically apoplectic with rage.

[You okay there, buddy?] I asked hesitantly. His face looked ready to pop like a balloon at any moment.

"Higher-end models of pickaxes in your world make it *easier* to Shard Crystals *faster*?!" His head might not have exploded, but his voice sure did. I winced in spite of myself, trying not to give away to everyone that I had an imaginary friend with me who could rupture eardrums. "There's an entire branch of Enchantments dedicated to helping tools pull Crystals, Herbs, Fruit and Skins whole and unblemished and *you*—you..." He buried his face into his hands, continuing to rant.

I caught what sounded like laments about his world being starved of Mana while we 'burned the garden of the Gods and laughed while we did it.' For the briefest of moments, I thought he might be right, but surely he'd misunderstood what Willa had meant. She was saying that the Mining Pick Enchants helped mine minerals not Crystals.

A smile came onto my face as Smegma continued to rant about idiotic Flesh Demons, and the state of his world. Seemed like 'big brain' had gotten it wrong—and I was perfectly content to let him think that.

134

Our group lapsed into silence after that. Allowing me to truly bask in Smegma's displeasure with our race. I hoped the other two didn't think my wide smile was too weird for the situation. I glanced around to make sure I wasn't getting strange looks. Willa was stewing in the memory of her debt, it appeared, while my dad was daydreaming.

For my part, when I wasn't laughing at Smegma's mood, I was rejoicing. I may have found the perfect market for the Miner's Picks that Smegma was selling. I scanned back to the Crafting Components and wondered if there was anything else in there that could be as valuable. Like the Herbalism Kit—could a Gardener get the same use out of it as a Miner and the picks?

My knee began jumping up and down in excitement, and my dad broke out of his waking dream to stare at my telltale 'jimmy leg.' "You're thinking of buying one, aren't you?"

The ATV now coming to a coasting stop saved me from answering. We must have made it through the gate and back into Windsor. The conversations went from controlled murmurs to excited exchanges. People took the opportunity that this provided to congratulate the injured man on his survival. Everyone stayed strapped into their seats but a song started up. It wasn't a song I was familiar with, and if I was honest, the song practically had no tune. It reminded me of Happy Birthday in a way, with a rote set of words that allowed you to insert someone's name into the jingle. The man's name was Silvia, and he managed to perk himself up enough to smile through the somewhat haunting melody.

Mining tales of Miners tells,

Of one who went to Mine and Fell,

For though they crossed the Line Within,

All Mines and Miners meet their Ends.

We take our Picks for Mining Licks,

To each our own, the Mining Tricks.

But, ho' today's a Mining Day!

And lo' the Miners come to Play!

The Miners come for Mining Well,

They leave their Ghost, to Mining Dwell.

But woe to those, the Mine it Picks

For lo' they go give Death a Kiss,

Who was Kissed amidst the Dark?

'Twas Silvia who played their Part!

Who took to Mine like it's a Sin?

'Twas Silvia who took the Win!

Who Fell that day, like it was Art?

'Twas Silvia who played the Part!

Mining tales of Miner's Tells,

Of one who went to Mine and Fell!

The song repeated until the ATV came to a stop and continued for a third round even as the hatch lowered. Even the Lynx's Hunters and Banks joined in, making me one of the few men or women not singing along. No one unstrapped until the third time through, even though the hatch had been fully dropped for about forty seconds at that point. Then, as if the ending of the song was a cue, people unstrapped and descended the ramp.

Some groups formed at the bottom of the ramp, and I could tell that these were the bar flies. The somewhat younger group of men mixing with the two-decade senior ones was a dead give-away. This was the afterwork crew who either didn't have responsibilities at home or were past those responsibilities. The second and more damning piece of evidence was that they all headed toward a pub that was easily visible across the road from the parking lot.

"Do ya be wantin' to head over for a pint at 'World's End' to celebrate Brodie's first day?" Willa asked.

I shook my head. "I'd really like to get home. I still need to call the school and drop this semester's courses. Then I'd like to go to the Hunter's Mall and grab some more appropriate clothes for tomorrow. I can't keep wearing civilian clothes under the loaner armor."

"Okay, but you two are joining me tomorrow whether you like it or not. No excuses!" Willa exclaimed and then jogged to catch up with the group.

Turning to my father, I raised a questioning eyebrow. "She goes for one beer most days. Says it clears the dust from her throat." I nodded but he changed the subject. "Are you really only going to buy clothes?"

I looked at him and then motioned to the car, trying to say we should talk on the drive back. He frowned but nodded. I grabbed the bag of loaned armor and my pickaxe, and together we moved to the trunk of the Ford Escort. In quick fashion, we were out of the armor and packed up. We both got into our seats and I was surprised to find my dad reaching across to snatch my hand.

He examined my left hand as his brow furrowed, then he absent-mindedly snatched my right and checked it too. After staring at it and then back to my left for a short few seconds, he looked up to meet my eyes. "Since when do you have the calluses of a veteran Miner?"

I looked at my own hands, not having to fake my confusion. Sure enough, I had rather large calluses that I knew for certain hadn't been there before. Just like my appearance, I took careful care of my hands. Sure, I'd had some callouses from the gym, but this was as my father alluded to: excessive.

"I've had them for a long time," I lied. "You know, weights and Muay Thai, Dad."

I wasn't sure why I couldn't tell my dad about my *Recovery* Skill yet, but I just didn't. If he heard about *Recovery*, I'd probably tell him about *Mental Fortitude* and then *Demonic Vault*—and I just wasn't sure how that would go.

Instead, I motioned for him to start the car, and he did, after a final skeptical look at my hands. I waited until we pulled out of the parking lot to start talking, which effectively distracted him from my hands. I used the time it took to navigate the Ford Escort through the parking lot to finalize the partially formed plan of what I wanted to say. Smegma didn't help as he offered suggestions that no human would ever take.

My final decision on the ATV ride back was not to tell my father the whole story just yet. I had begun by thinking I would confess everything that had happened since Morgan Hallsbrad assaulted me, but eventually landed on the complication—Smegma. I just couldn't be sure how my dad would react to me telling him I had a Demon-Imp that was going to sell me items from his 'destroyed' or slowly dying home world.

Religion—particularly Catholicism—was extremely prevalent in our part of the world. While my family weren't devout followers by any stretch of imagination, they still might feel the need to have an exorcism performed. Or consult 'experts.'

I just wasn't ready for that level of scrutiny. No, if I was honest, I didn't want this opportunity to be taken from me. So any risk of that was unacceptable.

"I know you said that it's a gamble," I started, and saw my dad's face morph into a deep disapproving frown. "But!" I added pointedly before he could get a word in. "I think that I Awakened a second Skill." The frown became numerous blinks and the car even slowed down as he grew slightly distracted.

"What?!" he asked, his voice excited but also unbelieving.

"Today when I was swinging the pickaxe, I could feel my Mana Pool draining. Then, on a particularly bad swing, I chipped off a bit of the metal, and that's where things got strange. The chipped piece kind of returned to the pickaxe, like it was magnetized. I thought I imagined it, but it happened a few more times throughout the day. I think I have a new Skill that repairs weapons, maybe even armor."

Sure, that was a lie, but it was what Smegma and I managed to come up with.

My dad screeched the tires as he pulled to a quick stop on the side of the road. Once the car jerked to a stop, he turned on the four-way blinkers and avoided looking at me. He breathed in deeply and then let the air out in a long, slow sigh. He scratched roughly at his beard and didn't look at me for the next several minutes as he continued his patterned breathing.

Finally, he turned on me, and I could see a glimmer of something in his eyes. "Brodie, you would be one of possibly one or two percent of the world's population with two Awakened gifts. Are you certain you aren't still just reacting to the Mana Theft?"

I nodded, having expected some sort of reaction like this. It was *extremely* rare to have two Awakened Gifts. Just as rare to re-Awaken, according to everything I read. Looking my father firmly in the eyes, I whispered, "I'm pretty sure, Dad."

"You heard Ms. Stovall, Son. It would be on par with winning the damn lottery to have re-Awakened outside of a Portal!" My dad argued one final time, his eyes staring earnestly into mine. When I didn't look away, he nodded slowly and took a deep breath, his eyes going unfocused for a moment.

This probably meant he was currently internalizing the 'bombshell' I just dropped on him. After a moment, he looked back up.

"That doesn't mean you need to be a Miner, Brodie!" he said, his voice animated in a way that wasn't quite excitement—more like agitation. "If you have another Skill, and that *particular* one, you could repair my pickaxe every night at home." This time the excitement was real and I smiled.

"Got 'em," Smegma said evilly. My smile slipped a bit. I wasn't sure I liked how much Smegma seemed to want me to lie—wanted me to do things that were morally ambiguous.

Still, this was exactly where we hoped my lie would lead, and realizing this allowed my smile to grow. Thinking of the hopeful destination turned the look devious.

"And Willa's," I added.

My dad demonstrated where the habit of my jimmy leg when I got excited came from, as his leg began bouncing under the steering wheel.

"Should we get you tested first?" he asked, and I quickly shook my head. I truly wasn't sure where I would rank now that I had three Skills of relatively high-rank and a Mana Pool.

The UNMH provided free surface scans of all Awakened, and I had already completed one to find out that I had an F-Rank Skill. That test was more of a quick aura scan. There were more in-depth tests, or rumors of them at least— for those who were scanned with Skill rankings higher than C they were complimentary. If you had money you could also pay for them supposedly. According to rumors, you could find out a little more about your Skill specifics, which made it extremely valuable for Combat Hunters.

138

"No, I think if I go buy one of those five-thousand-dollar picks you mentioned, I can prove it myself tomorrow. Plus, I don't know if it only works when I'm the one holding the pick. I don't think that's the case, it feels more like a mark I'm applying to the pick that slowly repairs it using ambient Mana. Still, I think slowly figuring it out through use will be way cheaper than spending twenty-five thousand on an Assessor."

"I guess that's true," my dad said sheepishly, some of his excitement seeming to escape from him. "If the Skill is strong enough, though, you should get it Assessed. Even D-Ranks get free tuition at lower end UNMH sponsored Academies!"

"If this Skill works the way I think it does, then I could go to school and start a business, right?" After that suggestion, it took a few minutes for my father to get a hold of his bouncing leg and be able to drive again.

The drive home was very pleasant after that if I ignored Smegma's snide comments. My dad spoke excitedly about future possibilities: if I actually had a secondary Repair Skill, about him starting his own Mining crew filled with nothing but Equipment Specialists, and about how my mother would never have to work again.

"If it is a repair Skill, do you think we should buy the picks and rent them to others? I would need to repair them or reapply whatever my Mana is doing each night, so…" I let my thoughts hang in the air.

"Not sure. If you need to repair them, that would be the easiest, and we wouldn't have to tell people about your Gift. Just say that it's for maintenance, or perhaps even use the excuse of replacing them. However, if people know about your Skill, we can also just charge them for repairs, but keep it more reasonable than if they went to an Enchanter or Blacksmith."

My heart hammered as I heard that suggestion. "I think I'd prefer to keep it hidden," I lied, further realizing that the lie was getting larger with every sentence. I consoled myself with the thought that I'd tell my parents the whole truth at some point.

My father helped me feel worse instantly when we pulled into the driveway. He stared pointedly at our front door and said, "That's true. Probably best to keep it hidden for now. However, I'm not the only one you need to convince."

I joined my father in imagining the upcoming conversation.

"Are you both afraid of Clara?" Smegma asked. "She's half the weight of both of you?"

I didn't humor the Imp with a reply and just continued to stare at the front door to our house. In a whisper, I asked, "Can you let me take a shower first?"

CHAPTER 16

Thursday, April 4th, 2069

"**I**s this why you asked Ms. Stovall about if things might get complicated if you were no longer an F-Rank?" My mother asked. Her expression was both disappointed and deadly serious. She, too, had been extremely skeptical at first about my 're-Awakening.' The odds were just too small.

Either way, I wasn't about to admit that I may be a Cannibal…

Unlike my father, once I managed to convince her it was *real*, she was taking the news of my re-Awakening with far less excitement. Her reminder of my court case and the possible trouble I was in sobered my father's excitement as well. He now wore an expression that was somewhat easy to read. He was trying to figure out why I seemed fine, even after everything I'd just been through.

I nodded in affirmation to my mother's question, while giving my father a disappointed look. I had wanted nothing more than five minutes to myself so I could shower—maybe use the Spent Mana Crystal—but that didn't seem to be in the cards. I'd even told my father that in the car, but I had barely made it to my room when I heard my mom's very dramatic gasp.

Smegma had begun laughing, and moments later, I'd heard my mother calling my name. My mother's next words echoed my fathers.

"It might be best if we had him reassessed," my mother said while looking at Dad. Since only one person at the table had gone to post-secondary school for Portal and Hunters affairs, and she was cutting me out of the conversation a bit, I felt heat rise from my chest.

"No," I said shortly. Both my parents looked at me with shocked expressions. My tone hadn't exactly been soft, and it wasn't often that I flat out refused something they suggested. Sighing, I explained, "It will only muddy the water. Right now, the case is of a—" I cut off just before mentioning the rank of the highest Skill I'd stolen from the man. I paused for a moment, trying to recall what Morgan Hallsbrad's Rank was. I didn't remember Ms. Stovall's words through the hot buzz of my frustration. Smegma helped me out. "—C-Ranked Awakened assaulting an F-Ranked. Cut and dry. If I suddenly became higher ranked, then my self-defense may get called into question."

My mother's face went red as her own anger was likely kindled. "He was a known criminal—who murdered so many people for their Skills! I don't think it will go that way."

She paused for a moment, studying me.

"How are you so calm about this?!" My mother demanded, tears forming in her eyes. I winced, my frustration dying in my chest as *Mental Fortitude* asserted itself.

"Sweetie, he's probably right." My dad saved me from answering my mother's question. "While we both think a Repair Skill won't change things, we don't know."

"The man who attacked Brodie was a murderer!" My mother said for the second time. My father stood up and placed both hands on her shoulders.

"That's true, honey—but we know nothing about the law. Why don't we tell Ms. Stovall after he confirms the Skill tomorrow?"

"Surely the Judge would take into account *when* the Skill Awakened!" My mother added, her voice growing higher in octave.

My anger simmered as they once again cut me out of the conversation. While they were making good points, it just didn't feel good to not have any say. I tried to put a lid on it, realizing that it wasn't intentional.

"We can't know that," I growled quietly, not fully managing to keep the aggravation in. "I agree we *might* want to consult Ms. Stovall and see what she thinks."

My mother stared first at me and then imploringly at my father. My father winced in a near mirror of my own, thanks to our similar genetics. "She does have a bit of a point, Son. Most Judges also have a *Truth Detection* Skill…"

I nodded. That was my greatest fear and why I wanted to keep this out of a courtroom. "You're actually making a case *against* telling her, Dad," I responded, pointing at him. "Keeping Ms. Stovall in the dark *may* be best. While client confidentiality still exists, so does *Illusory Truth*."

That had been covered in one of my introductory classes. The example the teacher used was of a particularly bad case of murders. A Hunter nicknamed 'Slaughter' had been running Portals with his Guild, Anarchy, for about five years before he was finally caught. The reason being is that he never spoke directly to someone with a *Truth-Seeking* Skill.

The UNMH courts had adopted the American's Fifth Amendment right— and he used it to have his lawyers speak on his behalf. Cleverly, Slaughter had always explained his falsehoods to his lawyer, who conveyed the incidents as 'Portal mishaps' on his behalf.

In fact, Hunter-death in Portals was more of a report than a trial. So he'd remained free, right up until the Anarchy Guild hired a lawyer with a *Truth-Seeking* Skill. There had just been too many incidents of Portal Mishaps surrounding Slaughter. The lawyer could tell that Slaughter wasn't telling the whole truth, but nothing more.

This was practically an admission of guilt to the Anarchy Guild, and they had to make a choice. Slaughter was a high-ranking Hunter that raised Anarchy's profile.

In the end, the Guild wanted to keep him on as a Solo Raider—choosing to keep him active in the field, but taking other Guild members out of his reach. However, both Anarchy and Slaughter got extremely unlucky. The Judge also had a *Truth-Seeking* Skill, and when the lawyer came in to claim the most recent death to be Portal related, the Judge knew it to be an omission of information.

It took a few more years for all the information in the case to be gathered, but when a survivor of Slaughter's attack was found, a media storm broadcast the case planet-wide. The entire Anarchy Guild, which operated in South Africa, was deemed criminal by the UNMH, and Slaughter was instantly put to the top of the UNMH Most Wanted List.

I could tell by my parents' faces that my use of the term was bringing back memories from ten years ago. The case was rather sensationalized, especially because the Guild and Slaughter were still at large. Everyone assumed they were hiding out in a Field somewhere in Africa, but despite their notoriety, no reports of their whereabouts were known to have been made.

"I feel like I'm missing something," Smegma said while looking between everyone from his place on the dining table's hanging light.

[There's an entire streaming documentary about it. I'll show you later,] I responded.

Silence continued to stretch at the table, and my parents looked between me and each other. Smegma hovered down from the light. "You could just buy an Obfuscation Ring," he said as he landed on the table in front of me. "It would hide one of your Skills from detection. You'd have to get a mid-grade since *Mental Fortitude* is an A-Ranked Skill, but I think it's only a hundred thousand mC in the *Demonic Vault* Shop."

Smegma tried to send a screen with the information, but I ignored it, which somehow minimized the window to a small red dot in the corner of my vision. I made a mental note to remember that piece of functionality. I desperately searched my brain for something to say to break this uncomfortable silence and thought I'd found something.

"Mom. Dad. You and I know that my new Skill Awakening had no impact on me defending myself from Morgan's Mana Theft," both my parent's faces drained of blood.

I swallowed and realized this was one of the first times I had said the term aloud since the Police Station, or maybe even before that. For a moment, I felt nauseous. A fire that I hadn't felt since that day erupted in my stomach. Thankfully, something seemed to contain it—like a ring of stones around a campfire. Heat still wafted from it, but it didn't allow the destructive part to escape.

"I did nothing wrong," I said, my voice hot. "Stressful situations can cause re-Awakenings, and that husker attacked me unprovoked. I won't let someone twist that to make me look like a bad guy."

I realized I was shouting and didn't continue. That hadn't been even close to the direction I was planning to go with the conversation, and frankly, I was surprised by it. Somewhere along the way, I must have stood up and I lowered myself back into my seat, my face feeling hot with the dueling emotions of embarrassment and anger.

Once seated, I looked pointedly at Smegma, my eyes wide, and he inferred the question I wanted to ask. "The *Mental Fortitude* Skill doesn't stop emotions, it just helps keep memories and situations from breaking you. Notice that you don't have any fear while talking about your assaulter? That's the Skill. Some say it contains strong negative emotions, but it doesn't simply delete them. They're still there, inside you. It's believed that the Skill relieves those emotions back into your psyche over time and that won't harm you, but they have to be expressed. Even the Skill can't keep it bottled up forever... Then everything just bubbles over, which is probably why you just shouted at your parents and it feels like it came out of nowhere."

My mother rushed over to my chair and hugged me. My dad stood and moved over as well, but only placed a hand atop my free shoulder, opposite my mother.

"We don't think you're the bad guy!" My mom blurted out, and I could hear the tears in her voice.

My anger slowly cooled—the *Mental Fortitude* Skill or my own calming breathing getting it under control.

I looked to my dad, who must have seen something in my eyes because he nodded. "You can head up to your room, shower, and then hit the Mall. I'll talk with your mother."

Maybe he felt slightly responsible since he'd been the one to blab about the second Awakening right after we got in the door. I regretted not immediately hopping in the shower. Still, I couldn't read the somber look on his face.

I gave him a tight-lipped smile but waited for my mother to stop squeezing me before I slowly stood up and hugged her back. As I hugged her, I apologized to both my parents, "I'm sorry I shouted. We can discuss again later if telling Ms. Stovall will be for the best."

Something in their expressions instantly made me feel better. They clearly didn't think I was shouting at them. "Don't keep everything all bottled up!" My mom answered my apology. "Don't hold it in—you're going to give yourself an aneurysm. We're always here to talk. And we weren't trying to make a decision without you."

Swallowing hard, I squeezed her tight, expressing that I wouldn't hold things in, but definitely *not* explaining that I was pretty sure that wasn't how aneurysms worked. The entire time, I couldn't help but wonder how I would be handling all of this without *Mental Fortitude*. That thought and Smegma's earlier comment brought me to the stark truth of the situation. I had a whole lot more than the *Demonic Vault* Skill to hide. After a few minutes of hugs and promises, I was free to return to my room.

It shouldn't be a surprise what my first question to Smegma was. "How high of a rank was *Mental Fortitude* again?"

"You originally said you'd gotten it at A-Rank," Smegma stated plainly without even looking at me.

My stomach fell through the floor and back to the table downstairs. I hadn't even considered how bad things could go if I was rescanned. While I was sure that the Awakened Assessment Machine wasn't exactly perfect, I knew it wouldn't be classifying me as an F-Rank if I possessed four Skills and one of them was A. *Wouldn't I then be classified as an A-Rank Awakened?*

Smegma landed on my desk lazily and slowly turned to look at me. I'd found my way to the floor, leaning my back against my bed frame. He stared at me and then shook his head while rolling his eyes. "You think that they're going to waste a mid to high-ranked Spent Mana Crystal on an F-Rank?" Smegma asked, and I shook my head. "So then what are you worried about?"

"As far as I know, people aren't aware that Spent Mana Crystals can be used to identify Skills," I began. Smegma gave me a condescending look and I rolled my eyes at him before continuing, "Even if we had them in abundance, which I don't think humans do, it isn't like someone would think to send their Mana into the thing for five minutes.

"No, what we have is a machine you stand in and it identifies your rank. I don't know what other machines lay deeper in, but I'm confident it isn't Spent Mana Crystals…"

"How?" Smegma said, looking interested.

"Huh?" I answered stupidly and then replayed the conversation and the question. "Oh, common people don't really know but it measures the magic energy coming off of you or something."

"So, it can't tell what your Skills are?" Smegma asked, sounding disgusted.

"Would I have needed a Spent Mana Crystal to see mine if it did?"

Smegma raised the ridge above his black eyes. Whether he was realizing that I had a point or if he was questioning my tone, I couldn't tell. "So, you're worried that this machine will somehow feel more energy coming off of you?"

I nodded. Smegma began tapping his teeth with a talon. After a moment, he returned his attention to me. "I'd have to see this machine, but that makes my concerns about discovery far smaller. It sounds like at best it's reading your Mana Runoff. Tell me, are there some people who are misclassified?"

"Yeah, quite a few, but it gets adjusted and caught by the more in-depth tests," I answered. "Most of those were the high-rank Hunters that the first machine couldn't read properly."

"*Ahhh*," Smegma said smugly. "A retest wouldn't force you to take the more in-depth tests?" I shook my head and Smegma smiled. "I think the machine's problem is an issue of Passive Skills versus Active. *Mental Fortitude*, for example, is a Passive Skill and gives off no external Mana Runoff or Signature. *Recovery* will only give off a Signature when you're healing. As for *Demonic Vault*, well, *I* am the magic energy Runoff and Signature. That and the windows. So, I would need to see this machine to be sure, but I think if I'm outside the machine, and you aren't accessing the windows, I would doubt that it could sense anything. Do you know if the people who were misread couldn't use their Skills while being tested or what it read?"

"Uhhh, I think they are read as Skill-less. Or, at least, that's what I think the Read-it forum on Jax claimed." I shrugged unhelpfully, not remembering something I'd read in passing properly. Smegma returned to thinking but this conversation brought me full circle to the Spent Mana Crystal I'd left on my dresser on the way out of my room. I slowly got to my feet and went to grab it. Then I moved to my office chair, which sat me in front of Smegma. He shook his head. "You know it doesn't matter what rank your Mana Pool Skill Card is right now, right? With me here, you can eventually upgrade it to something higher."

"I'm telling you, it's growing," I answered. "While it isn't full at the moment, I think I could probably get fifteen or sixteen points if I let it keep going."

He shrugged. "Even if that's true, it isn't like sixteen points of Mana is something to brag about."

"Husk you," I responded, allowing just a touch of my frustration from my discussion with my parents into my voice. "Earlier you told me that Mana Pools don't grow before Evolution. Now you're saying it doesn't matter if it did. Which one is it, you gaslighting son of a Greed?" The last bit I said teasingly, trying to lighten the mood and soothe my frustration.

"I am the proud son of a Felguard and an Imp, thank you very much!" Smegma retorted just as cheekily. "Just use the damn Crystal already and prove me right."

I changed my grip on the Spent Crystal to highlight my raised middle fingers, and then spun the chair away. With a deep breath, I mentally dove into myself. It took me about five minutes of struggling before I found the trick of connecting my Pool to what appeared to be a small black dot between my physical hands. It was the straw conduit trick again, but finding the object in my Mental Universe was a bit of mental gymnastics.

Thankfully, Smegma was patient—not!

"You know children on Crendalar Five can do this at birth?"

"Demon children…" I countered and was rewarded with a black, forked tongue stuck out in my direction.

Thankfully, my phone was on my desk table, and so while the five minutes of slow Mana seepage felt far longer than it should have, I could see the time and reaffirm that it was just my imagination.

A single blue dot spun inside the Crystal at the five-minute mark, and then it slowly grew and clarified. The blue Mana morphed to look like a red playing card with an elaborate design on the back. However, I couldn't make out the design or the front side of the card thanks to the distortion of the Crystal.

That problem didn't last for long and the Crystal shrank inwards, surprising me enough that I dropped it. By the time I thought of trying to catch it, two cards were left fluttering to the floor like pieces of paper. I stared at the fractal patterns on the back that I hadn't been able to make out through the Crystal. It was hard to describe.

The images seemed to change. The red-backed card seemed to always have the image of Imps, horned humanoids, a vault door or the like—and I guessed that one was the *Demonic Vault* Card. The second Card was green and seemed to depict scenes of a multitude of people and creatures healing from wounds, then somehow surviving curses or poison, and finally some images of super strong people? Eventually, the changing images made me close my eyes and look away.

Smegma saw my reaction and chuckled. "Disturbing, isn't it?"

I swallowed and nodded before picking up the Cards. Smegma motioned to the table, indicating I should put it down in a place we could both read them. I ignored him and he huffily floated to my shoulder.

Demonic Vault

(5)

Skill Type: Summons (#$^~|)

Skill Rank: High E-Rank (Evolv–Error!)

In exchange for Mana, the holder can Summon objects once owned by the Abyss Sect on Crendalar Five. This Skill comes with a guide and the ability to store Mana Points as Mana Coins.

—

Recovery
(4)
Skill Type: Self-Activating
Skill Rank: High C-Rank (Evolvable)
In exchange for vital energy, the Skill holder's body will heal at rapid speeds upon injury. Warning: This Skill will consume other body structures to prioritize your life if vital energies are insufficient.

Why wasn't there a Card for my Mana Pool Skill?

"Do I have to get another Spent Crystal to show my Mana Pool?" I asked, not really complaining but still sounding exasperated at the prospect of trying to take another Crystal home as a 'souvenir.'

Not to mention if this thing was random…

"No, that doesn't make any sense. It should have recognized all Skills below high C-Grade." Smegma hopped off the office table and hovered around near the floor, clearly looking for a third card. A smile broke onto my face after I scanned the floor as well and found nothing.

"Got anything to say?" I gloated.

"Yeah, let your Mana Pool fully refill, then tell me what you're at," Smegma answered excitedly. Since I had been hoping for him to say something along the lines of, 'I guess I was wrong,' this response and the excitement surprised me.

"Okay, so you believe me now?" I asked.

"Not yet, but I certainly don't think you have an F-Ranked Mana Pool either," Smegma answered but continued to look around on the floor of my room. "Turn out your pockets," he added after he still didn't find a third Card.

I once again flipped him the finger he was becoming so fond of.

CHAPTER 17

Thursday, April 4th, 2069

"Come on, just admit you're making this whole thing up," Smegma said as I drove the car into the parking garage for the Devonshire Mall. It had retained its name from before the Portal Advent but was drastically changed, according to my parents. Now it was a mall that catered exclusively to Hunters, Crafters, and Crystal Tech.

A growl was my only response to the Imp. After my shower, he'd refused to let the issue of my Mana Pool go. Even though I confirmed I could now hold sixteen points, which meant it was growing. His reason? A comparison to the E-Rank of 'his' *Demonic Vault* Card. How could my sixteen points of Mana be a Card that was higher than *him*?

"I'm not making anything up, and you said it yourself, you've never seen a growing Mana Pool before an Evolution. If you're so sure, why don't *you* tell me why my Mana Pool Card didn't show up after using the Spent Crystal and your Card did, if—whatever my Skill is— isn't a higher Rank than yours? So, just shut the husk up about it," I answered, annoyed.

The Imp narrowed its black eyes and began biting at its talons using the razor-sharp-looking fangs in its mouth. I slammed the door closed behind me after parking and getting out of the vehicle. Honestly, I didn't know what was going on, but to be constantly questioned by Smegma with the intention of catching me in a lie was grating.

I figured in time I'd just purchase or mine a mid-grade Spent Crystal and find out for myself. Then we'd both get an answer. My slammed car door didn't do enough to vent my anger, especially when Smegma just floated out of the windshield to follow me. He at least seemed to have gotten the hint and didn't pester me on the walk through the area. I made note of where I parked, 'Section D-2.'

The old, dusty and rusted Ford Escort would stand out pretty clearly if I just got myself in the right ballpark. I walked by numerous types of vehicles and marveled at the designs, colors, and price points of each. Many of them, I didn't even recognize and so couldn't estimate the expense, but I could just tell they weren't cheap thanks to the fact that they were clearly over-designed with comfort in mind.

Smegma floated into and out of a few cars. I debated about stopping him but didn't want him to return to pestering me, so I let him continue and thus was surprised when he exited a Teezla Model Z. Smegma asked, "What are the screens and strange mechanical devices that are in many of these vehicles?"

I frowned, wondering what Ether Tech component he was talking about before realizing what he must actually mean. Something that would be severely lacking in our family's ancient Ford Escort. "The computers, cameras and sensors?"

"Computers?" Smegma said, testing the word. "Is that the thing that showed the images in the cockpit of the ATV?"

"No, those are the cameras, and well, yeah, I guess there's also a computer to a lesser degree," I answered.

The ATV cockpit was a pretty special case since it didn't have any windscreens or windows. Instead, the thing was a literal moving tank that was piloted from feedback cameras mounted to the outside. I was told by a family friend, who was also a mechanic, that drilling the holes for the wires was a huge challenge for the engineers on materials like that. They needed special drill bits made from Sea Creature horns. Some people called it Unicorn Horn, but the creature resembled an oversized Narwhal more than a mythical horse.

It was a rare 'Monster' that seemed to have survived a Portal Break in the sea. Still, like the Evolved Narwhals, it hadn't suddenly started sinking freighters or blasting planes from the sky—like doomsday predictors seemed to claim would happen at some point. It was just a new species of whale, probably twice as large as a Blue Whale.

"I don't understand how an image can be transmitted mechanically," Smegma stated, interrupting my tangent, clearly wanting an answer. I gave him a tight-lipped smile, wanting to make him angry. It was mid-smile that I realized that my silence could perhaps do more.

"You should buy one from me, and your people could study it," I answered smugly.

"I'm sure there are books that will explain the concept better," Smegma said through narrowed eyes.

"Oh yeah? How are you going to interact with those?" I said with a far too casual shrug.

"I can interact with objects to a small degree," he countered hotly, but his spin and float away toward the mall doors made his answer slightly less reliable. My guess was he could interact with objects but at a cost. Perhaps he would be able to if I had more Mana…

Or he was simply lying—which was a distinct possibility, knowing him.

Which brought me full circle to him annoying me at my house and the entire car ride here. I glared at his back but followed his floating, flapping form into the mall.

The inside of the mall was as stunning as I remembered it being as a kid. The halls were all made of Portal Materials that had been turned into tiles and laid so well that the interior almost looked the way I imagined a Guild Hall might. Something akin to what old stories described Palaces and Mansions as.

It was lavish, to say the least.

I smiled, recalling my family coming here when I was in my teenage years. Not to buy anything, since we couldn't afford much, but to explore and play tourist. 'Staycation,' we'd called it.

The tiles merged into store fronts that were just as beautiful, and my smile only grew when I saw the Lion-head entrance for 'Hunter, Hunter, Hunter.' A store that specialized in mass-produced gear and weapons.

According to my parents, the 'Lion' on the front used to be considered the 'king of the jungle.' A creature that was an apex predator before the Portal disgorged creatures far more terrifying. Others called the creature a Manticore now-a-days since that creature was often found in B-Rank Portals.

[Float through some stores and see if there is anything that your people would value at five hundred mC,] I mentally said to Smegma. He shrugged and then floated into Hunter, Hunter, Hunter.

In seconds, he exited the store. "Is that supposed to be gear?" he said smugly, clearly conveying his races 'superiority.' I simply raised my eyebrow and motioned to the next store. "Fine, whatever. At least I'll be more sure of how primitive your race is."

I really hoped that Smegma was wrong as I walked down the center of the hallway. Soon the entry hall opened into the main area before the center of the floor vanished behind railings.

According to my parents, this mall used to be a single level but was now comprised of three floors. I looked up, hoping we wouldn't have to go up there for Smegma to find something. The third floor was for the most expensive and luxury stores only, and even the major brand three-leveled stores reserved their best gear for the upper floors.

I scanned down to one of the ends of the central hallway, which led to a 'Hudson's Bay Company,' one of the oldest stores in the world, but certainly the oldest in North America. This was one of those stores that contained three levels. According to my history class, the Hudson Bay Trading Company was originally something of a pirate entity trading in animal pelts in the late sixteen hundreds, but became the store HBC, which ironically enough still dealt in Monster Parts. I moved in that direction since stores like HBC were filled with items at some of the lowest prices, thanks to their buying power.

On the way we passed a Rootz, which likely could have been on the top floor just as easily as the second. Most Canadians had a pair of their extremely expensive sweaters or sweatpants from the brand—but only one even if it was their favorite thing to wear. They were just made so well and lasted so long, that you rarely needed another. I even had a pair that we'd picked up second hand from somewhere.

Smegma continued to float through stores, Rootz included, and each time he would come out with a sneer. In a few instances, that wasn't true, but he gave me a sign that told me that 'Snape's Potions' wasn't the answer to our search. I made it into HBC, and he rejoined me with a frown.

"I'll admit that some of the things I saw are interesting, but you'd need to spend five hundred thousand *dollairs* to earn five hundred mC." Smegma's mispronunciation of dollars amused me, but I didn't bother correcting him. Instead, his statement made my heart rate speed up. If that was the case, would I be able to buy something from him, like the Miner's Pick, and sell it for millions?

I thought back to just after seeing Silvia return from getting healed. I'd been thinking about options for making money, and it looked like many of them would be viable—with one small problem…

Could I trust Smegma?

My family's money problems might be over if I could, or if we could figure out a way to work together. Then again, how would I convince people to purchase something like that? I didn't exactly have a brand name buyers would trust, like Rootz, or HBC, for example. The simple answer would be to either make a company and build a reputation from the ground up or find a connection with an existing corporation. The second option had the obvious flaw of me being a nobody teenager with no business experience, who suddenly popped up with access to unseen and previously unknown goods and technologies. I'd be eaten alive.

The first option had similar flaws, however—I didn't know where to start. *If* I managed to get a foothold, somehow, in the various markets, great, but I couldn't handle any scrutiny—not yet. I also didn't delude myself, any success I created could and perhaps would paint a target on my back from all manner of powerful people.

Anonymity, experience, and a way of ensuring that I wasn't being taken advantage of by my intangible companion was what I needed.

So simple, right?

I held back a sigh. Frankly, I wasn't even opposed to an agreement where my portion of the profits was on the lower side of things—say a sixty-forty split. Ultimately, I just wanted to be informed, even if that knowledge was that I was being bent over the proverbial table. I could work with that. What I couldn't work with were the doubts and uncertainties. Were there such things as System-enforced Contracts? I'd have to look into it.

I motioned around myself, my smile fading. [Anything in here?]

Smegma raised his eyebrows and scanned the opulent design of the store. While the mall outside was stunning, the HBC was breathtaking. Display booths were set up in the aisles, where men and women dressed in suits or Hunter gear stood manning them. Each booth sold different wares, ranging from accessories to potions. Smegma moved first to the potions and pointed.

"How can they be selling the same potion for less?"

[I really don't have time to discuss competitive marketing with you, but Snape's Potions likely has a better product, overall. Maybe…] I wasn't sure of the truth to the statement.

"So, they just name the potion the same thing and don't have to disclose the effects?" he asked, clearly confused.

I moved up to examine the potion he was indicating.

Moderate Health Potion
Heals moderate injuries in moments.
Price: $50,000 Greenbacks

I saw his confusion but didn't get a chance to respond immediately as a girl dressed in 'Wizard' robes shuffled to greet me. "Welcome sir, can I pull anything out for you to take a closer look? Do you have any questions that need answering?"

Choosing to use her to explain the differences despite knowing most of them myself, I asked, "What's the difference between Minor, Moderate, and Major Health or Mana Potions?"

"Oh?" she answered, giving me an up and down. Her face morphed into a frown while her eyes narrowed in disdain, but her training must have kicked in because no negative emotions entered her voice as she explained. "Minor Healing Potions can heal all surface-level wounds, such as gashes, slashes, bruises, and even most fractures. Moderate Potions can repair most ruptured or damaged organs, limbs, and help recover from blood loss. Major Potions can repair practically any injury but traumatic injuries to the brain or heart."

"Ahh, thank you. I'm just browsing before my first Portal," I said in answer to her silence after the explanation. She scoffed and moved away from me, clearly offended by my presence now that I admitted I wasn't going to buy anything.

"What the actual husk does that mean?" Smegma said, his voice possibly more disdainful than the woman's. "So, you imbeciles just accept vague ass descriptions like that and buy these potentially lifesaving potions?"

[I'm confused. What should we be doing?]

In answer, a screen popped up in front of me.

Consumables
Moderate Healing Potion
Restores five thousand health over one minute.
Cost: 100,000 mC

It was my turn to be confused. That was probably less of a description than what the lady had said, but Smegma was claiming it was more specific. I moved into a section selling mass-produced Hunter Gear, and asked, [What in the husk does five thousand health mean?]

"By Asmodan! Are you husking kidding me?" Smegma asked.

We just stared at each other, both realizing that the other wasn't making a joke. Smegma broke the stalemate. "Wait, you don't have your health represented as a number?"

[I'm not exactly a high-ranking Hunter, but as far as I know, no, we don't have 'health bars.']

"But you have Mana Pools?" Smegma asked dumbly. I looked around before answering in the affirmative out loud. Smegma blinked his black eyes at me rapidly. "I don't understand. How do front liners like Tanks in your world get stronger?"

"Uhh," I began aloud before switching to a mental conversation as a particularly well-dressed man gave me a strange look. [Well, better gear for starters. Plus, usually they have a Skill that makes them harder to kill.]

"They don't get a Card that Awakens their Martial Power Pool, or Force Pool for Mages?"

I shook my head. [We don't get Cards, Smegma. Remember? Yet, I think there are a few Hunter's on SwiftGram who have revealed they had a stat, but I can't think of anyone who's said they have two, or with those names either.]

He shook his head and began slowly descending toward the floor. I mentally coughed at him as he distractedly began phasing through the tiles to the floor below. He shook himself again and then floated back up to my head height.

"This almost doesn't feel like the same System. We're going to need to start examining these things—no Cards? Well, except for the artificial ones we made with the Spent Mana Crystal, but that doesn't count." Smegma added the last bit in a whisper to himself and I let it go. Maybe there was a way to get these Skill Cards Smegma claimed could be formed from 'Shards' or came whole from bosses, but I certainly hadn't heard of them.

"Can we get back to the original reason we came?" I asked.

Smegma nodded and floated three booths away before he stopped and stared wide eyed at something. I had just exited the clothing racks and found him hovering there with his mouth hanging open. I slowly joined him to find Monster Cores on display. This didn't exactly seem like something that should be shocking to the Imp.

"These are un-enchanted Monster Cores?" Smegma asked.

[Uhh, yeah,] I said, looking between the shocked Demon and the mid-grade Cores on display. All of them were well out of my price range.

Smegma hovered closer to a blue one that almost looked like a bowling ball. The Monster's heart it came out of must have been massive. The spheres of Monster Cores got smoother, rounder and clearer the higher rank they were. The label on this one claimed it was high C-Rank, and thus it looked almost perfectly round, especially compared to the other D-Ranks it sat between.

Its price tag was five hundred thousand, which meant we were never getting it, but I didn't think we would need such a high-leveled one, based on the Imp's shock. I stepped back as the attendant of this room began moving toward the locked glass door to admit me. He sniffed in disdain as well, but I ignored it.

[Smegma, what is it?]

"I don't know." Smegma whispered.

[Do you want to go downstairs and look at some of the Cores I might be able to afford?]

"Yeah," he answered offhandedly. It took a few more mental prods to get him to come back to his senses and follow me to the escalators. I guess I could have just walked and have him pop in beside me—but that felt rude for some reason.

Unfortunately, the only thing I could afford for five thousand dollars was low F-Rank Cores. I guess I had been wrong in my estimates of twenty-five hundred starting, but I'd never had to buy one before. Still, to my surprise, Smegma offered five hundred mC for it. I tried to bargain up, of course, but Smegma was too smart to allow me to do that. He saw how much I paid for it, and he'd seen the prices above. According to him, five hundred mC for an unknown object was damn good.

"Plus, if it actually has value, I will pay you more for the next one," Smegma added when I seemed to still hesitate in the purchase.

152

[Which one do you want?] I asked sheepishly.

Smegma took a while to ponder, and I had the attendant down here, a woman in a business suit, pull out all the options so I could 'take a closer look' as I waited on his decision.

He eventually chose an orange one that looked like a somewhat rounded rock. I paid using my credit card before instantly walking out with the Core in an ornate box inside of a branded bag. I didn't even wait till I left the store to sell the low-grade F-Rank Salamander Core to Smegma for five hundred mC.

I wasn't proud to say I considered letting him go back into the store to procure a few more after that—but thankfully my conscience and the way *Demonic Vault* worked, not always allowing him to interact with objects, held me back.

We got back in the car, and I locked the doors. I was pretty sure no one would target me for a low-grade F-Rank Core, but just like my run in with 'The Shop,' you never really knew when someone might think you were an easy target.

Now in the safety of the vehicle, the excitement hit me fully. I now had two hundred mC more than I needed for the Miner's Pick!

CHAPTER 18

Thursday, April 4th, 2069

"**A**re you sure you want to purchase the Miner's Pick for ten thousand mC?" Smegma intoned dryly as he rolled his eyes.

"I just said I wanted it! What the husk is going on?"

"I'm required by the System and my sect to ensure that you didn't choose the wrong option," Smegma explained, still sounding upset with the process.

"Oh okay, yes then," I answered.

"Sorry, you have to say yes right after I ask the question. So, once again. Are you sure you want to purchase the Miner's Pick for ten thousand mC?"

"What if I say no?"

"Keep it up, and I'll pee on you in your sleep."

"Would that even work?"

"No, but you'd always know I'd done it—so, I figure it's still effective as a threat."

"Do you even pee?"

"Of course, I do! Wait—do I?" Smegma eyes unfocused as he seemed to try to recall if he'd peed since I'd 'Summoned' him. I cleared my throat, bringing him back to the moment. "Right. Are you sure you want to purchase the Miner's Pick for ten thousand mC?"

"Yes."

Smegma vanished. "Haha," I said pointedly. "Very funny."

No response came, and my smile of amusement slowly began to fall. Was he really gone or was he just hiding in the seat or under the car to come out and 'get me.' I replayed the moment he had seemed to vanish. Normally, I could see him move and this time I definitely hadn't.

"Husk, are you serious?" I asked the empty car. "Was this thing just a scam to make me buy an F-rank Monster Core?" That question obviously went unanswered but brought me full circle to another question that my too-calm mind highlighted for me. Had I just been imagining the Imp this whole time?

Now, I've just spent all my savings for a Core that is—gone.

I'd never really gotten any proof he was 'real,' had I? I recalled the interrogation and the vanishing Crystals from earlier that day. Surely that was—

Buyer's First Purchase detected.
You've unlocked the contribution system in the *Demonic Vault* Skill.
Current contribution = 10,000 points

Error. Contribution features unavailable.
Checking Skill OS…
Out of date.
Updating to 6.1.4…
Downloading…
Error. Insufficient Bandwidth to continue.
Contribution too low to increase Bandwidth.
Attempting smaller packet…5.0.18
Insufficient Bandwidth
Attempting smaller packet…4.3.4
Insufficient Bandwidth
Attempting smaller packet…3.2
Insufficient Bandwidth
Attempting smaller packet…2.0.0.1
Downloading…
Updating Demonic Vault.
Rebooting…

"Oh shit! I'd forgotten about this version-OS thing." Between one blink and the next, the screen was gone, and in the silence that followed I once again doubted my own sanity. My brain helpfully chugged along, far-too-calmly analyzing if I was crazy or not.

Of course, that's when I saw the people stopped in the parking garage staring at me—well no, not at *me* but at my car. Unbidden, I sank down in my seat while simultaneously looking around to try to figure out what drew their attention. A light knock on the passenger window surprised me enough that I jumped.

An older-looking woman holding a purse far too big for her was standing there looking concerned. She had grey hair cut in that short bob which was popular with the elderly. Her smile reminded me of my grandmother's, who'd passed away during a Portal Break when I was young. Unfortunately, the windows on the Escort weren't electric, so I climbed over the seat to manually roll it down a crack.

"Just making sure you're okay, sonny," she said. I stupidly stared at her as my brain continued looking for the reason everyone had looked over. A glance around showed people going about their return to cars or into the mall, which boded well.

She must have noticed my confusion because when I looked back, she had a big smile on her face. "Happy birthday," she said—which didn't help my confusion in the least.

"I'm sorry, what?" I asked.

"Your Awakening, sonny. You glowed brighter than the floodlights out here. Drew everyone's eye. From the light, I'd say you got a good one. So, happy birthday!"

My eyes widened and the smile on the lady grew bigger. It was not my birthday, but I could see the logic the old woman had followed. Everyone Awakened on their eighteenth birthday, and admittedly I looked eighteen or younger, even though I was twenty-one. With the Skill update, I must have glowed similarly to when that happened. The second part about how bright someone glowed to their Skill rank wasn't a proven fact, but a superstition many people held onto.

"Oh, thanks. And yeah, I'm fine—definitely wasn't a powerful enough Skill to have knocked me out. Bummer that!" The people who fell unconscious during Awakenings were all immensely powerful, so I figured it might be the right thing to say.

"Oh, don't worry about that—I've got a good feeling about your chances. Glad you're okay."

"Thanks again," I mumbled, unsure how to exit the conversation. The woman began rummaging in her purse a moment later and then pulled out a white rectangle. I only recognized it as a business card as she pushed it through the cracked window.

"Ayla Moody, Hunter Manager. Once you get Assessed, I'd love to chat with you," she said, her smile genuine without a hint of awkwardness. I guessed her embarrassment at 'cold-calling' Hunters likely had long since vanished if her job was managing them.

"Thanks, I'll keep you in mind," I answered as I took the card. She nodded, turned and simply walked toward the mall after that—which I greatly appreciated, since I didn't have to keep lying.

I rolled back up the window and was pushing myself back into the driver seat when Smegma popped back into existence. Or rather, what I first *thought* was Smegma. While the coloring was right and the demonic creature had similarities to the Imp from moments ago, it definitely wasn't the same.

My eyes wouldn't have been able to pull themselves away if something didn't try to push me into the seat—from the top of my thighs, no less. I started to scream as I looked down in panic—only to find a wooden handle of a Miner's Pick across my lap. I turned my scream into a coughing cheer and glanced over to the passenger window. Sure enough, Ayla was looking back over her shoulder.

I gave her a double thumbs up and faked a fist pump into the air. She smiled and kept walking. I breathed out heavily in relief before remembering the new killing machine in my car. My eyes locked back onto the muscular flying demon. "Ahhh… Smegma, is that you?"

I now could catalog all the differences. His skin before had been dark with some red hues underneath, or shining through. Now that red almost looked like decals on a vehicle. Where the arms were spindly before, there was now much more muscle. Even more than had been filled out from me connecting my Mana Pool.

This creature looked almost like a pint-sized black-and-red Goblin with wings.

"Of course, it's me, dumb-dumb," Smegma said in a familiar voice, and I sighed again in relief. Now knowing that it was Smegma, I chose to study the Miner's Pick—my brain no longer able to find a reason to curb my enthusiasm.

I hurriedly grabbed it in my hands and spun it. My enthusiasm shriveled up and began to crack, like wet mud in the scorching sun.

156

The wood of the handle was old and dry, and even spinning it threatened to imbed splinters into my hands. I stopped spinning the thing and looked it over more. The head wasn't rusty, but pockmarked, as if someone cleaned it with FF-fifty and sandpaper. Even the wedge that was hammered into the haft stuck up above the lip. I turned to look at Smegma, who was still studying his newly improved body.

"Hey, stop examining your new racing stripes. What the husk is *this*?" I asked, holding up the Miner's Pick. "*This* is supposed to be worth ten thousand mC?" I asked, my voice laced with the suspicions I felt. He was from a race of Demons, after all, and had just vanished and then reappeared 'stronger.' I couldn't get the thought out of my head that this whole thing was a scam. Had I been too naive?

Smegma slowly looked up from his self-admiration and saw what I was holding toward him. He rolled his eyes.

"Yes, the problem with the Self-Repairing Enchants placed on the weapon is that it instantly degrades the quality when first applied," Smegma said with a world-weary sigh, as if he was explaining that the stove could be hot to a child for the third time.

I tried not to let the state of the thing be a disappointment, I truly did. However, I didn't even want to spin the handle again, in case it gave me a magical splinter that festered and husking killed me. Who knew what kind of diseases Crendalar Five possessed?

Smegma must have inferred a question from my lack of response. "Don't worry, it will look brand new after a few days of use. Even now, it has some Penetration Enchants active, so it will be better than a standard Pickaxe."

"You do realize the problem this creates in my plan though, right?" I responded, trying desperately to figure out how I was supposed to allow others to swing the Pickaxe and watch it repair itself right in front of their eyes. Smegma went back to studying his biceps with his eyes and hands.

"All you have to do is hand them an already repaired one," Smegma countered. I bestowed upon him another withering stare. That was a very simple solution that I had already considered. The issue was how much time that would take. I couldn't exactly use every Pickaxe for a few days before giving it to someone else.

Well, I could—but that would put a huge damper on the big dreams I had. How long would that even take?

Wait—it wasn't like anyone knew how my new 'Skill' in Repair worked. Wanting to get Smegma's opinion, I asked, "Have you ever heard of a Skill that could put self-repair on an item?"

"Yeah, it's called Enchanting, nimwad," he answered without looking up from his stronger-looking taloned fingers, and I immediately felt stupid.

Blushing red, I changed my question. "Could something like a Self-Repair Enchant Skill exist? Husk—never-mind."

I saw my mistake almost as soon as the words left my mouth. *Of course it could exist, moron, you're holding an example right now. You don't* actually *have a Repairing Skill.* My realization along with the Imp's sudden smirk that indicated he was going to give that exact smart-ass answer were enough to get me back on track. Taking a deep breath, I put the car in drive. I would consider more options on my drive home.

I still hadn't come up with anything new by the time I pulled into the driveway and got out of the car. Smegma hadn't helped in the least, using the quick trip to thoroughly examine his new body.

As I approached my front door, all I could wonder was: Should I tell my family the whole story or make up more lies?

Instantly, I knew it was still too early to confess everything, and so I was left with the only other option. Still, all these lies were starting to feel like a precariously stacked Jengal Tower. When I opened the door, my father practically jumped off the couch to come greet me. I could see his excitement written clear across his face.

My mother slowly got to her feet off the couch behind him and followed in his wake. Sounding almost like a child on Christmas, my dad held up his hands and said, "Let's see what you got!"

It almost physically hurt to hold out the ancient-looking Pickaxe and watch his face fall. My stomach knotted as he took the Pick and examined it. "Not a bad thought," he said as some of the earlier excitement came back over his face. "If you can repair it, why not grab a used one on the verge of breaking. You save money and get a better product!"

My mother came over and winced as she figured out what the change in his tone was about, her eyes easily assessing the state of the decrepit-looking Miner's Pick. She frowned at it and then looked at me before asking the clear question I had been expecting. "But why does it still look like this if you can repair it?"

My father's eyebrows joined his hairline as he looked at me and then the wedge protruding from the top of the Pickaxe. "My Skill doesn't work the way I originally thought," I said, speaking the best lie I had planned on the drive home. "It turns out I put a self-repair stamp, or something like that, on it. Then it repairs itself as it mines Crystals, I think?"

"You don't know?" my dad said skeptically, then nodded before I could answer. "Right—new Skill. So? I guess that's the feeling you get when you try repairing it?"

I could only nod. "I mean, I'll know a bit more tomorrow."

My dad scratched his head and gave a look to my mother that seemed to be pleading. I wondered what exactly it was about, but I certainly had a few guesses. The most likely of which was that she disagreed with me spending my savings on a Pickaxe to begin with, and my current lackluster purchase wasn't exactly giving her confidence. I really didn't want to get involved with that argument if that was the case.

"I'm going to head to bed, my whole body aches from my first day. Any idea where the crew is working tomorrow?" I asked the last question to change the subject.

"We think we're heading back into the Detroit Field. The Dungeon we were in today was only half-cleared of Crystals by our team and has some other valuable Ores, so we're heading back. Plus, they need to make a trip out there for the Gardeners anyway. According to Willa, they only got about a tenth of the Herbs and Fruit out."

I nodded and yawned. I didn't try to fight the yawn since it helped my current plan of escape. "Alright, I'll see you in the morning then."

I gave both a hug, and they squeezed tighter than normal, clearly still concerned over my recent trauma. At that moment, I was even more desperate to stop telling lies—to admit everything—but the words caught in my throat. I'd wait just a bit longer and show them how valuable the *Demonic Vault* Skill was.

And maybe wait till my trial was finished…

Smegma didn't bother hovering around when I entered the house, and while I was pretty sure he was in my room already, I was somewhat relieved to find him there when I went upstairs. I was marginally confident he couldn't get himself into trouble, what with the whole incorporeal thing, but I wasn't willing to fully trust that sentiment.

Like a dog peeing on the carpet…

He flipped me the bird when he heard that surface thought.

"I hope you're happy. I'm lying to my parents now," I said to change the subject. He shook his head with an amused grin.

"Yes, because I'm the puppet master who forces you to do my bidding," he retorted and added an evil laugh along with a creepy three-fingered hand motion. I smirked, already having known my comment was unfair. I'd simply said it to start the conversation.

Because I *wanted* a conversation.

The silence that fell after Smegma's sarcasm disappointed me.

I sat down at my desk and pulled out my notebook. I made a note of two things: Monster Cores and Smegma's interest in them, and the lie I'd used to cover up the state of the Miner's Pick. As I made the second, I realized I'd left the new Pick in my father's hands when I made my escape. Part of me wanted to go get it because I wanted to test feeding it my personal Mana to see if it repaired. However, I wasn't sure that would be how it worked, so instead I asked, "Smegma, what would happen if I fed the Miner's Pick my personal Mana?"

"It would repair, but why in the hell would you do that?" He sounded incredulous. Another blush came over me. His question made me consider why I was wanting to test that. I simply wanted the Pick to look better when I brought it with me tomorrow. Seeing my flush, Smegma shook his head, "Just channel them to me for mC, let the Enchant on the Miner's Pick handle the rest tomorrow. Especially since you have to *Shard the Crystals*." The last bit was said with all the scathing commentary I'd heard multiple times throughout the day.

I flipped back a page in the journal instead of answering, reading my order of events for my plan. I'd now accomplished the first part, which was buying the Miner's Pick, but my second purchase of an E-Ranked Mana Pool was no longer required, at least not until I confirmed what sort of Mana Pool I had.

I crossed that part out.

"Should I prioritize buying a mid-grade Spent Mana Crystal?" I asked Smegma, hoping he would say yes.

"Husk no," he said. "You know as well as I do that you might get one of those in the coming weeks. Clearly you need to buy a Skill you can use in combat."

I flinched when Smegma suggested that. I wasn't against combat and becoming a Hunter, but the way Smegma suggested it seemed to indicate the idea of getting the Skill and immediately diving into Portals solo. "You know I can't get a Skill and immediately start farming Portals, right?"

"Why not?" Smegma countered. At my raised eyebrows, he explained, "With the right Skill you easily could solo F-Rank Portals."

"Me and what army?"

At that, Smegma snapped his fingers, bringing a red prompt up in front of me.

Necromancy Skill Card
Necromancy
(1)
Skill Type: Summons
Skill Rank: High D-Rank (Evolvable)
Summon slain creatures to act as your personal troops. Creatures suffer a fifty percent reduction in combat power and lose any Skills they possessed. For convenience, Summoned creatures are Summoned as Shadows to prevent diseases and smells from spreading.
Cost: 500,000,000 mC

"Yeah, 'cause five hundred million Mana Coins seems achievable…"

"That's just an example. I'm just saying you can definitely have an army!" Smegma countered.

I stood up and started my preparations for bed. I didn't want to admit it, but I really liked the idea of being able to Summon creatures to fight for me—becoming a Solo Hunter who could clear Dungeons by himself appealed to me in a way I hadn't felt before. I didn't bother writing down that pipe-dream, not yet at least.

Instead, I brushed my teeth, got into my pajamas, and climbed into bed.

My eyes flew open and I sat up, wide awake again. "Smegma, that Skill you showed me was High D-rank!"

"By golly-gosh," Smegma began with a fake, very fairy-tale-esque lilt to his voice. "I think you're right!"

"Can the sarcasm. Did the new version of OS give you access to more Skills?"

"Obviously," he answered dryly.

Sleep forgotten, I spent the next few hours scanning through the newest Skills. Turns out that a high D-Rank Mana Pool had two hundred and fifty Mana. No wonder my measly sixteen points raised questions.

Then what rank of Mana Pool does Smegma's Sect Leader have if its Pool is in the millions? I wondered to myself.

"Probably Extraordinary Rank," Smegma said offhandedly in response to my errant thought. I pointedly didn't think about the fact that I recalled *Demonic*

Vault starting in the Ex-Ranks. I didn't think Smegma would handle that information too well.

Eventually, my eyes felt heavy and without finding anything that changed my current plans, I fell into a fitful sleep.

My dreams, of course, betrayed my earlier thoughts—creating a movie of me as a Necromancer taking on Dragons like Abbas.

* * *

Greb-Shak looked at his new form again, and then at the sleeping child. His body was just a representation of changes that were far larger and more sweeping than mere physicality—as if that would have any bearing, anyway, with his incorporeal nature. Now that the human was asleep, he began examining his 'updated' memories.

First, was the obvious misconception he'd been operating under when the kid made the Mana connection. He could recall the team of researchers struggling to figure out that functionality—but landing on a happy coincidence. Where the curator's appearance would be based on Skill Rank. And clearly, they had been aiming to make Demonic Vault the highest they could.

So, what had happened?

It was strange. Earlier tonight, he could recall thinking he was mid-training for his role as a Demonic Trader when he was 'Summoned' early. Then, as if between one blink and another, he could remember ten additional years and his graduation from that 'program.' He could even recall him and other researchers discussing changes the 'System' made on Gelth, a planet that was still initiating after Crendalar Five had failed.

How had they discovered that? He couldn't remember. However, he knew that multiple planets went through initiation at the same time. Then reached their Tests for Evolution at different paces. He could even remember that they were making progress on the why of that—something to do with how many Portals were left open and for how long?

No, those were his speculations back then. He couldn't recall what the other Researchers discovered…

What exactly had happened at the moment Brodie purchased the Pickaxe? He checked his log but only saw the same notification that he'd minimized after discovering his new memories and body changes.

Demonic Vault Skill
(32)
Skill Type: Summons (#$^~|)
Skill Rank: Low D-Rank (Evolv-Error!)
As a Demonic Trader, you can offer the user of the Vault a choice of two of the following secondary effects.
Secondary Effect Options:
Achievements
Buffs

Classes
Crafter
Dungeon Lord
Extract
...

The list kept going but didn't explain what had changed. Greb-Shak began tapping a much harder and sharper black talon on his much larger and sharper teeth as he began looking through the options.

What would be best for Brodie? No, more importantly—what would be best for himself?

CHAPTER 19

Friday, April 5th, 2069

Those who said I would get used to following a B-Rank Hunter around were wrong.

"Or it's only been two days, dumb-dumb," Smegma assessed from above me, where he lazily backstroked meaninglessly through the air. The change to his body was already a bit disturbing, but the way the Goblin-Imp moved now spoke of a litheness that was usually reserved for the naturally athletic or highly gifted Hunters.

Still, his words barely stung this morning. *I was following Sturdy Jeral into battle with my newly purchased weapon.*

"Kid, you're husking delusional," Smegma said with a snort of laughter.

Again, I let the Demon's words slide off me. Sure, I was acting childish, but before he died I'd once heard my grandfather say that it is when you decide you've grown up that you truly have. Sure, it was just after he'd crop-dusted the whole living room and couldn't catch his breath from laughing—but I think the sentiment still held. *In the immortal words of the Great Theologian, Pan Peter, 'little boys should never be sent to bed. They always wake up a day older.'*

Smegma paused momentarily in the air before turning toward me. "This Pan Peter sounds like a quack. That's complete nonsense. You should burn his religious writings and remove him from your people's history before he infects people with his nonsense."

I chuckled at the Imp's literal interpretation of my joke and did nothing to correct him. Here's to hoping that one day that little 'fact' comes up in conversation and makes him look stupid. Was it petty? Sure, but it was *my* pettiness, and with how much the Imp annoyed me, I fed that shit like logs into a roaring fire.

"It's mostly the deeper caverns left today," my father said from my other side, which at least stopped Smegma from making another snide comment. "The deeper we go, the more chance the crew has of running into Slimes. Because of that, Sturdy Jeral and the two Archers with him are going to sweep each chamber more thoroughly before we start."

It took me a moment to register what those words meant. Chance of Monsters—slightly scary. Deeper caverns—much ominous. Hunter's fighting those Monsters in the deeper caverns—totally husking *epic!* And this time I had a warning of the sweep, so I could ask to watch from the front! Well, not from the *very* front, but maybe at the front of the Mining group, at least.

"Oh my god, you gotta stop going out half-cocked in the morning—I think you just spudded in your Mining gear," Smegma snidely added to the conversation.

[That's where you're wrong,] I sniffed, trying to force as much bravado into the thought as I could. [I never leave the house half-cocked. I only ever leave full-cocked, baby.]

I had the satisfaction of watching the Imp's facepalm.

"Just wait, Brodie!" Willa shouted, clearly seeing my excitement and matching it with the tone she used. "Watchin' a coordinated Hunting Team fight be somethin' ya never forget." I mentally stuck my tongue out at Smegma. See, I wasn't the only one excited.

"She's clearly faking it because she saw your O-face," Smegma grumbled.

[Who husking pissed in your Barlies this morning?] I asked.

"You eat that strange *serial* with piss in it?" Smegma asked, shocked. A moment later his face turned considering. "What effect does it have?"

Thankfully, Willa and my father had begun discussing some 'epic' fights they'd seen over the years—which, admittedly, I wanted to hear, but it did also give me time to confront Smeg.

[No, it means what is wrong with you, or what has got you upset?]

Smegma gave me a stare that felt to be weighing me before he shrugged. Then he physically stuck his tongue out, but just like with the drive to the Dungeon and this whole walk, something felt off with the Imp. Like there was something he was deciding whether or not to tell me.

I gave up. The allure of hearing about eye-witnessed epic battles pulled me back to the conversation at hand. "—then Derelict used his *Oil Slick* Skill an' dropped his cigarette. He just whispered 'boom' an' the whole floor went up like a gasoline-drenched bonfire."

Willa was using her hands to convey a great deal of the action, and seemed to excuse my far-off look as daydreaming because she smiled even wider when I tuned back in.

"Both your da' and I think that's where the line from Predatory X came from—ya know, the one where he be blowin' up a gas truck to create the updraft that destabilizes the flyin' alien superhero guy."

"That's not what I said, Willa. I said that movie came out years before we saw Derelict say it. Most likely he took that line from the movie!" My dad countered. "Still, it was pretty great." My father wore a look that told me he was having an internal war. He didn't want to glorify Mining, or likely even more so—Hunting, but also wanted to brag about the 'good' points of the job.

We finally reached a cavern still filled with Mana Crystals, and Jeral held up a gauntleted hand high—so that we could see it over his door of a shield. The Miners formed ranks and Willa helped me get into the right spot with a guiding hand on my elbow. The 'right spot' turned out to be at the front for a better view. I could literally hear my heart hammering in my ears as the three Hunters un-shouldered weapons and shields.

Jeral moved to the front and hugged the right wall, keeping his shield canted ever so slightly up and toward the wall. His legs were bent, loaded, and ready to react.

I held my breath.

The Archers began moving when Jeral was ten feet in front of them. Six armored Mana Banks, including Jeral's, separated from the Miners, almost seeming to be towed in their wake.

Still holding my breath, I studied the six individuals. They seemed to almost fade into the background when Hunters were so close. Each one seemed to move in step with the other five, and thanks to the similar armor, seemed to form three pairs of 'identical' individuals. For the first time in my life, I questioned my earlier dream of being where they were. Not because it was dangerous—but because it was hardly any different than what I was doing right now.

Watching…Then again, they were helping, while I was just watching…

Eventually, my screaming lungs forced me to gasp in a breath. Willa and my father gave each other amused looks and patted my shoulders. The silence was highlighted by their choice to not poke fun.

Smegma, on the other hand, had no such compunction. "Are you into a gag kink too? Really trying to pull out all the stops this morning, huh? You know, I might actually have something in the Shop here that you could use to—"

[How do you even know about some of these references? Is it because you heard about them and desperately needed to know more?] I retorted, still fixated on Jeral and the Hunting group. Smegma's silence at the retort almost felt like a victory, but I knew it had been a weak comeback. Almost like an 'I know you are, but what am I.'

I just couldn't give the Demon the attention a better retort would need.

Five minutes later, Jeral signaled an all clear and I frowned. "That was husking anticlimactic," I complained. However, it wasn't like there wouldn't be more caverns—

"Gary, Willa, Brodie, Fat Gary, and Miguel, you'll take this room." One of the Specialist Miners called. The way the other Miners looked outraged at my father, but then softened when my name was called, told me that the Specialist was doing my father a favor to keep me safe.

I seriously considered if there was a way to decline because I wanted—no *needed*—to see a fight, but those same softened looks told me that they would insist. *So, did I want to throw a fit in front of the Hunters?*

Nope, I did not.

"Good call, don't ever let the ones you love know how crazy you actually are," Smegma said.

[It's called chain of command, numb nuts. I swear to god, I will figure out how to un-Summon you if you keep this up.] Smegma paused then nodded to himself—almost seeming to come to a decision.

"Alright, fine. Once you start working, I'll tell you what's going on."

[Thanks, oh benevolent one.]

"You think you can clear your own starting point, Bro?" my father asked. I nodded and followed the group to the center of the cavern, careful of where I was placing my feet.

Willa began placing the post and hung her Light Stone before directions were assigned. I still felt a bit disappointed we didn't get to stay with the group and possibly see a fight, but I also couldn't wait to see my new Pick in action. Willa had scoffed at the thing when she saw it, but since my father had told her about my 'Skill' already, she gave a semi-compliment about how smart I was to purchase a worn-down but highly Enchanted Pick, instead of a somewhat serviceable low-ranked option.

Thankfully, both her and my father believed me when I told them it had a Penetration Enchant in it. Otherwise, they might have questioned the materials, or lack thereof.

Smiling, I raised up the Pick and brought it down on a particularly spiky Crystal to begin clearing my assigned section. A jolt of vibration went through my Monster-hide gloves and up my arms, making me wince. The Pick did crack the targeted Crystal but my flinch was for *expected* pain. Yesterday, my hands and arms had gone numb but then ached as I worked. Today, though?

It felt like I hadn't spent all day yesterday Mining for the first time in my life. My brain worked through the problem despite my surprise. [Holy shit, *Recovery* is healing muscle fatigue, blisters *and* delayed onset?]

"Finally figuring out why your hands were okay last night?" Smegma asked, sounding slightly amused. I kept Sharding out the circle I was going to work on, but mentally prodded him to elaborate. With a huff, he continued, "Yes, as you thought yesterday, *Recovery* was likely actively working all day as you Mined, last night and even now. Remember your dad's surprise when you had no blisters, and when you came running down the stairs for breakfast this morning?"

Blinking, I saw the interaction with my father and mother this morning in a new light. Was that why they were looking at each other so worriedly? Did they think I would be in so much pain that I might regret going to Mine in the first place?

[Of course,] I mentally said. [They were thinking the difficulty of this job might reaffirm the choice to stay in school.]

"Bingo," Smegma said sarcastically, but then called me back to task. "That's twelve Sharded already. Try to get a whole one now."

I did so and found the Pick's reverberations in my hands worsened when striking the rock beneath the Crystals, where the stem resided. However, the wood of the Pickaxe visibly grew healthier when I made contact with and shattered the glass-like stem.

[Is that accumulation or does the Pickaxe Repair faster from hitting the stem?] I asked over the noise of plinking glass, trying to understand why that particular strike seemed to provide more repairs to the Pick.

"How the husk would I know? Do I look like a lesser Demon—" Smegma paused and looked at himself. "—scratch that. I *do* look like a lesser Demon, however, I was never a Miner."

[Won't hurt to experiment, then,] I said as I resumed Sharding, after selling the intact Crystal and Mana inside for ninety-three mC. By the time I tried for my next intact Crystal, I was sure that Mining properly would give me better results. While Sharding was repairing the Pickaxe, it was barely noticeable. Still, much to Smegma's continued complaints of wastefulness, it was steady.

So, when I struck the next stem and saw the wedge sink in smoothly, I wasn't surprised. I *was* surprised when Smegma reminded me of his earlier words. "You haven't asked me to tell you what's going on yet…"

166

[Wow, do I need to ask for you to tell me? I figured you'd get on with it when you were ready...] I sent the mental image of a child throwing a tantrum and felt a thrill when Smegma gnashed his teeth audibly.

"Do you want to be a Ghast about it, or do you want to hear what I have to say?"

[First, what does that saying mean? Then, sure, go ahead...]

"Oh, for once you got caught with an idiom. I'm going to let this percolate. Enjoy my—"

[Something to do with wailing, I assume?]

"Husk you, Brodie. Just husk you," Smegma responded, his voice instantly less excited than a moment before. "Not that you deserve to be offered this choice, but when the *Demonic Vault* Skill Evolved yesterday, two choices were presented— here they are!"

That seemed a bit abrupt, but the screen popping up in front of me seemed to be all the explanation I needed.

Demonic Vault 2.0.0.1
Secondary Effect Skills
Extract
Upon death, this Skill may allow the *Demonic Vault* user to reclaim Skill Cards from a target's heart. *The target must have used Mana on the owner of *Demonic Vault* or be an Ally who shared Mana for the Skill to trigger.
OR

My eyes froze on the 'or' as the realization hit me. This Skill was what Morgan had been trying to trigger! This is what made him a Snatcher. This single Skill led to a killing spree up the east coast of the United States and eventually to me. My brain attempted to calm my emotions—tried to point out how good this Skill could be—but I knew I wouldn't be taking it.

I didn't want to turn into Morgan 'The Snatcher' Hallsbrad.

"Keep reading then, there's still the second option," Smegma said, sounding slightly pleased.

Wait, hadn't Smegma said *Demonic Vault* hadn't been the Skill—

"And it wasn't—it was one of these sub-Skills," Smegma said. It felt a lot like gaslighting to me, but I let it slide in favor of reading the other option.

OR
Overdraft
Skills and items can either Overcharge or Overflow.
Overcharge allows the item to increase its effects by 100%.
Overflow allows the excess Skill experience, Mana,
or power to be channeled to a person or object of the owner's choosing.
[Overflow chosen.]
Current Overflow target [Smegma]

Immediately, I was able to figure out why Smegma was pleased. However, a quick mental click brought me into the box with Smegma's name in it. Like a computer, it had a pull-down menu that allowed me to select other targets. Everything I currently wore, including my Pickaxe, was there. Most importantly though, *my* name was there.

I toggled the other selection box to *Overcharge* and found only the Pickaxe available as a target. Plus, a description that included a time limit of five minutes.

"Leaving it on me should upgrade the *Demonic Vault* or *Overdraft* Skill," Smegma mentioned, trying to sound offhanded. He wasn't a particularly good actor. I could tell that leaving it on him would also give the Demon something else. Maybe even a physical form?

Should I pick *Overdraft?* I still felt like I couldn't take *Extract*—not to mention, know how to make use of it. I wasn't going to start killing monsters anytime soon, right? That was the only lawful way I could see it being used.

Changing the target of *Overflow* to myself and then switching the Skill to *Overcharge*, I selected *Overdraft*. Immediately, I felt a connection form inside my Soul Universe. Still Sharding Crystals to stay discreet, I peeked into the space.

To my surprise, I found a Planet, or perhaps a Moon, revolving around the Sun that was *Demonic Vault*. Just touching it with a mental tendril seemed to bring with it an awareness that it was Overdraft.

The small Planet, because that's what it was, had two 'switches.' One allowed me to spin the planet in a circle, aligning a red volcanic side or a serene blue side. I could tell *Overcharge* was red and blue was *Overflow*.

How could I tell? Well, both sides had a small pedestal-like mountain that depicted something. One was my face carved into the cliff face, and the other was a Pickaxe. However, the red side was more of a volcano than a mountain and I could command it to erupt—or *Overcharge,* I supposed.

I mentally prodded it, and sure enough, my Mana flew into the *Demonic Vault* Skill as the volcano erupted in red energy. Smegma forced me to open my eyes when he squealed, "Wait, you put the target of *Overflow* to yourself? Why?"

Answering was put on hold when I saw the small red nimbus that surrounded the Pickaxe. My next swing was supposed to be the eighth Sharded Crystal, but I chose to try to get a full Crystal and test my new Skill. The Pick hit the ground and cut through it—before clicking into the stem. It felt the exact same as any other time I had used the Pick.

When I sold the full Crystal to Smegma, though, I got a full hundred and five mC. [Did I just get full price for that Mana Crystal?]

"I don't care. Why aren't you targeting me with *Overflow?* We could upgrade *Demonic Vault* and get more Skills!" Smegma shouted. I didn't bother responding, since he chose to ignore my question, and instead returned to Sharding. After five Crystals, he answered, "Yes, it seems like it was full price— almost no Mana loss. I'm assuming *Overcharge* doubled the Penetration Enchant on the Pick, which made it so your horribly aimed swing just broke through the additional rock it needed. Now, can you answer why I'm not targeted by *Overflow?*"

[If *I'm* the target, I can figure out what exactly *Overflow* is doing. If *you're* the target, I have to rely on you telling me what it's doing.]

"It's like you don't trust me," Smegma said sulkily.

[I really don't,] I mentally answered as I continued working.

Smegma stuck his tongue out at me and flew off to be alone. I shrugged; I may change the target to Smegma later if it really would help level *Demonic Vault*.

Five minutes later, the barely visible red aura around the Pickaxe faded, and I tried to swap the planet to *Overflow*. I found that I couldn't. What I discovered upon closer examination was that the red planet currently had a black moon beside it. The moon was slowly moving around the planet. I kept working as I periodically checked on my Mental Universe.

After an hour, according to my watch, the black moon vanished behind the planet, and I could spin it around again. Unfortunately, that coincided with our first break for lunch, and so I was forced to wait to try *Overflow*.

* * *

"Look at that," Willa said, as she examined my new Pickaxe at lunch time. "Some o' the pockmarks are already gone, Gary. Plus the handle be lookin' well maintained, if still old."

My dad smiled with a mouthful of ham sandwich. Well, ham or Wild Boar Monster. That was a tough distinction these days. Farm-raised Pork wasn't always cheaper than Monster Pork, and if I was being honest, the taste wasn't noticeably different either. I looked at my own sandwich and shrugged, even as my father said, "So, what do you think? Should we both go out and buy one tonight as well?"

My few bites of sandwich in my stomach instantly became poison that it wanted to eject. I don't think my stomach ever fell that quickly—like it was some sort of drop-zone amusement park ride. I began shaking my head before considering what type of answer I was going to give them. They both looked at me with concern.

"You're pale as a linen sheet, Brodie," Willa commented. "What's up?"

[Husk, husk, husk,] I thought desperately.

"Just tell them that you need to buy the Picks, or at least be with them. The repair mark doesn't work on all the gear you tested it on last night," Smegma gave me a probable lie, which I dutifully repeated.

"That's probably because some of what you held didn't need repairs, no?" my dad answered with an obvious piece of logic I clearly hadn't considered. I looked to Smegma, who shrugged. He clearly hadn't considered that either. *The prick.*

"I can't be sure that's the case. I tried it on everything I held and only found this one. So, maybe let me purchase them for you?"

"Oh, that be easy. Ya okay with him puttin' two on your credit card, Gary? I'll e-transfer ya the money tomorrow," Willa said to my dad.

I was already at two thousand mC this morning from sales of Mana Crystals, which meant if I pushed hard I might be able to afford another Miner's Pick tonight, but two?

"Just tell them you only found one or didn't find any that you could 'mark' after going to the mall tonight," Smegma gave the obvious solution. I nodded in relief as my esophagus slowly unclenched, allowing my somersaulting stomach to calm down. My half-eaten sandwich didn't look appealing at all anymore thanks to the rollercoaster of a conversation.

This was the problem with lies…

"I'll take a look tonight, then," I answered with a nod.

"I'll come with you," my dad said. I wanted nothing more than to close my eyes and swear at myself.

"I'd rather go by myself, if that's okay," I lied. "It was pretty hard to apply the mark to this one, and I don't want your preferences making me think I can force it onto something I can't."

My father nodded shallowly, which probably meant he was confused by my response, or slightly hurt by it. I didn't like either of those thoughts but couldn't really allow him to come with me, watch me *not* buy something, and then magically pull a Miner's Pick out of thin air…

"You got enough room on your credit card?" my dad asked, skeptically.

"Yeah, for sure. I paid it off immediately after yesterday…"

I could tell by the silence that followed that both Willa and my father found my insistence odd, but thankfully Willa eventually broke the uncomfortableness. "Let us be gettin' back to work, ya?"

Forcing the rest of my unappetizing sandwich down my throat, I dusted off my disgusting hands on my disgusting Miner's uniform and stood. This afternoon, it was just the three of us in this cavern since Fat Gary and Miguel were called to a deeper one a few minutes ago, which I suspected was my father's doing. He likely wanted to be able to talk freely like we just had, and to get Willa on board with his plans from the drive home the previous night.

I kind of wished he hadn't, now. Still, their conversation did flesh out my current plans a bit more. If I got my father a Miner's Pick tonight or tomorrow, and then Willa one on one of the following days, I'd have three people working to up the level of the Miner's Picks and collecting Mana that I could turn into Mana Crystals.

[How exactly do I turn the collected Mana into Crystals?] I asked Smegma as I moved to the area I had been Sharding through this morning.

"That small gem that I told you to take out of the base of the haft yesterday in the car. That's the Keystone. You just put that back in and it will create a Crystal. If the Pick has enough Mana stored."

[Okay, and how can I tell what level the item is at?] I asked.

"That's a bit more difficult," Smegma answered while biting one of his talons. "For that, you need to purchase a Scroll of Identification or have an Eye related Skill."

[How much are those?] I asked with a mental and physical sigh.

"Ten thousand mC," Smegma answered quickly. I felt my hands clench around the haft of the Pick. That was the same price as buying another Pick. Smegma smiled at my frustration. "It isn't like you need to know what level the Pick is at. It will keep leveling up and improving itself whether you know where it's at or you don't. At least, until it needs to Evolve…"

I swung down with a frustrated grunt, taking my feelings out on a Mana Crystal that shattered into pieces. A few jumped up and bounced off my safety glasses, telling me that I'd swung too hard. I didn't bother changing the force as I moved onto the next one. This sure was therapeutic.

Thus, it took me multiple Crystals and a reminder from Smegma to check on *Overflow* to remember it. After the reminder, I realized that I wasn't feeling anything that would hint at what it was doing. I'd kind of expected to feel, well, *something*. I took another mental trip to my Internal Universe and found the answer to my question.

Each time I struck with the Miner's Pick, a small white tendril left the *Demonic Vault* Skill and went off into the utter nothingness of space that surrounded the Skill. I had been hoping that *Overflow* would begin increasing my body's strength or something like that. Surely, that's what Smegma had been wanting to happen, or at least that's what I'd originally thought.

[I don't suppose you'll tell me what it's doing?]

"I think it's just *Overflowing* out into the darkness. Targeting yourself is probably impossible," Smegma answered far too quickly.

[Unlikely. I doubt there's zero benefit. I'll keep testing for now.] I responded dryly. For the next several hours, I was forced to put up with occasional sales pitches from Smegma for me to change the *Overflow* target. It became so frequent that I began using it for tempo.

* * *

"Mind if I try it on this deposit?" my dad asked.

I glanced at Smegma who shrugged. Since I hadn't asked my question yet, I mentally rolled my eyes. [If I *Overcharge* it, will it still work for him?]

"It should," Smegma answered sourly.

Wondering if my father would see the red aura, I said, "One sec, let me try something."

It took me a second to connect my straw to *Overcharge* again, but once I did, my Mana drained, and the red aura around the Pickaxe became visible again. Well, it drained my Mana and used the Skill once I spun the planet and commanded the volcano to erupt. My father just watched me patiently and I looked between the Pickaxe and him for a moment. "You don't see the red glow?"

"No, I see a much better-looking Pickaxe than I did this morning, though!" he said excitedly. "Did you just reapply your mark?"

I nodded before handing my slightly better-looking Pickaxe to my father. My only concern was that the Pickaxe might not get any Mana to repair itself from Ore deposits. However, Smegma's original shrug of indifference made me a bit less hesitant to let my dad try it.

He hefted the thing with a few flicks of his wrists before he adjusted his grip slightly. "Weight balance is better than last night, too."

He didn't wait for me or Willa, who stood watching, to respond before stepping up to the silvery vein of Ore in the cavern wall. His first swing buried deeply into the stone just above the upper part of the vein, and my father pulled the point back out and examined the Miner's Pick, pausing in his usual relentless swings. "Did you know it had a Guiding Enchant on it?"

171

I shook my head, and he shrugged before getting back to work. Instead of disturbing him, I turned to Willa. "What's a Guiding Enchant?"

"It's a Precision Enchantment, dumb-dumb, it was likely added as the thing was repaired," Smegma answered unhelpfully. I ignored him.

"Well, it ain't be super common on professional tools, but we be seein' it once or twice on a Specialist's Pick. So, I not be surprised ya don't know. Trajectory Assistance or a Guiding Enchant does what it be soundin' like. It be adjustin' a weapon strike to hit a more vulnerable spot on the target. In the case of Minin', it be shiftin' the trajectory to ensure ya don't ruin the Ore or Crystal's value." Willa spoke between the loud metallic pangs of my father's swings. Her voice was loud to be heard but she couldn't hide her excitement. "Can ya see if ya can get me one with that, too?" she added between the next swings.

"I'll try!" I shouted back, trying to be heard over the next pang of impact.

It took my dad about thirty minutes to get the silvery Ore out of the wall in large, clean sections. I spent that time looking at my mC count. The afternoon had gone better than the morning, allowing me to be at a total of just over twelve thousand Coins. We still had an hour left and I was somewhat anxious to get my Pick back from my father to see if I could collect some more to help get Willa a Pick sooner.

However, it wasn't meant to be. It turned out that there was a reason Willa and I could stand around watching my father work.

"All the Crystals are cleared out further down," a new Lynx Guild member said as he made piles of Sharded Crystals vanish into a large Prospector's Pack on his back. Or I guess I assumed that the pack was one of the spatial bags, he could have been using a Skill but I doubted that. "Is that Magna Steel?" he asked as he saw the pile of silvery Ore.

My father nodded while sporting a massive grin. "It sure is."

"Are one of you a Specialist?" he asked as he hurried to collect it.

"My son bought an Enchanted Pick last night. I used it for the deposit." My father answered while resting the Miner's Pick on a shoulder.

"Well, hopefully the value of the bonuses today will cover the cost of repairs—that thing looks ready to fall apart," the porter said and indicated the Pickaxe. Thanks to his comment, I noticed that the Pickaxe did in fact look like it had lost some ground on the repairs when my father swung it. My father un-shouldered it and winced as he studied it.

"Sorry, kid," he said sheepishly, handing it back.

"How much is Magna Steel worth?" I asked while I accepted the Miner's Pick back.

"Sixty thousand a pound," the Lynx Guild 'porter' answered quickly and began writing something out on a piece of paper. "You did manage to get eleven pounds here. Here's the receipt." He handed the paper to my dad, who nodded.

Willa and my dad waited for the porter to leave to look at me and the Pick I was examining. The haft and wedge looked far better than they had this morning, but the tip of the Pick didn't. The pockmarks were still mostly gone now, but the point was bent and battered nearly beyond recognition.

My dad winced and asked, "I didn't realize. Can your mark still work on it?"

"I think so. However, I think that means it only repairs when you use it on Crystals?" I answered, using the question as an excuse to add a bit more flesh to my lies.

My dad nodded and stroked his beard, even as Willa ran a hand over her forehead and into her hair. Hand still atop her head and tangled in her hair, she asked, "So, we'll have to balance the use of them between Crystals and deposits?" At my nod, she turned to my father. "Can we still claim to be Specialists with that limitation?"

"I think so. The Skilled Specialists can only do so many deposits a day. Why can't we?" My dad replied.

Willa frowned. "I'm not sure it works that way…"

"Either way, let's use our own Picks and try to get these other Ores out of the walls," my dad said in answer, pointing at a few other deposits in our small cavern.

By the end of the day, the Mining crew retained three hundred thousand dollars in bonuses, even after a few injuries and paid healings. That meant that each person could expect to take home an extra seventy-five hundred or so. That was right up until the Lynx guide reminded my father and the crew leaders about the healing the previous day. "What do you want to do? Pay from today's surplus or have the insurance take the hit."

I could tell that the guy was doing the crew a favor, since the leaders—my father amongst them—chose to take the hit on today's earnings rather than filing the report to insurance for the previous day. We still got just under a hundred thousand to split. Which meant each person would get around twenty-five hundred. I, of course, being new, only got five hundred. But both Willa and my father should get five thousand due to their experience—so it balanced out in our favor.

Well, in *their* favors, I supposed.

CHAPTER 20

Friday, April 5th, 2069

Just like that, I was back in another mall. This time I went to Tecumseh Mall, so I could keep up with my lie. I had told Willa and my father that I'd gone through a great deal of second-hand picks to find mine the previous day. I really just wanted to avoid any awkward questions tomorrow. Questions that would lead to more lies.

Strangely, my stories and subsequent lies weren't exactly what was weighing on me at this very moment. Not exactly.

No, it was the far bigger lie I was about to tell. I realized I needed to spend an appropriate amount of money at the mall and get my father and Willa to transfer the money to me later. That meant I had to buy something. I needed the receipt. That, of course, led to me needing to buy something from a store that sold Mining equipment, and depending on the itemization name on the receipt, it might even mean I needed to purchase a pick. A second-hand pick that was inferior to what I would get from the *Demonic Vault* store.

That was a huge waste.

Currently, I stood at the entrance contemplating how small lies were slowly growing into something that kind of bordered on a large moral gray area. Sure, I was providing my father with a Pickaxe that was worth much more than the five thousand-ish I was going to try to spend, but that didn't mean buying something else with his money was completely fine either.

"Gahhh," I grumbled.

"What are you so moody about?" Smegma asked as he floated out of a nearby store.

I looked around to make sure no one was giving me strange looks after my incoherent noise of frustration. Luckily, I was just inside the double doors of the mall's entrance and off to one side.

[I don't feel right about buying something with my dad's money. It feels dishonest.]

"Then don't buy something?" Smegma both answered and asked. His voice carried a question of my sanity.

[I need a receipt to show them! And they'll need a copy of it…]

"Okay, but who's saying you must keep the item you purchased. I've been seeing return counters in most stores, and many people seem to return items for their money back."

[Usually, secondhand things are final sale. Plus, there is still the problem that I'd have to do this twice,] I answered but began considering his proposal. His answer was surprising, considering he knew less about this world than I did, but I hadn't thought of it first. Then again, I was very close to the problem, which sometimes made it harder.

"In theory, you have ten thousand to spend, right?" Smegma asked, and my eyes narrowed but I nodded. "What if you purchase two used pickaxes, return them *instantly*, after a phone call, while still at the counter or something, and then buy a higher-grade Monster Core to sell using *Demonic Vault*."

My eyes narrowed this time. While the plan was fantastic, his slightly excited tone over the higher-grade Monster Core made me suspicious. I decided to treat his 'slyness' with some of my own. [I can't spend the whole ten thousand today, though. I don't have enough mC to purchase two Miner's Picks.]

"We won't know until you check what's available," Smegma countered. That response came far too quickly, which made me think my suspicions were correct.

[I guess you're right...] I mentally mumbled, hoping my internal voice carried the wary feel I was going for. I wasn't exactly an actor, but I'd had a few lessons thanks to my attempts to be a SwiftGram influencer.

Well, my continued attempts... I realized I should probably document my trip to the mall in some way to my SwiftGram followers. There was probably a Venice Vici Hunters store in here, right? I found it on the map while remaining silent. Smegma could read even my thoughts, so I needed to be extra careful. I didn't trust the Imp and wanted to wait to see what he'd say when we got to the Cores before I confronted him.

My slyness seemed to work because Smegma followed in my wake as I made my way to the third floor Venice Vici for a picture and then the Wallsmart store. Wallsmart was another long-standing chain with a ton of buying power, but much more importantly for me—it had a very lax return policy. I didn't bother with the second or third floor and made my way right to the first. There, I found the Monster Core section.

Like HBC, Wallsmart had a room that was enclosed with thick, likely magic-proofed, glass. The interior reminded me of an eyeglass store with small pegs sticking out from peg boards, atop which rested Monster Cores of all kinds. I pushed the button at the door and waited for the clerk inside to come greet me.

A young teenager, probably fresh out of high school, looked up at me and gave me an up and down before his face fell. I could tell that he didn't want to bother with me, but since our eyes had met, he didn't dare provide subpar customer service. Not at a place like Wallsmart, where a complaint could cost him his job. The only other sign I got that he was unwilling to get up and serve me was a glance to another section of the room, at two people standing there examining Cores. That's when I realized there were two clerks inside, and one was already helping another customer.

The teenager stood up and made his slow walk to the door. Just before he opened it, he fixed his face into a terribly fake smile. Did the idiot not realize that the whole front of the room was glass? He pushed a button beside the door and then swung it wide in an overly exaggerated gesture. "Welcome to Wallsmart Cores, what can I help you with today?"

"I'd like to take a look at the E-Grade Cores," I answered.

I debated acting a part, and perhaps treating him poorly in turn, but I had worked retail in the past. It wasn't pleasant at the best of times, and even worse if you worked on commission. On top of that, I didn't want to draw too much attention.

"Absolutely," the kid, whose name-tag read Brad, answered. His fake smile slipped slightly, and I couldn't tell if he was surprised or excited by the notion of me purchasing an E-Grade Core. "Follow me," Brad said, his voice finally revealing that he did have a bit of excitement now.

He led the way to the same wall the other customer was looking at, but instead of the far back corner, we approached the section nearer the doors. A glance at the descending prices of Cores that led to the other clerk told me that was the F-Ranked section. I guessed the excitement wouldn't last long when I saw the prices of the Portal Cores nearest the window. I moved down the row until I reached the section where Cores started at twelve thousand dollars.

A sigh came from behind me, but when I looked at Brad, his fake smile was firmly in place. I calmed my slight frustration at the kid's judgment by steadily breathing in and out through my nose. Mentally to Smegma, I practically shouted, [Are these going to be worth eight thousand mC?]

"I can't say for sure yet," Smegma started to say, and thanks to my frustration, I wasn't willing to play this game anymore.

[Husk off dude, you're as obvious as a virgin looking at his first pair of tits. I know that the one yesterday turned out to be worth more than you thought. So, I'll expect some extra mC due to that as well.]

"This one here is a Thunder-attuned Core from a Thunder Roc," Brad explained as he picked up the most expensive one on the row I was standing in front of. The price tag was a whopping twenty-two thousand. "It's great for Machine Enchanting. The thunder also lends itself exceptionally well to crafting Bombs or Paralysis Arrays."

"Alright, idiot," Smegma said, giving me a very pointed look. "If I'm being *honest*, I'm not sure just how valuable these Cores are. However, I did seem to gain a great deal of energy from *somewhere* after the purchase. So, maybe my sect sent that on as encouragement to buy more.

"Yet, as this other ugly ape just stated, they only have quite a bit of value in Crafting. That wouldn't be enough for eight thousand mC. It's the possible uses that would interest my people. There is a small chance that an Array could be created that would be powered by these Cores. The proposed Array could then create a field of dense Mana converted from the Cores. That doesn't—" Brad was staring at me as Smegma spoke, and by his slowly falling smile, he was getting impatient.

"I'm sorry but I'm not looking for something with Thunder attunement. I moved over here because this blue one looked like it could be Water, no?" I cut off Smegma, motioning to the cheapest E-Rank on the rack. Brad replaced the Thunder Roc Core and picked up the blue one I indicated.

He began explaining what it was, and I turned back to Smegma, who had paused in his rant. "As I was saying," he continued. "That doesn't mean that they will be valuable—in fact, you're probably just in a position to take advantage of us needing higher ranked Cores to test the theory. Now, if possible, a Portal Core…"

I didn't roll my eyes, because I figured Brad, who was telling me about the Blast Turtle Portal Core, might take that the wrong way. [Okay, well with the credit from the Core yesterday and the value of this Blast Turtle Core, could you get me eight thousand mC?]

"—I'd suggest going with something more firmly Water attuned if you are wanting to craft something for consumption. Because this is a Portal Core, it has a slight Earth attunement. That will likely make a Bottomless Water Skin create water with a muddy taste, for example. We have a Fresh Water Sea Jelly Portal Core that—"

"I can only do about five thousand," Smegma answered.

I waved a hand, stopping Brad from going to collect what I guessed was going to be a far more expensive Monster Core. He looked back at me, his fake smile somewhat falling away, even as his eyes looked hopeful. "This is a purchase that is being made with a group. Can you place the Blast Turtle Portal Core on hold for me?" His face began to fall further. "I just need to step out, check the prices on a few other things, and make a call to my partners to okay the spending."

"Yeah, yeah, go ahead, I'll have it waiting here for you," Brad said, his voice and face betraying his skepticism about my return.

I felt my cheeks get hot but turned and left, pushing the internal button on my way out. I wasn't even sure why I had made up the excuse, but for some reason I felt the need to let the teenager down easy. I guessed I still had hang ups from my retail job. Still, Brad's guilt trip made it worthless, which in turn made me upset. I would never have treated another person like that.

"Wait, wait—" Smegma shouted as I stormed off. "Surely, Willa and your father could spend a bit more money."

[Nope, we'll go with the buy and return option, and I'll just have to get Willa one tomorrow,] I answered, stomping away from the room. Thankfully, there were signs hanging from the roof here that directed me to the first floor Miner's Section of the store. I worried that in my current mood I might ask a little too sternly if I stopped a store clerk for directions.

"Hold up, if you were willing to promise a purchase of another Core later, I could treat the extra three thousand as a loan," Smegma hurriedly said. I glanced back at him over my shoulder. This asshole was still lying, wasn't he?!

[Nope, I'd rather not be in your debt,] I said and kept heading to the Mining section. Smegma didn't answer, which surprised me, but since I was serious in my response, I figured I'd let him stew.

A few minutes later, I turned a corner and found myself surrounded by familiar looking gear, as well as a great deal of pieces I hadn't seen before. One aisle had boots, pants, chest pieces, glasses, helmets, and gloves prominently displayed on hangers or shelves. These looked like the loaners I used the last two days, but where mine were old and worn, these practically shone. Plus, the smell of new leather that tickled my nose almost sold the gear for Wallsmart.

The next few rows had pickaxes hanging from metal pegs. I could tell that these were the mass produced un-Enchanted ones, like the gear, since they weren't behind panes of plastic like the following rows. This is also where I found equipment I hadn't seen on our job site. The opposite side of the row had baskets of wedges and hanging sledgehammers. I moved to the nearest basket and picked one out.

The tag claimed it was made from Thorium-Steel, which was an alloy that combined a tiny amount of Thorium with Iron to create a metal that was harder than its original parts. From my understanding, the Thorium took the place of the carbon that was used with Iron to make the far more common metal that was Steel. Still, I wondered why I hadn't seen these used when my father was attempting to get the 'True Gold' or when Willa was trying to crack Necrograph.

What sat beside the sledgehammers gave me the clue. Drill bits. Clearly made in different sizes that corresponded to the wedges I was studying. So, I guessed that you could drill holes and then widen them using the sledge. I only wondered why they weren't used with my dad's crew until I went to the next aisle. This one had the same gear, but it was Enchanted. The Wedges, and Drill Bits were far more expensive and made for higher grade metals—such as Necrograph. But on top of the purely metal pieces, there were Drills for sale here. Drills powered by Mana Crystal Engines.

Since I was on the first floor, these would be the 'cheapest' Drills and Bits available, and they were already starting at fifty thousand, which was more expensive than most gas-powered cars.

Whereas new Picks hung inside the case opposite, and they were also Enchanted. In comparison, they started at three-thousand dollars for a Pick with a Strengthening Enchant. The problem was that a simple Strengthening Enchant wouldn't do much to help a Miner, and the price of the new Picks only ramped up from there.

I also realized that buying all the drills, wedges and sledges needed would create a huge amount of equipment to lug around between jobs… I pictured myself carrying what equated to a truck bed full of the tools and felt my legs protest the imaginary torture.

Smegma scoffed at what he was seeing in my mind, but I didn't bother engaging with him. I already knew that he'd just have more insults for humanity.

Instead, I exited the row of new Picks and walked around until I found huge oak barrels. Sure enough, they were filled with used but still working Pickaxes. They were organized by barrels and there were only three. One thousand, three thousand and a five-thousand-dollar barrel. I scanned the contents and chuckled when I realized that each Pick had a single tag attached with one word on them, sometimes two but only in the five-thousand-dollar barrel.

None had Accuracy written on them, but the majority had Strengthening. Especially in the thousand-dollar options. Almost ninety-percent of them were Strengthening. Penetration was the next most popular and it dominated the second barrel, as well as some particularly dented ones in the first. The third most popular was something called Weight. At first, I thought they would be making the Axe heavier but when I lifted one, I found that it felt no different. Smegma chimed in with an explanation, "When you swing it, it will strike with greater force. That Enchantment should be called Momentum, but since weight is a component of force, I guess they aren't wrong."

178

I found two good options in the most expensive barrel. One was 'Weight+Strengthening,' the other was 'Penetration+Resistance,' which Smegma again explained, "Resistance means it will take less damage from Mana, and since most Ores and Crystals are hardened by Mana, it's more or less the same as Strengthening, which no—doesn't make *you* stronger, it makes the material of the Pick more resilient…"

I nodded and chose the one with Resistance. It seemed rarer based on it being the only one with that label on its tag. I started moving back to the cash register, when Smegma coughed politely. I just kept walking, which made him blurt out, "Okay, I can do eight thousand mC for the Blast Turtle Portal Core."

"Fifteen thousand, and you never try to pull this bullshit with me again, or no deal," I said quickly, spinning on the Imp.

"It's already a stretch to give you eight thousand, dumb-dumb," he said while glaring at me.

"See, here's the problem, and why I said you never pull this bullshit again. Whether you like it or not, we're stuck together—" a clerk peaked his head out of an aisle to see who was speaking so sternly to someone else. At his strange look, I pulled my phone from my pocket and made a gesture with it, pretending I was using it. I then walked away quickly as I continued, "—and if I can't trust your prices, this is going to be a huge pain in the ass. I know you are selling things I can't get here on Earth, but I need to be able to trust that you are giving me as fair a value on what I sell, or we'll have trouble down the road."

"You're upset that a Trader is trying to get the best margins he can?" Smegma countered, sounding incredulous.

[No, I'm not upset, I just don't want to play these games.] I switched back to internal dialogue due to the looks I was getting as I passed people. Even with my phone pressed against my head. [I don't like what it will lead to. These games degrade your trust with me. Right now, because of your actions, I'm wondering if the Cores are worth far more than you're claiming. Because of that suspicion, I'm considering buying this Pickaxe, returning it, and waiting until tomorrow night to get another one, but what if your people want, no *need*, another Core. Do you understand what I'm saying?]

"So, you're willing to pass up on the deal I'm offering you out of spite?"

[Spite? No, it's not spite at all. Do you really not understand what it means to be a merchant—what it *really* means? Our economic infrastructure is built on supply and demand, which in turn is built on the backs of merchants on a global scale—and in that game, your word and your reputation are everything. Right now, your reputation is Ghast shit to me.]

"Well, Ghast's don't actually-—"

[You're purposefully not getting my point. I don't trust you, and I won't do business with someone I can't trust. That's why I'm refusing your offer.]

Smegma began tapping talons on his teeth and I rolled my eyes. Sure enough, if the fifteen thousand I countered with required thought, he was trying to trim the margins in his favor. I spun again and began making my way back to the counter. Smegma stopped me by flying in front of me and holding up both hands.

"Wait, wait," he said, "I see your point, but I'm being honest with you. This thing could be worth nothing. I'm assuming my people will try creating an Array, but I have no real contact with them other than that surge of energy I felt." He paused for a moment to let that sink in—then continued, "Or these Portal Cores could be worth far more. It's a gamble and I can't make it recklessly. My people only have what you see in this shop, and I can't be giving it away because of an optimistic hope. We've lost so much already on those…

"Here's what I can do," Smegma continued after letting his last-stated whisper hang in the air in an attempt to garner my sympathy. "I'll give you eight-thousand now, and if I get another surge of energy from my people, I'll make up the difference later. However, at that time, you promise to come purchase higher grade ones. Deal?"

"Deal." I spun back around and headed back to the barrels. I grabbed the other Pickaxe I was considering and then made my way to the checkout. Ten thousand dollars was charged to my credit card. I snapped a picture of the receipt and then made my way across the store to the returns counter. I purposefully picked the checkout counter furthest from the returns so I was less likely to be questioned.

For another layer of security, I put my phone to my ear and began a fake conversation. At the end of which, I attempted to sound defensive. "I didn't know you had already bought two. I'm sorry, boss. I'm still at the store, so I'll return them, geeze!"

"What the husk are you doing?" Smegma asked, causing me to blush.

[Trying to make my reason for return seem legitimate!] I said.

"Oh, 'cause that guy following you is going to figure out your plan?"

[There's a guy following me?]

"No, you husking twat! No one *cares* what you're doing. They all have their own lives to live. Just return them and go buy the Core."

My cheeks grew hotter. He was probably right.

At the returns counter, the clerk claimed that all sales were supposed to be final, which caused me to suffer a small heart palpitation. Thankfully, she was kind and made an exception because of my story, the time stamp on the receipt, and the fact that I never left the store.

A quick walk later and I was back at the Cores section. The second clerk I saw before, this one with a name-tag that read 'Jeff,' opened the door.

"Welcome to Wallsmart Cores, what can I help you with today?" Jeff repeated the same greeting Brad had offered me earlier. He also rushed to open the door and greeted me with a far warmer smile. Still, if they were on commission, I shouldn't stiff Brad just because I liked Jeff more.

"I was in earlier, Brad put a Blast Turtle E-Rank Portal Core on hold for me," I said. Jeff nodded, even as his smile fell. However, his fell in a far different way than Brad's had. This wasn't insulting, but more an internal sadness that he would miss out on a new commission.

"Absolutely, I'll get that wrapped up for you, then?" Jeff turned the statement into a question with an intonation in his voice.

I nodded, and together we moved to the counter. Brad wasn't in the room, and I assumed he had finished for the night or gone on break. Jeff opened a drawer

180

and blinked. Then he opened multiple others and began scratching his head. "You said he put it on hold for you?"

I tilted my head in confusion, and then slowly turned to look at the wall that contained E-Rank Cores. There, in the exact same spot it had sat when I viewed it earlier, was the Blast Turtle Portal Core.

That piece of shit... Jeff had pulled out his cellphone as I made this discovery and made to search through his contacts as he said, "I'll just give him a quick call."

"Don't bother," I said and pointed to it on the wall. "It's right there, and I think you should take the commission."

"Oh, I'm sure it was just a mistake on his part, I couldn't do that—"

"I really think you can," I said, cutting him off again. "In fact, you'll be saving him from a complaint directly to your boss if you do." Jeff blinked in response and then seemed to connect the dots.

"Was he in a mood again?" he said sheepishly. I nodded and Jeff returned the nod. "Look, I know I should just shut my mouth and take the commission but Brad's going through some stuff. His girlfriend just left him because he isn't making enough, and his little sister is in the hospital. So, can I persuade you not to complain, and to let me put it in under his name?"

I sighed and nodded. As always, life was far more complicated than what was immediately apparent. Now I just hoped Brad would pull himself out of his slump.

Husking empathy...

CHAPTER 21

Saturday, April 6th, 2069

"I be needin' a copy of a physical receipt for taxes," Willa said as she spun her Miner's Pick in her hands. It looked almost identical to how mine had looked yesterday. However, if I was honest, my own still looked pretty beat up from my father's Mining of Magna Steel. I nodded to her and reached into my back pocket for my phone.

"The only issue is that my dad needs it as well, so I took a picture, is that okay?" I answered, feeling slightly sick to my stomach. Willa and I were waiting outside of a construction trailer for my father. He'd gone in to register the three of us as Specialists.

"Oh right. Ya, I guess that works. It be better ta have a picture since Gary would probably just lose the huskin' thing," Willa stated, her voice telling me that my father had lost important things in the past. "So, explain to me again how—" Willa looked around to make sure no one was nearby and lowered her voice to a whisper, "—this 'repair mark' of yours be workin'."

"It seems to only works when you're Mining Crystals. That's why mine looks like this after my dad went a bit too hard and extracted the entire eleven pounds of the Magna Steel vein," I held up mine, which currently sported a nearly flat spike and twisted spade. "So, in theory, the more Crystals we Mine, the better it will look. I also think Mining without Sharding repairs the thing faster, so maybe try keeping the Crystals whole if you can. It's kind of all a balance, I think…"

"That's not it at all," Smegma spat, but thankfully only I could hear him. "The real problem was that Magna Steel was too hard for the level of your Miner's Pick, and so while the metal had Mana in it—the damage far outstripped your Pick's level and durability."

I repeated Smegma's words to Willa as though they were simply speculation on my part.

"So, what? Keep it to one Ore deposit a day?" she asked, clearly looking for set parameters of use. Unfortunately, I didn't have an instruction manual. I mentally asked Smegma for help and then continued to repeat what he told me.

"In theory, it shouldn't break even if you use it right now on a magical Ore deposit. However, it will be far less effective as the metal warps out of shape. Still, no matter how bad the head gets, Mining some Crystals should slowly return it back to working order—even if the Enchants fail."

"What are you two whispering about over here?" asked a man I didn't recognize, as he walked toward the trailer door. He was wearing a pin-striped black suit with a metallic powder-blue collared shirt, tie, dress pants and shoes.

His jet-black hair was expertly styled, and he wore a pair of sunglasses that hid his eyes. The man didn't look particularly strong, which made me instantly realize he was neither a Hunter nor a Gatherer from the Portal team. Still, the way Willa jumped and then ducked her head respectfully to him made me take careful note. It also made me duck my head.

"What the husk are you doing?" Smegma asked.

[I don't know,] I answered, even as I saw Willa raise her head beside me. I joined her, following her lead. [The bow is a show of respect, and if Willa respects this man, I probably should too!]

"You're an idiot," Smegma said as Willa started to speak as well.

"—Specialists. We're trying a new strategy where we buy secondhand picks, sir." Willa's explanation was quick and concise. The fact that she called this man sir, and the way he was dressed, instantly clued me in on his identity. This was Jagger Vance, the CEO of Portals, Portal's, Portalz —aka the company I was currently working for, or P-Cubed.

"Oh? Trying your hand again, Willa?" he said with concern in his voice. He took off his sunglasses and gave Willa a less than caring look though. His eyes were a yellowish-brown in color and they were bloodshot, like he'd been out drinking last night. "You know I can't give you an advance on pay again, right?" Willa nodded sheepishly and scratched her hair just under the high ponytail. Seeing her acknowledgement, Mr. Vance turned to me. "You must be Gary's son?"

"Yes, sir," I responded, and quickly cut off since I didn't know what else I could say.

"I heard you're just joining us part time until the second semester of school starts?" Jagger asked directly.

"Yeah, I won't be here on Mondays," I answered immediately, feeling stupid. This man didn't need to know the specifics.

"Well, we're glad to have another body." Jagger began to walk by us but then eyed the Pick in Willa's hands. She tried to pull it close to her side and hide it from view, but it was clearly too late. "Please tell me that this isn't the Pickaxe you are becoming a Specialist with?" He then looked at mine, with its bent and mangled head, and sighed further. "Willa!" he exclaimed. "The kid might not know any better, but you? Are you trying to rob the company?"

"There always be a probationary period, Jag," Willa countered, some heat in her voice like she took offense to being told she was an idiot, or maybe the implication that she was a bad influence.

"Morning, Mr. Vance," my father said, his greeting accompanied by the squeal of the trailer door. "I see you're questioning Willa again."

"Morning Gary," Jagger responded quietly, his bloodshot eyes still on Willa. "I wasn't trying to upset her. I'm just surprised that you're part of the cockamamie scheme too…" He turned his head and narrowed his eyes at my father. I felt my brow furrow. What the husk was cockamamie?

Smegma was snickering from where he perched on a nearby parking sign.

"It's only crazy if it doesn't work," my dad said as he walked down the steps and extended a hand toward Jagger. Jagger's narrowed eyes looked at the proffered handshake with disgust. My father's face attempted to stay schooled in a happy grin, but I knew him, and he definitely wanted to either laugh or smile wickedly. Willa snickered from beside me, telling me which one it was.

"Good luck today, then!" Jagger spat and fled into the office.

Willa broke into actual laughter and my dad joined her with a much more muted chuckle. Seeing me scan between him, Willa, and the door that Jagger fled through, my father explained, "He's a bit of a clean-freak but also a firm believer in gentlemanly conduct. So," my father's face broke into the wicked grin that had been threatening for a while. "If you ever want to get him off your case, you just need to offer a dirty Miner-handshake."

"It be workin' all of the time, ninety percent of da time," Willa said jokingly but sobered a moment later. "Just don't be tryin' it if you be in actual trouble. His head might explode if it tried that level of moral computin'."

"So, we don't like him?" I whispered as we began making our way out of the trailer section and toward the Portal. They both nodded.

This morning, the Portal we were going into was inside the city. In fact, it was inside a high school, which was why a group of kids and some parents were across the street on the sidewalk. Someone had even erected a temporary fence for about five hundred yards in both directions to stop anyone from getting closer. The same temporary fence was set up around the perimeter of the school.

A few parents and kids held up signs, and I read them before reading them again. Some parents were protesting leaving the Portal open so long since their kids were out of school. While others held signs I was more used to viewing on the TV at Hunter Combat events. Signs like 'Beastmode have my babies!'

Maybe the ones holding those weren't parents...

"I guess this Portal was cleared by Lynx?" I said, connecting the sign with the Guild.

"Yep," my dad confirmed. "It's a red-sun desert inside. The Monster Corpses I've seen were all insectoid. However, our biggest concern is parasites in the cave we're trying for."

"Parasites?" I asked.

"Really?" Willa asked, looking at my father with concern. "Ya think it's a good idea to bring Brodie in there?"

My confusion only grew as my father's face paled. "What the husk is going on?"

"Hey! Language!" my dad said, sounding like the response was startled out of him. He looked me over. "Son, Willa makes a good—"

"You need to explain!" I said, cutting my dad off before he could finish the thought that would likely damn me to staying outside the Portal today.

"Parasites be a general term for things like leeches, mosquitoes or ticks, Brodie," Willa responded in his place. "However, they don't be feedin' on your blood, but your Mana Pool."

"Oh," I said in startled realization. "Ohh!" I said with a bit more emphasis. They were worried that it would bring back the trauma from my assault. "Don't they take care of most of the creatures before we go in, though?" I asked.

"They probably had a Fire Mage bathe each chamber in fire, sure, but Parasites aren't like Slimes. They're small and can easily hide in cracks or crevices to survive. In almost every operation with parasites, we'll get at least ten to twelve bites per Miner," my dad further explained.

"Then how do you all deal with it?" I asked, to which Willa slapped an imaginary bug on her forearm. I pointed to her. "You're saying they're exactly like mosquitos?" My dad looked at Willa and then me before nodding with a clenched jaw.

"So, I can kill them personally with a slap of my hand?" I asked, trying to press my point. I decided to focus on the ease with which Willa and my dad seemed to handle these Parasites, instead of trying to convince them I was over the assault.

Considering the attack happened on Monday, and it was Saturday, I doubted I could make that point.

"We can have him be workin' closest to the Light Stone, Gary," Willa said, making a case for me. I speculated that the Parasites must not like the light, based on her words.

"The problem is, if we go in there and have to call in a favor for an escort out, it will cut into everyone's bonuses." Gary pointed to the group of Miners we had been walking toward before we'd stopped to have this conversation.

"But if the three of us can mine one Ore deposit each, by the end of the day it will be increasin' the bonus, too! I know that be a risk I be wantin' took if I was given a choice," Willa countered again.

Since she seemed to be on my side now, I let her make the arguments for me. She knew far better which points to emphasize.

[Smegma, are Parasites really that bad?] I asked in an aside to my Demon-Imp trader.

He waved a hand to dismiss the question, like it was beneath him. "They're only bad if you don't find them. Eventually they suck you dry and lay eggs in your corpse."

[Husk!] I mentally said with a start, not having expected that response after the dismissive wave.

"That's exactly right." Smegma agreed. "In the worst cases, you get Husked and die, but I'd put that at about the same equivalent of your world's Darpin Awards. If you take yourself out of the gene pool like that, you pretty much deserve it."

Gary and Willa resumed their walk toward the other Miners, and I had to play back the end of their conversation to make sure I was meant to join them. Willa had won the argument, but by the not-so-subtle glances my father was giving me, he wasn't totally convinced. I pretended I didn't notice.

Thirty minutes later, we were led through the basement of the school and into a gymnasium. Atop the logo of a panther sat a red Portal. Our group, with three Lynx guides in the front, walked directly into it without pause. The change from the climate-controlled gym to the dry, arid heat made my first inhalation stutter. It felt like the air burned my esophagus and I coughed, which only irritated it more.

Willa, who was beside me, pulled up my mask for me as I was doubled over coughing. I didn't think it would help, but to my surprise the next inhalation, while hot, didn't feel like it was burning me from the inside. My exposed skin between my Miner's gear was another story, but it only felt like I would be coming home with a sunburn.

"It be the fine sand particles that cause the most problems," Willa explained. "They actually be hotter than da air. I should have been warnin' ya."

I shrugged and brushed off the implied apology, partly because I didn't want to risk wheezing out a response. I scanned the area for a moment but quickly lost interest in the endless red sand dunes that stretched out in every direction. Until my scan passed over Smegma, who was on the ground. Considering I had never seen him land on the actual ground so far, I paused. [You okay?]

"This is Crendalar One or Two," he said as his hand passed through the sand he was clearly trying to pick up.

[Does that mean your people might be here?] I asked, looking around anxiously.

"No, all the Demons on Crendalar One through Four died or escaped to Crendalar Five. All that's left are Monsters and baking sand." Smegma didn't look back at me, and his tone of voice gave me no hints to his mood. He'd simply stated it like it was a fact, but I couldn't help but think he was upset. Or, at the very least, unhappy with the situation.

I had questions but put them off. We'd be here all day, and I might get an opportunity to ask later. Smegma made me think I made the right decision when he changed the subject. "Is your Mana Pool full again?"

I'd woken up this morning to eighteen points of Mana to convert, and Smegma had told me that I should wait till it filled up each time from now on. That way we could better track its growth. [Nope,] I answered. [Sixteen points.]

"Okay." His words sounded odd as he stared off into the distance. "You should hold off on converting all of it while in the Mines." That last part sounded… ominous, and his next words only confirmed it.

"You might need the buffer if a Crendalarian Mana Leech latches on."

CHAPTER 22

Saturday, April 6th, 2069

I felt the Mana in my Pool start to course through my body just as I heard Smegma say, "Ankle." Peeling back the top of my boot, I squished the strange, segmented leech-like insect. This was the fourth one I'd killed, but the only one so far to succeed in biting me. So, when it died, it mildly exploded with red blood. My blood. I swallowed my nausea and pulled the things teeth out of my skin with a harder yank than I thought it should require.

[Can you—] I began to chastise Smegma on the late warning, when suddenly the world became purple, gray, black, red, green and shades of orange. Considering that a moment before I could only see a sphere of perhaps thirty feet around me, thanks to the Light Stone on a pole, and that everything had been a dusky brown, Mana-Crystal-blue, or the shimmering colors of metallic ores—this change shocked me. It took a disorienting moment of looking around to realize that the new vision was in many ways superior to my limited one from before.

As long as I was actually seeing well outside of the sphere of light... and not just hallucinating.

Thus, my instinctive closing of my eyes and shaking my head to clear it was nearly instantaneous. When I opened my eyes again, everything was back to normal. Smegma answered my unspoken chastisement, anyway, likely sensing my intent even though I'd cut off.

"I'll try to pay more attention, but that one was flung off Willa's Crystal as she Sharded it."

"What the husk was *that?*" I asked, my brain realizing that Smegma wasn't going to know, but my confusion needed an outlet.

"I basically just told you it was my bad," Smegma responded, and I winced realizing that not only had I exclaimed that out loud, but I'd also made the Imp think I was angry with him. Both Willa and my dad rushed to my side, as if I had just suffered some grievous wound.

"Are you okay?" they asked in near unison, sounding like a harmonizing band that was nearly ready for a performance.

My dad started to look me over and, of course, found the blood on my hands. Willa, in the meantime, had found the blood on my boot and then leg beneath. My dad continued, "Where did it get you? How long was it attached?"

Willa began pulling out antiseptic spray and gauze bandages. I began kicking my foot and waving my hands back and forth across my chest. "I'm fine. I'm fine. Stop it! It's just a bug bite..."

They, of course, didn't stop. My father grabbed both my shoulders and manhandled me to a sitting position on the somewhat-clear floor. The level of his superior strength was on display as he 'guided' me down. There were still a ton of F-Rank Shards under me, but thankfully my gloves and leather pants prevented me from being stabbed by any sharp ends. Willa sprayed on the antiseptic and I flinched. "I knew we shouldn't have brought you. God, what is your mother going to say when I tell her!"

"Would you two calm down?" I shouted, managing to startle them with the volume. Now that I had their attention, I pointed to the ankle and then my face. In a much more reasonable tone, I explained, "It was just a single bite and I got it before it even managed to get more than a single drop of Mana. It was nothing more than a big bloodsucking worm!"

Willa wrapped the bandage around my ankle with a practiced hand, before cutting it and tucking it in on itself. "That's good, then," she said. "I wouldn't want to be losin' my Pickaxe repair guy! They be hard to find."

I saw her attempt at lightening the mood and jumped on it with a good-natured chuckle. My dad, whose face had gone deathly pale, didn't manage to laugh but did manage a smile before he, too, tried to improve the atmosphere. "So, you won't be telling your mother?"

"Last time you said something similar, *you* were the one that went and tattled. All I wanted was the time for a shower, but noooo, as soon as we got in the house, you spilled all the details, not two minutes later!"

"Not *everything!*" my dad countered.

"I bet he did tell her everythin'. So, he still be the worst secret-keeper in the world, ya?" Willa asked.

"Have you been burned, too?" I asked.

Willa scoffed. "Let me tell ya one of many stories—"

"Come on, guys! I'm not that bad," my dad complained, cutting Willa off. He looked worried about what story Willa might share.

"So, you aren't going to immediately crumble and tell Mom when you get home?" I asked.

"Well, I mean, that's your mother and my wife we're talking about here, son…" he said after a few gaping-fish-mouthed nonsensical noises. Willa and I threw up our hands and started laughing. Smegma eyed the exchange without saying a word. Giving us a look like we were all idiots. "Whatever!" my dad added into our laughter, chuckling himself. "We better get back to work!"

"Don't worry, I be tellin' ya the story later," Willa whispered loud enough to be heard and my father began shoving her back to her abandoned Pickaxe. She began roaring with laughter and I had a few chuckles at my father's antics. It felt good to see him in his natural environment with a friend. Not that he wasn't the same man as a father and husband, but this good-natured ribbing wasn't something I was used to seeing him fall victim to.

I stood up and looked at Smegma. [Sorry, I didn't mean what I said as a hit against you—]

"Two more in the Shard pile you're sitting on," Smegma interrupted, tone serious, and suddenly my standing motion became a lot more hurried. I found the two segmented bugs on top of the Sharded Crystals, seeming to be in the very spot I'd just vacated. I used my boot to squish both, in two aggressive stomps.

My dad and Willa looked back over their shoulders, but I ignored them. This wasn't a sign of overreaction. There had been two Parasites.

[As I was saying, my exclamation was because my vision suddenly changed.] I happened to blink again as I mentally sent that thought to Smegma. Suddenly, the world went back to the odd purple overtones. [Holy shit, it happened again. It looks almost like the movie camera version of infrared or night vision or something.]

I purposefully didn't blink and began studying my surroundings. My father and Willa were lit up in red, orange, and green. I quickly looked away when I realized I could see the shape of Willa a bit *too*... well. Looking at my own hand, I saw the same pattern.

"What the hell are you talking about?" Smegma asked incredulously. "Did the bite from the insect really make you insane, like they think?" he motioned to my father and Willa.

[I'm not making this up. I can see all the heat signatures in this entire cavern.] I pointed out the two nearest Parasites and then squashed them with my boot. Then I turned my head to stare at Smegma. Only to find him not in the spot I thought he had been. I kept looking around. Mentally, I tried to send Smegma a mental image of what I was seeing, similar to how he could read my surface thoughts. I tried to *push* the image outward, however, I wasn't sure whether I'd succeeded or not.

"You really aren't making this up!" Smegma exclaimed from a place nearly atop me. I spun in the direction of the voice but again found no Smegma. "You really can't see me?" he asked, and it sounded like it came from the spot I was intently staring at. "Did you just get a new Skill down here in a Portal?"

I shrugged in response and then attempted to turn it off. A single blink and it was gone. Smegma popped into the space directly in front of my eyes between one blink and the next. I jerked back but managed to hide the action slightly at the last moment. Thankfully, both Willa and my father weren't looking at me.

I blinked again, expecting for the infrared to return. It didn't. [How do I turn it on and off?]

"Skills like that usually need an action paired with an intention," Smegma responded while stroking his pointy chin in thought. The next few blinks after his instruction, I managed to toggle the Skill on and off at will. Smegma floated down to the latest two newly dead parasites, still stroking his non-existent beard. "I wonder?"

[You wonder what?] I asked as I picked back up my Miner's Pick and began Sharding again. Smegma didn't answer right away, and I kept toggling on and off the infrared to ensure no other parasites were nearby.

I ended up killing one more that was approaching me when Smegma finally spoke again. "These things don't have eyes," he commented, sounding offhanded but floating to the newly squished corpse I'd just created. "What if they see using heat?"

Those two hints made my eyes shoot open wide. [I killed them. Just like Morgan Hallsbrad! Are you thinking I somehow inherited their Skill?]

"I'm still not sure if any of this is a product of *Demonic Vault*—or not. So, maybe? But these things don't have 'vision,'" Smegma began tapping his teeth with a talon. "So, you couldn't get a 'vision' related Skill from them. Unless—"

[Unless what?]

"Unless it isn't infrared vision, but something like *Heat Sense*. Try turning on the Skill but not focusing the intent to your eyes."

It didn't work, despite me trying numerous times. I kept working as I went, not wanting to alert Willa or my father.

Smegma, in time, shook his head. "Then, I guess you must have Awakened a new Skill due to stress…"

There was a part of me that was relieved at his pronouncement, and another part that was disappointed. While I didn't want to be a Cannibal, having the ability to consume Skills from Monsters that attacked me wasn't a bad thing. I shrugged between swings, trying to hide that piece of disappointment. It would have been nice to be special and use my will to resist the path of Morgan Hallsbrad.

Still, I was working toward getting Skills *plural*, right? I guess I was pretty special in some sense, after all. I decided to not Shard my next Crystal. I could really use another Spent Mana Crystal to identify what this new Skill was.

Smegma surprised me with a question, "Would you be up for an experiment?"

[What kind of experiment?] I mentally asked dubiously.

"Let another one bite you before you kill it," Smegma stated excitedly. "I want to see if you get another Skill. You know since you didn't go strobe light on us…"

His last contemplative sentence made me pause. I hadn't glowed—so maybe I had stolen a Skill? I wasn't keen on the experimenting idea, but the lingering excitement from the idea of being a Cannibal rekindled a bit and somewhat forced me to make a slow, reluctant nod. I kept working and watched in infrared as a single Parasite approached.

My body trembled as I let it crawl up my boot and then under the cuff. I felt the moment it bit me, thanks to being hyper aware of its location. I shocked myself by not flinching immediately. I further surprised myself when I let it have a single drop of Mana before I killed it.

Breathing heavier than I probably should be in the situation, I waited. I tried holding my breath despite my lungs screaming. Nothing happened. No change in my vision, and no burst of light either.

Smegma watched me closely and then sighed audibly when I didn't react. "Well, that was anticlimactic," he said sadly. "It was worth a try, though."

The lack of light was still strange. I clearly hadn't naturally re-Awakened. That or maybe the Skill was just really low level?

I continued working, managing to get a Mana Crystal out in one full piece before selling the Mana inside to Smegma. It was time to figure out what was going on. Over my shoulder to Willa and my father, I shouted, "Going to take a quick snack break."

They both grunted in affirmation, which allowed me to move back to the cooler with my low-rank Spent Mana Crystal and grab a granola from the exterior side pocket. I chewed mechanically while holding my hand atop the Spent Crystal and feeding it Mana. I had my back to my father and Willa, with the Crystal in my lap. I was also on the edge of the Light Stone, so I didn't worry about Willa or my father seeing.

A short five minutes later, I held three Cards in my hands. Two were instantly recognizable, since the patterns on the back were the same as the ones I'd seen in my room. The other, though, looked drastically different. It was a shiny green that reminded me of grass after rain, and the five swirls of orange that decorated the rest in evenly spaced sections reminded me of caricatures of the sun.

Smegma landed on my shoulder as I turned it over and blinked at the card title.

Heat Sensitivity
(11)
Skill Type: Passive-Intentional Activation
Skill Rank: Low E-Rank (Evolvable)
Users can make a body part sensitive to the energy fluctuations given off by heat. This Skill is primarily used on the eyes but can be applied to any body part.
Toggle the Skill on and off with a physical action and intention.

"So, it *isn't* a vision Skill!" Smegma exclaimed. As soon as I mentally read the description, I tried to activate the Skill on my body, just like I had earlier. This time, it worked without a single hitch. I could now feel the heat my body gave off, as well as the nearest heat sources within about thirty feet.

[Yeah,] I answered while scratching my head. [Although, I tried the same thing I did earlier, but this time it worked.]

Smegma gave me an intense look then began scratching his chin again. "In theory, that change could be because now you're certain of what the Skill can do. But try applying it to your eyes again."

I did so and the change this time was more evident. The tones my eyes were seeing were the same, but different. Now if I was looking at something that gave off a red hue, it had several different shades to it. The purple that the heat faded off to also had different tones. I could tell that each tone was trying to depict a different temperature, but without a legend or lookup table, I'd be guessing what each one was representing. Still, clearly red was the highest and black was the absence of heat.

[It's different,] I said offhandedly as I looked around. This time, something did appear where Smegma perched on my shoulder. It was very faint, but there was the smallest outline of purple so dark, it might have just been my imagination.

"Time for a few more experiments," Smegma said with perverted excitement. I shivered but nodded even as my heart sped up.

[Wait. You don't think that the little eleven next to the Skill tag was because…] But I knew that's exactly what he thought. Was I really willing to let these insects suck my Mana? My mental fortress seemed to claim I was not only willing but prepared…

Five bites later, it was lunchtime, and I had a new Spent Mana Crystal to use. Thankfully, Willa and my father ate lunch while studying the different Ore deposits in the room. From the overheard conversations, they were trying to decide which ones they might be able to mine. I ignored them as I mechanically shoveled my mother's famous lasagna into my mouth.

The second Spent Crystal vanished in a small display of light that made my father glance in my direction right near the end, but thankfully it was over by then, and the three Cards in my hand weren't visible in the semi-darkness.

I put the second *Demonic Vault* and *Recovery* cards in my chest pocket with the other ones and then hurriedly flipped the green card over. Sure enough, as Smegma suspected, it wasn't the same. Throughout the rest of the morning, I had let the bugs bite me and had kept using the Skill. I was aware that the Skill was showing me more shades of colors, and even heat sources further buried in the sandstone.

Heat Sense
(50)
Skill Type: Passive-Intentional Activation
Skill Rank: Peak E-Rank
Users can make a body part extremely sensitive to the energy fluctuations given off by heat. This Skill is primarily used on the eyes but can be applied to any body part.
Toggle the Skill on and off with a physical action and intention.

I toggled it on my body and thought I could now sense heat sources in about a ninety-to-one-hundred-foot bubble. Still, the ones far away got a bit jumbled. I reached out and dug through the nearby Shard pile to grab a parasite and squish it maliciously between two fingers.

"It's no longer Evolvable," Smegma said, and I nodded while showing him the bug.

[I noticed that, too. Which is why I'm not letting any more of these little huskers bite me.]

"What if they have another Skill, though?" Smegma countered but ruined it with a laugh. "Yeah, the last three were probably overkill," he admitted.

CHAPTER 23

Saturday, April 6th, 2069

"There isn't much in this chamber of high value," my father said as he came to rejoin me.

Willa followed behind but did point to one vein on a wall she'd been studying by herself. "Could be that it be havi' Shilver dust mixed amongst da True Silver."

I let the two discuss that as I studied the wall Willa mentioned. I toggled on my new heat vision and found a dark patch of stone. It had been too much to hope that my new Skill would be helpful.

"It likely be the most valuable deposit in da room, either way," Willa argued. "Plus, True Silver be softer…" They both looked to me and I nodded my agreement. "Words about how ya Skill be workin' *inserted here*," Willa said sarcastically.

"Oh," I whispered as my face grew hot. "Still figuring some of that out, but in theory, as the pick repairs, it will work better?" Willa blinked at me, her look telling me that was obvious.

"Well, you see," I began awkwardly. "Even Ores have Mana, so the mark should—"

"I think we get it, Son," my father said, saving me from my stumbling explanation. "Willa, stop giving Bro a hard time. You knew as well as I did that was how it worked."

Willa started laughing and even punched my father in the shoulder. "We don't even make decisions on what Ores to mine, kid," she said in my direction. "I just be pokin' fun."

"Well, as I said, I'd stick to only Mining one Ore vein today, and choosing a lower valued one, too," I countered, my voice infused with false confidence. "The Picks will only be better tomorrow for it."

Willa and my father nodded. It was just the three of us in this room, and thanks to my heat vision, there were practically zero Mana Leeches. I stood and squashed one of them that had inched closer as I ate.

"Get back to it?" I asked as I ground it with my foot. Willa and my father exchanged raised eyebrows.

"I be bitten a few times and am getting' the feelin' that my Mana is at about half. So, I'm gonna be sittin' to eat." Willa shivered before looking at my father, who nodded along with what she was saying. "Your kid be built different Gary."

I blinked, even as my dad shiver-shrugged and blushed. "I need some food and a break to let my Mana replenish, too. I got bit four times myself. You sure you don't need more time, Brodie?"

"Nah, I'll keep going and try to keep an eye out for Leeches near you," I answered, realizing that *Recovery* was likely playing a big role in my current energy levels. Either way I picked up my Pick to get back to work.

"As long as neither of us be gettin' Husked, everything should be—" Willa was cut off as a massive tremor shook the cavern. Echoing shouting accompanied the shaking floor. The shouts seemed to come from a far way off but bounced up the tunnel that led deeper into the caverns. Were they growing in volume?

"Uh, people are coming," Smegma said as the screaming grew—and now with the proximity, I could tell they were shrieks of horror. Ten Miners exited the tunnel at a dead sprint. Their faces were contorted into masks of terror as they continually looked back over their shoulders.

"What's going on?" my father shouted in a commanding voice.

"King Leeches!" someone nearest the front cried—and I instantly felt my father's strong hand, on my shoulder, he spun me toward the exit, then used his Pickaxe to crosscheck me with the handle and get me moving. Willa was already a few steps in front of me as the caverns gave another violent shake.

"What is a King Leech?" I asked as my father corralled me into a jog, then a sprint, both of us heading toward the exit.

"I'll tell you outside!" my father yelled. "Just run!"

"Wait!" Smegma shouted, flying after us. "Where are you going? Think of the Skill one of *those* could give you!"

I gave the Imp the finger with my one free hand, not caring if anyone saw or not. [I can't use a husking Skill if I'm dead!]

A few steps in, I was at a full sprint. It felt like running out of a building when the fire alarm was test screeching—but wondering if it was really necessary. However, considering that the current screeching screams were from seasoned Miners, I decided that my statement to Smegma held.

It was time to get the husk out.

Thankfully, we were the first cavern before the exit and so were outside in a short couple of minutes. The Miners that came from deeper stopped their shrieking in favor of gasping in air.

A Lynx Guild member who was stationed out front instantly asked, "What's going on? Is everyone okay?"

He directed the question at my father, who could only give the other Miners a look before saying, "King Leech, not sure where, but I felt the tremors."

"Husk," the guard exclaimed and then pulled a signal flair out of his pocket. A quick pull of a cord sent up a red ball of light as the guard grabbed a walkie talkie from his pocket. "Twenty-three, red flare. Trouble at the Mine, may need Excavators or our members with Earth Skills. Over."

"Guild Command. Assistance en route. Over." The radio chirped almost as soon as the man let go of his button.

"Can you explain what's going on?" I whispered to Willa. Searching the area, I didn't find Smegma but figured the Ghost-like Imp would be fine on his own. It wasn't like he could get far in any case. Actually, that last thought made me wonder if the invisible tether on my demonic little buddy got longer with the increase in the levels of *Demonic Vault*. I thought of a free-ranging Smegma,

194

popping his head in whatever shower or corner of the world he wanted to, and shuddered.

"King Leeches be rare. They be more a mix of a Worm and da small Leeches we be squishin' throughout the day. The problem is they be tunnelin' through walls, creatin' massive instability—" she was cut off again as another group of Miners streamed from the entrance.

"Anything to report?" the guard asked the first one of the twenty people.

"Four King Leeches surfaced in the cavern we were Mining in. Our team was second to last," one of the Miners answered even as he gasped for oxygen. "Jeral and the two Hunters were attempting to hold them in the cavern as we escaped, but the group of Specialists in the lowest cavern is trapped."

"I'm sure Jeral—" my father started saying but cut off as everyone outside of the Mining cave was shaken violently to the ground. My eyes closed unbidden as what felt like an invisible hand grabbed me and threw me into the sand. I opened them and turned on my *Heat Sense*. What I saw shouldn't have been surprising since I was on sand baked by the sun. My entire field of vision was varying hues of red except the cave, which seemed to be a mild yellow. That felt strange since I was looking at the sandstone rock—shouldn't it be…

The stone at the top was orange but the ground and mine itself grew darker, going purple, dark blue and then black.

"What the husk is *that* thing?" Smegma asked unhelpfully as the sandstone mine exploded.

No, as I watched, I realized it hadn't exploded but had been launched skyward with such force that sand shot into the air in a cloud. Many pieces of stone chipped off and bounced away. Behind the now-flying section of stone came a large, gray body.

"Oh shit!" Smegma said, seeming to realize what this creature was. "That's a husk-damned Sandworm."

Smegma and I watched it climb higher and higher, breaching into the sky with me on the ground and him floating in the air just above me. The hot sand started to fall creating a cloud that quickly started to obscure my vision. I felt that tickle in my throat and pulled up my mask.

"It's going to fall!" someone shouted, and as my heartbeat exploded in terror, I felt the strong hands of my father or Willa grab me and hoist me to my feet. I like the others left our Picks behind in the sand. Part of me wanted to go back for mine and at least Willa's and my fathers, but there wasn't time.

I immediately blinked my heat vision on, then off, realizing it wasn't helping in the situation—the Sandworm was a yellow-black, the falling sand a fading orange—and my regular vision would serve me better here. My father shoved me away from the huge dusky brown body that was slowly stopping its upward ascent.

Its body must have been at least two hundred yards into the air, and my far-too-calm brain finally translated the problem. It wasn't going to stay up there like a cobra ready to strike. It was coming down, and from the slight angle of its body, it was coming down in a direction not far off from the one we were all gathered. The shadow from the sun didn't help since it was cast out behind the creature.

My father seemed to have decided to sprint after the Hunter who, admittedly, was the only one strong enough to not be flung back and forth atop the shaking earth. Instead, the Hunter ran in a single, undeviating direction.

The ground continued to shake and buck under my feet, not helped in the least by the sand, making me realize the semi-staggering run everyone was making wasn't a choice. Clearly, the Hunter was far stronger or more practiced in these types of situations than the rest of the people.

"Brace!" someone yelled, and I had enough time to soften my knees before the sand leaped. Literally—the top layer of sand was suddenly at my knees, and I was watching it fall back to the ground, covering my shoes. I glanced back and found the Worm had hit the sand in a direction away from us.

Lucky. And not just because it missed us—it also missed the Picks…

As if someone was filming it in super slow-mo, the Worm slowly bent its back and got its head at an angle with the ground that it seemed to deem acceptable before sliding into the sandy ground like it was easing itself into a pool.

The whole group stayed deathly silent until nearly half of its visible body vanished. The thing's total length may have been anywhere from five hundred yards to over half, or even a mile long. It just kept bunching itself up and 'metering' itself forward in huge sections.

"What the hell was that?" I asked, directing the question to everyone present.

"It must have gotten in last night some time," Smegma answered. "It isn't a carnivorous creature and likely sensed the Mana Crystals. One thing's for sure— that thing is way above the ranking for this Dungeon."

"Miner!" the Hunter said, approaching the man who had 'reported' earlier. "Was Jeral near the entrance, following you, or in the deep cave when you last saw him?" The Hunter's face was pale—and I felt my own mirror his at the reminder. There had been people down there.

"He was nearly in the deepest cavern we were Mining in," the Miner responded before puking. "He was trying to get the Specialists out."

"You'll have to come with me to report to the Guildmaster," the guard said, even as a few other Miners emptied their stomachs.

A guiding hand from Willa told me that everyone was going to follow the guard, and I managed to get my semi-numb legs to start working. I couldn't help but wonder if this sequence of events was somehow planned. It just felt too coincidental.

"Nah, kid," Smegma said, his voice hard. "Those King Leeches likely felt the Worm coming and were trying to get out of the way—beast senses are keen. If Jeral had abandoned those Specialists in the deepest cavern, then he could have made it. Unfortunately, he wasn't that kind of man."

I could only look back over my shoulder as the massive body of the Worm continued to literally 'worm' itself into the sand again. The now-gravesite of one of our city's heroes.

CHAPTER 24

Saturday, April 6th, 2069

"**O**ur insurance isn't going to take a hit on this," Jagger Vance growled as he and a powerfully built giant of a man walked into a police trailer. All the surviving Miners, Gardeners, and Cleaners from his company sat around either on the sidewalk, curb or front lawn of the high school.

The Lynx Guild also formed its own group at the side parking lot of the building. They surrounded the police cars and even the trailer that Jagger had just entered.

"Want me to go see what they're talking about?" Smegma asked, causing me to blink. I nodded after a moment and the flying Goblin phased through a wall of the trailer a few moments later.

"Who was the man with Jagger?" I asked as I turned to my father. I could immediately tell he wasn't in a place to talk. His face was pale, and his eyes were unfocused. I spun to my other side and found Willa looking green but in a better place than my dad.

"That be the Lynx Guild Leader—Taz," she said simply, her voice sounding like she was faking a sick phone call. I could tell she wasn't faking anything. That she wasn't physically ill but simultaneously had her stomach turned in knots.

I wondered if I should be feeling the shock or illness the two currently were. While I was 'shocked' by the sudden death of the Hunters, Banks, and Miners, I hadn't exactly known any of them personally. I realized that I was trying to explain away how calm I felt but already knew the reason. *Mental Fortitude.* Just like after Morgan Hallsbrad's assault and death.

Simply put, it felt like months had gone by since the incident with the Worm instead of a few hours. So, why was I making up other reasons for my lack of reaction?

Because the more I went through, the more I didn't like the thought of a Skill messing with my mind—with my emotions.

Even now, *Mental Fortitude* was reigning that feeling of discomfort in, calmly collecting my thoughts, and directing my mind to what Willa had just said. That was the 'Tazmanian Devil,' the only known S-rank Hunter in the Windsor area. Thanks to that fact, it didn't take my Skill long, or much effort, to redirect my attention.

"Wait—that's him?" I asked in a whisper, trying to recall what he looked like. Sadly, I had been too focused on Jagger and the argument, to notice anything but his size.

Willa blinked once, and then a couple more times, her eyes coming into focus. Her face, still a little green, gained back a shade of color. I could tell the distraction helped because a small smile grew in the corner of her mouth as she started talking.

"When they be sayin' indestructible—they be meanin' it! Gary and I saw him pull out a Rakshasa Fang that be stuck in his chest. It had to have been hittin' his heart or lungs, an' Rakshasa poison literally be meltin' your guts. Taz just kept goin'. He almost doesn't be seemin' human when he be doin' stuff like that."

Where her voice normally would have been excited, this time it started out somewhat flat—but picked up a bit more as she continued. I turned to my father and saw that his face had regained some color and his eyes were now focused on his hands.

I tried a follow up, "Is it true that his armor also regenerates?"

"Not sure," Willa said as she scratched her head. "The gear he be wearin' into the Dungeon always be lookin' the same—an' there definitely would have been a massive hole or cuts in it that day. But that could also be the man buyin' multiple sets of the same armor. I'm inclined to be believin' the latter. Why would ya be needin' expensive armor if ya can recover from almost anythin'?"

"That's what they say online—that the armor being the same is him creating a narrative," I said offhandedly. "Do you know what's going on in there?" I asked as a follow up.

"They're coming to an agreement on fault and liability," my father growled. I was simultaneously startled to hear his voice so low and disgruntled, but also happy to hear him talking. "Once you enter a Dungeon, death is always a 'personal' liability. This is only the second time that workers and Hunters have died in the same incident…"

My father trailed off as his eyes started to lose focus again. I touched his shoulder, which brought his attention back to me. "What happened last time?"

My dad took a stuttering breath in and looked past me to Willa. I followed his gaze and saw her face morph into a sneer that clearly held disdain for the memory I was bringing up. My father's whisper brought my attention back around to him, "Last time, they laid off half the company…"

I could tell that was all the conversation I was going to be able to get out of him, as his eyes began trying to drill through the police trailer and likely through Jagger inside. A turn to Willa found a similar reaction, and so I let the conversation die, instead choosing to mentally ask Smegma, [What's going on in there?]

He zoomed through a wall and came back to my side. "The Guild Leader guy is strong-arming Jagger Vance into taking more than fifty percent responsibility for this."

[What?] I mentally asked. Clearly, the Sandworm hadn't been the Miners' fault. It hadn't been anyone's 'fault.'

"Yeah, according to that big blonde oaf, the Miners were causing too many shockwaves, which is what drew the Sandworm to the site. They also went 'too deep' and caused the King Leeches to grow defensive. He's claiming that if Jagger had older, more experienced Specialists, this wouldn't have happened."

198

Both my hands came up to my head and I ran my fingers slowly through my hair—trying to push and pull the words of Smegma out of my brain along with the sensation of my parting hair.

It didn't work.

[How the husk can they get away with that?]

"Well, I'd have to go back in there to be sure, but it sounded like the 'Tazmanian Devil—'" Smegma said the name very derisively, "—was subtly threatening to never hire Jagger's company again if he didn't take the hit. Want me to go back and keep listening?"

I nodded again and watched the Demon fly back into the trailer. It was about thirty more minutes of contemplative silence before Jagger Vance stormed out of the trailer. Since the first interruption, I'd left Smegma in the trailer and the Goblin-Imp followed after the storm that was Jagger.

"Senior staff with me!" Jagger commanded without even looking at the group of his employees. Willa and my father looked at each other before they both got up and walked in the man's wake.

My eyes followed them for a moment before I spun back to the trailer. I was just in time to see the back of Beastmode entering, even as Detective Flair exited. Our eyes met, and I groaned as recognition fluttered over his features. He started coming my way as Smegma was beginning to redirect from following Jagger, in my direction. I mentally told him to stop, to keep listening as I stood up to greet Flair.

"Brodie, what are you doing here?" Detective Flair asked, his tone sounding like a parent who found their child in a place they didn't belong.

"I joined my father since I didn't want to be at home alone all day," I answered. I was attempting to make the decision to work instead of taking time off, as 'directed,' somewhat more reasonable.

The Detective's eyes narrowed.

"So, let me get this straight. You believed that entering a Portal with your father would be better for your recovery than relaxing at home watching Webflick and surfing your SwiftGram?"

I held out my hands in a way to indicate everything that was going on around me. "It stopped me from thinking about it—until you just brought it up again. So, I would say it *was* working…"

"Right," Detective Flair said with skepticism but also a slight wince. "Still, with what I just heard in the command trailer, you seem relatively unbothered. So, what? Is this environment calming to you?"

"I was in the closest cavern the Mining group was working in. We vacated as soon as people started screaming and running by us. We weren't ever in any danger."

"No emotions for the people who died?" Detective Flair asked with a pointed look and a frown.

Did he expect me to be crying? I looked around me and found a few Miners doing exactly that. Maybe he did. I changed what I was going to say.

"Should I be an emotional wreck?" I gestured toward the Detective's unflappable expression. "I was certainly scared and definitely shocked by the speed at which it all happened. I've only been here for about four days, though.

Of the people who died, I think I only ever had a conversation with Sturdy Jeral. That alone should tell you how well I knew everyone. We lost one of Windsor's heroes today, Detective—one of my personal heroes. Of course I feel like shit. I'm just trying to keep it together."

"I guess that makes sense," Flair said but his tone said those words were platitudes. "It looks to me that you're doing a great job keeping it all together. Like a fifty-year veteran on the force. That's commendable."

His eyes flicked all over my face, looking for something. What? I couldn't have said, but I assumed he was cataloging my expression or lack of reaction. What was his problem?

"Well, I better get back to the Chief and fill out the paperwork," Flair said after he noticed I was studying him in turn. "Glad to see you're back on your feet." The last comment felt very off in sincerity. It made me feel like a criminal. Like he was saying, 'I'll be keeping an eye on you.'

As soon as he turned, I shivered. I knew I hadn't done anything wrong, but the man's scrutiny was making me very worried. *Illusory Truth* or not, it might be best to tell Ms. Stovall about my second Skill. Well, the story I'd concocted. My one worry there would be she'd insist on a re-Assessment and then what rank would I currently be…

"You know glaring at someone more powerful than you is kind of stupid, right?" Smegma said from behind me. I'd felt him pop back to my side sometime in the middle of the conversation with Flair, so he didn't surprise me.

[Yeah,] I began, even as I immediately stopped staring after the retreating back of the Detective. [What do you make of that conversation?]

"What conversation? He was clearly trying to get a read on you. Or do you think it's normal for people to push into sensitive topics like that?"

I thought back over the conversation and saw it in a new light. Other than the wince, Detective Flair had shown no reaction to my responses that clearly called him out on being a bit insensitive. However, did that mean Smegma was right? Was the man trying to feel me out?

[Maybe,] I admitted but countered, [He could just be trying to understand my choices.] Smegma fake-laughed and I gave him a truly withering stare. [Okay, *that's* unnecessary.]

Thankfully, my father and Willa both returned after that. To my surprise, Willa spoke to the whole crowd of Miners as she arrived. "We all be headin' into da office. Big meetin' room. Start be in forty-five minutes."

The further paling of faces told me that whatever was going to happen back at the office wasn't going to be pleasant.

"What's going on?" I asked my dad. He just shook his head and then motioned with a tilted neck toward the Ford.

Together we walked to the car, even as the other Miners made their way to their own.

"I came in with Brad," one of the Miners said as he was sitting on the grass. He had been crying, and after his statement, his face contorted into a mask of pain again. No tears came this time. Either because he was all cried out or because a new emotion was overwhelming him.

Whatever that emotion was, it couldn't be far from anger, if I was reading the reddening and contorting twitches of his face properly.

Willa went to his side and put a hand on his shoulder. In a consoling whisper, she said, "I'll take you to the office and then home."

CHAPTER 25

Saturday, April 6th, 2069

After placing the Picks in the trunk, and despite numerous attempts by me, my father remained moodily silent for the entire drive. To be fair, I didn't even realize that Jagger Vance had an office building that Gatherer's used. With the silence and disgruntled vibe from my father, I couldn't help but feel like we were heading to the principal's office or maybe an auditorium presentation on saying no to drugs?

Smegma thankfully filled me in on a bit more of what went on in the Lynx trailer. He couldn't tell me what Jagger had said to the Miners and other senior staff after because they'd gone further than a hundred yards, though.

At least that confirmed his 'chain' was still firmly in place.

"From what I could tell, Taz was strong-arming Jagger."

[You said that already, but like there must have been more to the threat, right?]

"Not really. That they wouldn't hire Portals, Portal's, Portalz again—and I guess Taz also hinted at stopping other strong Guilds, too. Horrible name for a company, just wanted to throw that out there. Is Jagger Vance slow of mind?"

[Wait, Taz—*the* Taz—threatened to have other Guilds not work with Jagger's company anymore if he didn't take more responsibility? Why?]

"No idea. Jagger was originally only willing to take ten percent of the blame. Or that was what they argued about. However, Taz essentially kept saying he was more than half responsible, and at the end of their 'negotiations,' that Jagger was sixty percent responsible?" Smegma explained, his voice sounding lost, which didn't help my own confusion.

Is it just about insurances taking a bigger hit? Sixty-percent liable means that the Miners insurance will pay out the majority of the claim. Or is it something else?

"How would I know?" Smegma answered my accidental mental questions. I tuned him out in favor of looking at the approaching warehouse. I could read the sign on the side and knew by its P-Cubed logo, along with the rather more obvious 'Portals, Portal's, Portalz' neon signage, that it was our destination.

Part of me felt sure my father wouldn't be this upset if the problem was only the Miner's insurance was taking a hit. I'd only been on the job for four days, and even I'd already seen the 'threat' of consequences when the man had been attacked by the Slime. While I was sure this incident, which involved the death of Specialist Miners and Hunters, was worse, I still couldn't believe my father's sullen silence was due to that alone.

Once parked, we waited for the majority of Miners to arrive before joining Willa, who was helping the man who'd driven in with Brad that morning out of her car. She had a Ford Ranger, which looked like it was being held together with rust and duct tape. I looked back at the Ford Escort and was shocked to find it holding its own against many of the other Miners' 'roadworthy' vehicles.

"Is that thing even legal to drive?" Smegma asked, and he zoomed around the truck. I had been about to ask the same question but held my tongue due to the stifling silence that hung over each and every Miner. It was almost like we were attending a funeral—well, that made a lot of sense. Friends and coworkers had just died—Detective Flair's reaction earlier, and my own inability to feel out the situation for what it was, worried me.

My dad began leading the way into the building and past the reception desk when the sound of slapping bare feet on the tiled floor made me swing my head around. My mother, in the same business outfit from this morning, which was currently looking far more wrinkled and worn than it probably should have after half a day's work, was running toward me in pantyhose-clad bare feet.

I turned in concern as I realized she wasn't slowing down enough. Thankfully, she wasn't a large woman and when her feet slid on the linoleum, I managed to catch her with a grunt and a forceful exhalation of all the air in my lungs. Before she could get a word in, I said, "Mom, I'm fine. Calm down."

She squeezed me tight enough that attempting to get my next breath of air became harder than it should have been. Two other arms joined the hug, and from the height, clothes and sandy dust I could see, I knew it was Dad.

Before I knew it, my mother and father had separated from me, and my father had smartly taken her into a nearby office before closing the door. I could hear her shouting from inside. About how I had been put in danger and how she could have lost us both.

Something felt like it was climbing up my throat. Still, even if I had been one of those Mana Banks that was traveling with the Lynx Hunters, I would have been at risk. Clearly, that job was a much higher risk since they hadn't made it out—so I also found a small seed of anger beginning to burn inside me at the situation.

I wanted to work in Portals. It wasn't like Miners were normally at risk. This had just been a freak accident—not to mention, we had been some of the first ones out. Standing outside the door of the office, listening to them argue about me and my safety, was grating to say the least. Part of me wanted to go in and stop them, but instead I just joined the straggling Miners and followed them to where I assumed the Meeting Room would be.

"Ahh, yes, that'll teach them," Smegma said unhelpfully.

[I'm not in the mood.]

"But why wouldn't you just tell them how you feel?" Smegma asked, sounding genuine in the question, which shocked me enough that I responded.

[I don't think my mom is actually as angry as she sounded. She was just worried and needed to vent some of that fear. She would likely be reacting the same way even if I had been in school today and only my dad had been at risk. Even if she *was* serious about locking me in my room for the rest of my life, she would be doing it out of love. So, it would be a really tough argument to have when emotions are running high. She wouldn't be able to see me as an adult in the moment. I'm her baby that needs her until she cools off a bit.]

"Okay, *Acclaxian*," Smegma said with a clear intonation in his voice, making it sound like he was calling me 'Freud' or some other psychologist. Luckily, it helped me understand what he was trying to say before he continued. "So, you don't think that they will decide to stop you from Mining or going anywhere near a Portal after this?"

[That isn't their decision to make,] I answered as I turned a corner. Two sets of double doors stood open on the right wall, and a straggler who had been three people in front of me was walking through the nearer of the two. I followed him in and immediately looked around for Willa. She was next to the man she'd driven here but had two spots saved beside her, which I assumed were meant for my father and me.

When I sat down, she gave me a nod and immediately looked for my father, so I explained, "He's arguing with my mom."

"Oh, poor Clara," Willa answered in a whisper while looking back at the doors. "Wish I could be helpin', but I be sure if my husband knew about da incident, he'd be difficult to be talkin' off his own ledge, too."

"I swear, you humans think too much about others," Smegma said. "Husk everyone else—and live for yourselves."

Licking my teeth, I considered the dichotomy of those two answers. Was asking my family to continue Mining as selfish as Smegma's response? My brain chugged along and analyzed that consideration before rejecting it. No, they weren't the same thing.

"Any idea what this will be about?" I asked, wanting to change the subject.

"I ain't huskin' jinxin' it. Let me just say I hope it isn't what happened last time," Willa answered cryptically. I stared at her, surely Jagger didn't plan to announce firing people this soon after the tragedy—right, both her and my father had been through something similar before. They'd said the last time there was a death, half the company had been laid off—and maybe it *had* happened in the meeting room…

My father sat down beside me, causing the chair to squeak and me to turn to look at him. His haggard expression changed what I wanted to say. "Everything okay?"

He gave me a chagrined smile. "You know I always side with your mother. Just going to say—good luck ever leaving the house again once you're home." I could tell by his tone that he was making light of something my mother had actually said. "She might even be putting a deadbolt on your bedroom door as we speak."

I rubbed the bridge of my nose. Did I have a headache or were my thoughts truly at war with each other?

Smegma didn't help the situation as he excitedly said, "Put your foot down and go on a Slaughter."

[A what now?] I mentally asked as I tried to understand just what type of bad advice I was getting.

"A Slaughter. You know, a quest. Kill as many Monsters and creatures that you can to prove you're a full-fledged Demon." Smegma sounded a bit fanatical as he exclaimed all of that, and I just let him have his moment—instead choosing to answer my father after too long a pause.

"It's been a rough week. Can you at least stop her from making any rash decisions until after my therapy on Monday?"

We met eyes for a long moment, but he eventually nodded. Which only really meant he would try. I knew who wore the pants in my parents' relationship—and it wasn't Dad when Mom got into one of her moods.

"Looks like everyone's here," Jagger said from a chair tucked back into the corner of the room. It was so tucked in that, until the man spoke, I hadn't seen him. Jagger wore a sour expression, but whether that was from the talks with Taz earlier, or what he was about to tell us, wasn't clear. He stood up and made his way to a movable podium that sat at the very center of the room. From my seat, I had to lean one way or the other to see around a poorly placed support beam.

"All remaining Specialists to the front," Jagger intoned. Everyone looked around the room, but no one stood. By the time I looked back to the front, Jagger was glaring right at me—no, not at me—at our group of three.

Husk, that's right. We'd signed up as Specialists just this morning. Willa and my father weren't far behind in recalling that fact because they stood up before I had the courage to get to my feet. Together, we made our way to the front of the room under Jagger's frowning scrutiny.

"As you can all see, we have three *Equipment* Specialists remaining and thirty-six Miners. Normally, that would be close to a good ratio, but since Enchanted Miner's Picks can break, the ratio needs to be about one Specialist to every five workers. As you can see, we need to hire more Specialists or we need to start laying people off."

"Well, that was husking blunt," Smegma added. The Demon actually understated that. I felt my mouth attempt to fall open at Jagger's words. He really was firing people right here—*right now!*

I looked around the room with wide shocked eyes from my place at the front and realized that everyone had already been expecting this. Thanks to *Mental Fortitude* I got control of myself and rubbed the bridge of my nose again. In theory, I could fix this problem by promising to buy a few more people Mining—

My father's hand on my shoulder drew my attention in his direction. He shook his head slightly, indicating he knew where my thoughts were going. Clearly, making this offer publicly wasn't going to work. Still, that didn't mean that people couldn't volunteer to purchase Enchanted Gear to keep their job and others, right?

No one stood to make that seemingly simple offer, though. My brow creased as my brain went into overdrive. Surely people would be willing to buy an expensive pick if it meant them plus five others could continue to work.

Nobody moved. I even got a few dirty looks from seated Miners. Like I was somehow a problem, instead of a reason five more people would keep a job.

"We'll do layoffs by seniority," Jagger said, his voice sounding frustrated but not remorseful. "If anyone has friends who could work as Specialists, let me know. Otherwise, each person laid off will get their job back based on seniority as I hire more Specialists and the ratio improves. I'm heading to my office, work it out amongst yourselves."

I blinked and Jagger was already exiting through a back door in the meeting room. My eyes stared at the closing door as I thought, [Is that it? Work it out amongst ourselves? What the husk?]

"What's wrong with that?" Smegma asked. "Now you can fight each other to the death to see who really wants it."

[That second part wasn't exactly needed. Surely you've realized that isn't how human society works.]

"You think so, huh?" Smegma said and I glanced at his hovering form without turning my head. The room was deathly silent other than the Demon's voice, which only I could hear. Smegma caught my look and elaborated. "You think Taz cared about the deaths in the Dungeon? He only cared about coming out on top over P-Cubed in negotiations. People with power don't give a husk about people who aren't stronger than them. That's the simple truth of the powerful, kid."

I looked around the room at a group of people that could easily solve the problem laid out before them. All they needed to do was form groups of six, pool money and buy one Specialty Pick between them. Then they could all work— instead…

"I've got a baby on the way; I can't afford to lose this job right now," the man who had come in with Brad cried—his face somehow so pale it looked almost blue.

That started the floodgates as many others proclaimed why they couldn't lose their jobs. The hierarchy of the group was on clear display as fifteen people stood up and walked to the front of the room through the midst of these cries. Fat Gary and Miguel were amongst this group.

These fifteen didn't say a word, which only made the situation worse as the pleas amplified in volume and severity. One man was going to lose his house if he didn't keep up with a payment plan. Another was fighting for custody of his children. The only other woman in the room claimed she had just put down first and last month's rent on an apartment, and this would ruin her. It was tough to judge the severity of each claim against another.

I turned to my father and whispered, "Why can't they just form groups of six—"

My father shook his head violently to cut me off, but it was too late. "Gary, surely your kid doesn't need to be here! Just give one of us his Pick—we'll pay you back with the first bonus."

"It will only break faster with him using it!" the man who lost Brad shouted. "He's only supposed to be a temp, right?"

The suggestions as to why I didn't need to keep my 'job' and my Miner's Pick only degraded from there, and I recognized that opening my mouth had been a bad choice. My father slammed a hand down onto the podium, causing a loud boom that shut everyone up.

"It looks like this is the division," he said into that silence. "Remember, if you know anyone who wants to be a Specialist, go talk to Jagger. I'll go let him know who's staying."

My father took my shoulder and steered me to the door Jagger left through in a hurry. Shouting broke out in our wake. Once we made it through the door, he said, "It's up to them, Brodie. As you can see, everyone has their own circumstances. Maybe there is a group of six close enough to trust each other, but I doubt it."

"How long will they be out of work?" I asked, my voice catching in my dry throat.

"Last time, it took six months to get everyone back."

"Can't they just join another crew?" I asked, hoping he would give me a more positive answer than the last.

"If they want to risk their lives, sure," was all he said.

Did he mean that, despite what happened today, P-Cubed had better safety precautions for their workers?

"That sounds like exactly what he's saying," Smegma said from somewhere behind me.

CHAPTER 26

Saturday, April 6th, 2069

My father left me at my mother's desk with instructions to drive home with her. He said he'd be a while handling paperwork, but I knew the real reason as soon as I saw her. She needed some more venting of the anxiety this incident had caused.

There was a simple solution to it, of course. I'd learned this method growing up. Whenever I saw a tear forming in her eye—I'd simply wrap her into a hug. When I had been smaller than her, it might have overwhelmed her with cuteness, but now I wanted to believe that it made her feel safe. Still, once we started driving, that tactic went out the window.

My mother's car was a two-seater since we had one and a half parking spaces at our rent-controlled townhouse. If the Ford Escort was a beater, then this was a rusty lawnmower by comparison. I wasn't even sure what year this thing was made. Still, despite it not having any of its logos remaining, I knew it was a Toyota Yaris.

"You can't go back in there! I can't lose you both," my mother said, her tone containing the bubbling, simmering anxiety she'd likely been dealing with since she'd first heard of the accident.

"Mom, we're both fine. Look, see, I'm right here," I said, waiting to get her attention. She managed a glance from the road as she coasted to a stop at a light.

She studied me with glassy eyes once she came to a full stop. "Brodie, you might think you're fine now, but what happens when the shock wears off? When you get older and this causes psychological issues? When you squander your intelligence and opportunity in school because Mining makes you money now?"

I couldn't help the huff of air that escaped my nose. That last bit was clearly a reach. I didn't have any current plans to stop attending school. Sure, if I got a Skill that could make me a Hunter, I might switch to a Hunter's track—but I didn't plan on stopping. Despite my clear humor at the situation, Smegma was studying me, and my mother, with intense scrutiny. And a frown.

Hurriedly, I responded to my mother before Smegma could get a word in. "Mom, stop it! I'm only out of school right now because Ms. Stovall suggested it. I've got my first session in therapy in two days, too. So, if there is a problem, won't whoever does that session find it?"

"Sweetie," my mom started her voice, seeming to be pleading, which didn't make sense until I saw the open tears on her cheeks. She was looking away now as she accelerated with traffic. "Why can't you just take some time off, and then go back to school next semester? Or if you have to work—maybe join a fast-food

208

restaurant chain or *like…* a Portal Material Distribution Center for experience? You could be a temp or a student on co-op, I'm sure!"

"*Mom!*" I let my complaint envelop that one word. "Those jobs might seem safer, but do you remember when the company Triple Threat accidentally brought back a Monster that was still alive. It killed all the workers in the warehouse and office building. Or how about Trip to Taco, which was serving ground King Cow, and a rampant bacteria turned them and practically the whole town into zombies?"

"There's protocols in place for stuff like that now!" she countered and I sighed.

"There's protocols in place for Mining, too," I grumbled.

She pulled the car into a parking lot with a quick jerk of her wheel that caused the car to complain with loud groans and squeals. Once sufficiently out of traffic, she slammed the brakes and mashed the four-ways button before spinning to stare at me. I absently noted that the four-ways weren't working properly due to the too quick pace of the clicking sound they made.

The tears that had been running down her cheek seemed to have evaporated in the heat of the flush that her anger brought on. She opened her mouth in what I assumed was going to be a shout, appeared to think better of it, and clicked her teeth together in a rush to clamp down whatever she had been about to say.

After a few deep inhalations and very loud exhalations, she said, "Brodie, I'm only wanting what's best for you. Surely, we can come up with a job or something you can do that's safe, right?"

My stomach twisted sideways in my abdomen. I wanted nothing more than to agree with her, but I couldn't. Not if I wanted to live my dream. Instead, I asked, "Mom, where do you think I would have been if I had become a Mana Bank?"

"Come on, Brodie, even if that happened, there is a higher chance of you being on some rich family's daughter's arm at parties than in Portals!"

"Even if that happened?" I questioned, feeling a surge of gut-wrenching nausea threatening to either cause me to vomit or scream incoherently. Thankfully, *Mental Fortitude* seemed to curb that desire and allowed me to get out the question I managed.

"Brodie, you know I support you in anything you want to do," my mom answered the somewhat rhetorical question. "I'm not saying that I didn't believe—I was trying to say that being a Mana Bank doesn't mean you'll work with active Hunters. There are other people, like Healers, who need Banks."

Her words did calm down whatever had been trying to claw its way out of my chest and stomach, but only served to morph the emotion I felt into sadness. "But that's what I wanted, Mom. I told you and Dad that. I want to be out there making a difference. Stopping things like what happened today!"

"Brodie!" my mom said, clearly ready to continue arguing.

"MOM!" Acidic bile gathered at the base of my throat as I shouted. "Don't you get it? Do you think these Portals are going to get *less* dangerous over time? It's common knowledge that they get stronger the longer they're open." The words spilled out of me.

Words and truths that had been burning away inside of me after meeting Smegma and learning of the fate of integrated worlds that failed to Evolve. There was a grinding, torrential fear churning inside me that couldn't be fully mitigated by even *Mental Fortitude.*

"If *we*, the '*Normies*,' don't try to help, then Hunters are going to get overwhelmed. Just look at what happened today. We lost one of the strongest Hunters in our area, Mom! He's the person who has provided us with the protection we've lived under. What happens if we keep losing more like him?"

I chose to exit stage left or in this case, rusty-passenger-door right. It was the only thing I could think to do that would stop more words I couldn't take back from spilling out of me. More theories and fears that were based on Smegma's words, with no grounding in current reality.

And if I was honest, this argument didn't feel like something I could win or even come out of feeling good about.

"Get back in the car, Brodie," my mom said as she rushed to take off her seat belt. "I'm sorry. I'll stop," she continued. I began walking around the side, then back of the car. Just as she got out of the driver's door, I closed the distance and wrapped her in a hug.

Squeezing her tightly, I whispered, "Mom, I understand you just want to keep me safe. Still, I'm the one who just went through these things. I'm the one who needs to decide if that means I need to stop. You want to protect me, and I want to protect you, too. But I think the best way to do that is helping the Hunters.

"I'm going to take the bus and think about that. Okay?"

She gently pushed on my biceps, and I ceded to it, allowing her to get me at arm's length. She looked up at me as tears resumed flowing down her cheeks. After a moment, she nodded and stopped the light pressure that was 'holding' me at arm's length. I wrapped her in another hug.

"Okay," she whispered into my chest. "I'll think about it too." She coughed or sobbed before changing the subject. "I'll start dinner. Are you going to come straight home?"

A small smile fought the corner of my mouth. I loved my mother. Even at times like this, where emotions could overwhelm her. Her slight shaking made me realize how much of a fight she was putting up against herself to say those words. To allow me the space to think. It meant a lot.

"Yeah, I may skip a bus or two, but I'll be home by five. Promise."

She pushed me away gently again and wiped a sweater sleeve across her face to collect the tears. "Okay, get out of here before I try to lecture you some more."

Smiling broadly now, I turned and walked away, moving to the sheltered bus stop that had prodigious enough graffiti that I wasn't sure I'd even be able to see out of the plexiglass panels. Still, it had a bench and no one around, other than the people in cars as they drove by. Why did I feel like I desperately needed that space?

"You weak humans are so husking *emotional!*" Smegma said, reminding me that he was present for that entire conversation. I wasn't sure whether I should be embarrassed or angry with him and instead settled on treating this like a conversation with Dave.

210

"Smegma, do Demon parents not care about their children?" I asked, wondering how a living creature seemed to be unable to understand a maternal instinct.

"Parents?" Smegma guffawed. "Sure, we have them, but we're born in clutches of thousands. Only the strong survive—otherwise, you're useless to the family. Parents?" he repeated his earlier sarcastic question again, this time not sounding amused. "I've never even been in the same room as the people whose genes I carry."

"That sounds awful," I whispered as I collapsed onto the bench. I glanced back to the parking lot and saw my mom's Yaris still sitting there with only one of the back two four ways blinking. I wanted to go back and try to console her but knew that would just devolve back into the argument we were having before.

Smegma distracted me again when he shouted, "Don't you pity me!"

I spun with a raised eyebrow and looked at him. He seemed to realize that I hadn't been meaning my words to come across in any derogatory way by the look on my face. He shut his mouth and after a tap of talon to teeth, said, "It isn't awful, though. It's our way of life."

"Fair," I said hurriedly, hearing the question Smegma seemed to be asking. "Just like how Demons seem to live by killing their siblings and being strong. Humans, with the capacity to only birth one offspring at a time—"

"Come on, I've seen trailers for a show where a woman had eight kids all at once!" Smegma interrupted.

"That's a show because of how insanely rare that is," I said while laughing. "Sure, some anomalies do happen. Like octuplets. But that particular 'miracle' was the result of artificial medical intervention. For the most part, humans have one child—one time a year or so. We have to protect those kids and help them grow up as best we can. Each couple usually tries to ensure their child or children can live their dreams."

There was a long pause before Smegma countered, "Then why is she trying to stop you from living yours?"

"Because she would rather me be *alive* than living my dream for a day and dead," I answered with a glance back to the parking lot. The Yaris was thankfully gone, which meant my mom was on her way home to her kitchen. I assumed I would arrive to a plethora of baked goods and overly extravagant dinner—just another of her coping mechanisms.

"So, your race is more like the Elves, then?" Smegma asked, and I spun back to him so quickly I felt my neck protest.

"What? Elves?" I said stupidly.

"Yeah, they're the race that lives on—" Smegma started before cutting himself off. "Lived on?" he repeated, sounding to be questioning not only the tense of the wording he used but also himself. "Uhhh, well, Elves are one of the races like Demons. They failed the System trials, too—I think?"

The fact that one of his taloned claws was grabbing a horn and pulling seemed a lot like pulling out one's hair in frustration. So, I smartly decided to let that topic die—for now, at least. "So, we're like them because we care for our offspring?"

"Well, they're more of the opposite extreme than you are, at least in comparison to us Demons. They rarely seem to procreate and when they do, it takes almost a decade of gestation."

"We call it pregnancy here on Earth," I informed the Demon. Then added, "So, like each of their offspring is practically sacred?"

"I think so?" he said, and I chose to change the subject as he brought his other hand up to his second small horn to start tugging.

"Ahh I see," I began. "Regardless, my mother would react that way to any situation that put me in danger. It's just what parents do. My dad was probably only so calm because he was there, but even then—I'm pretty sure that soon, if not already—he's going to realize that *I* was there. Did you see how pale he was? I bet that my safety, and how close that was today, was one of the first thoughts he had after the shock wore off."

"So, what are you going to do?" Smegma asked as he released his horns and focused his black eyes to regard me.

"First, I'm going to figure out what options I have," I said meaninglessly. Then, because it was Smegma, I admitted, "I have no husking idea."

"You were trying to sound cool there, weren't you?" he asked.

"Yep, did it work?"

"A little bit, till you ruined it."

"Well, husk you very much, then."

* * *

That night was exactly as I predicted. My mother had practically made a feast—even having stopped on her way home for more ingredients. The time by herself, and likely in large part to my father getting home before me, had helped her calm down. While I still caught worrying looks from her and my father in turn, they both seemed to have an unspoken agreement to let me decide on my own.

Unless it wasn't the *right* decision…

Smegma and I were up in my room now, and I was silently going over the gains from the day. Not only did I have over ten thousand mC, my Pickaxe and the other two I'd recently acquired were looking far better than they would have if we had used them on Ore veins. In fact, the first one I purchased seemed to be humming in my hands.

I brought up that feeling to Smegma.

"Oh, it's probably ready to extract a Crystal from, then," he said offhandedly as he 'lounged' on the bed.

Still, his words made me rush to my desk to grab the Keystone. Unfortunately, all three looked the same—and I wasn't willing to make the trip back and forth a bunch of times. So, I turned around and grabbed the pickaxe from where I'd leaned it against my lounge chair before rushing back. The second one I tried began to glow pink as I brought it up to the base of the handle.

I had a brief thought to stop and label each one but was too excited, and instead touched the Keystone to the handle base. The pink glow grew brighter until suddenly my entire vision went white. I blinked, and nothing changed. Then I tried closing my eyes for a longer period and opening them again. The change from strobing reddish-white lights to black-tinged red was the only thing that told me I hadn't just gone blind.

"What the husk, Smeg?" I asked. Then when he didn't immediately explain I added, "A warning would have been nice."

No response came, and my breathing grew heavier as my vision slowly returned. "Smegma?"

Nothing.

The first thing I saw as the world seemed to come back into focus was a familiar red box.

ERROR!

...

CHAPTER 27

Saturday, April 6th, 2069

Error!
This Enchantment has been destroyed and banned!
Assessing Criminal Case...
Three such items in possession.
Two unused.
First time offense.
Impossible to obtain Enchantment from earlier System
iteration.
Verdict: Not-Guilty
Compensating Party for destruction of Enchantment.
Scanning for appropriate Trade...
Overdraft Skill detected...
Funnel Enchant Chosen—Growth Grade.

...

My vision was just coming back into focus, and I caught up with the text that seemed to be writing itself out on the box. What any of it meant was beyond confusing, but one thing was for certain: the Enchant to create a Crystal that I had activated was banned and *illegal*. Illegal usually meant *enforceable*.

Did I want to meet the System's equivalent of police, FBI, CIA—what jurisdiction was I even in, exactly? Nevermind. The question was: did I want to meet the Cosmic or Divine or whatever-the-husk-level-of-power the System's law enforcement operated on? ...I immediately determined that no—no, I did not.

A heat began growing in my chest—coming right from where I knew my Mental Universe was. I took a quick scan of the room and realized Smegma wasn't visible or had once again popped out of existence, then I mentally dove into my Universe.

What I found certainly explained the uncomfortable building heat. Those wisps of energy that seemed to shoot off the *Demonic Vault* constellation was now a torrent. I followed the undulating banner of smoky blue energy and found it coalescing into a ball—where before it just evaporated. That ball was giving off the immense heat that had just then gone past uncomfortable to percolating.

I opened my mouth to scream but thankfully my throat was too dry to get more than a croak out before I thought better of it. My parents were right downstairs—and a scream would bring them running immediately. Surely my own Skill wouldn't kill me.

I just had to endure this. Right? *Right?*

System?!

Energy levels too high. Destruction of Host imminent.

...

Husk!

The pain cranked up a few more levels—making my already spotty vision grow black. I thought I might have been screaming already but realized that the lack of my parents hovering over me likely meant I wasn't. My whole body felt like one singular muscle—and it was currently experiencing an existential-level Charlie Horse tension. Beyond tension, actually. It was attempting to rip me in half like a stubborn piece of packaging.

Blackness consumed whatever thoughts I had, making them impossible to hold onto. The last thing I saw before the darkness fully closed in was.

Shunting...

* * *

Sunday, April 7th, 2069

"What the actual husk is going on?" Smegma asked, his voice panicked and high-pitched in a way that felt like nails on a chalkboard. My eyes opening and closing must have clued him in to the fact I was coming to.

Still, the sun streaming in my window through the blinds told me that I had passed out for more than a few minutes. I managed to tilt my head enough that my eyes could make out my alarm clock. It was Sunday, and thankfully early enough that my parents hadn't decided to come in and check on me.

So, only unconscious for a single night?

"It could be a week or even a husking year!" Smegma shouted, reading my unintentional sending. "I was thrown into the center of some black hole that was filling with Mana in the form of smoke. Then the smoke started to become puzzle pieces with sharp edges. At first, I didn't want to touch them but then I realized with the speed they were forming I was going to be sliced to—"

"Slow down," I croaked. "Whoa, man. I *just* woke up…"

"I almost died!" Smegma shouted. If the Demon-Imp breathed, I was pretty sure he'd be hyperventilating right about now.

Still, I couldn't look at him because it felt like if I tried to sit up, the back of my skull might fall off. My body was telling me that, after that happened, my brain would simply pool on the floor behind me. Smegma thankfully flew into view above my head and stared right into my eyes with his black orbs as he repeated, "I almost husking died!"

"So did I!" I choked out. "'Destruction of Host imminent,' okay? So get your shit together and tell me what happened." I immediately regretted raising my voice. Even the little bit of volume that I was currently capable of caused my head to attempt to implode. "I don't actually know what happened…" I groaned. "There was a System message. Something about an illegal Enchantment, and then another saying that I wasn't guilty—before the Enchant was changed to *Funnel Growth* something or other."

"What—does that even—are you sure?" Smegma said in a halting pattern of speech that highlighted just how out of place he currently felt. "You were *tried* by the System?" he finally added, his voice sounding so very fatalistic.

That got me to sit up. Had there been a chance of the System finding me guilty and then doing something like destroying *me*—instead of the Enchantment? It didn't seem like a far stretch, seeing how it still almost destroyed me even though I wasn't 'guilty.' Guilty of what? I had no idea. By all accounts, it wasn't like there was a Terms of Service agreement the world signed when the System decided to impose itself on our reality.

My increased headache reminded me why I was scared to sit up, but thankfully my brain wasn't actually in a puddle behind me. Slowly I got to my feet and went into a cabinet drawer looking for some ibuprofen or acetaminophen. I found both and chose to take two pills of each. Then I collapsed into my office chair and stared up at the ceiling—and Smegma, who once again chose to fly into my field of vision.

He helpfully commented, "Well, you *do* look like you almost died."

"Sure did. Somehow *Overdraft* went crazy and almost popped me like a balloon. Or maybe it was *Funnel?* I don't husking know.

"…Shunting," I whispered after a small break.

"What?" Smegma frowned. "What does that mean?"

"It was the last thing I saw before I passed out," I clarified. "There was a System message that said something about too much 'energy' and 'destruction of Host imminent'—I remember that part *very* clearly. But afterward, there was one last message. It just said: Shunting. That basically means 'to divert,' right? Did you see me have any kind of reaction after activating the Keystone? That's when things started to go sideways. After the 'System Trial,' as you called it, I started to feel this burning heat building inside of me before I got that last message and passed out. Do you think the excess energy was…"

Smegma nodded. "I saw your face start to grimace and your surface thoughts got… chaotic, and I was suddenly *there.*" The Imp shuddered. "I guess we know where the extra 'energy levels' went." He glanced over at the nearby desk and pointed. "The extra Mana must have been used to destroy the Keystones."

I reluctantly followed his gaze. There were two melted spots on my table—in the approximate spot where the Keystones for my dad's and Willa's Picks used to sit. The Picks didn't look any different—not from here at least. I hesitantly looked to my hand that had been holding the third and final Stone and found some very fresh skin on my palm and fingers. It was red enough that I would have thought I was badly sunburnt if it wasn't for the clues. The other Keystone had burned its way through my hand—but it looked like *Recovery* had taken care of that when I 'slept.'

216

"When did I become Wolferine?" I asked no one, still turning my hand back and forth. "My *Recovery* never worked like this. I mean, to heal a hole in my hand overnight? I didn't think it was that powerful. Not like that story about Taz pulling the Rakshasa Fang from his chest. My *Recovery* has only been good for keeping muscle fatigue and blisters away."

Smegma snorted, rolling his eyes.

I glared at him. "What?"

"*Recovery* prioritizes injuries that are life threatening or debilitating. So, muscle fatigue and blisters are definitely outside of that category. Plus, that's really a good thing. If *Recovery* always returned every injury you have back to normal—you'd never grow stronger or build those calluses. As for the comment about Taz—not a husking chance. If you got stabbed with a Rakshasa fang—you'd be a puddle of human slush."

"Oh." I nodded. "That makes sense. So, his *Recovery* Skill is stronger?"

This time it was Smegma that shrugged. "I can't even confirm he has *Recovery*. But whatever effect he used after pulling a Rakshasa fang from his chest... Well, I can guarantee it needs to be more powerful than a C-Rank Skill."

With that thought, I started considering how I was going to have to catch that Skill in action one day. The thought of cutting myself or something similar was disconcerting to say the least. My brain chose to deliberate on that thought and I was horrified to find it disagreed with my initial assessment. According to my train of thought, it might be worth it. I'd gain valuable knowledge from learning more about the Skill that could one day influence my very survival.

[Husk that!] I thought as I shivered. Was I even myself anymore? My own thoughts contradicting my gut feeling wasn't pleasant. It truly felt like I had somehow acquired a passenger or a new brain that was giving commentary on matters.

"Felhound style, too!" Smegma added, misinterpreting why I shivered and the direction of my thought. Then I chuckled when I realized the Demon had basically said husk something doggy-style in response. I filed that particular curse away. I might want to use that insult later.

Remembering the streaming energies I'd seen inside myself, I took a deep breath and exhaled slowly, no longer having any more excuses for not checking in and seeing what the damage was. I dove into my Mental Universe and found a new planet—or perhaps a moon this time, because it was smaller than *Overdraft*—circling the *Demonic Vault* Skill. It looked like a marble until I drew closer. Even as it grew, due to my proximity, it became clear that it wasn't truly large. I mentally prodded Smegma and said, "This is where the energies 'funneled.'"

I felt Smegma prodding at the planet before he said, "These are the same color as the sharp puzzle pieces I had to assemble. See how it all looks husking uniform! It took what felt like years to get it all together—what exactly is it?"

"I have no idea—maybe those screens would have told me but I kind of passed out."

"Pussy!"

"Dick!" I countered. "Do you think it's a new Skill or something?"

"I mean, what else could it be? It's in your Mental Universe and is an actual object. That or it's a tracker from the System to make sure you don't do anything bad. Husk, maybe it's a bomb."

"Oh, husk off!" I said but did take a good look at the metal globe-moon-planet-thing. Could it actually have technology inside to track me? Once I realized where my thoughts were going, I opened my eyes to stare at a smirking Smegma, "You know I husking hate you right?"

"Feeling's mutual, weakling." I shook my head at Smegma's response. It was so similar to what Dave might have said if he were an intangible System-induced companion. I realized that I was missing my best friend and shot off a quick 'Hey' from my phone.

It had been a week, and he had clearly seen me right after I was assaulted. I wondered why he hadn't reached out yet until I received a litany of five responses in a row.

Holy husk dude! I was starting to think you weren't allowed to have your phone. I was trying to give you space but…

If I didn't see you still posting to Swift I would have for sure marched my ass over to your house.

You doing okay?

What the husk happened? The cops only told me so much.

I chose not to immediately respond to those and instead asked Smegma the question I'd just thought of. "Does this mean I can't buy more Miner's Picks from the Store?"

"Oh, don't worry too much about that—the System *updated* the items, removing that and a few other Enchants. See, look."

Miscellaneous Professions Gear
Miner's Pick
(1)
Item Rank: Low F-Rank
Durability: Unlimited
Damage: 1-3 (x100% to Mineable minerals)
This Miner's Pick will use the Mana run-off from Crystal Mining to repair and strengthen itself, making it unbreakable. It will also Funnel excess Mana to Brodie Flacarada's Overdraft Skill.

Cost: 10,000 mC

"Does that mean that all excess Mana goes to whatever *Overflow* is doing?" I asked, even as I began distractedly sending updates to Dave. Did that mean that I needed to put as many of these things in as many hands as I possibly could? …Damn. Did I need to start my own Mining company? It would make providing 'standard equipment' easier and I'd have less explaining to do than if I suddenly pulled out dozens of these things and started handing them out like Halloween candy…

"Oh shit," Smegma said. "It probably does. It might be time to talk about changing *Overflow's* target again…"

"You're a flying rat."

"And you're a selfish pile of shit. Share the wealth."

"The same 'wealth' that nearly killed you?" I shot back.

Smegma stuck his tongue out. "Nearly killed you, too, tough guy."

I ignored the Imp as I finished my back and forth with Dave—eventually planning to meet him at the movies sometime later. I, of course, kept my new Skill to myself and everything to do with it as well, but honestly, if there was someone I wanted to tell, it was him.

CHAPTER 28

Monday, April 8th, 2069

My leg bounced nervously, and I looked around the small waiting room that was likely furnished with the attempt to look opulent. Unfortunately, it had either been designed sometime in the late nineteen hundreds or the budget for a city-run, union-affordable psychiatrists' office just couldn't buy furniture that matched.

Each individual piece of furniture or décor in the room looked like it had once been nice—or even that it would have been nice in a set—but thanks to each piece varying drastically in color, style and function, it just looked like my grandparent's house. When they had still been alive...

"Does the owner of this place not care for aesthetics?" Smegma asked. I nodded agreeably, having to wonder if it was the direction of my thoughts the Demon picked up on, or if he had been studying the room with the same disappointment I had. "It's almost like the designer just took anything he could get his hands on! For some reason, that bothers me!"

[Okay, I know why it bothers *me*, but why are you so upset?] I asked, hoping to see if my mood was truly the cause.

"Because this is clearly an attempt to appear more powerful than the owner truly is. First, they intentionally sit us in a room and we're made to wait—which is a perfect opportunity to flaunt wealth, power, or connections. Yet, this room is empty, has no prominent pictures of any meaning on the walls, and shows the total lack of wealth through the very act of attempting to flaunt it in such an ineffective manner." Smegma made a sound similar to a dog's disgruntled growl before scoffing.

So, I was definitely not the cause...

Then, to my surprise, he continued. "If one of these pieces was in this room and everything else matched, it would be a show of desire to reach above the current power strata the designer currently occupies. This!" Smegma practically shouted the word, scoffed again and then repeated it, "*This* is a total lack of care, and instead of showing a desire to grow, it shows the owner's belly. Like the person has given up on life or dreams or just anything!" Smegma finished with the sound of spitting, but I noticed nothing came out.

I looked around the room once again with new eyes. Sure, it didn't look good, but was it truly as bad as Smegma said? I pushed the cushion of the cracked, brown leather armchair I had chosen to sit in. It was comfortable—maybe that's what the psychiatrist had been going for. Psychiatrist... Was this entire room simply designed to have the sitter studying the space wondering what was going on with the decor? Was this some kind of hands-on psych test? Well, if it was, it was husking working—and apparently not just on humans, either.

Take the very next 'comfortable' chair for example. It looked like it would pepper my ass with its buttons. Plus, it was an off-white yellow that suggested it was likely stained. Each chair had similar issues—plus, there was a couch that looked like if someone sat in the center it might crack in half. Thankfully, someone exited the thick wood door that led into the office of the person I was here to see.

This man glanced my way then continued to the counter to talk with the receptionist. The room was small enough that I heard every word but easily dismissed their importance. He was just scheduling his next appointment. My eyes instead tracked toward the sound of the door opening for the second time.

In the open door stood a woman, with a clipboard that looked familiar. It was likely the same one that had the form I'd filled out on arrival. The woman had long dark brown hair that was braided and hung over a shoulder. It looked like it would reach her waist if it hung on her back. She had green eyes that studied the clipboard from behind large old wire rim glasses.

"Brodie Flack-a-rad-ish—oops—ah?" the woman sounded out. I stood and she looked away from the clipboard to smile at me. She then looked around before asking, "No parents today?"

My eyebrows rose before I could think to stop them. This woman was likely the same age as my mom and dad, meaning somewhere in her mid-to-late forties, but surely I had filled out my age on that form. Even as I wondered if I should be insulted, she seemed to catch herself. "Oh, twenty-one, sorry about that—I swear kids look younger and younger these days."

Not only seeming to decorate like an aged grandmother but speaking like one, too?

Her comment incited a questioning head tilt from me, but the woman had already spun around to head back into her office. She hadn't even looked up again from the clipboard or told me to come inside. Was I supposed to just sit back down?

"She reminds me of a distracted researcher," Smegma said, sounding oddly fond of whatever memory that thought had conjured. I glanced his way, and he shrugged before indicating he thought I should be following her inside.

The heavy wood door clicked closed just before I reached it, though—and I discovered that it was locked. Awkwardly, I turned back around and moved to my recently vacated chair. Surely she would have held the door till I was through it, if she wanted me to come in. I was halfway back to my chair when the sound of the door opening again made me spin around.

"Sorry, I totally forgot to tell you to come in, didn't I?" she said. "I was just reading over your circumstances. Come on in."

This time, she held the door, and I moved through it. As I passed, I noted her height, and found her to be very tall for a woman. She was hovering around the six-foot mark that was for sure. The office was similar to the waiting room in that its aesthetics were all over the place. Each bookshelf filled with thick hardcovers was made of a different wood, reached different heights, and seemed out of place because of it. The couch and armchair seemed to match, which was a blessing, but the coffee table was so scarred and battered that it looked like it was covered in dirt or from a kindergarten classroom.

I paused too long in the doorway and she directed me with a, "Please take a seat on the couch for this session."

I obeyed the tall psychiatrist and walked to the couch. I realized I hadn't gotten her name yet, but that was remedied when she took her seat. "Hello, Brodie, my name is Evelyn Treesong!"

Smegma distractedly hovered around the woman's chair and head. I tried to focus on her, but his breaking of eye contact made that difficult. Mentally, I shouted, [Stop that!]

"She has an Elven name," Smegma said, as if that was an explanation for his behavior. He did, thankfully, choose to fly off and examine the bookshelves.

"Hi, Ms—"

"Evelyn is fine for our sessions," she interrupted.

"Okay, nice to meet you, Evelyn," I corrected. An awkward pause followed, and it was long enough that Smegma decided to interject.

"Oh, this is going to be amusing!" he said as he sat on top of the tallest shelf. I glanced at him and found him miming eating something. That little husker…

"So, normally I'd start by getting you to retell all the events that brought you to me. In your own words. Are you up for that?" Evelyn said with a small frown that suggested she wasn't sure this was the appropriate course of action for me.

I shrugged, and at her insistent nod, told her the tale of the assault, Mana Connection, and then my previous week as a Miner. She asked a few questions that seemed to just be asking for more detail, but I suspected were actually her trying to gauge my emotions or distaste over a subject.

Why?

Because whenever I brought up 'The Shop,' she'd correct it to Morgan Hallsbrad—plus, she would ask me to go back over a spot in the story right after the correction. Like she was asking me to humanize the man, instead of calling him by his SwiftGram username.

Smegma continued to watch, giving clear signs and even comments that let me know how amusing he found this situation. I could tell that the Demon wasn't a believer in talking out problems.

"—then they laid off a bunch of Miners with years of experience and I 'kept' my part-time job. Everyone's acting like I should be sadder or hurt by what happened, but other than being shocked at how close I was to the Worm, I don't feel much. Sure, I liked Sturdy Jeral—"

"Just Jeral," Evelyn corrected.

"*Sturdy Jeral,*" I growled. "He earned that name fighting and dying for humanity. It's not a dissociation or a label to put him at a distance or whatever you think it is by trying to correct me. It's a name soaked in the blood of the Monsters he fought and the people he fought *for*, so don't try to take it away from him."

She raised both her hands, palms out as if to say 'okay, I surrender.' Her voice was soft as she asked the next question, while simultaneously writing something down in a small book in front of her. "So, tell me more about Sturdy Jeral."

"I liked Jeral," Feeling a bit bad for my outburst, I gave her a small concession, "he was nice, and clearly, he stayed behind to try to save the other Miners, which speaks very highly of his priorities, but I didn't actually know him, you know?"

"It sounds to me like you're the one who thinks you should be feeling more emotional about all the events that happened," Evelyn stated. I blinked and she pounced. "Why do you feel that your reaction isn't 'normal?'"

Swallowing the first answer, which would be the full truth about the *Mental Fortitude* Skill, I chose to say, "Everyone acts like I should be weeping, shell-shocked, curled up in the corner about all these things, or maybe even burning with all-consuming anger. Instead, I just feel upset that some of it happened to me, but ready to keep moving on with my life. Still, everyone in my life, including the police, seem to think I'm about to go bananas or something."

"*Is* the anger all-consuming or *do* you ever want to curl up and stop trying?" Evelyn asked, pulling pieces of what I said out to further examine them. She had been making small notes in a leather-bound journal the entire session and these questions incited a pause.

The silence allowed me to stop and really think about her question. I'd had a few moments where my anger had truly bubbled over—sure. But I'd been in control, I thought. I started with the second question since that was much easier to answer. "No, I've never wanted to stop trying. I want *more*. I was in school, but I'm not sure if the degree I was in will satisfy me, but I'd always been working toward helping the fight against Monsters, I dreamed of becoming a Mana Bank—"

"Why the past tense? Do you not feel like that's what you want anymore?"

Husk, that was a good question that would have been a really simple denial if I didn't have *Demonic Vault*. Now… no, I wanted to be more than a Mana Bank, I admitted. But how do I tell Evelyn about that without telling her the whole truth?

"Honestly, I want more than a degree or even being a Mana Bank. I always have but didn't have the opportunity to—"

"Interesting, so you have the capability now to reach for more?" she asked, her eyes seeming to shine with excitement. I stared at her for a long moment, trying to figure out if I should answer that question. Thankfully, a ding from her tablet that was on the battered coffee table interrupted any chance I might have had to answer.

"That's unfortunately the end of today's session, Brodie. I know today was a lot of you talking and only a few questions from me. There wasn't a lot of helpful advice, but I needed to understand a bit more before I said too much. I do think that the most important thing you need to hear right now is that everyone handles things like this differently. Don't try to conform to what society, the police, or your family think you should be doing. I'm going to email you some homework questions and some meditation exercises that should help you keep a lid on that 'all-consuming anger.' When's our next session?"

I ruminated on just how much she had inferred from my lack of responses, and tone or tense in others, as she picked up her tablet and scrolled through it.

She frowned at the screen after a moment and then chuckled lightly. "Looks like I have you for the next eight Mondays. Smells like you're being forced to be here."

"I think it's more of what you just talked about. Everyone thinks I need help to get through all this."

"Well," Evelyn said, sounding surprised. "You certainly have been through a lot, but by your very phrasing—you don't seem to think you need help. Very interesting." Her eyes continued to sparkle as she regarded me excitedly. "Okay, well please at least try the meditation and definitely answer all the follow-up questions. Next session, we'll try to see if you're right—that you don't need help."

I opened my mouth to protest her interpretation of my words multiple times as she spoke, but she kept talking over me. Plus, I didn't really disagree with the statement. Thanks to *Mental Fortitude,* I was probably healthier than I had been before the assault—mentally, at least.

So, instead of protesting now, I stood up and looked at the time. Ten thirty. I could still, in theory, make it to the Mine for the afternoon. That's when I remembered that I'd made the agreement with my parents to ask her advice on that front. "Oh, my parents want you to tell me if I can continue to Mine part time."

"That's not what I do, Brodie," she answered as she stood up, still studying me. "That is a choice you have to make."

"Can I tell them that you said I could?"

"You can tell them that I had no clinical objections to whatever you choose to do. In other words: you're cleared for duty. I stand behind any decision you make, as long as it isn't standing still and doing nothing."

I decided to join my father and Willa. Knowing that having one more Specialist there would justify the five others who hopefully were already inside the Portal.

CHAPTER 29

Monday, April 8th, 2069

"**B**rodie, are you absolutely sure you've Awakened a new ability after the assault?" Ms. Stovall asked. Through the phone, the tone of her voice sounded a hell of a lot like, *'Are you sure you want to tell me this before your court hearing?'*

After my meeting with the psychiatrist, I'd taken public transportation to the location of my father's cell phone. Sure, following his cell phone's location wasn't perfect, since the reception went out once inside the Portal, but the location tracker pinged his last location for me. Then, once I was in the general vicinity of the Mining team, it was easy to find the caution tape and temporary fences that attempted to keep the general public safe.

It hadn't even taken long, only about thirty minutes, to arrive at the University of Windsor's campus. It had, however, taken a few hours of talking to finally convince someone to call Jagger and confirm I worked with the Miners. Even then, the Mantis Guild had chosen to go inside and radio to the Mining team for further confirmation. Through that radio call, my father had embarrassingly 'reminded' me that I'd promised to talk to Stovall. So, here I was.

"Yes, at this point, I'm relatively sure," I answered after a loud exhalation.

"Do you know what it does?" Ms. Stovall followed up.

"Seems to repair equipment from Mana Spillage or something similar. I know that it can repair Mining Picks as long as they are Mining Crystalized Mana."

"So, it isn't a Combat ability?"

"Definitely not."

"Have you told anyone else about this?"

"Only my family and my *aunt Willa.*"

"By you stressing the word aunt, I can assume she isn't actually of blood relation?"

"You can."

"Alright, well the therapist did send me confirmation of your attendance, and while a new Awakened ability does slightly change the case, I don't think it will matter. The ability would not increase your capability to defend yourself and there is no evidence that you had the ability before the attack. I'm going to go ahead and continue on the current course of getting this dismissed before trial if I can, but if that isn't possible, we might have to get you re-assessed in preparation. Still, I don't think there's much to worry about."

"I'm also supposed to ask you if it's okay for me to continue Mining with my father for now," I dead-panned, half-expecting the answer I eventually got.

"What did the psychiatrist say?"

"That it's my decision."

"Then, what's your decision?" Ms. Stovall said with a chuckle, probably in large part to the exasperation in my previous answer.

"Thank you for your time, Ms. Stovall. Need anything else from me?"

"Not much right at this moment. I'd suggest you stay off SwiftGram. Maybe even make a post about needing some time. Other than that, once we get the pre-trial date, I'll have you in for some prep work. My suggestion is that you don't take the stand, but we should likely be ready just in case. Either way, you'll need to be in the pre-trial meeting thanks to the Hunter laws surrounding Judges' Skills. So, having an idea of how it will go will help you."

"Okay," I responded, letting the word carry all the confusion I had with it. The situation regarding what was definitely self defense confused me.

"Not to worry, Brodie. I'll get it thrown out before trial. Enjoy your Mining."

I was still blinking in confusion when I heard the other side of the line disconnect. That didn't feel reassuring.

"Why don't you just start saving enough Mana Coins to buy a truly powerful Combat Skill? Then they can't convict you," Smegma said in answer to my thoughts.

[That is not how our justice system works. They've convicted an S-Rank of crimes before.]

"Ahhh, but did they catch him?"

[Husk off, sky-rat,] I mentally answered.

Smegma guffawed, which at least made me smile. If there was one thing I was sure of, it was that I should have nothing to worry about in a trial over the death of Morgan Hallsbrad. He'd attacked me—and I'd defended myself. It was the truth, pure and simple.

"Unless someone twists the truth," Smegma said with a very disturbingly flat tone.

[Again, not how our justice system works.]

"Sure, it isn't." The Imp's sarcasm was on full display. "If there is one universal truth in any world—it's that power always corrupts. Let me ask you this, Mr. Lawyer: why do you think Ms. Stovall is going to prep you, if there is no chance of this going in a different way than expected?"

I walked to the Hunter who had gone into the Portal to radio my father earlier and gave him a quick update. He then made a motion for me to follow him and told me he would guide me to the site. The Portal wasn't visible unless inside the Quad, but the glow it gave off was. Deep ocean blue.

Waiting for Smegma to offer the Portal's destination didn't yield anything and so I asked, [Where does this one lead?]

"No idea. Despite how intelligent I look, I don't know everything."

[Ahhh, so that's why you don't know anything?] I countered. I caught the Imp flipping me the double three-fingered Demon birds from the corner of my eye and smirked.

Passing through this Portal felt a lot like being suddenly submerged in warm water, unable to breathe. Coming out the other side, I started gasping, and my guide did as well. We exchanged a look that conveyed the guide's dislike of this Portal and I suddenly felt bad for making him come in to radio my father.

My first glance away from the guide showed a similar environment to Agora. Simply put, it looked like a different rainforest. The ground was where the two differed. Agora had firm ground beneath a layer of moss and dead leaves.

The ground here? My feet squelched as I went to take my first step. I watched as my foot and ankle sunk under the semi-hardening mud. The smell of sulfur as my foot entered intensified, signaling my brain of the putrid odor this Dungeon exuded. It was so bad that I considered just leaving again.

"It isn't far from the entrance," the guide said while tying a bandana around his mouth and nose. That reminded me of my face-shield and I pulled it up. "This way," the guide continued and began walking.

To my surprise, his feet didn't squelch. I stared after the man as he strode above the mud. I must have made a noise because he turned back and chuckled. "Basic Hydrophobic Enchant—lets you walk on most surfaces that have high enough water content. The whole guild got them done when we heard what type of Dungeon this was."

"Do you have a spare set?"

"Nope. You'll just have to squelch it out." The man chuckled again, clearly impressed with his own joke. I shook my head and began to 'squelch.'

* * *

"You might want to check what this thing is," Smegma commented, startling me out of toggling on and off my heat vision. It didn't show me anything inside this Portal since there were no Mana Leeches.

I turned to look at the hovering Imp. He had his eyes closed and didn't appear to be indicating anything. "In your Mental Universe you dumb-dumb."

Oh, that made sense. I even likely knew what he was talking about. A quick check showed me that the metal-looking moon was growing.

Thanks to the few days I'd been Mining, I was able to keep working even when distracted. I scratched the side of my head but kept up my Sharding of low-rank Crystals. [Okay, so it's growing from Mining and *Overflow*—it's kind of what I expected, really.]

"I think it's been growing since you entered the Portal," Smegma answered, and I looked back at him. That didn't make sense, I just started Mining less than an hour ago. Where would the—

My eyes flew wide, and I stared to where my father and Willa were currently talking with another Miner. I knew they were discussing which Ores to try for, so didn't bother having Smegma listen in. Could it be?

[Smegma, pull up the Miner's Pick description.]

Miscellaneous Professions Gear
Miner's Pick
(1)
Item Rank: Low F-Rank
Durability: Unlimited

Damage: 1-3 (x100% to Mineable minerals)
This Miner's Pick will use the Mana run-off from Crystal
Mining to repair and strengthen itself, making it unbreakable. It
will also Funnel excess Mana to Brodie Flacarada's Overdraft Skill.
Cost: 10,000 mC

[Did their Picks change to Funnel to my Overdraft, too?] I thought, staring at the Picks currently in their hands. Sure, I'd had that dream earlier when reading it and considering starting my own Mining Company—but the confirmation…

"Only explanation I can think of. Now, you just need to figure out what this Skill is," Smegma said.

Shrugging, I finished Sharding the Crystal I was on. I was due for harvesting a full Crystal anyway, and maybe the new Skill would be low ranked.

In one strike, I managed to ping the next Crystal loose. I smiled. I was getting relatively good at this, if I did say so myself. Placing my hand on the Crystal, I sold the Mana inside and then waved to my father. Once he glanced over, I pointed to the cooler, indicating I was going to take a break for a snack.

"You just got here!" My father shouted across the cavern. A moment later, I heard all three of the Miners laughing. I was only left confused for a moment, thankfully. "Willa says you only have one way to grow—be careful."

"You can tell *aunt Willa* I kept that picture she loves from when she was pregnant," I shouted back.

The laughter of two people grew louder, while Willa made choking sounds. Thanks to no one currently Mining in our chamber, I heard her response to my father. "He don't actually be havin' that, right?"

This elicited more laughter from the men, while I sat down and pulled out a ham and swiss sandwich. I placed the Spent Mana Crystal strategically behind the cooler from the three and began channeling my Mana. My Pool was up to twenty-five points, which meant I was easily a mid E-Grade.

As I waited, I glanced back to my Pick, which I had traded with the spent Crystal, leaving the former in my Mining spot. Depending on what this Skill was, couldn't I supply an entire Mining crew with Picks and just infinitely level it up? I could feel my skin flush with the excitement that particular thought led to.

If Overflow had just created a Combat Skill—

"Stop daydreaming," Smegma interjected. "All that line of thinking can do is make you disappointed if it isn't something good."

[What's got your wings twisted?]

"That's a good saying. I'm going to steal that if I ever see my family again. Still, the reason my 'wings are twisted,' is because everything I know says you can only have a certain number of Skills. So, if this thing isn't powerful—and doesn't have the chance to become powerful—well, that's a waste."

I supposed it was. With *Demonic Vault*'s Store and my ability to somewhat *Cannibalize* Skills. I used the term *somewhat* because I could never have expected to get *Heat Sense* from some random superbugs and not, say, a Skill that made me super awesome at drinking blood or something. If there truly was a cap on the number of Skills, I'd need to be extremely specific on what Skills I got or figure out a way to reject a Skill if I didn't like it.

228

My imagination took over for a moment. I pictured being a Hunter, slaying monsters left and right to *Cannibalize* their skills, only to pick up the most random, worthless Skills until I reached my Skill cap—and that was it. Lamest superhero story ever.

Sighing, I considered the problem with the other option of buying what I truly wanted from *Demonic Vault.* I was, at a minimum, nine hundred and eighty thousand Mana Coins away from any of the just-above-crap options. More than five hundred million away from the awesome ones. So, at present all I could do was hope and plan for the future.

One of my thoughts in my daydream needed to be explored.

[Is there a way to reject or delete Skills once learned?]

"I want to say yes because it was possible to not select Skill Cards or remove the Cards from your Heart Deck on Crendalar Five. However, I can't even begin to guess what's going on with the current System. That Crystal Conjuring Enchant being banned and," Smegma shivered, "the updates for *Demonic Vault*; I really can't say for sure."

That seemed fair—

The Crystal glowed bright and then began shrinking into the stack of Cards. I fanned them out, hoping for something new. The red *Demonic Vault* Card was there, as was the green *Recovery.* Under that was a plain brown Card and then the multi-hued one that had been *Heat Sense.*

I glanced at the multihued one first. It was plain—looking like a playing card from an off-brand deck. When next to all three others, it just didn't have the changing pictures and three-dimensional appearance. A quick flip and a glance reminded me of my Heat Vision-esque Skill. While I still used it frequently, other than the time with the Mana Leeches, it hadn't proved to be overly useful.

One I'd likely delete if I truly had a Skill cap.

Shrugging, I put the Card back in the pile, which I then placed in a pocket. Then I moved on to studying the earthen-brown one. The back didn't have sheen to it, but did seem to have a hint of moving picture. Still, that moving just made it seem like a camera panning over rocks. All that just made the card look like a rock that had been shaped into a card.

I flipped it over and wasn't sure whether I should throw it away in disgust… another useless Skill.

Mining
(4)
Skill Type: Gathering
Skill Rank: Mid F-Rank (Evolvable)
As you Mine, you slowly improve your understanding of Minerals, Ores, and Crystals. As this Skill grows, this individual will notice improvements to all actions related to Mining.

Smegma started laughing. In between loud inhalations so he could continue, he crowed, "You better hope you can get rid of Skills."

I just stared at the card. The Skill wasn't horrible—and paired with the leveling Miner's Pick, I figured I would grow as a Miner exponentially over time. Still, with the fact that this was a part-time job; and my desperate dream to become a Hunter—this Skill just wasn't it.

Something I'd never have thought even a few weeks ago—not when I had a single Skill and only a fantasy of Awakening another. Now, I was going to desperately be searching for a way to possibly remove Skills?

Actual functioning Skills?!

CHAPTER 30

By the time we were done for the afternoon, I could tell that my Mining Skill was truly starting to show its value. How?

Well, I was swinging at a Red Copper vein and marveling at how easily the head of my Pickaxe cut through the metal. I was also celebrating how easily I was hitting the spots Smegma was pointing out.

Smegma, on the other hand, seemed far from impressed. "Great, now you can surgically cut metal out of a wall. We sure are going places!"

[Right, and you can phase through objects but can't go farther than a hundred yards. You're really helping me move up in the world.]

"Husk you, pipsqueak."

[You're smaller than me!]

"This isn't my real body. If I were in my *real* body, the pinky-talon on a toe is bigger than your cock!"

[You've really gotta stop watching me in the shower. Plus, I'm a grower, not a shower!]

"And you were probably showering in cold water, right?"

[Do you stay up watching TV or something? How do you know all these references…]

"Just admit that your puny brain can't compete with my quick wit."

[Never—did you ever figure out if you even have a dick in this form?]

"Low blow, asshole."

[No wonder you have penis envy.]

Smegma looked back at me with wide eyes, but his only response was to open and shut his mouth. I smiled as I forced Smegma to falter slightly, even as he floated to a new spot on the Red Copper deposit and pointed to the spot I should hit. This was probably the twentieth, or maybe twenty-fifth, such spot.

Dutifully, I struck, and as the Pickaxe head penetrated the metal, I felt a click as the tip contacted something further in. Each strike that Smegma had me make gave off this tactile sensation and I had a few suspicions as to what he was having me do. Five swings later and my suspicions were confirmed when a huge portion of the Red Copper slid free from the wall.

I jumped back from the slow moving 'rock' slide and watched as it hit the ground. Smegma smiled at me and I gave him the finger. [A warning next time would be nice.]

"If that hit you, you have no business dreaming of Hunting. Ever!"

[Fair point.]

"Now you should clean out the small stragglers with a few strikes—"

[Wait, something happened.] I pointed to a spot inside the hole left by the Red Copper. [Should I swing here?] I asked.

Smegma tapped his teeth, examined the area and nodded. "Yes, that is one of a few—" I cut him off by pointing out five more in quick succession. My vision was inundated with glowing blue spots. There must have been hundreds of them. "Did you figure out the method, now that you can see the embedded rocks?"

[No, I think the Mining Skill is showing me where to strike. But—] I let the word mentally hang as I looked at a Necrograph deposit a few feet to my left. [—it doesn't seem to work with any other deposits?]

Smegma continued to tap a talon on his tooth. I rolled the large piece of Red Copper out of the way and got back to work. After perhaps five minutes, Smegma said, "Your Skill in Mining has probably already grown two more times, but if five points was the threshold—maybe you can now see low-ranked Ore's Mining strategies?"

[Sure, my father and Willa decided to go for softer and easier-to-mine veins today, so we can keep the Picks strong, but isn't Necrograph one step above a rock?]

"A really, stupidly dense and hard rock, sure," Smegma confirmed. "Still, that doesn't make it easy to Mine."

[I didn't say it did. But it can't be one of the most expensive or valuable ones, right?]

"If I remember correctly, it ranks somewhere in the middle. Still, I don't think you're looking at this right."

[Why? Isn't Red Copper one of the least valuable?]

"Least valuable, no. It has a huge amount of uses and is in constant demand—*was* in constant demand on Crendalar Five. I'm saying you're thinking about this wrong because it isn't about the value of a deposit but the rarity. Value is set by supply and demand—so while every spawned Mine will have a Red Copper deposit, its value is still high because of all of its uses. Whereas things like Adamantite and Jade Copper rarely show up, are nearly impossible to Mine, but have almost no value."

I kept Mining the Red Copper even as I mentally questioned, [Why would something so rare have almost no value?]

"I thought you were in school for Dungeon Portal Materials. Surely you understand the invisible hand of supply and demand."

[I do, but either we never got to speak on those metals or they've yet to be successfully mined from a Dungeon?] I turned the last into a question, which Smegma answered with a casual shrug. He wouldn't know that answer either.

"Think of it like this: if only one person in the entire world can work with a metal, does that metal have value?"

[Depends on what that person could make with it.]

"Not really. Let's say that this person has no need to make something to sell. They are so proficient at their Engineering, Smithing or Jewel crafting, that they are wealthy beyond your wildest dreams. In essence, you have one person who can use this metal and a low supply of said metal."

[And that person never buys the metal—or if he does, he doesn't show what he makes with it!]

232

"Precisely."

I continued to Mine as I considered that little tidbit. It likely meant that there were plenty of metals that were being passed up but had truly astronomical values. However, not only did humans not have the ability to recognize their value, but we also didn't have the capacity to work with them. At least not yet…

****

"You got a bonus of three hundred dollars and are taking me out on a date?" Dave said skeptically.

"You really need to get better taste, Brodie," Smegma chimed in.

"Yeah, sure, a date. I always take my romantic interests to the VIP Cinemas and offer to buy them popcorn. You better make sure to put out later; it's part of the social contract. Now, do you want extra butter?"

"Yes, please, sugar daddy," Dave said comically. He added a 'swoon' for effect.

I rolled my eyes and turned to see the attendant attempting to not break into a smile. "It's okay, you can laugh," I said to her. "Clearly, I need better friends."

"With friends like that," the girl said while breaking into a beautiful smile and pointing at Dave, who was now batting his eyelashes. "Who needs enemies, right?"

"Hey!" Dave said sarcastically before switching it up and somehow going 'Casanova.' "Still, with a smile like that—maybe you'd let me show you—"

"Nope!" the girl said while laughing loudly. "Here's the popcorn with extra butter, greaseball!"

"Come on, let me take you out," Casa-nope continued trying. I laughed and was surprised to hear Smegma joining in. I glanced at the Imp and shivered. Was that a smile?

"Listen, butterball, maybe you should try to take after your friend here and spend less time in the books, and more time in the gym…"

I collected my own popcorn and thanked 'Laura' for her help and meaning it in more ways than one. As we walked away, both Smegma and Dave had comments.

"If you're going to let a chance like that go, I'm really going to start thinking you're batting for the other team," Dave said.

"Kid, I've been meaning to talk to you about how dense you are when it comes to the opposite sex," Smegma added.

"Husk you both," I said out loud, forgetting that Dave wasn't aware of Smegma. Thankfully, he misinterpreted.

"I hope you don't mean the same type of 'husking' for both me and her?" Dave responded while laughing.

"Can we just go watch The Making of a Hero, please!" I answered, exasperated.

"Husk yeah, we can," Dave answered. "Who are you most excited to see?"

"I don't know. Supposedly, they have never-before-seen footage from Gamonji in this," I answered, feeling my heart rate increase at the thought.

"I still think King Anubis is the GOAT, man, but I have to admit that Gamonji definitely died too early. That man totally has some great pieces of wisdom in the interviews I've seen."

"You've actually watched the full interviews?" I asked, knowing that he hadn't.

"You know what I mean, Brodie. The clips I see, paired with his Dungeon Recordings, make him a total badass. But, like, King Anubis has been raiding Dungeons for over two decades and is still going strong."

"He never conquered an S-Rank solo, though. Let alone six times."

"He's building to that—he's taking the safe approach. Unlike Gamonji, he wants to survive the attempt. Plus, if solo S-Rank clears makes a GOAT, why aren't you bringing up Mastiff Jones?"

"I don't want to have this argument. At least half of his eleven solo clears are from before the rating System existed as we know it today. Even Mastiff says that at least half of them would be B or A-Rank at best today."

"That's only because he trail-blazed and figured out the creatures' weaknesses!"

We continued arguing familiarly until the trailers started, followed by the movie. While it was more of a documentary than a true movie, I really enjoyed it. Especially the sections where it showed the current top five Hunters in the world and their daily routines.

It's one thing to dream of being a Hunter, but it was something else entirely to see how much goes into it. Sure, high-ranked Hunters had wealth, game, and notoriety, but the very best—the active double and triple S hopefuls—barely had time to enjoy it. They were too busy working in the gyms, running through tactic briefings, and managing Guilds to attend more than four or five events a year.

And even those were often canceled due to emergencies. The movie really painted the landscape of Hunters differently. Even Smegma grudgingly said, "These ones seem to be at least marginally better than those Snow Canaries and Housecats."

Still, it was Gamonji that stole the show.

"Did you know that his Mana Pool was over a hundred thousand?" Dave asked as we made our way to the car. I shook my head. This movie had just come out and rumors were being actively suppressed by AI software.

"Honestly, Hunters never reveal Skills, Stats or Mana capacity. It makes them vulnerable, or so they've always said. Do you think because Gamonji died, that his beneficiaries thought it was okay?"

"Husking must have, man. A hundred thousand! That's insane! Like, I'm only at thirty according to my Awakening reading. You have, what? Ten to twenty?"

"Yeah!" I answered, not revealing that my Pool was currently at thirty-one, and a step ahead of Dave's. "Still, what got me was when Gamonji said to Eleanor that his Pool started in mid B-Ranks! It really struck me, what he said about time and perseverance were what made people great, not god-given Skills."

"Husk yeah. Makes me want to form a Bank and get cracking! Too bad we're a dime a dozen, Bro." Dave started out excited but lapsed into a complaint about halfway through. I looked at him over the hood of the Ford Escort as he lowered himself into the passenger side. I could tell he wasn't depressed or angry over the statement, but also saw the loss of the excitement.

I got in my own side and started the car. "Hey, you never know what might happen, right?"

"Listen, at least you have your looks, Brodie. So, you might have a chance. Me? I'll be working in Canadian Portal Management, if I'm lucky."

I didn't mention that luck would have nothing to do with it, not with his family's connections. In fact, I had no doubt that his family would never let him occupy such an unglamorous job.

But I didn't say that, not wanting to remind my friend of the circumstances he was working hard to try to distance himself from.

The drive back to campus was a quiet affair after that. I don't know what Dave was thinking about, but I was quiet for a different reason. If I could purchase a Skill for people like Dave, surely I could change his life, right?

"You know you haven't even purchased one for yourself yet, right?" Smegma interrupted my thoughts, and I pursed my lips in frustration.

Unfortunately, he wasn't wrong…

CHAPTER 31

Tuesday, April 9th, 2069

"We'll be there, thank you," my father said as he hung up the phone. I raised an eyebrow over the rim of my morning coffee, and he explained. "That was Ms. Stovall's assistant. Your pre-trial hearing is set for next Monday. She says that you'll need to come in over the weekend to prepare a bit."

I must have made a face because my dad gave me a reassuring smile. "Don't worry, we've been on the phone most of the morning. She said that it is all very standard procedure. It's mostly about how not to react if something is said that you disagree with. You shouldn't even have to take the stand."

"It sure was nice of Ms. Stovall to have her assistant wake up early and get to the office to get us before work," my mom chimed in as she plated some scrambled Roc egg, toast and vegetables for all three of us. She took the small side plate, as usual, and left the big portions for my father and me.

I noticed mine seemed to have grown and smiled. I don't know why, but it felt good to get an equal portion to my father's. Not that I would have been eating it before, but since I'd started Mining, I really could see why my father needed the extra calories. I nodded to my dad and put on a fake smile as I picked up my phone and pulled up the SwiftGram app.

Sometime late last night, I'd realized that my online content was growing stale. While I still had plenty more pictures from my shoot to use, I also needed to create a path forward. A way to grow the account for what I may need it for in the future. What direction that path would be, or even what I might use my social media accounts for, I couldn't decide on. But I still might need the visibility they would offer, for *something...*

"Still thinking of trying the sob story approach?" Smegma asked lazily from his 'usual' spot above the hanging dining light. I mentally flipped him the bird because he had read my thoughts again. Yes, I was thinking of telling my followers what had happened. This all stemmed from Ms. Stovall's suggestion to put a post about needing time off. Now I was thinking of explaining how and why I was taking a semester off and Mining in Portals...

It was so much more interesting than the thirst-trap approach I was using—which also, clearly, hadn't been working. I had still only received 'offers' for one-time Mana Connections.

"Why not try combining the two?" Smegma suggested, his voice far more enthusiastic than I thought my current train of thoughts warranted.

I hesitated, sensing a trap, but mentally asked, [What do you mean?]

"Go with the Hot Mining Shirtless Calendar approach. You know, take a few pictures with the Pick slung over a shoulder—give the camera that pouty baby-bird look you do!" I once again mentally gave him the finger, but he continued as if he couldn't feel it. "Oh, what a great thought I just had! Include your dad, and Willa! Fat Gary, too! This could be a real thing. Rub some dirt on each other—"

[That's husking enough, asshole!] I interjected forcibly, finally getting the Imp to stop his enthusiastic, and clearly sarcastic, rant.

Once I was sure he was done, I returned to my initial thoughts of the morning and last night. *What direction should I take my SwiftGram? The real sticking point was—*

"You don't want to be a Mana Bank anymore…" Smegma finished my thought, his voice much more serious, and this time I only nodded my head slightly as I swallowed some rather tasteless Roc egg. While the Roc eggs were good sources of nutrients, they really lacked almost any flavor in comparison to normal chicken eggs. Of course, chickens were far rarer after the advent of Portals.

Why?

Well, according to first-year economics, a great deal of farmland had been overrun early on. Unfortunately, the population out in the 'countryside,' as it was once called, was just too sparse to feasibly send Hunters or the Military out there. Not when cities needed them more and had denser populations.

Now the countryside was called the 'Wilds,' simply because it needed to be thoroughly cleared of stray creatures before it could be settled again. Thus, why most humans survived on a combination of Farm and Portal products.

Still, some large organizations kept massive sprawling farms and produced 'old-world' goods, but they also set the prices. So, was the nostalgia of a breakfast omelet worth hundreds of dollars? Not to my parents, and certainly not to me since I'd never had one.

"Plus, you guys are husking poor," Smegma added.

[Thanks for that,] I responded, not exactly disagreeing with the statement but not liking the reminder. [We're considered middle class.]

"Yeah, bottom middle class. Like, I think your parents would still be living out of that junker RV they sold to your uncle, if they hadn't had you twenty-one years ago…"

I snorted into my coffee, admitting to myself and Smegma that he was certainly accurate in that alternate history. My parents had told me that a few times before. The RV was the one 'nice' thing they'd owned, and it was eight years old when they sold it, twenty-nine years old today. Everything else was secondhand or rented. Then again, my parents hadn't ever told me how they got the thing.

[I bet my parents procured it after the Advent,] I answered my own question.

"You mean stole," Smegma corrected.

[Stole is such a dirty word. Re-appropriated sounds better. Plus, can it be stealing if no one owns it?]

"That's the first smart thing you've ever said. Now, you're thinking like a proper Demon." Smegma grunted and allowed me to clear my plate as I continued to consider my next steps for my SwiftGram.

I wasn't sure that I liked Smegma's 'compliment' there, but I pushed the thoughts and feelings aside. By the time me and my father stood up to leave, I'd made the extremely important choice—to decide later.

I know, I know—smart, right?

Shaking my head at my own sarcasm, I got in the passenger side. I supposed I could be the one driving every second morning to give my dad a break, but he always knew where we were going. Me, on the other hand, I kind of felt like I was, well, a part-timer.

* * *

[What do you mean it's not going into the Mining Skill anymore?] I asked.

"You know that big metal moon in your Mental Universe? Well, *Overflow* is no longer feeding into it…" Smegma said very condescendingly.

[The lack of a penis in this form is really making you cranky…] I responded, even as I attempted to keep Sharding the F-Rank Crystals and peek into my Mental Universe.

"Maybe it's the lack of hormones?" Smegma retorted, and I chuffed out a small cough to hide a laugh.

Did Demons have testosterone and estrogen like humans or something totally different?

"We don't call them that, but I can tell by the contextual concept it's similar."

Putting aside Smegma's grudging answer to my casual thought, I watched as *Overflow* did, in fact, feed the white smoke into a place right beside the metal moon. Curious, but not expecting an actual answer, I rhetorically asked, [Where do you think it's going?]

"You know what would help?" Smegma said, and I rolled my eyes. "If you knew of a way to check on the Skill! Too bad that's *impossible.*"

[You really need a release buddy—you're all pent up.]

I thought back to the drawer in my desk where all the Cards from previous Spent Mana Crystals resided. I guess it wouldn't hurt to add four more to the stack. Still, this cave wasn't exactly easy to hide in. The problem wasn't exactly the size—it was about ten times larger than the largest cavern I'd seen since starting. No, the specific problem was that the size warranted keeping everyone in the same room.

A quick scan of my immediate surroundings showed two people already taking a quick break to eat something and another one stopping for water. While eighteen people in a large cavern like this didn't exactly mean someone's eyes would be on me—it did greatly increase those chances. My scan paused as something in the distance, behind the Miner drinking from a Snowman bottle, caught my eye.

It was the color that stopped me from continuing to scan the room. It was the same red as the shop window from *Demonic Vault*. Shouldering my Pick, I moved carefully over the Mana Crystals to the wall where the strange 'box'

238

seemed to be anchored. As I approached, I noticed that the plaque grew, and I also discovered two other places on other walls where similar boxes seemed to float.

Like a street sign from far away that finally comes into view after squinting, the letters inside the box became readable.

Fool's Gold
Rank: Low F
Quality: Very Low
Quantity: High

"Ahh, the True Gold caught your eye?" my dad said as I stopped walking away from the group.

"That's Fool's Gold," I answered absently.

"What? How can you be sure?" My dad blurted as he looked between the distant golden-colored Ore vein and me. His question startled me out of my musing with a jolt. I hurriedly tried to come up with an excuse but Smegma helpfully provided one.

"The sulfur smell," he explained, and I repeated. "I noticed it on that first day, when you tried your hand at Mining a 'True Gold' vein."

My dad pointed to my left, and I followed his finger to find another golden-colored vein—a smaller one. This one had no hovering box in front of it. "Okay, but that smell could be coming from plenty of other places. Even some trapped gasses."

This time, I didn't need much help from Smegma as I responded, "That's a bit of a misnomer. The smell of sulfur in propane and other natural gasses is artificially added in most cases so that you can detect it if there's a gas leak. Also, if the smell was coming from a gas pocket in here, then the sensors we brought would alert us, no?"

"That still doesn't mean that that one's Fool's Gold or if this one is, *or if both are*," my dad said, pointing between the two. Theoretically, he wasn't wrong, but if the hovering box was to be believed, I knew which one was false and which one was True Gold.

But how do I convince my father of that?

"I'm going to take a break to eat a sandwich. I'll walk around and take a closer look to see what other Ores are in here," I said with a shrug, deciding that I would keep thinking on what to say to convince my father and Willa as I checked out the cavern.

"Okay, take my Light Stone, and don't mine any of them till after lunch. Willa and I should discuss what our best options are." I didn't like that I wouldn't be included in those decisions but realized that they were far more experienced than I was. So, while it seemed that I could identify some veins of Ore, it made sense that they wouldn't think I had the experience to do so on sight.

Nodding, I turned on the Light Stone my father handed me and put it in a mesh pocket on the front of my borrowed Mining Gear. Then I went to the cooler and grabbed a sandwich before moving off to the next nearest hovering red box in the distance. Seeing me move away from the group, a Hunter from Snowbirds broke away and accompanied me, along with his Mana Banks.

"You a Specialist?" he asked, and I nodded. He then nodded and followed quietly. I wasn't even sure of his name but did a once over of the Mana Banks that followed the man. There were three of them and, where the ones for the Lynx Guild Hunter's wore armor, these three appeared to have dress clothes.

In fact, two were women and I didn't think their 'stylish' dainty slippers were exactly appropriate for a Portal, let alone a Mining cave inside one. Was that a slit in one of their black pants to expose smooth legs beneath? Do they think this is a fashion show?

"With the way they're giving the Hunter the husk-me eyes, they may just think there will be a muddy orgy later."

I snorted and then turned it into an excuse to pull up my mask. At the questioning look from the Hunter and Banks, I explained, "Sorry, just some dust," while pointing to the mask. Clearly, these three did believe that this was some sort of game. Even the Hunter looked like he wanted to be anywhere else but escorting me through a dark, Mana Crystal-filled cavern.

My brain couldn't help but compare them to Gamonji, or any of the other amazing Hunters I'd seen in the movie last night, and find them extremely lackluster. One of them, the only other male of the group, pulled his necklace out of his v-cut t-shirt as I watched. To my astonishment, it turned out that the necklace wasn't a simple religious symbol.

Smegma and I kept a side eye on him as he fiddled with the necklace and then held it to his nose before sniffing loudly. *Was that a drug?*

Smegma moved over and looked inside the man's necklace. "It's a white powder. Could be Awake Aid."

[What is that?] I asked, still leaning towards the man that I was pretty sure just snorted cocaine.

"An Alchemy product. It's made from bones of certain beasts. Stops the imbiber from falling asleep for about twelve hours."

I blinked in surprise. I was relatively certain the human race hadn't discovered that Alchemical product yet. I was also slightly concerned by the wording Smegma used. However, I wasn't curious enough to ask any further questions because there was a possibility he meant the phrasing. And that was a nightmare.

My answer to Smegma, though, was, [Yeah, well I'm pretty sure that was a drug. We call it cocaine, and it also will keep you awake. I think?]

"Really? I wonder if it's just a different name for the same thing?" Smegma responded, sounding truly interested in knowing the answer.

[Ahh, it isn't really a product from after the Advent. It's actually a drug from before…]

"Fascinating! So, you had Alchemy before the System?"

[Chemistry,] I clarified. [There might be some overlap between the two, but I'm neither a scientist nor a magician."]

"*Alchemist.*" Smegma sniffed in disdain. "Mages are something else entirely."

[Whatever.] I shrugged.

I explained what I could to the Imp, but was forced to admit my utter lack of knowledge multiple times as he tried to dig deeper into the production of drugs pre-System and now. The conversation distracted me enough that I reached the wall almost before I realized it and began reading the text I found there. The box just seemed to hang there in the air, which confused me. That also could have been a product of me not noticing an actual vein of Ore. I reached out and touched the 'stone' as I read the plaque.

Graphenite
Rank: High F
Quality: Very High
Quantity: Low

"Ohhh, that's *very* valuable," Smegma said as he either read the plaque or my thoughts.

[Really? It just looks like stone?]

"It is a kind of stone. Still, when you mix it into other metals, it can create far stronger alloys."

[So, it functions like carbon in steel?]

"Ummm. Sure?" Smegma answered, clearly trying to understand what I was talking about. He must have gotten enough from my thoughts because he did follow up with, "We called it BlackRock, but I think it's the same as a Mana-enriched version of your *carbon*."

The Hunter and his Banks were giving me strange looks as I felt around on what appeared to be slightly darker stone than the rest around it. I moved on, hurriedly scanning for my next red plaque.

Red Copper
Rank: Mid F
Quality: Low-Medium
Quantity: Medium

—

Tontin
Rank: Low F
Quality: Very Low
Quantity: Very High

—

Platinum Iron
Rank: High F
Quality: Very Low
Quantity: Very Low

That was all the floating red windows I could see in the massive cavern. I had long since finished my sandwich by the time I returned to the group and got back to Mining. I still hadn't thought of a good plan to convince my father to Mine the True Gold, but we had time.

Plus, I really wanted to find out what was going on with *Overflow*. So, to that end, I Mined a full Crystal—now a very easy task—and sold the Mana inside to Smegma. I left the clear Crystal on the ground as I kept working—my best chance to grab it was probably going to be at the end of the day.

Maybe I'd leave a few more strewn about and then ask for one to take home? Would other Miners want one if there were plenty? It would take a great deal of suspicion off me if they did. Well, suspicion from my father at least, if I wanted a second one of the 'souvenir' Crystals.

An hour later, it turned out I shouldn't have bothered.

Right after a swing into a Crystal stem, I felt a flush of heat that accompanied the strange pinging noise that came from breaking free a whole Crystal. The flush surprised me and caused me to stagger slightly. Yet, when I tried to firm my legs to correct the overbalance—I jumped unexpectedly.

What the husk?

It was all I could think as I literally left the floor on an angle and joined the pile of Sharded Crystals to my left.

"Did ya just Scrooge McDuck into a pile of Shards?" Willa asked from nearby. My 'flush' intensified as I blushed. I was sure I was bright red, but a screen in front of me was also distracting enough that I chose it over looking at Willa.

Strength Increased by 1.
Strength Stat Unlocked.
Stat Screen Unlocked.

Stats
Strength: 2
Locked.
Locked.
Locked.
Locked.
Locked.
Locked.

I waved distractedly at Willa since I could feel her staring.

"Sorry, I slipped," I said as I stood up. To Smegma, I repeated my earlier sentiment. [What the *husk* just happened?]

"There are two orbs currently circling the Mining Skill sphere, so I'm going to say that's probably where *Overflow's* been going…"

[But how?!]

"That's a *fantastic* question. Maybe a *Spent Mana Crystal* will help us figure it out," Smegma said, with particular emphasis on the part where he called me stupid. Well, he didn't really say it, but I heard it.

CHAPTER 32

Tuesday, April 9th, 2069

Mining
(10)
Skill Type: Gathering
Skill Rank: Peak F-Rank (Evolvable)
As you Mine, you slowly improve your understanding of Minerals, Ores, and Crystals. As this Skill grows, this individual will notice improvements to all actions related to Mining.
This Skill is multiplied by the Strength Stat.
Current max level reached until Evolution Condition is reached.

I turned the Mining Skill Card over in my hands, reading the final line for what felt like the hundredth time. I had nothing better to do as I waited for my father and Willa to come out of the Snowbirds' command tent. I guess I could go check on them as a Specialist who contributed to the bonuses we'd receive, but…

"Still bitter they wouldn't listen to you?" Smegma said while chuckling. "Pouting about it sure seems productive," he added, clearly twisting the screws on my mood.

[We could have gotten so much more of a bonus if they'd let me Mine the True Gold!] I complained.

"Yeah, and they wouldn't even let you mine the Graphenite—because why would they waste the one Ore deposit each Pick can mine a day on something that might just be stone!" Smegma faked my second complaint in a very insulting mimicry of my voice.

[Husk you sideways, dip-shit.]

"Whatever gets you off, dumb-dumb."

[Open the Shop,] I responded dejectedly, feeling like I was going to lose any exchange I had with Smegma in my current mood. It would be nice to look at something else, at least.

Demon Vault 2.0.0.1
Crendalar Five – Abyss Sect's Wares

<Skills>
Consumables

Weapons
Armor
Miscellaneous

Currency: 45,045 mC (Mana Coins)

Before I started scrolling, I allowed the current Mana Coins total to bring a smile to my face. However, it almost instantly made my mood sour again when I started searching through Skills. Just like before, every Skill cost astronomical amounts. Still, if I kept saving, by the end of the semester I'd be able to get something worth a million, I supposed.

The problem was that the million-coin Skills were pretty basic and F-rank—like *Aid* or *Firestarter*...

Wait—how much were some of the Skills I currently held worth?

Recovery Skill Card
Recovery
(1)
Skill Type: Passive
Skill Rank: Low C-Rank (Evolvable) (Reduce?)
Supercharge natural healing factors. Caution: this Skill will consume nutrients in the body to heal at dizzying speed; if nutrients are not available, it will consume body mass to prevent death, leaving the user severely malnourished. This can be offset by [Locked] Stat.
Healing speed can be increased by a factor of [Locked] Stat.
Cost: 250,000,000 mC

"Holy shit," I said, managing to turn it into an excited whisper at the last second. I'd, of course, started by reading the price. However, the more I read, the wider my eyes grew. First, I hadn't known of the side effect of the Skill I already possessed, which was slightly disturbing. But second, was the [Locked] Stat in the description. I had only now unlocked Strength and had to wonder if that was a factor for getting information on Stats, albeit Locked ones, in the description.

I looked at the Mining Card and focused on that second to last line. It also had a line about Stats it hadn't before. I was about to ask Smegma if that was the reason for the change in description when I thought of a better idea.

Necromancy Skill Card
Necromancy
(1)
Skill Type: Summons
Skill Rank: High C-Rank (Evolvable) (Reduce?)
Summon slain creatures to act as your personal troops. Creatures suffer a fifty percent reduction in combat power and lose any Skills they possessed. This debuff can be mitigated by [Locked]

**Stat. For convenience, Summoned creatures are Summoned as
Shadows to prevent diseases and smells from spreading.
Creature Stats can be increased by a factor of [Locked] Stat.
Cost: 1,000,000,000 mC**

Not only had the description of the Skill changed, but so had the price. It took me a moment to find the cause—mostly because I tended to skip over some of the short top lines. Thanks to the upgrade to *Demonic Vault,* a C-Rank Card was available. However, this also allowed me to find the 'reduce' hyperlink I'd missed on the *Recovery* Skill.

**Necromancy Skill Card
Necromancy
(1)
Skill Type: Summons
Skill Rank: High D-Rank (Evolvable) (Increase?)
Summon slain creatures to act as your personal troops.
Creatures suffer a fifty percent reduction in combat power and lose
any Skills they possessed. This debuff can be mitigated by [Locked]
Stat. For convenience, Summoned creatures are Summoned as
Shadows to prevent diseases and smells from spreading.
Creature Stats can be increased by a factor of [Locked] Stat.
Cost: 500,000,000 mC**

So, unlocking my Stat Screen was granting me more information? It was either that or the increase to *Demonic Vault.* Either way, that was definitely good news.

"Right, because this *new* information lacks the very essence that makes information helpful. How are you going to strategize and plan with this *new* knowledge that lacks the fundamental piece of hellish-damned information?" Smegma joked.

[Ahh, but what if I do have a plan?]

"Okay, since I can read your thoughts—I'm going to spoil your big husking reveal. Buying other tools will just be a waste of your Mana Coins."

[Fine. Since I'm starting to get to know you, and I can basically read your mind right now too, I'm gonna call you out. You just want me to save up and purchase a Combat Skill so I can start farming more efficiently…]

"You mean more *directly…* Okay, that's a fair assessment, but it doesn't mean that what I want isn't also what's best for you."

[It also doesn't mean that my plan also isn't best for both—"

"Husk yeah!" Willa exclaimed as she exited the command structure. Her cheer drew the eye of most of the surrounding Hunters, Miners, Gardeners, and support staff.

We were in a parking lot behind a Precise Superstore. It was large enough that the Portal, all the command trailers, tents and staff cars could easily fit.

Additionally, they even had a small section of the parking lot open to the public—so the store could stay open.

It seemed like an unnecessary risk to me, but the Snowbirds had fenced off the Portal with temporary barricades, I supposed. Still, by the crowd, this was either a crazy busy Precise Superstore or the presence of the Hunters and Portal was making it busier.

My dad exited after Willa with a wide smile on his face as well. I stood up and brushed off my pants, removing some dirt and leaves that clung to them. Willa, unsurprisingly, was the first to reach me. I didn't even have to ask for an explanation.

"We be able to hire back another fifteen of da laid-off Miners!" she squealed. I raised an eyebrow, *demanding* a bit more. "Oh, shut up!" she said and punched me in my arm. "I be gettin' ta the reason. With today's bonus and work, Jagger be thinkin' we be classified as full Specialists—"

"As long as we could guarantee to keep ourselves kitted out!" My dad interrupted, adding in a small but very important caveat. Still, I supposed with the Mining Picks—or my 'repair mark'—that wasn't a big worry for them.

"I always be sayin' that the biggest issue with da job is that individuals with Minin'-related Skills rarely have experience, and once they do, they be workin' with people like us no more!" Willa said excitedly, seeming to relish the fact that she was now the one who had experience and—through her equipment—those vaunted Mining Skills.

It didn't take me long to remember the laid-off Miner's looks in that meeting. I guessed that it would be pretty grating to watch as others came into the job with no experience and were treated better in every way.

My dad's smile grew wider, but what he said changed the topic, "We should get out of here—they're calling back in the full team to take on the Boss. They'll want the space to plan and park."

"Still…" my dad continued before anyone could say anything in response. "I think everyone could go for a beer, maybe a Dreaded Shredded too, don't you, Willa?" Willa's smile grew larger than my father's and I chuckled as he added, "I just need to call the boss and make sure that's okay."

I knew he wasn't talking about Jagger.

"Clara better be sayin' yes, Gary, I ain't had a Dread Shredded Monster Pepperoni Pizza in forever!" Willa crowed.

* * *

My father was only allowed to stay for a single beer, and no Pizza. Even though I could tell he wasn't in need of it, I was told to act as the designated driver. We'd laughed about it on the way home, even as my father enacted his plan to get the remaining ten members of the team their jobs back as well.

"Jarred, I'm telling you that you need to come back and work with me," my dad was saying. "Come over for dinner tonight and I'll tell you all about it." This invitation was the actual reason that Clara hadn't allowed my dad and I to eat Pizza. She was already cooking.

There was a long pause as my father listened. I could see his face fall slightly and realized that uncle Jarred was likely not as enthusiastic in his response as my father thought he should be. "Have I ever steered you wrong before?"

I sucked on a tooth as I took an advanced left turn and merged onto the highway.

"Okay, that's fine!" My dad said in response to more conversation I couldn't hear. "Bring the whole family on Sunday. I can't wait to see Ella and the kids."

There were a few more pleasantries about how much I'd grown, and a bit of a hiccup when my dad said I was taking a semester off, but otherwise, it seemed like they caught up with each other in about five minutes of conversation. Uncle Jarred was like Willa and not blood-related, but a very close friend of my father's. He'd worked at Portals, Portal's, Portalz in the past but left some time ago. I think I was a teenager at the time.

"You're sure you can find another Pick for him?" my dad asked.

"Yeah," I began, but hesitated. "I don't think he's going to be willing to go back into the Portals, though. Wasn't it the kids and Ella that made him leave in the first place?"

"They're older now, and from our last beer together, the family is really hurting for money—you know, with University coming up…"

My lips pursed from the reminder, but I nodded into the silence to show I understood, and I did. Jarred would be a third trustworthy member of our group—and its secret.

Yet, as my lie grew, and my dad kept bringing up my schooling, I couldn't call what I was experiencing a pleasant feeling either.

Immediately upon getting home, I shut myself in my room and began going through *Demonic Vault* again, looking up a few more Skills and their value.

Mining Skill Card
Mining
(1)
Skill Type: Gathering
Skill Rank: Low F-Rank (Evolvable)
As you Mine, you slowly improve your understanding of Minerals, Ores, and Crystals. As this Skill grows, this individual will notice improvements to all actions related to Mining. This Skill is multiplied by the Strength Stat.
Cost: 250,000 mC
—

Mental Fortitude Skill Card
Mental Fortitude
(1)
Skill Type: Passive Mind
Skill Rank: High C-Rank (Evolvable) (Reduce?)
Increase your mind's capacity to remain rational in the direst of situations. Create a barrier from mental attacks. Continue to

think of the best solution even when it seems impossible. This Skill will not improve [Locked] Stat, but [Locked] Stat will increase the strength of mental barrier by a factor of [Locked] Stat.
Cost: 2,500,000,000 mC

Since I couldn't see the description of my A-Ranked *Mental Fortitude*, I wrote the information on the last one down. It was somewhat interesting to see just how much I'd been 'given' for free—all because of a purchase of equipment and a choice in a sub-Skill.

"What? You think your dad is going to let you go Gather herbs on Monday?" Smegma asked, extremely sarcastically. I could tell he was still trying to persuade me away from my current plan. Still, it wasn't a Gathering-type of profession I was thinking about. "Oh, sure, so you're going to pick up Blacksmithing in your room and think that no one will bat an eyelash?"

That point did make me frown. That was the sticking point to all this. What could I purchase and perform cheaply and covertly? I scanned through the Miscellaneous Tools section—pretty sure I was likely missing a great deal of Crafting professions due to my lack of knowledge.

So I made a list as I went.

1. Tamer

2. Gardener

3. Tracker

4. Trapper

5. Builder

6. Performer

7. Musician

8. Merchant

9. Blacksmith

10. Tanner

11. Cleaner

12. Poison Expert

13. Fisher

14. ...

I stopped after that, not finding anything that I could do without a great deal of expense or time invested. Plus, any non-Gathering or Crafting profession tool was exponentially more expensive to purchase. *Still, Smegma had been right—*

"Of course I was, dumb-dumb"—and I hated to admit that. I couldn't just switch professions tomorrow. It would bring on too—

[Wait—] I thought-exclaimed pointedly at Smegma. [I'm a husking genius.]

"I mean, I'll admit that what you just thought of isn't half bad, but a *genius* is stretching things."

[The answer is perfect, though. It even goes along with our current story.]

"Perfect, until you realize that you don't know anyone you can trust in other trade jobs."

[Uncle Jarred, Willa, or my father probably do, though!]

"At this point, why don't you just start your own group?" Smegma said, his tone joking. "Wait—I wasn't serious," he added when his comment sparked my imagination on that topic once again.

Why *didn't* I start my own *company*? To Smegma, I intentionally added, [Where would I even start?]

"Maybe your dad knows someone to talk to," Smegma said, repeating the sentiment I had made earlier but more excitedly and sincerely. "If this works—wait—what about Skill limits?"

Husk!

CHAPTER 33

Sunday, April 14th, 2069

"Pass the 'potatoes,'" Jarred said from his spot at the foot of the table. The man had aged since I'd last seen him. That might have been unfair. It was just that my memory of Jarred and the slightly pudgy, balding man in front of me didn't match up. It was like someone had taken my uncle and treated him to an all-indulgent trip to a top-end resort where he didn't even have to stand up from his chair.

"Did I tell you about the article I was reading?" My mom said as she lifted the mashed Portal Potatoes, using the cork-insulator that it sat on to avoid burning her hands on the ceramic. She continued, clearly not expecting an answer. "They said that Portal vegetables and meats are actually much better for you than Earth equivalents."

Jarred moved to run his hand over his shaved head but changed midway to scratch at his own ear. Sheepishly, he said, "Sounds like they're trying to drive up prices, Clara."

"There were a whole bunch of doctors and Hunters that signed off on it," Clara said, looking to my father for support.

My father smiled sheepishly in response as well. "The doctors might have some codes of ethics, I'm not sure, but you know Gifted Hunters will sponsor anything if they give them enough money."

"Well, I guess I'm just being optimistic, then," my mom said with a pout. I chuckled, which earned me a glare. "You, too?" my mom asked, like she was truly saying, 'et tu, Brutus?'

That drew a laugh from my uncle and father. Still, she wasn't wrong, not really, so I added what I knew on the subject. "It isn't so much that it's 'better' for us or not. The one definitive is that there are 'alien' nutrients that may or may not be part of what empowers Skills or contributes to Awakenings. They also may be what causes people to come down with unique illnesses. Last I heard, there isn't an accepted study that proves the validity of either hypothesis."

"I haven't seen the kid in a few years and suddenly he's a genius," uncle Jarred said, clearly not intending to be condescending but failing. He wore a broad smile under his unkempt beard, and because of that, I managed to not misinterpret the words. He also followed it up quickly, telling me he understood the way his words could be misconstrued. "You must be coming close to finishing your third semester, right? Your Co-op is after the fourth, right?"

My father had already mentioned me taking time off in the car, hadn't he? I guessed uncle Jarred probably just forgot. Still, my smile morphed into a wince.

I had been planning to join either Portals, Portal's, Portalz or uncle Jarred's company to do my Co-op.

Although… Now that I thought about it, I just might be creating my own… business? Team? I didn't think there were any rules against doing something like that as a Co-op. In fact, if I had to guess, an entrepreneurial spirit would likely be encouraged. The world ran on small businesses, after all. I shook myself out of my thoughts as I remembered uncle Jarred's comment. I squirmed uncomfortably.

My mother's mouth curled as well, but it was my father who jumped to my rescue. "That's a loooonnnggg story, Jar. Right now, Brodie is taking a semester off. Remember, I told you about the Mana Theft…"

"Oh shoot, I totally blanked, Brodie. You just look so good and nonplussed about the whole thing. Then, it's just so easy to connect a young bloke like you to schoolin' that I sort of put my foot in it, didn't I?" Jarred offered as an explanation. I shrugged and decided to finally get this meal on track.

"It's hard to be upset when the situation Awakened a second Skill," I said leadingly and was damn pleased when I saw Jarred lean forward in his seat.

"A what now?!" he exclaimed, his eyes glittering with excitement on my behalf. "Anything good? Am I going to be an uncle to a drafted Hunter?"

And just like that, my mood soured again. Smegma's laugh rang in my ears as my mouth curled into a sneer again. My father took up the explanation, though. "Nothing that fancy, Jar, but it is very valuable with the right people around him."

"What does that mean?" Jarred asked skeptically. "Sounds like a sales pitch."

"Well, it kinda is one," my dad answered. "With his *Repair Mark*, Willa, Brodie, and myself all became Specialists. *Sustainable* Specialists…" My father let that statement hang in the air.

I smiled when Jarred's mouth opened and closed multiple times without voicing a response. My dad continued, his tone amused as well, "I actually called you to see if you want to join—"

"Gary!" Jarred said, his voice filled with exasperation. "You know Ella won't allow that." Ella hadn't made it to dinner tonight with the kids as originally planned. "She wants me in a safe office environment." Silence descended on the table at this pronouncement. For my part, I was nodding in understanding, but I could tell that wasn't the case for my mother and father.

It was a strange dichotomy to how they would treat me… Something was being left unsaid, because I doubted they would push a man further after he refused—not without a reason.

Dad didn't say a word. He simply hefted the Pick that he'd had resting at his side and laid it on the table in front of Jarred. The one he put there first was clearly my Pick because it was in far better condition than Willa's and my dad's. Why?

Well, I was assuming a lot, but my Mining Skill and its helpful guidance seemed to allow the Pick to take less damage.

Next, my father hefted his or Willa's up and set it next to the first. This one was in rough shape. Because of that, I assumed it was Willa's. She'd tried to Mine two veins today, and by all accounts, succeeded. Except for the state of her Pick.

The Pick was now in almost as poor a shape as it had been when my father used my first Pick to Mine.

"The first one looked worse than the second one here when we first got it, Jar. That's the god's-honest truth." Dad's voice was low, steady and filled with conviction. "This is what I'm offering."

Jarred's voice seemed to have gotten caught in his throat as he reached out and traced the lines and curves of both Pickaxes, his eyes wide. I watched his Adam's apple as he swallowed hard. He looked dazed. After a long moment, he shook himself. Blinking, he cleared his throat and gently pushed the Picks a couple of inches away from himself, as if in a symbolic effort to distance himself from them.

"You know I can't do this. God has a plan for us, Gary. Once the kids grow up and Ella can get back to work, we'll earn it off," Jarred said with a significant look in my direction as his cheeks went red. "Can you not bring this kind of stuff up in front of the kid, Gary?"

I looked around the table hoping for a hint as to what was going on.

"Your kids are already in school," my mother said, "and I've gotten Ella numerous interviews as an office administrator. I even know that a few places offered her the—"

"Clara, you don't understand. She wants to work but she just hasn't been able to make that transition with everything she does around the house and the volunteering at Church. You two only had the one kid, so you won't understand." Jarred sounded like he was almost reading from a script.

"You had twins, Jarred. They are the same age—go to the same school and can probably even attend the after-school program that Brodie went to."

"That costs more money, though!" Jarred shouted another interruption. "Ella staying home saves us about two thousand a month right there, plus she can cook and clean. Take care of the dogs. Don't even get me started on her Church duties. You know how much she does!"

"What is happening? Are these things really important?" Smegma asked as he hovered down in front of uncle Jarred, studying his red face.

[Honestly, yes and no, but I think there is a lot of underlying stuff that isn't being said. I'm struggling to understand what's happening here myself. But my parents wouldn't push this point if there wasn't a good reason. Plus, I've been to Jarred's house—it's never clean….]

My parents and Jarred had continued the 'discussion' as I responded to Smegma. "—extra two thousand a month isn't much if you come back to work as a Specialist. That's all I'm saying," my father stated.

"We're not trying to attack you, Jar," my mom added. "Or Ella. She can still be a stay-at-home mom, as long as you're making more money. Or, if you're both working and you rejoin Gary as a Specialist—you'll be out of debt in no time."

Debt? I looked back to uncle Jarred. I hadn't known…

"The only reason I'm still sitting here is because you've helped us out so many times!" Jarred answered, his voice threatening. I swallowed a lump in my throat. I had changed the mood of this dinner to this subject and felt a bit responsible for where this conversation had gone. *Still, I could tell that there were still a lot of things being left unsaid.*

"So, ask about it?" Smegma said, once again reading my thoughts.

Is a Demon-Imp a reliable touchstone in human society? Someone to take advice from?

"Certainly," Smegma answered my 'unspoken' questions again. "If you don't ask, they're going to keep skirting around it."

With a deep inhalation and audible exhalation, I drew the attention of the adults at the table. "Can you guys stop beating around the bush and explain what's really going on?"

Gary and Clara looked to Jarred. Jarred's face morphed multiple times, going red from indignant anger, then white and stricken from meeting my parents' gazes. Eventually I heard him whisper, "Come on, guys, it's his Aunt Ella. He doesn't need to know…"

"He's an adult now, Jarred. Plus, he's the one with the Skill that can get you back to Mining as a Specialist. Maybe even with bonuses to get enough money to get her some help," my mother said.

Jarred stood up and slammed both hands onto the table. "I'm not going to sit here for this. Husk you both!"

Jarred stormed out of the dining room and made quite a bit of unnecessary angry noise as he put his shoes on. My parents didn't bother getting up, and instead looked at each other sadly. The door slammed and a car stuttered its engine multiple times. After the ninth or tenth stuttered attempt at starting, I heard a car door slam and some rather prolific swearing.

At this point, my dad got up and went to go help uncle Jarred, leaving me and my mother at the table.

"What's going on?" I asked, trying not to listen to Smegma prompting me to ask that exact question.

"I'm not sure if I should be the one to tell you this. Your father and I don't even know the whole story."

"Mom!" I retorted.

"Okay, Brodie, but please don't judge Ella or Jarred. Okay?" I nodded and she took a deep breath before starting. "When the twins were born, Ella took her maternity leave. She was working at Rummage Portals in the same position Jarred is currently working."

My eyes narrowed slightly at the way this story was starting. A knot started to form in my stomach as I predicted the next line my mother said. "As the year of leave was coming to an end, she wasn't ready to go back to work—or maybe she wasn't ready to put the twins in daycare. Or both, I suppose.

"So, she extended the leave to eighteen months. That meant that she wasn't drawing a paycheck anymore, though, since she had already received her maximum allowance of salary from the Canadian Government. Still, with Jarred working as a Miner, they were able to make ends meet. Or so Jarred thought."

The way my mother said the last line made my already-knotted stomach attempt to backflip as well. "Every day that Jarred came home, there started to be Rainforest Boxes on his porch. At first, what Ella was buying was necessities for the kids. Things like diapers and new clothes. However, that didn't last as she started buying outfits that would only be worn once before they were never used again."

"Oh no," I mumbled, feeling physically ill now.

"We held an intervention. Your father, myself and Jarred. We even thought it had worked, that we'd convinced her to start buying secondhand clothes from thrift stores, salvation armies and checking the stuff at the Catholic Church. But all we really did was make her hide the addiction.

"She got her own credit card and started hiding her purchases in the basement. It was right around then that your uncle Jarred inhaled Shilver Dust by accident. He ended up in the hospital for an extended stay, fighting for his life. You'll probably remember some of that…"

"Yeah, he was really sick…" I answered, recalling those visits to the hospital and seeing uncle Jarred hooked up to tubes, machines and constantly visited by a Gifted Healer. "Is that what caused the debt?"

"No," my mother answered sadly, while someone else mirrored those words from the doorway behind me. I spun in the chair to see Jarred there, looking strung out, pale, angry and defeated. He continued, his eyes meeting mine, "That was covered by the Miner Union insurance, thankfully. It was my loss of income and Ella's continued spending that put us behind the eight ball."

"The what?" I asked.

"It's a saying from a sport that many people used to play in bars," my father said as he came into the room behind Jarred. With a hand on my Uncle's back, my father guided him back to his chair.

"It just means that we are now fighting an uphill battle to get ourselves out of debt. It didn't help that I didn't even know about the second credit card. Plus, Ella was beyond distraught at the thought of losing me in some freak accident. As you said, I was fighting for my life." Clearly, Jarred had been in the doorway for a bit.

I recalled my mother looking over my shoulder sadly once or twice as she'd recollected the story. Maybe she hadn't been 'looking' at the front door, but at Jarred.

"She insisted I take a safer job and even managed to talk her boss into letting me take over for her. She argued that spending a couple thousand on daycare, or even more for nannies, wasn't worth it and that she'd stay home. It seemed reasonable…" Jarred said the last bit while looking pleadingly at my mother and father.

"It was, Jarred," my mother said consolingly. "Her hiding her purchases and debt wasn't."

Jarred's shoulders raised and a flush swept over his pale face as he clearly fought with anger. By the cant of his head and his unfocused eyes, which were directed down at the table, I could tell he was angry at himself and not my mother.

My mother picked up the story as she saw my uncle grow tongue-tied. "It was about a year later that the creditors started hounding her, and by association, Jarred. By then, the credit card debt had reached over eighty thousand dollars."

Jarred nodded along and picked up the story again. "Yeah, we agreed to garnish my wages to ensure we didn't have to declare bankruptcy and end up on the street."

"It's been almost fifteen years since then, Jar. Do you mind if we ask what the debt is down to now?" My father asked.

Jarred swallowed hard and shook his head sadly. I could tell that what he was going to say wasn't going to be good. Drops of water hit the scratched and stained wood under his hung head, and he stuttered in a breath. My father got up and put a hand on each of Jarred's shoulders.

The physical touch seemed to allow Jarred to mumble, "Two hundred thousand."

"I thought if you paid your credit card debts, they were supposed to go down?" Smegma asked, clearly confused.

[They should. But one of the most evil inventions of my people is something called compound interest. It basically means that if you borrow money, then you owe back that much plus a little more. If you borrowed a lot, that 'little more' might not be so little, and tough to pay. It gets added to the original amount—which increases both how much you owe in total and the interest. My guess is that, without Ella working and the continued expenses of the kids, their debt has only grown.]

"*Husk…* That's a plot worthy of Beelzebub himself." Smegma breathed, seemingly awe-struck.

I choked, spraying water across the table. A coughing fit took me then, my eyes watering as I fought to get myself under control. [Husking *Beelzebub* is real? What the *actual* hu—]

A heavy hand slapped my back. "Woah there, Son. It's not that surprising. You're embarrassing the man. Get yourself under control," he scolded. "And you wonder why we don't include you in the 'adult talk.' Well, show us you can handle it."

I was so grateful for the excuse of spitting out my water that I didn't even mind my dad getting on to me like that. However, I still glared out of the corner of my eye at Smegma. [We are *definitely* going to talk about this later.]

The Imp just shrugged and nodded, seeming confused. I turned my attention back to the table.

"Yessir," I nodded emphatically. "Sorry, uncle Jarred, I was just surprised, that's all. I've never even seen that much money. Sorry."

Jarred waved it off, chuckling. "Don't sweat it, kid. I spit out my beer when my wife told me about the eighty thousand, so don't be so hard on yourself."

"And that's with the fifty thousand in loans you've taken from us, to pay back the government for Ella not returning to work?" My dad asked, trying and failing to keep his voice from sounding shocked.

"No. Luckily, it's not as bad as all that. The two hundred thousand is including the money I've borrowed from you and Willa. The credit card is still sitting at eighty thousand…"

"Surely, that means he'll join the crew, right?" Smegma asked, and I could only shrug.

This was a situation far deeper and more turbulent than I could dive into. *All I knew was that uncle Jarred needed help—and a lot of it.*

"Maybe Aunt Ella even more so," Smegma stated, clearly skimming my surface thoughts.

I could only nod.

CHAPTER 34

Monday, April 15th, 2069

"So, did you try the meditation or answering the questions I sent you?" Evelyn asked after a very lengthy greeting and current mood check. My wince conveyed my answer and she sighed. "You won't get as much out of these sessions if you don't at least try to work with me."

"I'm sorry. I've been pretty busy."

"Don't you have Sundays off?" She asked, clearly going over her notes from our previous session.

"Yes, well," I said while nodding. "Yesterday kind of became even more of a distraction than work because we had it off."

"More of a distraction? Have you been finding yourself distracted often?"

"Husk, this lady is amazing," Smegma said from his perch on the highest shelf. "She can twist anything you say into something else… I think I'm in love," That last bit was said while tossing up a small, white kernel into the air and catching it in his open mouth. Where had the husker gotten actual *popcorn* this time? Surely it wasn't real, or Evelyn would be questioning the floating bag…

"I didn't say that I, personally, was distracted—and I'd appreciate it if you stopped twisting my words. I don't like it. What I meant was that some things came up during my day off that took my time and attention. I went in for pre-trial prep work, which was just a bunch of 'sit there and don't react' training. Then, we had my uncle Jarred over for dinner and he, and my family, dropped a bombshell on me. So, yeah, I was pretty *distracted* all weekend."

"What about the nights after Mining?" Evelyn asked and I winced again. Sure, I could have spent those nights meditating and answering the emailed questions. But I had been looking through the Shop or talking with Smegma. That wasn't a distraction, was it?

"It was," Smegma stated, with a particularly loud crunch of popcorn. That popcorn had to be fake, right?

"I see," she said after my long silence. "I apologize for 'twisting your words.' Clearly, you haven't been distracted in the slightest and I'm just mistaken."

Smegma nearly squealed, shoving fistfuls more of the salty snack into his stupid pie-hole.

"Okay," I cleared my throat, desperately trying to not start screaming at my 'imaginary friend.' I just didn't think that would go well in therapy.

"Well, let's tackle some of the questions now then, shall we?" Evelyn asked. I nodded gratefully and Evelyn asked the first question, which was also the last question of her previous session.

"You said your dream to become a Mana Bank has morphed into something more. Why is that?"

I immediately cursed internally. I should have looked at these questions and answered them when I had time to think. Now, with my brain consumed with the pre-trial this afternoon and Jarred's predicament, I felt extremely put on the spot.

Still, I should be able to tell my psychiatrist the truth. Right? Wasn't there client confidentiality just like with Lawyers? Smegma encouraged me to ask her. So, I did.

"Yes, anything you tell me will stay between us. I do have to give general updates if asked, basically stating whether or not you've been attending, or if you need more counseling. Stuff like that."

"Okay," I answered with a nod. "When The Shop—sorry, Morgan Hallsbrad, assaulted me, I had a secondary Awakening."

"You did?!" Evelyn said, sounding shocked and excited, but forcing herself to maintain a level of professionalism. "Anything good?"

I considered for the briefest of moments about telling her the whole truth. Yet, there was one thing I'd 'learned' from Hollyhood on this matter. Shrinks and lawyers could break confidentiality if they believed someone was a threat to others or themselves.

So, would telling Evelyn about Smegma, and *Demonic Vault*, fall into that category? From my point of view, no, but from others? Maybe.

Eventually, I went with the concocted story I was telling everyone. I just couldn't be sure that telling Evelyn about my 'Demonic' Skill wouldn't lead to me in a shrink ward, or worse—Permanently Husked of all Skills. "I got a repair mark for equipment…"

"You can repair equipment?!" Evelyn said. Her excitement was still higher than I expected. I waved my hands in front of myself to try to explain that it wasn't that fancy.

"No, no. I can put a mark on equipment that allows it to pull ambient Mana in to repair itself."

"It doesn't pull 'ambient Mana'—the gear pulls—" Smegma began, even as Evelyn stood up and began to pace.

"So, you can place this mark on gear and it will just pull in Mana to repair itself. That's quite the valuable—"

"Sorry, I think I used the wrong term," I interrupted. "It pulls… 'spilled' Mana to repair itself?" I corrected, using the term Smegma was practically shouting from his popcorn-eating perch while laughing. "I'm not sure of the best way to describe it."

"What you're calling 'spilled Mana' is Mana given off by plants, creatures, minerals, Crystals and other stuff as they are being harvested?" I flicked my eyes over to Smegma before nodding. Evelyn returned to excitedly pacing. "That is a very valuable Skill, Brodie—and I assume you've been using it with Portals, Portal's, Portalz and your Mining?"

"Well, yes."

"And that's why you don't want to be a Mana Bank anymore? You've found a more lucrative vocation? So, you want to own a company now?" Evelyn grabbed her book and began madly scribbling notes even as her questions hung in the air.

"What? No," I said, which elicited a derisive laugh from Smegma.

"Wrong answer, kid."

"So, what is the new dream, Brodie?" Evelyn asked, making me realize what Smegma meant. Answering 'yes' to her previous question would have avoided this follow-up.

"I mean, yes, or… maybe. I don't know. I just haven't gotten that far yet. What I do know is that I can now grow my Mana Pool on my own. So, maybe in time I will still want to be a Mana Bank, or own a company, or smite *Demons* with my magically empowered gear…"

"Good one," Smegma commented.

"*Demons* are an interesting choice of Monsters to choose." Evelyn quickly made some notes, and Smegma's laughter cut off, leaving the room eerily silent in its absence. After she was done with whatever note she took, she returned to the points before my 'joke.' "I see. So, you feel like you're reassessing your previous dreams? Or are you in fact putting off thinking about them because of something else?"

"Something else? Like what?" I asked.

"Like a feeling that anything you want to do could be taken from you—without your permission." Evelyn sat back down in her chair with that statement, causing the leather to groan audibly. I ran my hand through my hair.

That was oddly specific. I assumed it was in reference to the assault. Morgan *did* try to take something away from me without my permission. Did I have any feelings like that? I shook my head and Evelyn nodded, even as she made a new note.

"No, I'm not sure that's it, exactly. I just know I can do more now—and I don't want to pigeonhole myself into something."

"Into something as *small* as owning a company, when you can do so much more?" Evelyn asked.

After a brief hesitation, I nodded. "Am I… broken? Is there some kind of 'Main Character' disorder out there that I've got? I just want to *do* more, to *be*… more."

Evelyn smiled. It was a smile full of softly spoken approval and a hint of rebuke. "No. You're not 'broken.' Everyone is the main character of their own story, Brodie Flacarada. Even you."

I blinked. "I… never thought about it that way. I mean, even with this Skill, I could probably get into the Crafting Classes at Phoenix University. Maybe learn some ways to apply it to Hunter's gear and still have it work when killing Monsters."

"So, the bottom line is that you want to help Hunters in the fight against Portals and Fields?" Evelyn asked. I nodded again and she made a note. "So, why do you think that Miners, Cleaners, Herbalists and the like aren't helping Hunters?"

I raised my hands defensively as I strongly denied Evelyn's accusation. "I never said that! I know that Gatherers help Hunters, too—I just…Well, I just want to be more hands-on?"

Evelyn smiled as she made a new note. "I think we're getting somewhere. Why do you feel you need to be more 'hands-on?'" I made a confused face and she changed the question. "If you had the ability to Enchant weapons with something that empowered them against Monsters—and then you sold that to Hunters—would that be enough?"

Now understanding what Evelyn was getting at, I shrugged, before licking my teeth and shaking my head. "No, that wouldn't be enough."

"Can you explain that?"

"I want to be in charge of my own destiny, I guess," I said, trying to feel my way to the bottom of the strange concept that Evelyn evoked in me. "I guess, with the re-Awakening, I want to be an actual Hunter now."

"Oh? Are you thinking of trying to be like ManIron or Cyborg?" she asked and I felt my eyebrows raise in consideration. With the 'repair mark,' that certainly would be a possibility. Still, the truth and my lie kind of lined up at that moment. So, I nodded.

Evelyn made some more notes and then asked a new question. "Why is being a Hunter or *directly* helping more important to you than providing value in some other way?"

Her question was punctuated by her tablet beeping, but other than reaching to click off the timer, she kept intently staring at me.

Seeing as I wasn't about to get off the hook this time, I said, "I think being a Hunter will make me powerful. It will put me in control of my own destiny. I can make it so that my family stops living from paycheck to paycheck—maybe even solve other issues, too."

Evelyn didn't ask a follow-up question and instead scribbled in her book. When she finished, she looked back up and met my eyes with an intensity I hadn't yet seen from her.

"This time, Brodie, I'm going to insist you follow the meditation exercises I sent—and answer my newest batch of questions. As you know, that timer marked the end of our session. So, I'll see you next Monday?"

"As long as I'm not dead or in jail," I said jokingly, but flushed when Evelyn tilted her head and made a new note.

Smegma laughed uproariously as he called me a bunch of variations of stupid, along with a *healthy* smattering of profanity.

* * *

"To the charge of second-degree manslaughter, how does Brodie Flacarada plead?" The Judge asked, the question appearing rote and clearly spoken often.

"Not guilty, Your Honor," Ms. Stovall said on my behalf.

We were currently inside the Judge's office and not in the far larger courtrooms I'd seen through various open doors. The building was clearly old, but the office—unlike the one I was in with Evelyn this morning—carried that age with a level of class and dignity that far outstripped the woman's mismatched furniture.

"This is more like it," Smegma said in response to my assessment of the furniture. "Everything matches—the books are boring but look ostentatious and expensive. This person clearly knows how to impress those who are visiting her chambers."

I of course ignored the Demon-Imp, tuning in to the two others in the room—the people I assumed were assigned to represent Morgan Hallsbrad.

There was something strange going on. Standing behind the chair was a well-dressed man in a suit comparable to Ms. Stovall's blouse and skirt. It was definitely not overly expensive but functional and well kept. Seated in the chair, however, was someone entirely different. I tried to remember the training Ms. Stovall put me through yesterday and kept my face neutral as I studied him.

The man wore a dark, shiny suit that screamed money. In fact, I was pretty sure that the material was made from Portal cotton and Monster wool and leather. It made the man look suave and dangerous. I didn't understand the reason for my feelings of apprehension until the Judge looked at the man standing nearby.

"Crown Attorney Markham, I assume you disagree with that, considering that Mr. Varnish is here?" Judge Dench said, sounding almost sarcastic. I fought a smile that threatened to break onto my face. It seemed that the Judge was already on my side.

"Yes, Your Honor," Markham responded, making a hand and arm gesture at the seated man, who fixed his expensive suit and stood up. He was easily as tall as me, if not taller. He carried that height with a lithe athleticism that almost made me shiver. His features were all sharp. His black hair and light brown eyes made him look even more intimidating. "As you already know—Mr. Varnish is here on behalf of the Larvae Guild to represent their member Morgan Hallsbrad. The Attorney General, along with the Supreme Court, has appointed him as a temporary Crown Counsel for this case."

Mr. Varnish was suddenly holding a leather portfolio, making me blink. Had he just pulled that from a Bag of Holding? I searched what I could see of him and didn't find anything overt that looked like one of the bulky bags I'd seen the Lynx Guild Member carrying in the Portals.

If the man didn't have a Bag, could he have a Ring, or something far pricier? He was wearing an expensive-looking watch, but no rings that I could see.

"Your Honor," Mr. Varnish said with a dip of his black, styled hair, interrupting my scrutiny of the man's jewelry. "On behalf of Her Majesty the Queen, we will prove that Mr. Flacarada used excessive force to defend himself, and in doing so, seized an opportunity that is highly beneficial to himself."

As instructed, I kept my reaction to another blink even as Smegma said, "What the husk is he talking about?"

"Your Honor, Morgan Hallsbrad had a gun and not only intended to use it but had a history of doing so in past murders." Ms Stovall said, clearly contradicting Mr. Varnish's attempt to paint me as somehow guilty.

I transferred my gaze to the judge, still trying to control my reactions. The judge was an older woman. Likely sixty or so. She had grey hair, styled in a bob. She wore a robe. Everything about her had a dignity and aura that seemed fair. I liked her immediately.

"I have to agree with Ms. Stovall, Mr. Varnish; Morgan Hallsbrad has been tied to multiple murders up and down the East Coast of the United States."

"That has been grossly misinterpreted, Your Honor." Mr. Varnish pulled out a piece of paper from the portfolio, not having to sort through it, and handed it to the Judge. She read it quickly, her eyebrows rising. As soon as she was finished, she handed it to Ms. Stovall. Mr. Varnish handed over the next page, again simply pulling it from the next in line. It felt like he was beyond prepared, which caused goosebumps to rise on my skin.

This time, when the Judge handed the next sheet to Ms. Stovall, she wasn't handed another. Instead, Mr. Varnish said, "As you can see, Morgan Hallsbrad was a private investigator hired by a fellow Guild member to investigate the death of a daughter while she was stateside. The next piece of paper further explains his visits to every victim of the crime, which is how the DNA evidence was accidentally transferred to the book."

Ms. Stovall snorted. "Judge Dench. The prosecuting counsel here would have you believe that Morgan Hallsbrad visited every single victim and *accidentally* had their DNA transferred onto the book—multiple times. If you don't mind my saying, Mr. Varnish here should go to Vegas if he's betting on those odds. Not only that, but none of this is proof that Brodie Flacarada used excessive force, Your Honor," Ms. Stovall interjected.

The Judge met Ms. Stovall's eyes, nodded, and then looked to Mr. Varnish, seeming to silently direct the question to him.

Mr. Varnish appeared unfazed. "It is my intention to not only prove Morgan Hallsbrad's innocence of these crimes but show that he approached Brodie Flacarada as a person of interest, with no ill intent."

"Your Honor, we aren't here to judge Morgan Hallsbrad. This pre-trial is to clear my client of any responsibility. May I remind the Court that Morgan Hallsbrad was a C-Ranked Awakened with a gun!"

"*Mister* Varnish," the Judge scowled. "I am going to have to side with Ms. Stovall on this. Morgan Hallsbrad is not on trial here. I will remind you that in this case you are representing the Attorney General and by association the Crowned Queen of England. It is not under your purview to 'prove' Morgan Hallsbad's guilt or innocence. Confine yourself to the actual case at hand:

"Brodie Flacarada claims that he was attacked by Morgan Hallsbrad with a gun, unlawfully Mana Connected, and defended himself, which resulted in the death of his attacker. Morgan Hallsbrad was a C-Ranked Awakened and in possession of a weapon.

"You have one question you need to answer: What possible reason would I have to allow you to take this to a trial against Mr. Flacarada?

"I will further remind you that Mr. Flacarada is innocent until proven guilty, which—as you know—means that the burden of proof that his claims are false are the primary focus for you to prove and *not* the innocence or guilt of Morgan Hallsbrad. Those murders occurred in the States and another Judge will be presiding over *that* case. Are we clear?"

I'll give it to Mr. Varnish. He smoothly bowed as if he were before the Queen herself. "Forgive me, Judge Dench. I misspoke. I only meant that I would use the proper evidence gathered in regard to Morgan Hallsbrad and use it only as it pertains to Mr. Flacarada's testimony in order to prove his guilt of excessive force with clear intent. Going forward, I may refer to Morgan Hallsbrad as 'my client,' as he is—by proxy—the extension of my current client's involvement in this case." He calmly straightened his suit, continuing on. "Your Honor, as I've already mentioned, Morgan Hallsbrad was a private investigator hired by a grandfather of one of the first victims. He was tracking the killer up the east coast, where he discovered a link to Brodie Flacarada. From what my employer knows, he was approaching Brodie peacefully to offer to discuss this issue when things went south."

Mr. Varnish handed over a small, leatherbound journal to the Judge. "In here you will find a detailed description of Morgan's findings from his investigation. The final pages highlight the link between Brodie and the case."

I tried and failed to stop my eyes from widening. I did manage to keep my mouth from falling open, but just barely. My eyes found Ms. Stovall, who was looking confusedly between Mr. Varnish and the Judge. Once the book was handed to her, she skipped to the final page, as the Judge had.

"Let me get this straight. Your client was tracking comments made by the SwiftGram Account he is suspected of owning? Then entered the country illegally to approach Brodie Flacarada after seeing a 'flame war' on one of his posts?" Ms. Stovall pulled a paper from her own pack and handed it to the Judge. "This is a document from Border Control, Your Honor. I have simplified it to individuals with last names starting with 'H,' and who entered the country through customs and border control, including all land-bound traffic and commercial flights up to a month before the assault."

Judge Dench flipped through two to three pages of the huge, stapled stack before looking dryly at Ms. Stovall and asking, "I assume I won't find Hallsbrad on here even outside of the appropriate alphabetical section?"

"That's correct, Your Honor. I believe that Morgan Hallsbrad *knew* he would succeed in killing my client. Why would he not? As the primary suspect in the Heartless Killer murders, he'd successfully accomplished it dozens of times up to that point. Knowing he would succeed, one of his concerns would be not leaving a trail indicating that he'd crossed the border into Canada at all—just pop over the border, kill an unknown-to-the-public college kid, and pop back over—leaving no tracks for law enforcement to follow. We know he's in the country right now—we have his body, for crying out loud! If this hearing was about me being required to prove that Morgan Hallsbrad crossed the border from the United States into Canada between March 27th and April 1st—I wouldn't be able to do it. How did he get here? I believe that this gives some insight on how the man has managed to remain at large for as long as he has. He is a ghost. As for the Prosecution's outlandish claims of goodwill and 'helpful' intentions, I have a further question for Mr. Varnish. Why did your 'client' Morgan Hallsbrad need to 'approach my client peacefully' with a weapon behind the trash cans of a darkened alleyway?" The skepticism in Ms. Stovall's voice was so thick I could nearly taste it.

Mr. Varnish didn't react to her comment and instead dutifully handed over another paper to the Judge, which she began to read instantly. The raise of her eyebrows conveyed confusion and shock to me, and her words furthered it. "The weapon at the scene had its serial number filed off and didn't contain a single fingerprint outside of Brodie Flacarada's?"

My brain stuttered. That was impossible. Smegma was staring at me, clearly reading my thoughts as they raced through my head. I'd looked down the barrel of the gun that *Morgan Hallsbrad* had been holding!

Ms. Stovall was reading through the page, her eyes tracing left to right as they climbed over the report multiple times. She looked up to the Judge quickly after what could have been a fifth or sixth perusal. "Your Honor, the fact that my client's fingerprints are on a gun that he didn't own isn't contradictory to events as told to the Court. He was held at gunpoint and used reasonable force to disarm a C-Ranked Awakened in possession of a deadly firearm."

"Ahem." The Prosecutor cleared his throat, handing over yet another document. "Disarmed? The police report here demonstrates only that *Mr. Flacarada* was in possession of the firearm and was commanded by officers arriving on the scene to drop the weapon. There is no evidence that it was taken from Mr. Hallsbrad. Unless the Court has any evidence of that claim?" Mr. Varnish asked the Judge.

Judge Dench turned and looked at Ms. Stovall, who flipped through a few pages on her desk before punching a finger into the bottom of one. "Yes, Your Honor. A video from the Transit Station captured Mr. Hallsbrad leading Brodie away at gunpoint."

"Okay, let me see it," Judge Dench stated as she held up her hand and simultaneously opened a laptop. Ms. Stovall flipped open her bag and pulled out a USB, consulted her page and then handed the USB stick to the judge.

"The file is TransitCamFootage2, Your Honor," she explained and the Judge nodded before clicking around.

Once Mr. Varnish could tell she was watching the video, he chimed in. "The important part is at ten fifty-five, Your Honor. You will no doubt notice that no gun is present."

His knowledge of the time in the video and quick direction to it made my head feel light. What was going on?

"What's he talking about?" Smegma said. "You told me the guy had a gun and you just remembered looking down the barrel."

[He husking *did*. I have no idea what's going on.]

There was a long silence, which was finally broken by the Judge looking up at Ms. Stovall. "Ms. Stovall. I'm afraid that while it does look like Morgan Hallsbrad has a hand either in a jacket pocket, or right beside his body, there is no obvious sign of a gun in this video. Do you have any other proof that Mr. Flacarada was held at gunpoint?"

"Your Honor, I also watched the tape and agree that the camera angle and distance from the scene in question isn't the best. However, with the footage of Morgan Hallsbrad's stance and my client's testimony, as well as the fact that it is undeniable that Mr. Hallsbrad led my client toward the same alleyway that my client had previously avoided, I believe there is enough probable evidence present to assume compulsion. Let me ask the Court two questions: Was there a gun present at the scene of the attack?" Ms. Stovall asked calmly.

"You know there was, Ms. Stovall." Judge Dench stated, sighing.

"*We* know there was because that weapon is part of evidence." Ms. Stovall turned her gaze on Mr. Varnish. "If the weapon was at the scene and not shown in this video, where was it? Furthermore, whose could it have been if not Morgan Hallsbrad's? Let's not forget, Judge Dench, Morgan Hallsbrad is the number one suspect in the Heartless Killer serial killings. Even after more than sixty-five killings—which evidence is adding to daily. Morgan Hallsbrad is the *number one* suspect in a case in which the killer was *never caught.* We have to seriously take the possibility that Morgan Hallsbrad was a capable, cunning killer who would likely be wearing gloves and heavily aware of the possibility of security cameras in public spaces. Logically, he wouldn't openly reveal the weapon we found at the scene.

"Additionally, Your Honor, as I alluded to before—we have numerous videos that show Brodie specifically avoiding that alleyway on his way to the transit station, and that Morgan Hallsbrad led him into it after approaching him. Why would my client willingly go with him into an area he'd just recently avoided, despite that path being the shortest route to and from where he was going?"

"Ms. Stovall, your logic that Morgan Hallsbrad possessed the gun and wore gloves are accusations that would need to be proven in court, if it cannot be clearly demonstrated during this hearing. I will also note that none of your assertions prove that Hallsbrad threatened your client with that weapon. Such accusations require proof. As for the factual evidence you've mentioned, I assume I can watch those videos?" Judge Dench said. Ms. Stovall consulted her list and then conveyed the relevant file names to the Judge. Mr. Varnish remained silent through the exchange, which made my skin crawl, even as my heart hammered apprehensively.

After another twenty minutes of silence, in which the Judge confirmed Ms. Stovall's proof, and I had to continually remind myself to breath, she turned to Mr. Varnish. "These videos, along with the campus map, do make a compelling argument that Brodie Flacarada was led against his will into an area he had previously avoided. I'm leaning toward Ms. Stovall once again, Mr. Varnish."

"This is why it is so important for me to show the Court Morgan Hallsbrad's innocence in regards to the Heartless Killer murders, Your Honor. If you'll permit me, I have further evidence that lends itself toward Morgan Hallsbrad's innocence of the accused assault and thus solidifies the story told in his case journal. This evidence may not show that Morgan peacefully approached Brodie Flacarada, but it certainly shows that he isn't the 'cold, cunning' killer he is being painted as by the Defense."

Mr. Varnish hadn't glanced at me once through this entire meeting with the Judge, but when the Judge glanced my direction, so did the man. I felt like a rabbit when a large wolf catches it in the open. I wanted to shiver but I held it back.

The Judge didn't convey much with that look, but to me, it felt like she was sad for me. I wondered why, right up until she held out a hand and said, "I'll read this evidence first, before I make the final decision, if it's relevant to this case."

The silence that stretched was broken only by Ms. Stovall fiddling with something in her pocket. It wasn't truly loud, but as the Judge read the manilla folder that had the word 'classified' stamped in red on it—it sure sounded loud.

The Judge sighed when she reached the end. "Mr. Varnish, I do believe that this evidence may be enough to clear Morgan Hallsbrad in the cases that the UNMH is bringing against him, but I do not believe that continued activity of a SwiftGram account named 'The Shop' after Morgan's death and new murders connected to the Heartless Killer in California mean that Brodie should be under any suspicion in the events of this case."

"That may be true, Your Honor, but that isn't for you to determine. One thing that this does neatly defeat, is Counselwoman Stovall's assertion that Morgan Hallsbrad is the primary suspect of the Heartless Killer murders, as well as her statements that he would act or behave as a hardened killer, with gloves, foreknowledge of public cameras and their locations. The 'cunning killer' that entered the country illegally? Come now. To that last point—I have here a flight manifesto that I prepared in advance against the potential of anyone questioning my client's entering the country unlawfully or with criminal designs." As he handed over this final sheet of thick, official-looking paper, I felt my throat constrict—tightening down and stopping my breathing from coming easy.

My breathing sounded loud in my own ears, but no one else even glanced at me.

Like a roofer with a nail gun, Mr. Varnish continued, puncturing my screaming lungs with his well-prepared, and extremely false, case. "The Larvae Guild, of whom Morgan Hallsbrad was an upstanding member, expedited his transportation across the Canadian border via private jet. These documents were disclosed appropriately to both the United States and Canadian Federal Aviation Administration. His entry into the country was validated and verified at the highest levels.

"As I also believe I've given the Court ample evidence to call into question the ownership of the weapon in evidence, it is my statement and assertion that Morgan Hallsbrad carried no such weapon on this flight, nor on his person at the time of meeting Mr. Flacarada, Your Honor. I, for one, am not convinced that it belonged to Morgan Hallsbrad at all. We only have Brodie's testimony that Morgan held the weapon for any length of time, and—as we already proved— there was no sign of Hallsbrad holding the gun in the videos, coupled with the fact that Mr. Flacarada was found by the police with the weapon in his hands, and his fingerprints were the only ones present on the weapon…"

This time when Mr. Varnish paused, I managed to suck in a breath only due to my biological need for oxygen. It came in, stuttering and loud, clearly going against my one day of 'don't react' training. What in the hell was going on? My eyes were already unfocused and I felt lost. Still, Mr. Varnish didn't relent.

"I believe that this is more than enough grounds for jurisprudence to be compelled to put this case in front of a panel of impartial peers." Mr. Varnish responded far too calmly.

I felt a small hand on my shoulder and with it came a rush of warmth. That's right, I still had Ms. Stovall. Surely this pre-trial wasn't going as poorly as it seemed?

"Your Honor, my client has gone through enough; surely we don't need to parade a victim in a public trial on top of everything else."

Judge Dench looked at the two lawyers and then met my confused, wide eyes. "Jury trials are only for criminal cases. You know that, Mr. Varnish. Your evidence is by majority circumstantial and has not met the prerequisite thresholds. I agree with Ms. Stovall that a victim should not be made to suffer further, Counselman. Unless you can present me with something more, I will move to weigh in on the evidence of Ms. Stovall's that supports self-defense."

"As you wish, Your Honor. I would like to enter into evidence video forty-seven. This video shows Mr. Flacarada getting into his car at the mall before going through a second, third, or perhaps even a *fourth* Awakening after the manslaughter."

The Judge blinked and looked at me, then Ms. Stovall, before holding out a hand toward Mr. Varnish. As Ms. Stovall had done with the transit cam footage, Mr. Varnish gave her a USB along with instructions on what video to open.

"I've clipped the video to save your time, Your Honor," he said to finish.

I felt my stomach, which felt like it couldn't twist any more, clench tight. I knew what video he must have. It was the one where I got in the car and purchased the first Miner's Pick—where everyone in the parking garage saw my car light up like it was struck by a flash-bang.

"Is this bad?" Smegma asked as he hovered close to me and looked into my eyes.

[I don't know? I don't see how a new Skill could change anything.] Even my mental voice sounded lost.

"Ms. Stovall, this clearly shows Mr. Flacarada undergoing an Awakening. Have you had him re-Assessed?"

I felt the slithering snake of my stomach somehow constrict further. I definitely was no longer an F-Rank Awakened. Just based on my Mana Pool, now sitting at forty-five points, moved me from peak F-Rank to high E-Rank. Sure, the growth was slowing down pretty significantly, but that paired with all of my existing and new Skills might put me anywhere from E to B-Rank if assessed. I fought my own face to stop from reacting as Ms. Stovall replied.

"I can neither confirm nor deny the presence of my client undergoing an Awakening. So far, I can see no relevance to this case whether it happened or not."

"Confirm nor deny?" Mr. Varnish drawled. "The evidence is right in front of your face. If what happened to your client in that car wasn't an Awakening, then what was it?"

"You tell me." Ms. Stovall retorted. "As Judge Dench stated earlier, the burden of proof is not on me in this pre-trial. It's on you, and until you prove to the Judge how this is relevant to the case, I refuse to possibly acknowledge anything that might unknowingly impact Mr. Flacarada either in this case or going forward."

Mr. Varnish looked appreciatively at Ms. Stovall. "Your Honor, the reason this is relevant is that the case is being presented as an F-Rank versus a C-Rank, but not only is Mr. Flacarada possibly far higher than C-Rank, I can prove that at the time of his death, Morgan Hallsbrad was no longer C-Rank."

"What do you mean, Mr. Varnish?" Judge Dench asked.

Once again, Mr. Varnish entered in new evidence and directed Judge Dench on where to find it. This time he also presented a paper to Ms. Stovall. She quickly read it over and a frown slowly grew into a scowl on her face.

"At autopsy, Mr. Hallsbrad was Skill-less and below F-Rank? How is this possible Mr. Varnish?" Judge Dench asked.

"We have our suspicions, Your Honor, but no proof. If Mr. Flacarada would like to go through a re-Assessment though and prove that he is still F-Rank, the Crown might be willing to grant self-defense as a verdict in the manslaughter case."

"Your Honor, the date of the video where my client allegedly underwent a secondary Awakening is a full two days after the altercation. Even if he did undergo another Awakening at that time, I fail to see how it has any bearing on the case."

"She is right, Mr. Varnish. Even if he is of a higher rank now, it doesn't mean he was then. Just like your client at autopsy being of lower rank doesn't exactly mean that he wasn't of higher rank during the assault."

"Then I must ask, Your Honor, if my client was Unskilled at the time of his autopsy, and—as Ms. Stovall here asserts—C-Ranked at the time of the alleged attack, then what happened to Morgan Hallsbrad's C-Ranked Skills in the intervening thirteen hours between the events on campus and the autopsy? That is not enough time for the Mana in a Pool to even fade."

"I see what you're implying, Mr. Varnish, but without further proof, I will not order Mr. Flacarada to be reassessed. I will, however, be stating clearly, Ms. Stovall—that in my assessment, the evidence of an apparent Awakening happening to Mr. Flacarada does appear to be potentially relevant to this case. So I'll ask you: what does this new Skill do, or what exactly was it that happened on this security footage, assuming this was not an Awakening at all?"

"Very well. My client did, in fact, experience a second Awakening during the events in the security footage. From my understanding, and his growing understanding, it repairs Mining Picks from 'spilled' Mana."

"So, Mr. Flacarada is able to capture Mana leakage from Minerals, Ores, Creatures and Flora?" Mr. Varnish asked.

Ms. Stovall glanced at me then back up to Mr. Varnish before she answered, "That isn't what I said, Mr. Varnish. From my understanding, his Skill can use the Mana Spillage from Mining Mana Crystals in particular to Repair a Pickaxe. That's our full understanding of the Skill at present."

"That's some excellent tip-toeing you're doing there, Ms. Stovall, and I commend you for it. However, the fact is that we now know that Mr. Flacarada has a Skill that siphons Mana and we only have his word that this Skill works solely on Crystals. What we also know is that there is a body that Mr. Flacarada has recently interacted with and whose ranking after death mysteriously dropped. I submit that he is not telling the full truth and he likely is able to capture spilled Mana from dead or dying humans as well. This is where we believe Morgan Hallsbrad's Skills went. The Crown believes that Brodie Flacarada may be a Cannibal or Snatcher."

"Holy shit, this guy is good," Smegma said, sounding impressed.

268

[Don't husking compliment him! Everything—] I hesitated before correcting myself, [—most of what he said is a lie, and you know it.]

"Yeah, I know it, but there is no way that anyone besides you and me can truly know that he's lying. That's why I said he's good."

"Ms. Stovall. Do you have any evidence that can prove beyond a reasonable doubt that Mr. Flacarada didn't use excessive force in self-defense so he could steal Morgan Hallsbrad's spilled Mana?"

Two muscles bulged on the side of Ms. Stovall's face, but after a moment she looked directly at the Judge and exclaimed, "Yes, Your Honor. There still remains a time discrepancy. The fact that this Skill didn't Awaken until two days *after* the assault. Is Mr. Varnish accusing my client of traveling back in time to 'steal' Morgan Hallsbrad's spilled Mana?"

"As I've already mentioned Judge Dench, this Awakening could be a third such, and does not need to be the only one that Mr. Flacarada has undergone. In this, I must ask the Court who else had access to Morgan Hallsbrad before, or immediately after, his death that had the potential to remove these Skills and possibly acquire them at a later date?"

Ms. Stovall's jaw clenched again as the Judge looked to her. "Your Honor, when Morgan Hallsbrad was taken to the hospital—he was taken there *alive*. There are *numerous* people who could have and did interact with him during that time. I was not aware of the loss or disappearance of Mr. Hallsbrad's Skills and therefore did not interview or investigate the circumstances around his death beyond the available medical reports. The autopsy was not available yesterday evening when my office requested the report. I'm not sure how Mr. Varnish was able to secure a copy when I was not." The man's bright smile didn't appear to be helping Ms. Stovall's mood. "The fact is that the implication that my client was the last person to interact with Morgan Hallsbrad before his death is far from the truth. However, without a proper investigation, I am unable to determine if—or under what circumstances—Mr. Hallsbrad may have lost his Skills during his time at the hospital."

Judge Dench sighed tiredly. "I'm afraid that lack of time or resources is not a valid argument, Ms. Stovall.

"Counselman Varnish. Counselwoman Stovall. In this preliminary hearing of the case of Brodie Flacarada vs The Crown Council appointed by the Attorney General and Supreme Court of Canada, I am—at this time—unable to determine the guilt or innocence of the defendant Brodie Flacarada beyond a reasonable doubt." Judge Dench said, her eyes locking onto mine. "I'm afraid I will have to send this to a private trial."

CHAPTER 35

Tuesday, April 16th, 2069

"**I**'ve got some more bad news," Smegma said as we began Mining the following day. It had been a rather long night of explaining the horrible news of the pre-trial to my family, over, and over again. So, Smegma uttering those words instantly put a spike of hot iron into my gut.

[What is it?] I asked as I pummeled an F-Rank Mana Crystal into Shards.

"Your Strength Stat didn't go up at all yesterday," Smegma grumbled, the simple statement sounding like a pronouncement of death by the tone of the Demon-Imp. I waited for more, even pausing in Mining to rub the back of my forearm over my forehead to clear the sweat.

Today's Dungeon was all underground. A cave System that was likely extremely deep on the 'planet' we currently were on. Why did I think that? Well, the heat that radiated from the rocks surrounding us suggested that we were closer to the core than we were to the surface. Or at least that's what the Lynx Guild believed.

Finally, I had enough and prompted, [And?]

"It seems you have to be present to receive the Mana Spillage from the Enchant," Smegma explained, his voice hysterical, like this news should send me into suicidal thoughts.

[Still not picking up what you're laying down, Champ.]

"Well, I mean you could have owned a business and just sat back as your Stats and Skills came pouring in, Chief."

I rolled my eyes. *Only a fat, lazy Demon-Imp—*

"Hey, that's totally uncalled for *bucko!*" The lazy Imp complained.

[Whatever, then stop eating all that buttery 'popcorn.' As far as 'bad' news goes—that's like a one on the Richter scale I'm currently reading from. The rest of the shit going on ranks around an eight. Just for reference…]

I continued to Shard when I realized something. It was something I probably should have asked Smegma a while ago. [Umm, Smegma, you probably know what all the locked Stats are right?]

"Took you long enough, but nope, not a clue, dumb-dumb," Smegma said as I set up to Mine a Perfect Crystal. I paused and looked pointedly at him, and he got the hint. "We didn't have a Stat called Strength. Crendalar Five had three primary 'Stats' and some hidden ones that only a few people possessed."

My Pick tinged into the soil and I felt the head hit the stem of the Crystal perfectly, severing the thing in a single swing. It felt good, brightening my mood, until I realized that Smegma wasn't going to offer further explanation—which admittedly annoyed me. [And those three Stats *were?*]

"What the husk do you care, you clearly have seven—" He growled. I glared at the Imp even as I sold the Crystal. "Ughhh. Whatever, fine. The three main Stats were Martial Power, Magic and Force. Do you need a description of what these Stats did, too?"

[That would be fantastic.]

"Why do you husking need to know when you don't have them?"

I gave the Demon a look. [Am I the only one listening to this conversation? You *just* said that you didn't know what the locked Stats are. Neither of us know if one of those locked Stats are one of the ones your people had. Sooo… it might be helpful for me to know what different Stats did in your world. Even if humans don't get the same Stats as Demons, there may be similar effects between the two.]

The Imp scowled after my 'gotcha' moment. "I guess I've got nothing better to do, anyway. Okay, Martial Power was the strength of body and came with a pool of energy we called Endurance. Some people also referred to it as Stamina. In essence, it was just a gauge of how long you could continue to physically exert yourself at a super-Demon level before your body became weakened. You follow me?"

I nodded, clearly understanding his point thanks to role-playing video games. Some of those possessed a stamina bar that you needed to let recharge from time to time. Smegma began picking his teeth with a taloned claw as he continued.

"The Magic Stat determined how powerful your Spells and Skills were, while also decreasing how much of your Mana Pool activation of said Skills would cost. It goes without saying that the resource pool for the Magic Stat was Mana. Finally, there's Force. This Stat was the least understood but also widely varied in use. Force could add damage to physical strikes, magic spells, be used for telekinesis and even served to create various Auras. Some could empower specific beings inside of it or just as easily weaken others. It manifested differently for each person, but you could train yourself to have it mimic what others did; if you understood the why."

About midway through Smegma's description I realized that, like he had thought, his description of Stats wasn't going to help me. Clearly, based on the operating System updates to *Demonic Vault*, the System had gone through many changes before arriving on Earth. *That of course begged the question of why it even needed to?*

"That's the million-Mana-Coin question," Smegma mumbled. "If you figure out why the System does what it does, please let me know." The second part was clearly meant to try to lighten the serious mood. Unfortunately, I had too much 'serious' on my mind, and Smegma's lame attempt at humor didn't break me.

"Okay, grouchy pants, I'll leave you alone then," Smegma whined before flying away through the cavern ceiling. I shook my head, not understanding why Smegma was pouting over my mood. "Cause you're a buzzkill," Smegma explained by poking his head through said ceiling.

[You really should stop reading my thoughts then, husktard,] I responded but got no response.

I had to assume this all stemmed from Smegma's bad news. I examined why it was such horrible news from Smegma's point of view and arrived at one conclusion. Smegma had been harboring a hope that I could become powerful quickly by giving people Enchanted Gathering Gear.

My head shook in exasperation. Nothing in this world was free. I'd learned that years ago when I started my Mana Bank to the stars Swiftgram account. Others had made it look easy, had made it seem like success was practically handed to them. I instantly discovered, and now intrinsically knew, that wasn't the case. It was the forward-facing facade of an iceberg of hard work.

The steady thump and tinging of my Pickaxe kept my thoughts company as I began thinking of the actual problems in my life. I was about to be on trial for second-degree manslaughter. I was innocent and knew it, so surely the jury would find the same thing, right?

I'd seen enough Hollyhood crime shows and real-life documentaries to know that wasn't always true. Yet, it was pretty far-fetched to think that Mr. Varnish was going to be able to prove that I killed Morgan Hallsbrad for his Skills. That absurdity raised a far more potent question. Who was behind Mr. Varnish? What was their goal?

Ruin some random college kid's life?

Maybe, but I doubted things were that simple.

Ms. Stovall, after the pre-trial, had been furious with her team and herself. I'd only heard a bit of the barrage she'd been starting as I left her office, but it seemed that Mr. Varnish replacing the State Prosecutor was a last-minute thing—and one that she felt they should have known about. That sudden last-minute change, though, led to a question. Why would someone like Mr. Varnish be brought in to take on a case like mine?

Morgan Hallsbrad had definitely *not* been a private investigator—despite whatever paperwork the Judge and Ms. Stovall were handed...

Plus Judge Dench was rumored to have a Truth Detection Skill. So, how could Mr. Varnish get away with lying? Smegma had pointed out the only conclusion to this the night before. He wasn't lying—but then who was feeding him *false* information.

I worked like that until lunch, my thoughts circling each other uselessly like a boy and girl at an eighth-grade dance. Every so often, Smegma mentally told me how pointless my maudlin was but I ignored the pouty Demon—even sending barbs back his way when I thought of a good one.

"Did ya hear?" Willa said excitedly as she looked between my father and me—both of us were eating our Portal-ham and American-singles sandwiches. I raised my eyebrows and looked at my father, who was smiling widely. I shook my head. "Jarred be comin' to work with us startin' tomorrow!"

"That fast?" I asked, my voice carrying my excitement and surprise.

"Yeah, Ella came around. Well, I'm sure it isn't that simple, but the important part is that Jarred is going to work with us—and Ella *may* be retaking her position as an office administrator."

"*May?*" I asked, attempting to mimic my father's tone when he said that word.

"She be *thinkin'* about it," Willa answered. I groaned and saw both of the adult's faces fall in unison. "Honestly, she probably be needin' a shrink even more than Brodie…"

"Willa!" My dad said, and I laughed at Willa's apologetic wince.

"Sorry, Brodie, I be puttin' my foot—"

"Willa, it's fine. Honestly, I only have to go to eight more sessions with Evelyn." Willa looked at me with narrowed eyes and then glanced at my father, seeming to look for permission. Which apparently she either got, or took his lack of noticeable response as an affirmative.

"How be you okay with all this, Brodie?" Willa voiced. I could tell that she had only concern for me in mind, and from the way that my father leaned in—he also wanted an answer to this question.

I guess that's why he'd not given Willa a shake of his head.

Taking a deep breath, I thought about the question, before finally sighing and saying, "I'm not really okay. I was fine with the assault because I beat the guy—protected myself from him. You know?" I got nods and clenched fists in response, and continued, "Now? Now, I'm really lost.

"How can the court send me to trial for defending myself?" I finished after a pause.

"Don't worry, Bro," my dad said, instantly reaching over to squeeze my shoulder. Hard. "They'll find you innocent."

Willa spoke instantly after my father finished. "Someone *did* die, Brodie. So, they gotta be doin' the due-digilence."

"Due-diligence," my dad corrected fondly.

I chose to point out the rather glaring flaw in their thoughts. "But then why did the Crown Prosecutor get switched with Mr. Varnish?"

"Did you be lookin' into him?" Willa asked.

I nodded but threw up both my hands to say that the internet had failed me, which was strange, considering that almost all top-tier lawyers had websites, SwiftGrams, Smilebooks, *and* JackedIn profiles. Ms. Stovall was a perfect example.

"Maybe he's new?" My dad suggested.

"Fat husking chance," Smegma commented from somewhere in the cavern. I licked my teeth and looked around for the Imp—pretending to be thinking.

"I don't think he's new. He was too well dressed and frankly, too good at his job. Ms. Stovall is excellent, but even she seemed surprised by how much effort this guy put into twisting the facts," I explained.

"Maybe he work for mob," Miguel added from his seat with Fat Gary.

I had kind of forgotten their presence because they had been so quiet. I looked at Miguel then and found him shrugging as he went back to eating, clearly conveying that it was just a thought. The fact that the man's brain went somewhere so dark likely told a story about his past, but that didn't make it any less possible. Right?

"It definitely fits," Smegma added.

My father scoffed and spoke simultaneously. "No way, Miguel. Come on, a mobster in Windsor? Why would they care?"

"I don't know," Fat Gary said, patting Miguel on the back. "This Haller guy was from the states right? Operated up the east coast, and ended in New York? Sounds possible. That or Cartel?" Fat Gary finished in a whisper.

Miguel shivered, and Fat Gary squeezed his shoulder, like my dad had done mine. I decided to change the subject. "Mob? Cartel? After the Advent we just started calling them Guilds, didn't we? Either way, I think this lawyer is pretty well funded, and whoever is behind him seems to want something out of this."

"How do you figure?" my dad asked.

"Well, even if you hired a private investigator to track a murderer, would you care if something happened to the guy?"

"That be dependin' on how long I be workin' with da' guy," Willa said. At the shocked looks she said, "What? I watch crime shows!"

"Even then, Morgan Hallsbrad was a piece of shit and is being tried for multiple counts of murder. Who would be willing to exonerate someone like that? Plus, why isn't Mr. Varnish representing him in any of those other cases?"

"He's not representing him in this case, either," My dad said, firmly.

"What do ya be meanin'? How would ya even be knowin' that?" Willa asked.

Dad scoffed. "Brodie's my son. His mail still comes to my house. I read the documentation on the case. Mr. Varnish is representing the Larvae Guild, not Morgan Hallsbrad."

I blinked. "The Judge said something exactly like that. She sort of—got onto Mr. Varnish and reminded him that he was representing the Guild and not Hallsbrad…"

"So, you be sayin' that someone be specifically targetin' your case?" Willa asked.

[I'm saying someone is specifically targeting *me*,] I mentally sent, refusing to admit that particularly terrifying truth in front of Fat Gary and Miguel. To the group, I just shrugged, which brought about a pretty profound silence.

"Why don't we start discussing which veins to tap?" My dad said, changing the subject. I allowed Willa and him to start assessing as Smegma flew down to hover beside me.

"You know, you should probably tell your family the whole truth at this point."

I reached up and ran a hand through my sweaty hair. This wasn't going to be a pleasant conversation.

CHAPTER 36

Tuesday, April 16th, 2069

"**W**hy is this one orange?" I whispered, far enough away from anyone else that I could speak to Smegma somewhat openly.

Shining Meteorite
Rank: Entry E-Unique
Quality: High
Quantity: Very Low

"It says 'Unique,' doesn't it," Smegma said haughtily.

"Okay, so it's a one of a kind or something?" I asked.

"That's what *unique* means," Smegma confirmed.

"So, it's both invaluable and valueless?" I whispered, matching Smegma's tone. The Imp was getting on my nerves ever since this morning. So, I decided to piss him off in turn. "Guess, I should 'pick' something else."

"First off, that was husking horrible! Don't pun. Second, it's motherhusking *unique!* Like hell you're going to just walk away."

"Hmm, nah, I'll just leave it for you to get."

"Low blow, dick-face," Smegma retorted but eventually sighed. "Look, I'm sorry for being in a bad mood—but you have to get why I'm put-out, right?" I gave the Imp a flat stare and he continued, "You're telling me that it wouldn't be awesome to just be gaining Strength constantly until you were totally OP. You could have a literal horde of Miners just farming the Strength Stat for you…"

[Awesome, sure, but shit is never that easy,] I switched to mental communication as I felt myself growing a bit frustrated. [Smegma, I would love to be a Hunter right now, but honestly, nothing is free. The *Mining* Skill planet isn't growing anymore. Plus, just look at the Pickaxes. They've stopped leveling, too.] I held out my Pickaxe, which looked far better than it had before but refused to become anything better than 'second-hand.' Still showing the Imp the tool, I added sourly, [Just like your billion-Coin Skills. So, let's pump the husking brakes and take things slow.]

"Okay. *Okay!*" Smegma responded, and added the second when I gave him a meaningful stare. "So, you'll Mine the *unique* husking mineral now?"

[I will if you tell me what you know about *unique husking minerals*.]

"Ugghhh. Fine. It's something that the System spawned specifically for someone in a given Dungeon. Because it's an Ore—it's most likely for a Miner or Blacksmith or even a Trader that deals with metals. Meaning it's most likely here for *you*." At my somewhat confused look, Smegma threw his hands in the air. "Remember I told you about System Opportunities. That *means*, this Ore is likely something that the System deems you qualify for and will either help you in the future or help you right husking now!"

[Was that so hard?]

"Honestly, who the husk wouldn't Mine a Unique Ore?" Smegma countered.

[I never said I wasn't going to Mine it. I just wanted to know what I was getting into.]

I glanced around me and deemed it safe to Mine the vein I wasn't supposed to be Mining. I looked at the Red Copper about ten feet to my left—the deposit I was *supposed* to be Mining—and then shrugged. It was close enough to keep up appearances.

Bringing up my Pickaxe, I held it aloft, getting ready to strike where the *Mining* Skill told me to. Nothing happened, and Smegma face-palmed.

"You are totally useless without your Skill. Here!" He said while pointing at a spot. I sent the Pickaxe through his head, totally missing the indicated area. "Wow. Just wow. Want to actually try, or shall I start dancing around for husking target practice."

[Why don't you put your head where you want me to strike?]

"Husking rude! Here!" He said seriously, and this time I followed his finger to strike the spot indicated.

The Pick bounced back and I almost dropped it due to the vibrations. [What the husk?]

"Okay, so this isn't like a normal vein," Smegma said as he began tapping a talon on his tooth and studying it more closely. "Ahh, yes, the rock immediately around it seems to have hardened. Is that a property of the metal?"

[Smegma,] I tried, but clearly the Imp was too deep in his own thoughts.

"So, if this Ore acts as some sort of reinforcement, maybe it is an ingredient that can be added to existing weapons and armor." The Imp scoffed after that thought and looked derisively at me, in my second-hand gear and just-slightly-better-than-second-hand Pickaxe. "What a waste—"

[Smegma!] I tried again and this time the Imp blinked and looked me in my eyes.

"Oh, sorry. Try striking it right in the center of the Ore."

[That's it?] I asked and Smegma both shook his head and shrugged excessively. Showing he had no idea, but also didn't appreciate me questioning his deduction.

Well then!

I swung sidearm, making sure the Pick sailed through a piece of the incorporeal Demon but still landed the point of the Pick dead center on the Ore. It wasn't a particularly hard swing, and thanks to my childishness, I expected nothing to happen.

Thus, when the entire point of the Pickaxe sunk into the Ore like it was mercury, I almost let go of the handle. Almost—only because I *couldn't* let go of the handle. My hands felt like they were open, but they were somehow not—like

276

the nerve endings were faulty. My eyes went wide just in time to watch the Ore turn into liquid metal and begin to move.

It didn't drip like a liquid should, but moved over the Pickaxe in an engulfing wave.

"Oh, so that's what it was here for," Smegma said. I wanted to glare at him and demand an explanation, but I couldn't peel my eyes away from the liquid metal that was flowing over and down the Pickaxe like an alien symbiote.

It made its way to the handle and kept coming, inching toward my hands. I tried to scream, but realized that my mouth, like my hands, wasn't listening. Were my eyes even wide? They felt like they should be, but despite my desperate commands to do something, *anything*—my body didn't listen.

Smegma caught my terror through my thoughts because he said, "Don't panic. It's going to Upgrade the Pickaxe. It must have reached a plateau, but you met all the requirements for an Upgrade."

That calmed me for all of fifteen seconds—before the liquid began seeping onto my husking *hands*.

"Oh, well—that's not what I expected," Smegma stated as he watched the liquid metal begin coating my fingers.

[You husking husk. Do something!] I mentally screamed.

"That just means that it's Upgrading something else, Brodie. Plus, what should I do? You want me to fly through you a couple times?"

Quickly, and with far too much glee, he did just that—latching onto my face and diving down into my body before his head burst out of my chest, his arms flailing as he screeched loudly. I knew I should never have let him watch that husking movie, but he just kept whining about how 'booooring' it was just watching me 'sleep all the time.' Eventually, I caved and left the Tablet open with a playlist of chosen movies and the volume turned down while I went to bed.

I resolved right then and there to figure out a way to punch this husker right in the face.

One day!

The liquid metal encased my hands, then my forearms, before making its way up my elbows to my biceps, where I felt the calm bubble of dissociation lent by my *Mental Fortitude* shatter. Surely it wasn't going to consume me—how much of this metal was there? The prompt had said that the quantity was 'very low.'

As if the thing was some sort of husked-up tentacle-porn-hentai bullshit— it made its way over my shoulders and up my neck toward my mouth. Which was conveniently slightly ajar and *paralyzed*.

[If this thing tries to get me to call it onii chan, I will burn down the world.] The thought came before I could stop it, and I quickly shifted to the topic I actually *wanted* to think about: [Smegma, if I survive this, I'm going to husking kill you.]

"You're going to have to get used to shit like this if you want to be a powerful Hunter," Smegma answered.

The cool sensation the metal was causing to ripple over my skin moved over my lips and then shot down my throat. It tasted exactly how I would have expected—like I was sucking on batteries. Thankfully, it seemed to speed up at that point and was almost instantly gone.

My body unfroze and the Pickaxe fell to the ground with a clatter and then a clank as first the wood, and then the metal, bounced off the stone. I retched, for obvious reasons, but somehow managed to stop myself from actually vomiting.

"It's inside your Mental Universe," Smegma said, distractedly—like he was also focused inside my Internal Universe as well.

I fell into myself, ignoring my convulsing stomach. Sure enough, inside my Mental Universe I was greeted with the rapey-alien-meteorite metal floating in strangely undulating patterns. Immediately I asked, [What's it doing?]

"Moving toward the *Mining* Skill, I think," Smegma answered.

I glanced at the *Mining* Skill and found it surrounded by five of the tiny moons that I thought represented my Strength Stat. Had my Strength Stat risen by three today?

I opened my eyes and checked it quickly, calling up my Stats page.

Strength Increased by 1.
Strength Increased by 1.
Strength Increased by 1.

Stats
Strength: 5
Locked.
Locked.
Locked.
Locked.
Locked.
Locked.

Confirming that the moons on the metal planet were in fact Strength Stats, and making a note that the Stat page kept a log, I dove back into my Mental Universe.

The slowly moving liquid-meteorite metal was just about to reach the *Mining* Skill when I returned. I held my breath, unsure what it was going to do. I was both anticipatory of something amazing and terrified of something terrible.

When the meteorite reached the first moon, it began to coat it. Very much like what it had just done to the Pickaxe and then my skin. Then in a flash, the same increase of speed occurred, and the metal planet became *more* metal. It almost looked like a silver pool from my vantage point.

What was that light, though? I scanned the Mental Universe, even as the light began to penetrate my eyelids. Wait—if it was penetrating my closed eyes, then it was *outside*. I opened my eyes just in time to see the telltale flash of Skill Awakening.

Or, as it turned out—Skill *Evolution*.

Of course, the flash got everyone's attention, which effectively gathered everyone around me, as if I had just screamed bloody murder. I was already beginning to fend off unspoken words of questioning when two things happened. First, I caught sight of my still-open Stat window.

Strength is doubled by Shining Meteorite.

Stats
Strength: 10
Locked.
Locked.
Locked.
Locked.
Locked.
Locked.

Secondly, two very loud, and very *echoing* bangs resounded through the floor of our chamber and the air. I looked to what was clearly the nearer of the two noises—and found the exit *closed*. I only say closed because it was clear a door had fallen from the ceiling of the space. *Door* wasn't an accurate description, but it was a piece of rock that was so smooth, and different from the rock around it, that it was just that out of place. Like a castle's portcullis in the movies—the one that falls straight down.

Dreading what I would see, I scanned to the other tunnel, the one that led deeper, and didn't find what I expected.

Well, that was mostly because my eyes never made it to the other tunnel. In the center of the cavern, amidst the scattered Shards of F-Ranked Crystals, something was moving. No, something was *forming*. I could see small pieces of loose dirt rolling toward the spot, even as it grew large enough to punch up through the small pile of Shards. It was only a small mound, but it was becoming ever larger.

"What the husk is that?" I asked, directing my question at Smegma but accidentally including everyone. The group followed my frantic gaze and also froze. Whatever they had been about to say was forgotten in the shock of finding a moving pile of rock and dirt.

My father found his words and actions first. He began shoving everyone toward the exit. "Let's get out of here. That sound could have been a cave—"

It was right then that his cajoling and spinning of others turned him around enough to see the 'door' that had fallen shut over the exit.

"Oh *husk*," he said as he began frantically spinning me toward the other tunnel.

"No point, Dad," I said as I allowed him to move me. I realized that if I wanted to, I could stand in place like a bolted down statue, and briefly wondered if that was due to my Strength Stat. Still, maybe that pile wasn't really anything—

"It's a low-rank Rock Golem or something similar," Smegma stated. "Normally, they wouldn't be aggressive, but I'm guessing that this one is going to be coming after you."

"Why the husk would a Rock Golem come after me?" I shouted, completely forgetting my current company. The group froze for the briefest of moments as they took in my words and then double-timed it to the tunnel that led deeper into the mines. The exit to the tunnel that we knew Hunters from Lynx were down.

"What was it you said before? 'Nothing is free?' Well, here you go, pal. Time to pay up." Smegma shook his head as if, had I *not* said anything, this wouldn't be happening.

"Everyone start working to break the cave-in," my dad shouted as we neared the 'door.' I nodded—surely we could break through the door with our Pickaxes.

Willa was the first to arrive, and with a sliding step, she used all of her strength and momentum to drive the Pickaxe into the center of the flat stone door with an overhand swing. The Pickaxe bounced back hard enough that she lost her grip and the Pick catapulted back the way we had come, landing midway between us and the now slightly humanoid-looking Rock Golem.

"That's a System Shield—you're going to have to kill the Boss, Brodie," Smegma said flatly, sounding slightly worried about my chances. But his assessment was correct—destroying the Golem was the only choice. I didn't even get to voice any questions before he responded, "It's a System Event. Those doors aren't going to be breakable or open until someone kills the Rock Golem. Since you're the only one with any chance against it, I'm voting for you!"

[Did you know this was going to happen when I tapped that vein?]

"No. This was my first time seeing a Unique material in person. I was a fighter and then a researcher…"

The mound now had distinct arms and legs and… Was that a head forming?

I rushed into my Mental Universe and flipped the *Overdraft* Skill to *Overcharge*, before applying it to my weapon. Well, to my Pickaxe…

"I'm going to try to distract it," I said but immediately felt my father's hands grab at my shoulders to pull me back.

This time, I didn't let him. He tried once with more strength and then gave up and yanked at me with everything he had. My shoes slid slightly on the stone but I didn't break my casual stance.

"I'm sorry, Dad, this is the only way," I whispered before twisting my body to place a hand in the center of his chest. Shoving him off his feet and removing his arms from around me, I began to rush at the almost fully formed Rock Golem. I could only hope that getting in a first strike would somehow help.

After all, I only had ten minutes on *Overcharge*.

CHAPTER 37

Tuesday, April 16th, 2069

"**C**harging a creature made of stone with a husking Pickaxe isn't going to work," Smegma shouted as he sped past my ear. I heard him. I chose to ignore him. It wasn't like I had other options. "Don't ignore me! At least gang up on it!"

My feet slid multiple times as I passed over a carpet of Sharded Crystals. Each footfall created a wind-chime-like tinkle of the things as they cascaded into each other. It was a strange battle hymn, and I might have truly considered that further if I had time. I needed to strike the Golem before it fully formed—that was my one advantage.

I saw a somewhat clear space in the Crystal carpet ahead and planted my foot into it before leaping the remaining eight or nine feet toward the Monster. Its head was just rounding enough to be considered an appendage as I bent my back and raised my *Overcharged* Pickaxe over my head.

Like sit ups in the gym, I started with my stomach and then shoulders before beginning to straighten my elbows, aiming a blow right at the center of the creature's smooth, rocky head. As if I was watching a drowning puppy in slow motion, the Golem's head moved out of range just as my pickaxe began to pick up speed.

What just happened?

"It's allowed to dodge, you husking moron," Smegma quickly spat, which actually helped me in that moment. I saw the one leg it had left behind, trailing the rest of its body as it swayed back defensively. I adjusted my trajectory minutely changing targets and aiming the still falling Pickaxe point at the place where the rock of the leg met the hip.

Hopefully, that was a weak point—

The Pickaxe slammed into the rock and drove through it. It was then that I realized I hadn't considered landing from my leap. That, and the contact of a swung Pickaxe with a rather dense rock, changed my body's trajectory.

All that to say, I was going to come down sideways.

Something hit my sternum, right upper chest, and arm simultaneously before my momentum changed. All those points instantly bloomed in traumatic pain. Then, instead of gravity alone being in control of my body, I suddenly had to deal with gravity *and* a backhand from a ton and a half of pure Rock Golem. Like a schooner in a crosswind, I sailed sideways and hit the ground with all the momentum of my jump and the Golem's blow.

[Good thing this bed of razor-sharp Crystals was here, really,] I mentally joked.

I felt some of the Crystals shift, absorbing the impact as others sliced and cut sharp, jagged lines across every exposed area of my body. I narrowly avoided my more sensitive areas by curling into a fetal position.

As soon as I came to a stop, I tried to pull in oxygen but felt my chest fight me on the action I'd accomplished several billion times since birth. I heard shouting, but my ears felt like they were filled with cotton.

Well, I guess this is the end—too bad I hadn't gotten a chance to buy one of the cool Skills from Smegma.

My struggle against my own lungs suddenly shifted in my favor, allowing me to pull in some air. However, it felt like I was sucking it through a constricted straw. My brain screamed at me to move, and that if I didn't, a Golem was going to stomp me into a pancake. My body, sans oxygen, wasn't complying. Again, I felt the struggle against my own air supply shift in my favor, and the straw became a hose.

With some oxygen now, my body managed a roll, which I thought, in that moment, had saved my life. Turns out I was wrong. I couldn't tell where the Golem was specifically because my eyes were filled with unshed tears of pain. But from noises that weren't right on top of me, I did manage to piece together that I wasn't in desperate danger. Thankfully, the rejuvenating oxygen also unfroze my brain enough to start hearing things. Was that the sound of Pickaxes at work?

"Get up, you husking moron. The others are barely managing to keep it grounded."

I quickly blinked my eyes, allowing some of the water to leak down my cheeks as I tried to focus on the direction of the sound. Sure enough, Willa, Fat Gary, Miguel and my father were all pummeling the creature as it lay on its back.

One of its legs was still standing with my Pickaxe embedded through it. My strike must have severed the limb, causing it to fall. In any other battle, that would have spelled the end. However, this was a Golem—and I could see the rocks gathering around its leg, as well as each of the small 'dings' Fat Gary, Willa, Miguel and my father were making.

Dings were the only word for them. My father and Willa, with the Enchanted Pickaxes, were managing to carve out bigger sections of rock from its arms and other leg, but I could tell they were all fighting a losing battle against its regeneration.

I croaked, "Grab my Pickaxe."

No one in the group moved.

With an effort of will, I heaved in a breath and pushed myself up to my feet. Thanks to the return of feelings, I could sense the warm, sticky sensation of my own blood liberally covering my arms and legs. I ignored it and shuffle-walked to the Golem's leg and my Pickaxe in the stone.

Heaving, I managed to 'King Arthur' that shit out of its 'sheath,' and I continued toward the downed Golem. My legs didn't have the strength to jump again, but I figured if I could take off another limb, then we could go back to whittling it down. Of course, that was when it swung an arm defensively. Everyone managed to step back and out of the path of the blow, but Miguel and Fat Gary's pickaxes didn't have the sense to dodge with them.

They broke with a scream of splintering wood.

One head sailed away harmlessly. The other punched me in the face. Stars exploded in my vision as I fell on the ground. Again.

"Are you husking kidding me?" Smegma shouted. "I'm going to laugh about that later, but without those two chipping away—it will be on its feet soon. Get up!"

Bracing with one hand in the Shards, I managed to get to my knees. Thankfully I still held my Pickaxe, but even from my knees, I wobbled. I put one foot under me and felt gravity shift to the left and then right. I shook my head and instantly regretted it as a migraine almost worse than the original one-ton punch from Mega-Rock over there came back with a vengeance.

With the migraine, however, came some semblance of balance, and I managed to get up onto unsteady feet. The leg I'd removed was only missing a 'shin' and foot now. I was two steps away and could tell that my involvement against its regeneration would be a close thing.

Fat Gary and Miguel were still swinging at the thing with the broken shafts of their pickaxes, but it wasn't doing anything. I hesitated for the briefest of seconds before mentally commanding Smegma to purchase two more Miner's Picks.

"Are you certain you want to purchase two Mining Picks?" he asked, his inflection reminding me that this was a rote question he had to ask.

[Husking yes. Are you kidding me with this?!]

Sure, there were probably more effective weapons in the shop, and I'm sure if I had time, I'd be overjoyed to scour the husking thing and find them. Time and questions about where the sudden Picks had come from, however, were not luxuries that I possessed at the moment. Two Miner's Picks fell at my feet, and I bent down to grab both in an unsteady grip. With a shouted "Miguel!" I threw them in an underhand lob in the two Miner's general direction.

Miguel looked up and snagged one from the air. The other landed on the flailing Golem and was quickly flung away as it waved its arms defensively from the continued barrage of Pickaxe blows. Thankfully, Fat Gary—a name I didn't bother shouting, 'cause it was simply too long for my addled brain—got the message and chased after the 'weapon.'

All of that happened in the span of a couple of seconds, which also let me close the remaining distance to the fallen Golem. Grinning, I brought my Pickaxe down on its still-whole leg. The Pick turned slightly in my hand, but with my added Strength, it still bit in deeply. I had a short-lived and manic question of whether my *Mining* Skill was providing its own level of assistance but pushed the thought aside. When I pulled back, I took the creature's entire quad with me.

Then I struck again and again. And again.

People began noticing that my Pickaxe, and my 'Strength,' was having the greatest effect and started shifting spots to allow me access to each limb. Fat Gary had rejoined the four of us at some point, but I just kept wailing down blows until all four limbs became lifeless stone on the floor beside a wiggling torso.

Then I began turning its head and torso into stone chips. The chest was far harder than the limbs and repaired at an increased pace. Still, it was a losing battle against my quickly deforming Pickaxe. That was when I saw why its torso was harder and prioritized in the regeneration process of whatever mind or will that animated the Golem.

A large brown orb became visible when I pulled back from one of the strikes that ripped an impressive chunk of the creature away. It looked like a mix between a shiny rock and metal. I'd seen pictures of these in Portal Materials' class. It was a Golem Core. The thing's weakness!

With a new target, I swung again and felt the Enchantments on the Pickaxe for precision guide the deformed point home. The sound of a ringing bell made my exhausted muscles tense, thinking that my tool had just been rebuffed from the rigidity of the Core. But that wasn't the case. The sound acted like the epicenter of a stone dropped into a pond—only it was the *room* that rippled, like waves in water.

Sharded Crystals bounced into the air as the wave passed under them. The strange, magical percussion caused me to stumble and then fall to a knee as it passed under me.

Afterward, I had a front row seat as the stone that made up the creature turned to dust—my muscles slackened and I fell to my ass, out of breath. Only then did I realize that I'd been held up by sheer adrenaline–and that was quickly fading. I saw the 'doors' turn to dust as well, before falling away as if they were simply an eddy in an unfelt wind.

The sound of coughing, shifting Crystals, and an odd thumping reached my ears as the four others fell to their asses as well. Well, I had assumed all four of the others. Until my father rushed to my side and shouted, "Are you okay? You're bleeding from everywhere. We need to get you to a Healer."

Others came into the room from the deeper caverns. They were covered in a layer of dirt that made the Hunters indistinguishable from the Miners unless you looked for the weapons. Well, that and their actions, I supposed. A team of three rushed toward us with another five Banks in their wake.

"Is this everyone that was in this chamber? Is everyone okay? What happened?" A man with a circular shield rapid-fire shouted.

My dad looked like he was going to indicate me and my need for a Healer, but I grabbed his wrist. He looked at me and I shook my head.

Insistently, I whispered, "I'm okay."

As soon as I had the brain capacity to check. I'd run my hands over the 'cuts' on my body—only to find them already closed. Sure, they were scabbed and sensitive, but closed. If I went to a Healer, they might just discover my *Recovery* Skill.

"Look at your Pickaxe and all the Ores near the walls," Smegma said.

I blinked meaningfully at my father and then turned slowly to look at the Pickaxe that was under the palm of my right hand. The shaft was now a dark-brown, polished wood. The head, which had been previously at risk of becoming nothing more than a hammer, was shining and sharp.

My father followed my gaze and his eyes widened. He lifted his own Pickaxe and found a similar sight. It was my turn to blink in surprise. I checked the other three Pickaxes and noticed that among them, only Willa's had changed. Fat Gary and Miguel's literally looked like hammers—or maybe round maces?

They had clearly flipped them around at some point, when the sharpened point of the pick had become worthless, to use the spade-side because even it was nearly bent ninety degrees.

Without looking away from the nearly destroyed 'new' Pickaxes, I said, "Everyone's okay. A Golem formed in the middle of the cavern."

"A *what?*" the Hunter shouted and then shifted his gaze to the Monster Core and Golem Core that sat in a pile of stone dust. "And you defeated it?"

My dad took over explaining the group effort. He left out my 'heroics,' thankfully.

Tired, I let the explanation fade into the background as I caught my breath.

"The wall!" Smegma demanded, reminding me of the second part of his earlier comment.

His insistence made me scan the wall where this had all started. More specifically, the Red Copper I had been told to Mine. As if I had done what I was told, the chunks of Red Copper Ore were stacked neatly in a pile. While I had hit my head—multiple times—I was sure I hadn't done that.

Scanning further, I found more stacks of Ores in a whole range of colors. When I say a 'whole range,' I mean *every* husking color of the rainbow. Almost every three or four feet, there was a pile of something. I sucked in a breath and pointed at a small stack of vibrant purple Ore.

"What is *that?*"

My question made everyone in the room turn to look at my finger. I had been meaning the question for Smegma, but something in my tone had instantly drawn everyone. Even the Miners who had been examining the piles of Ore nearer the hallway to the deeper caverns turned to look.

Everyone first stared at the purple Ore, which clearly hadn't been visible in the cavern before the fight, but soon people began looking at the green, blue, and orange Ores in turn. Each one hadn't been visible when we'd decided which valuable ones to tap.

"It's not just this cavern," Smegma said as he floated through the floor. "*Every* cavern in this place has been automatically tapped of all Ores."

Coughing, I relayed that in a roundabout way. "Is this the only cavern that this happened in?"

That sent the Miners nearest the tunnels running to the deeper caverns. Thanks to Smegma, I knew what they'd find.

My father had finished his explanation, or maybe I had interrupted him, because when I leaned back in satisfaction, I found his intense gaze locked on me—me and my bloody and ripped clothing.

I sat back up hurriedly and mouthed, "I'll tell you later."

His eyes bugged out and his mouth firmed.

But he nodded.

"You know what probably would have helped you find that Core faster?" Smegma said into the silence. "Your *Heat Sense* Skill."

[Super helpful tip, now that it's all over.]

"You can't help stupid. Idiot!" The Imp just always had to get the last word in.

CHAPTER 38

Tuesday, April 16th, 2069

Despite the somewhat insane events that happened in our cavern, no one questioned me. Not even as I carried out three Pickaxes—two nearly maces and one more elegant than the one I'd come in with. I think it was probably the fact that the porters had to make several trips outside and then back in to gather everything. They even requested the other Miners to help and lent them Bags of Minor Holding to assist in the task.

It turned out that all the Crystals in the caverns had also been Mined. Mined perfectly—without Sharding or, for that matter, any effort by anyone. The buzz from the Miners and Hunters was pretty loud and constant. Thus, probably why no one was questioning me. My father still insisted on taking me to a Healer. So, after I dropped the Pickaxes in the Ford Escort, I reluctantly complied to a quick once over.

A cold sensation traveled from my arm where the man's hand rested and moved through my body. Goosebumps broke out on my skin, but before I could brush the man's hand away from the uncomfortable sensation, he pulled it back. The sensation went with it.

"A fair bit of minor damage but nothing serious. I can Heal you if you think the discomfort is too great?" The man sounded like a sleazy salesman. I gave my father a pointed look and declined the expensive offer.

"What do you mean the entire Mine is cleared? Like this?" Jagger Vance shouted as he indicated a box filled with perfectly intact Mana Crystals. "Our contract was to Shard them. Who's responsible for this?"

My father winced and so did I. Jagger was clearly not yet aware of the circumstances, but I had a feeling he would still be upset after learning what had happened. My guess? Well, he had probably negotiated a certain cut but was now about to lose out on a huge profit. Especially with all the Ores added to the mix.

In essence, he'd sold us—his Miners—as three Specialists and thirty laborers, when we'd likely done the work of a hundred Specialists or more. I didn't feel the least bit bad for him. I did feel bad for all the bonus money we were going to likely miss out on. Of course, a bigger percentage for Portals, Portal's, Portalz didn't mean we'd receive larger bonuses.

My stomach grumbled, and I pushed the sensation aside. Surely we'd get something good for this, right?

Thankfully, the Healer did hand me a few protein bars, which let me know that my stomach rumble wasn't nerves—and was obviously audible.

Out of misplaced curiosity, I followed in the wake of my father and saw Willa join from another direction as I greedily scarfed down one of the bars. She wore a smile that was far too large, like a cat that caught a canary. Looking at me, she tried to whisper but practically screamed, "A whole unfound cavern be unblockin' in that sound-wave-thing. It be filled with D-Grade Crystals an' True Gold Ore. All of it be layin' on the ground, just ready to be collectin'!"

Jagger made choking sounds as his mouth opened and closed. Then he shouted, "I need to speak to Taz!" and rushed off.

All three of us watched him go, my father finding his voice first. "Do you think he'll be able to get more out of Taz?"

"Not a huskin' chance. *A contract is a contract.* It be his own words throwin' back at him. He be getting' a bit more for da D-Rank Crystals, since that be a standard—as be most of the Ore values. But they won't be payin' more for full Crystals after da fact." Willa's smile was heard in her voice, making it sound like she was happy that Jagger would be ripped off.

"If he negotiated for more, would we get bigger bonuses?" I asked.

Willa and my father's laughter was all the answer I needed.

"I really don't like that husking guy," Smegma commented as he popped back into space beside me. He had clearly tried to follow Jagger to Taz but had crossed out of range.

Shrugging in response to both him and the two fake hyenas, I said, "How much of a bonus do you think we'll get after that?"

"Enough ta huskin' retire!" Willa stated.

"There's no way," my dad countered. "Bonuses are capped at fifty thousand a person and two hundred thousand per Specialist. You can try to negotiate with Jagger, but I'm betting he'll give you the same response Taz is going to give him."

"A contract is a contract," they said together. Willa continued by herself after that, her smile falling. "Motherhusker! We be da ones who be riskin' our life against that Monster. We be da ones that be down there every day, and Jagger be da one ta pocket millions?"

"Maybe he'll use the money to hire more experienced Specialists?" My dad suggested, his voice telling me that wasn't likely.

"Sure, he be findin' some 'new' promising Miners, train them up and then sell 'em off for commission," Willa responded. Both my head and Smegma's jerked in her direction.

"What does she mean? Is he enslaving them?" Smegma asked. My brow furrowed more at his interpretation. I knew that wasn't the case, but it still sounded nefarious.

Willa thankfully got the hint from my reaction. "Once our new Specialist Miners be trained up, da boss over there be tradin' them ta a bigger team and continuin' to earn commission from their work. It be his 'business model.'"

She didn't really need to add the air quotes to the words with the tone she used, but it really drove home the point. This wasn't a Mining team that ever had a chance of 'training up.' I had never understood just how much of a dead end job my dad was working.

"You should offer to go cart Ores and Crystals up," Smegma suggested. "You won't be stealing what's worked by your hands."

I used a subtle tilt of my head to indicate the far-too-numerous crates that surrounded the entrance. [I doubt there's much left. But…]

"I want to go see what a D-Grade Crystal looks like," I said as an excuse and began walking toward the aforementioned, far-too-plentiful crates. Thankfully, my father and Willa chose not to follow me.

Once there, it was easy to ask a passing porter which box held the Crystals. It was also relatively easy to distinguish between Ores and Crystals, thanks in large part to the distinctive blue glow of Mana. The smiling woman I asked practically jumped for joy as she pointed out a group of crates that were set slightly aside from the others.

"Wonder if she knows she can only get fifty thousand?" Smegma asked.

[I doubt it makes a difference. While she might be disappointed in the cap, it will still be more than she or any of them have ever made before. It's likely why they signed a capped contract to begin with. Who thinks they'll actually get to those bonus numbers in a day?]

"It's a payday either way, even though someone else is becoming rich. Huh…" Smegma said, lapsing into semi-silence before interrupting himself with noises of contemplation as he hovered from open crate to crate.

I made it to one of about five crates that contained the blue glow of Mana and stared down at Crystals that definitely glowed with a purer light. Where the F-Rank Crystals had an almost salt-like quality to their crystalline edges, these were significantly clearer. There was still a hint of fog, but it was next to nothing compared with what I was used to seeing.

I reached into the crate and moved them around a bit, pretending to marvel at them. I saw a few Miners, and even Hunters, doing something similar at nearby crates. I sold the first one from a layer deeper in the crate.

"Wow, a hundred and twenty thousand Mana Coins from that. I left the Crystal if you want to try to keep it," Smegma said. I smiled and pulled out the Crystal, setting it on a corner of the crate where two edges met. Surely no one would mind if I took a souvenir.

I sold four more from this crate before grabbing the Spent Crystal and moving to another. Unfortunately, my first chosen crate was without people nearby, but the next few had others surrounding them. After a quick mental discussion with Smegma, I decided I couldn't risk it.

"You should buy a Ring or Necklace of Holding," Smegma suggested—his voice carrying with it a wickedness I found appropriate for the situation. With that, I could take multiple 'souvenirs'…

[What are my options?] I asked as I continued moving from crate to crate.

This section, which was set aside, clearly held the priciest wares. That and things that weren't identified yet. I came to that conclusion as I passed a crate of black Graphenite. It was the same color and texture as the deposit I hadn't been able to Mine a few days ago.

Plus, even out of the wall, it still held a nice little plaque to confirm what I was seeing. Two windows popped up in front of me, overlaying that plaque.

Miscellaneous Gear
Ring of Minor Holding

Grade: High F
A ring that has a space inside it of 8 feet cubed. Items can be Summoned into and out of this space by mental command. This ring is made with True Silver and can hold another Enchantment.
Cost: 250,000 mC

—

Necklace of Small Holding
Grade: High E
A necklace that has a space inside it of 125 feet cubed. Items can be summoned into and out of this space by mental command. This necklace is made with True Gold and can hold another two Enchantments.
Cost: 500,000 mC

[More space means more *misplaced* goods,] I mentally sent, matching Smegma's earlier nefarious tones. With that, I purchased the necklace and it flashed into existence, falling into my hand, which was over a Mana Crystal crate. The glow of the Mana hid the flash from most, but a few nearby Hunters gave me a glance.

I held up the Spent Crystal in my other hand and said, "Look what I found."

They dismissed me with a snort just as Smegma said, "Oh husk, not this shit again."

I turned in time to see the Demon-Imp pop out of existence. The last time that happened—oh shit!

Buyer's Contribution has crossed two thresholds.
Current contribution = 550,000 points
Error. Contribution features unavailable.
Checking Skill OS...
Out of date.
Updating to 6.1.4...
Downloading...
Error. Insufficient Bandwidth to continue.
Contribution too low to increase Bandwidth.
Attempting smaller packet...5.0.18
Insufficient Bandwidth
Attempting smaller packet...4.3.4
Contribution being consumed to increase bandwidth.
500,000 Contribution points consumed.
Downloading...
Updating Demonic Vault.
Rebooting...

My body lit up like I was hiding a floodlight in every cell. With blind eyes, I rapidly threaded my head through the necklace and then put the Spent Mana

Crystal inside. By the startled exclamations that surrounded me, I knew my earlier plan of thievery wasn't going to work anymore. I thought, for just a moment, I could make out the exact noise of my father's slapping shoes, but it wasn't his voice that I heard first.

"He just Awaken again," Miguel said. "He is one who land kill blowing on Golem!"

My father's voice was next, and it was accompanied by his hands. "You okay Brodie? Did you just get another new Skill?"

Still blind, I answered, "Can we get out of here?"

My father's hand lifted off my back for a brief second before he said something more. This one, not directed at me. "Willa, can you stay here and negotiate on behalf of all of us?"

I felt a slightly smaller, but no less strong hand, squeeze my bicep before Willa answered, "I will. Get Brodie home, Gary. Brodie, I be comin' over tonight for dinner, make sure Gary be tellin' Clara."

My vision slowly started returning as I *allowed* my father to guide me toward the car. I saw the faces of everyone in the parking lot. Not a single person I could find wasn't looking at me. I hoped that was my imagination, but I doubted it.

I couldn't help but think about how Mr. Varnish had already used that time in the car against me… What would he do with this?

CHAPTER 39

Tuesday, April 16th, 2069

"**Y**our son is trending all over social media," Ms. Stovall said. Her voice held an odd mixture of emotions. Excited, proud, worried, and nervous. In the time that it took my father and me to drive home, my follower count had doubled—then tripled—before I'd shut down notifications.

But not before I had seen the video. The video that was captioned, 'Is this the next S-Rank?'

The fact that my *Demonic Vault* Skill was still 'rebooting' left me without a touchstone—Smegma, in this case—to explain what had happened.

Surely more followers weren't a bad thing, though, right?

I'd spent two years of my life, many late-nights, and dedicated days of trial and error to growing a fan base. Now, all that hard work was bearing fruit—right?

Even I could tell I was only trying to convince myself...

Sitting around our small kitchenette table with Ms. Stovall, who had made an emergency trip to the house, didn't make my attempts to convince myself very effective. We'd even had to call Willa and let her know that dinner would have to wait. Probably a good thing, since both of my parents' expressions were serious, worried, and drained. They looked like they'd lost color and were now the traditional 'Canadian' pale, but that usually only occurred towards the end of winter, not in early spring.

"He's been trying to grow his followers for years," my dad said, mirroring some of my thoughts. "Surely, this will only help him in the long run?"

"I'll be honest here, Mr. Flacarada. I'm really not sure what this means. Normally, I would congratulate someone for the meteoric rise that's occurring, but in the midst of the trial—well, I assume your son told you about the pre-trial."

She said it matter of factly, like that was a foregone conclusion. I winced. I had, in fact, not worked up the courage to tell them the whole story. I figured I'd reveal the whole truth all at once, and them knowing about my 'Awakening' in the car would just be another piece to the explanation.

Everyone at the table was looking at me and saw my grimace—

"I guess he hasn't divulged the whole story. Brodie, I think it will mean more coming from you..." Ms. Stovall said. I could tell she was confused by the situation, and wanted an explanation herself, but felt my parents deserved the whole story more. It was probably also telling that I looked at Ms. Stovall for a long moment after she made her 'plea.' "Would you like me to give you some privacy?" she asked.

Both my parents shifted visibly in my peripherals, but I maintained eye contact with Ms. Stovall. She probably needed to know the whole truth to be effective at her job. Or at least that's what the TV shows depicted. Plus, she'd rushed over here as soon as she'd seen—almost arriving before my father and me. I gave a small shake of my head and then reaffirmed the motion by saying, "No, you should probably stay and hear this, too.

"This all started the night The Shop—uh, Morgan Hallsbrad attacked me," I started. My parents blinked at my admission, but Ms. Stovall gave a small nod of confirmation, like I had just confirmed her suspicions. More worried about what my parents thought, I turned and addressed them. "It isn't like I lied. There is just more to the story than I originally explained."

My mother gave me a soft look that made my stomach twist—I hadn't seen this particular look in a long while. I knew what would come next but didn't interrupt her. With a tone matching her look, my mother said, "Brodie, that's an omission and the same as lying in our house."

Tears threatened then, even as my windpipe seemed to suddenly have a grape in it. I knew that. I did, but it was also far more complicated than that. Wasn't it? Even now, the whole truth felt like something of a death sentence. Like I could see the plank extending off the edge of the ship and knew the waters we were treading weren't close to land—not to mention dark, sinister, and Monster-infested. I knew in my bones that those black waters held unknown and terrifying creatures beneath its depths.

"Ma—" my throat attempted to stop me from speaking the truth, constricting down as my brain urged it to stop. I cleared my throat and found a water bottle in front of me. The hand that retracted from the bottle was Ms. Stovall's, and I nodded to her in thanks. I took a sip, cleared my throat and tried again. "Mom, I know that but I think you'll agree it's a bit more complicated than that."

My voice still sounded slightly hoarse, but with that segue uttered, I took another sip of water and let the silence mount. A deep breath later, I began. "As I said, this all started when I was assaulted by Morgan Hallsbrad. He seemed to have a Skill that he was going to activate using my Mana Pool and Husking me."

My parents gasped at that, and I paused for another sip of water. "Thanks to the information from the cops, I think that Skill was either Cannibalistic or Snatcher in function. My current theory," I said, changing the topic before my parents could interject. "Is that he screwed up, somehow, somewhere, *because*—"

My throat again attempted to silence me, and my last word came out like a croak. Water, a cough and then I started again. "—because I'm pretty sure I inherited his Skills."

My mom's hands went to her mouth, and my dad's hands gripped the top of his head. A moment later, his eyes and head pivoted to me in a rush. "Wait, you got a *Repair Mark* Skill?!"

My brain went blank at the reminder of just how big my lie had snowballed. The silence was clearly answer enough because my dad said, "So, you didn't get a Repair Mark or not *just* a Repair Mark?"

"Gary!" My mom exclaimed. "I think you're missing the bigger point. Our son got a Skill that is *Cannibalistic* or *Snatcher* in origin."

My dad's face paled so much he looked like he was turning blue. I waved my hands back and forth in front of my face to get their attention—but also to deny the assumption. "That's where my theory kind of falls apart. You see, what I inherited is a Skill called *Demonic*—"

My mom fainted or at least became lightheaded enough to slide from her chair to the floor. My dad jumped up and checked on her. Ms. Stovall pulled out a phone, looking ready to call one-nine-nine. Whether it was to arrest me or help my mom was still unclear.

Husk!

Well, this was going almost exactly as I had feared. I was thankful to see my mother was still conscious, but her reaction just seemed to drive a stake deeper into my stomach. Should I have continued to lie? My too-calm brain, something I had grown pretty used to, logically explained how that wasn't possible after the events of the day.

The awareness of *Mental Fortitude* at work reminded me of just how much I'd changed. Just how much had happened in the two and a half weeks since the assault. With some mental coaxing, I managed to start speaking again. "It's called *Demonic Vault*."

My mother gasped, and I felt my stomach go from a twisted snake to one coiled and ready to strike. Thankfully I reigned myself in, probably with the help of *Mental Fortitude*. "Mom, you're going to have to stop reacting like that, or I'm going to have to stop telling the truth."

"Brodie!" My dad said, but I wasn't in the mood for him to blindly defend my mother's current responses.

"I get it. I do. But why do you think it's been so hard to tell you this right away?" I said and immediately felt bad as my mother started crying.

"You can't blame your mother for your lies, Brodie," my father said.

My nose sucked in a breath, but once again, I calmed myself enough to respond without raising my voice. "I'm just saying that this isn't making it easy for me to—"

Smegma popped back into existence right in front of me. Blocking my vision of my parents and the whole room. I had enough time to register that he'd grown again—and quite a bit, at that—before the screaming started.

My mom *did* faint then, even as my father tried to cover her with his body like a shield. Still, it was Ms. Stovall that I leaped toward, grabbing the phone and stopping her mid-dial. Shouting, "No, no, wait!"

The room devolved from there as Smegma said, "Husk, I can't believe I didn't even remember how to make myself visible to others."

"Could you maybe turn it off!" I shouted, even as Ms. Stovall attempted to interpose herself between me and the human-sized Demon with bat wings. "He's part of my Skill!" I shouted as my dad, not feeling claws in his back, began to crawl away while dragging my mother. "He's part of my Skill. He won't—no, he *can't* hurt anyone!"

"I mean, I can insult people enough to make them wish they were dead," Smegma stated evilly. Then he started cackling and I closed my eyes tight.

At least I could no longer say this was going the way that I thought it would.

* * *

"So, you're saying that the Earth is home to more than just humans?" Ms. Stovall asked Smegma. It had taken quite a while to calm things down, and quite a bit longer on top of that for my mother to wake up and be able to be in the same room as the Imp—well, full-sized Demon.

To call Smegma an Imp anymore just wasn't possible. His body was muscled and toned in a way that spoke of athletes of old, before the System. Those muscles looked honed for combat, but not in a brutish way. More like his body was made for long, drawn-out combat—for battles of endurance and survival. The color of his skin was still black with red, and his pupils, three talons and sharp teeth were the same as ever—but only his bat-like wings seemed to suggest he was anything other than a terrifying human with horns. He looked like a Felguard— well, it wasn't like I knew what a Felguard would look like, or an Imp for that matter. Maybe all Demons had bloody wings…

What surprised me most was just how human his face looked. Sure, he had defined cheekbones and a cranial ridge just under the start of his horns—but if his skin were just black without the red accents, his face would look like a cosplaying black man.

Smegma preened, telling me he was listening to my thoughts, and I rolled my eyes. Thankfully, he answered Ms. Stovall instead of verbally poking fun at me. "I can say, without a shadow of a doubt, that your world is definitely acting as an asylum for numerous failed races. It would be overrun and conquered if the System didn't have preventative measures against such things…"

"It would be what?" My mom squeaked.

"Conquered," Smegma stated firmly, clearly missing the reason for the question. "Don't feel bad. The Crendalar Cluster would have been conquered, too, if the System didn't have checks in place."

"I don't think she was asking for you to clarify," I said flatly. My mom was looking faint again, but thankfully Ms. Stovall coughed and returned Smegma's attention to her.

"Can you explain that a bit further for me? What checks does it have to stop—" she paused in her question, clearly looking for a polite word to describe Smegma.

"Demons? *Invasion?*" The Demon crowed happily. "Trust me, we aren't even the race you should be most worried about. But I digress. You want to know what the checks are?" Smegma paused, waiting for confirmation. At Ms. Stovall's nod, he smiled and I groaned. "You and every researcher under the stars, lady. We do know some of the more important ones, though."

"Like?" Ms. Stovall said with an emotionless, prompting voice.

"A Portal can only allow one member of a sapient race through, and they must be one rank lower than the Portal to pass through it. A higher ranked individual could go through, but then they would be forcibly reduced in power by the Portal, which means they'd lose Skills and the Stats they'd obtained without control over what they keep or lose. So, low-rank Portals can't be used to cross over by the truly powerful of other failed races without dire consequences. Well, they can, but they'd lose all that power. F-Rank Portals would send them here with no Skills for instance. Even then, the *one* is important. Even during a Portal Break, only one sapient can cross from their indigenous world, all others who try—

haven't been heard from again. These rules don't apply for races undergoing the Trials, of course."

"Indigenous world?" Ms. Stovall prompted.

"Where did you think the Portals were taking you? You think you show up onto some alien geography with multiple suns or moons or different constellations in the sky and that it's all—what? Some kind of hallucination?" Smegma asked derisively.

Ms. Stovall frowned but answered with a commonly held belief of humanity. "We believed that Portals took us to planes of existence outside of our own that are created to house the Monsters."

Smegma glanced at me and then around the room at the nodding heads of my father and mother. My mother froze when his black pupils crossed over her, but inhaled sharply after his gaze moved on. I sighed and moved to her back to rub her shoulders. While waiting for Smegma to contradict Ms. Stovall, I whispered, "Don't worry, Mom, he can't do anything to hurt you. I promise."

She raised a hand to rest atop mine on her shoulder and gave a weak squeeze.

"Again, words *can* hurt!" Smegma said but continued quickly, addressing Ms. Stovall. "I can't remember everything, but I do recall Brodie telling me that your race wasn't aware of any locals inside Portals. Partially, that could be because of your stigma against going inside at night, which I will admit is a good choice. The second, far more likely reason, is that they are *here* and actively hiding themselves."

"Why would they hide themselves if they're powerful and have greater knowledge of the System than us?" I asked.

"To avoid a purge," Smegma said. "Plus, anyone they sent over would be A-Rank at the highest. That's one of the biggest reasons that my Abyss Sect made this Skill. We were kind of hoping to give it to someone who was crossing over— so they would possess all of our knowledge and be powerful enough to—" Smegma coughed, glancing at my parents. Then, licking his shark-like teeth with a black forked tongue, mumbled, "Powerful enough to take over."

Everyone heard him. My father jumped to his feet and pointed an accusatory finger at the Demon. "So, you admit it. You're evil!"

CHAPTER 40

Tuesday, April 16th, 2069

Silence descended on the room at the pronouncement. The statement was so absurd that it startled a laugh from me. Ms. Stovall followed suit, and then even my mother chuckled once, before Smegma's *evil* cackle overrode us all. Four pairs of widened eyes turned on him.

Maybe my father wasn't too far off.

When Smegma was in control of himself again, he brushed black tears out of his eyes and said, "I don't think we are any *eviler* than you humans, Elves, Dwarves, Deep-dwellers or Mermen. I'm sure there are others I'm not remembering, but I can tell you that by and large, all life is the same. Just like you, we've all gone to war with each other over differences amongst our own race. Before the System, we've all had genocides and crusades. We've all got a history of evil dictators with hands soaked in the blood of the innocent and heroes who rise to oppose them.

"The only reason the Abyss Sect wanted to 'take over' Earth was for another chance to Ascend," Smegma finished, opening the door to more questions.

Which Ms. Stovall asked immediately, "Ascend?"

"Yeah, like I told Brodie—" All eyes turned to me, even my mother's, and she had to crane her neck back awkwardly to do so.

[Thanks a lot,] I mentally sent.

[You're welcome,] Smegma responded before continuing, "The System's goal and function—as far as anyone understands it—is to test a species. After an indeterminate amount of time, it will deem you humans 'ready' to take on the Seven Deadly Realm Trials. When it does that, only your race can compete. So, even if another race did conquer the planet, it would ultimately be meaningless to treat you humans poorly. You're our ticket to a higher Plane…"

"But only the few of you who crossed into our world could go?" I asked, seeing a flaw in the Demon's logic.

"If you were close to succeeding, word would be sent back to Crendalar, and you would find a steady stream of F-Rank or Unskilled refugees coming through each Portal that opens onto our world."

"But if only one person can go through each Portal, your whole race couldn't possibly cross over," my dad said skeptically.

"The goal isn't everyone. It's like lifeboats on a sinking ship. We'll send over anyone and everyone we can. Races that fail to Ascend aren't really living anymore—just slowly dying. Still, how many Portals are open worldwide at any given time?"

Ms. Stovall picked up her phone from where I'd put it on the table after everything had calmed down and the threat of her calling the police had subsided. She answered a moment later, after typing something onto the screen. "Estimates say a couple million."

"So, a million refugees a day," Smegma said. "Not just Demons, obviously. But even if only ten percent of the Portals lead to Crendalar—then hundreds of thousands of us could cross over with each cycle of opening and closing Portals."

"Well, isn't that lovely," Ms. Stovall said as she slumped back in her chair. "Surely, we need to tell the UNMH or our government about this…"

"What makes you think they don't already *know*," I asked.

"They do," Smegma added, confirming my suspicions. "It would be impossible for your race to not have met a single local of another planet in the twenty-plus years you've been working with the System."

"Can't you just communicate with your Sect and find out?" Ms. Stovall asked.

"Nope. This Skill has some flaws—communication being one of them. Theoretically, they were supposed to be able to communicate through pricing and therefore give me some information on what I'm buying, or they could increase items' prices for sale as well—but that hasn't happened, and I'm not sure why. Still, it's very limited, so I'm all by my lonesome."

"But you said there are other Demons already here," my mom whispered.

Smegma nodded knowingly. "Remember when I said that every race has internal wars and problems? Well, while I'm sure there are other Demons here, I'm not sure what faction they belong to, so you'll have to forgive me if I don't go advertising my whereabouts and existence."

"Isn't that a pleasant thought," Ms. Stovall said as she looked meaningfully at her phone, the door, and then even our TV. Only due to the sequence could I tell she was still considering trying to reveal this bombshell.

"You can't," I said quietly. Her head spun to focus on me so fast I thought she might be a Hunter.

"What do you mean I can't?" she asked.

"Client confidentiality," I answered. "All of this falls under that, right?"

She waffled. I could tell she was thinking that question through to its terminus, mostly because she spoke out loud to herself. "Client confidentiality can be broken if the information poses a threat to themselves or others. Surely the invasion of other species would put others in imminent danger."

"Nope," Smegma said. "The invasion has already happened. After twenty-plus years, other races have probably infiltrated deeply into every power structure you have. If there is a risk anymore, it's against Brodie, his parents, and you, if you try to upset that balance."

"Are you threatening me?" Ms. Stovall asked.

"I can't threaten even a hair on your head, lady," Smegma said dejectedly, sounding truly remorseful about that fact.

"He's just saying that we should be worried about what people will do to cover up the truth." I looked around the room, my eyes pleading after my excuse for the Demon. I wasn't really sure if that was what he was saying, but those were my own thoughts on the matter.

Ms. Stovall accepted my look and slowly lowered her phone back to the table face down. That was good enough for me. She did of course add to the gesture by saying, "Okay, I'm not a hundred percent convinced that this doesn't fall outside client confidentiality, but I'm willing to hold off revealing what we just heard for now.

"Still, speaking of clients, I came here to discuss the video and its effects on the case," she looked pointedly at Smegma. "Before you started telling the truth, and *he* showed up."

She turned Smegma's gender into a question and I couldn't help but realize I'd never really asked him about that. We had joked about his 'penis' envy, and he had questioned whether he could even piss. So, I had assumed, but hadn't really asked that question yet. Let alone had Smegma answer it.

He nodded in affirmation to Ms. Stovall, making me chuckle under my breath. I was going to make sure I poked more fun at him about his dickless state later. Smegma glared at me but didn't respond to my 'thoughts,' leaving the floor open to me. I took the hint and stopped laughing before I asked, "Well, I haven't checked my social media since I got home, but how bad is this?"

"When I got here, I was worried that Mr. Varnish would use this to further muddy the water. Now? Now, you've got me thinking a bit deeper."

"What do you mean?" My dad and mom asked in a slightly staggered unison.

"Well, if other races have infiltrated the governments, UNMH and other power structures of our world—who's to say that someone wasn't aware of what Morgan Hallsbrad's Skills were. If that person exists, wouldn't it make sense to hire a lawyer to find out more about the person who managed to one-up someone who had a literal Demon on his side?"

"Husk!"

"Language, Brodie," my mom said, sounding a bit more like herself.

"Sorry, Mom, but if that's the case, I don't only have a high-priced lawyer to worry about. I've also got whoever is behind him, too!"

"Yeah, another evil Demon," my dad said jokingly. The comment broke the seriousness once more with a few chuckles.

It also got my brain to unstick on the conspiracy of the whole thing and ask, "So, what should we do?"

"Well, let's say that the person behind Mr. Varnish is a Demon, for example. From what *Smegma* said—" Ms. Stovall said the Demon's name in such a way that let me know she found the choice I'd made somewhat distasteful. I winced as she continued, "—there are other races that would probably oppose his backer.

"The trick will be finding them," Ms. Stovall said after she'd let a small silence stretch.

"Well, I do have SwiftGram and a sudden surge in popularity," I mentioned. "Surely, that will help."

"You also have Evelyn Treesong," Smegma added, and everyone turned to stare at him. "You know, your therapist."

"We aren't questioning who she is!" I exclaimed and Smegma either got the hint or read my thoughts to figure out the reason for my incredulity.

"I did mention that she has an Elven name," Smegma retorted as if that was enough explanation.

"But now you're sure she is Elven?" I asked, my tone questioning the line of logic.

"No, but it's somewhere to start…"

"Right, so you want me to go in and ask my *psychiatrist* if she is an Elf?" I asked. "That will go well, I'm sure. She won't commit me to a high-dose medicated mental institution with a personalized straight jacket."

"You *can't* be crazy. Not with your A-Rank *Mental Fortitude*." Everyone was looking at me again in an instant, and I closed my eyes in exasperation as I sighed.

"I guess I should tell you all the Skills I have, *and* what the 'repair mark' really is," I said, and launched into the whole story I had been trying to tell but kept getting interrupted. This time at least, everyone let me speak without stopping me.

Except, Smegma. That thirsty Husker was a dick without a dick—through and through.

* * *

"So, you have access to a Shop that sells Skills, Profession gear, Weapons and Armor? Did I miss anything? Can anyone learn these Skills you purchase or just you? I'm assuming the Weapons, Armor and Gear can be used by anyone, based on the Mining Picks," Ms. Stovall shot-gunned out when I was finished.

"Uhhh—" I began but thankfully was saved by Smegma.

"That is something I'm not sure of," Smegma said, tapping a talon on his sharp teeth. I was happy to see everyone around the dinette shiver, just like I had done when I first saw the action. It really was disturbing to see the creature use one deadly killing instrument to pick at or tap another. "At first, I thought he could do whatever he wanted with the Skills, but with each update that *Demonic Vault* has gone through, I've had more rules of the current System shoved into my head."

"So, wouldn't that mean you would know whether I could give the Skill to other people or not?" I asked.

"Well, everything I know suggests you can. However, do you remember the *Mining* Enchant destroying itself and then bringing the System's disciplinary failsafes down on you?" He looked over at me. I nodded and a few others at the table, now in on the full story, did so as well. "Well, that's just one example of things the System has scrapped through iterations. Usually, it wants the people undergoing integration to get strong, so buying new Skills like this wouldn't be curtailed."

"But why would it destroy an Enchantment used to create a Crystal from the Mana Spillage during a task the Profession was intended to do?" I asked.

"Exactly," Smegma agreed. "There's just no telling what the System would or wouldn't do."

"Okay, but that doesn't stop him from buying Weapons or Armor and selling it for outrageous profit," Ms. Stovall said.

"I think you missed the part where Brodie said that everything combat-oriented is prohibitively expensive, and even after the updates, he can only purchase high B-Rank Skills or Equipment at the highest."

"Normally, I would agree with that, but you have also said that your people know far more about the System than we do. So, wouldn't your B-Rank Equipment be far stronger than what we can produce?"

Smegma went back to tapping a talon on his teeth. After a moment, he grumbled, "You aren't wrong, but Brodie doesn't have the connections in place to make sales like that without a middleman. Meaning he doesn't have access to the kind of resources he'd need to build up enough Mana Coins to make those kinds of purchases. Plus, suddenly coming out with the kind of things we're talking about would reveal this Skill, or at least hints of it, to others—" Smegma stopped mumbling to himself and looked pointedly around the room. "—Which didn't go over so well with all of you, and most of you are family. So, I'm guessing that we should keep quiet about everything that's happened in this kitchen. What do you think?"

Ms. Stovall's eyebrows climbed as her eyes widened in realization. Then she nodded and said, "I wouldn't tell anyone anything that was discussed in this room."

"Does that include the refugees-on-Earth part?" I asked.

She shrugged. "For now. Still, I think our earlier thought of looking for our own backers in this case is even more important now. If it's okay with you, Mr. Flacarada, I think it's time we hired a social media manager."

"You really think that's a good idea?" My father asked, clearly thinking that 'Mr. Flacarada' was referring to him. He realized, too, when Ms. Stovall transferred her gaze onto him. "Oh, you were asking Brodie. Sorry."

"I mean, we don't really have the money for that—"

"I think the bonus of four hundred thousand today should cover it," my father said. My mother, who hadn't heard that part of the story yet, gasped.

"You think *that's* big news. Your husband and son killed a—"

"Get husked, Smegma." I shouted, interrupting him and earning an intense stare from my mother.

"Brodie, do you want me to wash your mouth out with soap like you were five?" my mother asked pointedly. I didn't think that was totally fair—I'd just saved her from fainting again. Still, my head fell—I didn't like upsetting her.

Ms. Stovall saw my hangdog expression and saved me, thankfully.

"Well, if you have the money, you can pay upfront, or my office can. We will, of course, attempt to go after Morgan Hallsbrad's estate to recoup costs."

"Okay," I said. "When do we start?"

"Tonight," Ms. Stovall answered and reclaimed her face-down phone from the table with a fervent gleam in her eyes.

CHAPTER 41

Wednesday, April 17th, 2069

"First thing tomorrow morning, head over to Sparkle Legion," I read, including Smegma, and my parents in the 'conversation.' "After discussing your circumstances—she opened brackets here to tell me she didn't discuss anything confidential, just the broad strokes the public already has access to."

From the time stamp on the email, Ms. Stovall had gone back to her office after our meeting last night and likely worked through the night on my behalf. Of course, that also meant whoever I was meeting with today kept late hours, or she had talked to them early in the night before deciding on what 'package' we should be getting. I kept reading, wanting to know that decision myself.

"We believe you need more than just a simple campaign aimed at gaining followers. You need a narrative and the ability to tell your story to curry public opinion, and hopefully, if it comes to it—outrage on your behalf. I've got a weird feeling about everything that's been going on. The kind of hot-shot lawyer like Varnish should have never been called in for a case like this. Now that I know everything from the beginning, I think it will only work in our favor to have everything play out in the court of public opinion. Whoever is behind this, it's unlikely they want to draw attention to things, so that's exactly what we're going to do. You'll be meeting with Kristen Franzke and Geneva Agnos. They are a team I've worked with before, and are fantastic at their jobs.

"She then just lists the address and says I need the Full Sparkle Package, whatever that is…"

I was already pulling up the website to see what options Sparkle Legion had and what the chosen package offered. I scanned the title headers before arriving at the premium, best value, option—meaning it was the most expensive of the bunch.

My face obviously conveyed the sentiment because my dad whistled and asked, "That good?"

"Well, I don't know the name of the company, but it's their premium package. Remember I tried to get Aesir Living to work with me a few years back, but after the initial call they stopped picking up?"

"Yeah, your father and I were trying to figure out how we were going to be able to put up a thousand dollars a month for the videos they were going to help you shoot," my mother answered over her coffee.

Running my tongue over my incisor behind closed lips, I once again chose to not tell them that it was not a monthly fee. It was a thousand dollars for four videos, which could have lasted anywhere from four days to, at most, two weeks, and that would have been with me cutting the videos to make quick, attention-grabbing pieces in between the posts. Not to mention—a thousand dollars was Aesir's cheapest package. I think their premium was twenty-five hundred.

"Look here, they're going to write the scripts for videos, monitor the posts, adjust content, remaster audio and even color adjust. On top of that, they offer something called image Sparkle. It's a hyperlink."

I clicked it and heard my parents stand up to read over my shoulder. I flicked my hand and cast the screen onto the small TV, which turned the old contraption on. They made it to my back before I managed to use the slow technology to my favor. I stopped reading aloud though, allowing my parents to take in the information themselves.

"Does she think I need this?" I asked when I reached the bottom of the jot-notes-format description. The gist of it was that they were going to create a public-facing image for me that would counter any bad rumors. I scrolled back up and read the first line, "—we offer a targeted solution to targeted attacks."

"That's ominous, ooooooooooo," Smegma said, joining the conversation in his usual derisive terms. This time, since my parents could see and hear him, they gave him a wide-eyed look.

"I don't think sarcasm is the best approach here," my dad said, scolding the Demon like it was me. I smiled, hearing words from Gary that I hadn't heard since I was in my mid-teens.

Smegma made a rude gesture, and my mother scoffed. "We do not tolerate language like that in this house!"

"Language? I didn't say a thing. Besides, what are you going to do about it? I'm kind of stuck here, lady," Smegma answered. My mother narrowed her eyes, clicked her tongue, but then picked up her phone.

I started laughing, knowing that she was moogling a way to deal with the incorporeal Demon. I kind of even hoped she found something. It would be very helpful to have a punishment option for the little—never mind—the *large* shit.

His new size was going to take some getting used to.

To be honest, I'd woken in the early morning hours due to my bladder informing me it was time to be emptied. When I stood and made my way into the bathroom, I'd discovered a human-sized, winged Demon kneeling in the shower. He seemed to be speaking into a small, glittering crystal.

"Captain's log, day seventeen. Unfortunately, I am still stuck on this strange, backward planet. The primary dominant intelligent lifeforms have proven to continually defy the Galactic standard definition of 'intelligent,' however, and I fear something must be done. Let this log serve as a reminder to check the ship's computer for a more appropriate designation for local inhabitants. Unfortunately, I don't believe I will be able to make my way back until the Transporter has been repai—"

"What. The. Hell?" I gaped.

Smegma startled and the crystal vanished near-instantaneously as he leaped into the air, his body quickly disappearing through the ceiling. Seconds later, a scowling face pushed, upside-down through the ceiling's sheetrock. "What are you doing up? Don't you humans have some strange, sexual fetish for sunlight? Shouldn't you be sleeping?"

"What?" I blinked, baffled. "It's not—*we're* not… Hey! Don't change the subject. Have you been staying up watching StarTrip all night? I know I parental-locked the soap operas after they started giving you weird ideas about how humans' 'primary erogenous zone is betrayal,' but have some self-respect and at least watch Star Battle Galactica for God's sake. Now get the hell out, I need to take a leak, and unless you've picked up some kind of golden shower fetish, you're not going to want to hang around."

Smegma continued to glare at me as his fist slowly slid into view through the ceiling, once again holding the strange crystal. "Continuing Captain's log. The sanity of the local populace seems to be spiraling downward. I am beginning to see signs of irrational anger, paranoia, and confusion—*so* much confusion. I'm afraid that it is starting to look like the kindest thing we can do at this point is to put the rabble out of its misery. Document a reminder to Glass the planet once the Transporter has been repaired and we are safely back in orbit." As he spoke, he slowly withdrew back into the ceiling, the last bit of him to disappear was the hand that wasn't holding the crystal, which was sticking through the wall with the middle finger raised like a twisted take on the death of the Finalizer.

I rolled my eyes and did my business but couldn't help checking behind doors and even—I hate to admit it—under my bed before I was able to go back to sleep. It was embarrassing to admit, but when I'd first seen him there, hunkered down like a feral beast in the shower, I lost bowel control for the *tiniest* of instances and may have peed a little in my boxers. It didn't help that I'd heard my mother screech first thing in the morning as well—telling me that she had also discovered a bathroom 'Demon-Captain.'

There was a good possibility that was why she was in a bad mood.

"Guild Wars break out in the Middle East," the TV said from where it hung from the wall in front of our couch. Since the room was open concept, it was part of our dinette but also considered a separate room by the family. The morning news segment had just come on, and Fleece's face took over the screen. He looked dire due to his pronouncement.

My mother clicked around on her phone and the volume increased, allowing us to more clearly hear what Fleece said next, "—the primary target of a myriad of Guilds seems to be the Sayyad Guild. Who amongst these Guilds struck first in the conflict is a heated debate, but let's go to Echo in the field for more."

The screen changed to a large, zoomed-out view, showing a massive dome mid-construction. I frowned at the image. Why was it showing the Field Containment? A new shot was cut in, and Echo with a microphone came into clear resolution. "Thank you, Fleece. I'm here in Qatar at the only site currently considered safe by the UNMH. As soon as conflict broke out, the UNMH fortified this structure and issued a warning to all Guilds. Anyone who attacks the Field will become an enemy of the UNMH."

"What happened down there to start the conflict?" Fleece asked as his screen popped into place beside Echo.

"From what we know, Sayyad's compound, housing family members and children, was attacked sometime late last night. Visitors—women and children alike—were put to death before the Sayyad Guild was able to pull their members out of the Field to return home. Reports say that the Guild's Homestead is now free of all threats, but since six this morning, Sayyad has been active in its revenge."

"Please explain what you mean by 'revenge,' Echo?" Fleece encouraged.

"So far, there have been attacks on eight Middle Eastern Guild Buildings, Fleece. Each one has been executed with extreme prejudice and no quarter. We are unsure if these Guilds were even involved in the initial assault. Some local experts believe that Sayyad is taking this opportunity to clear out enemies while it has Carte Blanche."

Images flashed onto the screen as Echo spoke. Horrible images of high-rises ablaze. Of people leaping from upper windows as they burned. Even of children amongst the rubble. The images continued to play across the TV, and I grew nauseous.

"Why are they only showing the eight Guilds that Sayyad attacked and not the Sayyad Guild itself?" Smegma asked, tapping a talon to fang.

I blinked then looked back to the TV with narrowed eyes. Surely some of these images were of the Sayyad Homestead? From what little I knew of the term Homestead, it meant that the Guild had purchased a large plot of land and built it up with houses and stores. All the current images were of high-rises in ruins.

The screen returned to Fleece and not Echo, surprising me again. "Stay tuned throughout the day for further updates on the tragedy unfolding in and around Qatar. If that was already a bit too much stress for your morning, I suggest you turn off your TV if you live in California. It seems the Heartless Killer has struck again—the increased time between killings is likely due to the locale shift from the east coast to the west.

"Let's head to Ken in California to learn more—"

I closed my eyes tight against the words even as my mother hurriedly turned off the TV. Ken was just popping up on the screen as the TV blinked off. I took a few steadying breaths—trying to center myself before I looked up and said, "It's got to be a copycat or something. Don't worry—Ms. Stovall is handling it."

My dad and mom came over and wrapped me in a long hug. Smegma, of course, ruined it slightly by making noises of disgust—or, far worse, suggestions to simply kill Mr. Varnish, the A-Rank Lawyer.

My mother let up in her hug and spun on the Demon. "First, we do not make jokes like that in this house," she exclaimed, thankfully thinking Smegma wasn't serious about killing Varnish. I knew better. "Second, we handle our problems with love and care—and if you find that disgusting, go away."

Smegma stared at my mother pointedly for a long moment before continuing with the disgusted noises. My mother sniffed and rejoined the hug, giving up—for now. Eventually, his words and mocking became amusing, which helped snap me out of my mood. That or *Mental Fortitude* did…

"With all of this, I doubt we're making it to Mining today," I said to change topics. I got some weird looks because I'd not spoken about the killings or the War in Qatar but I shrugged them away. I asked, "Can you and Willa try to use the two *newer* Pickaxes today to repair them?"

My dad nodded but didn't look at me. Instead, his eyes followed Smegma as he 'subtly' floated toward my mom. From her smirk, I could tell she also noticed the Demon.

Just before he hovered around behind her, she clicked the side button of her phone and responded to my question, "What Pickaxes, Brodie?"

I felt my face break into a smile and said, "I got two new ones yesterday, but they got pretty beat up—umm, Mining Ore."

My mom's eyes narrowed again, and she dove back onto her phone. Knowing it wouldn't take her long to find an article that covered some of the events yesterday, I hurriedly said, "Dad, the attorney did say to meet up first thing this morning. Think we can get breakfast on the way?"

My dad nodded hurriedly and joined me in a 'brisk' walk out of the kitchen and back up our narrow stairs to change. I was back to the front door first, having not even considered what I was putting on. I'm sure my mentors in fashion over the years would threaten me with a knife if they heard, but I was trying to avoid a real knife.

"A *Golem*! A Golem was killed by five Miners!" My mom shrieked from the kitchen. I heard Smegma start cackling. "You better tell me you had no part in this, Gary!"

"Oh, your husband and son had more than a part in it," Smegma crowed. "Why, you should've been there. The way that Golem's fist shot out and *POW!* knocked Brodie something like *ten* kreebles—oh wait, you guys don't use kreebles, do you? I'm guessing it must have been, what—thirty feet or so, Brodie? Oh *man*, you should have seen the blood—"

I closed my eyes and mentally adjusted the meaning of 'first thing in the morning.' Surely breakfast and being in by nine-ish was fine...

Right?

* * *

"I needed a day off anyway," my dad said as he pulled into a spot beside a business high-rise. "Plus, this way I get to hear about all the things Sparkle is going to do for my son."

"Can we call it Legion if we're going to shorten it?" I asked morosely. This morning, reassuring my mother that I was okay and that stuff like sudden-death-by-Golem wasn't common in Portal Mines had taken all of my energy.

"I think Sparkle fits better," Smegma said from the backseat, where only I could see and hear him. It turned out that he could only turn it on or off—not be selective of who was included. So, since we were out in public and a human-sized, bat-winged Demon would cause a few commuters to join me in the loss-of-bowel-control department, Smegma was 'invisible.'

"You've talked enough today," I said angrily, confusing my father. I pointed to the back seat by way of explanation.

It was thanks in *huge* part to the Demon that we were late enough that my father had to call in 'sick.' The husker had literally egged on each and every one of my mother's over-the-top reactions. "I really hope the next Evolution in *Demonic Vault* makes you corporeal so I can punch you in the face!"

Smegma smiled evilly, reminding me of his sharp-ass teeth. I scanned down to his talons and decided internally to retract that wish. Smegma's smile was joined by a contented growl from deep in his throat. He'd heard that admission, it seemed.

"Let's head up," I said, my tone losing any heat it had held with Smegma and returning to morose.

The exterior of the building was old—like pre-System old, which immediately made me worried about what we were walking into. Still, with how expensive Aesir had been, I could get behind a cheaper brand that did the same thing. I guessed.

"Why is it such an ugly brown?" Smegma asked.

Now out of the car, I switched to mental communication to respond. [It's brick. Very old brick, at that. So, the color likely faded.]

"Are you saying that a large, checkered-brown building once had a *nice* coloring?" Smegma responded.

I didn't bother responding, considering that I somewhat agreed with the shit-stirrer. The lobby of the building wasn't much better, with a small entryway, drug store, and a coffee shop. The interior windows had bars on them for Selfless' sake.

A bulletin board with white plastic letters gave a rundown of businesses in the building and where to find them. Sparkle Legion was on the second floor— another small hit to their standing in my books. To be in a shitty building like this, and not even be in the penthouse…

We moved to the elevator bank, which was contrived of four ancient-looking contraptions that were divided into two per side, and pushed the up button, only to discover that the button didn't respond.

"Do you think the light is out?" My dad said.

"That guy behind the cardboard desk is sticking his nose a bit too high in the air," Smegma interjected. Since I was getting ready to respond to my dad, it took me a moment to find the desk Smegma mentioned.

It wasn't cardboard, but it *was* particle board. Clearly, someone had put together a cheap Rainforest or Aeki desk. The sign on top that read 'Security' in computer-generated font had a black marker underneath that added '& Information.' I took it all in, my eyes finishing on the very smug-looking worker. He was leaning back in his chair and had even gone as far as putting his feet up on the desk. The particle board bowed under his old but newly shined 'combat' boots.

"I think we need a card or permission to go *up*," I said, responding to my dad's earlier question. He'd also noticed the worker. I heard a resigned exhalation from him as he also realized we were going to have to deal with the man in the power-tripping station.

He did take the lead, though, which I appreciated. *We'd both had a long morning, but only I still had to listen to Smegma.*

Whether that was the reason or not, I chose to take it as such.

"Hey!" Smegma said, his voice filled with mock outrage. He even went as far as to hold a three taloned hand over his heart. "Okay, okay," he said, chuckling in response to my thought of 'point proven.'

306

"We're here to meet with Sparkle Legion," my dad said as we approached the 'counter.' The security guard ignored the statement, waiting until my father was directly in front of the desk before slowly taking his feet down and standing up.

"Can I help you with something?" he asked, overly sweetly.

"His smile looks like that of a snake's," Smegma commented.

[You two have a lot in common,] I thought at the Demon.

"Yes," my dad responded to the man. His tone was stiff, and I could see his hand open and close itself a few times to dispel frustration. "We are here to meet with Sparkle Legion."

"Oh, we have a company called Sparkle Unicorn here?" The man asked. "Let me just check the book and find out what floor they're on."

"That wasn't even close—this guy isn't only annoying but he's bad at it, too!" Smegma said.

"The second floor," my father said pointing at the sign. "And it's Sparkle *Legion.*"

"Oh, sorry, I didn't understand your accent," the security guard said smugly. My jaw clenched. We didn't have an accent, which meant the asshole was essentially calling out what area of town my father grew up in. I rolled my neck, dispelling my rising ire.

"Ahhh, here it is. Sparkle *Leg-on*, you'd think a company that worked on public image would make sure they spelled their name right in the directory." At this, I frowned. Even from here, I could see that each entry was handwritten in the same style. Plus, I could also see the 'I' he was skipping.

Still, the choice to insult a business in the building the man worked in seemed strange to me. My father's head tilted in confusion as well, but neither of us bothered responding, not wanting to engage the unpleasant man any more than necessary.

"Honestly," the security guard said in a conspirator's whisper, "I know a couple better options for public image if you want their contacts. From what I've heard, Sparkle Legion is going under."

There it was—the other shoe.

Why would he be bad-mouthing a business in his own building? A company that likely paid a portion of his salary. Because he had an angle.

My father looked at me questioningly, unsure how to respond to the offer. I shook my head, willing to trust Ms. Stovall and at least meet with Legion. To the security guard, I said, "We have an appointment, but if it goes poorly, we'll take you up on that."

"Sure, sure," the guard answered, giving me an up and down before addressing my father again. "Just remember, you want the best if you're going to spend hard-earned money. Someone like Aesir Living. My cousin works there, and she'll get you in right away."

"Could you make the call and let Kristen or Geneva know we're here?" I interjected, causing the guard to glance back at me. My dad stepped back slightly to show that he was 'standing by me' in that decision.

The man shrugged and handed over a keycard without making any phone calls. "It isn't like they have any other clients. Just head on up."

Reaching out, I took the card and spun away. Smegma made the comment I was feeling. "Did that seem off to you?"

I chose not to answer until we were behind the dinging elevator doors.

"That seemed *very* odd to me," I agreed, including my father in the conversation—even though he couldn't have heard the question.

"Me, too," Dad answered. "What possible reason could a security guard have for trying to poach clients?"

The ride up was short enough that I didn't get a chance to respond before the doors opened. The sliver of floor I could see made my response catch in my throat. It looked like a floor undergoing renovations. Cubicle walls were stacked off to one side, as were some office chairs, desks and even pizza boxes.

"Is this the right floor?"

My father, myself, and even Smegma checked the digital display to discover that this was, in fact, the second floor. I heard the sound of heels on carpet before I saw two women come into view. While they were only 'walking,' it was quick enough to tell me they were rushing to greet us.

Taking the initiative, I stepped out from the elevator and gave a slight wave to put them at ease. We weren't about to ride it back down and let dickish McGee down there have the satisfaction of being 'right.' We'd at least hear them out.

"You sure?" Smegma asked in response to my stubborn thought. "Dickish McGee may have a good reason for trying to get us better representation."

My dad stepped out but stayed firmly behind me, trying to show the women without speaking who they should be greeting first. I appreciated the gesture, knowing that most people would talk to him first due to age, even if they knew I was the 'client.'

"Brodie Flacarada?" One of the women simultaneously greeted and asked with her intonation. I nodded and they both broke into wide smiles. "Glad you made it past 'Security,'" she said.

Once the distance was closed, she extended her hand and said, "Welcome, introductions first. I'm Geneva Agnos, and this is Kristen Franzke—we're social media managers and are excited to start working with you."

Hesitantly, I reached out and shook her hand. "Thanks," I started slowly before deciding on a tack and continuing. "This is my father, Gary. You mentioned security, though. Does that mean you're aware of the guy downstairs trying to poach your clients?"

Kristen cursed under her breath and Geneva's face fell. I hadn't realized at first just how tired the two women looked. With make-up and their hair done up, I had taken them to look like well-dressed businesswomen. Now, I looked closer.

Geneva had dark red hair, bordering on brown. She wore a knee-length, black skirt and a pinstriped shirt that both accentuated her curves but made them business appropriate. All in all, she looked like a woman who was in control of her outward appearance. At least, she had looked that way when she was smiling. Now, with her face fallen into a frown, the dark circles under her eyes and frown lines were a bit *too* apparent.

I scanned my eyes over to Kristen and found the top of her blonde head. She was looking at the ground, and her pale skin was flushed from what little of it

I could see. She wore dress slacks and a white blouse that like Geneva were business appropriate but highlighted her figure. The outfit would have sparkled if she didn't distinctly lack that characteristic in the moment.

Geneva corrected her expression almost instantly when she saw my scrutiny and forced a smile. With a nod, she said, "Yes, we are aware. This is the eighth security guard that's taken the job. Strange how they all have nieces, cousins or nephews who work for our competitors…"

My eyes went wide.

"I smell a juicy story," Smegma crowed as he hovered around the two women. "Who do you think they pissed off?"

Frowning now, I sucked on my teeth. After the interaction downstairs, I was absolutely sure that the person they'd 'pissed off' was from Aesir Living. I took another look around the 'office,' seeing it in a new light.

I saw it for the fight that these two women were waging with a bigger company. Sure, they were losing—but they hadn't given up. My heart swelled on their behalf. I may later discover that it was misplaced, but I immediately felt a connection with the two.

I, too, was going up against someone who had too much money and powerful connections.

All I said, though, was, "Is there a place we can sit down to discuss strategy?"

Kristen's red face became visible again. There was a moment of hesitation displayed by them both before they broke into wide grins. Were those tears in their eyes?

"This way," Geneva said.

CHAPTER 42

Wednesday, April 17th, 2069

"**M**s. Stovall has caught us up on your situation. The very first thing we need to do is paint you as the victim in this," Kristen said, pulling up a slide on the projector. The slide showed a few viral SwiftGram personalities who had made their names by sharing stories that painted them as victims in one way or another. "These people here are examples of success for this strategy."

"I'm familiar with all of them," I answered but then followed up a bit more seriously. "Yet, none of them are on trial for murder."

"Self-defense!" Geneva corrected gently. "While that's true," she continued, "what we are looking at is proof that the formula works. The trick, if you will. Why did Jesse Barnes, for example, get to keep his house even though the bank foreclosed?"

"Well, he not only created enough public outcry toward the bank that they had to listen, but he also got enough in donations using FundMeNow," I answered.

Kristen nodded but chuckled a bit, letting me know I had missed something. She didn't leave me guessing for long. "No, Brodie. What he did, which led to all that, was share his story. He let people into his problems without oversharing or crying for help. He was a victim without the victim mentality."

She clicked the next slide and some of what she just said appeared on screen. "The formula here is telling the truth. Making sure you're aware of each public 'fact' and giving your audience an explanation. It's not about trying to ask for help, but just letting interested, concerned people into your life."

Geneva picked up the thread and continued, "The key is being aware of the public's lean on an issue and giving them your version. Remember, you're the victim, but we want to avoid the more negative connotations that come with that sort of label. You have a story of the events that people can't get anywhere else. Only *you* can tell them exactly what happened that night, and only *you* can share with them what you went through, before, during, and after."

"That's the problem, though," I said. "It would just be my retelling of a story that is being twisted by the opposing counsel."

"Not twisted well enough!" Kristen said while holding up a finger. "We spent the entire night going over the case, and it has several glaring facts that work in your favor. First, Morgan Hallsbrad currently is on trial in the United States for forty-six murders that span across the eastern seaboard of the country. Second, Mr. Varnish and his firm 'Black and White' are only taking on *your* case."

"How is that a fact that works in my favor?" I asked, not putting together the puzzle pieces.

"If used correctly," Geneva said as the slide flipped again. "We can paint this as a case of David vs Goliath. Of a hero who saved future victims and is now being prosecuted and persecuted unfairly. Then, we hopefully evoke the question of 'why is a high-powered firm from California representing Morgan Hallsbrad outside of their own country,' but has nothing to do with the much larger, ongoing case in the United States?"

"With enough fans looking into it, we might even be able to force a response," Kristen added to Geneva. The two seemed to work better together than Volt and Flair.

My face twisted into a frown. "Surely, me telling my story out of the blue isn't going to go over well."

"Definitely not, we've got a lot of work to do before then. This is the end game," Kristen stated. "First, we believe that the people will want to know what Skill you received. They'll want to know what you do. They'll want in on your day-to-day life and to feel as though, in some small way, they're a part of it."

"Okay?" I said, again pretty sure that showing myself Mining in Portals wasn't going to 'capture' people the way they described.

"I know what you're thinking." Geneva smiled and flipped the slide again. This one was titled 'Your Groomed Image.'

Smegma suddenly bolted forward. "She *does?* Is it a Skill? You think it's high ranked? Does she know about me?" He started wildly waving his hands in front of her face. "This is a strong illusion if she's from Crendalar Five…" He swung back to face me, his eyes wild. "BATTLE STATIONS! Get ready to launch Proton Torpedoes on my mark!"

[Dude. Calm down. It's just a saying on my world.] I struggled not to roll my eyes as both Geneva and Kristen were still looking directly at me. [It basically means 'I can tell by the look on your face what you must be thinking right now,' and she was right.]

"Aw." Smegma's ears somehow wilted. "That's lame. I was kinda hoping for… I don't know—something more exciting than all this Sparkle nonsense."

Biting my tongue, I worked my face into an expression of earnest interest as I looked toward the two women.

"People already know you're a Miner that just Awakened after a dangerous—and most importantly—lifesaving fight in a Portal. The buzz already exists, now you just need to use it. The question is what Skill you Awakened and how we're going to market it to fit your blue-collar persona."

"Blue-collar persona?" I asked, not getting the reference.

"Sorry," Kristen said and held up a phone. "I forgot that you haven't been online to see all the comments. Right now, you're being hailed as an 'everyman' hero. What we would call a 'one-of-us' reaction." She paused for a second and rummaged on her computer with the mouse pad before changing the slide to one that fit the discussion. "On that note, we think your photos and dream of becoming a Mana Bank fit but only as a sort of launchpad, and they need some trimming. I think we want more of an underdog-to-greatness arc for you."

"For example," Geneva said, edging in before I could say anything. "This picture here and that one there show you in 'tropical' locales. We think you should delete them. That's not relatable to the general public, and while we know that those are green-screened, the common man doesn't."

I blinked and immediately identified at least twenty other pictures with the same problem. Surely, people wouldn't actually think I went to these places just for a photo, right? I tried putting myself in someone else's shoes and realized the problem immediately. It didn't matter. People wouldn't click on the photos and see my descriptions or tags. They may just scroll through the thumbnails, just like I did on the first inspection of a person.

"And the one with a helicopter view will make it seem like I'm living a glamorous life," I concluded and saw both women's smiles grow.

"But we spent a good deal of money to get those photos taken and edited," my dad said, entering the conversation for the first time.

"Don't worry, Mr. Flacarada, we aren't suggesting never using them again. Here at Sparkle Legion, we work in phases. In phase one, we need to set Brodie's foundation. He needs to be an everyman who has been victimized and is continuing to be targeted. In phase two or three, we'll give the fans what we call a 'payoff.' Show them what they've accomplished for him.

"That's when we plan to put those back up but without the description saying it was a photo shoot. This will be your rags-to-riches story. We'll use them to create super-fans that will stay by your son's side for life."

"They're thinking in terms of 'fans for life,' and you're worried about getting locked up. The dichotomy is amusing," Smegma said, chuckling.

I held up a hand to get the women's attention back on me. "I think the focus should be on the trial. We'll deal with the other stuff if I don't end up in prison."

"Absolutely. We're fully onboard with that. That's why we're saying phase two or three. We're prepared for every possibility—" Kristen paused and looked flustered for a moment. "This plan helps you before, during, and after the trial…"

"Even if I go to jail?" I said, trying to save her from having to say it. She nodded sheepishly and flushed red.

"Exactly. Even if that happens, we'll make sure the public is up in arms…"

The rest of the meeting was spent getting to know me better and then brainstorming video ideas. In the end, the ladies said they wanted to take away what we'd done today and think about it, but they did hand me a 'Cannonball 360,' one of the best person mounted SwiftGram cameras for athletes and Hunters.

As Geneva handed it to me, she said, "Wear that as you Mine, and get some shots of coming home, eating dinner—that kind of thing. We'll clip out anything too personal, unflattering, or anything that would inadvertently dox you. No matter what we start with, you'll need some footage to clip together between expositions. Try to show the Mining Picks with the Repair Marks. Maybe even a before and after if you can manage it?"

I'd used the public lie with them for now, not wanting the whole world to react as my mother had. Then again, Willa hadn't made it for dinner to meet the *Demon* last night—so, that could be an *interesting* conversation.

"It can only hold about forty-eight hours of video on the internal memory, so upload the videos to this virtual drop-box once every two days." She held out a small card. "We'll handle the editing after that. Well, once we create a script. Also, as soon as you try out your newest Skill and know what it does, call us. Okay?"

"New Skill?" I asked, confused.

Her brows furrowed at the question. "The one you got in the video that just went viral? You lit up like the Fourth of July. Everyone's wondering what you got."

Momentarily shocked, I nodded and accepted the business card that held a scannable QR, which would likely take me to a digital dropbox. I had totally forgotten that, to the world, I'd had an Awakening and not an Evolution to an existing Skill.

"Oh! Everything's been so crazy that I'd nearly forgotten about that." They looked at me like I'd grown a second head. Right. Who's going to forget about gaining a Skill? "I was sort of… bleeding all over the place and just glad to be alive…"

Their looks of confusion transitioned to ones of concern and understanding. "Right," Kristen cleared her throat, seeming embarrassed. "It's easy to forget that the stuff in the video is real and not some movie about an action hero or something. Sorry. Are you… okay?"

"Everyone made it home alive and safe, so I'm better than okay. I'll make sure to let you guys know what I find out about the new Skill, though," I said into the awkward silence.

The silence grew and I was looking for a way to exit the conversation and office when my dad coughed.

"We'll let you ladies get back to work," he said and stood from the mesh-backed office chair. "Come on, Brodie."

Thanking the women, I got to my feet and they took the hint. Geneva and Kristen walked me and my father to the elevators before Geneva finally blurted, "We'll send you an email with the FileBox link as well, so don't worry about losing the card. In that email, we'll attach the contract. We'll need it signed before we start work."

My hand slapped my forehead involuntarily. Of course, a contract and agreement to work together. No wonder it had gotten so awkward there for a moment. Chuckling, I said, "No, you don't have to do that. I'll sign it right now."

Both women breathed a sigh of relief.

* * *

Greb-Shak, or rather the construct who retained Greb-Shak's memories, watched the proceedings of the night and day. While he joined the conversation at times, mostly when prompted to do so, he was distracted.

Firstly, because he wasn't alive. Not really. With his new memories gained from Evolving *Demonic Vault*, came the realization that he had sacrificed his body, Skills, and power to create the very Skill that linked him to Brodie. He could vividly recall making that decision with his team of researchers. Memories flashed through his mind of them selflessly sacrificing nearly their entire team of thirty of the Abyss Sect's most brilliant minds. He could also recall the mathematical error that he'd only noticed after the Ritual had begun. The System destroyed and banned out-of-date or obsolete Skills with each new integration, trying to 'better itself for the inhabitants' of the given tested world.

Greb-Shak sneered at that thought, knowing he disliked the System but not having all the memories to fully understand why. He did have one complaint he could still recall, though.

The System depicted itself as benevolent. As always updating itself for peak efficiency—to give the new world a 'better' chance at Evolution. The one memory Greb-Shak could recall was his feeling toward that sentiment. The System wasn't kind or benevolent, and new worlds weren't given the 'optimal' chance to Ascend.

No, new worlds were husking petri dishes.

He shook off that emotion, which stemmed from watching his people slowly erode. They had slowly transitioned from a society mostly adapted to the System, to one scorned by it. He shook his head and body vigorously to truly clear the rising disgust.

Back to his memory of the *Demonic Vault* Skill's creation.

Unfortunately, that was all he knew—they had started creating the Skill. Something went wrong and bam! Everything after that was blank. But he was here, and the Skill was functioning—albeit with some… *issues*.

So, surely it couldn't have gone entirely wrong, but without the ability to remember anything more… he was left pondering. Clenching his fist, he deliberately let his talons puncture the meat of his palm. It didn't bring him pain like it once would have, but the familiar action still helped calm him down.

The second distraction stemmed from a decision he had to make. A decision he had already made once but hadn't had the knowledge he currently possessed while doing it. He'd chosen sub-Skill options for Brodie, picking what would be best for him—not necessarily what was best for the Abyss Sect's champion. Admittedly, *Overdraft* wasn't the worst choice he could have made, but he could remember his tiny 'Imp' brain thinking that picking it would increase the *Demonic Vault* Skill faster…

Now, after the most recent Update and pulsing with new energy in his soul, he knew that there were so many better options. Also, offering Brodie *Extraction*— a Skill designed to take Skills from enemies—well, that wasn't optimal for the Abyss Sect or the kid. He wasn't out there hunting for beasts or his fellow humans to take their Skills, and the Sect didn't need new Skills—they needed Mana.

Admittedly, in that regard, Brodie's choice to Mine Crystals was actually working in the Sect's best interest. So, could Greb-Shak use that and cater the next sub-Skill choices in the right direction?

That was only his second distraction, and not the one that consumed most of his thoughts. The third, overwhelming problem stemmed from the first but was also entirely separate. What was the situation of the Abyss Sect? Of Crendalar Five? Of Demons in general? He had to admit that his earlier 'posturing' inside the meeting with that Stovall woman was just that. Sure, he did believe that other races were on this planet, but normally he wouldn't divulge that.

Except for this one all-consuming worry. Where *were* the Demons? They should be pretty husking obvious if they were on 'Earth.' His appearance was a bit unique—not many Felguards would ever consider bedding an Imp—and other Demons' appearances would certainly stand out amongst frail humans. The closest he could think of on his planet would have been the Orcs, or maybe the Hobgoblins. But even they would scream 'alien species' or 'Monster' to the inhabitants here.

So, his biggest worry of what happened to his Abyss Sect was compounded with the question of what happened to his entire people…

Brodie was downstairs discussing the day with his parents. He was clarifying some things that they didn't understand and conveying information from follow-up emails Geneva and Kristen sent. So, Greb-Shak was alone in the bedroom—well, in the shower specifically.

He liked the device. It was somewhat of a novel idea and looked relaxing to him. Crendalar was a planet filled with sand and limited water. So, their 'showers' consisted of body scrubs with sand. Sure, he couldn't interact with this shower, but he could imagine, and that relaxed him and let him think.

While he didn't approve of the practice of 'therapy' in general, he did admit that there were some things that had intrigued him during Brodie's discussion with the Evelyn 'Maybe Elven' Treesong. One of the more interesting ideas was organizing your thoughts into a journal or some systemized format. With how scattered his mind had been of late, he felt like getting the various ideas, fears, concerns, and vague, patchy memories into some kind of order would be beneficial.

The main problem with that idea was that he was incapable of writing, or otherwise seriously interacting with the world, but one thing he did have access to was the System-like notification windows of his Shop. He could massage some of the features that had been intended for custom ordering to create things like fake popcorn, or other objects. A bit more finessing and he'd created a functional notepad where he could organize his headspace.

He'd found that speaking his thoughts aloud, even to himself, seemed to help clarify them. Since the Shop was intentionally designed to be able to be operated through mental intent, he was able to dictate his notes to said notepad. After several nights binge-watching Star Trip—Ultra Deep Space Forty-Two— he'd found that the idea of the ship captain's log really appealed to him. He could interact with replicas of any item in his Shop—a feature that allowed him to showcase his wares to potential buyers. Among the items there, he'd found a small, crescent-shaped Spent Mana Crystal that resembled one of the communication devices among the members of the Starship Energize and used the replica of it as a focus for his attention.

Unfortunately, he'd been mortifyingly caught in the act the previous night. After the initial shock had passed, he'd taken up the policy of 'it's only awkward if you make it awkward,' and refused to be shamed. The shower was relaxing and the makeshift journal was, ughh… *therapeutic*, but he now had exactly what he needed: time, space, and a place to *think*.

He shook his head and muttered, "Yeah, 'cause I'm not chasing my own wings right now."

Sighing heavily, he decided to try taking a meditative breath, something that was wholly unnecessary in a body that didn't truly exist, but maybe, like the talons into his palm, the action would help calm him. It didn't really work, but it did reset his internal loop of distractions to the beginning.

"Well, there's only one problem that can be handled right now," he said to himself. "Two decisions to make that should help Brodie stay alive and grow. Maybe if he stays alive long enough, I'll find answers. Then again, if I make the wrong decisions, he could turn out like that Morgan guy and wind up getting himself husking killed."

If 'Smegma' had hair, he would have started pulling it out of his scalp like he'd seen that Jagger Vance do on a few occasions. Instead, he reached up and tugged on his horns worriedly…

CHAPTER 43

Friday, April 19th, 2069

"So, remember that talk we had about trust?" Smegma said as soon as I opened my eyes. My eyes were still foggy with sleep but they narrowed as I tried to focus in on the Demon. I found a dark silhouette that looked like it had wings and decided to transfer my apprehension onto it with the look. Had he gotten even bigger? I was going to have to either hit the gym or gain some kind of complex if he didn't knock that off—and soon. "I'm over here, dumb-dumb."

Smegma said this from near the window, which made me aware I was glaring at his overly enlarged shadow. "Good morning to you, too," I said dryly, attempting to cover the embarrassment. "So, what's all this about *trust*?"

"Well, I need to admit to something, but it requires a bit of backstory," Smegma responded. I could hear in his voice a bit of embarrassment, which surprised me. Had I ever heard that from the Demon before?

I sat up and moved to the edge of my bed before giving him a nod. "I'm not really sure where I should start, so bear with me, okay?" Another nod. "I'm not a living creature…"

He left that statement hanging in the air. I waited for more. When it didn't come, I said, "And?"

"Well, I *thought* I was a living creature when I first appeared with you," Smegma added, giving me a bit of context but leaving me confused as to the direction he was taking.

Why did his being alive or not matter?

I didn't interrupt, knowing he could see my confusion from my pursed lips and blinking eyes—not to mention what was going on with my surface thoughts. "It's an important distinction because it will help explain why I did what I did, later. Still, when I arrived, *Demonic Vault* was an out-of-date Skill, and the version of me you interacted with didn't have all the knowledge I do now."

"Meaning you're learning from being in our world?" I asked, trying to clarify his story a bit.

"No, well yes, but no for the purposes of this story. Each time the Skill has updated, I've gained more memories from my life on Crendalar Five. Some of those memories are just pieces of things I already knew, but they fill in and firm up the picture. Still, with this latest Update, I gained a huge chunk of memories back from when my team and I were creating this Skill."

I opened my mouth to cut in with a question, but Smegma held up a hand. "Wait, just a second. I now understand that it has multiple purposes. The Skill was meant to support my Abyss Sect as well as the recipient who Awakened with it."

"Okay," I said quietly. "I don't mean to burst your bubble, since you're being all serious and everything, but as far as I understood things—that's exactly what we knew the Skill did already." I followed up when Smegma stopped speaking. For the first time, I could see a bit of disappointment in the Demon's black eyes. Was it directed at me or himself? Since he was looking at the old carpet on the floor, I was leaning toward the latter.

"It's not, or rather—not exactly. That's why I'm telling you this. After the first Upgrade, I believed that this Skill was solely for the betterment of the Abyss Sect. That we would use it to essentially take over or strip this planet of resources and send them back home to continue living the life we did before our Ascension failure. I now understand that Crendalar Five failed to Ascend eons ago. While we wanted to gain some benefits for our people back home, it was just until we found the right life raft. This Skill was originally created for the inhabitants of Sective Agora, and I learned that something terrible happened during its creation."

His eyes lifted then to meet mine, and I was shocked by the depth of emotion they contained. In that look, I nearly felt as though I could read *his* surface thoughts. Smegma was scared, sad, hurt, and worried at a bare minimum. My skin broke out in goosebumps. This powerfully built, monstrous-looking creature was terrified. Sure, through context, I could tell he wasn't scared of anything from this world—but for him to be this shaken up highlighted the seriousness of this conversation.

I bit my tongue to stop from offering any meaningless speculation. Smegma didn't need my concern. This was clearly leading somewhere, and my guess was that I'd understand more of his emotions if I listened.

"Hey, I may not *need* your concern but…. Ahem… I do appreciate it." Smegma cleared his throat. "I take back all those things I said about you being a gaping asshole. You're totally not gaping, so… thank you."

"Wait, what?" I half-shouted, leaping up from my bed. "So I'm still an asshole, I'm just not a *gaping* one? Is that supposed to be a compliment? I mean, what do you even—" In the middle of my tirade, another thing he said struck me and I stumbled over my words. "Hold on. 'Take back *all those things* you said?' To who? When? …*How?* …WHY?"

Smegma's face was too studiously straight. He only acknowledged my outburst with a sage nod that seemed to say 'some day, young apprentice, you shall have the answers you seek.' I wondered if that would be before or after I figured out how to punch him in his stupid, dumb face.

"Before," he answered the unspoken question. "Far, *far* before, since that's never going to happen. Now stop distracting me. Where was I? Oh, that's right, making the Skill. I don't fully remember what happened during the Skill creation, but I do know that no response has really come back from the Abyss Sect on the Monster Cores we sold in terms of where they value them. At first, I believed that was because they'd already stocked up from my previous owner and didn't have any huge demand for them. Now, though? Now, I'm worried they might not even be alive anymore." His eyes never left mine. Something leaked from his eye. It

318

looked like over-used oil from an engine; it was so thick and black. It took me a moment to realize the Demon was crying.

"While I'm mostly sure that the Demonic race from the Crendalar Cluster has survived, I have no idea what changes they must have gone through in those long years. With this latest Update, I'm also aware of three other planets that failed the Ascension since Crendalar. Sective Agora was one of the planets directly after us, and it is home to the Elves. The Elves, like the humans, were all 'one race' but categorized themselves based on skin color, eye shape or color, and ear shape.

"One of the second planets after Crendalar was Slithera, a planet similar to Sective Agora in that it was vibrant in plant life, but different in two major ways. It had a great deal more water, both in its seas and on its 'land,' creating a higher water table and mostly swamp-like living areas. The people who lived in this world were Lizardkin—which was a caste-based culture. The older a Lizardkin lived, the more powerful their bodies became—starting from what they called Kobolds and growing to eventually be as large as a Felguard, which they called Dragonkins.

"The next planet was Uther's Edge, a planet so close to its own sun that its inhabitants lived underground, only venturing to the surface for resources for a few hours a day. You were Mining on it when you discovered the Shining Meteorite. The inhabitants of this world were Dwarves and categorized themselves by how deep into the earth they lived.

"Finally, one of the last planets I can recall taking the Trials after Crendalar was called Morgraine. It was a planet that contained high amounts of nitrogen in the atmosphere, similar to your own planet. However, from what I can remember, unlike the other races I've mentioned, the inhabitants of Morgraine breathed nitrogen, not oxygen like the others. This was considered very promising—since differences can lead to power.

"But that's all I can remember. Even the race of creatures on that planet eludes my memories. I can see on your face that you're questioning why I'm telling you all this, and what it has to do with my story."

I nodded with a half-grin, trying to apologize for my lack of patience. "Let me get to the point. Sometime after Sective Agora, and maybe even after Slithera, I realized that the most beneficial thing for the Demons of Crendalar is if the individual bestowed with *Demonic Vault* Ascends. Meaning that my primary goal should have been helping you become stronger... It may seem like shifting the focus from helping my Sect, or even on helping the bestowed person's world to Ascend, to focusing on the individual is a trivial thing, but it's not. Yes, if *you* Ascend, then by definition—your world Ascends with you. However, there are... paths that can be chosen that can serve specific goals more than others.

"Let's say, for example, that there's something we can do that weakens you but strengthens others on your world, or increases the number or strength of Awakened on your planet. That would seem like a great option toward helping your world Ascend as a whole, despite that benefit coming at your personal expense. Or maybe something much simpler. If my goal was primarily to help my Sect, maybe it makes sense to buy things from you as cheaply as possible and sell to you at the highest markup I can manage..."

He let that rather disturbing reminder hang in the air, allowing me to make the realization of what he was saying. My half-smile vanished, and I felt my empty stomach bubble with a simmering anger. I clenched my blankets in a fist and managed to ask my next question without raising my voice. "Are you saying that you have been ripping me off on Mana Coins?"

"No." Smegma shook his head vigorously. "Not that. Except for maybe the Monster Cores—" I started to feel angry and Smegma waved his hands. "I honestly still don't know on those, but I can assure you that Demonic Vault wouldn't have let me pay too much. Or too little!" he added hurriedly as my mood went thunderous again. "There are limits on both ends in place. More on the upper end, but—"

"Then, you've somehow made me weaker?" I asked, cutting him off from that tangent. My anger puttered the more he explained. I was failing to understand Smegma's point. However, I felt like he was trying to gently break bad news to me.

"Not really, no. I just was given a choice to make after the last Update— and I didn't consult you…"

"What *choice* did you make after the last Upda—" the *Overdraft* and *Extraction* options for sub-Skills came to the forefront of my mind. Had Smegma somehow offered me duds for Skills? "Wait, are you saying that *Overdraft* and *Extraction* were shit sub-Skills?"

"No, but you're on the right track. Those two Skills weren't the only options available," Smegma admitted. I leaned back on my bed, trying to understand why this conversation had built up so much. Smegma continued hurriedly, likely trying to head off an angry response from me. "I scanned through the options that were offered and picked two that would hopefully start making the Abyss Sect more Mana."

I licked my lips, flopping back down onto my bed as I started to piece together the tale and what Smegma was saying. Still, I didn't feel any anger toward him for some reason. I scratched at an itch above my ear before I responded. "Okay, sure—but they were still strong options?"

"Definitely, but I'll admit I knew you weren't going to take Extraction. So I essentially manipulated you into taking *Overdraft*."

"So… you 'manipulated' me into taking a Skill that has unlocked a Stat for me and helped my family?" Smegma made a face that told me I was correct but missing something. "Okay…What were the other options, then?" I asked, needing to understand what I missed out on before investing an emotional response into it.

My brain was clearly doing its too-calm logical deductions, but it was immensely hard to fault the Demon, considering the results. Not only had I destroyed a Rock Golem, I'd also gotten a Skill that could turn my families' and friends' lives around.

"I can't share the list with you. I've tried multiple times. It seems when we created this Skill, we wanted to have control over its development—so, we left the decision to the curator of *Demonic Vault*. Then he can offer the options individually to the user…"

"So, *you?*" I asked and Smegma nodded. Even more reason I couldn't get upset. He'd made a decision he was supposed to have made. Plus, if this was leading where I thought it was, he had now decided on including me in the next sub-Skill choices. "Does this mean we have another sub-Skill to choose?"

"Two, actually." I stood up from the bed and practically left the ground as my knees locked out.

Did I have two more sub-Skills to choose? I couldn't curb my excitement considering just how much *Overdraft* had done for me.

"So, is there a reason why you're including me in the decision this time?" I asked as I began to pace.

"I think I included other wielders in this decision before, so you probably would have been included either way. However, I've also reached a bit of a wall. I've been looking through the options all night. The problem is that I'm unable to decide what direction will lead to the best results. You know your world far better than I can, and even on the other side, I'm not sure what direction will allow you to discover more about the Abyss Sect. And keep you growing to challenge the Deadly Realm tests."

"Do you have it narrowed down, then?"

"I have several paths to choose from, but I don't know all of the variables—in fact, I'm not even sure I truly know *any* of the variables…"

Smegma and I stared at each other as I stopped my pacing. I scanned my room, my eyes eventually landing on my laptop. "I have to go to work today, but I could start transcribing what sub-Skills there are to my computer. Then later tonight we could go through them."

Smegma rubbed at a ridge on his head. "There are about two hundred options…"

"Well, shit. Then I guess we'll have to go over all the options tomorrow or the day after."

Smegma smiled widely, displaying his sharpened teeth, and I shivered a bit before joining the Demon. I should probably get started if there were that many choices.

* * *

"What da ya huskin' mean we not be gettin' our bonuses from yesterday?" Willa shouted.

The target of her ire was Jagger Vance. He hadn't looked happy before Willa had confronted him, either—so, now he just looked constipated and angry about it.

"It wasn't my choice, you selfish piece of shit!" Jagger shouted back.

"Oh, please be tellin' me how this ain't the fault of our *Greed* CEO? The same asshole that be Huskin' three Mana Banks before his da' cut him off?!"

Jagger's face went so red, he became a tomato. A very angry tomato. He jabbed a finger into Willa's chest and growled, "That is not the entire story, witch! If you speak another husking word about what you don't understand, I will have you out of my company so fast—it will make your head spin."

My dad, also beet red in the face, grabbed Willa's shoulder and pulled her back, only to take her place. "The whole Mining team will just leave if you don't hold to your contract terms, Jagger! Yesterday's haul likely made you hundreds of millions—"

"I've made husking *nothing!* Everything from the Dungeon yesterday was confiscated by the UNMH for an 'ongoing investigation.' What *investigation* they were talking about, the Windsor PD department hasn't seen fit to tell me! So, not only do I not have the Ores and Crystals—they've also taken the husking plants—and Monster parts!"

"What?" My dad asked as he involuntarily stepped back. "But if they take the Monster parts and plants, won't they be reducing the value?"

"Yes, they are, and they wouldn't even concede anything to Taz, you know—*the S-Ranked Hunter? God among men?* You tell me, if he's getting stiffed, what do you think I can do about it? The answer is—*not much.* I've got my lawyers on it, but they've said that the powers that be are keeping their mouths shut tighter than a Hellclam!"

"Surely, ya can be frontin' us some money?" Willa said, her voice carrying a hint of her earlier heat. I would probably say it had transitioned to a complaint.

"For all I know, they will never return any of the material. The only thing I am left with right now is the expenses. There were at least *eight* unknown Ores in there and just as many stacks of unknown materials that presented as rocks. If I front you the money and get nothing back—then I'm out almost a million dollars!"

"What should we be doin', then?" Willa asked, her voice now entirely devoid of anything other than pleading.

"Just keep working—if they return the Ores, I'll immediately make good on the bonuses. In the meantime, I'm sure you can earn some more bonuses with your fancy new Picks."

I looked down at the Pick in my hand, realizing that Jagger believed we had all gone out and preemptively 'spent' the bonus on new gear. I had to admit that the Picks did give that impression. I looked over to my right, at uncle Jarred. He was looking back and forth between the speakers while holding the mirror-image of the original Miner's Pick from the Shop. Well, a particularly bad specimen of the original Miner's Pick.

He currently had one of the untransformed Picks I'd purchased during the Rock Golem fight, leaving me with one remaining. Which I had left in the car—unable to bring myself to hand it out with everything that was going on. *There was just too much of a chance of it ending up in the hands of Mr. Varnish—*

I froze.

[You think it was Mr. Varnish that seized the Ore?] Smegma asked, his voice mirroring my surprise at my own revelation.

To stop any further argument on that matter, just in case others made that connection, I rushed forward and grabbed my dad. "He's right," I said. "Let's just get to work and see what happens…"

Jagger was still upset with our little group of 'Specialists,' and his wide, angry eyes fixated on me for a moment. That was all it took for him to discover something. "Is that a camera?" he shouted. "You know that any recording equipment must be cleared by the site super, right Gary?"

I could tell he was trying to find any avenue for some quick revenge, but unfortunately, he had landed on something that was truly going to hurt me if he took it away. I looked helplessly up at my father, who blinked first at me and then at the Cannonball 360 camera on loan from Sparkle Legion.

He got the hint and put on a fake smile before turning to address Jagger. "Jagger, he's a kid and this is for a project for his second year of school—when he goes back."

Jagger's face softened a bit, but he still shook his head. "I don't care! The level of liability a camera brings into a Portal is too high to ignore. It always turns into people in comfortable office chairs second guessing decisions of people who were in the thick of a dangerous situation. If the kid wants to bring in a camera, he has to sign all the proper forms!"

"Well, that should be fine—" my dad began but saw my paling face.

"Oh shit," Smegma said, reacting to my continued worrying about the source of our problems and not the conversation. The loss of the recording inside the Portal would hurt us even more if I was right…

"Good, then go talk to the super and leave me the husk alone." Just as we turned to leave, Jagger shouted, "Willa!" which drew all of us up short. Willa, of course, more so than the rest of us. She turned back to Jagger and he motioned her to follow him. "You will be getting a write-up for insubordination before you go anywhere!"

Willa looked back to us and rolled her eyes in a way that told us all that she'd been through this song and dance before. My dad's cough sounded suspiciously like an attempt to cover a laugh. The group split, though. Willa followed Jagger into his trailer and my father led the way to what I assumed would be the super's trailer.

It wasn't a trailer, just a beat-up, old Dodge Caravan. Sure, it was in better shape than my mom's car but just barely. The man inside practically guffawed when we asked him for permission to bring the camera inside. Turns out the forms were supposed to be printed by the home office and brought onsite. Of course, the super didn't know where they were—so, he requested we wait to start recording until we were inside the Mine—because he couldn't guarantee that the Gecko Guild, the group that owned the Dungeon, would want images of the terrain or possible creatures to be leaked.

I waited until we were alone again before I voiced my earlier concern. "Dad, what if the confiscated Ores and Crystals has something to do with my trial?"

My dad stared at me, his face paling with each second. He gasped in a lungful of air when he realized he'd forgotten to breathe.

"Surely, a self-defense case wouldn't—"

"I think it's pretty clear that Mr. Varnish, or whoever is behind him, is trying to make this a bit bigger than a self-defense case…" I countered.

"I feel like I've stepped into a TV show," Jarred said. "Would either of you care to explain what the hell is going on?"

My dad looked a bit too shaken up to speak, so I took up the duty of explaining the situation to Jarred. He knew some of the story, thanks to my father, but learning about the massive value of confiscated Ores and the escalating self-defense-to-manslaughter trial definitely shook him up as well.

"You didn't actually kill him for his Skills, though," Jarred said when I finished. He didn't really make it a question, but I could hear it all the same. And so did my dad, as he was startled out of his shock.

"Jarred," he crowed, "that's my son!"

"I haven't talked to the kid in years. I'm just making sure!" He answered, even as he looked to the pavement at his feet. We all let that direction in conversation drop after that. Each of us likely having similar if entirely different thoughts about it.

I distracted myself by looking around. Today the Portal was inside a Catholic Church—which made the whole thing highly political. I wasn't totally aware of why, but the Vatican wasn't exactly powerless before the Advent, and just as any organization with a vast population base and wealth, I doubted they'd gotten *weaker* in the intervening years. I could tell that the mood of everyone was subdued as we waited to be escorted inside. I had to wonder if the Gecko Guild, which was a pretty small entity, was somehow related to the Church.

I figured they must be, since the Catholic Church had both the pull and the money to have their own team if they wanted it. Or multiple teams. I think there were something like over a billion baptized Catholics across the world. That was a lot of Awakened stock to pull from.

My dad's phone ringing beside me cut off my conversation with Smegma discussing the Church, its beliefs and why I believed the Gecko Guild was contracted to or outright owned by them.

"Morning, honey—" my dad said before the speaker blared in his ear and cut him off. It was loud enough that I heard the first couple words and could make out my mother's voice.

"None of the cards are working! I can't even get—" that was all I heard before my father stood up straight and moved away from the group.

CHAPTER 44

Thursday, April 18th, 2069

Smegma, ever curious, followed my dad and relayed what he could hear of the conversation. Which was enough to understand what was happening. My parent's financial accounts were all frozen. My mother had been unable to purchase a cup of coffee on her way to work today. I frowned. Surely this didn't have anything to do with—

My phone rang in my pocket, and I distractedly fished it out before glancing at the screen. Disaster Dave…

With a lot of hesitation, I sent it to voicemail. I would call him back once I had a better handle on what the husk was going on—

My phone immediately began ringing again, and the caller was, unsurprisingly, Disaster Dave. This time I picked it up—a little annoyed.

"Dave, I'm kind of in the middle of—"

"Well, I'm *also* kind of in the middle of something!" Dave shouted over me. "The police just showed up at school and escorted me out of husking class, Brodie."

"*What?*" I hissed as my lungs seemed to clench in my chest.

"Yeah, I'm currently being held for questioning!" Dave shouted. I waited, but other than heavy breathing, Dave seemed to have gone silent.

I asked the obvious, thinking I already knew the answer since he had called me, but needing the confirmation all the same. "Questioned about what?"

"The night that you *murdered* Morgan Hallsbrad," Dave said, stressing the word he would never have used to describe the events from his previous knowledge of events.

"You know that Greed jumped me, right?" I responded, pleadingly. I needed Dave to be on my side—I hadn't realized how much I needed it until this moment—as my heart beat erratically and felt like it wanted to claw its way into my stomach.

"Of course, I husking do, but the police won't let me go and that's the wording they're using. They haven't confiscated my phone or placed me under arrest, and have *assured* me that I'm merely 'detained,' but they also just said they can hold me for questioning for up to twenty-four hours. They keep saying thinly veiled things about spending my night in holding. But, like, they're making it out to be worse than the drunk tank, Brodie. I'm man enough to admit they're scaring me."

"Hold on, I'm going to three-way-call my lawyer," I said placatingly, my stomach was both relieved that he was safe and bubbling with rage at my friend's response. I expertly pushed a couple of buttons on my smartphone and soon could hear the ringtone.

"I'm already on the phone with your father—" Ms. Stovall said as a greeting.

Hearing the dismissal that line of conversation would lead to, I blurted, "The police are detaining my friend Dave for questioning related to the night of the assault. He's on the other line."

"Okay, are you near your father to let him know he'll be on hold longer or should I jump over and inform him?" Ms. Stovall asked.

Glancing around, I couldn't see my dad and assumed he'd retreated to the privacy of the Ford. "You should jump over and tell him. I can't see him."

A moment later, she was back and ready to be linked in with Dave. I clicked the combine calls and introduced the two.

"Okay, I'll send an associate down to the station immediately, Dave. From this point on, you tell them that you won't answer any more questions without a lawyer present—understand?"

"Yes, ma'am."

I heard a huff of complaint at what I assumed was Dave's use of the word 'ma'am,' but a moment later Ms. Stovall was talking again. "Okay, I have to get back to the call with Brodie's father. Sit tight for now. My associate will bring you back to our offices once she arrives and gets you released. Brodie—I'd start heading to the car. Neither you nor your father will be working today."

"Okay," I said and heard her click off the line. I glanced at the screen and confirmed Dave was still on. "I guess I'll see you at Ms. Stovall's office," I said as a way to follow up.

Dave thanked me a bit too liberally for something I felt was a situation I was wholly responsible for, which made me uncomfortable. Not to mention that if he made just one call to his powerful family—they'd get him off just as quickly. I figured I would have to take him out for some pho or sushi to make up for it. Wait—I couldn't do that if my accounts were also locked...

After hanging up the phone, I pulled Willa aside and explained what was happening. She immediately checked her financial apps and sighed in relief when she still had access. Jarred stood nearby looking at me, then Willa, and then in the direction he knew my father had parked.

"Wow, this is pretty intense," I heard him say as I started to walk away.

"Brodie ain't be outright sayin' it, but I be thinkin' the bonuses be withheld due to him," Willa whispered back. My teeth and fists clenched as my eyes watered. It felt like I was a Cursed Item. Something that seemed good for the people who found it at first but was now causing them endless problems.

Just to be sure of my assumption, I pulled out my phone and opened my banking app. Sure enough, I needed to 'call my financial institution' to resolve some sort of problem.

When I got into the car, my dad was off the phone and staring blankly out the front windshield. He glanced at me as I slammed the car door, then put the key in the ignition and started it without saying anything. Just after he put it into drive, he said, "We have to go by the home office and pick up your mother."

That was it. I felt frustrated, disappointed and angry. I wasn't even sure what I wanted him to do—but I definitely knew I wanted more than this. Still, my *Mental Fortitude* worked overtime to point out just how illogical that thought was— so, I managed to bite my tongue before saying anything I'd regret.

Instead, I gave a red-faced, fist-clenched, nod.

* * *

"You're going to have an aneurism," Smegma said unhelpfully. I glared at him as my body shook from how tightly every muscle was clenched.

I'd thought I was disappointed and upset when my father couldn't do anything—well, now I was doubly so when Ms. Stovall seemed to also not have a solution. Wasn't that her job?

Dave sat beside me, shrunk in on himself. My father and mother were across from me and were pale as they heard Ms. Stovall carefully dictate the next steps forward. "Your family will get a stipend of about a thousand dollars to cover food, and—"

"Our monthly rent is double that alone—how are we going to keep our *house*?" My mom asked, her face impossibly paling further.

"That thousand-dollar figure was just for food," Ms. Stovall cut back in. "What I had been about to say was that; I have a meeting with Judge Dench tomorrow to flesh out exactly the budget you need to live. This is just a temporary prepaid credit card. So, what I need you two and Brodie to do is come up with the exact amount of money you need per month. Put in about a thousand dollars of leeway, so we can allow Mr. Varnish to knock it down to an amount commensurate with the kind of pressure he's attempting with this stunt. This should only be a temporary freeze regardless—based on what I was informed of, they are looking for a lump-sum payment that would indicate Brodie was paid to kill the 'private investigator.'"

"Was it Mr. Varnish who also seized all the materials from the Portal?" My dad asked, his voice smaller than I'd ever heard.

"Yes. That, unfortunately, is a separate issue. I will bring it up tomorrow, but other than the expirable goods, I doubt I will be able to get the Judge to release what Mr. Varnish will no doubt be claiming as evidence."

"Evidence of what, exactly?" I asked, confused.

"Likely," she sighed, "evidence that you are capable of destroying Boss-class Monsters and are therefore more powerful than you've been letting on, and helping to invalidate any claim on being out-classed in the confrontation with Hallsbrad. It would further weaken your self-defense plea in regards to the degree of force you used to protect yourself."

I didn't like where this was heading. "What do the items and materials have to do with anything?"

"They don't. Not really. But there is some plausible argument that, with the unidentified nature of some of the materials, that something there could have some possible bearing on the situation." She shrugged. "The truth is that confiscating everything complicates your life and those around you, and if it can strip you of your pillars of support, you're potentially going to be in a weaker position socially, emotionally, mentally, or any number of areas, when going into your trial."

I cursed, gritting my teeth in frustration.

"Language," my mother whispered half-heartedly.

"What about me?" Dave whispered urgently.

"The cops know that they have to come to my offices to request for you to come in if they want to question you further—so, you should be able to return to your life." At Ms. Stovall's words, Dave swallowed and then proffered his phone. I could tell that SwiftGram was open and could read the headline.

'Phoenix Academy class interrupted by Police involved in murder investigation…' As if that wasn't bad enough, he flipped to another app, and I saw a message that I'd read on my own phone. Call your banking institution for more information. Dave's accounts were also seized.

We were currently sitting in a large meeting room that could easily seat twenty people but only contained the five of us. The table was heavy oak, and the chairs were beyond comfortable. The only thing I didn't like was that the walls surrounding us were all glass—it made me feel like a fish in a tank. An assistant knocking on said glass and all of us turning to look at the noise didn't help the feeling.

Smegma chuckled and added, "Dance puppets, dance!"

The comment almost startled a laugh from me, which actually did wonders to unclench my muscles and relax me. Ms. Stovall excused herself but was back in a moment before any conversation could break out. She was holding a yellow post-it and looking right at me.

"Brodie, Mr. Varnish would like to have a settlement meeting this afternoon at his offices," Ms. Stovall conveyed, her voice confused, but I could see her collecting herself. "It's likely a good idea to at least go and see what he wants—I doubt he'll show us any of his cards, but you never know."

"Can we also attend?" My parents asked in near unison.

"That's up to Brodie. He's an adult—so, you aren't required to be there."

That was a harder decision that the casual question they'd asked made it out to be. While I wanted them there for support—would they reveal something accidentally? I hated that was where my too-calm mind went. I nodded to my parents, not allowing my cynical mind to win. They both should and could attend. I needed to trust the people I loved and cared for. However, my father cursed under his breath a moment later.

"I've already taken yesterday off work." My dad said, clearly frustrated. "And with two Specialists missing… I think it's going to have to be just your mother and you, Brodie. Is that okay?"

My too-calm mind tried to alter my original decision once again. My mother was the one most likely to accidentally slip up. I clenched my jaw. I wouldn't let *Mental Fortitude* make me a different person. I nodded, even as Ms. Stovall handed over a card to my parents, which I assumed was the promised stipend. "Don't worry too much. With this meeting request, I can roughly guess what Mr. Varnish is doing. This strong-arm tactic is common when you want to spook the defendant and then try to reach a favorable agreement. The only oddity here is that you aren't really a defendant, and he should know that—so, what he's after, I can't say."

I told Dave I would call him after the meeting, intending to share with him exactly what happened. All of it! My friend still seemed shaken up, and he was also the only one in the room that wasn't continuously glancing around. I knew that was because everyone else knew Smegma was around and invisible.

It was definitely time to change Dave's status from outside of this little group and finally bring him into the fold. If there was anyone I should trust—

I walked out of the room, intending to invite him to my parents' place later. Now, there was just a meeting with the man who had quite literally turned my life upside down since he'd entered it.

Husking Mr. Varnish.

* * *

The building the GPS led us to, had no parking anywhere near it. Forcing the group to park a few hundred yards away and walk.

"Good afternoon, Mrs. Flacarada. Brodie," Mr. Varnish said, greeting us at the door. The man was in a silver suit that looked like it was for anything but business. While it had a tie, and undershirt, and all the accouterments of a traditional suit—it was also clearly freaking *Armor.*

"Is he expecting an attack?" Smegma asked. I very pointedly didn't glance at the Demon but did convey the question all the same.

"My suits are always multipurpose. As an A-Rank Awakened, I can't say where my day might take me. Do you like it?" Mr. Varnish asked, his tone conversational. "I can give you the card of the Crafter who designed it." I raised an eyebrow and glanced first at my mother, who looked as lost as I was, and then at Ms. Stovall, who was appraising Mr. Varnish in a new way.

"An A-Rank?" She said, giving voice to the question that was written across her scrutiny. "Why are you practicing law if you are also called upon to deal with Portals and Fields?"

"Ahh, trying to fish for information, Ms. Stovall?" Mr. Varnish asked with a wide smile. "I must disappoint you in that regard," he continued as his smile became more neutral. With a wave of his hand, he ushered us into the building— which, unlike Ms. Stovall's, was a standalone.

Ms. Stovall's offices, like Sparkle Legion, were inside a high-rise. Admittedly, Ms. Stovall's were far more extravagant and better staffed, but this building was strange. It had no exterior markings, and from the outside, it could easily be mistaken for a warehouse. Only the doors, which we had just been greeted at, gave away that it was something more.

Two solid wood doors that stood about fifteen feet in height adorned the street-side of the 'warehouse's' sheet metal. While I could see a glimpse into the building from the open door when Mr. Varnish greeted us, walking in still had my breath catch in my chest.

There was a small entry chamber that couldn't be more ostentatious. Every piece of furniture, down to the plants, were clearly Portal products. *Matching* Portal products. Clearly, this was meant to be a waiting room, since it had a large Castenork Desk with a secretary behind it. I could tell it was Castenork because of the epoxy that had been used to seal all the small holes in the 'spongey' wood.

Castenork was most like cork, but far harder and more durable. The finished product of a desk had a spotted pattern that was admittedly stunning with its light brown and black patterns. The chair she sat in looked more like a throne with wheels than it did an office seat. Honestly, I'd seen leather armchairs in magazines that didn't look that comfortable.

"I think that's Bovine hide," Smegma said, also staring at the chair. "All of them are."

I nodded. The color of the leather was just too foreign to be from earth cows. Bovine was a term now used exclusively to describe creatures that resembled cows in Portals. Things like Minotaurs or massive Bulls. Or anything in between.

The Demon's words made me scan the rest of the seats, and I immediately felt myself comparing the matching chairs and tables to Evelyn Treesong's waiting room. This was definitely a display of wealth and status even when compared to Judge Dench's office—and I had no doubt Smegma approved. Mr. Varnish walked slowly enough that we got plenty of time to 'get a feel' for the place.

Once through the side doorway consisting of more epoxied Castenork, it didn't get better. The lights in this area weren't even electric. No, instead, each office was surrounded by glowing Mana Crystal Glass—something I didn't even know existed until… right now.

"Are those Mana Crystals?" My mom asked as I swallowed the lump in my throat. They didn't just *look* like Mana Crystals. From the relative lack of any visible frosting in the glow—they were high-rank Mana Crystals that had been somehow converted into glass and lighting.

"Yes, they are," Mr. Varnish answered. "We're still trying to figure out how to add tint to the glass, since we would love to personalize the colors more, but it makes up for our lack of windows."

"You say 'ours,' do you mean 'Black and White' or the company you work for?" Ms. Stovall asked, trying once again to mine some information. Mr. Varnish just chuckled as he continued to lead the way down the hallway. We soon arrived at a meeting room like Ms. Stovall's, but surrounded by Mana Crystal glass, which I had to admit I liked far better. Even as we approached, I couldn't see anything of the internal layout. Same with the offices, I realized, as I looked back to the nearest closed door.

When the door did open, I was greeted with ten people, most seated on the same side of the table. A table made of Portal Ore and Mana Crystal Glass—I immediately felt out-gunned. What the husk did these guys want?

CHAPTER 45

Thursday, April 18th, 2069

"It appears we come understaffed," Ms. Stovall commented, her voice cold. I could tell there was a threat of something in those words, but I couldn't have said what.

"Not to worry, Ms. Stovall, these two here are a clerk and reporter that Judge Dench sent over. Those two are Ashley Laurent and Jasmine Bell, my co-counsels." Mr. Varnish continued around the table, introducing people.

I will admit that I had dismissed the court clerk and reporter, simply due to the lack of polished dress when compared to the other individuals around the table. I gave them a brief glance now but moved on to Ashley and Jasmine. The former was a red-headed woman in a white blouse, and the latter a brown-skinned woman with beautiful curls and a matching white blouse.

Smegma also followed the introductions. "I'm pretty sure that's some type of Portal Spider silk."

I ignored him as Mr. Varnish moved on. "This is Mr. Jacob, he's here on behalf of Morgan Hallsbrad's business." Mr. Varnish pointed out a man who was getting on in years but clearly still had a great deal of wealth, based on what he was wearing. Mr. Jacob appeared bored, which was odd if he had any sort of positive relationship with Morgan Hallsbrad.

"Why? 'Cause you killed him?" Smegma asked without a hint of tact.

[You know damn well it was self-defense.]

"These two are Aurome and Seleff, two active Hunters from the Larvae Guild, which Morgan was a member of." Mr. Varnish finished his introductions with the only two men in the room that seemed to give off a more intense aura than the A-Ranked Hunter-Lawyer himself did.

Aurome was in a t-shirt and jeans, which should have been even more out of place than the reporter and clerk, but instead only served to make him fit in even more with the wealth and power on display. He had long black hair that was pulled into a bun atop his head, and while his features were oriental in origin, his eyes blazed a feral blue. Whether that was an effect of the Mana Glass or just his natural eye color, I couldn't tell. The reason I considered the gaze feral could also be due to the man's massive frame. Simply put—he was huge.

Seleff, on the other hand, wore a robe. I would have called it a bathrobe, without a sash, but for the metallic rainbow glint that ran over the purple material every time I shifted my gaze. After looking closer and seeing that it was of similar materials as Mr. Varnish's suit, I was forced to mentally call the thing Armor, and with the funny matching beret and glasses, I thought he might be attempting to look the part of a wizard. I didn't think I'd ever seen a man as pale-skinned as he was, that wasn't an albino.

Since I lived in Canada, where the sun took a six-month vacation, that was saying something.

"The way the wannabe wizard is looking at you makes me uncomfortable," Smegma said. I turned my head back to Seleff and saw him give a small head shake to Aurome beside him. Clearly, that was meant to convey something, but I couldn't tell what.

"—as you can see, Ms. Stovall, everyone here is involved in this case in one way or another." Mr. Varnish finished. I realized then that the court reporter and clerk were the only two seated 'neutrally' at the foot of the table. So, at least we were only outmanned by two *more* people.

"It's not like you can complain," Smegma said. "If you had the money, I'm sure you'd also have a whole team of lawyers."

[That's just it, though. Who's paying the bill for *this*? The Larvae Guild? Mr. Jacobs?] I mentally thought, [Something is off.]

"I could have told you that right after this guy showed up in the pre-trial. Still, you're right. Why is he showing you these connections and hidden cards? Although, the man in charge doesn't have to be in the room. In fact, they are definitely, unequivocally not present. Whoever's behind this, they're clearly comfortable pulling strings from the darkness."

"I'll grant you that everyone can be said to have some stake in things here, but it does seem slightly improper, Mr. Varnish," Ms. Stovall said, still not moving to take a seat. "Especially since I'm yet to receive an offer to go over."

We'd discussed this a bit on the drive over. According to Ms. Stovall, it was more common to send an offer to someone first so they could come in with an idea of what they wanted in order to settle a given dispute. At Ms. Stovall's best guess, this should be a lowball offer from Morgan Hallsbrad's estate to try to keep hold of more wealth. Still, I had been able to tell from her tone that something was off. I could even infer what.

Who went to all this trouble for a bit more wealth to be held from a victim?

"Please, have a seat," Mr. Varnish said, clearly ignoring Ms. Stovall in favor of directing his words toward my mother and I. Neither of us moved. "Suit yourselves," Mr. Varnish said as he moved to take an empty chair in the very center of the metal table, right between his two co-counsels. "Ashley, why don't you tell them the offer?"

Ashley theatrically pulled a piece of paper from one of her many overly large manilla folders. I would have rolled my eyes if I wasn't so interested in what she was going to say. "If Brodie Flacarada pleads guilty to Second-Degree Manslaughter, we're willing to commute his sentence to one year of Guild Arrest. That means—"

My mother's gasp was the first thing that cut into the offer. My stomach clenched as she did so, my earlier worries about her presence somehow highlighted by that gasp.

"Now hold on a second," Ms. Stovall stated, cutting over my mother's slight squeal and Ashley's 'settlement' offer. "This is a cut and dry case of self-defense. You might have managed to get this through the pre-trial, but you have no evidence that can prove this wasn't an accidental killing or justifiable homicide in self-defense."

"I'm clearly missing something here." Smegma frowned. "Is a year of 'Guild Arrest' really that big of a deal?"

[It's something generally reserved for the most dangerous and powerful Awakened criminals.] I glared across the table. [Think about it. You've got a weapon in the form of a very dangerous person. Do you destroy the weapon?]

"Ah," Smegma nodded, seeming to understand. "No. You put the weapon in the hands of your warriors and point it at some Portal or other. I take it that the survival rate of 'Guild Arrest' is rather low? You were worried about *years* of this—prison. So, to be immediately against a year under some 'Guild,' I'm guessing…"

[No.] I frowned. [You nailed it. The survival rate is terrible. Generally not at the beginning of an Awakened's 'arrest,' but the closer to the end of the term, mysteriously, the higher the rate of death.]

"Makes a morbid kind of sense, I suppose." Smegma shrugged. "Do you release the dangerous criminal, or 'take care' of them before they can be released back into the civilian population?"

It did make a terrifyingly efficient type of sense, one that I had no desire to submit myself to.

The whole table except my mother, who was breathing heavily, stayed silent after Ms. Stovall's statement. So, she continued, "If this is what you had us drive out here for, we'll be leaving immediately. I want this on record that the opposing counsel called us here to make spurious offers. Good day."

Mr. Varnish simply smiled and stood up. "As you wish, Ms. Stovall. I'll see you out, but remember this offer is only good for twenty-four hours. After that, we will begin digging deeply into every facet of Brodie's life."

Ms. Stovall looked toward my mother and me. I was staring at Seleff and Aurome. Something was nagging at me about their presence and the subtle exchange between them. I couldn't shake the feeling that *they* were why this settlement offer was happening. Had they simply wanted to get me in a room with them? That didn't fit since they hadn't really done anything since I'd arrived… Except the 'wizard' looked at me through those glasses of his, and then… Why did he shake his head at Aurome?

[Can you tell if there's anything special about the wizard's glasses? Or maybe if he's cast some sort of spell? I get the feeling that they're here to look for something, but the only thing I have with me is…]

"Me." The Demon finished thoughtfully. "They could be magical. Not *that* magical if they're supposed to spot me and can't. It could possibly be looking for some kind of energy signal, or may even be some sort of advanced tool for telling them a person's ranking."

[What?] My eyes widened. [You think something like that exists?]

"Pfft. Do *you* think that the best, most state-of-the-art technologies are the ones out in the public for everyone to use? Of course it's possible."

[So, what do you think it means that he shook his head at his scary, hulking buddy over there?]

The Demon shrugged. "No clue. You're right about one thing, though," Smegma said, adding to my thoughts. "As soon as you get out of here, find out what this Larvae Guild is."

I nodded to Ms. Stovall in answer to her unspoken question, telling her that I was ready to leave. I was somewhat surprised my mother hadn't already done so, but quickly realized how pale and shaken up by the 'offer,' or perhaps more accurately—at the veiled threat, she already was. I put a hand on her back to get her attention and then motioned to the door with a jerk of my neck.

A sudden thought struck me. I leaned over to Ms. Stovall and whispered quickly into her ear. She leaned back a moment, studying my face. I nodded.

She cleared her throat. The people around the table turned to look at her. "You said my client had twenty-four hours to decide to either accept or reject the settlement offer?"

Mr. Varnish raised a not-unpleased eyebrow. "Why, yes. Of course. Would you like to take a copy with you?"

"We would, thank you," she caught my eyes once more, and I nodded again. "We would like to step outside to personally deliberate over the details. It's… rather crowded in here."

Mr. Varnish chuckled smoothly. "By all means, take as much time as you like. I assure you, all of the chairs are beyond comfortable, and I'll have our staff come by to offer refreshments in a moment."

I felt bad that my actions only seemed to make my mother more unsteady on her feet, but I had a reason for asking this.

[Smegma, stay behind in this room as long as you can. See if they talk about anything once we leave. Mainly those two.]

Mr. Varnish politely led Ms. Stovall, my mother, and me out of the room.

* * *

There was an extremely long moment of silence in the room after Brodie, Ms. Stovall and Clara left. It stretched out until the first person moved—likely lasting five minutes.

"They've rejected the offer," a female voice said over a device at the center of the table. Likely one of those comp-doer things.

Then everyone still in the room began to move, standing up, or walking around. In the case of two of the individuals they began packing up belongings. The two that everyone kept glancing at were the ones introduced as Aurome and Seleff—further lending, at least to Greb-Shak, that they were the ones with the most power.

"So, he didn't inherit *Demonic Vault?*" Seleff asked Aurome in a whisper meant only to carry to his Guildmaster. It was in a different language as well, but through the magic of the System it was easily translated for Greb-Shak. He also noticed that Seleff had waited till the Guild Reporter and Clerk left the room.

Aurome licked his lips before a half-smile came onto his face. Greb-Shak could tell that the man was both excited and delighted by something. That was the type of smile he'd seen on numerous peoples' faces when they manipulated events, results, or others to get their way.

334

"He may not be a Cannibal at all, but seeing him…" Aurome responded, his voice deep and guttural in a way that conveyed power to Greb-Shak. The man didn't bother whispering. "I'm starting to see why Morgan went after him. He has the aura of a Monster. It's small right now, but even I felt twinges of bloodlust from it when he looked at us at the end. What was the boy's highest known Skill?"

"*Mental Fortitude* was his highest."

"Do we have any information on what Brodie originally Awakened with?" Aurome asked in English, and people around the table practically jumped out of their seats in their hurry to find papers.

A tug at Greb-Shak's naval was all the warning he got before he popped into existence halfway between the building and the SUV Ms. Stovall had driven them here in.

[Anything?] Brodie asked as soon as he appeared. Greb-Shak studied the human. The aura of a Monster?

He smiled to himself as he responded, "That Seleff guy can somehow read one of your Skills. From context, I think it's your most powerful Skill. They were specifically looking for *Demonic Vault*, I think, but *Mental Fortitude* is higher because of…" he shrugged. Those memories, if they existed, hadn't come back to him yet.

[So, they wanted an excuse to get me in a room and read my Skills? Why wouldn't they just wait for the trial? Or bump into me accidentally?]

"No clue, dumb-dumb. Did you figure out where this Larvae Guild is from?"

[No. They don't have a website or listing I can find on the UNMH database. There's some chatter about them on Read-it, but the threads were locked with minimal activity. One post claimed they're from Europe, which makes some sense with the Pre-Trial.]

Greb-Shak considered telling him about the absurdity of the last thing he heard but chose to leave it. Brodie thinking that this Aurome man thought of him as a monstrous potential, or 'Monster' period, wouldn't immediately help anything anyway.

* * *

Dave moved his food around his plate with his fork as the table continued to discuss what was going on in the case. I watched him doing it, trying to put myself in his shoes. I could tell he was not happy with something but what exactly that was, I couldn't say. Then again having the entire truth sprung on him by me, might be the problem…

He'd probably tell me in time once he collected his thoughts and digested through the bombshells I'd dropped on him. Not to mention the clearly visible hulking Demon with wings.

I managed to tune back in just as Ms. Stovall finished saying "—a threat, for sure."

I mentally replayed the conversation and realized she was talking about Mr. Varnish's final words to us as he moved to escort us out to the car. A big reason we'd left so 'quickly.' My dad picked up the thread she left hanging. "So, you're thinking it's going to get worse?"

"I would be prepared for it to, yes. That offer to commute Brodie's 'sentence' wasn't completely fabricated, but for them to make it shows some of their intentions in this case. Since the trial date isn't set yet, my offices can't start looking through what they have, but I think their goal is to make life so bad that you might be willing to plead out to make them stop. That or I'm missing something…"

"You're missing something," Smegma said with his usual lack of decorum. "Those two from the Larvae Guild just wanted Brodie in the room for some reason. I was able to stay behind and listen in for a few moments. We discussed it on the drive back from your office. We have to assume that Seleff can see people's Skills in certain contrived circumstances. I figure it's either those weird-ass glasses he was wearing, or maybe he has a Skill with circumstantial activation?"

"Do those exist?" Ms. Stovall asked. Smegma blinked at her and then around at the table before face palming.

"Yes, they exist. For example, he could have something like a *Diplomacy* Skill, which would trigger only if two parties are sitting down to discuss the terms of a deal. Then he might get extra information on the other side of negotiations or something. The fact that you all aren't aware of how to even see your Skill Cards is unreal."

"Wait—Skill Cards? Does he mean see our Skills without going to the UNMH and spending outrageous amounts of money?" Dave exclaimed as he perked up.

I started to nod but then realized I had a Spent Mana Crystal in my Necklace of Holding. With everything that had happened since I'd stolen it—I'd forgotten. I continued my nod with a small stutter, one that Dave didn't miss. I shrugged to my friend and then said, "I don't think discussing this more without a trial date is going to do much. I'm going to head upstairs with Dave and fill him in on some of the… other stuff."

I could tell my parents weren't thrilled that I was excusing myself from further speculations, but Ms. Stovall stood up and said, "Brodie has a point. I'll make sure to get your accounts unfrozen tomorrow, or at least get a proper monthly amount allocated for living expenses. I'll also look into the Larvae Guild through legal channels and figure out why they aren't registered with UNMH. Brodie, it's even more important that we get some videos uploaded to SwiftGram—so tomorrow, make sure you wear your camera."

Nodding, I motioned for Dave to stand up as I did. Together, we headed up to my bedroom. Dave snaked his way into my office chair when I was holding the door open for him. I gave him a look before sitting on the floor with my back leaning against the footboard on my bed. "You seemed distracted after Smegma showed himself to you."

Dave's smile fell and he scanned the room for the Demon. When he located him, he shuddered for a moment but then cleared his throat. "I'm sorry. I know I shouldn't be jealous but—"

He cut off mid-sentence and stared at the carpet, clearly looking for words. When he looked back up, he gave a shrug that said he hadn't found the right words, but he was going to try. "I just wish it had happened to me, is all." At my frown, he hurried to explain. "Sure, there's a lot of bad shit going on in your life

336

but to have a Skill like *that*. Husk, Brodie—you could become a world-renowned Hunter—probably even a Ranker."

"Yeah, that's not how it's worked so far," I said flatly, letting some of what I was feeling from the last few days enter my voice. Even to my own ears, my voice sounded weary—exhausted even.

"Well, it could," Smegma said. At my sigh, he continued. "What Brodie didn't explain is just how expensive Skills are. So, while it *could* work like that—he would need astronomical amounts of money. But, Mr. Mopey, there is another rather big possibility he didn't mention."

"What's that?" Dave asked, still sounding a bit hurt and jealous, but responding to Smegma's prompting due to the friendly ribbing in it.

"He may be able to purchase Skills for others as well!"

"We're not sure about that!" I shouted, cutting off Dave's excitement before it could mount. I only half-succeeded, so I changed the subject as well, "Smegma and I actually have a couple things to go over. Wanna help?"

Dave nodded a bit too vigorously. It made me smile and I motioned for Dave to pass me my school laptop from where it rested on the bookshelf. As soon as he looked away and stood up, I snaked the chair back from him. He made a small, annoyed grunt of protest but then pulled over a bedside table to sit on. He had been in my room enough to feel at home, and we'd used this exact setup for a few projects in first year.

"Which option did we finish with?" Smegma said lazily, which caused both Dave and I to look over. The Demon had chosen to lie on my bed—which was a pointless gesture, sure, but just seeing Smegma on my covers made my skin crawl. I couldn't even have told you why I was adverse to the Demon's choice of locations to hover, but maybe it was the way he lay on his side with his hand resting against the side of his head as if to say 'paint me like one of your French girls.' Goosebumps raised on my skin unbidden.

I froze for long enough that Smegma glanced at me, just as I realized what else was disturbing about the view. I had never really taken a closer look at Smegma's feet before. Now, I was aware of another deadly weapon the creature possessed.

And this was a race that failed to Ascend?

I shivered before shaking myself out of the moment and glancing at my screen.

"You had just given me the information on *Finder*, but give me one sec as I catch Dave up with the options." I spent the next twenty minutes going through the twelve sub-Skill options Smegma had already conveyed to me, giving Dave the brief descriptions Smegma had relayed. Dave's excitement returned once he realized what exactly he was helping with. I could tell he was still disappointed, and slightly jealous, but an inner focus I'd come to know in first year overrode those emotions—either channeling them into something productive or truly countering the negative energies.

Dave asked questions—that's just who he was. It was why I liked him so much. The proto-typical skeptic, he was never a hundred percent sold on anything. Just as an example, there was a contingent of people that believed the Monster invasions were a government conspiracy but had no real facts to support it. I'd seen Dave have a totally rational conversation with a man about it, in which he just asked pointed questions that continually poked holes in the wild theory.

In the end, the man hadn't changed his views on the topic, but I could tell he was flustered.

Simply put, Dave had a great mind for things like this. A thought process that looked at the presented information and dissected it in ways mine didn't. We spent another forty minutes, bringing the time spent up to an hour total, with him doing just that. By the end of it, I was smiling—I had needed this.

A friend, and a peer to talk with.

Smegma, of course, was annoyed. Whether it was because he hadn't thought of some possibilities Dave brought up, or because he wasn't being relied upon by me as heavily for speculations about each sub-Skill, I couldn't say. But I did know at least one thing.

Dave had started by asking questions of Smegma and eventually stopped. Why?

Well, Smegma was only given a sub-Skill and a paragraph of a description. He didn't *have* more information. After five answers to that effect, Dave had started speculating without including the Demon.

On second thought, I guess I knew the reason Smegma was unhappy.

CHAPTER 46

Thursday, April 18th, 2069

"So, we've narrowed it down to four options?" Dave reiterated. Yawning, I moused over to the 'keeper' page on the Accel Sheets app I was using. It was one in the morning, and we hadn't taken a single break from our current *mission*. Since my mouth was occupied with a second, larger yawn, I held up five fingers to convey the correction.

"What was the fifth again?" Dave asked.

"Buffs, Classes, Crafter, Merchant and Titles," I answered sleepily.

"Oh right, Merchant was because you would get a percentage of Mana Coins for every sale you make in real-world Greenbacks?" Dave asked, trying to recall the speculation he'd made a few hours before.

"That's not how it's going to work," Smegma said haughtily. "The description states it will allow Brodie to buy and sell equipment from other System-approved merchants using accumulated 'worldly wealth.' That single sentence makes it clear to me."

"Clear in what way?" Dave asked, not trying to upset the Demon but clearly succeeding since he was questioning him *again*.

"If the System is involved, then *Demonic Vault* isn't the Skill that will be affected. He can already buy and sell wares from the Abyss Sect—so why would you assume that means he'd get Mana Coins, which is a currency we developed."

"I'm simply speculating that he will either gain access to other Merchants outside of the Abyssal Sect that will accept our world's Greenbacks, or somehow *if Demonic Vault* is the approved Merchant, some real-world wealth will somehow transfer over."

"*Abyss* Sect," Smegma said pointedly. Dave nodded his head at the correction. Then snapped his fingers as if he'd thought of something.

"If it's the latter, it could work by funneling the Mana to your Sect or something, so both sides win. From what we've discussed tonight, the System doesn't seem to be unfair."

Smegma went quiet. I couldn't quite tell if it was because of his concern over his Sect or if Dave's logic had made him truly reconsider. Still, I didn't want either one of them making the hard decision that this choice was the best. My gut instinct was telling me the exact opposite, in fact.

"I still don't think this is the right choice," I said. "To make this a viable Skill, I would need to start a business where I'm selling and buying materials. Not only is that unfeasible at this specific moment, I doubt it will ever be possible. Becoming a conglomerate or powerhouse in the sales world isn't easy. I'd need connections to powerful people, Guilds and more."

"At a bare minimum, you'd need powerful backers or a substantial amount of capital to even get started," Dave added.

"Exactly. Imagine me trying to compete with HBC or Wallsmart or even larger companies. I'd get blown out of the water."

"Not if you're offering something unique," Smegma said quietly. The tone in his voice made me pause. At the silence that statement brought, Smegma looked up with his black eyes. Seeing mine and Dave's undivided attention, he quickly said, "You've said that getting new Skills in this world doesn't work the same as Crendalar Five. You don't get Card Shards that can be collected and combined into a given Skill. I can now recall that the System changed Skill acquisition quite heavily with each new integration. So, while I am sure there is a method to get new Skills out there—it either hasn't been discovered yet, or it is being kept a secret by the rich and powerful."

"But what if Brodie can actually buy Skills from *Demonic Vault* and transfer them to others!" Dave added excitedly. "Now, he's selling something that is currently unique and powerful. Once word gets out, individuals will come to Brodie. Then he wouldn't need backers or multiple powerful connections. He'd just need to start with one and use word of mouth." Dave clicked his tongue—a sure sign he had thought of an argument to his own point. "There are still some rather glaring unknowns in that," he began disappointedly. "First, I doubt Greenbacks will convert directly over to Mana Coins. So, you'd be asking the first buyer to purchase in Mana Crystals to ensure that you can get a Skill from the shop."

"More than just that. If this was possible, wouldn't Morgan Hallsbrad— with an *actual* business called 'The Shop'—have been selling Skills? Also, someone with access to that amount of Mana Crystals is already going to be A-Rank or higher," I added, seeing where Dave was headed.

"Good point on Morgan, but he may not have taken the Merchant sub-Skill, or better yet—how do we know he *wasn't* selling Skills? But back to the Skill sales. You aren't even sure that the Skills in the Shop will be transferable. But let's say they are—let's further say you have a Skill that someone with the proper funds would want because it would add to their arsenal in a meaningful way. What's the highest rank you currently have access to, Smegma?" Dave asked.

"High B," Smegma said proudly.

"What's the cheapest B-Rank skill?" I asked, letting my voice carry the weariness I felt.

"Half a trillion Mana Coins…" Smegma replied dejectedly.

My inhalation became loud as I tried and failed to hold onto the budding excitement that their conversation had ignited in me. On my exhalation, I was back to my earlier exhausted equilibrium. "Okay, so we'll revisit Merchant later?"

"Another fallacy. Just because you've gotten access to a sub-Skill with each Upgrade doesn't mean you will on the next one," Dave joked.

I ignored him pointedly by motioning to the first of the Skills listed on the 'keeper' page. "What do we think about Buffs?"

"It's great for others," Dave replied, even as he chuckled at his own joke. "I really don't love it. Just like Merchant, if you were going to start your own business, it would be pretty fantastic. Or if you were a Hunter and it worked as we speculate—again, fantastic. Right now…"

Dave left that hanging and I nodded. The paragraph we knew about the Skill seemed to be about me sharing my Stats or Skills with others in a radius around me. That had been what drew us to putting it in the 'keeper' section. What if I could share my *Mining* Skill with all the Miners in the Portal? Or if I gained a powerful Skill from *Demonic Vault* and could give it to other Hunters. Hell, even sharing my *Recovery* would be a huge boon for any Hunting team.

However, what would that gain me right now? Nothing. I didn't own the Mining Team. So, increased production would only benefit Jagger and the Guild who hired him. Attempting to join a Hunting party was even less beneficial for me. It stemmed back to the problem I'd faced when wanting to find a permanent Mana Bank partnership.

Just applying to join a Team as an untested F-Rank was going to be difficult, if not outright impossible. That or it would likely put me in a horrible situation where I'd be slaved out to possible Greeds. I shuddered at the thought.

"Next is Classes," I pointedly said, changing the topic with no room for more debate.

"Enables a Class bestowal by the System," Smegma said simply, either recalling the simple description or reading it again.

"It sure is lacking in description," Dave agreed. "But there are a few things I think are inferred by the wording." I nodded, seeing the implication I believed he was mentioning.

"By the System?" I asked to confirm. Dave nodded, and Smegma did as well.

"This sub-Skill has the possibility for the greatest immediate effect. But it could also be a huge dud."

"Dud?" Smegma asked.

"It means that it could be worthless."

"Ahhh," Smegma said but then shook his head. "No, the System, while the bane of worldly existence, has always been somewhat fair. If something is bestowed by the System, it is powerful and earned. Like the unique Ore that Brodie got."

"Okay?" Dave questioned. "Here's another question, then. Why did Brodie earn the unique Meteorite thing that spawned a Golem that almost killed him?"

I laughed at the chippy add-ons Dave tacked on to his question. Smegma narrowed his eyes, unsure if Dave was poking fun at him, the System or Brodie. "I haven't been able to confirm it yet, but I think his *Mining* Skill was ready to Evolve and the Meteorite was an Evolution catalyst—a huge waste, I might add, that you used it for a Rank F to E Evolution, but there's no guarantee the System would have presented you with another opportunity. Also, if you use the mid-rank Crystal in your necklace, you could confirm this theory!"

"Right, right," I said as I pulled the mid-ranked Spent Mana Crystal out of the Necklace of Holding. I'd put off doing so immediately upon getting upstairs, not wanting to distract Dave, myself or Smegma from the task of sorting through sub-Skills. Now that we had them narrowed down, it was probably the right time.

"That's a Mana Crystal?" Dave asked. I nodded and he frowned. "Why don't I see clear Mana Crystals often?"

"Because your idiot race breaks them into tiny pieces and then burns them to extract the Mana," Smegma practically cursed.

"Wait—so that's why we haven't discovered the uses of them yet, and why there aren't many whole Crystals on the market?" Dave said, growing excited again. At my look, he elaborated. "From my understanding, you can create these at will?" Pursing my lips at his tone, I nodded.

"I'm rethinking the Merchant option," Dave explained. "This is a far simpler product that you could create endlessly. Everyone down to the elderly would want to buy one—if just for the novelty of knowing their inborn Skill."

"You're suggesting I undercut the UNMH market on Skill appraisal?" I asked skeptically.

"Husk," Dave said, his excitement dying on the word like a fly in a zapper. "I was simply thinking that it would be something that would sell endlessly, giving you hundreds of millions of transactions, which goes directly to the Skill description, but you're right. That only works if you're still alive."

I could tell, like me, Smegma was thinking the original concept through because he was tapping a talon on his teeth. I shelved the issue for now and began channeling Mana into the Crystal. "Regardless, I'll at least try to grab one for you tomorrow."

Dave's face broke into a smile, and he turned away with his cheeks flushing. We both silently made a point of studying the screen and descriptions of the sub-Skills until the Mana Crystal glowed brightly enough to distract us.

Thinking of finally learning what my Mana Pool Skill was had me holding my breath.

The very first Card on top was something new. A picture of a shimmering wall that grew old, was rebuilt, crumbled, and then became bigger flashed over its aquamarine backing. It changed to other images, but I ignored them, since I believed I knew what this was. I turned it over, glanced at the title, confirming *Mental Fortitude*, and then put it aside to stare at the next Card.

It was red and orange, with 'cracks' of black running through it. The decal reminded me of cooling magma. At first, I was distracted enough not to see all the images that the Card created in the pattern. Then, because the image pulsed, I saw one. Mostly because one expects a heart to beat, I supposed.

The cracks resolved in my mind into dark, black metal chains that seemed to constrict around the organ. Swallowing against my newly dry mouth, throat and lips, I slowly turned over the card.

[Locked] Dragon Heart
(31)
Skill Type: Secondary Pool, Skill Steal
Skill Rank: High B-Rank (Evolvable)
A dragon heart is one of the most mysterious organs in existence. While it can act as a Mana, [Locked], and [Locked] Pool,

it is so much more. Each Dragon Heart has its own unique properties and sub-Skills, depending on the Dragon it comes from. Dragon Heart's effects are multiplied by [Locked] and [Locked] stats.
Sub-Skills:
Mana Pool – 45/50
Skill Copy and Cannibalism
[Locked]
[Locked]
[Locked]
…

The list of locked sub-Skills continued until there were eight listed. Since I couldn't stop staring at the Card, I double-counted, just to be sure. "What in the—" I tried to say, but it was more of a croak than a sentence. I swallowed again, wetting my throat before trying once more. "What in the world?"

No answer came and I looked over my shoulder to find Dave and a Demon both staring at the Card with wide, shocked eyes. My gaze snapped Dave out of his stupor first.

"What the hell?!" he said, mirroring my own sentiment.

That exclamation got Smegma to start. "By the Horned!" he said, using a curse or reverent prayer I'd never heard him utter before.

My throat had gone dry again, and smartly, I swallowed before I tried to speak this time. "Do Dragon Skills exist?"

"Until this exact moment?" Smegma stammered. "I would have said no…"

"But now?" Dave asked, and I could hear the smile in his voice before even glancing at him.

"Get husked," Smegma said playfully, going as far as to chuckle at himself. "Still, if I'm reading this right—then you don't have an actual Mana Pool. That's why it started in the F-Rank and has been growing. Plus, the *Skill Copy & Cannibalism* ability must have unlocked—"

"Yeah," I said, quickly cutting him off before he could sour the mood. There would be plenty of time for that later. Right now, I was marveling at the potential this Skill had and wanted to stay on that topic. "How is this Skill B-Ranked? It seems insanely strong. If this is what the System considers B-Rank, then I have no idea what an S-Rank Skill would even look like. Also, it seems to suggest that there are two other 'pools of power.' Do you know what they are, Smegma?"

"It's B-Ranked right *now*—with your Mana Pool and *Skill Cannibalism* unlocked. We don't know what rank it will end up once all those sub-Skills are available. As for the various resource pools? I have a guess. Remember when I told you about the three Stats on Crendalar, and the pools the Cards unlocked?"

"Oh!" I said, looking at the locked options again. So, I could unlock Force and Martial Power Pools through my Dragon Heart…

I paused as my own heart stuttered over the word 'my.' I could feel a surge of warmth start in my chest at the thought. It was *my* Skill. Something I had been embarrassed by in the past, when I'd thought it was an F-Rank.

Now, it had suddenly morphed into something I was *proud* of. Something that, by the reaction of Smegma, made me rare and unique—possibly as much or even more so than the *Demonic Vault* Skill.

That pride dried up when a sudden realization soured the mood. "Is this why Morgan Hallsbrad came after me?"

Smegma's widening eyes were answer enough.

CHAPTER 47

Thursday, April 18th, 2069

"What if Morgan Hallsbrad was a Skill broker?" Smegma said while scratching his ear. "But instead of buying the Skills from the Shop, he had the *Extraction* sub-Skill and was taking powerful Skills from people."

"You're thinking he had *Extraction* and *Merchant?*" Dave said as he pulled up the information on *Extraction*. With wide eyes, he then pulled up a browser window and moogled the murders that had plagued the eastern coast of the United States. I couldn't speak for Smegma or Dave, but the growing pit in my stomach told me they were onto something.

"Ahh, but a lot of the dead were F to D-Ranked," Dave said after a quick pass over an article.

"Excuse me if I don't have faith in your world's publicly available measurement standards," Smegma answered as he gestured to me. I began to nod in agreement before freezing—

"No, Dave's still got a point. Why would Morgan attack people that were rated as F-Rank? Wouldn't it be more likely that he targeted me by coincidence? Or that the actual Heartless Killer is now in California like the news said?"

"Let's assume Morgan is the Heartless Killer and that the California killings are the work of a copy cat. Okay?" Dave suggested, clearly building momentum in a thought process.

I nodded, wanting to see where he was going.

"What if someone he worked for could read Skills?" Dave returned to his earlier counter, his voice sounding like he was still thinking through the theory. "Like the guy you said was at the meeting with Mr. Varnish!"

Smegma's black eyes widened as he pointed to Dave in acknowledgement. "Exactly! If you're right that Hallsbrad was after you for your Skill, then that means someone had to know either what your Skill actually was, or its true ranking. There may be many others, including these other victims, with Skills that would show up as low on the broadly available public ranking equipment. You've said there is a more in-depth version that can clarify and more accurately assess skills. So, was Morgan targeting people who were assessed incorrectly but had yet to be scanned by a more precise technology—but had been covertly ranked by an identification Skill. The Skill *Diplomacy* I mentioned wouldn't work because of the requirements—but if someone had *Eyes of Truth* or similar…"

"*Eyes of Truth?*" I interjected.

"It's a Skill that can see information about the target. At low ranks, it showed us Crendalarians the names of targets. Then as it ranked up, it would start to give more information—like Mana, Force or Martial Power figures. Eventually, even listing the target's Skills and information." Smegma paused for a moment, looking distant, then added, "But it was prohibitively difficult to rank up."

"Still, it doesn't have to be the same Skill," Dave said, taking up the string Smegma had left hanging. "If we're right, all the owner of the Skill has to do is pass by these targets, see their Skills, and mark them as something more valuable than the UNMH believed. We can't prove any of this—for example, where would this person have come across Brodie?"

Up to that moment, I had felt like the threads of a mysterious tapestry were being untangled and woven together to paint a picture—but with Dave's last line, they started to knot back up. Right up until I actually replayed what I had been doing the days leading up to the attack. The long days waiting in line to see Arnando.

With a brush of my wrist, I took back my laptop's mouse-pad from Dave and entered my own search. The dates for Arnando's photoshoots came up and I resized the window to place it beside the article's list of homicide victims.

My heart started beating rapidly, thumping in my ears as I felt my feet and hands go numb. The dates mostly coincided—each occurring within a few days following the shoot, while only some locations did.

However, my family had driven to Toronto for the shoot, and the attack had happened in Windsor. So, the location could be in the vicinity…

The room was silent as I pulled up a map and checked some of the locations. I started dropping pins and stared as the pattern began to snap into place. Some of the dates weren't perfect because two or three victims fell inside the range of the shoot.

"Husk me!" Dave hissed. "It's Arnando!"

That statement bounced me out of my shocked stare and allowed me to hear some of my own thoughts on the matter. "I doubt it," I said. "Why would a world-renowned photographer be involved in something like this? He shouldn't need the money…"

"That's true. It might not be him specifically, but how many staff members were at the shoot? How many other participants?" Dave asked.

Smegma had been staring between the screen and me, staying quiet. Every so often he would vigorously scratch at his head—like there was something there he wanted to remember but couldn't. "We should probably show this to that Stovall woman," he said, breaking his silence. "Maybe she can pull some strings to investigate the picture shoot guy."

I nodded at Smegma but then returned to Dave's point. "Well, there were thousands, for sure—so if it's a 'participant' it would be pretty easy to hide amongst the crowd."

Dave held up a finger. "But would there be a list of people who got pictures taken multiple times over every event?"

I shook my head. "This time, you've presented the fallacy," I said jokingly. "He wouldn't have to get pictures taken at each event. Just be in line or milling about for a few days. There were so many people there, I don't think I would recognize anyone, other than the people who immediately surrounded me."

"What if the Skill has requirements like *Diplomacy*, though?" Smegma countered. "Like the guy had to use a tool or circumstance to read people's Skills. Was there anyone acting oddly?" Smegma paused but then sheepishly added, "Other than paying absurd sums for images of themselves…"

"You just couldn't let the chance to comment go, could you?" I said distractedly over Dave's guffaw. My mind was buzzing as it tried to pull memories from my peripherals on the days leading up to the photoshoot. I could recall some assholes arguing with each other over saving spots. A woman breaking down into hysterics because she'd woken up with acne on the morning she was supposed to head in.

Nothing stood out as odd to me—until I recalled that moment with the drunken man as I'd left. It had been around noon, and while people could drink whenever they wanted, it wasn't like this was a Hunter Mixed Martial Arts event and he was tailgating. Plus, his yellowing skin and eyes suggested he spent a good deal of time in that state…

Did it fit? I conveyed the interaction to Smegma and Dave, silencing the two, who had both begun taking turns poking fun at my 'life choices.'

I amended an earlier thought that had only included one of them. Who needed enemies with *friends* like them?

"Being drunk? That would certainly be an odd requirement." Smegma stated and questioned simultaneously, making it clear my discovery didn't convince them.

"It's somewhere to start," Dave said. "Put this all in an email to Ms. Stovall. Let her and her team sort through it for now. Even if you don't find the Skill-Identifier guy, you've already shown that the attack was premeditated. That should drastically strengthen your self-defense case, right?"

I shook my head almost instantly. Already seeing how Morgan's presence would be explained away. "They're claiming he was a private eye investigating the murders. So, they could just say he knew this information, right? Discovered it in his investigation?"

"Sure, but there's a huge hole in that excuse. You've been to a single one of these photoshoots. So, why would he suspect you? Why would he even know about you at all?" Dave countered and I felt my eyebrows rise in appreciation. I nodded and opened up an email to Ms. Stovall.

Another thought struck me. A few of them, in fact. Was this information beneficial to me? How much more information would Ms. Stovall or the courts need to know about this? I tried to think like Varnish, a man that was being fed twisted facts or chose them specifically to help bring the case to his outcome. I imagined him there, in the courtroom before the judge. If this information came out, he'd point out that I was more powerful than I'd let on and weaken my case that I was an F-Ranked attacked by a C-Ranked.

Not only that, but after the information came out that my Skill was more powerful than initially thought, what kinds of questions would *that* bring up? Would I be compelled to answer? If it was required to disclose how I came across the knowledge that my Skill was undervalued, would I have to admit that I had a method of identifying Skills? That I knew *what* my Skills were and be forced to admit that Varnish was right and I was a Skill Cannibal?

Should I tell Ms. Stovall after all? My mind continued to whirl. Okay. Let's assume that whoever hired Morgan was and still is after me and is the one behind Varnish being put on the case. That means that they knew about my Skill—at least to some extent. I didn't know if my Cannibalism trait only unlocked in the life-or-death confrontation with Morgan, but I could only pray that it did. If that were the case, then it couldn't have been passed onto the employer and therefore be handed over to Varnish to skewer me…

No. I groaned. That didn't work either. Varnish basically called me out as a Skill Cannibal in the pre-trial based on secondary evidence. So the truth is already on the table, even if Varnish only thought he was using the accusation as a scare tactic, but it could have been that he already knew. I blew out a breath.

Alright, let's assume the worst.

Varnish knows everything and reveals it at the worst time during the trial to paint me as a Skill Cannibal who—through whatever convoluted series of events that the terrifying lawyer concocted—targeted *Morgan*, instead of the other way around. I could imagine the shocked look on Ms. Stovall's face as that little bomb was dropped in the courtroom… No. She needed to know—if only to be prepared for the possible eventuality.

An hour later, I'd put everything I could think of into the email, and the three of us sat silently—thinking over the bombshell of a discovery we'd just made. Dave of course couldn't let the moment of appreciation last. "We should be husking detectives!"

"Definitely," I agreed flatly. "I hear it's the new big thing. Even serial killers are getting into that line of work. What do you think, Smeg? Want to be the Watson to my Sherlock?"

"Yeah, right. The Police need you two like I need a body," Smegma said derisively even as he started laughing. Me and Dave exchanged a look and smirked.

"Why? So you can touch yourself?" Dave began.

"Oh, actually that could be huge for your little PDA problem," I added.

"PDA?" Dave asked.

I nodded. "Public Display of Aggression." I turned back to the frowning Demon. "What he's saying does make sense. I've always told you a good wank will make you less grumpy—"

Smegma growled, which cut me off—and simultaneously caused me and Dave to erupt in laughter. I might have felt bad for the Demon if he wasn't always doing shit like this to me. A moment later, he even joined in with our laughter.

"Okay, can we get back to sub-Skills, now?" Smegma said a bit too quickly, clearly wanting to change the subject. I nodded and opened back up my Accel Spreadsheet.

"I think we were talking about Classes before we discovered my new Skill—oh shit!" I picked the stack of Cards up from my desk and flipped to *Mining*.

Mining
(11)
Skill Type: Gathering
Skill Rank: Low E-Rank (Evolvable)

As you Mine, you slowly improve your understanding of Minerals, Ores, and Crystals. As this Skill grows, this individual will notice improvements to all actions related to Mining. This Skill is multiplied by the Strength stat.

Two parts of the Card stood out to me, and I pointed at the bottom where the line 'Current max level reached until Evolution Condition is reached' was missing. Then at the rank. "You were right, Smegma, it leveled up."

"I know I was right. I'm a genius!"

"At touching yourself at night," Dave chimed in, which caused me to snort while trying to remain serious. Smegma transferring a menacing black-eyed stare to my friend broke me, and I started laughing again.

"Oh, you'll both pay for this," Smegma whispered, but again quickly shifted the topic. "So, Classes?!"

"Right, right," I responded mirthfully.

"I think you have to take it," Dave stated, surprising Smegma and me.

"What? Why?" I answered, instantly sobered by the level of confidence in my friend's tone. I knew Dave was smart, so surely he had a reason.

"If the System is going to give you a Class, and you have Skills called *Dragon Heart* and *Demonic Vault*—isn't it likely that you'll get a husking epic Class?"

"Not how it works," Smegma interjected quickly. "He also has *Mining, Mental Fortitude,* and *Recovery* Skills—" Either my wince or my mental scream warned Smegma because he cut himself off.

Dave was staring at the Cards in front of me. I realized I hadn't told him the names of my other inherited Skills. I handed him the Cards and he pursed his lips as he accepted them. I could feel the waves of suppressed jealousy from him as he flipped through. It was one thing knowing I had multiple Skills and another to see them—on literal display.

After he finished, he neatly stacked the Cards but refused to look up. A strange click sounded, and it took me a few words into what he said to realize he'd clicked his tongue. "I still think you have to take Classes. *Mining* is low rank when you compare it to the top four. One C-Rank, two B-Ranks, and an A-Rank would have to have more input on what the System grants—surely."

He still hadn't looked up from the Cards in his white-knuckled hands. I realized he was fiercely fighting off his internal jealousy. I also realized that the silence wasn't likely to be helping, so I hurried to answer. "I'm not the expert on the System, but that logic makes sense."

"He's right, but only if the System is taking all of the Skills into consideration with the Class choice. It could be using your actions to select it. If that's the case, what do you think you'll be doing for the next weeks, months, and years?"

"Mining," I said but Smegma's comment seemed to have also roused Dave.

"Sure, but your logic is circular. Should he wait until he is a Hunter to take Classes?"

Smegma shrugged while showing his three-fingered palms, the gesture saying 'of course.'

"First off, he needs a foundation, and Mining is as good as any. Secondly, it says 'Classes'—plural. What if there's a 'Gathering' Class and a 'Combat' Class available? It's sound enough logic! There are entire video game genres in our world with that sort of thing as a core feature. That's why it's so circular. How long will it take him to buy one of your Skills if he doesn't take a good sub-Skill to help him? I would argue that becoming a Miner Class would still get him to his goal of a Hunter faster..."

"He's not wrong," Smegma said, turning to me. "We're also not the ones making the final decision."

I let my mouth fall open and my eyes widened as I pointed at the Demon. "Did you just admit you might be wrong?"

"Oh, get husked! I swear I will turn invisible again and make you repeat everything I husking say!"

That got a laugh out of Dave and then, shortly after, myself. This time, I brought us back to task. "Let's go over Crafter and Titles to cover our bases."

"If you take Crafter, I think it would be better to take Merchant," Dave said as he pointed to the description on the screen.

"Grants the Skill *Crafting*. *Crafting* will allow the user to make items from all *Crafting* Skills. However, it will only grant knowledge based on Stats associated with said Skill, no matter the level of *Crafting*," I read aloud, then added my two cents, "Not to mention I only have Strength unlocked. So, if I'm reading this right, I might gain a high F-Rank Blacksmith Skill—if that's even based on Strength..."

"Still, it isn't like you can't unlock more Stats," Smegma countered, looking uninterested. I could tell he was playing devil's advocate and didn't actually want me to take the Skill. It had only made the list because of the Merchant sub-Skill after all.

"Moving on," I said pointedly and saw Smegma smirk. "Titles..."

"This is instantly both the most promising and the riskiest sub-Skill," Smegma said, sounding excited. "I think it will pair well with Classes in the way Merchant and Crafter do. However, none of us have ever heard of a System Title before, including me—and that's saying something in my case."

Dave and I looked at each other pointedly again, both probably thinking the same thing—'Did the System award a Title for touching yourself?' Smegma gave us both the middle finger, having read my thoughts, but he continued, "So Titles might be extremely complicated to acquire, which would likely make them more powerful as well..."

"What if you just take one sub-Skill for now?" Dave suggested.

"You just said that I need to take Classes to become a Hunter faster. Surely taking two sub-Skills follows the same premise?" I responded.

"I'm not saying *not* to take two—I'm just saying take one—see how it functions and then reassess. Smegma's right. 'Titles' has the potential to pair with what we *assume* Classes will do, but who's to husking say?"

I pointed to my friend in acknowledgment and then looked to Smegma, who nodded introspectively. That was good enough for me. "So, Classes then?"

"Classes," Dave and Smegma said in unison.

"Alright, Smegma, let's lock in the choice. Push the button!" I said. Smegma reached out into thin air, clearly adding the motion to dramatize the moment.

CHAPTER 48

Thursday, April 18th, 2069

"Smegma? Nothing happened," I said after waiting what felt like an entire minute.

"Of course nothing happened, you moron, I haven't done anything. It's asking me to confirm my choice, and I'm reading through the terms of service."

"Oh, just click accept, those never get enforced," Dave said, his nonchalance at his admittance a bit worrisome. If Smegma wasn't in my peripheral vision, I wouldn't have noticed his incredulous stare that I hoped matched my own. Dave looked at me and then Smegma, "What? They don't!"

"No, you likely just haven't broken one yet…" I said as if speaking to a child.

Smegma looked at me and a lightbulb seemed to go off behind his eyes. "Who cares about the 'terms of service' you humans have husking created? This is the *System*! It has infinite resources and punishes *all* transgressions. Ever heard the saying dick around and find out?"

"No, that term doesn't husking exist," Dave said sourly.

"Well, it did on Crendalar. You know what it got changed to?"

"Smegma, you do realize I just learned about other planets today, right?" Dave answered.

"It was rhetorical, asshat! The saying changed after the System arrived and it became, dick around and lose the dick!"

I grabbed my member unconsciously from the tone and pointedness that Smegma used. When I looked back to Dave, he was doing the same.

"Exactly, stupid child. If you ever get terms of service from the System, read them carefully…"

"Gotcha," Dave said, risking his precious man parts to un-cup them and fire a finger gun in confirmation at the Demon. "A story from experience…" Dave whispered, and Smegma glared at him. Dave winced but couldn't hide his chuckle.

"Would you like for me to accept on Brodie's behalf and he can just lose his dick?" Smegma growled. We both sat in silence after that *threat*, waiting for Smegma to finish. I was beyond glad that Dave stopped distracting Smegma.

"Nothing too worrisome—basically just says you can't have two Skills if one is given by a Class. The only problematic line says that once a Class is selected, it can't be changed until the allotted time period, and if a new Class is selected before that time, you will lose all Skills and ranks of any Skills associated with the Class."

"Why is that worrisome?" Dave asked before I could.

"Well, it doesn't really say what that time period *is*. Still, it's more about losing the Skills. It means that the first Class you choose might be one you can't change out of."

"But these Classes still come with Skills!" Dave said.

"Can't or shouldn't?" I said as a follow up, even as Smegma talked over us both.

"It does seem like a very powerful sub-Skill, and that's what worries me. There is no way to know. Like, if Brodie chooses a Class in Mining, and because of the Skill, he is able to create an amazing life for himself—then he may never change Classes because he grows comfortable and doesn't want to lose the Skills he's gained and grown."

"First, it mentions a time limit, so it won't be *forever*. Second, that's still a good outcome, you goober!" I exclaimed in exasperation. "Now accept and move on."

"Oh, husk," Smegma said. "It takes two sub-Skill slots."

"Really?" Dave asked, seeming to be torn between whether Smegma was joking or not.

"Why would I make that up?"

"Cause you're a *goober*!" I enunciated the word for the second time.

"Do you even know what that is? 'Cause I have no idea," Smegma said.

"Me either, man," Dave intoned with a look of concern. "You really should have just called him a Greed-pig or something, man. You trying to watch your language or something?"

"My parents are home, so yes," I said.

"Well, you've probably failed multiple times already. Well…" Dave retorted, then tried to think back on our conversation. "Maybe not?"

"Who gives a shit?" Smegma said. "They're just sounds you're making with your mouth…"

"His mom gets offended…" Dave explained.

"Okay, but isn't being offended by something a choice?" Smegma asked, sounding seriously confused by the explanation.

"Yeah, and she chooses to be offended by bad language," I answered. "And we kind of live in her house…"

"So, you'd get kicked out for making noises a family member finds distasteful?" Smegma asked and began tapping on his teeth in thought. "We Demons killed our siblings quite often and some parents even praised them for it."

"How does that even *remotely* compare to—? You know what? Nevermind. Can we just move on?" I asked, not wanting to get into a discussion about the differences between Crendalar and Earth.

"So, I'm still choosing it?" Smegma said, snapping out of his tangent.

"It's only sounding more powerful to me," Dave said, chiming in with his two Mana Shards.

"Agreed," I said.

Smegma shrugged and then popped out of the air. There was a literal noise that accompanied his disappearance.

"Very funny, Smegma. Where is he?" Dave said.

"Actually, he vanishes when stuff happens with the Skill. This is probably not a joke since I also can't see him," I answered.

Smegma flew through the floor, back into the space he'd previously occupied, flipping Dave and I the double birds before vanishing again.

"Is he actually gone this time?" Dave asked.

I held my breath and shrugged—unsure how I'd missed him phasing through the floor the first time. No response to Dave's question came, mentally or otherwise.

A way to check occurred to me and I dove into my Mental Universe. There, I found movement around the *Demonic Vault* Skill. A planet was slowly growing around the sun that was the *Vault* Skill. It appeared to be golden in color, and I could see a ring of some kind forming around it as well. Whether the golden ring of debris was feeding the planet's growth or being created as well was tough to tell.

"He's definitely gone this time," I answered.

"Any idea how long it will take for him to come back?" Dave asked and I re-entered my Mental Universe.

I took my time assessing the growing golden planet. At the speed it was going, it would take weeks to get to the size of the *Overdraft* planet. Maybe only a few days to get to the *Mining* Moon?

"Ahhhh," I said while still observing. "It looks like it'll be a while."

"What's 'a while?'" Dave asked.

"Enough time to sleep on it?" I answered.

"Oh shit, is it already past two in the morning? You mind if I crash here? I kind of don't want to be seen on campus right now, anyway…" For the first time since earlier in Ms. Stovall's office, I heard the worry in Dave's voice over the day's events.

"Do you want to talk about it?" I asked.

"Honestly, no. I know I'm overreacting, but every time I think about going back to that class and seeing the students' faces again—" Dave shivered. I swallowed a lump in my throat—somewhat knowing a muted version of that. It was a worry I'd had after the assault on campus—right up until I 'inherited' *Mental Fortitude*.

"Even if it isn't me, you should talk to someone about it."

"Like you and your shrink?" Dave began and then shook himself before holding up both hands. "That came out wrong. I'm actually curious if it's helping. I didn't mean to be derisive. I'm just husking pissed this shit happened to me."

I waved away the apology his words contained but didn't outright say. "Honestly, I think my *Mental Fortitude* is helping more, but yeah—it has been kind of nice talking to her about it. I have another session in a few days. I could ask her if she'd see you."

"I don't have the money for that, Brodie, and you know I don't want to ask my parents."

Dave's parents had kind of been an off-limits topic since I'd met him in first year. So, I let that drop and suggested, "Maybe you could sue the police department for unlawful actions or something?"

Dave tilted his head back and forth a few times, waffling on that thought. Then his neck jerked back up and he stared at me. "Do you think maybe I could become a Specialist Miner as well?"

"Umm, honestly, it's kind of as easy as handing you one of the Shop's Miner's Pickaxes and making sure you balance out smashing Mana Crystals to keep it repaired, but are you *sure* you'd want to? Would your parents be okay with it?"

"Not forever, nah, but maybe for a semester like you. Plus, if I drop out now I could still get a full refund for classes…" Dave answered. He wasn't looking at me and seemed to refuse to meet my eyes, which told me he wasn't sure of his decision. It was also why I started when he jerked his head up to look me straight in the face for a second time. "You haven't said it outright to your parents, or me, but you're stealing from the job site to buy the Picks aren't you?"

My jaw clenched so fast and hard that I heard my teeth click closed. Dave chuckled and continued, "Thought so. Your dad might suspect something too but doesn't want to say it. Anyway, maybe I can help?"

At my twisted mouth, he hurried to say. "If it helps you buy Skills faster, it may get me a Skill faster, too, if you can transfer them like we're hoping…"

"Okay, but I can't guarantee that you'll be hired. It isn't like it's my company."

"I mean, with what you are doing for Portal's Cubed or whatever, it kind of should be."

I laughed even as my logical brain pointed to the fact in Dave's joke. I'd had that thought myself numerous times. Sure, there were some complications here and there, but why couldn't I start my own Mining Company?

Deciding a nod was a sufficient answer, I stood up and pulled out a foam mattress cover from my closet. It was only for a twin, but we'd kept it after I got a new bed so someone could take the floor without being too uncomfortable.

"Bro. That's *so* sweet of you to take the floor for your esteemed guest. I'm touched." Dave wiped a fake tear from the corner of his eye.

"Get husked, Dave!" I answered, and we laughed softly as we went through a familiar routine where we both got ready for bed. The fact that Dave had a toothbrush here in a drawer should explain how often we'd done this last semester.

"I'm starting to feel like your girlfriend, man," Dave said as he pulled out some pajamas that were also left from a previous sleepover. "You really should have had a pretty lady over by now—you know, with the way you look."

"Yeah, 'cause that will go over well. Hey, let me introduce you to my parents—now let's go upstairs. It's why I kept pestering you to borrow your room…"

"No hanky-panky on my bed, bud."

"Oh, so you finally are admitting you're still a virgin."

"First," Dave said with a raised finger, "I never claimed to not be a virgin. But second, it's none of your husking business!"

The night continued like that until we were both laying down. I couldn't speak for Dave, but I was asleep almost instantly. It had been a long day.

* * *

Friday, April 19th, 2069

"You're fired," Jagger said, pointing at me as soon as I stepped out of our car. It was so sudden and abrupt that I looked behind me just to be sure he hadn't meant someone else. Dave stared at me with wide eyes.

Spinning back in a hurry, I asked, "What? Why?"

Even as my dad shouted, "What the husk do you mean, Jagger?"

"He's fired, Gary! That's what I mean. He's the reason they confiscated our goods. And someone at the WPD said if I kept him around, it would just keep happening!"

Willa, who had gone red in the face, slammed her Pickaxe into the parking lot. "Ya be meanin' the 'goods' that be only available 'cause he be killin' that Golem an' savin' the lives of your workers? Those goods? If you even be thinkin' about pullin' a stunt like this, we be gettin' the Union involved."

"First, you'll be paying for repairs of this asphalt. Second, he is still in his probationary period, so getting the Union involved won't change the fact that he's fired. Done. Finito. Kaput. Go be someone else's problem, kid. Let your father and angry aunty make money because you're just costing me."

My father's face looked like he had just eaten something sour, but he still placed a restraining hand on Willa's shoulder. It didn't look like he was forced to pull her back, which was at least somewhat of a blessing. However, his next words made me blink and replay them.

"Then we all quit." In the mental replay of that moment, I realized that he had been speaking on behalf of the Specialists and not the whole crew. However, that seemed like one and the same thing, based on how Jagger started stuttering.

"You can't do that," Jagger eventually got out, even as his face morphed to resemble something reptilian. "You can't afford to live without this job, especially if your wife loses hers too."

The creak of clenched fists on leather, Pickaxe handles, and straight popping knuckles was audible in the silence—as everyone who had been in earshot reacted to that threat. My father's eyes grew so hard I stepped back from beside him. I had never seen him like this.

It was a mood beyond anger. Not hot, but deadly cold. If that stare had been directed at me, I believed in that moment I would have frozen solid. Jagger noticed the temperature change too and tried to match my father's look but failed. Probably because my father growled, "*Watch* me, you piece of shit."

Or perhaps it was because uncle Jarred and Willa simultaneously said, "I'm done with this bullshit!"

And then again, maybe it was the look of the milling crowd. 'Shocked' was a mild descriptor of some of the faces. Aghast, maybe?

I stared around and swallowed to wet my throat as I rushed to my father's side. "Dad, you can't—"

"I can. I will not let anyone *threaten* my family. Let's go, guys."

Willa, Jarred and my dad spun in sync—like it was a practiced action. That of course left me and Dave staring at Jagger. Thankfully, his glare was on my father's back, which gave us time to spin and take a few jogging steps to catch the retreating adults.

"You'll regret this, Gary! No one is going to hire you in this town, and you can't afford to live anywhere better." There was a pause before Jagger yelled after us again, "Even if you find a job, I'll outbid the company on every contract they try for!"

My father literally shook because he was clenching his fists around his Pickaxe so tightly. I also noticed two hands on his back—one from Jarred and the other from Willa—to stop him from turning back.

The exit was a bit anticlimactic because we had been literally a step or two from the car when Jagger had 'ambushed' me.

"Meet at Miners Incorporated?" Willa suggested when she realized that we were already at the Ford Escort. Everyone nodded and the group split up. Dave, myself, and my father jumped into the Ford, and the exit was made even more sad when the car didn't start on the first or second try.

Thankfully, the third time was the actual charm—and it gave my dad time enough to calm down. I wasn't sure what would happen if he slammed the accelerator. My guess was that the engine might fall out, and with how tense I still felt, I didn't really want to find out just how embarrassing that would be.

Thankfully we didn't have to find out…

* * *

"That slimy *see you next Tuesday!*" Willa hissed. Everyone at the table nodded their heads, clearly knowing who she was talking about.

"It makes total husking sense," my dad said. "You two should go get your jobs back. I can't have both your families suffering because of my outburst."

"*Your* outburst?" Jarred said. "I wouldn't work for that snake if he doubled my wage. No—even if he tripled it."

I looked to Dave, who was somewhat shrunken in on himself again. As the newest Specialist, he hadn't offered anything to any discussions all day. For that matter, neither had I. With that realization, I took a stuttering breath to convey a similar sentiment to my father—but a hand atop mine where it rested on the old, stained oak table drew me up short.

Willa squeezed my hand hard enough to make me jump.

"Hey, what the hell?"

"No, Brodie. We ain't be goin' to get our jobs back. Plus, your mom be on her way here. We all be movin' to a new city together if we huskin' have ta. If that asshole be thinkin' he be ownin' us, it be better for us all to get out, right?" Willa ended by looking at the other three at the table.

Everyone but Dave nodded. He still clearly had the option to return to school on Monday, and I wouldn't blame him. It seemed like getting involved with me right now meant throwing your life into a blender.

"Why don't you all start your own company?" Dave asked so quietly that I barely heard him. Silence only broken by the bartender cleaning glasses followed his whisper, and I realized everyone in the pub had heard him. Not that there were many people here.

"It ain't be possible?" Willa said. "Right, Gary?"

My dad nodded sadly. "We don't have the capital for it. Willa and I considered it a long time ago—but we needed at least half a million."

"Not to mention if the police are seizing assets, they'll likely block a corporation bid," Jarred added.

"Can we get Ms. Stovall to intercede on something like that?" I asked.

"Maybe?" My dad said, "But that doesn't solve the problem of the capital."

"Well, between the three of us, aren't we owed six hundred thousand?" I countered. My dad blinked and looked at Willa. She was open mouthed and staring at me. I quickly added, "It's your money, Willa. I'm just saying—we could have the capital."

"I mean," Willa stammered. "I kind of be needin' that money, but if it be meanin' we could cut an asshat like Jagger out, then surely we all be making more, right?" She asked, looking at Jarred and my dad.

"That's only if Jagger pays you the bonuses," Jarred said softly. The table went silent as everyone's heads fell. Then he looked to Willa. "Plus, even if you manage to start a company, it doesn't mean you'll be making more money," he explained before further dampening the mood. "Not to mention, we won't have connections to large Guilds either. So, there would be a ton more danger and lower percentages. You'd need a building too, right? We have no idea what the overhead on a company like Portals, Portal's, Portalz is…"

"Actually, we do," my mom said as she strode from the closing door toward us. She was carrying a dark brown box, which indicated she had emptied her desk. However, when she slammed it down on the table and pulled out a folder from the top, I realized what it must contain. "I've been managing their books and inputting their contracts for years. I'd say I've got a pretty good idea of how to run the backend, as well as a rather *extensive* client list."

"How much did you hear?" My dad asked, pointing at the doorway.

"Just Jarred's thoughts, but I had the same thought after you called to warn me. I took copies of all my draft work since everything else is the intellectual property of P-three. I realized halfway here that we wouldn't have the money to hire lawyers to create contracts—or even the ability to secure a loan either, but I assume you all thought of a way to at least scrounge up the funds?"

"Not really," I admitted. "We have a thought—you know the bonuses that we are owed…"

My mom smiled at me appreciatively. "With some work, we might be able to get a loan with that as collateral. Right?"

"Who be sayin' that Jagger will still be payin' us them bonuses?" Willa asked quietly, repeating Jarred's earlier thought.

The whole table sighed heavily. My mom said the obvious, "He has to, though. It's in the contracts you all signed."

"That doesn't mean he'll make it easy, though," My dad answered.

"Husk!" My mom swore.

I gasped. Dave gasped. Everyone else smiled at the two of us.

My mom never swore!

CHAPTER 49

Friday, April 19th, 2069

"Employment Insurance will cover Clara," Ms. Stovall said. "Unfortunately, you walking out on the job is going to make it hard for me to get the Union involved, Gary."

"He threatened Clara in front of everyone!" My father exclaimed.

"We'll try to get you a lawyer to handle a case against him, and with sworn testimonies, I might be able to convince the Union to cover your salary, Gary. But you realize that what legal coverage you have is already being used up with your son." Ms. Stovall's face was deadly serious, making everyone stay silent. My dad sighed sadly as she turned to Willa, including Jarred and Dave with a hand gesture. "You three have no recourse. You weren't threatened, and you two are under probation. Yes, Jarred, even though you're returning to the Union."

The glass-windowed meeting room went quiet, and I looked around searching everyone's faces. Dave was the most expressive, likely thinking about returning to school on Monday. Jarred was the next person showing his feelings— looking both empathetic and furious with those of us around the table. Willa was a strange mix of emotions, hard to read but for a few. Anger, certainly, from the red flush and piercing gaze, maybe some stubbornness too? Then there was something that might have been fear or nervousness in the set of her shoulders, looking ready to hunch forward in defeat.

As I said—it was a strange mix.

My father met my eyes and nodded. Why had he done that?

I stared at him and he spun his hand in a circle, indicating I should get moving—What? When it clicked, I flinched back in my chair. He wanted me to tell her about the plan to start a Portal Mining Company?

"Ummm," I stammered, managing to get all eyes focused on me, which didn't help. "We were—" I coughed and managed to get my voice to come out solid again. "—We were thinking that we should start our own crew. Maybe even leverage our bonuses from the other job, if we're able…"

"Why *wouldn't* you be able to leverage your bonuses?" Ms. Stovall asked. The question shocked me enough that I looked to my dad and Willa.

"Cause the court be confiscatin' everythin' as evidence?" Willa said in both question and exclamation.

"And Jagger isn't paying the bonuses?" Ms. Stovall responded with widening eyes as she began scribbling on a legal pad. "He is required by contract to pay out the bonuses regardless of if the goods sell." She went to a side table, clicked a button, and said into an intercom. "John, bring in the Union contracts!"

She turned back around to see all of us staring at her. "It's in the contract. I'll have to check the exact verbiage, but Jagger can't withhold bonuses if I'm right. It's a clause to stop him from holding onto Metals or Ores and claiming they didn't sell—to avoid paying the workers."

A sigh of absolute relief left the lungs of three people around the table. Smiling, I turned to Dave. "At least the Unique opportunity and killing the Golem won't go completely to waste!"

"Wait—" Ms. Stovall pointed at me. "Say that again!"

"Say what again?" I asked.

"Did you say that the Ore haul was triggered by a *Unique* situation?" Ms. Stovall asked very pointedly.

"Uhh? Well, yeah—" I answered and saw everyone around the table look at me with wide eyes. I realized I hadn't yet admitted this part to everyone—I was just assuming they knew. "My new Skill was ready for Evolution—and I found something called Shining Meteorite. When I struck it with the Pickaxe—"

"New Skill? Evolution?" Willa and Jarred mouthed at each other. I realized they still weren't in on the whole story yet.

"You didn't say it was *Unique!*" My dad semi-shouted over them. His volume was a mix of excitement and concern. "How do you know it was Unique?"

"Uhhh," I answered 'smartly.' This would have been a good time to have Smegma here to help me come up with a lie. As it was, I figured a semi-truth wouldn't hurt. "My *Skill*," I began, stressing the word to let the people fully aware of the *Demonic Vault* Skill make the connection. I felt bad for Willa and Jarred but figured I would include them eventually. "I managed to Awaken an F-Rank *Mining* Skill, which grew from the rank of low F to high but stopped. I'd *heard* somewhere that sometimes the System gives people opportunities to Evolve Skills or gain Stats, and the *Mining* Skill allows me to see what some Minerals and Ores are called.

"Oh, and their ranks," I added when people looked confused.

"How many Skills do you be havin'?" Willa asked.

"Umm," I began, thinking of *Dragon Heart* and *Demonic Vault*. Did that count as a single Skill or multiple because of all the sub-Skills? Technically, was *Demonic Vault* a Skill under *Dragon Heart* because it was what had 'stolen' it? "Depending on how Skills are classified, you could consider me to have one or as many as seven."

"What?!" My dad exclaimed loudest, drowning out everyone else in the room, who all uttered similar sentiments. All but Dave.

"Does that include—?" Dave started to ask but I cut him off.

"Yep! Anyway, it was a Unique Ore for sure. And I can confirm that my *Mining* Skill Evolved after it." I turned back to Ms. Stovall, half-desperate to keep Dave from spilling the beans on my new Class Skill that was still forming. Let's just stick with one mind-blowing revelation at a time, shall we? "Why did you ask about that?"

"All Unique Experiences and kills in Portals belong to the person who received them, unless they have signed a contract with the Guild as a Hunter. In this case, you were a worker who got attacked by a Monster and killed it—so we can definitely claim the Golem Heart and Monster Core as your loot—well, you and the people who were involved—it's all of your loot. However"—she held up an emphatic finger—"a Unique Encounter triggered by an *individual* rewards the individual with all the benefits that derive from it. I assume that the Golem and all the Ores *Mining themselves* out of the walls were part of it?"

I nodded and pointed out to the parking lot below. "Any Pickaxe that was in good repair also changed upon defeating the Golem. The Golem spawned after I struck the Meteorite, and the gong when I struck his heart was what caused the Ores to Mine themselves. I think?"

Ms. Stovall began furiously scribbling. After a moment, she looked up, "How many Specialists were in the Mine?"

"Just us three," my father answered despite the question being directed at me.

"And how many veins could you have all tapped in a perfect scenario with the tools you had with you?"

"We be doin' one per day at that point, but we could be managin' two each if they not be hard Ores. Or we be doin' two difficult ones if we be comfortable doin' more damage to our Picks than we could be repairin' from workin' Mana Crystals in one shift," Willa answered this time.

"Okay, so best case scenario—six deposits." Ms. Stovall confirmed as she continued scribbling.

When John came into the room with a folder, she tapped the table next to her and then said, "John, we'll need my husband in here, if you don't mind."

"John two-point-oh, coming right up."

"Mr. Stovall, please," Mrs. Stovall said with a bit of exasperation. I couldn't tell what was bothering her with John calling her husband by the shared name, but from John's smile, I could tell it was not something that worried him.

"As you wish, Mrs. Stovall, I'll send the big guy in!" He said and fled the room. I couldn't help but laugh at Mrs. Stovall's rolled eyes. I thought perhaps I was starting to understand the situation. Mr. Stovall probably didn't care for formalities, whereas Mrs. Stovall did. It made me like them both more.

Mr. Stovall for letting his coworkers call him by his name, and Mrs. Stovall for allowing the joking to happen with minimal reaction. It humanized her even more. That wasn't the only reason for my Cheshire smile. I truly had just gotten the canary—

"Don't get too far ahead of yourself, Brodie," Mrs. Stovall said. Then she smiled herself. "I personally suggest that we settle with Portals, Portal's, Portalz. If your end goal is to start a company, it will get you the capital faster. It will also let Jagger Vance keep a good chunk of the money, which will probably make him fight less when faced with the possibility of losing everything."

"Wait," I said, confused. "I think I'm missing something here. Jagger complained that his contract with the Snowbird or Lynx Guild meant that he was getting stiffed on any real benefit from the extra materials. So, that means that Jagger doesn't have the biggest stake here when it comes to those materials and Ores potentially belonging to me. How is that going to affect everything—if it's not us versus Jagger Vance but us versus an entire Guild?"

The door swung open and a big, tall man entered. When I say big, I don't mean overweight, but I also don't mean gym muscled. Because he was tall, he carried his weight well—and by the size of his shoulders, I could tell a great deal of that weight was muscle. It was probably something that girls at school would call the perfect dad bod. It was a physique built to keep them warm at night but also get shit done when it was needed. His smile and manner of dress immediately marked him as jovial and happy.

"Hey, cupcake—" he began jokingly but stopped midway through when *Mrs.* Stovall raised an eyebrow threateningly. "What's got you asking for the big guns?"

"They need a lawyer who specializes in Portal Law, but you'll need to take a commission on winnings only. I hoped you'd have time," Mrs. Stovall replied, and I could hear the sarcasm building. "You know, since this case shouldn't go to court."

"Oh!" John responded. "Why's that?"

"Well, first of all, it will be a bit of a joint effort. I'll be working to get the court to release some seized Ores and materials. They're being held as evidence in a murder that happened weeks before. You'll be negotiating with Mr. Vance, and Taz from *Lynx* to settle with twenty percent after paid bonuses and your fees."

"Ahh, so you're giving me the easy task?" John responded mockingly, even as he pulled out a chair. As he sat down, he asked, "This isn't a conflict of interest?"

"Not according to the definition, which is all we really care about. We don't represent Portals, Portal's, Portalz, but the Miner's Union."

John nodded and then rolled his chair to a side desk to get a legal pad and pen. "Okay, fill me in."

Mrs. Stovall primarily did the talking, helped at times by the group and me. At the end, John had a page and a half of notes. He, unfortunately, was wearing a frown. "How can you prove that it was a Unique Encounter to Evolve your Skill?"

"Umm?" I questioned back.

"Does Ore normally Mine itself?" Dave said, speaking for the first time. Everyone around the room looked at him and nodded in agreement, but John scratched his five o'clock shadow.

"It certainly does not, but that could be seen as a product of defeating the Golem—which I could also use to claim the Ore as loot!" John had started stoically but quickly grew more excited. "Either way, the Ore and materials would belong to Brodie. Of course, a Unique Encounter would be better, though. Do you have an Awakening record with your Skill before the event?"

I shook my head and Mrs. Stovall winced.

"I can see by my wife's reaction you haven't. May I ask why?"

"Well, now that you fall under client confidentiality as well, you certainly can," Mrs. Stovall said lovingly. "However, Brodie, is there anyone in this room who doesn't currently know everything?"

My eyes found Willa and Jarred's. "Only two, but I've been meaning to tell them."

"Okay, *Smegma,*" Mrs. Stovall said the name distastefully, clearly understanding the meaning behind it, and held her hands out to the side theatrically. When no Demon popped into existence, she looked at me questioningly.

"Ahhh," I sputtered. "He's kind of… missing at the moment. He'll be back though." I turned to Willa and Jarred. "You'll just have to believe us when I say that I have a Skill called *Demonic Vault*, and with it, I have something of a snippy Demonic butler that follows me around *mostly* invisibly."

Jarred's face morphed into a distasteful look as he mouthed 'Demonic' to himself. Still, after a quick moment, he shrugged with a firmed mouth and seemed to tune back into Dave, who was now speaking.

"It's a good thing he isn't here to hear you say that," Dave said, chuckling. "He's more of the Skills' curator. Maybe… point of interaction? Sentient interface? Something like that."

Jarred's face seemed to grow less wary with each normal interaction of those who'd met Smegma.

I shrugged, while chuckling myself. "Either way, despite how dangerous he looks, he isn't actually in our plane of existence and can only verbally inflict damage."

John looked at Mrs. Stovall. "Shami, is he for real?"

"I've seen the bat-winged, horned annoyance myself. Honestly, I think the Demon said it was the spawn of an 'Imp' and a 'Felguard.'"

"Holy crap. It's like Dragons of the Coast!" John exclaimed, almost standing from his chair as he leaned toward me. "You think he'll be back, right? I want to see this thing. It's going to be badass inspiration for when I'm DMing!"

"You guys still play that game?" Jarred asked, confused and slightly alarmed. Whether that was from Smegma's description or the 'game' he mentioned, I wasn't sure.

"We do. It's online, for the most part, but my main group has found that almost every creature in the game has roots in these Portal Monsters. It's rather uncanny. That's why I wanted to see—"

"I can tell you right now that it doesn't look anything like I expected," Mrs. Stovall said, her own excitement matching her husband's. "Still, I can't wait to see how you use the likeness one day!"

Eventually the group got back to business, and Mrs. Stovall filled John in on the problems that had arisen because of Mr. Varnish. "I'm only telling you this in case he tries to put a spanner in your case as well."

"Other than the shoddy excuse that it could conceivably be 'evidence,' he doesn't have much to stand on. Make sure you argue Slim Shot versus Righteous Guild. If they plan to hold the evidence back, then the court needs to at least put up twenty percent of its value in cash for the use of the aggrieved. That usually gets them to smarten up."

"I will. Although I'm hoping Carterman versus Rainbow Stars will be enough. That's the only case I can think of where the court held evidence from a Portal in the wake of an alleged crime. However, in that situation, the evidence spoke directly to a stolen item. In this case, I think Mr. Varnish will try to claim that Morgan had a *Mining* related Skill that was also 'stolen'—however, I've gone through everything and there is no record of it. So, the Judge would be able to tell. Unless he pulls something new from the heavens…"

"You sound like you don't need my help," John said humbly and stood from the chair. "I'll start putting some motions together and serve Jagger with everything tonight or tomorrow. Don't worry, Brodie, if Jagger is sensible, we should have this all taken care of this week."

John left and Mrs. Stovall turned to me as she also stood. "As John says, most of the evidence and legal ownership stuff should be straightforward. At least for the purposes of acquiring capital to start a company. As for the murder trial, you should talk to Sparkle Legion again and let them know about the changes going on."

I glanced down at the camera that was still on my chest. It was still recording. And I'd turned it on when I'd gotten in the car this morning.

"Holy shit!" I said, realizing that not only was this conversation on it, but so were Jagger's threats. "This thing recorded Jagger firing me."

Mrs. Stovall's smile grew *very* large. "I'll let John know what you have—*after* you talk to Legion. I think you might get more than we originally thought. However, Geneva and Kristen might want to use some of the footage for sensationalism. You've been unjustly persecuted, after all. So, let's start with them."

Mrs. Stovall began collecting her papers into bundles and Dave spun to me. "Can I come with you to Sparkle Legion?"

"Hell yeah! We'll have to cut up the footage a bit—" I said as I motioned at the group and tried to include what we'd just talked about. "But I'll call them now to see if they're available."

They were.

CHAPTER 50

Friday, April 19th, 2069

"Yeah, just stand there with the school in the background," Kristen said. It felt kind of awkward staring at the Phoenix Academy across the street, but at least Dave was beside me.

"Why do I suddenly feel like a Japanese schoolgirl shooting for her OnlyFriends?" I complained, trying to burn off the nerves of being back *here*. Honestly, the nervousness wasn't because of the attack. I was surprised by that. It was because I realized that I felt like I'd come so far from my old life as a mild-mannered college student, and I didn't want to get sucked back in—as if the school was some blackhole waiting to swallow me up.

Kristen snorted while trying to contain laughter. "Stop it. You're making the camera shake."

We'd arrived at Legion just to be ushered toward a computer and shown a video. It was a masterfully edited piece from news and other sources—starring Morgan Hallsbrad. They'd left some scenes in that were just fillers, meant to depict examples of what they wanted to add—and this was one of them. Clearly, Mrs. Stovall had already informed them of a great deal.

"How are you feeling about maybe taking us through what happened in the alley?" Kristen asked, her voice filled with concern. It was still sunny outside, but even if it were dark, I doubted the alley would be able to cause me any fear with *Mental Fortitude*. So, I shrugged, and then pointed to the campus housing Dave stayed in.

"We can start at Dave's place since that's where I was before it all went down."

"Perfect!" Kristen exclaimed with excitement but then modulated her tone a bit. "But if it gets to be too much, we can stop at any time."

"Too bad you deleted those messages and blocked The Shop," Dave said. "It would have been a good piece to add—since it's part of SwiftGram."

"We don't want to promote that it was on the Gram that he was targeted. The video would get taken down faster than we can upload," Kristen corrected. "Plus, we *could* get them if we really wanted. We've decided to use a fake, third-party program and just make it look like they were chatting there."

"Good thinking, plus I have the screenshots saved on my phone. Want them for context?" I replied, realizing I had been on the same wavelength as Dave. Kristen and Geneva had thought this through a lot more than we had. I airdropped the pictures to them, hoping I would have been intelligent enough to arrive at the same conclusion if I'd been editing the footage.

That or my brain power was a bit preoccupied with studying the school and rehashing what had happened here. Yes, with *Mental Fortitude,* I was spookily calm and logical, but even the sound of the bus brought images of the events that happened near the transit station.

A chill ran up my spine as I relived some of those memories, but it was because of my recollection of the fear I'd felt in that moment. Not because of anything I was feeling now. We went up to Dave's room, where he was still roommate-less, and he gave a quick tour before we posed for some shots of us watching TV.

Sitting there, Dave asked, "Won't the waning daylight make it a bit off?"

"I'll adjust the lighting to look like night. It's why I pulled the blinds and turned the lights on, too. The next bit will be more of a retelling, and I'm really not sure how much of it we can use, but it will be good to have for future snippets and advertisements if this video gets the traction we're hoping for."

That wasn't the subtlest of hints, so I took it. "Well, after seeing the news about a serial killer in New York, I decided not to take the shortcut back. I'll show you."

We walked the campus, heading through the quad and seeing the jubilant, tired, and free students along the way. I found it strange. To think I would be with them having lunch or heading to class if…

A few students called out to Dave, distracting me enough to snap me out of my spiraling thoughts. Still, even the ones who also knew me didn't wave. I wasn't sure if I should feel hurt by that until Dave said, "I would have mentioned it earlier, but you look different, man. Like stronger and taller or something."

I laughed. "I'm the same height I always was, and I've actually just been Mining—no gym."

"Dude, your arms are jacked, if nothing else. It's part of the reason I wanted to get in on the whole Mining plan with you," Dave responded with a wink and flex. Kristen smirked behind us while leveling the Cannonball 360 camera in our general direction.

It was difficult to have a normal conversation after realizing everything was on film, and I could tell Dave had seen it too. Still, we didn't have to go far to arrive at the doors that led to the campus' wide sidewalks. I moved through the moderate traffic of students before arriving near the exact spot that Morgan had 'ambushed' me. I turned to the alley behind me and could almost see his shadowy figure step into the lamplight.

I stretched my neck and jaw, feeling them tighten up at the recollection. Then I began my story. I paused numerous times as my memory of the events made me picture it again. Still, the replays had no sharp edges, which I was thankful for.

By the faces of Kristen and Dave, though, the pauses made it seem like I was traumatized, which could only be a good thing for the video. I knew enough about acting to lean into it here and there, not embellishing the story, but making sure I replayed the emotions I had felt in that moment—a gun leveled at me, threats of Husking being thrown around, actually being assaulted and Mana Connected.

I was exhausted, mentally and emotionally, when I finished. Kristen dropped us back at the house in her somewhat older Volkswagen Bug. Even as she coasted to a stop in front of my driveway, she was looking at me with sympathetic eyes. "I'm going to get this up tonight or tomorrow morning. Be ready to respond to messages, and set up a CashPal account—send me the link for donations."

"I've already got one because I was hoping for some donations from my Swift a while back. I think I got a hundred bucks, actually."

"Perfect, let me take a quick picture of the QR code and the link, then."

Kristen didn't elaborate on the possibilities of me getting any money from this, but I could tell she was staying silent so I didn't get my hopes up. You just never knew with Swift. Geneva and Kristen might be fantastic at their jobs, but having a video go viral needed a bunch of factors that no one could control—even if the people behind the video were the very best at their jobs.

Walking in the door, I wasn't prepared for the group of excited people speaking over each other in my far-too-small kitchen. It seemed like my father and mother had made some phone calls. Fat Gary and Miguel were there, along with a good portion of the other Miners I'd seen over the two and a half weeks I'd worked with Portals, Portal's, Portalz.

The conversation stopped when Dave and I walked in, but only to give us a quick acknowledgement and continue. Dave and I stood in the doorway listening, and it was as I suspected. This had to do with the prospect of us starting a new company. It also turned out that, without Specialists, Jagger had lost the job they were on today and once again 'temporarily' laid off the non-Specialists.

Everyone seemed excited to leave P-three. Probably because, right now, all the pieces were lined up—like a bit of a perfect storm.

That mood lasted until we received a phone call from Mr. and Mrs. Stovall. They were coming over, and their tones didn't sound like it was to deliver good news.

Because of confidentiality, we were forced to excuse everyone but Dave, Willa, Jarred, my mother, father, and me for the meeting. Mrs. Stovall looked between everyone, but Mr. Stovall just stared at me. After a moment, he said, "Were you aware you unearthed about twelve new Minerals, Ores and materials?"

My head shook before I thought twice. Then I realized I needed a bit more of an answer and said, "Well, I did see a bunch of colored Ores I'd never seen or heard of, but I wouldn't have been able to say they were 'new.'"

"Did you also know that the Portal closed after your encounter? Even without the Lynxes defeating the Boss?"

I stared at him wide-eyed, even as I let my much more emphatic shaking head give answer. He continued, "The Lynx Guild had been certain this was a Permanent Portal. And an F to E-Rank Permanent Portal is basically a money-printing machine, not to mention a fantastic training ground for their recruits."

"Why are you bringing all this up?" Dave asked.

John nodded and hiked a thumb over his shoulder, indicating the people outside of this room. Not the Miners that just left but the world in general. "Well, the UNMH has staked their claim on the new materials and Ores. They've also expressed interest in the Golem Core and Heart."

"That's great news! They'll pay top dollar—right?" My dad said, his tone going from excited to confused as the Stovalls' faces fell.

"It *is* great news, but the prestige and top dollar—maybe even his hatred toward you all—has Jagger hiring big name attorneys. He's going to turn this into a fight, which could be great for us in the long run. Precedence will be in our favor, but as soon as he files, the evidence will be frozen in place till the trial ends. Due to the contention of ownership, the Crown also won't put any money up anymore."

"In a way, Mr. Stovall's filing hurt my case," Mrs. Stovall concluded. "While I can go after Jagger for the bonuses—my guess is he will try to bundle everything together under this case to avoid paying you. It seems like something he'd do out of spite."

My father explained what had just happened with Jagger losing the contract and laying off all his Miners. Mrs. Stovall nodded to herself when he finished. "That would certainly do it. Jagger has basically lost an entire arm of his company, which he relies on to get contracts. None of the big Guilds like to hire piecemeal if they can help it. Why have Cleaners from x, Miners from y and Herbalists from z if you can get them all from P-three."

"But surely he'll need money to hire Specialists, then?" My mom suggested.

"Well, in the long term, sure—he's going to need to rehire, which takes time. But if you're hoping to wait him out or put him in a financial bind then… Nah, he has the capital without it. So, he'll just go into his own accounts if needed. He can survive this easily. The problem is—can you all?" John said, looking at us in concern.

"How long are we talkin' here?" Willa asked. Jarred nodded along with her.

"If the courts are expedient—which they never are—at minimum, a month. If this drags on—which will certainly be Jagger's tactic—as long as a year."

Jarred whistled at John's timeline.

"Ain't no way I can be makin' it that long without a job and that bonus," Willa said, and Jarred joined in right on her heels with the same admission.

"Us either," my mom and dad said. "Do we have any recourse?" My mom finished.

"Not yet, but there's a few avenues we can explore," Mrs. Stovall said. "Don't get your hopes up, but we might be able to try to get per-diem payments against the value of the Ores. The problem is that they would come from a third party, and you'd all be paying out the nose for them."

Everyone leaned forward but John coughed politely. "Additionally, it's a bit of a gamble. We're pretty sure that you'll end up with possession of the Ores, but if you don't, you'd owe back that value…"

"There's no other way?" I asked.

"Sure," John began, "there are several, but they are all either even more distasteful than this or long shots."

"What do you mean?"

"Mr. Varnish seems to want something from you, Brodie. If you figure out what it is, then maybe we can get him to not only let off the gas, but also help you."

Another head shake, but this time I was joined by most of the people around the table. Even Mrs. Stovall.

"He wants Brodie to plead guilty, *Mr.* Stovall." I could tell she wanted to say John but changed it out for a very pointed, almost barbed use of the professional address. "He was clearly acting in self-defense."

"As I said, it's distasteful, but I think the 'plead guilty' portion might be a play to get the second part of the offer," John said slowly.

"The community service under the Larvae Guild?" My mom asked. "Where do they even operate?"

"Europe," John admitted and everyone around the table made wide-eyed looks between John and me.

I shook my head.

"I figured, but you asked. The other way would be to start renting the Pickaxes you can purchase. It would—"

"I only have the five of them and can't buy anymore for a bit. Not without Smegma. Also, I don't want to start giving them out. What if someone discovers that it isn't really a Repair Mark. It's already risky having only people I trust use them…"

"So, we should go with the third-party, per-diem option then? Should I be asking for everyone here or just the Flacaradas?" Mrs. Stovall asked.

Everyone looked at me, and it took me a second to realize why. Technically, I owned all the Ores, not them. So, they needed my permission.

"I assume this means that the bonuses will also be impossible to get, at least in the short-term, if it's going to likely get tied up in this whole mess with the Mining materials?" I asked.

John and Mrs. Stovall nodded.

I made a gesture to include the Miner's that had just left. "Then I vote for everyone here for per-diem, and they still get their bonuses," I said without hesitation.

"Okay, we'll do our best," John said with a fond smile. He pushed off our kitchen table as he stood. "Probably a good idea to wait on the bonuses, though. If we leave Jagger with a percentage, he will still be required to pay them—just saying."

I nodded to the large man, taking his suggestion. Sure, I wanted everyone paid their bonuses, but if they already were going to get them from Jagger, I was greedy enough to want to keep more money for our new business.

CHAPTER 51

Monday, April 22nd, 2069

My phone's buzzing woke me up, and I growled in frustration. I normally wasn't bothered by the thing. Most days, I was able to sleep through almost anything—however, if my half-awake brain was to be believed, this wasn't the first time the husking thing had gone off. I silenced it and passed back out even as Dave, sleeping on the spare bed again, thanked a higher being for me finally realizing and shutting it down.

* * *

Almost everyone sat at the breakfast table, our house somehow becoming the morning meeting spot now that we were *all* out of a job. I wondered if Willa had explained the situation to her family....

My guess was Jarred was not here this morning, because he was doing exactly that.

"I couldn't sleep at all these last few nights," my mother complained as she dished out scrambled Roc eggs onto plates. How she managed to cook for Willa, Dave, my father and I from our fridge was almost magical—she must have predicted that this would happen. When she finished serving I even saw one more helping, likely meant for Jarred. I couldn't recall a conversation about our house being the unofficial gathering place at the pub? "I really don't think Brodie should be doing this." She said this last bit to my father despite me sitting right there.

"Mom, I'm at the table!" I complained and then countered with, "Also Mr. and Mrs. Stovall are pretty confident that we have precedence behind us in this case."

Dave, who had been staying here all weekend, put up a hand to forestall a response and even talked through a mouthful of eggs when he realized he couldn't hold it back until he swallowed. "Either way, if you start a company with the money, even if you don't get the Ore, you'll have the ability to pay it off in time. It takes money to make money. Right?"

My father, who had been the one about to respond, made a 'waffling' gesture with his head, moving his neck back and forth. "Ahhh, maybe. You heard John and Mrs. Stovall yesterday. We likely won't get the big contracts from large Guilds. We'll be forced to scrum it out with the other start-ups."

"What if we give an offer to Taz and the Lynx Guild to keep some of the Ores?" Dave suggested.

I blinked, having not considered leveraging the windfall that were the Ores in that way. To my surprise, my father shook his head. "Nah. First, the big Guilds

370

don't really 'need' money from a single low Ranked Portal's Mine. Otherwise, wouldn't they have the Specialists down there everyday till it was cleared out? How many Portals do you think Guilds like Lynx clear weekly?"

"At least one to two," Dave suggested. Both Willa and my father chuckled, shaking their heads.

"One or two *a day*," my dad answered. "Snowbirds and Lynx in particular have about ten different teams going at any one time. That's the only reason a company like P-Cubed can survive. The best ranked Portals get sent the best Gathering Companies. It's one of the reasons P-Cubed rarely ends up in anything above F-Rank Mines or Gardens. It's why we'll likely only get hired by those small Guilds with a new company."

My mother gasped, which made me and Dave stop focusing on Willa and my father to see what had happened. I'd been expecting her to perhaps have spilled some eggs or maybe burned herself. Instead, I found her pale and scared. "Gary! You can't work for the small Guilds again; it was part of our agreement!"

"What's going on?" I asked, trying not to sound patronizing or belittling of my mother's reaction. She wasn't usually one to overreact, but this certainly seemed like one to me.

"You've seen how dangerous Mining can be," my dad explained. I narrowed my eyes and nodded, waiting for further explanation. "Well, with the small Guilds, you should multiply that by at least two."

"Moogle says it's ten times as dangerous!" My mom added right atop his words.

"That's from Infopedia, and I wouldn't trust it. Still, I can't argue that it's not more dangerous. Brodie, Dave, have either of you ever seen a low-ranked Guild in operation?" my dad asked.

"Do the movies count?" Dave asked. I realized what he meant as well. It was a popular plot where an F-Ranked Hunter joined a low-ranked Guild and helped them rise through opposition to the upper Ranks, changing the lives of everyone and getting the girl. A chuckle escaped my mouth as I thought about how the girl always seemed to not understand her powers until the hero came along.

Then *bam*—she was really an S-Rank.

"I doubt it be like Comet Risin'," Willa said through fits of giggles. Dave flushed red and became fascinated with his eggs.

"It is nothing like how Hollyhood depicts it, at least not in Windsor," my father confirmed. "There are reasons it is widely considered more dangerous to work for lower ranked Guilds. Most F to D-Ranked guilds use firearms inside Dungeons and have only one or two truly Skilled Hunters. Because of that, they rarely thoroughly clean out Mines, even if they send a protection team in with you. Now, remember—you're in a Mine—filled wall to wall, floor to ceiling with highly bullet-reflective materials called rocks. You wind up just as likely to get shot by them as killed by a Monster in a dangerous situation."

"And they never have Healers!" My mom added, seeming to be speaking from experience. At mine and Dave's raised eyebrows, she pointed to my father. "Gary used to roll with a low-ranked Guild as one of those suicidal gun-jockeys. It was before we met and I put a stop to it."

My father grabbed her hand and she leaned in for a kiss. Dave and I let them have their moment and ate some eggs in the meantime. Still, I could feel my disappointment and anger simmering at the admission.

When my father resurfaced, he coughed to bring our attention back. "That's when we made the agreement. I became a Miner as long as I could work for a big corporation."

"How come you never told me this?" I demanded. This whole time, I'd been dreaming of being a Hunter and he'd never even shared that he used to kind of be one.

"It was a different time back then, Brodie. I joined up under the propaganda that 'every little bit helped,' taking the risk to protect others. Nowadays, things are much more stable, and while the low rank Guilds still operate, they are pretty ineffective. They're more of a militia than an organized force like Lynx or Snowbirds."

"Still, you two always discouraged me from becoming a Hunter and barely allowed me to try to become a Bank," I countered. "That's pretty hypocritical." My *Mental Fortitude* didn't allow me to be too upset, but I still felt hurt by my parents' actions.

"Brodie, I was in those Portals—it was dangerous, and frankly terrifying, and I never Awakened a Skill under duress. You think I was going to let my kid gamble with his life for a chance at a Skill?" My dad answered, his own anger evident.

Heat rose in my chest, but thankfully my mind pushed it down. It told me that he was coming from a place of love and even had me replaying his words with a different meaning. He had nearly died, and by the sounds of it—numerous times.

"Either way," Dave cut in, clearly trying to diffuse, "now you have multiple Skills that will open any door you want in the future, so you have even less need to become a Hunter if your goal is gaining Skills."

My father and I stared at each other for a moment longer before I nodded, accepting his reasoning but not entirely happy with it. Just because he had given up on his dream didn't mean—I cut that thought off. It sounded like he was forced to give up on his dream, and without that, I probably wouldn't be here…

Husking *Mental Fortitude*—I *wanted* to be upset, but it already felt like I'd known about this for months and come to terms with it. It was both eerie and gratifying in this moment. It wasn't like I would have stayed angry for long—I just wished I'd known sooner. It was just another example of my parents trying to push me to become an office worker.

More of my parents trying to protect me… like *parents*—I corrected. I'm sure Evelyn would have a field day with this information later today.

"Okaaayyy, totally changing that subject—my earlier point still stands. As long as you start a business, you should be able to pay off the debt in time," Dave said, cutting in once again and dispelling any further awkwardness. "Plus, didn't you say you can buy other tools? Like Gardening Trowels, Sheers or Skinning Knives?"

"I can. However, I know nothing about those trades. For that matter, I knew barely anything about Mining. Like, there are so many more tools in the mall shops I wouldn't even know where to begin—"

"Ahh, you mean the wedges and sledges?" My dad said, sounding like he was using a term that was common and also described the drills, bits, etc. I nodded at him and he smiled. "Mining does have the cheapest overhead to enter, but most other unskilled trades don't have to deal with tool breakage. So—while there are more tools to purchase—many Cleaners and Gardeners slowly accumulate a set and stick with that for years. Many family men or women don't bother upgrading, either.

"Just like Mining, there are Specialists with better tools or Skills to handle tougher hides or plants that are either dangerous or easily destroyed when trying to Harvest. Clara and I discussed me moving to Gardening in the past. It's simply easier to slowly become a Specialist in that field. However, since everyone becomes one if they stay long enough—the pay is only slightly better than Mining. Way fewer bonuses, too."

"What—why?" I asked, meaning the bonuses.

My mom took over the explanation from there. "There aren't that many plants that sell for high prices. Ores for weapons and manufacturing are always in demand, and Hunters will pay a lot—but most of the plants and meats are sold to grocery stores. The hides of Monsters can sell for a great deal, but it has the same problem as Mining. If they are tough enough for armor, then you need a Specialist to Harvest them."

"I'm assuming there's some nuance there," Dave mumbled around a forkful of egg. My mom and dad nodded but my father held up a hand.

"All that to say, I bet you could get by with just trowels and skinning knives to cover the Gathering and Harvesting department at first," he said while changing his held-up hand to a pointing finger. "It just might work, and offering a 'total package' type of solution for Guilds would certainly be working towards better contracts…"

"Then we would need even more start-up capital," I said. "If we could start with Mining and build up to the others, there's a good chance…" I still couldn't bring myself to tell my dad and mom I'd been stealing Mana Crystals from the jobs. Then I realized it might actually be the perfect time with them both currently at odds with P-Cubed.

"There's one thing I still haven't told you two—" at their concerned looks, I hurried to add, "or anyone, well, except Dave." I could tell that didn't help. I took a moment to collect myself and then made the admission. "I've kind of been stealing Mana and some Mana Crystals from each job to pay for the Picks."

My mom's mouth fell open, but my father's only reaction was slightly raised eyebrows, comically widening eyes and a bit of a smirk. He clearly already knew or at least suspected. I addressed my mother with what I said next. "The currency for the *Demonic Vault* Skill isn't Greenbacks. It's Mana Coins. To get them requires offering up Mana in exchange for the currency at a one-to-one ratio. I can't get them in any other way."

"When you say Mana and Mana Crystals—is there a difference?" Dave asked as my mother plopped heavily into a seat beside my father.

I kept my eyes on her out of concern as I answered. "Well, the Crystals have Wild Mana inside them. So, I can sell the Mana inside and keep the Spent Mana Crystal. It's how I identified my Skills the other day. Remember?"

"Oh right," Dave said, sounding like he had asked the question on my parents' behalf. A glance got me a wink, telling me that he had. "The Wild Mana is why people can't use the Mana inside the Crystals like their Pools, right?"

The table chuckled, hearing his sarcastic tone, and all being let in on his earlier play-acting at not remembering. It was a well-known fact that Mana Crystals couldn't be used as a source of Mana for a Hunter. Well, they could—if the Hunter wanted to have his Skill burned out.

The laughter slowly died away, and in its wake, I could feel my mother struggling with my admission.

"Under the circumstances, I can't say he did anything wrong, honey," my father said while grabbing my mom's shoulder comfortingly.

"It's still theft!" My mom hissed.

"From a dickwad," my dad responded, which startled a laugh out of me and Dave. My mom looked at him with shock written across her face and then let her head drop as she joined in with a small chuckle of her own.

"You aren't wrong," she mumbled. I could tell that the thought of us not being contracted to low-ranked Guilds for long was helping her.

"Out of curiosity," Willa said sweetly, "what be happenin' to that five thousand dollars I be payin' you?"

"Uhhh," I stuttered as she and my father grew intensely interested in me and my reddening face. I started waving my arms to forestall them from jumping to conclusions. "I really did spend it on Monster Cores to sell to Smegma! When he gets back, he'll tell you!"

"Yeah, right!" Dave said, then realized how that came out, mirroring me in crossing his arms quickly back and forth to stop people from misinterpreting. "I meant the little shit will likely say the exact opposite if it gets Brodie in trouble."

Willa and my father looked at me seriously for a long moment but eventually nodded their heads. It was like they were saying, 'We'll trust you for now.' It was a very serious look, which made me tense—right up until Willa cracked a grin and punched me in the arm.

* * *

"So, you've discovered that your parents had lives before you came along, and that they even sacrificed parts of them on your behalf?" Evelyn asked, her word choice was pointed and intentional.

"Yeah, I mean I'm not upset about the fact that he was a Hunter. I'm just kind of disappointed he, or they, chose to keep that from me even though they knew my dream."

"Disappointed?" Evelyn asked, seeming to be badgering. I felt a twinge of irritation and instantly knew what she was going for. This was her trying to see if I was 'sugar-coating' my reaction.

I simply shrugged. "I was angry for a moment but realized they did it out of love. That they just want what's best for me."

374

"That's a very mature reaction," Evelyn said as she made some notes. "How long would you say it took you to calm down and reach that conclusion?"

Another shrug. "Couple of seconds? No more than half a minute?"

Evelyn's eyes narrowed slightly, but she made a note and schooled her features so quickly I almost thought I imagined it. "Let's get into why you were sent to me then, shall we?" I nodded and she continued with multiple questions. "How do you feel now that you are facing a trial? How are you handling the fact that it has become so public?"

I blinked, trying to interpret the question. It felt like it was worded strangely, but in the end, I decided to take it at face value. "Well, I know I didn't do anything wrong—so I'm not overly worried about the trial. I don't love the fact that people I don't know may see news from the trial or case reports in retrospect and form opinions without all the facts, I guess? But it is going to be a closed-door trial from my understanding."

Evelyn blinked this time, her vivid green eyes studying my face between each eye closure. "Is that why you are trying to control the narrative?"

This time, my head tilted along with my noticeable confusion. My *therapist* shouldn't know about the marketing team I'd hired. She explained a bit further. "You know, with SwiftGram and SmileBook."

Ah. So, she didn't know about Sparkle Legion specifically, but she noticed the changes in my social media presence and was clearly smart enough to deduce what we were going for. "Oh, well, kind of. That's mostly a company we hired to try to sway public opinion before the trial starts. It's what Mrs. Stovall suggested, and what Sparkle Legion will be working toward."

"This F-Rank stopped a C-Rank criminal who's killed dozens of people? I call bullshit!" Evelyn read off her book.

My head flinched back from her involuntarily before I realized she wasn't voicing her thoughts.

"What was that?" I asked slowly.

"It's one of probably a dozen negative comments on the video you posted last night," Evelyn explained.

My eyes widened and I began digging into my pocket for my phone. Evelyn must have made the connection because she asked, "You didn't know?"

By the time she'd finished her question, I'd seen the screen notifications. Fourteen thousand notifications… "What the husk?"

"Please don't swear in my sessions, Brodie," Evelyn scolded. Her tone pulled my attention from the screen. She sounded a lot like my mother in that moment.

"How do I have fourteen thousand notifications?" I asked as I opened SwiftGram and checked the post. "Twelve million views?"

"How come you didn't know?" Evelyn countered my questions.

"I silenced my phone last night 'cause it woke me up. Then this morning, Dave and I went right down for breakfast—I didn't even pick up my phone off the charger until my dad and I left to come here."

"Well, this is unexpected. How do you feel right now?" Evelyn asked, her pen poised to start furious note-taking.

I took a moment, leaning back in my chair and thinking about the question. How did I feel? There was certainly a spark of concern—especially with the highlighted negative comment, but…

Mostly, I felt excited. Finally, I had a viral video. That flame of excitement puttered in the wind of reality, though. The reason I wanted the viral video was so I could use it to become a Mana Bank. Now that viral video was letting the world know I was on trial for manslaughter. I couldn't say I loved fourteen million people knowing and judging that.

But I hadn't watched the video…

"I'm kind of excited," I explained. "I've always been looking to get a post to go viral. I'm also worried since I haven't watched the video—"

"Worried?" Evelyn asked as she scribbled away. She had to be noting more than my words—I hadn't said much.

"Well, I assume they depict me well, but since I haven't seen it, and there are negative comments…" I let that thought hang in the air and listened to Evelyn's pen on her page. It didn't take long before she looked up at me. She seemed to be expecting more.

"Uhhh, I feel okay?" I tried.

"You sound like I just told you that the weather will be nice tomorrow," Evelyn pushed.

I raised both hands palm up, not sure what more she wanted. I already said I *was excited*, didn't I?

Evelyn took a deep breath and sighed it out. "I'm confused, Brodie. Your dream was to become a Mana Bank because you couldn't be a Hunter. Now, you're knocking on the door of becoming famous, which *should* get you a Bank Partner, and you seem unconcerned. Plus, you seem only mildly interested in how it will affect your trial…"

"Well, I trust what Mrs. Stovall and Sparkle Legion are trying to do?" I said, making it a question.

"These are rather big events, though. Life-changing. Is there something new going on in your life that currently has your focus?" Evelyn tried.

After a moment, I gave a shallow nod and looked to the floor. "Kind of. We're thinking of starting our own Mining Company."

"Okay!" Evelyn exclaimed. "And you're downcast because?"

"Well, we were going to use our withheld bonuses for startup capital, then—" I explained the situation in detail. Evelyn's eyes grew wider and wider, and she took pages of notes. It also exhausted almost the remainder of our session as she dug deeper into my feelings about each occurrence.

"I don't know. I'm pretty bummed out about how hard it all seems to be. Like, is nothing easy?" I explained in answer to her asking about how the court's withholding the money made me feel. "It's like every*thing* and *body* is against the group of us little people. You know?"

Evelyn nodded sagely. "It is an unfortunate truth," Evelyn intoned, sounding like she was speaking from experience. "The wealthy and strong suppress the weak. Just remember that sometimes it isn't intentional. Sometimes, they do it with a similar motivation as your parents did—to protect.

Unconsciously, they make a decision that takes things away without necessarily meaning to. Like the UNMH and the Ores."

"Are you saying that Mr. Varnish and Jagger are somehow doing this accidentally?"

"No, not at all. They sound like jackasses. I just don't want you to get *completely* jaded," Evelyn said with a smile.

I couldn't help but laugh. When our mirth died, Evelyn said, "Have you worked on your meditation? Any notable spikes in emotions?"

"No," I admitted guiltily and then added, "but also no on the second one." I could tell that it didn't make it better.

"Maybe we should try something else since I don't see a journal here with you. I'm going to start a text group with you, okay? I'll check in daily…"

"Sure, I might not get back to you right away if I'm in a Portal."

"Or if you silence your phone," Evelyn chuckled and indicated my phone, which was still held in my hand, and the climbing notifications.

"I did just realize I can probably just silence the app…" I agreed and stood up. "I'll see you next week?"

"Good session today, Brodie. I hope things start turning your way," Evelyn said as she, too, stood and turned toward her desk.

As I walked to the door, I stopped.

Things turning my way? Words came out of my mouth unbidden. "What do you think I should do if they don't?"

A deep silence settled across the room and I nearly turned around to see the expression on the woman's face, but I was still locked in my own thoughts of what might come in the future.

Finally, a soft, concerned tone answered me that rose every hair along my arms and the back of my neck.

"Survive."

CHAPTER 52

Monday, April 22nd, 2069

I'll admit I started scanning through the comments before I even watched the video. Partially because I wanted to wait and have the first viewing with Dave, if possible. But probably more so because I was vain and needed to know what people were saying. Or perhaps I just was too eager, and this was my coping mechanism for—

Nope. *Mental Fortitude* and my logical brain firmly diagnosed me as vain. Honestly, this Skill was beyond frustrating.

From my peripherals, I could see my father giving me the side eye and a look I had long since learned was one of concern. I ignored it for now. He'd get an explanation along with my mom and Dave. Willa and Jarred, too, if they were at my place.

DailyGrind: This kid deserves some sort of medal not a trial!

5111 Likes

Replies—352

Rebecca Delayney: Wait, you can be tried for murder when someone was trying to kill you? Da husk is going on.

752 Likes

Replies—492

Anders Mole: Surely this is fake news. An F-ranked stopped a C-rank Suspected Serial Killer? Fat chance.

123 Likes

Replies—2001

Grim Men Guild: Check your CashApp. This scumsucker killed a sibling of a member. We've pooled some money and sent it on. Great work!

3521 Likes

Replies--121

L33T P3N15: My man did a no-hit run on the last boss. Bro is clearly hacking! Someone check his computer!

2971 Likes

Replies--1473

I blinked. Not only was the most negative comment I'd found so far just disbelief in the feat itself, it looked like people were arguing for me in the replies. Still, it was the mention of sent cash that had me stopping.

Opening my CashPal, I found five hundred dollars sitting there. No money from Grim Men, though—so, I felt a little disappointed. Still, the five hundred was made up from a large amount of five to twenty-dollar donations. I shrugged and closed out of the app. While it was fresh on my mind, I shot a group message off to Geneva and Kristen, thanking them for posting the video. I had two missed calls from them, though, and chose to instead dial them back.

"Morning, Brodie," Geneva said, leaving no space to follow up as she continued. "We're at your house already. You two on your way back?"

"Uhh, yeah," I answered dumbly.

"Perfect. We'll see you soon. Since you hadn't yet commented, we thought a watch party might be in order."

"That sounds perfect. Is everyone there?"

"That or on the way. Your mom, Willa and Dave are filling us in on the startup you're working on. With their permission, we're recording. I've got to go. See you soon."

"What was that?" My dad asked as the line disconnected. I pulled the phone away from my ear and looked at it, dumbfounded.

"Sparkle Legion is at the house. I think they're interviewing Mom, Dave and Willa?"

"Ahh, what did you call that? B-roll?"

"Well, yeah, that's the name of stuff that might not get used—but Geneva said it's about the company startup…"

"Huh? We aren't even sure that's going to happen," my dad answered.

"Exactly, but there was something about her voice—like she was really excited about it."

"Maybe it's something to do with the firing?"

"The faster you get home, the sooner we'll find out!"

"Kid, if I push down on the gas pedal anymore, we'll be Bintstoning it home."

"What's a Bintstone?" I asked.

"Oh my god, I never showed you BedRack, I'm either really old or failed you as a parent. Suffice it to say, my foot will go through the floor if I push down the pedal any harder."

The Ford Escort hiccuped to emphasize his point.

* * *

"—now the boy who survived is being tried for manslaughter and the opposing counsel is claiming Morgan 'The Shop' Hallsbrad was only a private eye. Like and follow to stay up to date on this incredible story!"

The video ended and I stared at the suggested content that popped up as the screen faded to a dark off-gray. There was a link in the video comments, and just from the number of likes, I could guess I'd gained more followers than I had before the video—probably a great deal more. Geneva closed her laptop with a broad grin and the room fell into silence as we all processed it in our own ways.

Mrs. Stovall was the first to respond. "That was fantastic Mrs. Agnos, Mrs. Franzke. Superb work as always." She had been a bit of an unexpected arrival, at least for me. I looked at Mrs. Stovall, trying to figure out why she seemed so serious even in her praise.

"Yeah, that was husking fantastic," Dave exclaimed, his voice filled with the kind of excitement I expected from everyone. Mrs. Stovall probably had news about the case and requests, I supposed. My excitement fell a bit as I realized it probably wasn't good news.

I only realized I was staring at Mrs. Stovall when the silence grew. Everyone was looking at me, waiting for a response. Everyone but Mrs. Stovall. I forced a smile onto my face and addressed Geneva and Kristen first. "That was better than I could have ever dreamed of." Then I turned back to Mrs. Stovall. "What's going on, Mrs. Stovall?"

She winced. "That obvious?"

"Well, I'd have expected some excitement from you since this was all your idea."

She gave a small smile and nod but immediately grew serious again. "I've got some great news, but also some bad news. I'm going to start with the good news."

I, for one, didn't miss how she downgraded great to good, but she continued without waiting for confirmation.

"We've managed to get a few companies to show interest in the Ores—especially with the UNMH offering top dollar for the unknown materials. So, you'll basically have your pick of lenders." She paused for a moment, everyone knowing that what was about to follow would sour the first part. Otherwise, she wouldn't be so serious. "The best we could do is one cent on the dollar up front, and it's from the Larvae Guild. Everyone else is bidding lower, and Mr. Stovall and I both don't like that their name is even in the ring. It just feels like they have another play."

She let that hang in the air, and I blinked. She was still frowning deeply. "There's more isn't there?"

She sighed. "The Union Benefits are about to run out and we won't have access to sue the Hallsbrad estate until after all the trials finish. I've pulled Mr. Stovall in to help start putting that together, but having him and I working on two different cases—along with Sparkle Legion—is burning the funds faster than anticipated. John is working on commission in the Portal Ownership case, but the offers just aren't as high as expected. So, he's been forced to pull back a bit. John and I were discussing options this morning…" She once again let the sentence hang in the air, but her look at Geneva and Kristen gave everyone context for what had been the final decision.

"You've got to stop paying for Sparkle?" I said, voicing the conclusion I had reached.

Geneva and Kristen wore bright smiles despite the news. Even as Mrs. Stovall nodded dourly at my pronouncement, I transferred my attention to Sparkle Legion. "You don't seem upset about that?"

I couldn't help the apprehension in my voice. Maybe the video had taken a ton of resources and wasn't getting the response they wanted. Maybe they were pumping advertisement dollars into it, and that was why it had so many views. Maybe—

"You might want to check your CashPal, Brodie," Kristen said with a chuckle.

I pursed my lips and narrowed my eyes. I began pulling my phone from my pocket as I gave an answer. "I did on the way home. It's got five hundred dollars, and I doubt that's enough to keep you two! Not with the video I just saw."

Their smiles didn't waver, which I found strange. Dutifully, I pulled up the app. The balance had climbed to a thousand, but that wasn't exactly wealth. I turned the screen to both women, biting back the 'I told you so' and keeping my face devoid of expressions that might convey it. They had worked hard and honestly—if I ever had enough money in the future, I would hire them in a second.

I'm sure I failed, but despite my face's expression of disbelief, their expressions only grew more amused. They looked at each other and then Kristen said, "You'll want to check the *pending* donations."

The phone spun in my hands so fast I knew the laughter that followed from them was at my expense. I didn't care. It sounded like they weren't worried about getting fired, and that could only mean—

Right at the top of the screen was a donation for five hundred thousand dollars. From the Grim Men Guild. My mouth fell open as I scanned past it and saw a donation of ten thousand, then a thousand. It kept going and I scrolled through quickly, trying to keep a mental amount but failing after the donation numbers stopped being whole amounts. Why so many people were sending one thousand, three hundred and thirty-seven dollars and thirty-six cents was beyond me. However, on a quick count, there were at least forty with that sum.

"What's going on?" My dad and mom said together, picking up on my facial expressions. Everyone else was also studying me, waiting for a response.

Closing my mouth to wet my tongue, I croaked, "Therccckk." I closed my mouth again, swallowed and salivated for a moment before starting again. "There's probably seven hundred thousand dollars in donations here."

"More than we expected, but not more than we thought would come in over time," Geneva said as the people around the table all reacted. My mom and dad stood up abruptly, Dave whooped and slammed hands onto the table, Jarred wore a proud fatherly smile, and Willa shouted, "We be startin' the company!"

Mrs. Stovall coughed politely after Willa's exclamation. "I am going to be the devil's advocate here. Brodie, I don't think you should use this money to start your company. You should probably put it aside to pay for Sparkle Legion, your friends' salary replacement, and us Lawyers. Otherwise, you're back to taking cents on the dollar from the Ores. It's your money and your choice, though."

For the first time since he arrived, I wished Smegma was here. I wasn't sure what his opinion would be, but I felt like he would have some valuable input. Instead, it was just me. I figured a company would, in time, get me more Mana Coins, and that could cascade to something huge, but so could winning the ownership of all these Ores and getting top dollar…

"Mrs. Stovall, how much is the Larvae Guild offering?" I asked.

"Well, the Ore is valued at seven and a half million on the low end. So, you'd only get seventy-five thousand—so basically a pittance—with a contract to make up ten percent of the difference in value later, if you win the case. According to experts, it could be worth as much as seventy-five million, which means you'd get seven and a half million at ten percent, but no matter who we talk to, they aren't willing to take the risk that you will be the one who ends up with legal possession of the materials. Partially because the UNMH has staked the claim, meaning they will get the unknown Ores at their estimated values. Secondly, Mr. Stovall and I believe someone is manipulating the bidding or putting out false information—"

"We can help with that! Propaganda is sort of our thing," Geneva said instantly. "Do you think they would let us get in to see all the materials? It would be great to have a shot of it all for our next video anyway."

Mrs. Stovall nodded even as she scratched her head. Her voice finally gained an ounce of excitement, "That might help if they're sowing misinformation about the Ores. And we should be able to get permission to send in a team to catalog everything for our records. We'll likely be fined a bit for releasing information on the contents, but it won't be that bad since, until proven otherwise, we have legal standing that they are Brodie's property. It might be our best play. Let me talk to Mr. Stovall and see what he thinks. Don't start the company until I get back."

"How long are you going to be gone?" My dad said from where he had been pacing behind his chair.

"A few hours at most," Mrs. Stovall laughed. "It was just a saying."

She left the room in as close to a jog as her heels would let her.

"So, now that she be gone, we be startin' the business, right?" Willa said immediately upon her leaving. My head swiveled to her in concern till I saw the huge joking smile. "Just joshin'. Still, I don't be thinkin' any of us be wantin' to leech off ya, Bro. So, think about it. Maybe we can be budgetin' or takin' loans or somethin'."

My dad and mom looked at me, their faces concerned until they were finished reading my expression. Then they both broke into grins that felt loud enough that I could almost hear their thoughts. It likely mirrored my own.

"Willa, Jarred, and even you, Dave—let's see what we can do, but until this money runs out—what's mine is yours."

Jarred waved his hands for a moment and opened his mouth, likely to protest, but my mom cut him off. "No way, Jarred. You quit your other job to work with P-Cubed 'cause we said it would be good for you. You aren't saying no. Still, I'm with Mrs. Stovall—why not use this money to fund the open cases and your friends, then when we get the Ores, we can start a company with multiple branches from the outset—and really stick it to Dicker Wimp."

It was clearly a play on Jagger Vance, which made me smile. She wasn't one for swearing, and this was clearly an attempt to still insult the man without calling him too severe of a name.

"Wouldn't it be best to start a company right away, though?" Dave said seriously, causing the mood in the room to change.

"Honestly, it might be the best choice—"

"No!" Jarred, my mother and father said in unison. Willa looked at them with a frown, which Dave and I mirrored.

"What do you mean 'no?'"

Jarred looked to my dad, who nodded at him, before looking at the three of us. Geneva and Kristen were staying out of the conversation for now and just recording. Instantly, I became a bit self-conscious, but my dad broke me out of it with his next words. "Maybe you'll all listen this time if we give you more details. Jarred…"

"Working with small Guilds is a cluster-husk, Brodie. It's always run by some idiot hopped up on what limited power he husking has, and if that sounds bearable—let me tell you—it ain't. Almost every run back in our Hunter days we lost Tradespeople, right?"

My mom frowned at Jarred's language but let it go. My dad nodded, which also prompted Jarred to continue. "At the time, I didn't think much of it because we clearly tried our best, and all the people who died knew the risks. We all did. Now that I've seen the way top-tier Guilds run things, there just isn't a comparison you'd understand. Think Hunter Wars but it's a pro team against—I don't know—a group of high schoolers with basic training."

"That bad?" Dave said, aghast.

"You were a Hunter too?" I asked incredulously right on top of him.

"He was but got out a bit sooner than I did," my dad explained. "I told him not to tell you. Let's not get into that…" My dad cut off abruptly and made a head motion to the camera.

"Actually, I think it would be good footage," Kristen said. Geneva nodded along but my father shook his head.

"It's family issues, and the line needs to be placed somewhere, ladies."

The tone he used was the same one he'd lectured me with in the past when I'd been gushing out ideas to gain followers on the Gram. At the time, I hadn't thought he was right. Now, after my experience with Morgan, I was far less confident in my *naive* assessment from merely a year before. Geneva conceded the point with a polite dip of her head but kept recording.

"So, we're waiting for the—"

Mrs. Stovall came back into the house without knocking, which surprised everyone. Partially because of the noise the screen door made, but mostly—at least for my part—because it hadn't taken her long at all.

"We chatted in the car," she explained breathily. "Mr. Stovall is on his way to do some budgeting. There just might be a way to fund Sparkle, us, and start your company—if you keep it to a Mining branch only."

My parents and Jarred winced, but the rest of the people in the room grew excited. My dad of course was the first to speak up. "The risk just isn't worth it, Brodie."

To my surprise, it was Geneva that responded. "With the videos we're going to make, I think the risk will be mitigated quickly."

"How so?" my mom asked skeptically.

"Well, you know how P-Cubed gets ahead by offering multiple arms of Gatherers under a single contract?" Kristen replied. My mother acknowledged Kristen's words with a nod and a casual affirmation. "Well, what if we can offer publicity by a famous SwiftGram, and SmileBook star?"

"I don't know," my father said. "Guilds surely won't care—"

"I'm going to stop you right there, Mr. Flacarada," Mrs. Stovall said. "I can tell you that the best Guilds in the world and area care *very* much about social media."

"So, this could actually work?" My mom and Jarred said after looking at each other.

"Not instantly, but after we get some footage!" Geneva crowed excitedly.

"John seemed to think so also," Mrs. Stovall answered, and I realized that she used his name, forgetting her insistence on formality. She must be very excited or happy.

Looking around the table, I realized she wasn't the only one.

<u>End of Volume 1</u>

AFTERWORD

Hello everyone. Ryan DeBruyn here again.

I just wanted to thank everyone who has read this far. I hope that means you enjoyed the story. Please if you have time rate and review it. I can't tell you how much us Indie Authors need that.

This next part is a bit of repetition from the Foreword, but I want to make sure everyone sees it.

<u>For anyone reading on Royal Road, or Patreon</u>: Please note that while the story contained in these pages are similar, they are not the same. Only the book you just read can be considered Canon for the series. Everything else is just a rough draft.

Still, I hope the people supporting me over on Patreon are enjoying the conclusion to Book Four. Keep reading after the bloopers for links to Royal Road or Patreon to continue your journey if you're desperate for more!

BLOOPERS

"I'm sorry dad, this is the only way," I whispered before twisting my body to place a hand in the center of his chest. Shoving him off his feet and removing his arms from around me, I began to rush at the almost fully-formed Rock Golem. I could only hope that getting in a first strike would somehow help.

After all, I only had ten minutes on *Overcharge*.

"Um, Brodie?" Smegma called out, zipping up behind me. "Before you die, hopelessly fighting a System-induced armored death machine…" Somehow Smegma's voice sounded hesitant, but his words caused me to stumble briefly before I caught myself.

However, I nearly fully face-planted at his next words.

"What's an oni-chan?"

* * *

We continued arguing familiarly until the trailers started, followed by the movie. While it was more of a documentary than a true movie, I somewhat enjoyed the fights.

There was also one Hunter it focused on that bothered me, but I shook off my disbelief choosing to focus on the amazing four other Hunters that I knew were total badasses.

It's one thing to dream of being a Hunter, but it was something else entirely to see how much went into it. Sure, high ranked Hunters had bankrolls, rizz, and chicks or dudes throwing themselves at their feet, but the very best—the active double and triple S superstars, barely got time to enjoy that fame. They were too busy slinging iron, strategizing or ordering around Guild-mates to enjoy their massive popularity.

Total bummer, that.

And even the days they planned to go boozin' were often canceled due to Emergencies. The movie really painted the landscape of Hunter's as a total grind—making me rethink my desire to be one.

"Still, why does that one bald guy in the Yellow Sweat Suit make it seem so easy?" Smegma asked. "Plus he's always going shopping and just doing what he wants. I'll admit his punch sounds impressive."

I growled, "SightArma is a total fake. The online Read-it forum's claim he just claims the kills of other Hunters. I don't know why they even focused a section on him. He should be C-rank or B-rank at the highest!"

* * *

"You can't blame your mother for your lies, Brodie," my father said.

My nose sucked in a breath but once again I calmed myself enough to respond without raising my voice. "I'm just saying that this isn't making it easy for me to—"

Smegma popped back into existence right in front of me. Blocking my vision of my parents, and the whole room. I had enough time to register a huge leather jacket with a giant 'T-Birds' stitched in white—the Imp had grown?

Smoke curled from his lip as he turned to look at me. In two fingers he held a cigarette, but that wasn't the most surprising thing. Between two black horns he had red hair. Not just any hair—

His dark red hair was styled in the Pompadour. A look popularized by Elvis. The red hair shone with grease, and as my family around the table went silent he preferred a pink leather jacket in my direction, but then seemed to think better of it—and leaned toward Mrs. Stovall.

"*Sandy?*" He said his voice still high-pitched despite his size increase. Then he coughed slightly and his voice deepened as he said, "What are you doing here?"

My mother stood up and pointed an angry accusing finger at the Demon. Her face flushed red, and I wondered how she'd gone from nearly faint to apoplectic. Before I could say anything she shouted, "You're making her a Pink Lady?"

ROYAL ROAD

This story is also being posted to Royal Road. If you have a moment head on over and give it a follow, favorite and a rating. It would really help me out.

Royal Road

MINERS MONOPOLY

Volume 2

By Ryan DeBryun

Without morals, the powerful and wealthy can do whatever they want. That's a hard truth for an aspiring Hunter to learn.

Brodie attempts to navigate his induction into the world of the multi Skilled, and discovers just how complicated and convoluted that can be. Even a small step from equipment Specialist Miner to company owner is fraught with challenges. Especially when you have to work with **low ranked Guilds**.

The complications only grow when the *Awakening procedures* of the UNMH are off limits to him due to a certain Demonic Skill issue. Brodie must navigate the hurdles of his legal trial **with a literal growing Demon on his shoulder**. At least Smegma doesn't have any morals either.

Can Brodie prove to the top clans that Abyss: Portal Services and Management has what it takes to thrive?

Coming soon!

ALSO BY RYAN DEBRUYN

Equalize - Book 1 of Ether Collapse Series
Excise - Book 2 of Ether Collapse Series
Earthdom - Book 3 of Ether Collapse Series
Equatorial - Book 4 of Ether Collapse Series

* * *

Tech Duinn - Book 1 of Ether Flows Series
Edda Gaia - Book 2 of Ether Flows Series

* * *

Starred Tower - System Misinterpret Book One
Endarkened Spire - System Misinterpret Book Two

ABOUT THE AUTHOR

Follow <u>Ryan DeBruyn</u>, or join his <u>Guardian's of The Grotto</u> Facebook group to stay up to date on new releases.

Visit Amazons Author Page

<u>Ryan DeBruyn</u>

RISE OF MANKIND : AGE OF STONE

By Jez Cajiao

In all the games Matt has played, Dungeons are places to raid, places you dream of conquering, but when the world is stripped of electricity, and the first mana-twisted beasts start to prowl, the games all come to an end...

Matt's just an ordinary guy, but when he's beaten, robbed, and left for dead, bleeding out at the bottom of a gully, it all has to change as he grasps frantically at his only chance for survival, coming as it does in the form of a glowing, dangerously pulsing light.

With his reality forever altered, Matt must quickly find a suitable place to deploy the Dungeon Core, fighting his way through the hundreds of people between him and safety, because if he doesn't do it soon, a Core Detonation will solve all of his problems for him… permanently.

Welcome to the New World.

Experience a dark apocalyptic LitRPG Dungeon Core tale, Matt is a normal guy, pushed into terrible situations, and without anyone to hold his hand and explain the system. This is a weak-to-strong tale about doing what's right, not what's easy, in a nightmarish world. Fans of Dungeon Core stories, progression fantasy and strategy real time expansion games are sure to love it.

Order Now!

THEFT OF DECKS

By Lars Machmüller

When the deck is stacked against you? Change the game!

In the frontier town of Isarn, Chase will never be more than the lowly Darkborn thief he is. Banned from training, banned from acquiring better cards, if the Lightborn had their way, he'd be banned from life itself.

He's not alone though, and the one thing he and his friends have is determination. Losing a hand to a brutal punishment only fueled his obsession to get access to his own amazing, reality-bending cards.

That is the path to power and a future for them all. Nobody cares where you came from when you're rich enough. For now, though, they're facing both established powers, churches and age-old prejudices. It's time to get to work, and if the Lightborn won't share and play nice?

Sometimes the only way to get dealt a better hand is to steal the whole damn deck!

Buy on Amazon

QUEST ACADEMY

By Brian J. Nordon

A world infested by demons.
An Academy designed to train Heroes to save humanity from annihilation.
A new student's power could make all the difference.

Humans have been pushed to the brink of extinction by an ever-evolving demonic threat. Portals are opening faster than ever, Towers bursting into the skies and Dungeons being mined below the last safe havens of society. The demons are winning.

Quest Academy stands defiantly against them, as a place to train the next generation of Heroes. The Guild Association is holding the line, but are in dire need of new blood and the powerful abilities they could bring to the battlefront. To be the saviors that humanity needs, they need to surpass the limits of those that came before them.

In a war with everything on the line, every power matters. With an adaptive enemy, comes the need for a constant shift in tactics. A new age of strategy is emerging, with even the unlikeliest of Heroes making an impact.

Salvatore Argento has never seen a demon.
He has never aspired to become a Hero.
Yet his power might be the one to tip the odds in humanity's favor.

Buy on Amazon

WANDERING WARRIOR

By Michael Head

A divine quest to deliver justice.
One year to accomplish his mission.
After nineteen planets, there's something different about this one.

James Holden has reached the maximum level there is for a human. That's perfect, since he's the only one of his kind. A wandering warrior, without control of his destination, tossed between universes by gods who've failed to tell him why. James is the lone Judge on a new world in need of someone to balance the scales. He isn't afraid to do so with extreme prejudice. As the Chief Justice, he has to right the wrongs the innocent can't fix themselves.

As James quickly discovers, the roots of corruption run deep. Guilds choose to protect themselves rather than the people. Monsters roam the wilderness unchecked. Judgment is usually a decision between right and wrong, but nothing is ever that simple. This time, being the strongest human won't be enough to punish the guilty. James might have to recruit some new blood, even if he prefers to work alone.

On his twentieth world, he is going to win, no matter the cost. James will have to find a way to break past the limits of the system if he's going to have a chance at making a difference.

Buy on Amazon

KNIGHTS OF ETERNITY

By Rachel Ní Chuirc

When Zara awoke in chains she thought she'd gone mad.

She was Zara the Fury - mistress of flame and fear. Her name was whispered across the land, from ramshackle taverns to the royal court. Even the heroic Gilded Knights thought twice before crossing her path.
She was feared—*respected.*
Now she was curled up on a dirt floor on her fiancé's orders. Valerius, leader of the Gilded, mocks her cries for help. And the kingdom is on the brink of war over the missing Lady Eternity…
But that wasn't why Zara thought she had gone mad.
The reason why is that the last thing she remembered was blood, an arcade screen, and the gun that changed everything.

But no chains can hold the Fury, and when she gets out?
The world is going to *burn.*

Buy on Amazon

SCARLET CITADEL

By Jack Fields

Gormon Hughes is 19, thin as a broom, and has—not for the first time in his life—been swept into the path of trouble. Poor, recently heartbroken, and indebted to the sort of people who file their teeth into needle points and devour wriggling bloated spiders for fun, Hughes sets his sights on salvation.

That salvation is the Scarlet Citadel, a wealthy organization of pageant fighters, monster hunters, and secret keepers. With the aid of strange oracles, rare good fortune, and a unique power that bubbles like champagne in the core of Hughes' being, he must join the Citadel and advance himself.

But the ladder of progression is harsh and dark. The rungs are slippery.

And falling means disaster…

Buy on Amazon

<u>LITRPG!</u>

To learn more about LitRPG, talk to other authors including myself, and to just have an awesome time, please join the LitRPG Group

www.facebook.com/groups/LitRPGGroup

FACEBOOK

There's also a few really active Facebook groups I'd recommend you join, as you'll get to hear about great new books, new releases and interact with all your (new) favorite authors! (I may also be there, skulking at the back and enjoying the memes…)

https://www.facebook.com/groups/LitRPGlegion/

https://www.facebook.com/groups/GamelitSociety

https://www.facebook.com/groups/LitRPG.books

https://www.facebook.com/groups/LitRPGforum/